Prof. Name

AND QUIET FLOWS

THE DON

AND

Quiet Flows

THE DON

By MIKHAIL SHOLOKHOV

TRANSLATED FROM THE RUSSIAN BY
STEPHEN GARRY

VINTAGE BOOKS
A Division of Random House
NEW YORK

VINTAGE BOOKS

are published by

Alfred A. Knopf, Inc. AND *Random House, Inc.*

Nor with the plough is our dear glorious earth furrowed,
Our earth is furrowed with the hoofs of horses,
And our dear glorious earth is sown with the heads of Cossacks;
Our gentle Don is adorned with youthful widows;
Our gentle father Don is blossomed with orphans;
The waves of the gentle Don are rich with fathers' and mothers'
    tears.

O thou, our father, gentle Don!
Oh, why dost thou, gentle Don, flow so troubledly?
"Ah, how should I, the gentle Don, not flow troubledly?
From my depths, the depths of the Don, the cold springs beat;
Amid me, the gentle Don, the white fish leap."

OLD COSSACK SONGS

CONTENTS

KEY TO
PRINCIPAL CHARACTERS

MELEKHOV, PROKOFFEY. A Cossack.

MELEKHOV, PANTALEIMON PROKOFFIEVICH, son of Prokoffey.

MELEKHOVA, ILINICHNA. Wife of Pantaleimon.

MELEKHOV, PIOTRA PANTALIEVICH. Son of Pantaleimon and Ilinichna.

MELEKHOV, GREGOR (GRISHKA). Son of Pantaleimon and Ilinichna.

MELEKHOVA, DUNIA. Daughter of Pantaleimon and Ilinichna.

MELEKHOVA, DARIA. Wife of Piotra.

KORSHUNOV, GRISHAKA. A Cossack.

KORSHUNOV, MIRON GREGORIEVICH. Son of Grishaka.

KORSHUNOVA, MARIA LUKINICHNA. Wife of Miron.

KORSHUNOV, MITKA MIRONOVICH. Son of Miron and Maria.

KORSHUNOVA, NATALIA. Daughter of Miron and Maria, afterwards Gregor's wife.

ASTAKHOV, STEPAN. A Cossack.

ASTAKHOVA, AKSINIA. Wife of Stepan.

BODOVSKOV, FIODOT. A Cossack.

KOSHEVOI, MISHKA. A Cossack.

KOSHEVOI, MASHUTKA. Mishka's sister.

Principal Characters

SHAMIL, ALEXEI, MARTIN, and PROKHOR. Three Cossack brothers.

TOKIN, CHRISTONIA (CHRISTAN). A Cossack.

TOMILIN, IVAN. A Cossack.

KOTLIAROV, IVAN ALEXIEVICH. Engineer at Mokhov's mill. A landless Cossack.

DAVID. Worker at Mokhov's mill.

FILKA. A shoemaker.

STOCKMAN, OSIP DAVIDOVICH. A locksmith and Bolshevik.

VALET. Scalesman at Mokhov's mill.

MOKHOV, SERGEI PLATONOVICH. Merchant and mill-owner.

MOKHOVA, ELIZABIETA. Mokhov's daughter.

MOKHOV, VLADIMIR. Mokhov's son.

LISTNITSKY, NIKHOLAI ALEXIEVICH. Landowner and retired general.

LISTNITSKY, EUGENE NIKHOLAEVICH. Son of Nikholai Listnitsky.

BUNCHUK, ILIA. A soldier volunteer, Bolshevik, and machine-gunner.

GARANZHA. A Ukrainian conscript.

GROSHEV, EMELIAN. A Cossack.

IVANKOV, MIKHAIL. A Cossack.

KRUCHKOV, KOZMA. A Cossack.

ZHARKOV, YEGOR. A Cossack.

ZYKOV, PROKHOR. A Cossack.

SHCHEGOLKOV. A Cossack.

URIUPIN, ALEXEI. Nicknamed "Tufty." A Cossack.

ANIKUSHKA. A Cossack.

BOGATIRIEV. A Cossack.

SENILIN, AVDEICH. Nicknamed "Bragger." A Cossack.

GRIAZNOV, MAKSIM. A Cossack.

KOROLIOV, ZAKHAR. A Cossack.

KRIVOSHLIKOV, MIKHAIL. Secretary of Don Revolutionary Committee.

Principal Characters

LAGUTIN, IVAN. A Cossack. Member of Don Revolutionary Committee.

PODTIELKOV, FIODOR. Chairman of Don Revolutionary Committee.

POGOODKO, ANNA. Jewish student and Bolshevik.

BOGOVOI, GIEVORKIANTZ, KHVILICHKO, KRUTOGOROV, MIKHALIDZE, REBINDER, STEPANOV: Members of Bunchuk's revolutionary machine-gun detachment.

ABRAMSON. A Bolshevik organizer.

GOLUBOV. A captain and commander of Don revolutionary forces.

ALEXIEV. Czarist general.

KORNILOV. Czarist general.

ATARSHCHIKOV. Lieutenant in Cossack regiment.

IZVARIN. Captain in Cossack regiment.

KALMIKOV. Captain in Cossack regiment.

MERKULOV. Lieutenant in Cossack regiment.

CHUBOV. Lieutenant in Cossack regiment.

PART I

Peace

PEACE

Chapter 1

THE Melekhov farm was right at the end of Tatarsk village. The gate of the cattle-yard opened northward towards the Don. A steep, sixty-foot slope between chalky, grass-grown banks, and there was the shore. A pearly drift of mussel-shells, a grey, broken edging of shingle, and then—the steely-blue, rippling surface of the Don, seething beneath the wind. To the east, beyond the willow-wattle fence of the threshing-floor, was the Hetman's highway, greyish wormwood scrub, vivid brown, hoof-trodden knotgrass, a shrine standing at the fork of the road, and then the steppe, enveloped in a shifting mirage. To the south a chalky range of hills. On the west the street, crossing the square and running towards the leas.

The Cossack Prokoffey Melekhov returned to the village during the last war with Turkey. He brought back a wife—a little woman wrapped from head to foot in a shawl. She kept her face covered and rarely revealed her yearning eyes. The silken shawl was redolent of strange, aromatic perfumes; its rainbow-hued patterns aroused the jealousy of the peasant women. The captive Turkish woman did not get on well with Prokoffey's relations, and before long old Melekhov gave his son his portion. The old man never got over the disgrace of the separation, and all his life he refused to set foot inside his son's hut.

3

Prokoffey speedily made shift for himself; carpenters built him a hut, he himself fenced in the cattle-yard, and in the early autumn he took his bowed, foreign wife to her new home. He walked with her through the village, behind the cart laden with their worldly goods. Everybody from the oldest to the youngest rushed into the street. The Cossacks laughed discreetly into their beards, the women passed vociferous remarks to one another, a swarm of unwashed Cossack lads called after Prokoffey. But, with overcoat unbuttoned, he walked slowly along as though over newly ploughed furrows, squeezing his wife's fragile wrist in his own enormous swarthy palm, defiantly bearing his lint-white, unkempt head. Only the wens below his cheekbones swelled and quivered, and the sweat stood out between his stony brows.

Thenceforth he went but rarely into the village and was never to be seen even at the market. He lived a secluded life in his solitary hut by the Don. Strange stories began to be told of him in the village. The boys who pastured the calves beyond the meadow road declared that of an evening, as the light was dying, they had seen Prokoffey carrying his wife in his arms as far as the Tatar mound. He would seat her, with her back to an ancient, weather-beaten, porous rock, on the crest of the mound; he would sit down at her side, and they would gaze fixedly across the steppe. They would gaze until the sunset had faded, and then Prokoffey would wrap his wife in his coat and carry her back home. The village was lost in conjecture, seeking an explanation for such astonishing behaviour. The women gossiped so much that they had no time to hunt for their fleas. Rumour was rife about Prokoffey's wife also; some declared that she was of entrancing beauty; others maintained the contrary. The matter was set at rest when one of the most venturesome of the women, the soldier's wife Maura, ran to Prokoffey on the pretext of getting some leaven; Prokoffey crawled into the cellar for the leaven, and Maura had time to notice that Prokoffey's Turkish conquest was a perfect fright.

A few minutes later Maura, her face flushed and her kerchief awry, was entertaining a crowd of women in a by-lane:

"And what could he have seen in her, my dears? If she'd only been a woman, now, but she's got no bottom or belly; it's a disgrace. We've got better-looking girls going begging for a husband. You could cut through her waist, she's just like a wasp. Little eyes, black and strong, she flashes with them like Satan, God forgive me. She must be near her time, God's truth."

"Near her time?" the women marvelled.

"I'm no babe! I've reared three myself."

"But what's her face like?"

"Her face? Yellow. Unhappy eyes—it's no easy life for a woman in a strange land. And what is more, women, she wears—Prokoffey's trousers!"

"No!" The women drew their breath in abrupt alarm.

"I saw them myself; she wears trousers, only without stripes. It must be his everyday trousers she has. She wears a long shift, and below it you see the trousers, stuffed into socks. When I saw them my blood ran cold."

The whisper went round the village that Prokoffey's wife was a witch. Astakhov's daughter-in-law (the Astakhovs lived in the hut next to Prokoffey's) swore that on the second day of Trinity, before dawn, she saw Prokoffey's wife, straight-haired and barefoot, milking the Astakhovs' cow. From that day the cow's udder withered to the size of a child's fist; she gave no more milk and died soon after.

That year there was unusual mortality among the cattle. By the shallows of the Don the carcasses of cows and young bulls littered the sandy shore every day. Then the horses were affected. The droves grazing on the village pasture-lands melted away. And through the lanes and streets of the village crept an evil rumour.

The Cossacks held a village meeting and went to Prokoffey. He came out on the steps of his hut and bowed.

"What good does your visit bring, worthy elders?" he asked.

Dumbly silent, the crowd drew nearer to the steps. One drunken old man was the first to cry:

"Drag your witch out here! We're going to try her. . . ."

Prokoffey flung himself back into the hut, but they caught him in the porch. A sturdy Cossack nicknamed Lushnia knocked Prokoffey's head against the wall and exhorted him:

"Don't make a sound, not a sound, you're all right. We shan't touch you, but we're going to trample your wife into the ground. Better to destroy her than have all the village die for want of cattle. But don't you make a sound, or I'll smash your head against the wall!"

"Drag the bitch into the yard!" came a roar from the steps A regimental comrade of Prokoffey's wound the Turkish woman's hair around one hand, pressed his other hand over her screaming mouth, dragged her at a run through the porch, and flung her beneath the feet of the crowd. A thin shriek rose above the howl of voices. Prokoffey sent half a dozen Cossacks flying, burst into the hut, and snatched a sabre from the wall. Jostling against one another, the Cossacks rushed out of the porch. Swinging the gleaming, whistling sabre around his head, Prokoffey ran down the steps. The crowd shuddered and scattered over the yard.

Lushnia was heavy of gait, and by the threshing-floor Prokoffey caught up with him; with a diagonal sweep down across the left shoulder from behind he clave the Cossack's body to the belt. Tearing out the stakes of the wattle fence, the crowd poured across the threshing-floor into the steppe.

Some half-hour later the crowd ventured to approach Prokoffey's farm again. Two of them crept cautiously into the porch. On the kitchen threshold, in a pool of blood, her head flung back awkwardly, lay Prokoffey's wife; her lips writhed tormentedly back from her teeth, her gnawed tongue protruded. Prokoffey, with shaking head and glassy stare, was wrapping a squealing, crimson, slippery little ball—the prematurely-born infant—in a sheepskin.

Prokoffey's wife died the same evening. His old mother had pity on the child and took charge of it. They plastered it with bran mash, fed it with mare's milk, and after a month, assured that the swarthy, Turkish-looking boy would survive, they carried him to church and christened him. They named him Pantaleimon after his grandfather. Prokoffey came back from penal servitude twelve years later. With his clipped, ruddy beard streaked with grey and his Russian clothing he did not look like a Cossack. He took his son and returned to his farm.

Pantaleimon grew up darkly swarthy and ungovernable. In face and figure he was like his mother. Prokoffey married him to the daughter of a Cossack neighbour.

Thenceforth Turkish blood began to mingle with that of the Cossacks. That was how the hook-nosed, savagely handsome Cossack family of Melekhovs, nicknamed "Turks," came into the village.

When his father died, Pantaleimon took over the farm; he had the hut rethatched, added an acre of common land to the farmyard, built new barns, and a granary with a sheet-iron roof. He ordered the tinsmith to cut a couple of cocks from the odd remnants and had them fastened to the roof. They brightened the Melekhov farmyard with their carefree air, giving it a self-satisfied and prosperous appearance.

Under the weight of the passing years Pantaleimon Prokoffievích grew stouter; he broadened and stooped somewhat, but still looked a well-built old man. He was dry of bone, and lame (in his youth he had broken his leg while hurdling at an Imperial review of troops), he wore a silver half-moon ear-ring in his left ear, and retained the vivid raven hue of his beard and hair until old age. When angry he completely lost control of himself, and undoubtedly this had prematurely aged his corpulent wife, Ilinichna, whose face, once beautiful, was now a perfect spider-web of furrows.

Piotra, his elder, married son, took after his mother: stocky and snub-nosed, a luxuriant shock of corn-coloured hair, hazel eyes. But the younger, Gregor, was like his father: half a head taller than Piotra, some six years younger, the same hanging hook-nose as his father's, bluish almonds of burning irises in slightly oblique slits, brown, ruddy skin drawn over angular cheekbones. Gregor stooped slightly, just like his father; even in their smile there was a common, rather savage quality.

Dunia—her father's favourite—a long-boned, large-eyed lass, and Piotra's wife, Daria, with her small child, completed the Melekhov household.

Chapter 2

Here and there stars were still piercing through the ashen, early-morning sky. A wind was blowing from under a bank of cloud. Over the Don a mist was rolling high, piling against the slope of a chalky hill, and crawling into the cliff like a grey, headless serpent. The left bank of the river, the sands, the backwaters, stony shoals, the dewy weeds, quivered with the ecstatic, chilly dawn. Beyond the horizon the sun yawned and rose not.

In the Melekhov hut Pantaleimon Prokoffievich was the first to awake. Buttoning the collar of his cross-stitched shirt as he went, he walked out on the steps. The grass-grown yard was coated with a dewy silver. He let the cattle out into the street. Daria ran past in her undergarments to milk the cows. The dew sprinkled over the calves of her bare, white legs, and she left a smoking, beaten trail behind her over the grass of the yard. Pantaleimon Prokoffievich stood for a moment watching the grass rising from the pressure of Daria's feet, then turned back into the kitchen.

On the sill of the wide-open window lay the dead-rose petals of the cherry blossoming in the front garden. Gregor was asleep face-downward, his hand flung out back uppermost.

"Gregor, coming fishing?" his father called him.

"What?" he asked in a whisper, dropping one leg off the bed.

"We'll row out and fish till sunrise," Pantaleimon proposed.

Breathing heavily through his nose, Gregor pulled his everyday trousers down from a peg, drew them on, tucked the legs into his white woollen socks, and slowly drew on his shoes, turning out the infolded flaps.

"But has Mother boiled the bait?" he hoarsely asked, as he followed his father into the porch.

"Yes. Go to the boat. I'll be after you in a minute."

The old man poured the strong-smelling, boiled rye into a jug, carefully swept up the fallen grains into his palm, and limped down to the beach. He found his son sitting restively in the boat.

"Where shall we go?" Gregor asked.

"To the black cliff. We'll try around the log where they were lying the other day."

Its stern scraping the ground, the boat settled into the water and broke away from the shore. The current carried it off, rocking it and trying to turn it broadside on. Gregor steered with the oar, but did not row.

"Why aren't you rowing?" his father demanded.

"We'll get into the middle first."

Cutting across the swift main-stream current, the boat moved towards the left bank. Muffled by the water, the crowing of cocks reached them from the village. Its side scraping the black, gravelly cliff rising high above the river, the boat hove to in the pool below. Some forty feet from the bank the peeled branches of a sunken elm emerged from the water. Around it turbulent flecks of foam eddied and swirled.

"Pay out the line while I'm tying her fast," Pantaleimon whispered. He thrust his hand into the steaming mouth of the jug. The rye scattered audibly over the water, just as though someone had whispered in an undertone: "Shick." Gregor strung some swollen grains on the hook and smiled.

"Fish, fish! There are fish both large and small here," the old man ordered.

The line fell in spirals into the water and tautened, then slackened again. Gregor set his foot on the end of the rod and fumbled cautiously for his pouch.

"We'll have no luck today, Father. The moon is on the wane," he remarked.

"Did you bring the tinder?"

"Aha!"

"Give me a light."

The old man began to smoke and glanced at the sun, stranded on the farther side of the elm.

"You can't tell when a carp will bite," he replied. "Sometimes he will when the moon is waning."

The water lapped noisily around the sides of the boat, and a four-foot carp, gleaming as though cast from ruddy copper, leaped upward, doubling his broad, curving tail above the water. Granular sprinkles scattered over the boat.

"Wait now!" Pantaleimon wiped his wet beard with his sleeve.

At the side of the sunken tree, among the branching, naked boughs, two carp leaped simultaneously; a third, smaller, writhed in the air and struggled stubbornly close to the cliff.

Gregor impatiently chewed the wet end of the twine. The misty sun was half up. Pantaleimon scattered the rest of the bait and, glumly pursing his lips, stolidly watched the motionless end of the rod.

Gregor spat out the end of his cigarette, wrathfully watching its rapid flight. He inwardly cursed his father for awakening him so early. Through smoking on an empty stomach his mouth reeked like burnt bristles. He was about to bend and scoop up some water in his palm, but at that moment the end of the line feebly swayed and slowly sank.

"Play him!" the old man breathed.

Starting up, Gregor seized the rod, but it bent in an arc from his hand, and the end disappeared violently into the water.

"Hold him!" Pantaleimon muttered as he pushed the boat off from the bank.

Gregor attempted to lift the rod, but the fish was too strong, and the stout line snapped with a dry crack. Gregor staggered and almost fell.

"Now you can drink!" his father cursed, just failing to catch the line as it slipped across the gunwale.

Smiling agitatedly, Gregor fastened a new line to the rod and threw out the end. Hardly had the lead touched bottom when the end of the rod bent.

"There he is, the devil," Gregor grumbled, with difficulty holding in the fish, which was making for the middle current.

The line cut the water with a loud swish, raising a sloping, greenish rampart behind it. Pantaleimon picked up the bailer-handle in his stumpy fingers.

A great red and yellow carp rose to the surface, lashed the water into foam, and dived back into the depths.

"Strike till it stings your hand! No, wait!" Gregor exclaimed.

"Hold him!" his father cried.

"I am holding him!"

"Don't let him get under the boat!"

Taking breath, Gregor drew the carp towards the side of the boat. The old man thrust out the bailer, but with its last strength the carp again disappeared into the depths.

"Raise his head! Make him swallow some air and he'll be quieter!" Pantaleimon ordered.

Once more Gregor drew the exhausted fish towards the boat. Its nose struck against the rough side, and it lay there with gaping mouth, its orange-golden fins flickering.

"We've won!" Pantaleimon croaked, lifting the fish in the bailer.

They sat on for another half-hour. But they had no more battles with carp.

"Wind in the line. They won't leap again today!" the old man said at last.

Gregor pushed off from the bank. As he rowed he saw from his father's face that he wished to say something, but Pantaleimon sat silently gazing at the huts of the village scattered under the hill.

"Look here, Gregor—" he began uncertainly, pulling at the knot of the sack beneath his feet. "I've noticed that you and Aksinia Astakhova . . ."

Gregor flushed violently and turned his head away. His shirt collar cut into his muscular, sunburnt neck, pressing out a white band in the flesh.

"You watch out, young man," the old man continued, now roughly and angrily. "Stepan's our neighbour, and I won't allow any playing about with his wife. That kind of thing can lead to mischief, and I warn you beforehand. If I see you at it I'll whip you!"

Pantaleimon twisted his fingers into his gnarled hand and watched the blood ebbing from his son's face.

"It's all lies!" Gregor snarled, and gazed straight into his father's eyes.

"Silence!"

"What if people do talk—"

"Hold your tongue, you son of a bitch!"

Gregor bent to the oars. The boat leaped forward. The water rocking behind the stern danced away in little scrolls.

They remained silent until, as they were approaching the shore, his father reminded Gregor:

"You look out, don't forget what I've said, or from today I'll stop your little game. Not a step will you stir outside the yard!"

Gregor made no answer. As he beached the boat he asked:

"Shall I hand the fish to the women?"

"Take and sell it to Mokhov the merchant," the old man said more gently. "You can have the money for tobacco."

Biting his lips, Gregor followed his father, his eyes wrathfully gnawing the back of the old man's head. "Try it, Father! I'm going out tonight even if you hobble me!" he was thinking.

At the farm gate he ran into his old friend Mitka Korshunov. Mitka was playing with the end of his silver-studded belt as he walked along. His round, yellow eyes gleamed greasily in their narrow slits. His irises were long like a cat's, giving him a shifty and evasive look.

"Where are you off to with the fish?" Mitka asked.

"We caught it today. I'm going to sell it to Mokhc v."

With a glance Mitka estimated the weight of the fish.

"Fifteen pounds?" he guessed.

"And a half. We weighed it on the steelyard."

"Take me with you. I'll do the selling for you," Mitka proposed.

"Come on, then."

"And what do I get?"

"You needn't fear. We shan't quarrel over that," Gregor laughed.

Mass was just ended, and the villagers were scattering through the streets. The three brothers nicknamed Shamil came striding down the road side by side. The eldest, one-armed Alexei, was in the middle. The tight collar of his army tunic held his veiny neck erect, his thin, curly, pointed little beard twisted provokingly sideways, his left eye winked nervously. His carbine had exploded in his hands at the shooting-range many years previously, and a piece of the flying iron had ploughed into his cheek. Thenceforth his left eye had winked in season and out of season, and a blue scar furrowed across his cheek to bury itself in his tow of hair. The left arm had been torn off at the elbow, but Alexei was past master at rolling a cigarette with one hand. He could press his pouch against his chest, tear off the right quantity of paper with his teeth, would bend it into a trough-shape, rake up the tobacco, and roll the cigarette almost before you realized what he was doing.

Although he had only one arm he was the finest fighter in the village. His fist was not particularly large as fists go—the size of a calabash—but if he happened to get annoyed with his bullock when ploughing and had mislaid his whip, he would give it a blow with his fist and the bullock would be stretched out over the furrows, blood streaming from its ears. And there it would lie. The other brothers, Martin and Prokhor, resembled Alexei down to the last detail. They were just as stocky and broad-shouldered, only each had two arms.

As he came up with Mitka and Gregor, Alexei winked five times in succession.

"Selling your load?" he asked.

"Want to buy it?" Gregor replied.

"How much do you want for it?"

"A couple of bullocks, and a wife thrown in."

Winking violently, Alexei waved the stump of his arm.

"You're a funny lad! He-he-he! A wife thrown in! And you'll take the offspring, too?"

"Clear off, or there will be some Shamils missing!" Gregor snarled.

In the square the villagers were gathered around the church palings.

In the middle of a ring of people a grizzled old man, his chest covered with crosses and medals, was waving his arms about.

"My old grandfather Grishaka is telling one of his tales about the Turkish war," Mitka directed Gregor's attention with a glance. "Let's go and listen."

"While we're listening to him the carp will start stinking and swell," Gregor objected.

In the square behind the fire-cart shed rose the green roof of Mokhov's house. Striding past the shed the two lads approached the steps. The balustrade was ornamented with wild vine entwined in the railings. On the steps lay a speckled, lazy shade.

"See how some folk live, Mitka!" Gregor said.

"A handle, and gilt, too!" Mitka sniffed as he opened the door leading to the veranda.

"Who is there?" someone called from the other side of the door.

Suddenly smitten with shyness, Gregor went in. The tail of the carp dragged over the painted floorboards.

"Whom do you want?"

A girl was sitting in a wicker rocking-chair, a dish of strawberries in her hand. Gregor stared silently at the full, rosy, heart-shaped lips embracing a berry. Raising her head, the girl looked the lads up and down. The berry rested patiently in the warm lips.

Mitka came to Gregor's help. He coughed and asked:

"Want to buy some fish?"

Her lips opened to admit the berry and then smiled swiftly, almost imperceptibly.

"Fish? I'll tell you in a moment."

She rocked the chair upright and, rising, shuffled off in her embroidered slippers. The sun shone through her white dress, and Mitka saw the dim outline of full legs and the broad, billowing lace of her underskirt. He was astonished at the satiny whiteness of her bare calves; only on the cushioned little heels was the skin milkily yellow.

"Look, Grishka, what a dress! Like glass! You can see everything through it," he said, nudging the carp instead of Gregor.

The girl came back through the door leading to the corridor and sat down gently on the chair.

"Go into the kitchen!" she ordered.

Gregor tiptoed into the house. When he had gone Mitka stood blinking at the white thread of the parting dividing the girl's hair into two golden half-circles. She studied him with saucy, restless eyes.

"Are you from the village?" she asked.

"Yes."

"Whose son are you?"

"Korshunov's."

"And what is your name?"

"Mitka!"

She attentively examined her rosy nails and with a swift movement tucked up her legs.

"Which of you caught the fish?" she continued her cross-examination.

"My friend, Gregor."

"And do you fish, too?"

"When I feel like it."

"With fish-hooks?"

"Yes."

"I'd like to go fishing some time," she said after a silence.

"All right, I'll take you if you want to."

"How is it to be done? Really, are you serious?"

"You must get up very early," Mitka declared.

"I'll get up, only you'll have to waken me."

"I can do that. But how about your father?"

"What about my father?"

Mitka smiled. "He might take me for a thief. The dogs will have to be baited!"

"That's simple! I sleep alone in the corner room. That's the window," she pointed with her finger. "If you come for me knock at the window and I'll get up."

The sound of Gregor's timid voice and the thick, oily tones of the cook came brokenly from the kitchen. Mitka was silent, fingering the tarnished silver of his belt.

"Are you married?" she asked, warming with a secretive smile.

"Why?"

"Oh, I'm just curious."

"No, I'm single."

Mitka suddenly blushed, and she, playing with a smile and a little twig from the hothouse strawberries scattered over the floor, queried:

"And are the girls fond of you, Mitka?"

"Some are, some aren't."

"You don't say. . . . And why have you got eyes like a cat?"

"A cat?" Mitka was now completely abashed.

"Yes, that's just it, they're cat's eyes."

"I must have got them from my mother. I can't help it."

"And why don't they marry you, Mitka?"

Mitka recovered from his momentary confusion and, sensing the hidden sneer in her words, twinkled the yellows of his eyes.

"My wife hasn't grown up yet."

She raised her eyebrows in astonishment, bridled up, and rose from her seat. Her fleeting smile lashed Mitka like a nettle.

There was the sound of feet ascending the steps from the street. Shuffling softly along in his capacious kid boots, the master of the house, Sergei Platonovich Mokhov, carried his corpulent body with dignity past Mitka.

"Want me?" he asked as he passed, without turning his head.

"He's brought some fish, Papa," the girl replied.

Gregor came out with empty hands.

Chapter 3

The first cock had crowed when Gregor returned from his evening out. From the porch came the scent of over-sour hops and the spicy perfume of chickweed.

He tiptoed into the hut, undressed, carefully hung up his Sunday striped trousers, crossed himself, and lay down. A golden, criss-crossed pool of moonlight lay on the floor. In the corner under em-broidered towels was the tarnished lustre of silvered ikons, from the shelf over the bed came the droning hum of agitated flies.

He would have fallen asleep, but in the kitchen his brother's infant started to cry. The cradle began to creak like an ungreased cartwheel. He heard his brother's wife, Daria, mutter in a sleepy voice:

"Sleep, little brat! Neither rest nor peace do I get with you!" She quietly crooned a lullaby to the child.

As he dozed off under the measured, soothing creak, Gregor re-membered: "Why, tomorrow Piotra goes off to the camp. Daria will be left with the baby. . . . We'll have to do the mowing without him."

He was aroused from sleep by a prolonged neighing. By its tone he recognized Piotra's army horse. Helpless with sleep, his fingers were slow in buttoning up his shirt, and he almost dropped off again under the flowing rhythm of Daria's song:

> "And where are the geese?
> They've gone into the reeds.
> And where are the reeds?
> The girls have pulled them up.
>
> And where are the girls?
> The girls have taken husbands.
> And where are the Cossacks?
> They've gone to the war."

Rubbing his eyes, Gregor made his way to the stable and led Piotra's horse out into the street. A flying cobweb tickled his face, and his drowsiness unexpectedly left him.

Along the Don lay a slantingly undulating, never trodden track of moonlight. Over the Don hung a mist, and above it a starry grain. The horse set its hind hoofs down cautiously. The drop to the water was bad going. From the farther side of the river came the quacking of ducks. A sheat-fish turned and darted over the water above the mud by the bank, hunting at random for smaller fry.

Gregor stood a long time by the river. The bank exuded a dank and sickly rottenness. A tiny drop of water fell from the horse's lips. A light, pleasant void was in Gregor's heart, life was good and free from care. The red-tailed dawn was pecking up the starry grain from the dove-coloured floor of heaven.

Close to the stable he ran into his mother.

"That you, Grishka?" she asked.

"And who else should it be?"

"Watered the horse?"

"Yes," he answered shortly.

Carrying some dried dung for fuel, his mother ran back to the hut, her withered bare feet slapping on the ground.

"You might go and wake up the Astakhovs. Stepan said he would go with our Piotra," she called.

The morning rawness set a spring stiffly quivering in Gregor. His body tingled with prickles. He ran up the three echoing steps leading to the Astakhovs' hut. The door was on the latch. Stepan was asleep on an outspread rug in the kitchen, his wife's head on his breast.

In the greying twilight Gregor saw Aksinia's shift wrinkled above her knees, and her birch-white, unashamedly parted legs. For a moment he stood gazing, feeling his mouth going dry and his head bursting with an iron clangour.

His eyes wandered. In a strange, hoarse voice he called:

"Hey! Anyone here? Get up."

Aksinia started out of her sleep.

"Oh, who's that?" She hurriedly began to fumble with her shift, and in drawing it down, her bare arm was entangled in her legs. A little drop of spittle was left on her pillow; a woman's sleep is heavy at dawn.

"It's me. Mother sent me to wake you up."

"We'll be up in a minute. We're sleeping on the floor because of the fleas. Stepan, get up, do you hear?" By her voice Gregor guessed that she felt awkward, and he hastened to go out.

Thirty Cossacks were going from the village to the May training camp. Just before seven o'clock wagons with tarpaulin covers, Cossacks on foot and on horseback, in sailcloth shirts and carrying their equipment, began to stream towards the square.

Gregor found Piotra standing on the steps, hurriedly stitching a broken rein.

His father, Pantaleimon, was attending to Piotra's horse, pouring oats into a trough.

"Not finished eating yet?" Piotra asked, nodding towards the horse.

"He's hungry," his father replied deliberately, testing the saddle-cloth with his rough palm. "Let even a crumb stick to the cloth and it will chafe the animal's back into a sore in one march."

"When he's finished eating, he must have a drink, Father."

"Gregor will take him down to the Don," Pantaleimon answered.

Gregor took the high, raw-boned Don horse with a white star on its forehead, led it outside the gate, and resting his left hand lightly on its withers, vaulted on to its back and went off at a swinging trot. He tried to rein the horse in at the descent to the river, but the animal stumbled, quickened its pace, and flew down the slope. As he flung himself back and almost lay along the animal's spine, Gregor saw a woman with pails going down the hill. He turned sharply off the path and dashed into the water, leaving a cloud of dust behind him.

Aksinia Astakhova came swinging down the slope. When still some little distance away, she shouted to him:

"You mad devil! You almost rode me down. You wait, I'll tell your father how you ride."

"Now, neighbour, don't get angry. When you've seen your husband off to camp maybe I'll be useful on your farm," he replied.

"How the devil would you be useful to me?"

"When mowing-time comes you may yet be asking me," Gregor smiled.

Aksinia dextrously drew a full pail of water from the river and pressed her skirt between her knees away from the wind.

"So they're taking your Stepan?" Gregor asked.

"What's that to do with you?"

"What a spitfire! Can't I ask?"

"Well, they are taking him, and what of it?"

"So you'll be left a grass-widow?"

"Yes!"

The horse raised its lips from the water and stood gazing across the Don, its forefeet treading the stream. Aksinia filled her second pail, hoisted the yoke across her shoulders, and set off up the slope. Gregor turned the horse and followed her. The wind fluttered her skirt and played with the fine fluffy curls on her swarthy neck. Her flat embroidered cap flamed on her heavy knot of hair, her rose coloured shirt, gathered into her skirt at the waist, tightly embraced her back and shoulders. As she climbed the slope she bent forward, and the hollow between her shoulders showed clearly beneath her shirt. Gregor watched her every movement. He badly wanted to renew the talk with her.

"You'll be missing your husband, won't you?" he asked.

Aksinia turned her head and smiled without halting.

"And how else? You get married!" She spoke pantingly. "Marry and you'll know whether you miss your friend or not."

Gregor brought the horse level with her and gazed into her eyes.

"But other wives are glad when their husbands go. Our Daria will grow fat without her Piotra," he remarked.

"A husband's not a leech, but he sucks your blood all the same. Shall we be seeing you married soon?" she asked.

"I don't know, it depends on Father. After my army service, I suppose."

"You're still young; don't get married."

"Why not?"

"It's nothing but sorrow." She looked up under her brows and smiled grimly without parting her lips. For the first time Gregor noticed that her lips were shamelessly greedy and swollen. Combing his horse's mane with his fingers, he replied:

"I've no desire to get married. Someone loves me already as I am."

"Have you noticed anyone, then?"

"What should I notice? Now you're seeing your Stepan off . . . ?"

"Don't try to play about with me. I'll tell Stepan."

"I'll show your Stepan. . . ."

"Mind you don't cry first, my brave one!"

"Don't alarm me, Aksinia!"

"I'm not alarming you. Let other girls hem your tear-wipers, but keep your eyes off me."

"I'll look at you all the more now."

"Well, look then."

Aksinia smiled pacifically and left the track, seeking to pass round the horse. Gregor turned the animal sideways and blocked the road.

"Let me pass, Grishka."

"I won't."

"Don't be a fool. I must see to my husband."

Gregor smilingly teased the horse, and it edged Aksinia towards the cliff.

"Let me pass, you devil! There are people over there. If they see us what will they think?" she muttered. She swept a frightened glance around and passed by, frowning and without a backward look.

Piotra was saying good-bye to his family on the steps. Gregor saddled the horse. His brother hurried down the steps and took the reins. Scenting the road, the horse fretted and chewed the bit. With one foot in the stirrup, Piotra said to his father:

"Don't overwork the baldheads, Father. Come autumn, we'll sell them. Gregor will need an army horse, you know. And don't sell the steppe grass; you know yourself what hay there'll be in the meadow this year."

"Well, God be with you. It's time you were off," the old man replied, crossing himself.

Piotra flung his bulky body into the saddle and adjusted the folds of his shirt in his belt at the back. The horse moved towards the gate. The sabre swung to the rhythm of the motion, and its pommel glittered dully in the sun.

Daria followed with the child on her arm. Wiping her eyes with her sleeve, his mother, Ilinichna, stood in the middle of the yard.

"Brother! The pasties! You've forgotten the pasties! The potato pasties!" Dunia ran to the gate. "He's left his pasties behind," she groaned, leaning against the gate-post, and tears ran down her greasy, burning cheeks on to her jacket.

Daria stood gazing under her hand after her husband's white, dusty shirt.

Shaking the rotting gate-post, old Pantaleimon looked at Gregor. "Take and mend the gate, and put a new post in." He stood in thought a moment, then communicated the news: "Piotra's gone."

Through the wattle fence Gregor saw Stepan getting ready. Aksinia, bedecked in a green woollen skirt, led out his horse. Stepan smilingly said something to her. Unhurriedly, in lordly fashion, he kissed his wife, and his arm lingered long around her shoulder. His sunburnt and work-stained hand showed coal-black against her white jacket. He stood with his back to Gregor; his stiff, clean-shaven neck, his broad, somewhat heavy shoulders, and, whenever he bent towards his wife, the twisted end of his light-brown moustache were visible across the fence.

Aksinia laughed at something and shook her head. Sitting as though rooted in the saddle, Stepan rode his black horse at a hurried walk through the gate, and Aksinia walked at his side, holding the stirrup and looking up lovingly and thirstily into his eyes.

With a long, unwinking stare Gregor watched them to the turn of the road.

Towards evening a thunder-storm gathered. A mass of heavy clouds lay over the village. Lashed into fury by the wind, the Don sent great foaming breakers against its banks. The sky flamed with dry lightning, occasional peals of thunder shook the earth. A vulture circled with outspread wings below the clouds, and ravens croakingly pursued him. Breathing out coolness, the clouds passed down the Don from the east. Beyond the water-meadows the heaven blackened menacingly, the steppe lay in an expectant silence. In the village the closed shutters rattled, the old people hurried home, crossing themselves. A grey pillar of dust whirled over the square, and the heat-burdened earth was already beginning to be sown with the first grains of rain.

Shaking her braided tresses, Dunia ran across the yard, clapped fast the door of the chicken-house, and stood in the middle of the yard with nostrils distended like a horse scenting danger. In the street the children were kicking up their heels. Eight-year-old Mishka, his father's absurdly large peaked cap drawn over his eyes, was spinning round and piercingly chirruping:

> "Rain, rain, go away,
> We're going off for the day,
> To pay God our vow
> And to Christ to bow."

Dunia enviously watched Mishka's scarred bare feet brutally trampling the ground. She, too, wanted to dance in the rain and to get her head wet, so that her hair might grow thick and curly; she, too, wanted to stand on her hands like Mishka's friend in the roadside dust, at the risk of falling into the nettles. But her mother was watching and angrily moving her lips at the window. With a sigh

she ran into the house. The rain was now falling heavily. A peal of
thunder broke right over the roof and went rolling away across the
Don.

In the porch Pantaleimon and perspiring Gregor were hauling
a folded drag-net out of the side room.

"Raw thread and a pack-needle, quick!" Gregor called to Dunia.
Daria sat down to mend the net. Her mother-in-law grumbled as she
rocked the baby:

"You're beyond belief, old man! We could go to bed. Light costs
more and more, and yet you go on burning it. What are you up to
now? Where the plague are you going? And you'll get drowned into
the bargain, the terror of the Lord is in the yard. Hark how it shakes
the house! Lord Jesus Christ, Queen of Heaven! . . ."

For a moment it became dazzlingly blue and silent in the kitchen;
the rain could be heard drumming on the shutters. A clap of thunder
followed. Dunia whimpered and buried her face in the net. Daria
signed the cross towards the windows and door. The old woman
stared with terrible eyes down at the cat rubbing itself against her
legs.

"Dunia, chase this cat away," she exclaimed. "Queen of Heaven,
forgive me my sins. . . . Dunia, turn the cat out into the yard! Stop
it, unclean power! May you . . ."

Dropping the net, Gregor shook with silent laughter.

"Well, what are you grinning at? Enough of that!" his father
shouted at him. "Hurry with your mending, women. I told you the
other day to see to the net."

"And what fish do you expect to catch?" his wife stammered.

"If you don't understand, hold your tongue! The fish will make
for the bank now, they're afraid of storms. I fear the water will be
turned muddy already. Run, Dunia, and see whether you can hear
the watercourses running."

Dunia edged unwillingly towards the door.

Old Ilinichna would not be repressed. "Who's going to wade with
you? Daria mustn't, she may catch cold in her breast," she persisted.

"Me and Gregor, and for the other net—we'll call Aksinia and another of the women."

Dunia ran in, out of breath. Drops of rain hung trembling on her
lashes. She smelt of the dank, black earth.

"The courses are roaring like anything," she panted.

"Put on your coat and run to Aksinia," her father told her. "If she'll go, ask her to fetch Malashka Frolova, too."

Dunia quickly returned with the women. Aksinia, in a blue skirt and a ragged jacket belted with rope, looked shorter and thinner. Exchanging laughs with Daria, she took off her kerchief, wound her hair into a tighter knot, and throwing back her head, stared coldly at Gregor. As corpulent Malashka tied up her stocking, she said hoarsely:

"Have you got sacks? True God, we'll stir up the fish today."

They all went into the yard. The rain was still falling heavily, the puddles frothed and crawled in streams down towards the Don.

Gregor led the way down to the river.

"Aren't we near the landing-place yet, Gregor?" his father asked after a while.

"Here we are."

"Begin from here," Pantaleimon shouted, attempting to drown out the howling wind.

"Can't hear you, grand-dad," Malashka called throatily.

"Start wading, for God's sake," he replied. "I'll take the deep side. . . . The deep—I say. Malashka, you deaf devil, where are you dragging to? I'll go out into the deeps. . . . Gregor! Let Aksinia take the bank!"

A groaning roar from the Don. The wind was tearing the slanting sheet of rain to shreds. Feeling the bottom with his feet, Gregor waded up to his waist into the water. A clammy cold crept into his chest, drawing tightly in a ring round his heart. The waves lashed his face and tightly screwed-up eyes like a knout. The net bellied out and was carried off into the deeps. Gregor's feet, shod in woollen socks, slipped over the sandy bottom. The net was dragged out of his hand. Deeper, deeper. A sudden drop. His legs were carried away. The current snatched him up and bore him towards the middle of the stream. With his right hand he vigorously paddled back to the bank. The black, swirling depths frightened him as never before. His feet joyously found the muddy bottom. A fish knocked against his knee.

Again the net heeled over and slipped out into the depths. Again the current carried the ground away from under his feet, and Gregor swam, spitting out water.

"Aksinia, you all right?" he called.

"All right so far," he heard her answer.

"Isn't the rain stopping?"

"The fine rain's stopping and a heavy rain beginning."

"Talk quietly. If my father hears he'll go for me."

"Afraid of your father, too?" she sneered.

For a moment they hauled in silence.

"Grishka, there's a sunken tree by the bank, I think. We must get the net round it."

A terrible buffet flung Gregor far away from her.

"Ah—ah!" Aksinia screamed somewhere near the bank. Terrified, he swam in the direction of her call.

"Aksinia!"

Wind and the flowing roar of the water.

"Aksinia!" Gregor shouted again, going cold with fear. He struck out at random. He felt something slipping beneath his feet and caught it with his hand—it was the net.

"Grishka, where are you?" he heard Aksinia's tearful voice.

"Why didn't you answer my shout?" he bawled angrily, crawling on hands and knees up the bank.

Squatting down on his heels, he tremblingly disentangled the net. The moon peeled out of a slash of broken cloud. There was a restrained mutter of thunder beyond the water-meadows. The earth gleamed with moisture. Washed clean by the rain, the sky was stern and clear.

As he disentangled the net Gregor stared at Aksinia. Her face was a chalky white, but her red, slightly upturned lips were smiling.

"As I was knocked against the bank," she said, "I went out of my mind. I was frightened to death. I thought you were drowned."

Their hands touched. Aksinia attempted to thrust hers into the sleeve of his shirt.

"How warm it is up your arm," she said mournfully, "and I'm frozen."

Someone came running along the bank. Gregor guessed it to be Dunia. He shouted to her:

"Got the thread?"

"Yes. What are you sitting here for? Father sent me for you to come at once to the point. We've caught a sackful of sterlet." Unconcealed triumph sounded in her voice.

With teeth chattering, Aksinia sewed up the holes in the net. Then, to get warm, they ran at full speed to the point.

Pantaleimon was rolling a cigarette with scarred fingers swollen by the water; he danced and boasted:

"The first time, eight fish; and the second time—" he paused and silently pointed with his foot to the sack. Aksinia stared inquisitively: from it came the swishing sound of stirring fish.

"Well, we'll wade in once more up to our knees, and then home. In you go, Grishka; what are you waiting for?" his father asked.

Gregor stepped out with numbed legs. Aksinia was trembling so much that he felt her movement at the other end of the net.

"Don't shake!"

"I'd be glad not to, but I can't get my breath."

"Listen! Let's crawl out, and damn the fish!"

At that moment a great carp bored through the net like a golden corkscrew. Gregor hurried and folded the net over it. Aksinia ran out on to the bank. The water splashed on the sands and ran back. A fish lay quivering in the net.

"Back through the meadow?" she asked.

"The wood is nearer," Gregor replied.

Frowning, Aksinia wrung out her skirt, flung the sack over her shoulder, and set off almost at a trot. Gregor picked up the net. They had covered some two hundred yards when Aksinia began to groan:

"I've no strength left."

"Look, there's a last year's haystack. You might get warm inside it," he suggested.

"Good! While I'm getting home I might die."

Gregor turned back the top of the stack and dug out a hole. The long-lying hay smelt warm and rotten.

"Crawl into the middle. It's like a stove here," he told her.

She threw down the sack and buried herself up to the neck in the hay. Shivering with cold, Gregor lay down at her side. A tender, agitating scent came from her damp hair. She lay with head thrown back, breathing regularly through her half-open mouth.

"Your hair smells like henbane—you know, the white flower," Gregor whispered, bending towards her. She was silent. Her gaze was misty and distant, fixed on the waning, crescent moon.

Taking his hand out of his pocket, Gregor suddenly drew her head towards him. She tore herself away fiercely and raised herself from the hay.

"Let me go!" she demanded.

"Keep quiet!"

"Let me go, or I'll shout."

"Wait, Aksinia!"

"Daddy Pantaleimon!"

"Have you lost yourselves?" Pantaleimon's voice sounded quite close, from beyond a clump of hawthorn bush. Grinding his teeth, Gregor jumped out of the haystack.

"What are you shouting for? Are you lost?" the old man questioned as he approached.

Aksinia stood by the haystack adjusting her kerchief, steam rising from her.

"We're not lost, but I'm all but frozen," she answered.

"Look, woman, there's a haystack, warm yourself," the old man told her.

Aksinia smiled as she stooped to pick up the sack.

From Tatarsk to Sietrakov—the training-camp centre—it was some forty miles. Piotra Melekhov and Stepan Astakhov rode in the same covered wagon. With them were three others from their village: Fiodot Bodovskov, a young Kalmyk-faced and pock-marked Cossack, Christonia Tokin, a second reservist in the ataman's regiment of Life Guards, and the artilleryman Ivan Tomilin. After the first halt for food they harnessed Christonia's and Astakhov's horses to the wagon, and the other horses were tethered behind. Christonia, strong and crack-brained like all the men of the ataman's regiment, took the reins. He sat in front with bowed back, shading the light from the interior of the wagon, urging on the horses with his deep, rumbling bass voice. Piotra, Stepan, and Tomilin lay smoking under the tightly stretched tarpaulin cover. Bodovskov walked behind.

Christonia's wagon led the way. Behind trailed seven or eight others, leading saddled and unsaddled horses behind them. The road was noisy with laughter, shouts, songs, the snorting of horses, and the jingling of empty stirrups.

Under Piotra's head was his bag of biscuit. He lay twirling his tawny whiskers.

"Stepan!" he said.

"Eh?"

"Let's have a song."

"It's too hot. My mouth's all dried out."

"There are no taverns anywhere near, so don't wait for that!"

"Well, sing up. Only you're no good at it. Your Grishka now, he can sing. His isn't a voice, it's a pure silver thread."

Stepan threw back his head, coughed, and began in a low, tuneful voice:

> "Hey, the ruddy, flushing sunrise
> Early came up in the sky."

Tomilin put his palm against his cheek and caught up the refrain in a thin, wailing undertone. Smiling, Piotra watched the little knots of veins on his temples going blue with his efforts.

> "Young was she, the little woman
> Went for water to the stream."

Stepan, who was lying with his head towards Christonia, turned round on his elbow:

"Christonia, join in!" he ordered.

> "And the lad, he guessed her purpose,
> Saddled he his chestnut mare."

Stepan turned his smiling glance towards Piotra, and Piotra added his voice. Opening wide his heavily bearded jaws, Christonia roared in a voice that shook the tarpaulin cover.

> "Saddled he his chestnut mare,
> Overtook the little woman."

Christonia set his bare foot against the singletree and waited for Piotra to begin again. Closing his eyes, his perspiring face in shadow, Stepan affably sang on, now dropping his voice to a whisper, then causing it to ring out metallically.

> "Let me, let me, little woman,
> Water my mare in the stream."

And again Christonia joined in with his alarming howl. Voices from the neighbouring wagons took up the song. The wheels clashed on their iron frames, the horses snorted with the dust. A white-winged peewit flew up from the parching steppe. It flew with a cry into a hollow, watching the chain of wagons, the horses kicking up clouds of white dust with their hoofs, the men, in white, dusty shirts, walking at the edge of the road.

Stepan stood up in the wagon, holding the tarpaulin with one hand, beating a rough time with the other, and sang on; Fiodot Bodovskov whistled; the horses strained at the traces; leaning out of the wagon, Piotra laughed and waved his cap; Stepan, gleaming with a dazzling smile, impudently swung his shoulders; along the road the dust rolled in a cloud. Christonia jumped out of the wagon in his unbelted, over-long shirt, his hair matted, and, wet with sweat, did the Cossack dance, whirling in a swinging circle, frowning and groaning and leaving the monstrous, spreading marks of his bare feet in the silky grey dust.

They stopped for the night by a barrow with a sandy summit. Clouds gathered from the west. Rain dripped out of their black wings. The horses were watered at a pond. Above the dike dismal willows bowed before the wind. In the water, covered with stagnant duckweed and scaled with miserable little ripples, the lightning was distortedly reflected. The wind scattered the raindrops as though showering largesse into the earth's swarthy palms.

The fettered horses were turned out to graze, three men being appointed as guards. The other men lit fires and hung pots on the singletrees of the wagons.

Christonia was cooking millet. As he stirred it with a spoon, he told a story to the Cossacks sitting around:

"The barrow was high, like this one. And I says to my dead father: 'Won't the ataman stop us for digging up the barrow without his being asked?' "

"What is he lying about?" asked Stepan, as he came back from the horses.

"I'm telling how me and my dead father looked for treasure. It was the Merkulov barrow. Well, and Father says: 'Come on, Christonia, we'll dig up the Merkulov barrow.' He'd heard from his father that treasure was buried in it. Father promised God: 'Give me the treasure and I'll build a fine church.' So we agreed and off we went. It was on common land, so only the ataman could stop us. We arrived late in the afternoon. We waited until nightfall and then set to work with shovels at the summit. We began to dig straight down from the top. We'd dug a hole six feet deep; the earth was like stone. I was wet through. Father kept on muttering prayers, but believe me, brothers, my belly was grumbling so much. . . . You know what we eat in summer: sour milk and kvass. My dead father, he says: 'Pfooh!' he says, 'Christan, you're a heathen. Here am I praying, and you can't keep your food down. I can't breathe for the stink. Crawl out of the barrow, you ——, or I'll split your head open with the shovel. Through you the treasure may sink into the ground.' I lay outside the barrow and suffer with my belly, and my dead father—a strong man he was—goes on digging alone. And he digs down to a stone plate. He calls me. I push a crowbar under it and lift it up. Believe me, brothers, it was a moonlight night, and under this plate was such a shine—"

"Now you are lying, Christonia," Piotra broke in, smiling and tugging at his whiskers.

"How am I lying? Go to the devil, and to the devil's dam!" Christonia gave a hitch to his broad-bottomed trousers and glanced around his hearers. "No, I'm not lying. It's God's truth! There it shone. I look, and it's charcoal. Some forty bushels of it. Father says: 'Crawl in, Christan, and dig it up.' I dig out this rubbish. I went on digging till daylight. In the morning I look, and he—there he is."

"Who?" asked Tomilin.

"Why, the ataman, who else? He happens to come driving by. 'Who gave you permission?' and all the rest of it. He lays hold of us and hauls us off to the village. We were called before the court at Kaminskaya the year before last, but Father, he guessed what was coming and managed to die beforehand. We wrote back saying he was not among the living."

Christonia took his pot with the boiling millet and went to the wagon for spoons.

"Well, what of your father? He promised to build a church; didn't he do it?" Stepan asked when he returned.

"You're a fool, Stepan. What could he build with coal?"

"Once he promised, he ought to have done it."

"There was no agreement whatever about coal, and the treasure . . ." The flames of the fire shook with the laughter that arose. Christonia raised his head from the pot, and not understanding what the laughter was about, drowned all the rest with his heavy roar.

Aksinia was seventeen when she was given in marriage to Stepan Astakhov. She came from the village of Dubrovka, from the sands on the other side of the Don.

About a year before her marriage she was ploughing in the steppe some five miles from the village. In the night her father, a man of some fifty years, tied her hands and raped her.

"I'll kill you if you breathe a word, but if you keep quiet I'll buy you a plush jacket and gaiters with galoshes. Remember, I'll kill you if you . . ." he promised her.

Aksinia ran back through the night in her torn petticoat to the village. She flung herself at her mother's feet and sobbed out the whole story. Her mother and elder brother harnessed horses to the wagon, made Aksinia get in with them, and drove to the father. Her brother almost drove the horses to death in the five miles. They found the old man close to the field camp. He was lying in a drunken sleep on his overcoat, with an empty vodka bottle by his side. Before Aksinia's eyes her brother unhooked the singletree from the wagon, picked up his father by the feet, curtly asked him a question or two, and struck him a blow with the iron-shod singletree between the eyes. He and his mother went on beating steadily for an hour and a half. The ageing and always meek mother frenziedly tore at her senseless husband's hair, the brother used his feet. Aksinia lay under the wagon, her head covered, silently shaking. They carried her father home just before dawn. He lay bellowing mournfully, his eyes wandering around the room, seeking for Aksinia, who had hidden herself away. Blood and matter ran from his torn ear on to the pillow. Towards evening he died. They told the neighbours he had fallen from the wagon.

Within a year the matchmakers came in a gaily bedecked wagonette to ask for Aksinia's hand. The tall, stiff-necked, well-proportioned Stepan approved of his future bride, and the wedding was fixed for the autumn.

The day was frosty and ringingly icy. Aksinia was installed as young mistress of the Astakhov household. The morning after the festivities her mother-in-law, a tall old woman doubled up with some female complaint, woke Aksinia up, led her into the kitchen, and, aimlessly shifting things about, said to her:

"Now, dear little daughter, we've taken you not for love, nor for you to lie abed. Go and milk the cows, and then get some food ready. I'm old and feeble. You must take over the household, it will all fall on you."

The same day Stepan took his young wife into the barn and beat her deliberately and terribly. He beat her on the belly, the breast, and the back, taking care that the marks should not be visible to others. After that he neglected her, kept company with flighty grass-widows, and went out almost every night, first locking Aksinia into the barn or the room.

For eighteen months, so long as there was no child, he would not forgive her his disgrace. Then he was quieter, but was niggardly with caresses and rarely spent the night at home.

The large farm with its numerous cattle burdened Aksinia with work; Stepan was lazy and went off to smoke, to play cards, to learn the latest news, and Aksinia had to do everything. Her mother-in-law was a poor help. After bustling around a little, she would drop on the bed and, with lips tight-drawn and eyes gazing agonizedly at the ceiling, would lie groaning, rolled into a bundle. Throwing down her work, Aksinia would hide in a corner and stare at her mother-in-law's face in fear and pity.

The old woman died some eighteen months after the marriage. In the morning Aksinia was taken in travail, and about noon, an hour or so before the child's entry into the world, the grandmother dropped dead by the stable door. The midwife ran out to warn tipsy Stepan not to go into the bedroom and saw the old woman lying with her legs tucked up beneath her. After the birth of the child Aksinia devoted herself to her husband, but she had no feeling for him, only bitter womanly pity and force of habit. The child died within the year. The old life was resumed. And when Gregor Melekhov crossed Aksinia's path she realized with terror that she was attracted to the swarthy youngster. He waited on her stubbornly, with bulldog insistence. She saw that he was not afraid of Stepan, she felt that he would not hold back because of him, and without consciously desiring it, resisting the feeling with all her might, she noticed that on Sundays and week-days she was attiring herself more carefully. Making pretexts to herself, she sought to place herself more frequently in his path. She was happy to find Gregor's black eyes caressing her heavily and rapturously. When she awoke of a morning and went to milk the cows she smiled and, without realizing why, recalled: "Today's a happy day. But why? . . . Oh, Gregor—Grishka." She was frightened by the new feeling which filled her, and in her thoughts she went gropingly, cautiously, as though crossing the Don over the broken ice of March.

After seeing Stepan off to camp she decided to see Gregor as little as possible. After the fishing expedition her decision was still further strengthened.

Chapter 4

Some two days before Trinity the distribution of the village meadow-land took place. Pantaleimon attended the allotment. He came back at dinner-time, threw off his boots with a groan, and noisily scratching his weary legs, announced:

"Our portion lies close to the Red Cliff. Not over-good grass as grass goes. The upper part runs up to the forest, it's just scrub in places. And speargrass coming through."

"When shall we do the mowing?" Gregor asked.

"After the holidays."

The old wife opened the oven door with a clatter and drew out the warmed-up cabbage soup. Pantaleimon sat over the meal a long time, telling of the day's events, and of the knavish ataman, who had all but swindled the whole assembly of Cossacks.

"But who's going to do the raking and stacking, Dad?" Dunia asked timidly. "I can't do it all by myself."

"We'll ask Aksinia Astakhov. Stepan asked us to mow for him."

Two mornings later Mitka Korshunov rode on his white-legged stallion up to the Melekhov yard. A fine rain was falling. A heavy mist hung over the village. Mitka leaned out of his saddle, opened the wicket, and rode in. The old wife called to him from the steps.

"Hey, you rapscallion, what do you want?" she asked with evident dissatisfaction in her voice. The old lady had no love for the desperate and quarrelsome Mitka.

"And what do you want, Ilinichna?" Mitka said in surprise, as he tied his horse to the balustrade of the steps. "I want Gregor. Where is he?"

"He's asleep under the shed. But have you had a stroke? Have you lost the use of your legs that you must ride?"

"You're always sticking in your spoke, old lady!" Mitka took umbrage. Smacking an elegant whip against the legs of his polished boots, he went to look for Gregor and found him asleep in a cart. Screwing up his left eye as though taking aim, Mitka tugged at Gregor's hair.

"Get up, peasant!"

"Peasant" was the most abusive word Mitka could think of using. Gregor jumped up as though on springs.

"What do you want?" he demanded.

Mitka sat down on the side of the cart, and scraping the dried mud off his boots with a stick, he said:

"I've been insulted, Grishka."

"Well?"

"You see, it's . . ." Mitka cursed heavily. "He's a troop commander, he says." He threw out the words angrily, not opening his mouth, his legs trembling. Gregor got up.

"What troop commander?"

Seizing him by the sleeve, Mitka said more quietly:

"Saddle your horse at once and come to the meadows. I'll show him! I said to him: 'Come on, Your Excellency, and we'll see.' 'Bring all your friends and comrades,' he said, 'I'll beat the lot of you. The mother of my mare took prizes at the officers' hurdle-races at Petersburg.' What are his mare and mother to me? Curse them! I won't let them outrace my stallion!"

Gregor hastily dressed. Choking with wrath, Mitka hurried him up.

"He has come on a visit to the Mokhovs. Wait, what is his name?

Listnitsky, I think. He's stout and serious-looking and wears glasses. Well, let him! His glasses won't help him; I won't let him catch my stallion!"

With a laugh, Gregor saddled the old mare and, to avoid meeting his father, rode out to the steppe through the threshing-floor gate. They rode to the field at the top of the hill. Close to a withered ash horsemen were awaiting them: the officer Listnitsky on a clean-limbed, handsome mare, and seven of the village lads mounted bareback.

"Where shall we start from?" The officer turned to Mitka, adjusting his pince-nez and admiring the stallion's powerful chest muscles.

"From the ash to the Czar's Lake."

"Where is the Czar's Lake?" Listnitsky screwed up his eyes short-sightedly.

"There, Your Excellency, close to the forest."

They lined up the horses. The officer raised his whip above his head.

"When I say three. All right? One—two—three."

Listnitsky got away first, pressing close to the saddle-bow, holding his cap on with his hand. For a second he led all the rest. Mitka, with face desperately pale, rose in his stirrups—to Gregor he seemed insufferably slow in bringing the whip down on the croup of his stallion.

It was some two miles to the Czar's Lake. Stretched into an arrow, Mitka's stallion caught up with Listnitsky's mare when half the course had been covered. Left behind from the very beginning, Gregor trotted along, watching the straggling chain of riders.

By the Czar's Lake was a sandy hillock, washed up through the ages. Its yellow camel-hump was overgrown with sandwort. Gregor saw the officer and Mitka gallop up the hillock and disappear over the brow together, the others following. When he reached the lake the horses were already standing in a group around Listnitsky. Mitka was sleek with restrained delight, his every movement expressive of triumph. Contrary to his expectation, the officer seemed not at all disconcerted. He stood with his back against a tree, smoking a cigarette, and said, pointing to his foam-flecked horse:

"I've raced her a hundred and twenty miles. I rode over from the station only yesterday. If she were fresh, you'd never overtake me, Korshunov."

"Maybe," Mitka said magnanimously.

Gregor and Mitka left the others and rode home around the hill. Listnitsky took a chilly leave of them, thrust two fingers under the visor of his cap, and turned away.

As he was approaching the hut, Gregor saw Aksinia coming towards him. She was stripping a twig as she walked. When she noticed him she bent her head lower.

Gazing straight before him, Gregor almost rode her down, then suddenly touched up the peacefully ambling mare with his whip. She sat back on her hind legs and sent a shower of mud over Ak' sinia.

"Oh, you stupid devil!" she exclaimed.

Turning sharply and riding his excited horse at her, Gregor asked: "Why don't you pass the time of day?"

"You're not worth it!"

"And that's why I sent the mud over you. Don't hold your head so high!"

"Let me pass!" Aksinia shouted, waving her arms in front of the horse's nose. "What are you trampling me with your horse for?"

"She's a mare, not a horse."

"I don't care; let me pass."

"What are you getting angry for, Aksinia? Surely not for the other day, in the meadow?"

Gregor gazed into her eyes. Aksinia tried to say something, but abruptly a little tear hung in the corner of her black eye, her lips quivered pitifully. Shudderingly choking, she whispered:

"Go away, Gregor. I'm not angry—I—" and she went.

The astonished Gregor overtook Mitka at the gate.

"Coming out for the evening?" Mitka asked.

"No."

"Why, what's on? Or did she invite you to spend the night with her?"

Gregor wiped his brow with his palm and made no reply.

All that was left of Trinity in the village farms was the dry thyme scattered over the floors, the dust of crumpled leaves, and the shrivelled, withered green of broken oak and ash branches fastened to the gates and stairs.

The haymaking began immediately after Trinity. From early morning the meadow blossomed with women's holiday skirts, the bright embroidery of aprons, and coloured kerchiefs. The whole village turned out for the mowing. The mowers and rakers attired themselves as though for an annual holiday. So it had been from of old. From the Don to the distant alder clumps the ravaged meadowland stirred and pulsed.

The Melekhovs were late in starting. They set out when all but half the village were already in the meadow.

"You sleep late, Pantaleimon Prokoffievich," the perspiring haymakers clamoured.

"Not my fault—the women again!" the old man laughed, and urged on the bullocks with his knout of rawhide.

At the back of the cart sat Aksinia, her face completely wrapped up to protect it from the sun. From the narrow slits left for her eyes she calmly and severely stared at Gregor, seated opposite her. Daria, also wrapped up and dressed in her Sunday best, her legs hanging between the rungs of the wagon-side, was giving her breast to the child dozing in her arms. Dunia danced alongside, her happy eyes scanning the meadow and the people met along the road.

Drawing the sleeve of his cotton shirt over his fists, Pantaleimon wiped away the sweat running down from under the visor of his cap. His bent back, with the shirt stretched tightly across it, darkened with moist patches. The sun pierced slantingly through a grey scrawl of cloud and dropped a fan of misty, refracted rays over the meadow, the village, and the distant, silvery hills of the Don.

The day was sultry. The little clouds crept along drowsily, not even overtaking Pantaleimon's bullocks dragging along the road. The old man himself lifted and waved the knout heavily, as though in doubt whether to strike their bony flanks or not. Evidently realizing this, the bullocks did not hasten their pace and slowly, gropingly set forward their cloven hoofs. A dusty-gold and orange-tinged horsefly circled above them.

"There's our strip." Pantaleimon waved his knout.

Gregor unharnessed the weary bullocks. His ear-ring glittering, the old man went to look for the mark he had made at the end of the strip.

"Bring the scythes," he called out after a moment, waving his hand.

Gregor went to him, treading down the grass and leaving an undu-lating track behind him. Pantaleimon faced towards the distant bell-tower and crossed himself. His hook-nose shone as though freshly varnished, the sweat lingered in the hollows of his swarthy cheeks. He smiled, baring his white, gleaming teeth in his raven beard, and, with his wrinkled neck bent to the right, swept the scythe through the grass. A seven-foot half-circle of mown grass lay at his feet.

Gregor followed in his steps, laying the grass low with the scythe. The women's aprons blossomed in an outstretched rainbow before him, but his eyes sought only one, white with an embroidered border; he glanced at Aksinia and renewed his mowing, adjusting his own to his father's pace.

Aksinia was continually in his thoughts. Half-closing his eyes, in imagination he kissed her shamelessly and tenderly, spoke to her in burning and speechless words that came to his tongue he knew not whence. Then he dropped this line of thought, stepped out again methodically, one—two—three; his memory urged up frag-ments of the past . . . sitting under the damp hayrick . . . the moon over the meadow . . . rare drops falling from the bush into the puddle . . . one—two—three. . . . Good! Ah, that had been good!

He heard laughter behind him. He looked back: Daria was lying under the cart, and Aksinia was bent over her, telling her something. Daria waved her arms, and again they both laughed.

"I'll get to that bush and then I'll drop my scythe," Gregor thought. At that moment he felt the scythe pass through something soft and yielding. He bent down: a little wild duckling went scurrying into the grass with a squawk. By the hole where the nest had been, an-other was huddled, cut in two by the scythe. He laid the dead bird on his palm. It had evidently only come from the egg a few days previously; a living warmth was still to be felt in the down. With a sudden feeling of keen compassion he stared at the inert little ball lying in his hand.

"What have you found, Grishka?"

Dunia came dancing along the mown alley, her pigtails tossing on her breast. Frowning, Gregor threw away the duckling and angrily renewed his mowing.

After dinner the women began to rake the hay. The cut grass

sunned and dried, giving off a heavy, stupefying scent. Dinner was eaten in haste. Fat meat and the Cossacks' stand-by, sour milk: such was the entire repast.

"No point in going home!" Pantaleimon said after dinner; "we'll turn the bullocks to graze in the forest, and tomorrow as soon as the dew is off the grass we'll finish the mowing."

Dusk had fallen when they stopped for the day. Aksinia raked the last rows together and went to the cart to cook some millet mash. All day she had laughed evilly at Gregor, gazing at him with eyes full of hatred, as though in revenge for some great unforgettable injury. Gregor, gloomy and brooding, drove the bullocks down to the Don for water. His father had watched him and Aksinia all day. Staring unpleasantly after Gregor, he said:

"Have your supper and then guard the bullocks. See they don't get into the grass! Take my coat."

Daria laid the child under the cart and went into the forest with Dunia for brushwood.

Over the meadow the waning moon mounted the dark, inaccessible heaven. Moths sprinkled around the fire like early snow. The millet boiled in the smoky field-pot. Wiping a spoon with the edge of her underskirt, Daria called to Gregor:

"Come and have your supper."

His father's coat flung around his shoulders, Gregor emerged from the darkness and approached the fire.

"What has made you so bad-tempered?" Daria smiled.

"He doesn't want to watch the bullocks," Dunia laughed, and sitting down by her brother, she tried to start a conversation. But somehow her efforts were unsuccessful. Pantaleimon sipped his soup and crunched the under-cooked millet between his teeth. Aksinia ate without lifting her eyes, smiling half-heartedly at Daria's jokes. Her burning cheeks were flushed troubledly.

Gregor was the first to rise; he went off to the bullocks.

The fire burned low. The smouldering brushwood wrapped the little group in the honey scent of burning leaves.

At midnight Gregor stole up to the camp and halted some ten paces away. His father was snoring tunefully in the cart. The unquenched embers stared out from the ash with golden peacock's eyes.

A grey, shrouded figure broke away from the cart and came

slowly towards Gregor. When two or three paces away, it halted. Aksinia! Gregor's heart thumped fast and heavily; he stepped forward crouchingly, flinging back the edge of his coat, and pressed the compliant, fervently burning woman to himself. Her legs bowed at the knees; she trembled, her teeth chattering. Gregor suddenly flung her over his arm as a wolf throws a slaughtered sheep across its back and, stumbling over the trailing edges of his open coat, ran pantingly off.

"Oh, Grishka, Grishka! Your father . . ."

"Quiet!"

Tearing herself away, gasping for breath in the sour sheep's wool of the coat, abandoning herself to the bitterness of regret, Aksinia almost shouted:

"Put me down. What matter now? . . . I'll go of my own accord."

Not like an azure and blood-red blossom, but like wayside henbane is a woman's belated love.

After the mowing Aksinia was a changed woman: as though someone had set a mark, burned a brand on her face. When other women met her they snarled spitefully and nodded their heads after her. The maidens were envious, but she carried her happy, shameful head proudly and high.

Soon everybody knew of her liaison with Gregor Melekhov. At first it was talked about in whispers—only half-believed—but after the village shepherd had seen them in the early dawn close to the windmill, lying under the moon in the low-growing rye, the rumour spread like a turbid tidal wave.

It reached Pantaleimon's ears also. One Sunday he happened to go along to the Mokhovs' shop. The throng was so great that no more could have crowded through the door. He entered, and everybody seemed to be making way for him. He pushed towards the counter where the textiles were sold. The master, Mokhov, took it upon himself to attend to the old man.

"Where have you been all this long while, Prokoffich?" he asked.

"Too much to do. Troubles with the farm."

"What? Sons like yours, and troubles?"

"What of my sons? I've seen Piotra off to camp, and Grishka and I do everything."

Mokhov divided his stiff, ruddy beard in two with his fingers and significantly glanced out of the corners of his eyes at the crowd of Cossacks.

"Oh, yes, old lad, and why haven't you told us anything about it?" he asked.

"About what?"

"How do you mean, what? Thinking of marrying your son, and not one word to anybody!"

"Which son?"

"Why, your son Gregor isn't married."

"And at present he doesn't show any sign of marrying."

"But I've heard that your daughter-in-law's going to be—Stepan Astakhov's Aksinia."

"What? With her husband alive. . . . Why, Platonich, surely you're joking? Aren't you?" Pantaleimon stuttered.

"Joking? But I've had it from others."

Pantaleimon smoothed out the piece of material spread over the counter, then, turning sharply, limped towards the door. He made straight for home. He walked with his head bowed as usual, pressing his fingers into his fist, hobbling more obviously on his lame leg. As he passed the Astakhovs' hut he glanced through the wattle fence: Aksinia, swaying from the hips, spruce and looking younger than ever, was going into the hut with an empty bucket.

"Hey, wait!" he called, and pushed through the wicket gate. Aksinia halted and waited for him. They went into the hut. The cleanly swept earthen floor was sprinkled with red sand; on the bench in the corner were pastries fresh from the oven. From the kitchen came the smell of fusty clothes and sweet apples.

A large-headed tabby cat came up to make a fuss of Pantaleimon's legs. It arched its back and rubbed itself against his boots. He sent it flying against the bench and shouted:

"What's all this I hear? Eh? Your husband's traces not yet cold, and you already setting your cap at other men! I'll make Grishka's blood flow for this, and I'll write to your Stepan! Let him hear of it! . . . You whore, your bitch of a mother didn't beat you enough. Don't set your foot inside my yard from this day on. Carrying on with a young man, and when Stepan comes, and me, too . . ."

Aksinia listened with eyes contracted. And suddenly she shamelessly swept up the edge of her skirt, enveloped Pantaleimon in the smell of women's clothes, and came breasting at him with writhing lips and bared teeth.

"What are you to me, old man? Eh? Who are you, to teach me? Go and teach your own fat-bottomed woman! Keep order in your own yard! You limping, stump-footed devil! Clear out of here, don't foam at me like a wild boar, you won't frighten me!"

"Wait, you fool!"

"There's nothing to wait for! Get back where you came from! And if I want your Grishka, I'll eat him, bones and all! Chew that over! What if Grishka does love me? You'll punish him? . . . You'll write to my husband? Write to the ataman if you like, but Grishka belongs to me! He's mine! Mine! I have him and I shall keep him. . . ."

Aksinia pressed against the quailing Pantaleimon with her breast (it beat against her thin jacket like a bustard in a noose), burned him with the flame of her black eyes, overwhelmed him with more and more terrible shameless words. His eyebrows quivering, the old man retreated to the door, groped for the stick he had left in the corner, and waving his hand, pushed open the door with his bottom. Aksinia pressed him out of the porch, pantingly, frenziedly shouting:

"All my life I'll love him! Kill him if you like! He's my Grishka! Mine!"

Gurgling something into his beard, Pantaleimon limped off to his hut.

He found Gregor in the kitchen. Without saying a word, he brought his stick down over his son's back. Doubling up, Gregor hung on his father's arm.

"What's that for, Father?" he demanded.

"For your goings-on, you son of a bitch!"

"What goings-on?"

"Don't soil your neighbour! Don't disgrace your father! Don't run after women, you hound!" Pantaleimon snorted, dragging Gregor around the kitchen as his son tried to snatch away the stick.

"I'm not going to let you beat me!" Gregor cried hoarsely, and setting his teeth, he tore the stick out of his father's hand. Across his knee it went and—snap!

"I'll whip you publicly. You accursed son of the devil! I'll wed you to the village idiot! I'll geld you!" his father roared.

At the sound of fighting the old mother came running. "Pantaleimon, Pantaleimon! Cool down a little! Wait!" she exclaimed.

But the old man had lost his temper in earnest. He sent his wife flying, overthrew the table with the sewing-machine on it, and victoriously flew out into the yard. Gregor, whose shirt had been torn in the struggle, had not had time to fling it off when the door banged open and his father appeared once more like a storm-cloud on the threshold.

"I'll marry him off, the son of a bitch!" He stamped his foot like a horse and fixed his gaze on Gregor's muscular back. "I'll drive tomorrow to arrange the match. To think that I should live to see my son laugh in my face!"

"Let me get my shirt on, and get me married after," Gregor retorted.

"I'll marry you! I'll marry you to the village idiot!" The door slammed, the old man's steps clattered down the stairs and died away.

Beyond the village of Sietrakov the carts with tarpaulin covers stretched in rows across the steppe. At unbelievable speed a white-roofed and neat little town grew up, with straight streets and a small square in the centre where sentries kept guard.

The men lived the usual monotonous life of a training camp. In the morning the detachment of Cossacks guarding the grazing horses drove them into the camp. Then followed cleaning, grooming, saddling, the roll-call, and muster. The staff officer in command of the camp bawled stentoriously; the military commissary bustled around; the sergeants training the young Cossacks shouted their orders. They were assembled behind a hill for the attack, they cunningly encircled the "enemy." They fired at targets. The younger Cossacks eagerly vied with one another in the sabre exercises, the old hands dodged the fatigues.

About a week before the break-up of the camp Ivan Tomilin's wife came to visit him. She brought him some home-made cracknel, an assortment of dainties, and a sheaf of village news.

She left again very early in the morning, taking the Cossacks' greetings and instructions to their families and relations in the village. Only Stepan Astakhov sent no message back by her. He had fallen ill the evening before, had taken vodka to cure himself, and was incapable of seeing anything in the whole wide world, including

Tomilin's wife. He did not turn up on parade; at his request the doctor's assistant let his blood, setting a dozen leeches on his chest. Stepan sat in his undershirt against one wheel of his cart (making the white linen casing of his cap oily with cart grease) and with gaping mouth watched the leeches sucking at his swollen breasts and distending with dark blood.

Tomilin approached. He winked.

"Stepan, I'd like a word with you," he said.

"Well, get on with it."

"My wife's been here on a visit. She left this morning."

"Ah. . . ."

"There's a lot of talk about your wife in the village."

"What?"

"Not pleasant talk, either."

"Well?"

"She's playing about with Gregor Melekhov. Quite openly."

Turning pale, Stepan tore the leeches from his chest and crushed them underfoot. He crushed them to the very last one, buttoned up his shirt, and then, as though suddenly afraid, unbuttoned it again. His blenched lips moved incessantly. They trembled, slipped into an awkward smile, shrivelled and gathered into a livid pucker. Tomilin thought Stepan must be chewing something hard and solid. Gradually the colour returned to his face, the lips, caught by his teeth, froze into immobility. He took off his cap, smeared the grease over the white casing with his sleeve, and said aloud:

"Thank you for telling me."

"I just wanted to warn you. . . . You won't mind. . . ."

Tomilin commiseratingly clapped his hands against his trousers and went off to his horse. Stepan stood for a moment staring fixedly and sternly at the black smear on his cap. A half-crushed, dying leech crawled up his boots.

In ten more days the Cossacks would be returning from camp.

Aksinia lived in a frenzy of belated, bitter love. Despite his father's threats, Gregor slipped off and went to her at night, coming home at dawn.

For two weeks he had strained like a horse striving beyond its powers. With lack of sleep his brown face was suffused with a blue tinge, his tired eyes gazed wearily out of their sunken sockets. Aksinia went about with her face completely uncovered, the deep pits under her eyes darkened funereally, her swollen, slightly pouting, avid lips smiled troubledly and challengingly.

So extraordinary and open was their mad association, so ecstatically did they burn with a single, shameless flame, neither conscience-stricken nor hiding their love from the world, that people began to be ashamed to meet them in the street. Gregor's comrades, who previously had chaffed him about Aksinia, now silently avoided him or felt awkward and constrained in his company. In their hearts the women envied Aksinia, yet they condemned her, malevolently exulting at the prospect of Stepan's return and pining with bestial curiosity.

If Gregor had made some show of hiding the liaison from the world, and if Aksinia had kept her relations with Gregor comparatively secret, the world would have seen nothing unusual in it. The village would have gossiped a little and then forgotten all about it. But they lived together almost openly, they were bound by a mighty feeling which had no likeness to any temporary association, and the villagers held their breath in filthy expectation. Stepan would return and cut the knot.

Over the bed in the Astakhovs' bedroom ran a string threaded with decorative empty white and black spools. The flies spent their nights on the spools, and spiders' webs stretched from them to the ceiling. Gregor was lying on Aksinia's bare, cold arm and gazing up at the chain of spools. Aksinia's other hand was playing with the thick strands of hair on his head. Her fingers smelt of warm milk; when Gregor turned his head, pressing his nose into Aksinia's armpit, the pungent, sweetish scent of woman's sweat flooded his nostrils.

In addition to the wooden, painted bedstead with pointed pinecones at the corners, the room contained, close to the door, an iron-bound, capacious chest holding Aksinia's dowry and finery. In the corner was a table, an oleograph with General Skoboliov riding at a flapping banner dipped before him, two chairs, and above them ikons in miserable paper aureoles. Along the side wall were hung fly-blown photographs. One was of a group of Cossacks, with tousled heads, swelling chests decorated with watch-chains, and drawn sabres: Stepan with his comrades in army service. On a hook hung Stepan's uniform. The moon stared through the window and uncertainly fingered the two ornamental white knots on the shoulder-straps.

With a sigh Aksinia kissed Gregor on his brow between the eyes. "Grishka, my love," she said.

"What is it?" he asked.

"Only nine days left. . . ."

"That's not so soon."

"What am I to do, Grishka?"

"How am I to know?"

Aksinia restrained a sigh and again smoothed and parted Gregor's matted hair.

"Stepan will kill me," she half-asked, half-declared.

Gregor was silent. He wanted to sleep. With difficulty he forced open his clinging eyelids and saw right above him the bluish depths of Aksinia's eyes.

"When my husband returns, I suppose you will give me up. Are you afraid?" she asked.

"Why should I be afraid of him? You're his wife, it's for you to be afraid."

"When I'm with you I'm not afraid, but when I think about it in the daytime I'm frightened."

Gregor yawned and said:

"It isn't Stepan's return that matters. My father is talking of getting me married off."

He smiled and was going to add something, but beneath his head he felt Aksinia's hand suddenly wilt and soften, bury itself in the pillow, and after a moment harden again.

"Who has he spoken to?" she asked in a stifled voice.

"He's only talking about it. Mother said he's thinking of Korshunov's Natalia."

"Natalia—she's a beautiful girl. Too beautiful. . . . Well, and you'll marry her. I saw her in church the other day. Dressed up she was. . . ."

"Don't talk to me about her beauty. I want to marry you."

Aksinia sharply pulled her arm away from under Gregor's head and stared with dry eyes at the window. A frosty, yellow mist was

in the yard. The shed cast a heavy shadow. The crickets were chirruping. Down by the Don the bitterns boomed; their deep bass
tones came through the window.

"Grishka!" she said.

"Thought of something?"

Aksinia seized Gregor's rough, unyielding hands, pressed them to
her breast, to her cold, deathly cheeks, and cried:

"What did you take up with me for, curse you! What shall I do?
Grishka! . . . I am lost. . . . Stepan is coming, and what answer
shall I give him? . . . Who is there to look after me?"

Gregor was silent. Aksinia gazed mournfully at his handsome
eagle nose, his shadowed eyes, his dumb lips. . . . And suddenly a
flood of feeling swept away the dam of restraint. She madly kissed
his face, his neck, his arms, the rough, curly black hair on his chest,
and while gathering her breath, whispered (and Gregor felt her
body trembling):

"Grishka—my dearest—beloved—let us go away. My dear! We'll
throw up everything and go. I'll leave my husband and all else, so
long as you are with me. . . . We'll go far away to the mines. I
shall love you and care for you. I have an uncle who is a watchman
at the Paromonov mines; he'll help me. . . . Grishka! Say just one
little word!"

Gregor lay thinking, then unexpectedly opened his burning
Asiatic eyes. They were laughing, blinding with derision.

"You're a fool, Aksinia, a fool! You talk away, but you say nothing
worth listening to. Where shall I go to away from the farm? I've got
to do my military service next year. . . . I'll never stir anywhere
away from the land. Here there is the steppe, and something to
breathe—but there? Last summer I went with Father to the station.
I almost died. Engines roaring, the air heavy with burning coal.
How the people live I don't know; perhaps they're used to it!"
Gregor spat out and said again: "I'll never leave the village."

The night grew darker outside the window, a cloud passed over
the moon. The frosty yellow mist vanished from the yard, the
shadows were washed away, and it was no longer possible to tell
whether it was last year's brushwood or some old bush that loomed
darkly beyond the fence outside the window.

In the room also the shadows gathered. The knots on Stepan's
uniform faded, and in the grey, stagnant impenetrability Gregor

failed to see the fine shiver that shook Aksinia's shoulders, nor her head pressed between her hands and silently shaking on the pillow.

After the visit of Tomilin's wife Stepan's features noticeably darkened. His brows hung over his eyes, a deep and harsh frown puckered his forehead. In his sullen, seething rage Stepan carried his burden of sorrow like a horse bearing a rider. He talked but little with his comrades, began to quarrel over trifles, and would hardly look at Piotra Melekhov. The threads of friendship which had previously united them were snapped. They returned home enemies.

They set out for their village in the same group as before. Piotra's and Stepan's horses were harnessed to the wagon. Christonia rode behind on his own horse. Tomilin was suffering with a fever and lay covered with his coat in the wagon. Fiodot Bodovskov was too lazy to drive, so Piotra took the reins. Stepan walked along at the side of the wagon, lashing off the purple heads of the roadside thistles with his whip. Rain was falling. The rich black earth stuck to the wheels like grease. The sky was an autumnal blue, ashy with cloud. Night fell. No lights of any village were to be seen. Piotra belaboured the horses liberally with the knout. And suddenly Stepan shouted in the darkness:

"You, what the—you—! You spare your own horse and keep the knout on mine all the time."

"Watch more carefully! The one that doesn't pull is the one I whip up."

Stepan did not reply. They rode on for another half-hour in silence. The mud squelched beneath the wheels. The rain pattered noisily against the tarpaulin. Piotra dropped the reins and smoked, mentally reviewing all the insulting words he would use in the next quarrel with Stepan.

The wagon suddenly jolted and stopped. Slipping in the mud, the horses pawed the earth.

"What's the matter?" Stepan took alarm.

"Give us a light," Piotra demanded.

In front the horses struggled and snorted. Someone struck a match. A tiny orange ring of light, then darkness again. With trembling hands Piotra held the fallen horse down by the bridle.

The horse sighed and rolled over, the centre shaft groaned. Stepan struck a bundle of matches. His own horse lay with one foreleg thrust to the knee in a marmot's hole.

Christonia unfastened the traces.

"Unharness Piotra's horse, quickly," he ordered.

At last Stepan's horse was lifted with difficulty to its feet. While Piotra held it by the bridle, Christonia crawled on his knees in the mud, feeling the helplessly hanging leg.

"Seems to be broken," he boomed. "But see if he can walk."

Piotra pulled at the bridle. The horse hopped a step or two, not putting its left foreleg to the ground, and whinnied. Drawing on his greatcoat, Tomilin stamped about bitterly.

"Broken, is it? A horse lost!" he fumed.

Stepan, who all this while had not spoken a word, almost seemed to have been awaiting such a remark. Thrusting Christonia aside, he flung himself on Piotra. He aimed at his head, but missed and struck his shoulder. They grappled together and fell into the mud. There was the sound of a tearing shirt. Stepan got Piotra beneath him and, holding his head down with one knee, pounded away with his fists. Christonia dragged him off.

"What's that for?" Piotra shouted, spitting out blood.

"Don't drive off the road, you serpent!"

Piotra tore himself out of Christonia's hands.

"Now, now! You try fighting me!" Christonia roared, with one hand holding Piotra against the wagon.

They harnessed Bodovskov's small but sturdy horse with Piotra's. Christonia ordered Stepan to ride his horse, and himself crawled into the cart with Piotra. It was midnight when they arrived at a village. They stopped at the first hut, and Christonia begged a night's shelter.

Bodovskov led the horses in. He stumbled over a pig's trough thrown down in the middle of the yard, and cursed vigorously. They led the horses under the roof of the shed. Tomilin, his teeth chattering, went into the hut. Piotra and Christonia remained in the cart.

At dawn they made ready to set out again. Stepan came out of the hut, an ancient, bowed woman hobbling after him. She followed him under the shed.

"Which one is it?" she asked.

"The black," sighed Stepan.

The woman lay her stick on the ground and with an unusually

strong, masculine movement raised the horse's damaged leg. She felt the knee-cap carefully with her fine, crooked fingers. The horse set back its ears and reared on its hind legs with the pain.

"No, there's no break there, Cossack. Leave him and I'll heal him." Stepan waved his hand and went to the cart.

"Leave him or not?" the old woman blinked after him.

"Let him stay," he replied.

"I yearn after him, old woman! I'm pining away in my own eyes. I can't put tucks into my skirt fast enough. When he goes past the yard my heart burns. I'd fall to the ground and kiss his footprints. Help me! They're going to wed him off. . . . Help me, dear. . . . Whatever it costs, I'll give you. . . . My last shirt I'll give you, only help me!"

With luminous eyes set in a lacework of furrows the old crone Drozdikha looked at Aksinia, shaking her head at the girl's bitter story.

"Whose is the young man?"

"Pantaleimon Melekhov's."

"That's the Turk, isn't it?"

"Yes."

The old woman chewed away with her withered mouth and dallied with her answer.

"Come to me very early tomorrow, child, as soon as it is getting light. We'll go down to the Don, to the water. We'll wash away your yearning. Bring a pinch of salt with you."

Aksinia wrapped her face in her yellow shawl and crept cautiously out through the gate. Her dark figure was swallowed up in the night. Her steps died away. From somewhere at the end of the village came the sound of singing.

At dawn Aksinia, who had not slept a wink all night, was at Drozdikha's window.

"Old woman!" she called.

"Who's there?"

"It's me, Aksinia! Get up!"

They made their way by side-turnings down to the river. By the waterside the sand stung icily. A damp, chilly mist crept up from the Don.

Drozdikha took Aksinia's hand in her own bony hand and drew her towards the river.

"Give me the salt. Cross yourself to the sunrise," she told her.

Aksinia crossed herself, staring spitefully at the happy rosiness of the east.

"Take up some water in your palm and drink. Hurry!"

Aksinia drank. Like a black spider the old woman straddled over a lazily rolling wave, squatted down, and whispered:

"Prickly chilliness, flowing from the bottom. . . . Burning flesh. . . . A beast in the heart. . . . Yearning and fever. . . . By the holy cross, most holy, most immaculate Mother. . . . The slave of God, Gregor . . ." reached Aksinia's ears.

Drozdikha sprinkled some salt over the damp sand at her feet and some more into the water, then gave the rest to Aksinia.

"Sprinkle some water over your shoulder. Quickly!"

Aksinia did so. She stared sadly and spitefully at Drozdikha's russet cheeks.

"That's all, surely?" she asked.

"Yes, that's all."

Aksinia ran breathlessly home. The cows were lowing in the yard. Daria, sleepy-eyed and flushed, was driving her cows off to join the village herd. She smiled as she saw Aksinia run past.

"Slept well, neighbour?" she asked.

"Praise be!"

"And where have you been so early?"

"I had a call to make in the village."

The church bells were ringing for matins. The copper-tongued clanging rang out brokenly. The village herdsman cracked his stock-whip in the side street. Aksinia hurriedly drove out the cows, then carried the milk into the porch to strain it. She wiped her hands on her apron and, lost in thought, poured the milk into the strainer.

A heavy rattle of wheels and snorting of horses in the street. Aksinia set down the pail and went to look out of the front window. Holding the pommel of his sabre, Stepan was coming through the wicket gate. Aksinia crumpled her apron in her fingers and sat down on the bench. Steps up the stairs. . . . Steps in the porch. . . . Steps at the very door. . . .

Stepan stood on the threshold, gaunt and estranged.

"Well—" he said.

Aksinia, all her full, buxom body reeling, went to meet him.

"Beat me," she said slowly, and stood sideways to him.

"Well, Aksinia—"

"I shan't hide. Beat me, Stepan!"

Her head sunk on her breast, huddled into a heap, protecting only her belly with her arms, she faced him. Her eyes stared unwinkingly from their dark rings, out of her dumb, fear-distorted face. Stepan swayed and passed by her. The scent of male sweat and the bitter pungency of road travel came from his unwashed shirt. He dropped on the bed without removing his cap. He lay shrugging his shoulders, throwing off his sword-belt. His blond moustaches hung limply down. Not turning her head, Aksinia glanced sidelong at him. Stepan put his feet on the foot of the bed. The mud slowly slipped from his boots. He stared at the ceiling and played with the leather tassel of his sword.

"Had breakfast?" he asked.

"No. . . ."

"Get me something to eat."

He sipped some milk, wetting his moustache. He chewed slowly at the bread. Aksinia stood by the stove. In a burning terror she watched her husband's little gristly ears rising and falling as he ate.

Stepan slipped away from the table and crossed himself.

"Tell me all, dear," he curtly demanded.

With bowed head Aksinia cleared the table. She was silent.

"Tell me how you waited for your husband, how you defended a man's honour. Well?"

A terrible blow on the head tore the ground from Aksinia's feet and flung her towards the door. Her back struck against the doorpost, and she groaned heavily.

Not only a limp and feeble woman, but lusty and sturdy men could Stepan send flying with a well-aimed blow on the head. Whether fear lifted Aksinia or whether she was moved by a woman's vital nature—she lay a moment, rested, then scrambled on to all fours.

Stepan had lit a cigarette and was standing in the middle of the room yawning as she rose to her feet. He threw his tobacco-pouch on to the table, but Aksinia was already slamming the door behind her. He chased after her.

Streaming with blood, Aksinia ran towards the fence separating their yard from the Melekhovs'. Stepan overtook her at the fence.

His black hand fell like a hawk on her head. The hair slipped between his fingers. He tore at it and threw her to the ground.

What if a husband does trample his own wife with his boots? One-
armed Alexei Shamil walked past the gate, looked in, winked, and
split his bushy little beard with a smile; after all, it was very under-
standable that Stepan should be punishing his lawfully wedded
wife. Shamil wanted to stop to see whether he would beat her to
death or not, but his conscience would not allow him. After all, he
wasn't a woman.

Watching Stepan from afar, you would have thought someone
was doing the Cossack dance. And so Gregor thought, as through
the kitchen window he saw Stepan jumping up and down. But he
looked again and flew out of the hut. Pressing his fists against his
chest, he ran on his toes to the fence. Piotra followed him.

Over the high fence Gregor flew like a bird. He ran at full speed
into Stepan from behind. Stepan staggered, and turning round,
came at Gregor like a bear.

The Melekhov brothers fought desperately. They pecked at
Stepan like carrion-crows at a carcass. Gregor went several times to
earth, sent down by Stepan's knuckles. Sturdy Piotra was stout by
comparison with the stiffer-jointed Stepan, but he bent under the
blows like a reed before the wind, yet remained on his feet.

Stepan, one eye flashing (the other was going the colour of an
under-ripe plum), retreated to the steps.

Christonia happened to come along to borrow some harness from
Stepan, and he separated them.

"Stop that!" He waved his arms. "Break away or I'll report it to the
ataman."

Piotra cautiously spat blood and half a tooth into his palm and
said hoarsely:

"Come on, Gregor. We'll catch him some other time."

"Don't you try lying in wait for me!" Stepan threatened from the
steps.

"All right, all right!"

"And no 'all right' about it or I'll pull your guts out, soul and all."

"Is that serious or joking?"

Stepan came swiftly down the steps. Gregor broke forward to
meet him, but pushing him towards the gate, Christonia promised
him: "Only dare and I'll give you a good hiding."

Chapter 5

"Tell Piotra to harness the mare and his own horse," Pantaleimon ordered Gregor as, solemn as a churchwarden at Mass, and sweating like a bull, he sat finishing his soup. Dunia was vigilantly watching Gregor's every movement. Ilinichna, bobtailed, and looking important in her lemon-yellow Sunday shawl, a motherly anxiety lurking in the corners of her lips, said to the old man:

"Get some more down your neck, Prokoffich. You're starving yourself."

"No time to eat," he replied.

Piotra's long, wheaten-yellow moustaches appeared at the door. "Your carriage is ready, if you please!" he announced.

Dunia burst into a laugh and hid her face in her sleeve.

Ilinichna's shrewd widow cousin, Aunty Vasilisa, was to go with them as matchmaker. She was the first to nestle herself into the wagonette, twisting and turning her head, laughing, and displaying her crooked black teeth beneath the pucker of her lips.

"Don't show your teeth, Vasilisa," Pantaleimon warned her. "You'll ruin everything with your gap. Your teeth are set all drunk in your mouth; one one way and one the other. . . ."

"Ah, Dad, I'm not the bridegroom to be. . . ."

"Maybe you're not, but don't laugh, all the same."

Vasilisa took umbrage, but meantime Piotra had opened the gate. Gregor sorted out the smelly leather reins and jumped into the driver's seat. Pantaleimon and Ilinichna sat side by side at the back like two youngsters, with no room to give or take.

Gregor bit his lips and whipped up the horses. They pulled at the traces and started off without warning.

"Look out! You'll catch your wheel!" Daria shrilled, but the wagonette swerved sharply and, bouncing over the roadside hummocks, rattled down the street.

Leaning to one side, Gregor touched up Piotra's lagging horse with the whip. His father held his beard in his hand, afraid that the wind would catch and carry it away.

"Whip up the mare!" he cried hoarsely, bending towards Gregor's back. With the lace sleeve of her jacket Ilinichna wiped away the tear that the wind had brought to her eye and winkingly watched Gregor's blue satin shirt fluttering and billowing on his back. The Cossacks along the road stepped aside and stood staring after them. The dogs came running out of the yards and yelped under the horses' feet.

Gregor spared neither whip nor horses, and within ten minutes the village was left behind. Korshunov's large hut with its plank-fence enclosure was quickly reached. Gregor pulled on the reins, and the wagonette suddenly stopped at the painted, finely fretted gates.

Gregor remained with the horses; Pantaleimon limped towards the steps. Ilinichna and Vasilisa sailed after him with rustling skirts. The old man hurried, afraid of losing the courage he had summoned up during the ride. He stumbled over the high step, knocked his lame leg, and frowning with pain, clattered up the well-swept stairs.

He and Ilinichna entered the kitchen almost together. He disliked standing at his wife's side, as she was taller by a good six inches; so he stepped a pace forward and, removing his cap, crossed himself to the black ikon.

"Good health to you!" he said.

"Praise be!" the master of the house, a stocky, tow-haired old man replied, rising from the bench.

"Some guests for you, Miron Gregorievich," Pantaleimon continued.

"Guests are always welcome. Maria, give the visitors something to sit on."

His elderly, flat-chested wife wiped non-existent dust from three stools and pushed them towards the guests. Pantaleimon sat down on the very edge of one and mopped his perspiring brow with his handkerchief.

"We've come on business," he began without beating about the bush. At this point Ilinichna and Vasilisa, pulling up their skirts, also sat down.

"By all means; on what business?" The master smiled.

Gregor entered, stared around him and greeted the Korshunovs. Across Miron's freckled face spread a vivid russet. Only now did he guess the object of the visit. "Have the horses brought into the yard. Get some hay put down for them," he ordered his wife.

"We've just a little matter to talk over," Pantaleimon went on, twisting his curly beard and tugging at his ear-ring in his agitation. "You have a girl unmarried, we have a son. Couldn't we come to some arrangement? We'd like to know. Will you give her away now, or not? And we might become relations?"

"Who knows?" Miron scratched his bald spot. "I must say, we weren't thinking of giving her in marriage this autumn. We've our hands full with work here, and she's not so very old. She's only just past her eighteenth spring. That's right, isn't it, Maria?"

"That will be it."

"She's the very age for marriage," Vasilisa joined in. "A girl soon gets too old!" She fidgeted on her stool, prickled by the besom she had stolen from the porch and thrust under her jacket. Tradition had it that matchmakers who stole the girl's besom were never refused.

"Proposals came for our girl away back in early spring. Our girl won't be left on the shelf. We can't grumble to the good God. . . . She can do everything, in the field or at home . . ." Korshunov's wife replied.

"If a good man were to come along, you wouldn't say no," Pantaleimon broke into the women's cackle.

"It isn't a question of saying no." The master scratched his head. "We can give her away at any time."

The negotiations were on the point of breaking down. Pantaleimon began to get agitated, and his face flooded with beet juice, while the girl's mother clucked like a sitting hen shadowed by a kite. But Vasilisa intervened in the nick of time. She poured out a flood of quiet, hurrying words, like salt on a fire, and healed the breach.

"Now, now, my dears! Once a matter like this is raised, it needs to be settled decently and for the happiness of your child. Even Natalia—and you might search far in broad daylight and not find another like her!—work burns in her hands! What a capable woman! What a housewife! And for her, as you see for yourselves, good folk"—she opened her arms in a generous sweep, turning to Pantaleimon and bridling Ilinichna. "He's a husband worthy of any. As I look at him my heart beats with yearning, he's so like my late husband, and his family are great workers. Ask anyone in these parts about Prokoffich. In all the world he's known as an honest man and a good. . . . In good faith, do we wish evil to our children?"

Her chiding little voice flowed into Pantaleimon's ears like syrup. He listened, pulling the little tufts of black hair from his nostrils with his middle and index fingers, and thinking rapturously: "Ah, the smooth-tongued devil, how she talks! You can get what she's driving at! Another woman would stun a Cossack with her many words. . . . And this from a petticoat!" He was lost in admiration of Vasilisa, who was fulsomely praising the girl and her family as far back as the fifth generation.

"Of course, we don't wish evil to our child," Maria declared.

"The point is it's early to give her in marriage," the master said pacifically, beaming with a smile.

"It's not early, true God! Not early," Pantaleimon rejoined.

"Sooner or later we have to part with her," the mistress sobbed, half-hypocritically, half in earnest.

"Call your daughter, Miron Gregorievich, and let's look at her."

"Natalia!"

A girl appeared timidly at the door, her swarthy fingers fiddling with the gathering of her apron.

"Come in! Come in! She's shy," the mother encouraged her, smiling through her tears.

Gregor looked at her.

Bold grey eyes under a dusty black scarf. A shallow, rosy dimple in the elastic cheek. Gregor turned his eyes to her hands: they were large and marred with hard work. Beneath the short green jacket embracing the strong body, the small, maidenly, firm breasts rose and fell, outlined naïvely and pitifully; their sharp little nipples showed like buttons.

In a moment Gregor's eyes had run over all of her, from the head to the arched, beautiful feet. He looked her over as a horse-dealer surveys a mare before purchase, thought: "She'll do," and met her eyes, directed stubbornly at him. The simple, sincere, slightly embarrassed gaze seemed to be saying: "Here am I all, as I am. As you wish, judge of me." "Splendid!" Gregor replied with his eyes and a smile.

"Well, that's all." Her father waved her out.

As she closed the door behind her, Natalia looked at Gregor without attempting to conceal her smile and her curiosity.

"Listen, Pantaleimon Prokoffievich," Korshunov began, after exchanging glances with his wife, "you talk it over, and we'll talk it over among the family. And then we'll decide whether we'll call it a match or not."

As he went down the steps, Pantaleimon slipped in a last word: "We'll call again next Sunday."

Korshunov remained deliberately silent, pretending he had not heard.

Only after he learned of Aksinia's conduct from Tomilin did Stepan, nursing his pain and hatred in his soul, realize that, despite his poor sort of life with her, he loved her with a dreary, hateful love. He had lain in the wagon at night, covered with his coat, his arms flung above his head, and thought of how his wife would greet him on his return home. His eyes veiled with their black lids, he had lain thinking over a thousand details of his revenge.

From the day of his homecoming an unseen spectre dwelt in the Astakhovs' hut. Aksinia went about on tiptoe and spoke in whispers, but in her eyes, sprinkled with the ash of fear, lurked a little spark left from the flame Gregor had kindled.

As he watched her, Stepan felt rather than saw this. He tormented himself. Nights, when the drove of flies had fallen asleep on the crossbeam, and Aksinia had made the bed, he beat her, his hairy hand pressed over her mouth. He demanded shameless details of her relations with Gregor. Aksinia tossed about on the hard bed and could hardly breathe. Tired of torturing her soft body, he passed his hand over her face, seeking for tears. But her cheeks were burningly dry.

"Will you tell?" he demanded.

"No!"

"I'll kill you!"

"Kill me, kill me, for the love of Christ! This isn't life. . . ."

Grinding his teeth, Stepan twisted the fine skin, all damp with sweat, on her womanly breast. Aksinia shuddered and groaned.

"Hurts, does it?" Stepan said jocularly.

"Yes, it hurts."

"And do you think it didn't hurt me?"

It would be late before he fell asleep. In his sleep he clenched his fists. Rising on her elbow, Aksinia gazed at her husband's face, handsome and changed in slumber. Throwing her head back on the pillow, she whispered to herself.

She hardly saw Gregor now. She happened to meet him once down by the Don. Gregor had driven the bullocks down to drink and was coming up the slope, waving a switch and watching his steps. Aksinia was going down to the Don. She saw him and felt the yoke of the buckets turn cold in her hands and the blood boil in her veins.

Afterwards, when she recalled the meeting, she found it difficult to convince herself that it had really happened. Gregor noticed her when she was all but passing him. At the insistent scrape of the buckets he raised his head, his eyebrows quivered, and he smiled stupidly. Aksinia gazed right through his head at the green waves of the Don and beyond to the ridge of sandy headland.

"Aksinia!" he called.

She walked on several paces and stood with her head bent as though before a blow. Angrily whipping a lagging bullock, he said without turning his head:

"When is Stepan going out to cut the rye?"

"He's getting ready now."

"See him off, then go to our sunflower patch and I'll come along after."

Her pails scraping, Aksinia went down to the Don. The foam serpentined along the shore in an intricate yellow lacework on the green hem of the wave. White seagulls were hovering and mewing above the river. Tiny fish sprinkled in a silver rain over the surface of the water. On the other side, beyond the white of the sandy headland, the grey tops of ancient poplars rose haughtily and sternly. As Aksinia was drawing water she dropped her pail. Raising her skirt, she waded in up to her knees. The water swirled and tickled her calves, and for the first time since Stepan's return she laughed quietly and uncertainly.

She glanced back at Gregor. Still waving his switch, he was slowly climbing the slope. With eyes misty with tears Aksinia caressed his strong legs as they confidently trod the ground. His broad-legged trousers, gathered into white woollen stockings, were gay with crimson stripes. On his back, by one shoulder-blade, fluttered a strip of freshly torn dusty shirt, and through the hole showed a triangle of swarthy flesh. With her eyes Aksinia kissed this tiny scrap of the beloved body which once had been hers; the tears fell over her pallid, smiling lips.

She set her pails down on the sand to hook them on to the yoke and noticed the traces of Gregor's boots. She looked stealthily around: no one in sight except some boys bathing from the distant strand. She squatted down and covered the footprint with her palm, then rose, swung the yoke across her shoulders, and hastened home, smiling at herself.

Caught in a muslin mistiness, the sun was passing over the village. Beyond the curly flock of little white clouds spread a deep, cool, azure pasture. Over the burning iron roofs, over the deserted dusty streets, over the farmyards with their parched, yellow grass, hung a deathly sultriness.

As Aksinia approached the steps, Stepan, in a broad-brimmed straw hat, was harnessing the horses to the reaping machine. He flung his sailcloth coat over the front seat and took up the reins.

"Open the gate," he told her.

As she did so, she ventured to ask:

"When will you be back?"

"Towards evening. I've agreed to reap with Anikushka. Take the food along to him. He'll be coming out to the fields when he's finished at the smith's."

The wheels of the reaping machine squeaked, and carved into the grey plush of the dust. Aksinia went into the hut and stood a moment with her hand pressed to her head, then, flinging a kerchief over her hair, ran down to the river.

"But supposing he returns? What then?" the thought suddenly burned into her mind. She stopped as though she saw a deep pit at her feet, glanced back, and sped almost at a run along the river-bank to the meadows.

Fences. Gardens. A yellow sea of sunflowers outstaring the sun. The pale green of potato plants. There were the Shamil women hoeing their potato-patch, their bowed backs in rose-coloured shirts. Reaching the Melekhovs' garden, Aksinia glanced around, then lifted the wattle hasp and opened the gate. She followed the path along to the green thicket of sunflower stems. Stooping, she pressed into the midst of them, smothering her face with golden pollen, and lifting her skirt, sat down on the ground.

She listened: the silence rang in her ears. Somewhere above her was the lonely drone of a bee. For perhaps half an hour she sat thus, torturing herself with doubt. Would he come? She was about to go and was adjusting her kerchief when the gate scraped heavily.

"Aksinia!"

"This way," she called.

"Aha; so you've come, then!" Rustling the leaves, Gregor approached and sat down at her side.

Their eyes met. And in reply to Gregor's mute inquiry she broke into weeping.

"I've no strength. . . . I'm lost, Grishka."

"What does he do?"

Wrathfully she tore open the collar of her jacket. On the rosy, girlishly swelling breasts were numerous cherry-blue bruises.

"Don't you know? He beats me every day. He is sucking my blood. . . . And you're a fine one. Soiled me like a dog, and off you go. . . . You're all . . ." She buttoned her jacket with trembling fingers, and, frightened lest he was offended, glanced at Gregor, who had turned away.

"So you're trying to put the blame on me?" he said slowly, biting a blade of grass.

"And aren't you to blame?" she cried fiercely.

"A dog doesn't worry an unwilling bitch."

Aksinia hid her face in her hands. The strong, calculated insult came like a blow.

Frowning, Gregor glanced sidelong at her. A tear was trickling between her first and middle fingers. A broken, dusty sun-ray gleamed on the transparent drop and dried its damp trace on her skin.

Gregor could not endure tears. He fidgeted in disquiet, ruthlessly brushed a brown ant from his trousers, and glanced again at Aksinia. She sat without changing her position, but three runnels of tears were now chasing down the back of her hand.

"What's the matter? Have I offended you? . . . Aksinia! Now, wait! Stop, I want to say something."

She tore her hands from her face. "I came here to get advice. What did you come for? It's bitter enough as it is. And you—I didn't come to fasten myself on you. Don't be afraid," she panted.

At that moment she really believed that she had not come to

fasten herself on Gregor, but as she had run along by the Don she had vaguely thought: "I'll talk him over! Who else am I to live with?" Then she had remembered Stepan and had obstinately shaken her head, driving away the troublesome thought.

"So our love is done with?" Gregor asked, and turned on to his stomach, supporting himself on one elbow and spitting out the rosy petals of the flower he had been chewing.

"How, done with?" Aksinia took alarm. "How?" she insisted, trying to look into his eyes.

He turned his eyes away.

The dry, exhausted earth smelt of moisture and sun. The wind rustled among the sunflower leaves. For a moment the sun was darkened, overcast by a fleeting cloud; and over the steppe, over the village, over Aksinia's moody head, fell a smoky shadow.

Gregor sighed—his sigh was like that of a horse with a sore throat —and lay on his back, warming his shoulders against the hot soil.

"Listen, Aksinia," he began slowly, "I've—got—an idea. I've been thinking . . ."

Through the garden came the creaking sound of a cart, and a woman's voice: "Gee up, baldhead!"

To Aksinia the call seemed so close that she dropped full length to the ground. Raising his head, Gregor whispered:

"Take your kerchief off. It shows up. . . . They mayn't have seen us."

She removed her kerchief. The burning breeze wandering among the sunflowers played with the wisps of golden down on her neck. The noise of the cart slowly died away.

"And this is what I've been thinking," Gregor began again. Then, more animatedly: "What's done can't be undone. Why try to fix the blame? Somehow we've got to go on living. . . ."

Aksinia listened anxiously, breaking a stalk in her hand as she waited. She looked into Gregor's face and caught the dry and sober glitter of his eyes.

"I've been thinking, let us put an end to . . ."

Aksinia swayed. Her fingers contorted and her nostrils distended as she awaited the end of the sentence. A fire of terror and impatience avidly licked her face, her mouth went dry. She thought he was about to say: "put an end to Stepan," but he vexatiously licked his writhing lips and said:

". . . put an end to the story. Eh?"

Aksinia stood up and, pressing through the swaying, yellow heads of the sunflowers, went towards the gate.

"Aksinia!" Gregor called in a strangled voice. The gate scraped.

He threw off his cap so that the crimson band should not be seen, and stared after Aksinia. It was not she that he saw—it was not her usual virile, swinging walk—but another, an unknown and a stranger.

Immediately after the rye was cut, and before it could be carried to the barns, the wheat ripened. In the clayey fields and on the slopes the parching leaves turned yellow and wilted into tubes, and the stalks withered.

The harvest was good, everybody joyfully remarked. The ears were full, the grain heavy and large. But since the spring the grain had been affected by a drought coming from the east, so the stalks were short and the straw worthless.

After talking the matter over with Ilinichna, Pantaleimon decided that if the Korshunovs agreed to the match, the wedding would have to be postponed until the 1st of August. He had not yet called on the Korshunovs for an answer; first the harvesting had to be done, and then he had waited for a convenient holiday.

The Melekhovs set out to begin reaping on a Friday. Pantaleimon stripped a wagon and prepared the under-frame for carrying the sheaves. Piotra and Gregor went to the fields to reap. Piotra rode and Gregor walked alongside. Gregor was moody, and knobs of flesh went quivering up from the lower jaw to his cheekbones. Piotra knew this to be a sure sign that his brother was seething and ready for a quarrel, but, smiling behind his wheaten moustache, he set to work to tease Gregor.

"God's truth, she told me herself!" he declared.

"Well, what if she did?" Gregor muttered, chewing the down of his moustache.

"'As I'm on my way back from town,' she says, 'I hear voices in the Melekhovs' sunflower patch.'"

"Piotra, stop it!"

"'Yes, voices. And I glance through the fence. . . .'"

Gregor blinked, and he went grey. "Will you stop it, oi мn', you?" he demanded.

"You're a queer lad! Let me finish!"

"I warn you, Piotra, we shall come to blows," Gregor threatened, falling behind.

Piotra raised his eyebrows and turned round in his seat to face Gregor.

"'. . . I glance through the fence, and there I see them, the two lovers, lying in each other's arms!' she says. 'Who?' I asked, and she answers: 'Why, Aksinia and your brother.' I say . . .'"

Seizing the handle of a pitchfork lying at the back of the reaping machine, Gregor flung himself at his brother. Piotra dropped the reins, leaped from his seat, and sprang in front of the horses.

"Pah, the devil!" he exclaimed. "He's gone crazy! Pah! Just look at him. . . ."

Baring his teeth like a wolf, Gregor threw the pitchfork at his brother. Piotra dropped to his hands and knees, and flying over him, the pitchfork buried its points a couple of inches into the earth and stuck upright, whanging and quivering.

Scowling, Piotra caught at the bridles of the startled horses and swore lustily. "You might have killed me, you swine!"

"Yes, and I would have killed you!"

"You're a fool, a mad devil. You're your father's son all right, you true Turk."

Gregor pulled the pitchfork out of the ground and followed after the reaping machine. Piotra beckoned to him with his finger.

"Come here! Give me that pitchfork," he ordered.

He passed the reins into his left hand and took the pitchfork by the prongs. Then with the handle he struck Gregor across the spine.

"A strap would have been better," he grumbled, keeping his eyes on Gregor, who had leaped away. After a moment or two they lit cigarettes, stared into each other's eyes, and burst into peals of laughter.

Christonia's wife, who was driving home along another road, had seen Gregor attack his brother. She stood up in her wagon, balancing precariously on the rye sheaves; but she could not see what happened, as the Melekhovs' reaping machine and horses were between her and the brothers. Hardly had she reached the village street when she cried to a neighbour:

"Klimovna! Run and tell Prokoffievich the Turk that his boys have been fighting with pitchforks close to the Tatar mound. Gregor

jabbed Piotra in the side with the fork, and then Piotra gave him—
The blood poured out. It was horrible!"

Meantime the brothers had begun reaping. Piotra was growing
hoarse with bawling at the tired horses, and Gregor, his dusty foot
resting on the crossbar, was pitchforking the swathes off the reaper.
Reaping was in progress all over the steppe. The blades of the machines rattled and groaned, the steppe was spotted with swathes
of corn. Mimicking the drivers, the marmots whistled in the hollows.

"Two more lengths and we'll stop for a smoke!" Piotra shouted
above the noise of the machine. Gregor nodded. He could hardly
open his parched lips. He gripped his pitchfork closer to the prongs
in order to get a better leverage on the heavy swathes and breathed
spasmodically. A bitter perspiration poured down his face and stung
in his eyes like soap. Halting the horses, they had a drink and a
smoke.

"There's someone riding a horse pretty hard along the road,"
Piotra remarked, shading his eyes with his palm.

Gregor stared, and raised his eyebrows in astonishment.

"It's Father, surely?"

"You're mad! What could he be riding? We've got both horses
here."

"It's him! God's truth, it's Father."

The rider drew nearer, and after a moment he could be seen
clearly. "Yes, it's Father!" Piotra began to dance in anxious surprise.

"Something happened at home," Gregor gave expression to the
thought troubling them both.

When still a hundred yards away, Pantaleimon reined his horse in.
"I'll thrash you, you sons of a bitch!" he yelled, waving his leather
whip above his head.

"What on earth—!" Piotra was completely flabbergasted, and
thrust half his moustache into his mouth.

"Get the other side of the reaper! By God, he'll lash us with that
knout; while we're getting to the bottom of it he'll whip our guts
out." Gregor smiled, putting the machine between himself and his
father.

The foaming horse came over the swathes of grain at a trot. His
feet knocking against the horse's sides (for he was riding bareback),
Pantaleimon shook his whip. "What have you been up to out here,
you children of the devil?" he demanded.

"We've been reaping, as you can see." Piotra swept his arms around, nervously eyeing the whip.

"Who's been sticking which with the fork? What have you been fighting about?"

Turning his back on his father, Gregor began in a loud whisper to count the clouds.

"What fork? Who's been fighting?" Piotra looked his father up and down.

"Why, she came running, the daughter of a hen, and shrieking: 'Your boys have stuck each other with pitchforks.' Eh? What do you say to that?" Pantaleimon shook his head ecstatically and, dropping the reins, jumped off his horse. "I borrowed a horse and came out at a gallop. Eh?"

"Who told you all this?" Piotra asked.

"A woman!"

"She was lying, Father. She must have been asleep in her wagon and dreamt it."

"A petticoat again!" Pantaleimon half-shouted, half-whistled, slobbering down his beard. "That hen, Klimovna! My God! Eh? I'll whip the bitch!" He danced with rage.

Shaking with silent laughter, Gregor kept his eyes fixed on the ground. Piotra did not remove his eyes from his father, who was stroking his perspiring brow.

Pantaleimon danced to his heart's content and then calmed down. He took the seat of the reaping machine and reaped a couple of lengths, then mounted his horse and rode back to the village. He left his forgotten whip lying on the ground. Piotra picked it up and swung it appraisingly, remarking to his brother:

"We'd have had a bad time, young man. This isn't a whip! It would have maimed you, brother. It could cut your head clean off."

The Korshunovs had the reputation of being the richest family in the village of Tatarsk. They had fourteen pairs of bullocks, horses, mares from stud farms, fifteen cows, innumerable other cattle, a flock of several hundred sheep. Their iron-roofed house was as good as that of Mokhov the merchant: it had six panelled rooms. The yard was paved with new and handsome tiles. The garden covered a good three acres. What more could man want?

So it was rather timidly and with secret reluctance that Pantaleimon had paid his first visit to the Korshunovs to propose the match. The Korshunovs could find a much richer husband than Gregor for their daughter. Pantaleimon knew this and was afraid of a refusal. He did not like to go begging to Korshunov, but Ilinichna ate into him like rust into iron, and at last she overcame the old man's obstinacy. So he drove one day to the Korshunovs' for an answer, heartily cursing Gregor and Ilinichna and the whole wide world.

Meantime, beneath the painted iron roof of the Korshunovs' hut a burning dissension had arisen. After the Melekhovs' departure Natalia declared to her father and mother:

"If Gregor loves me, I'll never wed another."

"She's found herself a bridegroom, the idiot," her father replied. "Only he's as black as a gypsy. My little berry, I didn't want you to have a husband like that."

"I want no other, Father." The girl flushed and began to weep. "You can take me to the convent otherwise."

"He's too fond of walking the streets, he's a woman-chaser, he runs after grass-widows," her father played his last card.

"Well, let him!"

Natalia, the eldest daughter, was her father's favourite, and he had not pressed her into a marriage. Proposals for her hand had been plentiful, some coming from distant villages, from rich, Old Believer Cossacks. But Natalia had not taken to any of the prospective bridegrooms, and nothing had come of them.

In his heart Miron liked Gregor for his Cossack skill, his love of farming and hard work. He had picked him out among the crowd of village youths when Gregor had won the first prize in the horse-races, but he thought it a little humiliating to give his daughter to a poor man, one, moreover, who had gained a bad notoriety.

"A hard-working lad and a good-looking," his wife whispered to him at night, stroking his freckled, hairy hand. "And Natalia has quite lost her heart to him. . . ."

Miron turned his back to his wife's cold, withered breast and snorted angrily:

"Dry up, you turnip! God has taken away your reason. Good-looking!" he stuttered. "Will you reap a harvest off his mug? It's a come-down for me to give my daughter to the Turks!"

"They're a hard-working family and comfortably off," his wife whispered, and moving closer to her husband's back, pacifyingly stroked his hand.

"Hey, the devil! Get away, can't you? Leave me a little room! What are you stroking me for as if I was a cow with calf? And you know what Natalia is! She'd fall for anything in trousers."

"You should have some feeling for your child," she murmured right into his hairy ear. But Miron pressed himself against the wall and began to snore as though falling off to sleep.

The Melekhovs' arrival for an answer caught the Korshunovs in confusion. They came just after matins. As Ilinichna set her foot on the step of the wagonette she nearly overturned it, but Pantaleimon jumped down from the seat like a young cockerel.

"There they are! What devil brought them here today?" Miron groaned, as he looked out of the window.

"Good health!" Pantaleimon crowed, stumbling over the doorstep. He was at once abashed by the loudness of his own voice and attempted to amend matters by stuffing a good half-pound of his black beard into his mouth and crossing himself unnecessarily before the ikon.

"Good day," Miron replied, staring at them askance.

"God is giving us good weather."

"Praise be, and it's lasting."

"The people will be a little better off for it."

"That's so."

"Ye-e-es."

"Ahem."

"And so we've come, Miron Gregorievich, to find out what you have come to among yourselves—whether we are to make a match of it or not."

"Come in, please; sit down, please," Maria welcomed them, bow-ing and sweeping the floor with the edge of her long, pleated skirt.

Ilinichna sat down, her poplin coat rustling. Miron Gregorievich rested his elbows on the new French cloth of the table, and was silent. The French cloth was adorned with pictures of the late Czar and Czarina in the corners, while in the centre were the august Imperial Princesses in white hats, and the fly-blown Czar Nicholas Alexandrovich.

Miron broke the silence.

"Well . . . we've decided to give our daughter. So we shall be kinsmen if we can agree on the dowry."

At this point, from somewhere in the mysterious depths of her glossy, puff-sleeved jacket, and apparently from behind her back, Ilinichna drew out a great loaf of white bread and smacked it down on the table. For some unknown reason Pantaleimon wanted to cross himself, but his withered talon fingers, set to the appropriate sign and raised half the requisite distance, suddenly changed their form. Against its master's will the great black thumb slipped unexpectedly between the index and middle fingers, and this shameless bunch of fingers stealthily slipped behind the open edge of his blue overcoat and drew out a red-headed bottle.

Blinking excitedly, Pantaleimon glanced at Miron's freckled face and caressingly slapped the bottle's broad bottom.

"And now, dear friends, we'll offer up a prayer to God and drink and talk of our children and the marriage agreement," he proposed.

Within an hour the two men were sitting so close together that the greasy rings of Melekhov's beard were groping among the straight red strands of Korshunov's. Pantaleimon's breath smelt sweetly of pickled cucumbers as he argued over the amount of the marriage settlement.

"My dear kinsman," he began in a hoarse whisper.

"My dearest kinsman," he repeated, raising his voice to a shout.

"Kinsman," he roared, baring his great, blunt teeth. "Your demands are far too heavy for me to stand. Think, dear kinsman, think how you are trying to shame me. Gaiters with galoshes, one; a fur coat, two; two woollen dresses, three; a silk kerchief, four. That means ruin to me."

Pantaleimon opened his arms wide. Miron drooped his head and stared at the French cloth, flooded with spilt vodka and pickled cucumber water. He read the inscription written in a sportive scroll at the top: "The Russian Autocrats." He brought his eyes lower. "His Imperial Majesty and Sire Emperor Nicholas. . . ." A potato-skin lay over the rest. He stared at the picture. The Emperor's features were not visible, an empty vodka bottle stood on them. Blinking reverently, Miron attempted to make out the style of the rich uniform with its white belt, but it was thickly covered with slippery cucumber seeds. The Empress stared self-satisfiedly out of a broad-brimmed hat, surrounded by the circle of insipid daughters. Miron felt so affronted that tears almost came to his eyes. "You look very proud now, like a goose staring out of a basket, but wait till you have to give your daughters away to husbands, then I shall stare, and you'll flutter," he thought.

Pantaleimon droned on into his ear like a great black bumble-bee. He raised his tearfully misty eyes and listened.

"In order to make such a gift in exchange for your, and now we can say our, daughter—these gaiters and galoshes and fur coats—we shall have to drive a cow to the market and sell it."

"And do you begrudge it?" Miron struck the table with his fist.

"It isn't that I begrudge it—"

"Do you begrudge it?"

"Wait, kinsman!"

"And if you do begrudge it—the devil take you!" Miron swept his perspiring hand over the table and sent the glasses to the floor.

"A cow sold from the yard!" Pantaleimon shook his head.

"There has to be a gift. She has a dowry chest of her own, and you take heed of what I say if you've taken to her. That's our Cossack custom. That's how it was of old, and we stick to the old ways."

"I do take heed!"

"Take heed!"

"I do take heed!"

"And let the youngsters fend for themselves. We've fended for ourselves, and we live as well as anybody. Let them do the same!"

The two men's beards mingled in a varicoloured weave. Pantaleimon began to eat a juiceless, shrivelled cucumber and wept with mixed, conflicting feelings.

The kinswomen were sitting locked in an embrace on a chest, deafening each other with the cackle of their voices. Ilinichna burned with a cherry-coloured flush; Maria was green with vodka, like a winter pear caught by the frost.

"Two such children you won't find anywhere else in the world. She'll be dutiful and obedient and will never say a word to contradict you," said Maria.

"My dear," Ilinichna interrupted her, supporting her cheek with her left hand and holding her left elbow in her right hand, "so I've told him, I don't know how many times, the son of a swine. He was getting ready to go out the other Sunday evening and I said to him: 'When will you throw her over, you accursed heathen? How long have I got to go on standing this shame in my old age? That Stepan will stop your little game one fine day!' "

Mitka stared into the room through the door crack, and below him Natalia's two younger sisters whispered to each other. Natalia herself was sitting in the farther room, wiping her tears on the tight sleeve of her jacket. She was afraid of the new life opening before her, oppressed by the unknown.

In the front room the third bottle of vodka was finished; it was decided to bring the bridegroom and the bride together on the 1st of August.

The Korshunovs' hut hummed like a beehive with the bustle of preparations for the wedding. Underclothes were hurriedly sewn for the bride. Natalia sat every evening knitting her bridegroom the traditional gloves and scarf of goat's wool. Her mother sat till dusk bent over a sewing-machine, assisted by a hired sempstress. When Mitka returned with his father and the hands from the fields, he did not stop to wash or pull off his heavy farming boots, but went to keep Natalia company. He found great satisfaction in tormenting his sister.

"Knitting?" he would ask briefly, nodding at the scarf.

"Yes; what of it?"

"Knit away, you idiot; but instead of being grateful to you, he'll break your nose."

"What for?"

"Oh, I know Gregor; he's a friend of mine. He's that sort, he'll bite and not say what it's for."

"Don't tell lies. You think I don't know him."

"But I know him better. We went to school together."

Natalia grew angry, choked down her tears, and bent a miserable face over the scarf.

"But the worst of all is he's got consumption. You're a fool,

Natalia! Throw him over! I'll saddle the horse and ride over and tell them. . . ."

Natalia was rescued from Mitka by Grandfather Grishaka, who came into the room, groping over the floor with his knobbly stick and stroking his hempen-yellow beard. Poking his stick into Mitka's side, he asked:

"What are you doing here, eh?"

"I came to pay a visit, Grand-dad," Mitka said apologetically.

"To pay a visit? Well, I tell you to get out of here. Quick march!"

Grand-dad Grishaka had walked the earth for sixty-nine years. He had taken part in the Turkish campaign of 1877, had been orderly to General Gurko, but had fallen into disfavour and been sent back to his regiment. He had been awarded the Cross of St. George and two medals for distinction under fire at Plevna and Rossitz. And now, living with his son, enjoying the universal respect of the village for the clarity of his mind, his incorruptible honesty, and his hospitable ways, he was spending his few remaining years turning over memories.

In the summer he sat from dawn till dusk on the ledge in front of the hut, drawing his stick over the ground, his head bowed. The broken visor of his cap threw a dark shade over his closed eyes. The black blood flowed sluggishly through the fingers curved over his stick, through the swollen veins on his hands.

"Are you afraid to die, Grand-dad?" Natalia would ask.

The old man twisted his withered neck as though working it free of the stiff collar of his uniform coat and shook his greenish-grey whiskers.

"I wait for death as I would for a dear guest. It's time—I've lived my days, I've served my Czars and drunk vodka enough in my day," he replied with a smile.

Natalia would stroke her grandfather's hand and leave him still bowed, scraping in the earth with his stick. He took the news of Natalia's approaching marriage with outward calm, but inwardly he grieved and was furious. At table Natalia always gave him the choicest pieces; she washed his linen, mended and knitted his stockings, his trousers and shirts. And so when the old man heard the news, he gave her harsh, stern looks for a couple of days.

"The Melekhovs are famous Cossacks. I served in the same regiment as Prokoffey. But what are his grandsons like? Eh?" he asked Miron.

"They're not too bad," Miron replied evasively.

"That Gregor's a disrespectful lad. I was coming from church the other day and he passed me without a word of greeting. The old men don't get much respect these days. . . . Well, so long as Natalia likes him . . ."

He took almost no part in the negotiations; he came out of the kitchen and sat down at the table for a moment or two, drank a glass of vodka, and then, feeling himself getting drunk, went off again. For two days he silently watched the happy Natalia, then evidently softened in his attitude.

"Natalia!" he called to her. "Well, my little granddaughter, so you're very happy, eh?"

"I don't rightly know, myself, Grand-dad," Natalia confided.

"Well, well! Christ be with you. God grant . . ." and he bitterly and spitefully upbraided her. "I didn't think you'd be going off while I was alive . . . my life will be bitter without you."

Mitka was listening to their talk, and he remarked:

"You're likely to live another hundred years, Grandfather. And is she to wait all that time? You're a fine one!"

The old man turned almost purple with anger. He rapped with his stick and feet. "Clear off, you son of a bitch! Clear off, I say! You devil's demon! Who told you to listen?"

The wedding was fixed to take place on the first day after the feast. On the Day of the Assumption Gregor came to visit his future bride. He sat at the round table in the best room, shelled sunflower seeds and nuts with the bride's girl friends, then drove away again. Natalia saw him off. Under the roof of the shed, where his horse was standing saddled with a smart new saddle, she slipped her hand into her breast, and flushing, gazing at him with eyes expressive of her love, she thrust a soft little bundle, warm from her breast, into his hand. As he took the gift, Gregor dazzled her with the whiteness of his wolfish teeth, and asked:

"What is it?"

"You'll see. I've sewn you a tobacco-pouch."

Gregor irresolutely drew her towards himself, wanting to kiss her; but she held him off forcefully with her hands against his chest, bent herself back, and turned her eyes fearfully towards the window of the hut.

"They'll see us!" she whispered.

"Let them!"

"I'm ashamed to!"

Natalia held the reins while he mounted. Frowning, Gregor caught the stirrup with his foot, seated himself comfortably in the saddle, and rode out of the yard. She opened the gate and stood gazing after him. Gregor sat his horse with a slight list to the left, dashingly waving his whip.

"Eleven more days," Natalia mentally calculated, and sighed and smiled.

Chapter 6

The green, spike-leafed wheat breaks through the ground and grows; within a few weeks a rook can fly into its midst and not be seen. The grain sucks the juices from the earth and comes to ear, it swells with the sweet and scented milk; then it flowers and a golden dust covers the ear. The farmer goes out into the steppe and stands gazing, but cannot rejoice. Wherever he looks, a herd of cattle has strayed into the corn; they have trodden the laden grain into the glebe. Wherever they have thronged is a circle of crushed wheat; the farmer grows bitter and savage at the sight.

So with Aksinia. Over her feelings, ripened to golden flower, Gregor had trodden with his heavy, rawhide boots. He had sullied them, burnt them to ash—and that was all.

As she came back from the Melekhovs' sunflower garden Aksinia's spirit grew empty and wild, like a forgotten farmyard overgrown with goose-grass and scrub. She walked along chewing the ends of her kerchief, and a cry swelled her throat. She entered the hut and fell to the floor, choking with tears, with torment, with the dreary emptiness that lashed through her head. But then it passed. The piercing pain was drawn down and exhausted at the bottom of her heart.

The grain trampled by the cattle stands again. With the dew and the sun the trodden stalks rise; at first bowed like a man under a too heavy burden, then erect, lifting their heads; and the days shine on them and the winds set them swinging.

At night, as she passionately caressed her husband, Aksinia thought of another, and hatred was mingled with a great love in her heart. The woman mentally planned a new dishonour—yet the old infamy; she was resolved to take Gregor from the happy Natalia, who had known neither the bitterness nor the joy of love. She lay thinking over her plans at night, with Stepan's heavy head resting on her right arm. Aksinia lay thinking, but only one thing could she resolve firmly: she would take Gregor from everybody else, she would flood him with love, she would possess him as before she had possessed him.

During the day Aksinia drowned her thoughts in cares and household duties. She met Gregor occasionally and would turn pale, proudly carrying her beautiful body that yearned so after him, gazing shamelessly, challengingly into the black depths of his eyes.

After each meeting Gregor was seized with yearning for her. He grew angry without cause, and poured out his wrath on Dunia and his mother, but most frequently he took his cap, went out into the back yard, and chopped away at the stout brushwood until he was bathed in perspiration. It made Pantaleimon curse:

"The lousy devil, he's chopped up enough for a couple of fences. You wait, my lad! When you're married you can chop away at that! That'll soon take it out of you!"

Four gaily-decorated pair-horsed wagonettes were to drive to fetch the bride. A crowd of village folk in holiday attire thronged around them as they stood in the Melekhovs' yard.

Piotra was the best man. He was dressed in a black frock-coat and blue-striped trousers, his left arm was bound with two white kerchiefs, and he wore a permanent, unchanging smile under his wheaten whiskers.

"Don't be shy, Gregor," he said to his brother. "Hold your head up like a young cock!"

Daria, as slender and supple as a willow switch, attired in a woollen, raspberry-coloured skirt, gave Piotra a nudge.

"Time you were off," she reminded him.

"Take your places," Piotra ordered. "On my wagon five and the bridegroom." They climbed into the wagonettes. Red and triumphant, Ilinichna opened the gates. The four wagonettes chased after one another along the street.

Piotra sat at Gregor's side. Opposite them Daria waved a lace handkerchief. The ruts and bumps interrupted their voices raised in a song. The crimson bands of the Cossack caps, the blue and black uniforms and frock-coats, the sleeves bound with white kerchiefs, the scattered rainbow of the women's kerchiefs, the gay skirts, and muslin trains of dust behind each wagonette made a colourful picture.

Gregor's second cousin, Anikhy, drove the bridegroom's wagonette. Bowed over the tails of the horses, almost falling off his seat, he cracked his whip and whistled, and the perspiring horses pulled harder at the tautened traces.

"Get a move on!" Ilia Ozhogin, the bridegroom's uncle on his mother's side, roared as he tried to overtake them with the second wagonette. Gregor recognized Dunia's happy face behind his uncle's back.

"No you don't!" Anikhy shouted, jumping to his feet and emitting a piercing whistle. He whipped up the horses into a frenzied gallop. "You'll fall!" Daria exclaimed, embracing Anikhy's polished top-boots with her arms. "Hold on!" Uncle Ilia called at their side, but his voice was lost in the continual groan and rattle of the wheels.

The two other wagonettes, tightly packed with men and women, drove along side by side. The horses were decorated with red, blue, and pale rose pompons, paper flowers, and ribbons woven into their manes and forelocks. The wagonettes rumbled over the bumpy road, the horses threw off flakes of soapy foam, and the pompons on their wet, foaming backs danced and ruffled in the wind.

At the Korshunovs' gate a horde of urchins was on the look-out for the cavalcade. They saw the dust rising from the road and ran into the yard bawling:

"They're coming!"

The wagonettes came rattling up to the gate. Piotra led Gregor to the steps, the others followed behind.

The door from the porch to the kitchen was shut fast. Piotra knocked.

"Lord Jesus Christ, have mercy on us!" he intoned.

"Amen!" came from the other side of the door.

Piotra repeated the words and the knock three times, each time receiving the same answer.

"May we come in?" he then asked.

"By all means."

The door was thrown open. The parents' representative, Natalia's godmother, greeted Piotra with a curtsy and a fine, raspberry-lipped smile. "Take this for your health's sake, best man!" she said, handing him a glass of bitter, overfresh kvass. Piotra smoothed his whiskers, drank it down, and spluttered amid a general restrained laugh:

"Well, you've made me welcome! You wait, my blackberry, I'll not treat you like that. I'll make you pay for it!"

While the best man and Natalia's godmother were competing in a duel of wits, the relatives of the bridegroom were brought three glasses of vodka each, in accordance with the marriage agreement.

Natalia, already attired in her wedding dress and veil, was behind the table, guarded by her two sisters. Maria held a rolling-pin in her outstretched hand, and Aggripina, a challenging fervour in her eyes, shook a poker. Sweating, and slightly intoxicated with vodka, Piotra bowed and offered them a fifty-kopek piece in his glass. But Maria struck the table with her rolling-pin.

"Not enough! We shan't sell the bride!" she declared.

Once more Piotra offered them a pinch of small silver in the glass.

"We won't let you have her!" the sisters said firmly, elbowing aside the downcast Natalia.

"Here, what's all this? We've already paid and overpaid," Piotra protested.

"Back you get, girls!" Miron ordered, and smilingly pressed towards the table. At this signal the bride's relatives and friends seated around the table stood up and made room for the newcomers.

Piotra thrust the end of a shawl into Gregor's hand, jumped on to a bench, and led him to the bride, who had seated herself beneath the ikons. Natalia took the other end of the shawl in her moist and agitated hand, Gregor sat down beside her.

There was a champing of teeth around the table; the guests tore the boiled chicken into pieces with their hands, afterwards wiping them on their hair. As Anikhy chewed at a handful of chicken the yellow grease ran down his bare chin on to his collar.

With a feeling of self-pity Gregor stared first at his own and Natalia's spoons tied together by a handkerchief, then at the vermicelli smoking in a bowl. He badly wanted to eat, his stomach was rolling over with hunger. But the marriage custom forbade.

The guests ate long and heartily. The smell of resinous masculine sweat mingled with the more caustic and spicy scent of the women. From the skirts, frock-coats and shawls, long packed in chests, came the odour of naphthaline.

Gregor glanced sidelong at Natalia. And for the first time he noticed that her upper lip was swollen and hung like the peak of a cap over her under lip. He also noticed that on the right cheek, below the upper jaw-bone, was a brown mole, and that two golden hairs were growing out of the mole; and for some reason this irritated him. He recalled Aksinia's slender neck with its curly, fluffy locks, and he had the feeling that someone had dropped a handful of prickly hay down his back. He bristled and with a suppressed feeling of wretchedness watched the others munching, chewing, and smacking their lips.

When he got up from the table someone, breathing the sour scent of wheaten bread over him, poured a handful of grain down the leg of his boot in order to protect him against the evil eye. All the way back to his own hut the grain hurt his feet; moreover, the tight collar-band of his shirt choked him and in a cold, desperate fury Gregor muttered curses to himself.

On its return the procession was met by the old Melekhovs. Pantaleimon, his silver-streaked black beard glistening, held the ikon, and his wife stood at his side, her thin lips set stonily.

Beneath a shower of hops and wheat grain Gregor and Natalia approached them to receive their blessing. As he blessed them tears ran down Pantaleimon's face, and he frowned and fidgeted, annoyed that anyone should be witness of his weakness.

The bride and bridegroom went into the hut. Daria went to the steps to look for Piotra and ran into Dunia.

"Where's Piotra?" she demanded.

"I haven't seen him."

"He ought to go for the priest, and he's nowhere to be found, curse him!"

She found Piotra, who had drunk more vodka than was good for him, lying in a cart, groaning. She seized him like a kite a lamb. "You've overeaten, you image! Get up and run for the priest!" she raged.

"Clear off! Who are you ordering about?" Piotra protested.

With tears in her eyes Daria thrust two fingers into his mouth, gripped his tongue, and helped him to ease himself. Then she poured a pitcher of cold well-water over him, wiped him as dry as she could, and took him to the priest.

Less than an hour later Gregor was standing at Natalia's side in the church, clutching a wax candle in his hand, his eyes wandering over the wall of whispering people around him, and mentally repeating the importunate words: "I'm done now. I'm done now!" Behind him Piotra coughed. Somewhere in the crowd he saw Dunia's eyes twinkling; he thought he recognized other faces. He caught the dissonant chorus of voices and the droning responses of the deacon. He was fettered with apathy. He walked round the lectern, treading on the down-at-heel shoes of Father Vissarion; he halted when Piotra gave a gentle tug at his frock-coat. He stared at the flickering little tongues of candle-flame, and struggled with the sleepy torpor which had taken possession of him.

"Exchange rings!" he heard Father Vissarion say.

They obeyed. "Will it be over soon?" Gregor mutely asked, as he caught Piotra's gaze. And the corners of Piotra's lips twitched, stifling a smile. "Soon now." Then Gregor kissed his wife's moist, insipid lips, the church began to smell foully of extinguished candles, and the crowd pressed towards the door.

Holding Natalia's large, rough hand in his, Gregor went out into the porch. Someone clapped his hat on his head. A warm breeze from the east brought the scent of wormwood to his nostrils. The cool of evening came from the steppe. Lightning flickered beyond the Don, rain was coming; outside the white church fence, above the hum of voices he heard the inviting and tender tinkle of the bells on the restive horses.

The Korshunovs did not arrive at the Melekhovs' hut until after the bridegroom and bride had gone to the church. Pantaleimon went several times to the gate to see whether they were coming, but the grey road, lined with a growth of prickly thorns, was completely deserted. He turned his eyes towards the Don. The forest was turning a golden yellow. The ripened reeds bent wearily over the Donside marshes. Blending with the dusk, an early autumnal, drowsy, azure haze enwrapped the village. He gazed at the Don, the chalky ridge of hills, the forest lurking in a lilac haze beyond the river, and the steppe. At the turn beyond the crossroads the fine outline of the wayside shrine was silhouetted against the sky.

Pantaleimon's ears caught the hardly audible sound of wheels and the yapping of dogs. Two wagonettes turned out of the square into the street. In the first sat Miron with his wife at his side; opposite them was Grand-dad Grishaka in a new uniform, wearing his Cross of St. George and his medals. Mitka drove, sitting carelessly on the box and not troubling to show the foaming horses his whip.

Pantaleimon threw open the gate, and the two wagonettes drove into the yard. Ilinichna sailed down from the porch, the hem of her dress trailing in the dust.

"Of your kindness, dear friends! Do our poor hut the honour of entering." She bent her corpulent waist in a bow.

His head on one side, Pantaleimon flung open his arms and welcomed them: "We humbly invite you to come in!"

He called for the horses to be unharnessed and went towards the newcomers. After exchanging greetings they followed their host and hostess into the best room, where a crowd of already half-intoxicated guests was sitting around the table. Soon after their arrival the newly married couple returned from the church. As they entered, Pantaleimon poured out a glass of vodka, tears standing in his eyes.

"Well, Miron Gregorievich, here's to our children! May their life be filled with good, as ours has been. May they live happily, and enjoy the best of health."

They poured Grandfather Grishaka out a large glass of vodka and succeeded in sending half of it into his mouth and half behind the stiff collar of his uniform. Glasses were clinked together. The company drank and drank. The hubbub was like the noise of a market. A distant relation of the Korshunovs, Koloveidin, who was sitting at the end of the table, raised his glass and roared:

"It's bitter!"

"Bitter! Bitter!" the guests seated around the table clamoured after him.

"Oh, bitter!" came the response from the crowded kitchen.

Scowling, Gregor kissed his wife's insipid lips and sent a venomous glance around the room. A crimson fever of faces. Coarse, drunkenly muddy glances and smiles. Mouths chewing greedily, slobbering on the embroidered tablecloth. A howl of voices.

Koloveidin opened wide his gap-toothed mouth, and raised his glass:

"It's bitter!"

"Bitter!" the cry was taken up once more.

Gregor stared hatefully into Koloveidin's mouth and noticed the livid tongue between his teeth as he cried the word: "Bitter!"

"Kiss, little chicks!" Piotra spluttered.

In the kitchen Daria, flushed and intoxicated, began a song. It was taken up by the others and passed into the best room. The voices blended, but above all the rest rose Christonia's rumble, shaking the window-panes.

The song ended, eating was resumed.

"Try this mutton!"

"Take your hand away, my husband's looking."

"Bitter! Bitter!"

In the kitchen the groaning floor shook, heels clattered, and a glass fell to the floor; its jangle was lost in the general hubbub. Across the heads of those sitting at the table Gregor glanced into the kitchen. The women were dancing now, to the accompaniment of shouts and whistles. They shook their ample bottoms (there was not a thin one there, for each was wearing five or six skirts), waved lace handkerchiefs, and worked their elbows in the dance.

The music of the three-tiered accordion sounded imperatively. The player began the tune of the Cossack dance. A shout went up:

"A circle! Form a circle!"

"Squeeze up a bit!" Piotra demanded, pushing the women aside.

Gregor roused himself and winked at Natalia. "Piotra's going to dance the 'Cossack'! You watch him!"

"Who with?" she asked.

"Don't you see? With your mother."

Maria Lukinichna set her arms akimbo, her handkerchief in her left hand. Piotra went up to her with mincing steps, dropped to his haunches and rose again, and returned backward to his place. Lukinichna picked up her skirt as though about to trip across a damp meadow, picked out the tempo with her toe, and danced amid a howl of approbation, kicking out her legs like a man.

The accordion-player accelerated the tempo. But Piotra kept pace with the music, dancing with incredibly small steps, then with a shout dropped to a squatting position and danced around, smacking the palms of his hands against the legs of his boots, biting the ends of his moustache in the corner of his mouth. He swung his knees in and out at great speed; his forelock tossed on his head.

Gregor's view was blocked by the crowd at the door. He heard only the shouts of the drunken guests and the continual rattle of the iron-shod heels, like the crackle of a burning pine board.

Then Miron danced with Ilinichna; they stepped out seriously and with their accustomed businesslike air. Pantaleimon stood on a stool watching them, dangling his lame leg and clicking his tongue. Instead of his legs his lips and ear-ring danced.

Others not so expert tried to dance the Cossack and other difficult dances. But the crowd shouted at them:

"Don't spoil it!"

"Smaller steps! Oh, you—!"

"His legs are light enough, but his bottom gets in his way."

"Oh, get on with it!"

Long ere this Grandfather Grishaka was completely drunk. He embraced the bony back of his neighbour on the bench and buzzed like a gnat in his ear:

"What year did you first see service?"

His neighbour, an old man stunted like an ancient oak, replied:

"1839, my son!"

"When?" Grishaka stuck out his ear.

"1839, I told you."

"What's your name? What regiment did you serve in?"

"Maxim Bogatiriev. I was a corporal in Baklanov's regiment."

"Are you of Melekhov's family?"

"What?"

"Your family, I asked."

"Aha! I'm the bridegroom's grandfather on his mother's side."

"In Baklanov's regiment, did you say?"

The old man gazed at Grishaka with faded eyes and nodded.

"So you must have been through the Caucasian campaign?"

"I served under Baklanov himself and helped in the Caucasian conquest. We had some rare Cossacks in our regiment. They were as tall as the guards, but stooped a little, long-armed and broad-shouldered. That's the men we had, my son! His Excellency the dead general was good enough to give me the cat for stealing a carpet. . . ."

"And I was in the Turkish campaign. Eh? Yes, I was there." Grishaka threw out his sunken chest, jingling with medals.

". . . We took a village at dawn, and at midday the bugler sounded the alarm," the old man continued without heeding Grishaka.

"We were fighting around Rossitz, and our regiment, the Twelfth Don Cossack, was engaged with the janizaries," Grishaka told him.

"As I was in a hut the bugler sounded the alarm. . . ."

"Yes," Grishaka went on, beginning to get annoyed and angrily waving his hand. "The Turkish janizaries wear white sacks on their heads. Eh? White sacks on their heads."

". . . The bugler sounded the alarm, and I said to my comrade: 'We'll have to retreat, Timofei, but first we'll have that carpet off the wall.'"

"I have been decorated with two Georges, awarded for heroism under fire. I took a Turkish major alive." Grandfather Grishaka began to weep and bang his withered fist on his neighbour's spine. But the latter, dipping a piece of chicken in the cherry jelly, lifelessly stared at the soiled tablecloth and mumbled:

"And listen what sin the unclean spirit led me into, my son! I'd never before taken anything that wasn't mine, but now I happened to see that carpet, and I thought: 'That would make a good horse-cloth.'"

"I've seen those parts myself. I've been in lands across the sea as well," Grishaka tried to look his neighbour in the eyes, but the deep sockets were overgrown with a shaggy bush of eyebrows and beard. So he resorted to craft. He wanted to win his neighbour's attention for the climax of his story, and he plunged into the middle of it without any preliminaries: "And the captain gives the order: 'In troop columns at the gallop! Forward!' "

But the old Baklanov regiment Cossack threw back his head like a charger at the sound of the trumpet and, dropping his fist on the table, whispered: "Lances at the ready; draw sabres, Baklanov's men!" His voice suddenly grew stronger, his faded eyes glittered and burned. "Baklanov's boys!" he roared, opening wide his toothless yellow jaws. "Into attack—forward!"

And he gazed at Grishaka with a youthful and intelligent look and let the tears trickling over his beard fall unwiped.

Grishaka also grew excited:

"He gave us this command and waved his sword. We galloped forward, and the janizaries were drawn up like this," he drew an irregular square on the tablecloth with his finger, "and firing at us. Three times we charged them. Each time they beat us back. Whenever we tried, their cavalry came out of a little wood on their flank. Our troop commander gave the order and we turned and went at them. We smashed them. Rode them down. What cavalry in the world can stand up against Cossacks? They fled into the wood; I see their officer just in front of me, riding on a bay. A good-looking officer, black-whiskered. He looks back at me and draws his pistol. He shot, but he missed me. I spurred my horse and caught up with him. I was going to cut him down, but then I thought better of it. After all, he was a man too. I seized him round the waist with my right arm, and he flew out of the saddle. He bit my arm, but I took him all the same. . . ."

Grishaka glanced triumphantly at his neighbour, but the old man's great angular head had fallen on his chest and he was snoring comfortably.

Chapter 7

Sergei Platonovich Mokhov could trace his ancestry a long way back.

During the reign of Peter I a State barge was travelling down the Don to Azov with a cargo of biscuit and gunpowder. The Cossacks of the little robber town of Chigonak, nestling on the bank of the upper Don, fell on the barge by night, destroyed the sleepy guards, pillaged the biscuit and gunpowder, and sank the vessel.

The Czar ordered out soldiers from Voronezh, and they burned down the town of Chigonak, ruthlessly put the guilty Cossacks to the sword, and hanged forty of them on a floating gallows, which, as a warning to the unruly villages, was sent sailing down the Don.

Some ten years later the spot where the hearths of the Chigonak huts had smoked began again to be inhabited. At the same time, on the Czar's instructions, a secret agent, a Russian peasant named Mokhov, came to live there. He traded in knife-hafts, tobacco, flints, and the other odds and ends necessary to the Cossacks' everyday life. He bought up and resold stolen goods, and once or twice a year journeyed to Voronezh, ostensibly to replenish his stocks, but in reality to report to the authorities on the state of the district.

From this Russian peasant, Nikitka Mokhov, descended the merchant family of Mokhovs. They took deep root in the Cossack earth; they multiplied and grew into the district like a sturdy field bush, reverently preserving the half-rotten credentials given to their ancestor by the Governor of Voronezh. The credentials might have been preserved until this day but for a great fire which occurred during the lifetime of Sergei Mokhov's grandfather. This Mokhov had already ruined himself once by card-playing, but was getting on his feet again when the fire engulfed everything. After burying his paralytic father, Sergei Platonovich had to begin afresh, starting by buying bristles and feathers. For five years he lived miserably, swindling and squeezing the Cossacks of the district out of every kopek. Then he suddenly jumped from "cattle-dealer Seriozhka" to "Sergei Platonovich," opened a little haberdashery shop, married the daughter of a half-demented priest, received no small dowry with her, and set up as a retail dealer in linen goods. Sergei Platonovich began to trade in textiles at just the right moment. On the instruction of the army authorities, about this time the Cossacks were migrating in entire villages from the left bank of the Don, where the ground was unproductive and sandy, to the right bank. And instead of having to journey thirty miles or more for goods, they found Sergei Mokhov's shop, packed with attractive commodities, right on the spot. Sergei extended his business widely, like a three-tiered accordion, and traded in everything requisite to simple village life. He even began to supply agricultural machinery. Evidently his trading yielded the quick-witted Sergei considerable profit, for within three years he had opened a grain elevator, and two years after the death of his first wife he began the construction of a steam flour-mill.

He squeezed Tatarsk and the neighbouring villages tightly in his swarthy fist. There was not a hut free from debt to Sergei Mokhov. Nine hands were employed at the mill, seven in the shop, and four watchmen: all together twenty mouths dependent on the merchant's pleasure for their daily bread. He had two children by his first wife: the girl Elizabieta and the sluggish, scrofulous Vladimir. His second wife, Anna, was childless. All her belated mother-love and accumulated spleen were poured out on the children. Her nervous temperament had a bad influence on them, and their father paid them no more attention than he gave his stable-hand or cook. His business activities occupied all his time. The children grew up uncontrolled. His insensitive wife made no attempt to penetrate into the secrets of the child mind, and the brother and sister were alien to each other, different in character and unlike their parents. Vladimir was sullen, sluggish, with a sly look and an unchildish seriousness. Liza, who lived in the society of the maid and the cook (the latter a dissolute, much too experienced woman), early saw the seamy side of life. The women aroused an unhealthy curiosity in her, and while still an angular and bashful adolescent she had grown as wild as a spurge.

The impatient years slipped by. The old grew older and the young grew green of leaf.

Vladimir Mokhov, a slender, sickly yellow lad now in the fifth class of the high school, was walking through the mill yard. He had recently returned home for the summer vacation, and, as usual, he had gone to look at the mill and jostle among the crowd. It ministered to his vanity to hear the respectful murmur of the Cossack carters:

"The master's heir. . . ."

Carefully picking his way among the wagons and the heaps of

dung, Vladimir reached the gate. Then he remembered he had not been to see the power plant and turned back.

Close to the red oil-tank, at the entrance to the machine room, Timofei, the mill-hand, Valet, the scalesman, and Timofei's assistant, David, were kneading a great ring of clay with bare feet, their trousers turned up above their knees.

"Ah! Here's master!" the scalesman jokingly greeted him.

"Good afternoon. What is it you're doing?"

"We're mixing clay," David said with an unpleasant smile, with difficulty drawing his feet out of the clinging mass. "Your father is careful of the rubles and won't hire women to do it. Your father's stingy," he added.

Vladimir flushed. He suddenly felt an invincible dislike for the ever smiling David and his contemptuous tone.

"What do you mean, 'stingy'?"

"He's terribly mean," David explained with a smile.

The others laughed approvingly. Vladimir felt all the smart of the insult. He stared coldly at David.

"So you're—dissatisfied?" he asked.

"Come into this mess and mix it for yourself, and then you'll know. What fool would be satisfied? It would do your father good to do some of this. It would give him a pain in the belly," David replied. He trod heavily around the ring of clay, kneading it with his feet, and now smiling gaily. Foretasting a sweet revenge, Vladimir turned over a fitting reply in his mind.

"Good!" he said slowly. "I'll tell Papa you're not satisfied with your work."

He glanced sidelong at the man's face and was startled by the impression he had caused. David was smiling miserably and forcedly, and the faces of the others were clouded over. All three went on kneading the clay in silence for a moment. Then David tore his eyes away from his muddy feet and said in a wheedlingly spiteful tone:

"I was only joking, Volodia."

"I'll tell Papa what you said." Affronted, with tears in his eyes for his father and himself, Vladimir walked away.

"Volodia! Vladimir Sergeivich!" David called after him in alarm, and stepped out of the clay, dropping his trousers over his bespattered legs.

Vladimir halted. David ran to him, breathing heavily.

"Don't tell your father! Forgive me, fool that I am. True God, I said it without thinking."

"All right, I won't tell him," Vladimir replied with a frown, and walked on towards the gate.

"What did you want to say that for?" Valet's bass voice reached his ears. "Don't stir them up and they won't trouble you."

"The swine!" Vladimir thought indignantly. "Shall I tell Father or not?" Glancing back, he saw David wearing his everlasting smile and decided: "I will tell him!"

Vladimir went up the stairs of the house. Over him swayed the leaves of the wild vine, thickly enlaced in the porch and veranda. He went to his father's private room and knocked. Sergei Platonovich was sitting on a cool leather couch, turning over the pages of a June magazine. A yellow bone paper-knife lay at his feet.

"Well, what do you want?"

"As I was coming back from the mill—" Vladimir began uncertainly. But then he recalled David's dazzling smile, and gazing at his father's corpulent belly, he resolutely continued:

"I heard David, the mill-hand, say . . ."

Sergei Platonovich listened attentively to his son's story, and said: "I'll fire him." He bent with a groan to pick up the paper-knife.

Of an evening the intelligentsia of the village were in the habit of gathering at Sergei Mokhov's house. There was Boyarishkin, a student of the Moscow Technical School; the teacher Balanda, eaten up with conceit and tuberculosis; his assistant and cohabitant, Martha Gerasimovna, a never-ageing girl with her petticoat always showing indecently; the postmaster, a bachelor smelling of sealing-wax and cheap perfumes. Occasionally the young troop commander Eugene Listnitsky rode over from his father's estate. The company would sit drinking tea on the veranda, carrying on a meaningless conversation, and when there was a lull in the talk, one of the guests wound up and set going the host's expensive inlaid phonograph.

On rare occasions, during the great holidays, Sergei Platonovich liked to cut a dash: he invited guests and regaled them on expensive wines, fresh caviar, and the finest of hors-d'œuvres. At other times he lived frugally. The one thing in regard to which he exercised no self-restraint was the purchase of books. He loved reading and had a mind quick to assimilate all he read.

The two village priests, Father Vissarion and Father Pankraty, were not on friendly terms with Sergei Platonovich. They had a long-standing quarrel with him. Nor were they on very amicable terms with each other. The fractious, intriguing Father Pankraty cleverly perverted his fellow human beings, and the naturally affable, syphilitic widower Father Vissarion, who lived with a Ukrainian housekeeper, held himself aloof and had no love for Father Pankraty because of his inordinate pride and intriguing character.

All except the teacher Balanda owned their own houses. Mokhov's blue-painted house stood on the square; right opposite, at the heart of the square, straddled his shop with its glass door and faded signboard. Attached to the shop was a long, low shed with a cellar, and a hundred yards farther on rose the brick wall of the church garden and the church itself with its green, onion-shaped cupola. Beyond the church were the whitewashed, authoritatively severe walls of the school, and two smart-looking houses, one blue, with blue-painted palisades, belonging to Father Pankraty; the other brown (to avoid any resemblance), with carved fencing and a broad balcony, belonging to Father Vissarion. Then came another two-storeyed house, then the post office, the thatched and iron-roofed huts of the Cossacks, and finally the sloping back of the mill, with rusty iron cocks on its roof.

The inhabitants of the village lived behind their barred and bolted shutters, cut off from all the rest of the world, both outside and inside the village. Every evening, unless they were paying a visit to a neighbour, each family shot the bolts of their doors, unchained their dogs in the yards, and only the sound of the night watchman disturbed the silence.

One day towards the end of August, Mitka Korshunov happened to meet Elizabieta Mokhov down by the river. He had just rowed across from the other side, and as he was tying up his boat he saw a gaily decorated, light craft skimming the stream. The skiff was being rowed by the young student Boyarishkin. His bare head glistened with perspiration, and the veins stood out on his forehead.

Mitka did not recognize Elizabieta in the skiff at first, for her straw hat threw her face into shadow. Her sunburnt hands were pressing a bunch of yellow water-lilies to her breast.

"Korshunov!" she called, as she saw Mitka. "You've deceived me."

"Deceived you?"

"Don't you remember, you promised to take me fishing?"

Boyarishkin dropped the oars and straightened his back. The skiff thrust its nose into the shore with a scrunch.

"Do you remember?" Elizabieta laughed as she jumped out.

"I haven't had the time. Too much work to do," Mitka said apologetically as the girl approached him.

"Well, then, when shall we go fishing?" she asked as she shook his hand.

"Tomorrow if you like. We've done the threshing and I've got more time now."

"You're not deceiving me this time?"

"No, I'm not!"

"I'll be waiting for you. You haven't forgotten the window? I'm going away soon, I expect. And I'd like to go fishing first." She was silent a moment, then, smiling to herself, she asked:

"You've had a wedding in your family, haven't you?"

"Yes, my sister."

"Whom did she marry?" Then, without waiting for an answer, she smiled again mysteriously and fleetingly. "Do come, won't you?" Once more her smile stung Mitka like a nettle.

He watched her to the boat. Boyarishkin impatiently pushed off, while Elizabieta smilingly gazed across his head at Mitka and nodded farewell.

When the boat was well out, Mitka heard Boyarishkin quietly ask:

"Who is that lad?"

"Just an acquaintance," she replied.

"Not a love affair?"

Mitka did not catch her answer above the creak of the rowlocks. He saw Boyarishkin throw himself back with a laugh, but could not see Elizabieta's face. A lilac ribbon, stirring gently in the breeze, hung from her hat to the slope of her bare neck.

Mitka, who rarely went fishing with rod and line, had never

prepared for the occasion with such zeal as on that evening. When he had finished he went into the front room. Grandfather Grishaka was sitting by the window, with round, copper-rimmed spectacles on his nose, studying the Gospels.

"Grand-dad!" Mitka said, leaning his back against the door-frame.

The old man looked at him over his spectacles.

"Eh?"

"Wake me up at the first cock."

"Where are you off to so early?"

"Fishing."

The old man had a weakness for fish, but he made a pretence of opposing Mitka's designs.

"Your father said the hemp must be beaten tomorrow. There's no time to laze around."

Mitka stirred from the door and tried strategy.

"Oh, all right, then. I wanted to give you a treat, but as there's the hemp to be done, I won't go."

"Stop, where are you off to?" The old man took alarm and drew off his spectacles. "I'll speak to your father. You'll go. I'll give you a call."

At midnight the old man, his linen trousers held up with one hand and his stick gripped on the other, groped his way down the stairs and across the yard to the barn. Mitka was sleeping on a rug in a corn-bin. Grishaka poked at him with his stick, but could not rouse him for some time. At first he poked lightly, whispering:

"Mitka! Mitka! Hey, Mitka!"

But Mitka only sighed and drew his legs up. Grishaka grew more ruthless and began to bore into Mitka's stomach with the stick. Mitka woke up suddenly and seized the end of the stick.

"How you do sleep!" the old man cursed.

The lad made his way quietly out of the yard and hurried to the square. He reached the Mokhovs' house, set down his fishing tackle, and on tiptoe, so as not to disturb the dogs, crept into the porch. He tried the cold iron latch. The door was shut fast. He clambered across the balustrade of the veranda and went up to the casement window. It was half-closed. Through the black gap came the sweet scent of a warm, womanly body and unfamiliar perfumes.

"Elizabieta Sergeevna!"

Mitka thought he had called very loudly. He waited. Silence. Supposing he was at the wrong window! What if Mokhov himself was asleep in there! He'd use a gun!

"Elizabieta Sergeevna, coming fishing?"

If he'd mistaken the window there'd be some fish caught all right!

"Are you getting up?" he asked, irritatedly, and thrust his head through the window opening.

"Who's that?" a voice sounded quietly and a little alarmed in the darkness.

"It's me, Korshunov. Coming fishing?"

"Ah! One moment!"

There was a sound of movement inside. Her warm, sleepy voice seemed to smell of mint. Mitka saw something white and rustling moving about the room. After a while her smiling face, bound in a white kerchief, appeared at the window.

"I'm coming out this way. Give me your hand." As she squeezed his hand in hers she glanced closely into his eyes.

They went down to the Don. During the night the river had risen, and the boat, which had been left high and dry the evening before, was now rocking on the water a little way out.

"I'll have to take off my shoes," Elizabieta sighed.

"Let me carry you," Mitka proposed.

"No, I'd better take my shoes off."

"Carrying you would be pleasanter."

"I'd rather not," she said, with embarrassment in her voice.

Without further argument Mitka embraced her legs above the knees with his left arm and, lifting her easily, splashed through the water. She involuntarily clutched at his stout neck and laughed quietly.

If Mitka had not stumbled over a stone used by the village women when washing clothes, there would not have been a brief, accidental kiss. She groaned and pressed her face against Mitka's lips, and he came to a halt two paces away from the boat. The water swirled over the legs of his boots and chilled his feet.

Unfastening the boat, he pushed it off and jumped in. He rowed standing. The boat gently breasted the stream, making for the opposite bank. The keel grated on the sandy shore. Without asking permission he picked the girl up in his arms and carried her into a clump of hawthorn. She bit at his face, scratched, screamed faintly once or twice, and feeling her strength ebbing, she wept angrily, but without tears.

They returned about nine o'clock in the morning. The sky was wrapped in a ruddy yellow haze. A wind was dancing over the river, lashing the waves into foam. The boat danced over the waves, and the ice-cold, sprinkling drops struck Elizabieta's pallid face and clung to her lashes and the strands of her hair. She wearily screwed up her dreary eyes and listlessly broke the stalk of a flower in her hands. Mitka rowed without looking at her. A small carp and a bream lay at his feet. His face wore an expression of mingled guilt, content, and anxiety.

"I'll take you to Semionov's landing-place. It will be nearer for you," he told her as he turned the boat into the stream.

Along the shore the dusty wattle fences pined in the hot wind. The heavy caps of the sunflowers, pecked by sparrows, were completely ripe and were scattering swollen seeds over the ground. The meadowland was emeralded with newly springing young grass. In the distance stallions were kicking up their heels; the burning southerly wind blew across the river.

As Elizabieta was getting out of the boat, Mitka picked up a fish and held it out to her.

"Here, take your share of the catch," he said.

She raised her eyebrows in astonishment, but took the fish.

"Well, I'm going," she replied.

Holding the fish suspended by a twig, she turned miserably away. All her recent assurance and gaiety had been left behind in the hawthorn bush.

"Elizabieta!"

She turned round, concealing her surprise and irritation. When she came closer, annoyed at his own embarrassment he said:

"Your dress at the back—there's a hole in it. It's quite small. . . ."

She flamed up, blushing down to her collar-bone. After a moment's silence Mitka advised her:

"Go by the back ways."

"I'll have to pass through the square in any case. . . . And I wanted to put my black skirt on," she whispered with regret and unexpected hatred in her voice.

"Shall I green it a bit with a leaf?" Mitka suggested simply, and was surprised to see the tears come into her eyes.

Like the rustling whisper of a zephyr the news ran through the village. "Mitka Korshunov's been out all night with Sergei Platonovich's daughter!" The women talked about it as they drove out the cattle to join the village herd of a morning, as they stood around the wells, or as they beat out their washing on the flat stones down by the river.

"Her own mother is dead, you know."

"Her father never stops working for a moment, and her stepmother just doesn't trouble."

"The store watchman says he saw a man tapping at the end window at midnight. He thought at first it was someone trying to break in. He ran to see who it was and found it was Mitka."

"The girls these days, they're in sin up to their necks. They're good for nothing."

"Mitka told my Michael he is going to marry her."

"He forced her, they say."

"Ah, my dear, a dog doesn't worry an unwilling bitch!"

The rumours finally came to the ears of Mokhov himself. They struck him like a beam falling from a building and crushing a man to the ground. For two days he went neither to the store nor to the mill.

On the third day Sergei Platonovich had his dappled grey stallion harnessed into his droshky and drove to the district centre. The droshky was followed by a highly lacquered carriage drawn by a pair of prancing black horses. Behind the coachman Elizabieta was sitting. She was as pale as death. She held a light suitcase on her knees and was smiling sadly. At the gate she waved her glove to Vladimir and her stepmother.

Pantaleimon Prokoffievich happened to be limping out of the store at the moment, and he stopped to ask the yardman:

"Where's the master's daughter going?"

And Nikita, condescending to the simple human weakness, replied:

"To Moscow, to school."

The next day an incident occurred which was long the subject

of talk down by the river, around the wells, and when the cattle
were being driven out to graze. Just before dusk (the village herd
had already returned from the steppe) Mitka went to see Sergei
Platonovich. He had waited until evening in order to avoid people.
He did not go merely to make a friendly call, but to ask for the
hand of Mokhov's daughter, Elizabieta.

He had seen her perhaps four times, not more. At the last meeting the conversation had taken the following course:

"Elizabieta, will you marry me?"

"Nonsense!"

"I shall care for you, I'll love you. We have people to work for
us; you shall sit at the window and read your books."

"You're a fool!"

Mitka took umbrage and said no more. That evening he went
home early, and in the morning he announced to his astonished
father:

"Father, arrange for my wedding."

"Cross yourself!" Miron replied.

"Really, Father; I'm not joking."

"In a hurry, aren't you? Who's caught you, crazy Martha?"

"Send the matchmakers to Sergei Platonovich."

Miron Gregorievich carefully set down the cobbling tools with
which he was mending harness and roared with laughter.

"You're in a funny vein today, my son."

But Mitka stood to his guns, and his father flared up: "You fool!
Sergei Platonovich has a capital of over a hundred thousand rubles.
He's a merchant, and what are you? Clear off or I'll leather you
with this strap."

"We've got twelve pairs of bullocks, and look at the land we own.
Besides, he's a peasant, and we're Cossacks."

"Clear off!" Miron said curtly.

Mitka found a sympathetic listener only in his grandfather. The
old man attempted to persuade Miron in favour of his son's suit.

"Miron," old Grishaka said, "why don't you agree? As the boy's
taken it into his head. . . ."

"Father, you're a great baby, God's truth you are! Mitka's just
silly, but you're . . ."

"Hold your tongue!" Grishaka rapped his stick on the floor.
"Aren't we equal to them? He ought to take it as an honour for a

Cossack's son to wed his daughter. We're known all around the
countryside. We're not farm-hands, we're masters. Go and ask
him, Miron. Let him give his mill as the dowry."

Miron flared up again and went out into the yard. So Mitka
decided to wait until evening and then go to Mokhov himself. He
knew that his father's obstinacy was like an elm at the root: you
might bend it, but you could never break it. It wasn't worth trying.

He went whistling as far as Mokhov's front door, then grew
timid. He hesitated a moment and finally went through the yard
to the side door. On the steps he asked the maid:

"Master at home?"

"He's drinking tea. Wait."

He sat down and waited, lit a cigarette, smoked it, and crushed
the end on the floor. Mokhov came out, brushing crumbs off his
waistcoat. When he saw Mitka he knitted his brows, but said·
"Come in."

Mitka entered Mokhov's cool private room, feeling that the
courage with which he had been charged so far had been sufficient
to last only to the threshold. The merchant went to his table and
turned round on his heels: "Well?" Behind his back his fingers
scratched at the top of the table.

"I've come to find out—" Mitka plunged into the cold slime of
Mokhov's eyes and shuddered. "Perhaps you'll give me Elizabieta?"
Despair, anger, fear, all combined to bring the perspiration in
beads to his face.

Mokhov's left eyebrow quivered, and the upper lip writhed
back from the gums. He stretched out his neck and leaned all his
body forward.

"What? Wha-a-at? You scoundrel! Get out! I'll haul you before
the ataman! You son of a swine!"

At the sound of Mokhov's shout Mitka plucked up courage.

"Don't take it as an insult. I only thought to make up for my
wrong."

Mokhov rolled his bloodshot eyes and threw a massive iron ash-
tray at Mitka's feet. It bounced up and struck him on the knee. But
he stoically bore the pain and, throwing open the door, shouted,
baring his teeth with shame and pain:

"As you wish, Sergei Platonovich, as you wish, but upon my
soul—who would want her now? I thought I'd cover her shame. But

now—a dog won't touch a gnawed bone."

Pressing his crushed handkerchief to his lips, Mokhov followed on Mitka's heels. He barred the way to the main door, and Mitka ran into the yard. Here the master had only to wink to Yemelian, the coachman, and as Mitka was struggling with the stout latch at the wicket gate, four unleashed dogs tore round the corner of the barn. Seeing Mitka, they sped across the yard straight at him. He had not had time to turn round when the foremost dog was up at his shoulders with its teeth fastened into his jacket. All four rent and tore at him. Mitka thrust them off with his hand, endeavouring to keep his feet. He saw Yemelian, his pipe scattering sparks, disappear into the kitchen and heard the door slam behind him.

At the steps, his back against a drain-pipe, stood Sergei Platonovich, his white, hairy fists clenched. Swaying, Mitka tore open the door and dragged the bunch of clamorous, hot-smelling dogs after him on his bleeding legs. He seized one by the throat and choked it off, and passing Cossacks with difficulty beat off the others.

Chapter 8

The Melekhovs found Natalia of great use on the farm. Although he was rich and employed labourers, her father had made his children work. Hard-working Natalia won the hearts of her husband's parents. Ilinichna, who secretly did not like her elder daughter-in-law, Daria, took to Natalia from the very first.

"Sleep on, sleep on, little one! What are you out so early for?" she would grumble kindly. "Go back to bed, we'll manage without you."

Even Pantaleimon, who was usually strict in regard to household matters, said to his wife:

"Listen, wife, don't wake Natalia up. She'll work hard enough as it is. She's going with Grishka to plough today. But whip up that Daria. She's a lazy woman, and bad. She paints her face and blacks her brows, the bitch."

Gregor could not grow accustomed to his newly married state;

within two or three weeks he realized with fear and vexation that he had not completely broken with Aksinia. The feeling which, in the excitement of the marriage, he had dismissed with a contemptuous wave of the hand had taken deep root. He thought he could forget, but it refused to be forgotten, and the wound bled at the memory. Even before the wedding Piotra had asked him:

"Grishka, but what about Aksinia?"

"Well, what about her?"

"Pity to throw her over, isn't it?"

"If I do, someone else will pick her up!" Gregor had smiled.

But it had not worked out like that. As, burning with his youthful, amorous ardour, he forcedly caressed his wife, he met with only coldness and an embarrassed submission from her. Natalia shrank from bodily delights; her mother had given her her own sluggish, tranquil blood, and as he recalled Aksinia's passionate fervour Gregor sighed:

"Your father must have made you of ice, Natalia."

When he met Aksinia one day, she laughed and exclaimed:

"Hello, Grishka! How do you find life with your young wife?"

"We live!" Gregor shook her off with an evasive reply and escaped as quickly as possible from Aksinia's caressing glance.

Stepan had evidently made up his quarrel with his wife. He visited the tavern less frequently, and one evening, as he was winnowing grain in the threshing-floor, he suggested, for the first time since the beginning of the trouble:

"Let's sing a song, Aksinia!"

They sat down, their backs against a heap of threshed, dusty wheat. Stepan began an army song, Aksinia joined in with her full, throaty voice. Gregor heard the Astakhovs singing, and while he was threshing (the two threshing-floors adjoined) he could see Aksinia as self-assured as formerly and apparently happy.

Stepan exchanged no greeting with the Melekhovs. He worked in the threshing-floor, occasionally making a jesting remark to Aksinia. And she would respond with a smile, her black eyes flashing. Her green skirt rippled like rain before Gregor's eyes. His neck was continually being twisted by a strange force which turned his head in the direction of Stepan's yard. He did not notice that

Natalia, who was assisting Pantaleimon repair the fence, intercepted his every involuntary glance; he did not see Piotra, who was driving the horses round the threshing-circle, grimacing with an almost imperceptible smile as he watched his brother.

From near and distant threshing-floors came the sound of threshing: the shouts of drivers, the whistle of knouts, the rattle of the winnowing drums. The village had waxed fat on the harvest and was threshing in the September warmth that stretched over the Don like a beaded snake across the road. In every farmyard, under the roof of every hut, each was living a full-blooded, bitter-sweet life, separate and apart from the rest. Old Grishaka was suffering with his teeth; Mokhov, crushed by his shame, was stroking his beard, weeping, and grinding his teeth; Stepan nursed his hatred for Gregor in his heart and tore at the shaggy blanket with his iron fingers in his sleep; Natalia ran into the shed and fell to the ground, shaking and huddling into a ball as she wept over her lost happiness; Gregor sighed, oppressed by gloomy presentiments and his continually returning pain; as Aksinia caressed her husband she flooded her undying hatred for him with tears. David had been discharged from the mill and sat night after night with Valet in the boiler-shed, while Valet, his evil eyes sparkling, would declare:

"David, you're a fool! They'll have their throats cut before long. One revolution isn't enough for them. Let them have another 1905, and then we'll settle scores. We'll settle scores!" he threatened with his scarred finger, and with a shrug adjusted the coat flung across his shoulders.

And over the village slipped the days, passing into the nights; the weeks flowed by, the months crept on, the wind howled, and, glassified with an autumnal, translucent, greenish-azure, the Don flowed tranquilly down to the sea.

One Sunday at the end of October, Fiodot Bodovskov drove to the district village on business. He took with him four brace of fattened ducks and sold them at the market; he bought his wife some cotton print and was on the point of driving home when a stranger, obviously not of those parts, came up to him.

"Good afternoon," he greeted Fiodot, putting his fingers to the edge of his black hat.

"Good afternoon," said Fiodot inquiringly.

"Where are you from?"

"From a village."

"And which village is it you're from?"

"From Tatarsk."

The stranger drew a silver cigarette-case out of his pocket and offered Fiodot a cigarette. "Is yours a big village?" he asked.

"Pretty large. Some three hundred families."

"Any smiths there?"

"Yes." Fiodot fastened the rein to his horse's bit and looked distrustfully at the man's black hat and the furrows in the large white face. "What do you want to know for?" he added.

"I'm coming to live in your village. I've just been to the district ataman. Will you take me back with you? I have a wife and a couple of boxes."

"I can take you."

They collected the wife and the boxes and set out on the return journey. Fiodot's passengers sat quietly behind him. Fiodot first asked for a cigarette, then he queried:

"Where do you come from?"

"From Rostov."

"Born there?"

"Yes."

Fiodot twisted himself round to study his passengers more closely. The man was of average height, but thin; his close-set eyes glittered intelligently. As he talked he smiled frequently, his upper lip protruded over the lower. His wife, wrapped in a knitted shawl, was dozing.

"What are you coming to live in our village for?"

"I'm a locksmith. I'm thinking of starting a workshop. I can do carpentry too."

Fiodot stared suspiciously at the man's plump hands, and, catching his gaze, the stranger added:

"I'm also an agent for the Singer Sewing Machine Company."

"What is your name?" Fiodot asked him.

"Stockman."

"So you're not Russian, then?"

"Yes, I'm a Russian. But my grandfather was a German by birth."

In a brief while Fiodot had learned that Osip Davidovich Stockman had formerly worked at a factory, then somewhere in the Kuban, then in the South-Eastern Railway workshops. After a while the conversation flagged. Fiodot gave his horse a drink at a way-side spring, and, drowsy with the journey and a good meal, he began to doze. He fastened the reins to the wagon and lay down comfortably. But he was not allowed to go to sleep.

"How's life in your parts?" Stockman asked him.

"Not so bad, we have enough to eat."

"And the Cossacks generally, are they satisfied?"

"Some are, some aren't. You can't please everybody."

"True, true," the man assented, and went on with his questioning. "You live pretty well, you say?"

"Pretty well."

"The annual army training must be a trouble, eh?"

"Army training? We're used to it."

"But the officers are bad?"

"Yes, the sons of swine!" Fiodot grew animated and glanced fearfully at the woman. "Our authorities are a bad lot. . . . When I went to do my service I sold my bullocks and bought a horse, and they rejected him."

"Rejected him?" Stockman said with assumed amazement.

"Right off. His legs were no good, they said. I argued with them, but no, they wouldn't pass him. It's a shame!"

The conversation went on briskly. Fiodot jumped off the wagon and began to talk freely of the village life. He cursed the village ataman for his unjust division of the meadowland and praised the state of affairs in Poland, where his regiment had been stationed. Stockman smoked and smiled continually, but the frown furrowing his white forehead stirred slowly and heavily, as though driven from within by secret thoughts.

They reached the village in the early evening. On Fiodot's advice Stockman went to the widow Lukieshka and rented two rooms from her.

"Who is that you brought back with you?" Fiodot's neighbour asked him as he drove past.

"An agent."

"What kind of angel?"

"You're a fool, that's what you are. An agent, I said. He sells machines. He gives them away to the handsome ones, but to such fools as you, Aunty Maria, he sells them."

Next day the locksmith Stockman visited the village ataman. Fiodor Manitskov, who was in his third year as ataman, turned the newcomer's black passport over and over, then handed it to the secretary, who also turned it over and over. They exchanged glances, and the ataman authoritatively waved his hand:

"You can stay."

The newcomer bowed and left the room. For a week he did not put his nose outside Lukieshka's hut. He was to be heard pounding with an axe, preparing a workshop in the outdoor kitchen. The women's interest in him died away; only the children spent all day peeping over the fence and watching the stranger with an unabashed animal curiosity.

Some three days before the Intercession of the Holy Virgin, Gregor and his wife drove out to the steppe to plough. Pantaleimon was unwell; he leaned heavily on his stick and wheezed with pain as he stood in the yard seeing them off. As Ilinichna wrapped Natalia in her jacket she whispered:

"Don't be long away; come back soon."

Her slender waist bent under the weight of a load of damp washing, Dunia went past on her way to the Don to rinse the clothes. As she went by she called to Natalia:

"Natalia, in the red glade there is lots of sorrel. Pull some up and bring it home."

The three pairs of bullocks dragged the upturned plough out of the yard. Gregor, who had caught a cold while fishing, adjusted the handkerchief bound round his neck and walked along at the roadside, coughing. Natalia walked at his side, a sack of victuals swinging on her back.

A transparent silence enveloped the steppe. Beyond the fallow land, on the other side of the rolling hill the earth was being scratched with ploughs, the drivers were whistling; but here along the highroad was only the blue-grey of low-growing wormwood, the roadside clover, and the ringingly glassy, chilly heaven above, criss-crossed by flying threads of natural-coloured web.

After seeing the ploughers on their way Piotra and Daria made ready to drive to the mill. Piotra sifted the wheat in the granary,

Daria sacked it and carried it to the wagonette. Pantaleimon harnessed the horses.

When they arrived at the mill they found the yard crowded with wagons. The scales were surrounded by a dense throng. Piotra threw the reins to Daria and jumped down from the cart.

"How soon will my turn be?" he asked Valet, the scalesman.

"You're the thirty-eighth."

Piotra turned to fetch his sacks. As he did so he heard cursing behind him. A hoarse, unpleasant voice barked:

"You oversleep and then you want to get in before your turn. Get away, Hokhol,[1] or I'll give you one."

Piotra recognized the voice of "Horseshoe" Yakob. He stopped to listen. There was a shout from the weighing-room and the sound of a blow. The blow was well aimed, and an elderly, bearded Ukrainian, with his cap crushed on the back of his head, came tumbling out through the doorway.

"What's that for?" he shouted, holding his cheek.

"I'll wring your neck, you son of a whore!"

"Mikifor, help!" the Ukrainian shouted.

"Horseshoe" Yakob, a desperate, solidly built artillery-man, who had earned his nickname because of the horseshoe marks left by the kick of a horse on his cheek, came runnning out of the weighing-room, rolling up his sleeves. Behind him a tall Ukrainian in a rose-coloured shirt struck hard at him. But Yakob kept on his feet.

"Brothers, they're attacking Cossacks!" he cried.

From all sides Cossacks and Ukrainians, who were at the mill in large numbers, came running. A fight began, centring in the main entrance to the mill. The door groaned under the pressure of the struggling bodies. Piotra threw down his sack and went slowly towards the mêlée. Standing up in the wagonette, Daria saw him press into the middle of the crowd, pushing the others aside. She groaned as she saw him carried to the mill wall and flung down and trampled underfoot.

Mitka Korshunov came running round the corner from the machine-room, waving a bar of iron. The same Ukrainian who had struck at Yakob from behind burst out of the struggling crowd, a torn sleeve fluttering on his back like a bird's broken wing. Bent double, his hands touching the ground, he ran to the nearest wagon

1 *Hokhol:* familiar name for Ukrainians.

and snatched up a shaft. The three Shamil brothers came at a run from the village. One-armed Alexei fell at the gate, catching his feet in reins lying abandoned on the ground. He jumped up and leaped across the cart-shafts, pressing his armless sleeve to his breast. His brother Martin's trousers came out of their socks; he bent down to tuck them in, but a cry floated high over the mill roof, and Martin straightened up and tore after his brothers.

Daria stood watching from the wagon, panting and wringing her hands. Sergei Mokhov ambled past, pale and chewing his lips, his belly shaking like a round ball beneath his waistcoat. Daria saw the Ukrainian with the torn shirt cut Mitka down with the shaft, only himself to be sent headlong by one-armed Alexei's iron fist. She saw Mitka Korshunov, on his hands and knees, sweep Mokhov's legs from under him with the iron bar, and she was not surprised. Mokhov threw out his arms and slipped like a crab into the weighing-shed, there to be trodden underfoot. Daria laughed hysterically, the black arches of her painted brows broken with her laughter. But she stopped abruptly as she saw Piotra; he had succeeded in making his way out of the swaying, howling mob and was lying under a cart, spitting up blood. With a shriek Daria ran to him. From the village Cossacks came hurrying with stakes; one of them carried a crowbar. At the door of the weighing-shed a young Ukrainian lay with a broken head in a pool of blood; bloody strands of hair fell over his face. It looked as though he was departing this pleasant life.

Herded together like sheep, the Ukrainians were slowly being driven towards the boiler-shed. There was every prospect of the fight ending seriously, but an old Ukrainian had an inspiration. Jumping into the boiler-shed, he pulled a flaming brand out of the furnace and ran towards the granary where the milled grain was stored: eighteen tons and more of flour.

"I'll set it afire!" he roared savagely, raising the crackling brand towards the thatched roof.

The Cossacks shuddered and came to a halt. A dry, boisterous wind was blowing from the east, carrying the smoke away from the roof of the granary towards the group of Ukrainians. One spark in the dry thatch, and the whole village would go up in flames.

A brief, stifled howl of rage arose from the Cossacks. Some of them began to retreat towards the mill, while the Ukrainian, waving the brand above his head and scattering fiery rain, shouted:

"I'll burn it! I'll burn it! Out of the yard!"

Horseshoe Yakob, the cause of the fight, was the first to leave the yard. The other Cossacks streamed hurriedly after him. Throwing their sacks hastily into their wagons, the Ukrainians harnessed their horses; then, standing up in their wagons, waving the ends of the leather reins around their heads, whipping up their horses frantically, they tore out of the yard and away from the village.

Standing in the middle of the yard, his eyes and cheeks twitching, one-armed Alexei cried:

"To horse, Cossacks!"

"After them!" the cry was taken up.

Mitka Korshunov was on the point of dashing out of the yard, and the other Cossacks were about to act on the advice. But at that moment an unfamiliar figure in a black hat approached the group with hasty steps and raised his hand, crying:

"Stop!"

"Who are you?" Yakob asked.

"Where did you spring from?" another demanded.

"Stop, villagers!"

"Who are you calling villagers?"

"The peasant! Give him one, Yakob!"

"That's right, close up his eyes for him!"

The man smiled anxiously, but without a sign of fear. He took off his hat, wiped his brow with a gesture of ineffable simplicity, and finally disarmed them with his smile.

"What's the matter?" he asked, waving his hat at the blood by the door of the weighing-shed.

"We've been fighting the Hokhols," one-armed Alexei replied peaceably.

"But what for?"

"They wanted to get in ahead of their turn," Yakob explained.

"One of them would have set fire to the place in his desperation," Afonka Ozierov smiled. "The Hokhols are a terribly bad-tempered lot."

The man waved his hat in Ozierov's direction. "And who are you?" he asked.

Ozierov spat contemptuously and answered, as he watched the flight of the spittle:

"I'm a Cossack. And you—you're not a gypsy, are you?"

"You and I are both of us Russians."

"You lie!" Afonka declared deliberately.

"The Cossacks are descended from the Russians. Do you know that?" the stranger declared.

"And I tell you the Cossacks are the sons of Cossacks."

"Long ago," the man explained, "serfs ran away from the landowners and settled along the Don. They came to be known as Cossacks."

"Go your own way, man!" Alexei advised, restraining his anger. "The swine wants to make peasants of us! Who is he?"

"He's the newcomer living with cross-eyed Lukieshka," another explained.

But the moment for pursuit of the Ukrainians was past. The Cossacks dispersed, animatedly discussing the fight.

That night, in the steppe some five miles from the village, as Gregor wrapped himself in his prickly linen coat he said querulously to Natalia:

"You're a stranger, somehow! You're like that moon, you don't warm and you don't chill a man. I don't love you, Natashka; you mustn't be angry. I didn't want to say anything about it, but there it is; clearly we can't go on like this. I'm sorry for you; we've been married all these days, and still I feel nothing in my heart. It's empty. Like the steppe tonight."

Natalia glanced up at the inaccessible, starry pastures, at the shadowy, translucent cloak of the clouds floating above her, and was silent. From somewhere in the bluish-black upper wilderness belated cranes called to one another with voices like little silver bells. The grass had a yearning, deathly smell. On the hillock glimmered the ruddy glow of the dying camp-fire.

Gregor awoke just before dawn. Snow lay on his coat to the depth of three inches. The steppe was hidden beneath the freezing, virginal blue of the fresh snow; the clearly marked tracks of a hare ran close by where he was lying.

For many years past if a Cossack rode alone along the road to Millerovo and fell in with Hokhols (the Ukrainian villages began

with Lower Yablonska and stretched for some fifty miles, as far as
Millerovo), he had to yield them the road or they would set upon
him. So the Cossacks were in the habit of driving to the district
village in groups, and then they were not afraid of falling in with
Hokhols on the steppe and exchanging invective:

"Hey, Hokhol! Give us the road! You live on the Cossacks' land,
you swine, and you don't want to let them pass!"

It was not pleasant for the Ukrainians, who had to bring their
grain to the central granaries at Paramonov on the Don. Fights
would break out without cause, simply because they were Hokhols,
and as they were Hokhols the Cossacks had to fight them.

Hundreds of years previously a diligent hand had sown the seeds
of national discord in the Cossack land, and the seed had yielded
rich fruit. In the inter-racial struggles the blue blood of the Cossacks and the crimson blood of the immigrant Muscovites and
Ukrainians were poured out liberally over the Don country.

Some two weeks after the battle of the mill a district police
officer and an investigating official arrived in the village. Stockman
was the first to be cross-examined. The investigator, a young official
from the Cossack nobility, asked him:

"Where were you living before you came here?"

"At Rostov."

"What were you imprisoned for in 1907?"

"For disorders."

"Hm! Where were you working then?"

"In the railway workshops."

"What as?"

"Locksmith."

"You're not a Jew, are you? Or a converted Jew?"

"No. I think—"

"I'm not interested in what you think. Have you been in exile?"

"Yes, I have."

The investigator raised his head, and chewed his lips. "I advise
you to clear out of this district," he said, adding in an undertone:
"and I'll see that you do."

"Why?"

"What did you say to the Cossacks on the day of the fight at
the mill?" he answered with a question.

"Well . . ."

"All right, you can go."

Stockman went on to the veranda of Mokhov's house (the authorities always made the merchant's house their headquarters), and although a frown furrowed his brow, he glanced back at the door with a smile.

Chapter 9

Winter came on slowly. After some days the snow melted and the herds were driven out to pasture again. For a week a southern wind blew, warming the earth; a late, straggling green sprang up over the steppe. The thaw lasted until St. Michael's Day, then the frost returned and snow fell, and the gardens by the Don, through the fences, were criss-crossed with the marks of hares' feet. The streets were deserted.

Just after the snowfall a village assembly was held to arrange for the allotment and cutting of brushwood. Long before the hour fixed for the meeting the Cossacks crowded around the steps of the village administration in their sheepskins and greatcoats, and the cold drove them inside. Behind a table, at the side of the ataman and the secretary, the respected village elders were gathered; the younger Cossacks squeezed together in a group and muttered out of the warmth of their coat collars. The secretary covered sheet after sheet of paper with close writing, while the ataman watched over his shoulder, and a restrained hum arose in the chilly room.

"The hay this year . . ."

"You're right. The meadow hay is good, but the steppe hay is all clover."

"What about the wood-cutting?"

"Quiet, please!"

The meeting began. Stroking his beard, the ataman called out the names of the families and their assignments of wood.

"You can't fix the wood-cutting for Thursday." Ivan Tomilin attempted to shout down the ataman.

"Why not?"

"On Thursday half the village will be going out to bring in hay."

"You can leave that till Sunday!"

"The better the day . . ." A howl of derision arose from the assembly.

Old Matvey Kashulin leaned across the rickety table and pointed his smooth ash stick at Tomilin.

"The hay can wait! You're a fool, brother! And that's that! You . . ."

"You've got no brains to boast about, anyway . . ." one-armed Alexei joined in. For six years he had been quarrelling with old Kashulin over a piece of land. Every spring Alexei asserted his right to it, but each time Kashulin ploughed it up again.

"Shut up, St. Vitus!"

"Pity you're so far away, or I'd give you something to remember me by," Alexei stormed.

The ataman banged the table with his fist.

"I'll call the militia in in a moment if there isn't silence." When order was restored, he added: "Wood-cutting will begin on Thursday at dawn."

"A fine time!" "God grant it!" arose the jeering remarks.

"And one other thing: I've received an instruction from the district ataman." The village ataman raised his voice. "Next Saturday the youngsters are to go to be sworn in at the district ataman's office. They are to be there by afternoon."

Pantaleimon Prokoffievich was standing by the window nearest the door. At his side Miron Gregorievich was sitting on the window-sill, screwing up his eyes and smiling into his beard. Close by them the younger Cossacks were crowded, winking and smiling at one another. In the middle of their group, the fur cap of the ataman's regiment thrust back on his smooth bald head, his unageing face everlastingly blushing like a ruddy winter apple, stood Avdeich Senilin.

Avdeich had served in the ataman's Life Guards and had come back with the nickname of "Bragger." He had been one of the first in the village to be assigned to the ataman's regiment. While he was on service a strange thing had happened to him, and from the very first day of his return he had begun to tell astonishing stories of his extraordinary adventures in Petersburg. His astounded listeners at first believed him, drinking it all in with gaping mouths, but then they discovered that Avdeich was the biggest liar the village had ever produced, and they openly laughed at him. But he was not to be abashed and did not cease his lying. As he grew old he began to get annoyed when nailed down to a lie and would resort to his fists; but if his listeners only laughed and said nothing he grew more and more fervent in his story-telling.

Avdeich stood in the middle of the room, rocking on his heels. Glancing around the assembled Cossacks, he observed in a ponderous bass voice:

"Speaking of service, these days the Cossacks aren't at all what they were. They're small and good-for-nothing. But—" and he smiled contemptuously—"I once saw some dead bones! Ah, they were Cossacks in those days!"

"Where did you dig the bones up, Avdeich?" smooth-faced Anikushka asked, nudging his neighbour.

"Don't start telling any of your lies, Avdeich, with the holy days so near." Pantaleimon wrinkled up his nose. He did not like Avdeich's bragging habits.

"It isn't my nature to lie, brother," Avdeich replied truculently, and stared in astonishment at Anikushka, who was shaking as though with fever. "I saw these dead bones when we were building a hut for my brother-in-law. As we were digging the foundations we came to a grave. The arms were as long as this—" he extended both arms wide—"and the head was as big as a copper."

"You'd better tell the youngsters how you caught a robber in St. Petersburg," Miron suggested as he rose from the window-sill.

"There's nothing really to tell," Avdeich replied, with a sudden attack of modesty.

"Tell us, tell us, Avdeich!" arose a shout.

"Well, it was like this." Avdeich cleared his throat and drew his tobacco-pouch out of his trouser pocket. He poured a pinch of tobacco on his palm and stared around his audience with eyes beaming. "A thief had escaped from prison. They looked for him everywhere, but do you think they could find him? They just couldn't. All the authorities were beaten. Well, one night the officer of the guard calls me to him. 'Go into that room,' he says. 'His Imperial Majesty is in there. The Sire Emperor himself wants to see you.' Of course I was taken aback a bit, but I went in. I stood at attention, but he claps me on the shoulder and says: 'Listen,' he says, 'Ivan Avdeich, the biggest thief in our Empire has escaped. Look for him and find him or never let me set eyes on you again!' 'Very good, Your Imperial Majesty!' I said. So I took three of the best horses in the Czar's stables and set out. I rode all day and I rode all night, until on the third day I came up with the thief near Moscow. I take him into my coach and haul him back to Petersburg. I arrive at midnight, all covered with mud, and go straight to His Imperial Majesty himself. All sorts of counts and princes tried to stop me, but I march on. Yes. . . . I knock at the door. 'May I come in, Your Imperial Majesty?' 'Who is it?' 'It's me,' I said, 'Ivan Avdeich Senilin.' I heard a noise in the room and heard His Majesty himself cry out: 'Maria Fiodorovna, Maria Fiodorovna! Get up quickly and get a samovar going, Ivan Avdeich has arrived.' "

There was a roar of laughter from the Cossacks at the back of the crowd. The secretary, who was reading a notice concerning a lost animal, stopped in the middle of a sentence, and the ataman stretched out his neck like a goose and stared hard at the crowd rocking with laughter.

Avdeich's face clouded and his eyes wandered uncertainly over the faces before him.

"Wait a bit!" he said.

"Ha-ha-ha!"

"Oh, he'll be the death of us!"

"Get a samovar going! Avdeich has arrived! Ha-ha-ha!"

The assembly began to break up. On the trampled snow outside the administration hut Stepan Astakhov and a tall, long-shanked Cossack, the owner of the windmill, were stamping about to get themselves warm.

When Pantaleimon returned from the meeting he went at once to the room which he and his wife occupied. Ilinichna had been unwell for some days, and her swollen face reflected her weariness and pain. She lay propped up on a plump feather bed. At the sound of Pantaleimon's footsteps she turned her head; her eyes rested on his beard, damp with his breath, and her nostrils dilated. But the old man smelt only of the frost and the sour sheepskin. "Sober today," she thought, and contentedly laid down her knitting-needles.

"Well, what of the wood-cutting?" she asked.

"They've decided to begin on Thursday." Pantaleimon stroked his beard. "Thursday morning," he added, sitting down on a chest at the side of the bed. "Well, feeling any better?"

"Just the same. A shooting pain in all my joints."

"I told you not to go into the water," Pantaleimon fumed. "There were plenty of other women to steep the hemp. . . . And how's Natalia?" he asked suddenly, bending towards the bed.

There was a note of anxiety in Ilinichna's voice as she replied: "I don't know what to do. She was crying again a day or two ago. I went out into the yard and found someone had left the barn door wide open. I went inside, and she was standing by the millet-bin. I asked her what was the matter, but she said she only had a headache. I can't get the truth out of her."

"Perhaps she's ill?"

"I don't think so. Either someone's given her the evil eye, or else it's Grishka. . . ."

"He hasn't been with that . . . You haven't heard anything, have you?"

"What are you saying, father?" Ilinichna exclaimed in alarm. "And what about Stepan? He's no fool! No, I haven't heard anything."

Pantaleimon sat with his wife awhile longer, then went out. Gregor was in his room sharpening hooks with a file. Natalia was smearing them with pork grease and carefully wrapping each in a separate rag. As Pantaleimon limped by he stared inquisitively at her. Her yellow cheeks were flushed like an autumn leaf. She had grown noticeably thinner during the past month, and there was a new unhappy look in her eyes. The old man halted at the door. "He's killing the girl!" he thought as he glanced back at Natalia bowed over the bench.

"Drop that, the devil take it!" the old man shouted, turning livid with his sudden frenzy. Gregor looked at his father in astonishment.

"I want to sharpen both ends, Father."

"Drop it, I tell you! Get ready for the wood-cutting. The sledges aren't ready at all, and you sit there sharpening hooks," he added more quietly, and hesitated at the door, evidently wanting to say

something else. But he went out. Gregor heard him giving vent to
the rest of his anger on Piotra.

A good two hours before dawn on the Thursday, Ilinichna got
up and called Daria: "Get up! Time to light the fire!"

Daria ran in her shift to the stove and struck a light with the
flint.

"Get a move on with it!" Piotra hurried his wife as he lit a
cigarette.

"They don't go and wake that Natashka up! Am I to tear myself
in two?" Daria fumed.

"Go and wake her up yourself," Piotra advised her. But the advice was unnecessary, for Natalia was already up. Flinging on her
jacket, she went out to get fuel for the fire.

The kitchen smelt of fresh kvass, harness, and the warmth of
human bodies. Daria bustled about, shuffling in her felt boots;
under her rose-coloured shift her little breasts quivered. Her married life had not soured or withered her. Tall and slender, supple
as a willow switch, she was as fresh as a young girl.

Dawn broke before the meal was ready. Pantaleimon hurried
over his breakfast, blowing on the thick porridge. Gregor ate
slowly, his face clouded, and Piotra amused himself with teasing
Dunia, who was suffering with toothache and had her face
bound up.

There was the sound of sledge-runners in the street. Bullock
sledges were moving down to the Don in the grey dawn. Gregor
and Piotra went out to harness their sledges. As he went Gregor
wound a soft scarf, his wife's gift, around his neck. A crow flew
overhead with a full, throaty cry. Piotra watched its flight and remarked:

"Flying to the south, to the warmth."

Behind a rosy little cloud, as gay as a maiden smile, a tiny slip
of moon gleamed dimly. The smoke from the chimneys rose in
columns, reaching towards the inaccessibly distant, golden slip of
the young moon. The river was not completely frozen over opposite the Melekhovs' hut. Along the edges of the stream the ice
was firm, and green with accumulated drift snow. But beyond the
middle, towards the Black Cliff, the ice-holes yawned sombre and

menacing out of the white snow.

Pantaleimon drove off first with the old bullocks, leaving his
sons to follow later. At the slope down to the river-crossing Piotra
and Gregor caught up with Anikushka. He was walking at the side
of his bullocks, and his wife, a stocky, sickly woman, held the
reins. Piotra called out to him:

"Hello, neighbour, surely you're not taking your woman with
you?"

Anikushka smiled and turned to talk to the brothers.

"Yes, I am, to keep me warm," he replied.

"You'll get no warmth from her, she's too lean."

"That's true; and I feed her with oats, but still she doesn't
fatten!"

The three drove on together. The forest was laced with rime, and
of a virgin whiteness. Anikushka went in front, lashing his whip
against the branches overhead. The needly and crumbling snow
fell in showers, sprinkling over his wife.

"Don't play about, you devil!" she shouted at him as she shook
the snow off.

"Drop her into the snow," Piotra advised.

At a turn of the road they met Stepan Astakhov, driving two
yoked bullocks back towards the village. His curly hair hung
below his fur cap like a bunch of white grapes.

"Hey, Stepan, lost your way?" Anikushka exclaimed as he passed.

"Lost my way be damned! We swung over, and the sledge struck
a stump and snapped a runner in two. So I've got to go back."
Stepan cursed and his eyes suddenly darkened as he passed
Piotra.

"Left your sledge behind?" Anikushka asked, turning round.

Stepan waved his hand, cracked his whip, and gave Gregor a
hard stare. A little farther on, the group came to a sledge abandoned in the middle of the road. Aksinia was standing by it. Holding
the edge of her sheepskin with her hand, she was gazing along
the road in their direction.

"Out of the way or I'll drive over you. You're not my wife!"
Anikushka snorted. Aksinia stepped aside with a smile and sat
down on the overturned sledge.

"I'd take you along, but I've got my own wife with me," Anikushka explained as he drove by.

As Piotra came up to her he gave a quick glance back at Gregor, who was some distance behind. Gregor was smiling uncertainly, anxiety and expectation expressed in all his movements.

"What, sledge broken?" Piotra asked.

"Yes," she replied, and rising to her feet, turned away from Piotra towards Gregor. "Gregor Pantalievich, I'd like a word with you," she said as he came up to her.

Asking Piotra to look after his bullocks for a moment, Gregor turned to her. Piotra laughed suggestively and drove on.

The two stood silently regarding each other. Aksinia glanced cautiously around, then turned her humid black eyes again to Gregor's face. Shame and joy flamed in her cheeks and dried her lips. Her breath came in sharp gasps.

At a turn in the road Anikushka and Piotra disappeared behind the brown oak trunks.

"Well, Grishka, it's as you wish, but I've no strength left to live without you," she said firmly, and pressed her lips together in expectation of his answer.

Gregor made no reply. The silence fettered the forest in its grip. The glassy emptiness rang in his ears. The smooth surface of the road, polished with sledge-runners, the grey rag of sky, the dumb, mortally drowsy forest. . . . A sudden cry of a raven near by seemed to arouse Gregor from his momentary lethargy. He raised his head and watched the bird winging its silent flight. Unexpectedly to himself he said:

"It's going to be warm. He's flying towards the warmth." Starting, he laughed hoarsely. "Well—" He turned his intoxicated eyes to Aksinia and suddenly snatched her towards himself.

During the winter evenings a little group of villagers gathered in Stockman's room at Lukieshka's hut. There were Christonia, and Valet from the mill, ever smiling David (now three months a loafer), the engine-man, Ivan Alexievich Kotliarov, occasionally Filka the cobbler, and always Misha Koshevoi, a young Cossack who had not yet done his regular army service.

At first the group played cards. Then Stockman casually brought out a book of Nekrasov's poetry. They began to read the volume aloud, and liked it. Then they went on to Nikitin, and about

Christmas-time Stockman suggested the reading of a dog-eared, unbound and well-bethumbed brochure. Koshevoi, who had been to the church school, read aloud from it as he contemptuously glanced through the greasy pages.

"You could make vermicelli of it, it's so greasy!" he said in disgust.

Christonia roared with laughter; David smiled dazzlingly. But Stockman waited for the merriment to die away and then said:

"Read it, Misha. It's interesting. It's all about the Cossacks."

Bending his head over the table, Koshevoi spelt out laboriously: *Short History of the Don Cossacks,* and then glanced around expectantly.

"Read it!" Kotliarov, the engine-man, ordered.

They laboured through the book for three evenings, reading about the free life of the past, about Pugachov, Stenka Razin and Vasily Bulovin. Finally they came down to recent times. The unknown author poured scorn on the Cossacks' miserable existence, he jeered intelligently and powerfully at the authorities and the system, the Czar's government, and the Cossackry itself, which had hired itself out to the monarchs as their bodyguard. The listeners grew excited and began to quarrel among themselves. Stockman sat at the door smoking a pipe and smiling.

"He's right! It's all true!" Christonia would burst out.

The engineer Kotliarov was steeped to the backbone in Cossack traditions, and he defended the Cossacks vigorously, his bulging round eyes glittering:

"You're a peasant, Christan, your Cossack blood's a drop in a bucket. Your mother was mated with a peasant from Voronezh."

"You're a fool, you're a fool, brother!" Christonia replied vigorously.

"Shut up, peasant!"

"And aren't the peasants just as much men as you?"

"They're peasants, made of bast and stuffed with brushwood."

"When I was serving in Petersburg, brother, I saw many things," Christonia said. "Once it happened that we were on guard at the Czar's palace, inside the rooms and around the walls outside. We rode around, two this way and two that. When we met we used to ask: 'All quiet, no risings anywhere?' and then we'd ride on. We weren't allowed to stop and talk. And they chose us for our looks;

when we had to take our turn on guard at the doors, they chose each pair so as they should be alike in their faces and their figures. The barber once had to dye my beard because of it. I had to take a turn at guard duty with some Cossack whose beard was a bay colour. They searched all through the regiment and there wasn't another like him. So the troop commander sent me to the barber to have my beard dyed. When I looked in the glass afterwards my heart almost broke. I burned, absolutely burned!"

"Yes, Christonia, but what's all this to do with the question? What were you going to tell us?" Kotliarov interrupted him.

"About the people. I was just telling you I once had to take a turn on guard outside. We were riding along, me and my comrade, when some students came running round the corner. As soon as they saw us they roared: 'Ha!' and then again: 'Ha!' We hadn't time to call out before they had surrounded us. 'What are you riding about for, Cossacks?' they asked. And I said: 'We're keeping guard, you let go of the reins,' and clapped my hands on my sword. 'Don't distrust me, Cossack, I'm from Kamienska district myself, and I'm studying in the university,' one said. We start to ride on, and he pulls out a ten-ruble piece and says: 'Drink to the health of my dead father.' And he draws a picture out of his pocket. 'Look, that's my father,' he says, 'take it as a keepsake.' Well, we took it, we couldn't refuse. And they went off again. Just then an officer comes running out of the back door of the palace with a troop of men. 'Who was that?' he shouts. And I tell him students had come and begun talking to us, and we had wanted to sabre them according to instructions, but as they had set us free we had ridden off. When we went off duty later, we told the corporal we'd earned ten rubles and wanted to drink them to the health of the old man, showing him the portrait. In the evening the corporal brought some vodka, and we had a good time for a couple of days. Then it turned out that this student had given us the portrait of the chief rebel of Germany. I had hung it above my bed; he had a grey beard and was a decent sort of man, looked like a merchant. The troop commander saw it and asked: 'Where did you get that picture from?' So I told him, and he began to roar: 'Do you know who that is? He's their ataman Karl—' Drat it, I've forgotten his name. What was it . . . ?"

"Karl Marx?" Stockman suggested with a smile.

"That's it, Karl Marx," Christonia exclaimed joyfully. "But we
drank the ten rubles. It was the bearded Karl we drank to, but we
drank them!"

"He deserves to be drunk to." Stockman smiled, playing with his
cigarette-holder.

"Why, what good did he do?" Kotliarov queried.

"I'll tell you another time, it's getting late now." Stockman held
the holder between his fingers and ejected the dead cigarette-end
with a slap from the other hand.

After long selection and testing, a little group of ten Cossacks
began to meet regularly in Stockman's workshop. Stockman was
the heart and soul of the group and went straight towards the end
he had in mind. He ate into the simple understandings and concep-
tions like a worm into wood, instilling repugnance and hatred
towards the existing system. At first he found himself confronted
with the cold steel of distrust, but he was not to be repulsed.

On the sandy slope of the left bank of the Don lies the centre
of Vieshenska, the most ancient of the district centres of the upper
Don, transferred from the town of Chigonak, which was destroyed
during the reign of Peter the Great, and renamed Vieshenska. It
was formerly an important link along the great waterway from
Voronezh to Azov.

Opposite Vieshenska the Don bends like a Tatar bow, turns
sharply to the right, and by the little village of Bazka majestically
straightens again, carries its greenish-blue waters over the chalky
feet of the hills on the west bank, past the thickly clustered villages on the right and the rare hamlets on the left, down to the
sea, to the blue Sea of Azov.

Vieshenska stands among dunes of yellow sands. It is a bare,
unhappy village without gardens or orchards. On the square stands
an old church, grey with age, and six streets run out of the square
in lines parallel with the river. Where the Don bends towards
Bazka a lake, as broad as the Don at low tide, runs like a sleeve
into willows. The far end of Vieshenska runs down to this lake,
and on a smaller square, overgrown with golden prickly thorn, is
a second church, with a green cupola and green roof, standing
under the green of the willows.

Beyond the village, to the north stretches a saffron waste of sands, a miserable pine plantation, and groves flooded with rust-coloured water. Here and there in the sandy wilderness are rare oases of villages, meadowland, and a grey scrub of willows.

One Sunday in December a dense crowd of fifteen hundred young Cossacks from all the villages in the district was assembled in the square outside the old church. Mass ended, the senior sergeant, a brave-looking, elderly Cossack with long-service decorations, gave an order, and the youngsters drew up in two long, unequal ranks. Followed by his staff, the ataman entered the church enclosure, dressed according to form and wearing a new officer's cloak, his spurs jingling.

Falling back a pace or two, the senior sergeant swung on his heels and shouted:

"By the right, quick march!"

The two lines filed through the wide-open gate, and the church rang to the cupola with the sound of tramping feet.

Gregor paid no attention to the words of the oath of allegiance being read by the priest. By his side stood Mitka Korshunov, his face contorted with the pain of his tight new boots. Gregor's up-raised arm grew numb, a jumbled train of thought slipped through his mind. As he passed under the crucifix and kissed the silver, damp with the moisture of many lips, he thought of Aksinia, of his wife. He had a fleeting vision of the forest, its brown trunks and branches lined with white down, and the humid gleam of Aksinia's black eyes beneath her kerchief. . . .

When the ceremony was ended they were marched out into the square and again drawn up in ranks. Blowing his nose and stealthily wiping his fingers on the lining of his coat, the sergeant addressed them:

"You're not boys any longer now, you're Cossacks. You've taken the oath and you ought to understand what it means and what you've sworn to do. You're grown up into Cossacks now and you must watch over your honour, obey your fathers and mothers, and so on. You were boys, you played about, you may even have played tipcat in the road, but now you must think about your future service. In a year's time you will be called up into the army." Here the sergeant blew his nose again, brushed his hands, and ended, as he drew on his fur gloves: "And your father or mother must think about getting you your equipment. They must provide you with an army horse, and . . . in general. . . . And now, home you go and God be with you, boys."

Gregor and Mitka picked up the rest of the lads from their village, and they set off together for Tatarsk.

It was dusk when they reached the village. Gregor went up the steps of the hut and glanced in at the window. The hanging lamp shed a dim yellow light through the room. Piotra was standing in its light with his back to the window. Gregor brushed the snow off his boots with the twig broom at the door and entered the kitchen amid a cloud of steam.

"Well, I'm back," he announced.

"You've been quick. You must be frozen," Piotra replied in an anxious and hurried tone.

Pantaleimon was sitting with his head bowed in his hands, his elbows on his knees. Daria was spinning at the droning spinning-wheel. Natalia was standing at the table with her back to Gregor and did not turn round on his entry. Glancing hastily around the kitchen, Gregor rested his eyes on Piotra. By his brother's agitatedly expectant face he guessed that something had happened.

"Taken the oath?" Piotra asked.

"Ah-ha."

Gregor took off his outdoor clothes slowly, playing for time and turning over in his mind all the possibilities which might have led to this chilly and silent welcome. Ilinichna came out of the best room, her face expressing her agitation.

"It's Natalia!" Gregor thought as he sat down on the bench beside his father.

"Get him some supper," his mother said to Daria, indicating Gregor with her eyes. Daria stopped in the middle of her spinning-song and went to the stove. The kitchen was engulfed in a silence broken only by the heavy breathing of a goat and her newly-born kid.

As Gregor sipped his soup he glanced at Natalia. But he could not see her face. She was sitting sideways to him, her head bent over her knitting-needles. Pantaleimon was the first to be provoked into speech by the general silence. Coughing artificially, he said:

"Natalia is talking about going back to her parents."

Gregor wiped his plate clean with his bread and said nothing.

"What's the reason?" his father asked, his lower lip quivering—
the first sign of a coming outburst of frenzy.

"I don't know," Gregor replied as he rose and crossed himself.

"But I know," his father raised his voice.

"Don't shout, don't shout!" Ilinichna interposed.

"Yes, there's no cause for shouting." Piotra moved from the window to the middle of the room. "It all depends on love. If you want
to, you live together; if you don't, well—God be with you!"

"I'm not judging her. Even if she was a wanton hussy and sinful
in the sight of God, still I'd not judge her, but that swine there—"
Pantaleimon pointed to Gregor, who was warming himself at the
stove.

"Who have I done wrong to?" Gregor asked.

"You don't know? You don't know, you devil?"

"No, I don't."

Pantaleimon jumped from his seat, overturning the bench, and
went right up to Gregor. Natalia threw down her stocking, the
needles clattered to the floor. At the sound a kitten jumped down
from the stove and began to play with the ball of wool.

"What I say to you is this," the old man began slowly and deliberately; "if you won't live with Natalia, you can clear out of this
house and go wherever your feet will carry you. That's what I say
to you. Go where your feet will carry you," he repeated in a calm
voice, and turned and picked up the bench.

"What I say to you, Father, I don't say in anger." Gregor's voice
was jarringly hollow. "I didn't marry of my own choice, it was you
who married me off. And I have no feeling for Natalia. Let her go
back to her father if she wants to."

"You clear out yourself."

"And I will go!"

"And go to the devil!"

"I'm going, I'm going, don't be in a hurry." Gregor stretched out
his hand for his short fur coat lying on the bed, distending his
nostrils and trembling with the same boiling anger as his father.
The same mingled Turkish and Cossack blood flowed in their veins,
and at that moment their resemblance to each other was extraordinary.

"Where are you going?" Ilinichna groaned, seizing Gregor's arm. But he forcibly threw her off and snatched up his fur cap.

"Let him go, the sinful swine! Let him go, curse him! Go on, go! Clear out!" the old man thundered, throwing the door wide open.

Gregor ran out on to the steps, and the last sound he heard was Natalia's weeping.

The frosty night held the village in its grip, a needly powder was falling from the inky sky, the ice on the Don was cracking like pistol-shots. Gregor ran panting out of the gate. At the far end of the village, dogs were barking in chorus; yellow points of light shone through the frosty haze.

He walked aimlessly down the street. Astakhov's windows sparkled like diamonds through the darkness.

"Grishka!" he heard Natalia's yearning cry from the gate.

"Go to hell, you fickle bitch!" Gregor grated his teeth and hastened his steps.

"Grishka, come back!"

He turned into the first cross-lane and for the last time heard her distant, bitter cry:

"Grishenka, dearest! . . ."

He swiftly crossed the square and stopped at a fork in the road, wondering with whom he could spend the night. He decided on Misha Koshevoi. Misha lived with his mother and sister in a lonely straw-thatched hut right by the hill. Gregor entered their yard and knocked at the tiny window.

"Who's there?"

"Is Misha in?"

"Yes, who is it wants him?"

"It's me, Gregor Melekhov."

After a moment Misha, awakened from his first sleep, opened the door.

"You, Grishka?"

"Me."

"What do you want at this time of night?"

"Let me in, and I'll tell you inside."

In the porch Gregor seized Misha by the elbow and whispered:

"I want to spend the night with you. I've fallen out with my people. Have you got room for me? Anywhere will do."

"We'll fix you up somewhere. What's the row all about?"

"I'll tell you later."

They made Gregor a bed on the bench. He lay thinking, his head wrapped in his sheepskin to muffle the snores of Misha's mother. What was happening at home now, he wondered. Would Natalia go back to her father or not? Well, life had taken a new turn. Where should he go? And the answer came swiftly. He would send for Aksinia tomorrow and go with her to the Kuban, far away from the village . . . far away . . . away.

His sleep was troubled by the approaching unknown. Before he finally dropped off he tried hard to recall what it was that oppressed him. In his drowsy state his thoughts would flow easily and smoothly, like a boat downstream, then suddenly they would come up against something, as though the boat had struck a sandbank. He wrestled with the baffling obstacle. What was it that lay across the road?

In the morning he awoke and at once remembered his army service. That was it! How could he go away with Aksinia? In the spring there was the training camp, and in the autumn the army draft.

He had some breakfast and called Misha into the porch.

"Misha, go to the Astakhovs' for me, will you?" he asked. "Tell Aksinia to go to the windmill this evening after dark."

"But what about Stepan?" Misha stammered.

"Say you've come on some business or other."

"All right, I'll go."

"Tell her to be sure to go there."

In the evening Gregor went and sat down by the windmill. He lit a cigarette. Beyond the windmill the wind was stumbling over withered cornstalks. The torn linen flapped on the motionless sails. He thought it sounded like a great bird winging around the mill and unable to fly away, and it was unpleasant and disturbing. Aksinia did not come. The sun had set in the west in a fading, gilded lilac, the wind began to flow freshly from the east, the darkness overtook the moon stranded among the willows. Above the windmill the sky was deathly dark, with blue streaks. From the village came the last sounds of the day's activities.

He smoked three cigarettes in succession, thrust the last butt into the trodden snow, and gazed around in anxious irritation. There was no one in sight. He rose, stretched himself, and moved towards the light twinkling invitingly in Misha's window. He was approaching the yard when he stumbled into Aksinia. She had evidently been running: she was out of breath, and the scent of the winter wind, or perhaps of fresh steppe hay, came from her cold mouth.

"I waited and waited and thought you weren't coming," he said.

"I had to get rid of Stepan."

"I'm frozen through you, you accursed woman!"

"I'm hot, I'll warm you." She flung open her wool-lined coat and wrapped herself around Gregor like hops around an oak.

"Why did you send for me?" she asked.

"Wait, take my arm. There are likely to be people around here."

"You haven't quarrelled with your people?"

"I've left them. I spent the night with Misha. I'm a homeless dog now."

They turned off the road, and Gregor, sweeping away the drift-snow, leaned against a wattle fence.

"You don't know whether Natalia has gone home, do you?" he asked.

"I don't. . . . She'll go, I expect."

Gregor slipped Aksinia's frozen hand up the sleeve of his coat, and squeezing her slender fingers, he asked:

"And what about us?"

"I don't know, dear. Whatever you think best."

"Will you leave Stepan?"

"Without a sigh. This evening, if you like."

"And we'll find work somewhere, and live somehow."

"I'll sleep with the cattle to be with you, Grishka. Anything to be with you."

They stood close together, each warming the other. Gregor did not want to stir; he stood with his head towards the wind, his nostrils quivering, his eyelids closed. Her face pressed into his armpit, Aksinia breathed in the familiar, intoxicating scent of his sweat; and on her shamelessly avid lips, hidden from Gregor's eyes, trembled a joyous smile.

"Tomorrow I'll go and see Mokhov. He may be able to give me work," Gregor said, gripping Aksinia's moist arm above the hand.

Aksinia did not speak, nor did she raise her head. The smile slipped from her face like a dying wind, anxiety and fear started to her dilated eyes like a frightened animal. "Shall I tell him or not?" she thought, as she remembered that she was pregnant. "I must tell him," she decided, but immediately, trembling with fear, she drove away the terrible thought. Her woman's instinct divined that this was not the moment to tell him; she realized that she might lose Gregor for ever; and uncertain whether the child leaping beneath her heart was Gregor's or Stepan's, she temporized and did not tell him.

"What did you tremble for? Are you cold?" Gregor asked, wrapping her in his coat.

"I am a little. . . . I must go, Grishka. Stepan will come back and find me not there."

"Where's he gone?"

"I took him along to Anikey to play cards."

They parted. The agitating scent of her lips remained on Gregor's lips: the scent of the winter wind, or perhaps the intangible scent of rain-sprinkled steppe hay.

Aksinia turned into a by-way, bowed and almost running. By a well, where the cattle had churned up the autumn mud, she stumbled awkwardly, her foot slipping on a frozen clod; and feeling a lacerating pain in her bowels, she caught at the fence. The pain died away, but in her side something living, turning, knocked angrily and strongly time and again.

Next morning Gregor went to see Mokhov. Sergei Platonovich had just returned from the shop and was sitting in the dining-room, sipping strong, claret-coloured tea. Gregor left his cap in the ante-room and went in.

"I'd like to have a word with you, Sergei Platonovich," he said.

"Ah, Pantaleimon Melekhov's son, isn't it? What do you want?"

"I've come to ask whether you could take me on as a workman."

As Gregor spoke, the door creaked and a young officer in a green tunic with a troop commander's epaulets entered. Gregor recognized him as the young Listnitsky, whom Mitka Korshunov had outraced the previous summer. Sergei Platonovich gave the officer a chair and turned back to Gregor.

"Has your father come down in the world, that he is putting his son out to work?" he inquired.

"I'm no longer living with him."

"Left him?"

"Yes."

"Well, I'd gladly take you on, I know your family to be a hard-working lot, but I'm afraid I haven't any work for you to do."

"What's the matter?" Listnitsky inquired, pulling his chair up to the table.

"This lad is looking for work."

"Can you look after horses? Can you drive a pair?" the officer asked as he stirred his tea.

"I can. I've had the care of our own six horses."

"I want a coachman. What wage do you require?"

"I'm not asking for much."

"In that case go to my father at our estate tomorrow. You know the house? At Yagodnoe, some eight miles from here."

"Yes, I know it."

Gregor went to the door. As he turned the handle he hesitated and said:

"I'd like to have a word with you in private, sir."

Listnitsky followed Gregor out into the twilit passage. A rosy light filtered dimly through the Venetian glass of the door leading to the balcony.

"Well, what is it?" the officer asked.

"I'm not alone." Gregor flushed darkly. "I've a woman with me. Perhaps you can find something for her to do?"

"Your wife?" Listnitsky inquired, smiling and raising his eyebrows.

"Someone else's wife."

"Ah, so that's it, is it? All right, we'll fix her up as cook for the servants. But where is her husband?"

"Here in the village."

"So you've stolen another man's wife?"

"She came of her own accord."

"A romantic story! Well, don't fail to come tomorrow. You can go now."

Gregor arrived at Yagodnoe at about eight the next morning. The great house stood in a broad valley, and was surrounded by a brick wall. Outbuildings straggled over the yard: a wing with a tiled roof, the date 1910 picked out with tiles of a different colour; the servants' quarters, a bath-house, stables, poultry-house, and cattle-shed, a long barn, and a coach-house. The main building was old, and nestled in an orchard. Beyond the house rose bare poplars and the willows of the meadows, empty crows' nests swinging in their brown tops.

As he entered the yard Gregor was welcomed by a pack of Crimean borzois. An old lame bitch was the first to snuff at him and follow him with drooping head. In the servants' quarters a cook was quarrelling with a young, freckled maid. Sitting in a cloud of tobacco-smoke at the threshold was an old bowed man. The maid conducted Gregor to the house. The anteroom smelt of dogs and uncured pelts. On a table lay the case of a double-barrelled gun and a fringed game-bag.

"The young master will see you," the maid called to Gregor through a side door.

Gregor looked anxiously at his muddy boots and entered. List-nitsky was lying on a bed under the window. The officer rolled a cigarette, buttoned up the collar of his white shirt, and remarked:

"You're in good time. Wait; my father will be here in a minute."

Gregor stood by the door. After a moment or two there was the sound of footsteps in the anteroom, and a deep bass voice asked through the door:

"Are you asleep, Eugene?"

"Come in," Listnitsky replied.

An old man wearing a black Caucasian cloak entered. Gregor gave him a stealthy glance. He was immediately struck by the fine hooked nose and the white, tobacco-stained arch of whiskers. Old Listnitsky was tall and broad-shouldered, but gaunt. Beneath the cloak a long coat of camel-hair hung on him. His eyes were set close to his nose.

"Papa, here is the coachman I spoke to you about," Eugene re-marked.

"Whose son is he?"

"Pantaleimon Melekhov's."

"I knew Prokoffey, he was in the army with me. I remember Pantaleimon, too. Lame, isn't he?"

"Yes, Your Excellency," Gregor replied, mentally recalling his father's stories of the retired General Listnitsky, a hero of the Russo-Turkish war.

"Why are you seeking work?" the old man inquired.

"I'm not living with my father, Your Excellency."

"What sort of Cossack will you make if you hire yourself out? Didn't your father provide for you when you left him?"

"No, Your Excellency."

"Hm, that's another matter. You want work for your wife as well?"

The younger Listnitsky's bed creaked heavily. Gregor turned his eyes in that direction and saw the officer winking.

"That's right, Your Excellency," he answered.

"Without any 'Excellencies.' I don't like them. Your wage will be eight rubles a month. For both of you. Your wife will cook for the yard and seasonal workers. Is that satisfactory?"

"Yes."

"Come along tomorrow morning. You will occupy the room the previous coachman had. And now quick march. Be here at eight."

Gregor went out. On the far side of the barn the borzois were sunning themselves on a patch of ground bare of snow. The old bitch followed Gregor a little way with head still drooping mournfully, then turned back.

(Natalia)

That same morning Aksinia finished cooking early. She raked out the fire, washed the dishes, and glanced out of the window looking on to the yard. Stepan was standing by the wood-pile close to the fence bordering on the Melekhovs' yard. The left-hand corner of the shed was tumbling down, and he was selecting posts suitable for its repair.

Aksinia had arisen with two rosy blushes in her cheeks and a youthful glitter in her eyes. Stepan noticed the change, and as he was having breakfast he could not forbear to ask:

"What's happened to you?"

"What's happened?" Aksinia echoed him.

"Your face is shining as though you had smeared yourself with butter."

"It's the heat of the fire," and turning round, she glanced stealthily out of the window to see whether Misha Koshevoi's sister was coming.

But the girl did not arrive until late in the afternoon. Tormented with waiting, Aksinia started up, asking:

"Do you want me, Mashutka?"

"Come out for a moment," the girl replied.

Stepan was combing his hair before a scrap of mirror fixed above the stove. Aksinia looked at him nervously.

"You aren't going out, are you?" she asked.

He did not answer immediately, but put the comb into his trouser pocket and picked up a pack of cards and his pipe, lying on the stove ledge. Then he said:

"I'm going along to Anikushka's for a while."

"And when are you ever at home? You spend every night at cards. You're not going to play for points?"

"Enough of that, Aksinia. There's someone waiting for you."

Aksinia went out. Mashutka welcomed her with a smile and a droop of her eyelashes.

"Grishka's come back," she said.

"Well?"

"He told me to tell you to come along to our hut as soon as it's dark."

Seizing the girl's hand, Aksinia drew her towards the outer door.

"Softer, softer, dear! Did he tell you to say anything else?"

"He said you were to get your things together and bring them along."

Burning and trembling, stepping from foot to foot like a mettlesome horse, Aksinia turned and glanced at the kitchen door:

"Lord, how am I to—so quickly? Well—wait; tell him I'll be along as soon as I can. . . . But where will he meet me?"

"You're to come to our hut."

"Oh, no!"

"All right, I'll tell him to come out and wait for you."

Stepan was drawing on his coat as Aksinia went in. "What did she want?" he asked between two puffs at a cigarette.

"Oh, she came to ask me—to cut out a skirt for her."

Blowing the ash off his cigarette, Stepan went to the door. "Don't wait up for me," he said as he went out.

Aksinia ran to the frosted window and dropped to her knees before the bench. Stepan's footsteps sounded along the path trodden out in the snow to the gate. The wind caught a spark from his cigarette and carried it back to the window. Through the melted circle of glass Aksinia caught a glimpse of his fur cap and the profile of his face.

She feverishly turned jackets, skirts, and kerchiefs—her dowry—out of the great chest and threw them into a large shawl. Panting, her eyes wandering, she passed through the kitchen for the last time and, putting out the light, ran on to the steps. She fastened the kitchen door by the chain. Someone emerged from the Mele-khovs' hut to see to the cattle. She waited until the footsteps had died away, then ran down to the Don. Strands of hair escaped from her kerchief and tickled her cheeks. Clutching her bundle she made her way by side lanes to the Koshevois' hut, her strength ebbing, her feet feeling like cast iron. Gregor was waiting for her at the gate. He took the bundle and silently led the way into the steppe.

Beyond the hut Aksinia slowed her pace and caught at Gregor's sleeve. "Wait a moment," she asked him.

"What is there to wait for? The moon will be late tonight, so we must hurry."

"Wait, Grishka!" She halted, doubled up with pain.

"What's the matter?" Gregor turned back to her.

"Something—in my belly. I carried too much away with me." She licked her dry lips and clutched at her bowels. She stood a moment bowed and miserable and then, poking her hair under her kerchief, set off again.

"You haven't asked where I'm taking you to. I might be leading you to the nearest cliff to push you over." Gregor smiled in the darkness.

"It's all the same to me now. I can't go back." Her voice trembled with an unhappy smile.

That night Stepan returned at midnight as usual. He went first to the stable, threw the scattered hay back into the manger, removed the horse's halter, then went to the hut. "She must have gone out for the evening," he thought, as he unfastened the chain. He entered the kitchen, closed the door fast, and struck a match. He had been in a winning vein that evening and so was quiet and drowsy. He lit the lamp and gaped at the disorder of the kitchen, not divining the reason. A little astonished, he went into the best room. The

open chest yawned blackly. On the floor lay an old jacket which
Aksinia had forgotten in her hurry. Stepan tore off his sheepskin
and ran back to the kitchen for the light. He stared around the
best room, and at last he understood. He dropped the lamp, tore
his sabre down from the wall, gripped the hilt until the veins
swelled in his fingers, raised Aksinia's blue and yellow jacket on
its point, threw the jacket up in the air, and with a short swing
of the sabre cut it in two as it fell.

Grey, savage, in his wolfish yearning he threw the pieces of old
jacket up to the ceiling again and again; the sharp steel whistled
as it cut them in their flight.

Then, tearing off the sword-knot, he threw the sabre into a
corner, went into the kitchen, and sat down at the table. His head
bowed, with trembling fingers he stroked the unwashed table-top
time after time.

Troubles never come singly.

The morning after Gregor had left home, through Getka's care-
lessness Miron Korshunov's pedigree bull gored the throat of his
finest mare. Getka came running into the kitchen, white, distracted,
and trembling.

"Trouble, master! The bull, curse him, the damned bull!"

"Well, what about the bull?" Miron asked in alarm.

"He's done the mare in. Gored her. . . ."

Miron ran half-undressed into the yard. By the well Mitka was
beating the red five-year-old bull with a stick. The bull, his head
down and dewlap dragging over the snow, was churning up the
snow with his hoofs and scattering a silvery powder around his
tail. He would not yield before the drubbing, but danced about
on his hind legs as though intending to charge. Mitka beat him
on his nose and sides, cursing the while and paying no heed to the
labourer who was trying to drag him back by his belt.

Miron Gregorievich ran to the well. The mare was standing by
the fence, her head drooping and a fine shiver running over her
body. Her heaving flanks were wet with sweat, and blood was
running down her chest. A rose-coloured wound a hand-breadth
deep and revealing the windpipe gaped on her neck. Miron seized
her by the forelock and raised her head. The mare fixed her glazing

eyes on her master as though mutely asking: "What next?" As if in answer to the question Miron shouted:

"Run and tell someone to scald some oak bark. Hurry!"

Getka ran to strip some bark from a tree, and Mitka came across to his father, one eye fixed on the bull circling and bellowing about the yard.

"Hold the mare by her forelock," his father ordered. "Someone run for some twine. Quickly!"

They tied string round the mare's upper lip so that she should not feel the pain, and then washed the wound. With freezing fingers Miron threaded raw thread through a darning-needle and sewed up the edges, making a neat seam. He had hardly turned away to go back to the house when his wife came running from the kitchen, alarm written large on her face. She called her husband aside:

"Natalia's here, Gregorich! . . . Ah, my God!"

"Now what's the matter?" Miron demanded, his face paling.

"It's Gregor. He's left home!" Lukinichna flung out her arms like a rook preparing for flight, clapped her hands against her skirt, and broke into a whine:

"Disgraced before all the village! Lord, what a blow! Oh! . . ."

Miron found Natalia standing in the middle of the kitchen. Two tears welled in her eyes, her cheeks were deeply flushed.

"What are you doing here?" her father blustered as he ran into the room. "Has your husband beaten you? Can't you get on together?"

"He's gone away!" Natalia groaned, and she swayed and fell on her knees before her father. "Father, my life is blighted. . . . Take me back. . . . Gregor's gone away with that woman. . . . He's left me. Father, I've been crushed into the dust!" she sobbed, gazing imploringly up at her father's grey beard.

"Wait, wait now. . . ."

"I can't go on living there! Take me back!" She crawled on her knees to the chest and dropped her head on her arms. Tears at such a time are like rain in a May drought. Her mother pressed Natalia's head against her skirt, whispering soothing, motherly words; but Miron, infuriated, ran out to the steps:

"Harness two horses to the sleigh!" he shouted.

A cock pattering importantly around behind its hen on the steps took alarm at the shout, jumped away, and fluttered agitatedly off towards the barn, squawking indignantly.

"Harness the horses!" Miron kicked again and again at the fretted balustrade of the steps until it was hopelessly ruined. He returned to the kitchen only when Getka hurried out from the stables with the pair of horses, harnessing them as he went.

Mitka drove with Getka to the Melekhovs' for Natalia's possessions. In his abstraction Getka sent a young pig in the road flying. "Maybe the master will forget all about the mare now," he was thinking, and rejoiced, letting the reins hang loose. "But he's such an old devil, he'll never forget," and Getka brought the whip-lash hard down across the horses' backs.

Chapter 10

Eugene Listnitsky held a commission as troop commander in the ataman's Life Guard regiment. Having had a tumble during the officers' hurdle races and broken his left arm, when he came out of the hospital he took a furlough and went to stay with his father for six weeks.

The old general lived alone in Yagodnoe. He had lost his wife while driving in the suburbs of Warsaw in the eighties of the nineteenth century. Revolutionaries had attempted to shoot the Cossack general, had missed him, but had killed his wife and coachman. Listnitsky was left with his two-year-old son, Eugene. Soon after this event the general retired, went to live at Yagodnoe, and lived a lonely, harsh life.

He sent his son Eugene to the Cadets' corps as soon as the lad was old enough, and occupied himself with farming. He purchased blood stock from the Imperial stables, crossed them with the finest mares from England and from the famous Provalsky stables, and reared a new stock. He raised cattle and livestock on his own and rented land, sowed grain (with hired labour), hunted with his borzois in the autumn and winter, and occasionally locked himself into the hall and drank for a week on end. He was troubled with a stomach complaint, and his doctor had strictly forbidden him to swallow anything; he had to extract the goodness from all his food by mastication, spitting out the residue on a silver tray held by his personal servant, Benyamin.

Benyamin was a half-witted, swarthy young peasant, with a shock of thick black hair. He had been in Listnitsky's service for six years. When he first had to wait on the general he could not bear to watch the old man spitting out the chewed food. But after a time he grew accustomed to it. After some months he thought as he watched his master chewing the white meat of a turkey: "What a waste of good food! He doesn't eat it himself, and my belly is turning over with hunger. I'll try it after he's finished with it." After that he made a practice of carrying the silver tray into the anteroom when his master had dined, and there hurriedly gulping down all that was left. Perhaps it was for this reason that he began to grow fat and double-chinned.

The other inhabitants of the farm were the maid, the pock-marked cook, Lukeria, the ancient stableman, Sashka, and the shepherd, Tikhon. From the very first Lukeria would not allow Aksinia to help in the cooking for the master, and Aksinia was set to work washing the floors of the house three times a week, feeding the innumerable fowls, and keeping the chicken-house clean. Gregor spent much of his time in the spacious stables with Sashka, the stableman. The old man was one mass of grey hair, but everybody still familiarly called him Sashka. Probably even old Listnitsky, for whom he had worked more than twenty years, had forgotten his surname. In his youth Sashka had been the coachman, but as he grew old and feeble and his sight began to fail he was made stableman. Stocky, covered with greenish-grey hair, with a nose that had been flattened by a stick in his youth, he wore an everlasting childish smile and gazed out on the world with twinkling, artless eyes. The reverend, apostolic expression of his face was marred by his broken nose and his hanging, scarred underlip. Sashka was fond of vodka, and when he was in his cups he would wander about the yard as though he were master. Stamping his feet, he would stand beneath old Listnitsky's bedroom and call loudly and sternly:

"Mikolai Lexievich! Mikolai Lexievich!"

If old Listnitsky happened to be in his bedroom he would come to the window.

"You're drunk, you scoundrel!" he would thunder.

Sashka would hitch up his trousers and wink and smile. His smile danced right across his face.

"Mikolai Lexievich, Your Excellency, I know you!" He would shake his lean, dirty finger threateningly.

"Go and sleep it off!" his master would smile pacifyingly.

"You can't take in Sashka!" the stableman would laugh, going up to the railings of the fence. "Mikolai Lexievich, you're like me. Me and you—we're like fish in the water. You and me—we're rich, ah!" Here he would fling his arms wide open to show how rich. "We're known by everybody, all over the Don district. We . . ." Sashka's voice would suddenly sound miserable and surreptitious: "Me and you—Your Excellency, we're good to everybody, only we've both got rotting noses."

"What with?" his master would ask, turning purple with laughter.

"With vodka!" Sashka would stamp out the words, winking and licking his lips. "Don't drink, Mikolai Lexievich, or we'll be ruined, you and me. We'll drink everything away."

"Go and drink this away!" Old Listnitsky would throw out a twenty-kopek piece, and Sashka would catch it and hide it in his cap, crying:

"Well, good-bye, general."

"Have you watered the horses yet?" his master would ask with a smile.

"You lousy devil! You son of a swine!" Sashka would turn livid and in his anger would stutter and shake as though with the ague. "Sashka forget to water the horses? Eh? If I was dying I'd still crawl for a pail to water the horses. And he thinks . . ."

The old man would march off fuming at the undeserved reproach, cursing, and shaking his fist. Everything came naturally to him, even drinking and his familiarity with his master. He was irreplaceable as a stableman. Winter and summer he slept in the stables, in an empty stall. He was ostler and blacksmith; he cut grass for the horses in the spring and dug up medicinal roots on the steppe and in the valleys. Bunches of dried herbs, remedies for all the various horse ailments and diseases, hung high up on the stable walls.

Winter and summer a fine tingling aroma hung like a spider's web about the stall in which Sashka slept. Hay packed as hard as a board, covered with a horse-cloth and his coat, smelling of horse sweat, served as mattress and bedding to his plank bed. The coat and a sheepskin were all the old man's worldly goods.

Tikhon, a healthy and dull-witted Cossack, lived with Lukeria and was needlessly jealous of her and Sashka. Regularly once a month he would take the old man by the button of his greasy shirt and lead him aside.

"Old man, don't you set your cap at my woman," he would say.

"That depends. . . ." Sashka would wink significantly.

"You ought to be ashamed of yourself at your age. . . . And you a doctor, too; you look after the horses . . . you know the Holy Book!"

"I like them pockmarked. Say good-bye to Lukeria, I'll be taking her away from you. She's like a currant pudding. . . ."

"Don't let me catch you or I'll kill you!" Tikhon would say, sighing and drawing some copper coins out of his pocket.

Life mouldered away in a sleepy torpor at Yagodnoe. The estate lay in a valley remote from all frequented roads, and from the autumn onward all connection with the neighbouring villages was broken. In the winter nights the wolf packs emerged from their forest lairs and terrified the horses with their howling. Tikhon used to go to the meadow to frighten them off with shot from his master's double-barrelled gun, and Lukeria would wait in suspense for the sound of the shot. At such times her imagination transformed bald-headed Tikhon into a handsome and desperately brave youth, and when the door of the servants' quarters slammed and Tikhon entered, she warmly embraced his frozen old bones.

In summer-time Yagodnoe was alive until late in the evening with the sound of labourers' voices. The master sowed some hundred acres with grain of various kinds. Occasionally Eugene came home and would wander boredly through the orchard and over the meadow or sit all the morning with rod and line by the lakeside. Eugene was of medium height and broad-chested. He arranged his hair Cossack-fashion, brushing it on the right side. His officer's tunic was always a perfect fit.

During the first ten days of Gregor's life on the estate he was frequently in the young master's company. One day Benyamin came smiling into the servants' quarters and announced:

"The young master wants you, Gregor."

Gregor went to Eugene's room and stood at the door. The master pointed to a chair. Gregor seated himself on the very edge.

"How do you like our horses?" Listnitsky asked.

"They're good horses. The grey is very good."

"Give him plenty of exercise, but don't gallop him."

"So Grand-dad Sashka told me."

Screwing up his eyes, the young master said:

"You have to go to the training camp in May, don't you?"

"Yes."

"I'll speak to the ataman about it. You won't need to go."

"Thank you, sir."

There was a momentary silence. Unbuttoning the collar of his uniform, Eugene scratched his womanishly white breast.

"Aren't you afraid of Aksinia's husband taking her from you?" he asked.

"He's thrown her over; he won't take her back."

"How do you know?"

"I saw one of the men from the village the other day, and he told me Stepan had said so to him."

"Aksinia's a fine-looking woman," Listnitsky remarked thoughtfully, staring over Gregor's head and smiling.

"Not bad," Gregor agreed, and his face clouded.

During the last few days of his furlough Eugene spent a great deal of his time in Gregor's room. Aksinia kept the little room spotlessly clean and made it gay with feminine gewgaws. The officer chose times for his visit when Gregor was occupied with the horses. He would first go into the kitchen and stand joking with Lukeria for a minute or two, then would pass into the farther room. One day he sat down on a stool, hunching his shoulders, and fixed a shamelessly smiling gaze on Aksinia. She was embarrassed by his presence, and the knitting-needles trembled in her fingers.

"Well, Aksinia, how are you getting on?" he asked, puffing at his cigarette until the room was filled with blue smoke.

"Very well, thank you." Aksinia raised her eyes, and meeting Eugene's transparent gaze silently telling of his desire, she turned crimson. She replied disconnectedly to his questions, avoiding his eyes and seeking an opportunity to leave the room.

"I must go and feed the ducks now," she told him.

"Sit a little longer. The ducks can wait," he smiled, and continued to ply her with questions concerning her past life, while his crystal-clear eyes pleaded obscenely.

When Gregor came in, Eugene offered him a cigarette, and went out soon after.

"What did he want?" Gregor asked Aksinia, not looking at her.

"How should I know?" Remembering the officer's look, Aksinia laughed forcedly. "He came in and sat there, just like this, Grishka" (she showed him how Eugene had sat with hunched back), "and sat and sat until I was sick of him."

"You made yourself pleasant to him, of course?" Gregor screwed up his eyes angrily. "You watch out, or I shall send him flying down the steps some day."

Aksinia gazed at Gregor with a smile on her lips and could not be sure whether he was speaking in jest or earnest.

Chapter 11

The winter broke during the fourth week of Lent. Open water began to fringe the edges of the Don; the ice, melting from the top, turned grey and swelled spongily. Of an evening a howling noise came from the hills, indicating frost according to the time-honoured saying, but in reality presaging the approaching thaw. In the morning the air tingled with the light frost, but by noon the earth was bare in patches, and in the nostrils was a scent of March, of the frozen bark of cherry trees, and rotting straw.

Miron Gregorievich leisurely made ready for the ploughing season, spending his days under the shed sharpening the teeth of the harrows and preparing for the thaw. During the fourth week of Lent old Grishaka fasted. He returned blue with cold from the church and complained to his daughter-in-law, Lukinichna:

"The priest starved me. He's no good. He's as slow as a carter with a load of eggs."

"You'd have been wiser to have fasted during Passion Week; it's warmer by then," she told him.

"Call Natalia," he replied. "Let her make me a pair of warmer stockings."

Natalia still lived in the belief that Gregor would return to her; her heart waited for him and would not listen to the warning whisper of sober reason. She spent the nights in a weary yearning, tossing on her bed, crushed by her undeserved and unexpected shame. Another woe was now added to the first, and she awaited its sequel in a cold terror, casting about in her maiden room like a shot lapwing in a forest glade. From the earliest days of her return home her brother Mitka began to give her queer glances, and one day, catching her in the porch, he asked frankly:

"Are you still yearning after Grishka?"

"What has it to do with you?"

"I want to help you get rid of your pain."

Natalia glanced into his eyes and was terrified by what she saw there. Mitka's green cat's eyes glittered and their slits gleamed oilily in the dim light of the porch. Natalia slammed the door and ran to her grandfather's room, standing and listening to the beating of her heart. Two days later Mitka came up to her in the yard. He had been turning over fresh hay for the cattle, and green stalks of grass hung from his straight hair and his fur cap.

"Don't torture yourself, Natalia. . . ."

"I'll tell Father," she cried, raising her hands to protect herself.

"You're an idiot! What are you shouting for?"

"Go away, Mitka! I'll go at once and tell Father. What eyes you make at me! It's a wonder the earth doesn't open and swallow you up. Don't come near me, Mitka," she pleaded.

"I won't now, but I'll come at night. By God, I'll come!" he replied.

Trembling, Natalia left the yard. That evening she made her bed on the chest and took her younger sister to sleep with her. All night she tossed and turned, her burning eyes seeking to pierce the darkness, her ears alert to the slightest sound, ready to scream the house down. But the silence was broken only by the snores of Grishaka sleeping in the next room and an occasional grunt from her sister.

Mitka had not got over the shame of his recent attempt at marriage, and he went about morose and ill-tempered. He went out every evening, and rarely arrived home again before dawn. He formed associations with women of undesirable reputation in the village and went to Stepan Astakhov's to play cards for stakes. His father watched his behaviour, but said nothing.

Just before Easter, Natalia met Pantaleimon Prokoffievich close to Mokhov's shop. He called to her:

"Wait a moment!"

She halted. Her heart yearned as she saw her father-in-law's face, mournfully reminding her of Gregor.

"Why don't you come and see us sometimes?" the old man asked her diffidently, avoiding her eyes as though he himself had been guilty of some offence against her. "The wife is longing to see you. . . . Well, perhaps you will come some day?"

Natalia recovered from her embarrassment. "Thank you," she said, and after a moment's hesitation (she wanted to say "Father") she added: "Pantaleimon Prokoffievich. I've been very busy at home."

"Our Grishka—ah!" the old man shook his head bitterly. "He's tricked us, the scoundrel. How well we'd have got on together!"

"Oh, well, Father"—Natalia spoke in a high-pitched, grating voice—"clearly it wasn't to be."

Pantaleimon fiddled about embarrassedly as he saw Natalia's eyes fill with tears. Her lips were pressed together to restrain her desire to weep.

"Good-bye, my dear," he said. "Don't grieve over him, the son of a swine! He's not worth the nail on your little finger. Maybe he'll come back. I'm thinking of going to see him, but it's difficult."

Natalia walked away with her head sunk on her breast. Pantaleimon stood dancing from foot to foot as though about to break into a run. As she turned the corner Natalia glanced back; the old man was limping across the square, leaning heavily on his stick.

As spring approached, the meetings in Stockman's workshop were held less frequently. The villagers were preparing for the field

work, and only Ivan Alexievich, the engine-man, and Valet came
from the mill, bringing David with them. On Maundy Thursday
they gathered at the workshop in the early evening. Stockman was
sitting at his bench, cleaning a silver ring made from a fifty-kopek
piece. A broad bar of rays from the setting sun streamed through
the window. The engine-man picked up a pair of pincers and turned
them over in his hand.

"I had to go to the master the other day to ask about a piston,"
he remarked. "It will have to be taken to Millerovo, we can't mend
it here. There's a crack in it as long as this." Ivan Alexievich measured the length on his little finger.

"There's a works at Millerovo, isn't there?" Stockman asked,
scattering a fine silver rain as he filed the coin.

"A steel-foundry. I had to spend some days there last year," Ivan
replied.

"Many workers?"

"Some five hundred."

"And what are they like?" The words came deliberately from
Stockman.

"They're well off. They're none of your proletariat, they're muck."

"Why is that?" Valet asked.

"Because they're too well off. Each has his own little house, his
wife, and every comfort. And a good half of them are Baptists into
the bargain. The master himself is their preacher, and they suck one
another's noses, and the dirt on them is so thick you couldn't scrape
it off with a rake. Well, and I went to Sergei Platonovich," Ivan
Alexievich continued his story, "and he had company with him, so
he told me to wait outside. I sat down and waited and heard them
talking through the door. Mokhov was saying there was going to
be a war with the Germans very soon; he had read it in a book.
But someone else said there couldn't be a war between Germany
and Russia, because Germany needed our grain. Then I heard a
third voice; I found out afterwards it was that of the officer, old
Listnitsky's son. 'There will be a war,' he said, 'between Germany
and France, over vineyards, but it's nothing to do with us.' What
do you think, Osip Davidovich?" Ivan asked, turning to Stockman.

"I'm no good at prophecies," Stockman replied, staring fixedly
at the ring in his hand.

"Once they do start we'll have to go. Like it or not, they'll drag

us there by the hair," Valet declared.

"It's like this, boys," Stockman said, gently taking the pincers out of the engine-man's hands. He spoke seriously, evidently intending to explain the matter thoroughly. Valet sat himself comfortably on the bench, and David's lips shaped into an "O," revealing his strong teeth.

In definite, well-chosen words Stockman outlined the struggle of the capitalist states for markets and colonies. When he had finished, Ivan Alexievich asked anxiously:

"Yes, but where do we come in?"

"Your heads will ache for the drunken orgies of others." Stockman smiled.

"Don't talk like a child," Valet said venomously. "You know the saying: 'The master tugs at the leash, but the dog shakes its head.' "

"And what was Listnitsky visiting Mokhov for?" David changed the subject.

"He was on his way to the station. Yes, and here's some more news. When I went out of the house I saw—who do you think? Gregor Melekhov! He was standing outside with a whip in his hand."

"He's Listnitsky's coachman," David explained.

It was getting late, and Ivan Alexievich initiated a general movement to depart. Stockman accompanied his guests to the gate, then locked up the workshop and went into the hut.

Gregor returned on Palm Sunday from his journey with Eugene to the station. He found the thaw had eaten away the snow; the road had broken up within a couple of days.

At a Ukrainian village some twenty miles back from the station he all but lost his horses as he was crossing a stream. He arrived at the village early in the evening. During the previous night the ice of the rivulet had broken and floated away, and the stream was swollen and foaming with muddy brown water. The tavern at which he had stopped to feed the horses on the way out lay on the farther side of the stream. The water might easily rise still higher during the night, and Gregor decided to cross.

He drove to the point where he had crossed over the ice on the outward journey and found the stream had overflowed its banks.

A piece of fencing and half a cartwheel were eddying in the middle. There were fresh traces of sledge-runners on the bare sand at the edge. He halted the horses and jumped down to look at the marks more closely. At the water's edge the tracks turned a little to the left and disappeared into the stream. He measured the distance to the other side with his eyes: fifty yards at the most. He went to the horses to see that the harness was in good order. At that moment an aged Ukrainian came towards him from the nearest hut.

"Is there a good crossing here?" Gregor asked him, waving his reins at the seething brown flood.

"People crossed there this morning."

"Is it deep?"

"No. It might flow into the sleigh."

Gregor gathered up the reins and, holding his knout ready, urged on the horses with a curt, imperative command. They moved unwillingly, snorting and snuffing at the water. Gregor cracked his whip and stood up on the seat.

The bay on the left shook its head and suddenly pulled on the traces. Gregor glanced down at his feet; the water was swirling over the front of the sleigh. At first the horses were wading up to their knees, but suddenly the stream rose to their breasts. Gregor tried to turn them back, but they refused to answer the rein and began to swim. The tail of the sleigh was swung round by the current, and the horses' heads were forced upstream. The water flowed in waves over their backs, the sleigh rocked and pulled them back strongly.

"Hey! Hey! to the right!" the Ukrainian shouted, running along the bank and waving his three-cornered cap in his hands.

Savagely raging, Gregor incessantly shouted and urged on the horses. The water foamed in eddies behind the dragging sleigh. The runners struck against a jutting pile, the remains of the bridge which had been swept away overnight, and the sleigh turned over with extraordinary ease. With a groan Gregor plunged in headfirst, but he did not lose his grip of the reins. He was dragged by the edges of his sheepskin, by his feet, drawn with gentle insistence, rocking and turning over and over at the side of the sleigh. He succeeded in clutching a runner, dropped the reins, and hauled himself along hand over hand, making his way to the singletrees. He was about to seize the iron-shod end of the singletree when one horse, in its struggle against the current, lashed out with its hind leg and struck him on the knee. Choking, Gregor threw out his hands and caught at the traces. His body fierily tingling with the cold, he managed to reach the horse's head, and the animal fixed the maddened, mortally terrified gaze of its bloodshot eyes right into his dilated pupils.

Again and again he grasped at the slippery leather reins, but they eluded his fingers. Somehow he managed at last to seize them. Abruptly his legs scraped along ground. Dragging himself to the edge of the water, he stumbled forward and fell in the foaming shallows, knocked off his feet by the horses' breasts.

Trampling over him, the horses tugged the sleigh violently out of the water and halted a few paces away, exhausted, shuddering, and steaming. Unconscious of any pain, Gregor jumped to his feet; the cold enveloped him as though in unbearably hot dough. He was trembling even more than the horses, feeling that he was as weak on his legs as an unweaned infant. He gathered his wits and, turning the sleigh on to its runners, drove the horses off at a gallop to get them warm. He flew into the street of the village as though attacking an enemy and turned into the first open gate without slackening his pace.

Fortunately he had chanced upon a hospitable Ukrainian, who sent his son to attend to the horses and himself helped Gregor to undress. In a tone permitting of no question he ordered his wife to light the stove. Until his own clothes were dry Gregor stretched himself out on top of the stove in his host's trousers. After a supper of cabbage soup he went to sleep.

He set off again long before dawn came. A good eighty-five miles of travel lay before him, and every minute was precious. The untracked confusion of the flooded spring steppe was at hand; every little ravine or gully had become a roaring torrent of snow-water.

The black, bare road exhausted the horses. Over the hard road of the early morning frost he reached a village lying three miles off his route and stopped at a crossroad. The horses were smoking with sweat; behind him lay the gleaming track of the sleigh-runners in the ground. He abandoned the sleigh and set off again, riding one horse bareback and leading the other by the reins. He arrived at Yagodnoe in the morning of Palm Sunday.

Old Listnitsky listened attentively to his story of the journey and went to look at the horses. Sashka was leading them up and down the yard, angrily eyeing their sunken flanks.

"How are they?" the master asked. "They haven't been overdriven, have they?"

"No. The bay has a sore on the chest where the collar has rubbed, but it's nothing."

"Go and get some rest." Listnitsky indicated Gregor with his hand. Gregor went to his room. But he had only one night's rest. The next morning Benyamin came and called to him:

"Gregor, the master wants you. At once."

The general was shuffling about the hall in felt slippers. Only after Gregor had coughed twice did he look up.

"Ah, yes! Go and saddle the stallion and my horse. Tell Lukeria not to feed the dogs. They're going hunting."

Gregor turned to leave the room. His master stopped him with a shout:

"Do you hear? And you're going with me."

Gregor led the saddled horses to the palisade and whistled to the dogs. Listnitsky came out, attired in a jerkin of blue cloth and girdled with an ornamental leather belt. A nickel cork-lined flask was slung at his back; the whip hanging from his arm trailed behind him like a snake.

As he held the rein for his master to mount, Gregor was astonished at the ease with which old Listnitsky hoisted his bony body into the saddle. "Keep close behind me," the general curtly ordered as he gathered the reins in his gloved hand.

Gregor rode the stallion. It was not shod on the hind hoofs, and as it trod on the shards of ice it slipped and sat on its hindquarters. It called for strong use of the bridle, for it arched its short neck and glanced askance at its rider, trying to bite his knees. When they reached the top of the hill from Yagodnoe, Listnitsky put his horse into a fast trot. The chain of hounds followed Gregor; one black old bitch ran with her muzzle touching the end of the stallion's tail. The horse tried to reach her by falling back on its hindquarters, but the bitch dropped behind, giving Gregor a yearning, grandmotherly glance.

They reached their objective, the Olshansky ravine, in half an hour. Listnitsky rode through the undergrowth along the brow of the ravine. Gregor dropped down into the valley, cautiously avoiding the numerous holes. From time to time he looked up, and through the steely blue of a straggling and naked alder grove he saw Listnitsky's clearly defined figure standing in the stirrups. Behind him the hounds were running in a bunch along the undulating ridge. Pulling off his glove, Gregor fumbled in his pocket for some cigarette paper, thinking to have a smoke.

"After him!" a shout came like a pistol-shot from the other side of the ridge.

Gregor raised his head and saw Listnitsky galloping along with upraised whip.

"After him!"

Crossing the rushy and reedy bottom of the ravine, slipping along with body close to the ground, a shaggy, dirty brown wolf was running swiftly. Leaping the bed of the stream, it stopped and, turning quickly, caught sight of the dogs. They were coming after it stretched in horseshoe formation, to cut it off from the wood at the end of the ravine.

With a springy stride the wolf made for the wood. The old bitch came almost straight towards it, another hound behind her. The wolf hesitated for a moment, and as Gregor rode up out of the ravine he lost sight of it. When next he had a good view from a hillock, the wolf was far away in the steppe, making for a neighbouring ravine. Gregor could see the hounds running through the undergrowth behind it, and old Listnitsky riding slightly to the side, plying his horse with the butt of his whip. As the wolf reached the ravine the hounds were beginning to overtake it, and one was almost on top of the hunted animal.

Gregor put his horse into a gallop, vainly trying to see what was happening ahead of him. His eyes were streaming with tears, and his ears were deafened by the whistling wind. He was suddenly possessed by the excitement of the hunt. Bending over his horse's neck, he flew along like the wind. When he reached the ravine neither wolf nor dogs were to be seen. A moment or two later Listnitsky overtook him. Reining in his horse sharply, he shouted:

"Which way did they go?"

"Into the ravine, I think."

"You overtake them from the left. After them!" The old man dug his heels into his horse's flanks and rode off to the right. Gregor dropped into a hollow, and with whip and shout rode his horse hard for a good mile. The damp, sticky earth flew up under the hoofs, striking him on the face. The long ravine bent to the right and branched into three. Gregor crossed the first fork and caught sight of the dark chain of hounds chasing the wolf across the steppe. The animal had been headed off from the heart of the ravine, which was densely overgrown with oaks and alders, and was now making for a dry, brush- and thistle-covered valley.

Rising in his stirrups, and wiping the tears from his eyes with his sleeve, Gregor watched them. Glancing momentarily to the left, he realized that he was in the steppe close to his native village. Near by lay the irregular square of land which he and Natalia had ploughed in the autumn. He deliberately guided the stallion across the patch, and during the few moments in which the animal was sliding and stumbling over the clods the zest for the hunt died to ashes within him. He now calmly urged on the heavily sweating horse and, glancing round to see whether Listnitsky was looking, dropped into an easy trot.

Some distance away he could see the empty camping-quarters of ploughers; a little farther off three pairs of bullocks were dragging a plough across the fresh, velvety soil.

"From the village, surely. Whose land is that? That's not Ani-kushka, is it?" Gregor screwed up his eyes as he recognized the man following the plough.

He saw two Cossacks drop the plough and run to head off the wolf from the near-by ravine. One, in a visored, red-banded cap, chin-strap under his chin, was waving an iron bar. Suddenly the wolf squatted down in a deep furrow. The foremost hound flew right over it and fell with its forelegs tucked beneath it; the old bitch following tried to stop, her hindquarters scraping along the cloddy, ploughed ground; but unable to halt in time, she tumbled against the wolf. The hunted animal shook its head violently, and the bitch ricocheted off it. Now the mass of hounds fastened on the wolf, and they all dragged for some yards over the ploughed land. Gregor was off his horse half a minute before his master. He fell to his knees, his hand on his hunting-knife.

"There! In the throat!" the Cossack with the iron bar cried in a voice which Gregor knew well. Panting heavily, he ran up and lay down at Gregor's side and, dragging away the hound which had fastened on the hunted animal's belly, tied the wolf's forelegs with a cord. Gregor felt under the animal's shaggy fur for its windpipe and drew the knife across it.

"The dogs! The dogs! Drive them off!" old Listnitsky cried as he dropped from his saddle.

Gregor managed with difficulty to drive away the dogs, then glanced towards his master. Standing a little way off was Stepan Astakhov. His face working strangely, he was turning the iron bar over and over in his hands.

"Where are you from, my man?" Listnitsky turned to Stepan.

"From Tatarsk," Stepan answered after a momentary hesitation, and he took a step in Gregor's direction.

"What's your name?" Listnitsky asked.

"Astakhov."

"When are you going home, my lad?"

"Tonight."

"Bring us that carcass." Listnitsky pointed to the wolf with his foot. "I'll pay whatever it costs." He wiped the sweat from his purple face with his scarf, turned away, and slipped the flask off his back.

Gregor went to his stallion. As he set foot in the stirrup he glanced back. Trembling uncontrollably, Stepan was coming towards him, pressing his great, heavy hands against his chest. He walked up to the horse and seized the stirrup, pressing himself right against the stallion's side.

"You're looking well, Gregor!" Stepan said.

"Praise be!"

"What are your thoughts about it? Eh?"

"What is it I'm to think about?"

"You've carried off another man's wife—and you're having your will of her?"

"Let go of the stirrup."

"Don't be afraid! I won't beat you."

"I'm not afraid. Stop that talk!" Gregor flushed and raised his voice.

"I shan't fight you today; I don't want to. . . . But mark my words, Grishka; sooner or later I shall kill you."

" 'We shall see,' said the blind man!"

"Mark my words well. You've brought shame on me. You've castrated my life as if I was a pig. You see there—" he stretched out his hands palms-upward. "I'm ploughing, and the Lord knows what for. Do I need it for myself? I could shift around a bit and get through the winter that way. It's only the dreariness of it all that gets me down. You've brought terrible shame on me, Gregor."

"Don't complain to me. I shan't understand. The full man doesn't understand the hungry."

"That's true," Stepan agreed, staring up into Gregor's face. And suddenly he broke into a simple, boyish smile which wrinkled the corners of his eyes into tiny furrows. "I'm sorry only for one thing, lad, very sorry. You remember how the year before last we boxed together at Shrovetide?"

"No, I don't."

"Why, it was when the single men fought the married, do you remember? And how I chased after you? You were thinner then, a green rush as against me. I spared you that time, but if I'd hit you as you were running away, I'd have split you in two. You ran quickly, all springy-like; if I'd struck you hard on the side you wouldn't have been alive in the world today."

"Don't grieve over it, we may yet come up against each other."

Stepan rubbed his forehead with his hand as though trying to recall something. Still holding the stirrup with his left hand, he walked alongside the stallion. Gregor watched his every movement. He noticed Stepan's drooping flaxen moustaches, the heavy scrub of his long unshaven chin. His dirty face, marked with whiter runnels of sweat, was sad and strangely unfamiliar. As he looked Gregor felt that he might well be gazing from a hilltop at the distant steppe veiled in a rainy mist. A grey weariness and emptiness ashened Stepan's features. He dropped behind without a word of farewell. Gregor touched up his horse into a canter.

"Wait a bit. And how is—how is Aksinia?"

Knocking a lump of earth off his boot with the whip, Gregor replied:

"Oh, she's all right."

He halted the stallion and glanced back. Stepan was standing with his feet planted wide apart, chewing a piece of twig between his teeth. For a moment Gregor had a feeling of immeasurable pity for him, but jealousy rose uppermost. Turning in his saddle, he shouted:

"She doesn't yearn for you, don't worry!"

"Is that so?"

Gregor brought the whip down between his horse's ears and rode away without replying.

The night before Easter Sunday the sky was overcast with masses of black cloud, and rain began to fall. A raw darkness enveloped Tatarsk. At dusk the ice of the Don began to crack with a protracted, rolling groan, and crushed by a mass of broken ice, the first floe emerged from the water. The ice broke suddenly over a length of three miles and drifted downstream. The floes crashed against one another and against the banks, to the sound of the church-bell ringing measuredly for the service. At the first bend, where the Don sweeps to the left, the ice was dammed up. The roar and scraping of the moving floes reached the village. The lads had gathered in the church enclosure. Through the open doors came the muffled tones of the service, light streamed gaily through the windows, while outside in the darkness the lads surreptitiously tickled and kissed the girls and whispered dirty stories to one another.

From the Don came a flowing whisper, rustle, and crunch, as though a strongly-built, gaily-dressed woman as tall as a poplar were passing by, her great, invisible skirts rustling.

At midnight Mitka Koshunov, riding a horse bareback, clattered through the Egyptian darkness up to the church. He tied the reins to the horse's mane and with a smack of the hand on her flanks sent her back home. He listened to the sound of the hoofs for a moment; then, adjusting his belt, he went into the church. At the porch he removed his cap, bent his head devoutly, and thrusting aside the women, pressed up to the altar. The Cossacks were crowded in a black mass on the left; on the right was an azure throng of women. Mitka found his father in the front row and, seizing him by the elbow, whispered into his ear:

"Father, come outside for a moment."

As he pressed out of the church through the dense curtain of mingled odours, Mitka's nostrils quivered. He was overwhelmed by the vapour of burning wax, the stench of women's sweaty bodies, the deathly odour of clothes brought out only at Christmas and Easter-time, the smell of damp leather, naphthaline, and other indistinguishable scents.

In the porch Mitka put his mouth close to his father's ear and said: "Natalia is dying."

On Good Friday the women gathered in the hut of Korshunov's neighbour Pelagea Maidannikov for a talk. Her husband, Gavrila, had written from Lodz that he was trying to get furlough for Easter. Pelagea had whitewashed the walls and tidied up the hut as early as the Monday before Easter, and from Thursday onward she waited expectantly, running to the gate and standing at the fence, straight-haired and gaunt, the signs of her pregnancy showing in her face. Shading her eyes with her palm, she stared down the road. Perhaps he was coming! She was pregnant, but lawfully so. Gavrila had returned from his regiment the previous year, bringing his wife a present of Polish chintz. He had spent four nights with his wife, and on the fifth day had got drunk, cursed in Polish and German, and with tears in his eyes had sat singing an old Cossack song about Poland. His friends and brothers had sat with him, singing and drinking vodka before dinner. After dinner he had said good-bye to his family and had ridden off. And from that day Pelagea had begun to watch the hem of her skirt.

She explained to Natalia Korshunov how she came to be pregnant. "A day or two before Gavrila arrived, I had a dream," she said. "I was going through the meadow, and I saw our old cow in front of me, the one we sold last August. She was walking along, and milk was dripping from her teats. Lord, I thought, how did I ever come to milk her so badly? Next day old woman Drozdikha came for some hops, and I told her my dream. And she told me to break a piece of wax off a candle, roll it into a ball, and to take and bury it in some cow-dung, for misfortune was watching at the window. I ran to do as she said, but I couldn't find the candle. I had had one, I knew, but the children had taken it or else the cockroaches had eaten it. Then Gavrila arrived, and the misfortune with him. Before that I had gone for three years without trouble, and now look at me!" She thrust her fingers into her belly.

Pelagea fretted while waiting for her husband. She was bored with her own company, and so on the Friday she invited her women neighbours to come and spend the evening with her. Natalia came with an unfinished stocking, for when spring came Grand-dad Grishaka felt the cold all the more. She was unnaturally full of high spirits and laughed more than necessary at the others' jokes, trying to hide her yearning for her husband from them. Pelagea was sitting on the stove with her bare, violet-veined legs dangling, and bantering the young and shrewish Frossia.

"How was it you beat your husband, Frossia?" she asked.

"Don't you know how? On the back, on the head, and wherever I could lay my hands on him."

"I didn't mean that, but why you did it."

"I had to," Frossia answered unwillingly.

"If you were to catch your husband with another woman would you keep your tongue quiet?" a gaunt woman asked deliberately.

"Tell us all about it, Frossinia."

"There's nothing to tell."

"Don't be afraid, we're all friends here."

Spitting out a sunflower-seed husk into her hand, Frossia smiled. "Well, I'd noticed his goings-on for a long time, and then someone told me he was at the mill with a loose woman from across the Don. I went out and found them by the—"

"Any news of your husband, Natalia?" another woman interrupted, turning to Natalia.

"He's at Yagodnoe," she replied in a whisper.

"Do you expect to live with him or not?"

"She might expect to, but he doesn't," their hostess intervened. Natalia felt the hot blood surging to her face. She bent her head over her stocking and glanced from beneath her eyelids at the women. Realizing that she could not hide her flush of shame from them, she deliberately, yet so clumsily that everybody noticed it, sent the ball of wool rolling from her knees and then bent down and fumbled with her fingers over the cold floor.

"Spit on him, woman! He would only be a yoke to you," one woman advised her with unconcealed pity in her voice.

Natalia's artificial animation died away like a spark in the wind. The women's conversation turned to the latest scandal, to tittle-tattle and gossip. Natalia knitted in silence. She forced herself to

sit on until the party broke up, and then went home turning over
an unformulated decision in her mind. Shame for her uncertain
situation (for she still would not believe that Gregor had gone
for ever, and was ready to forgive him and take him back) drove
her on to a further step. She resolved to send a letter secretly to
him, in order to learn whether he had gone altogether or whether
he was changing his mind. When she reached home she found
Grishaka sitting in his little room reading an old leather-bound,
grease-stained copy of the Gospels. Her father was in the kitchen
mending a fish-net. Her mother had put the children to bed and
was asleep on the stove. Natalia took off her jacket and wandered
aimlessly from room to room. She stopped for a moment in her
grandfather's room, staring listlessly at the pile of devotional books
under the ikons.

"Grand-dad, have you any paper?" she asked him.

"What sort of paper?" Grishaka asked, puckering his forehead
into frowns.

"Paper to write on."

The old man fumbled in a Psalter and drew out a crumpled
sheet of paper that smelt strongly of incense.

"And a pencil?"

"Ask your father. Go away, my dear, and don't bother."

She obtained a stump of pencil from her father and sat down
at the table, laboriously formulating her long-pondered thought
and evoking a numb, gnawing pain in her heart.

Gregor Pantalievich,

*Tell me, will you, how I am to live, and whether my life is quite
lost or not. You left home and you didn't say a single word to me.
I haven't done you any wrong, and I waited for you to untie my
hands and to say that you have gone for good, but you've gone
away and are as silent as the grave.*

*I thought you had gone off in the heat of the moment, and waited
for you to come back, but I don't want to part you. Better one
should be trodden into the ground than two. Have pity at last and
write. Then I shall know what to think, but now I stand in the
middle of the road.*

Don't be angry with me, Grishka, for the love of Christ.

Natalia

Next morning she promised Getka vodka and persuaded him to ride with the letter to Yagodnoe. Moody with expectation of his promised drink, Getka led a horse into the yard and, without informing Miron Gregorievich, rode off to Yagodnoe.

He returned in the afternoon. He brought with him a piece of blue sugar-bag paper, and as he drew it out of his pocket he winked at Natalia.

"The road was terrible. I got such a shaking that it upset my kidneys," he informed her.

Natalia read the letter, and her face turned grey. The four words scribbled on the paper entered her heart like sharp teeth rending a weave.

Live alone.

Gregor Melekhov

Hurriedly, as though not trusting her own strength, Natalia went into the house and lay down on her bed. Her mother was lighting the stove for the night, in order to have the place tidy early on Easter Sunday morning and to get the Easter curd cake ready in time.

"Natalia, come and give me a hand," she called to her daughter.

"I've got a headache, Mamma; I'll lie a little longer."

Her mother put her head in at the door. "A fine time to fall sick," she remarked.

Natalia licked her cold lips with her dry tongue and made no reply.

She lay until evening, her head covered with a warm woollen shawl, a light tremor shaking her huddled body. Miron Gregorievich and Grishaka were about to go off to church when she got up and went into the kitchen. Beads of perspiration shone on the strands of her smoothly combed hair, her eyes were dim with an unhealthy, oily film.

As Miron Gregorievich buttoned up the long row of buttons on his trousers he glanced at his daughter. "You've fallen ill suddenly, daughter. Come along with us to the service."

"You go; I'll come along later," she replied.

The men went out. Lukinichna and Natalia were left in the

kitchen. Natalia went listlessly backward and forward from the
chest to the bed, looked with unseeing eyes through the heap of
clothing in the chest, painfully thinking of something, her lips
whispering. Lukinichna thought she could not make up her mind
which clothes to wear, and with motherly kindness she suggested:

"Wear my blue skirt, my dear. It will just fit you. Shall I get it
for you?"

"No, I'll go in this!" Natalia carefully drew out her green skirt
and suddenly remembered that she had been wearing it when
Gregor first visited her as her future bridegroom, when he had
shamed her with a flying kiss. Shaking with sobs, she fell breast-
forward against the raised lid of the chest.

"Natalia, what's the matter?" Her mother clapped her hands.

Natalia choked down her desire to scream and, mastering herself, laughed with a grating, wooden laugh.

"I'm all unwell today."

"Oh, Natalia, I've noticed."

"Well, and what have you noticed, Mamma?" she cried with
unexpected irritation, crumpling the green skirt in her fingers.

"You're not well at all; you need a husband."

"Enough of that talk; I've had one!"

She went to her room, and quickly returned to the kitchen,
dressed, girlishly slender, her face an azure pallor, a mournful flush
in her cheeks.

"You go on, I'm not ready yet," her mother said.

Pushing a handkerchief into her sleeve, Natalia went out. The
wind brought the rumble of the floating ice and the scent of the
damp thaw to her nostrils. Holding up her skirt in her left hand,
picking her way across the pearly-blue puddles, she reached the
church. On the way she attempted to recover her former comparatively tranquil state of mind, thinking of the holiday, of everything vaguely and in snatches. But her thoughts turned straight
back to the scrap of blue sugar-bag paper hidden at her breast,
to Gregor and the happy woman who was now condescendingly
laughing at her, perhaps even pitying her.

As she entered the church enclosure some lads barred her way.
She passed round them and heard the whisper:

"Whose is she? Did you see?"

"It was Natalia Korshunov."

"She's ruptured, they say. That's why her husband left her."

"That's not true. She got playing about with her father-in-law, lame Pantaleimon."

"Ah, so that's it! And that's why Gregor ran away from home?"

Stumbling over the uneven stones, followed by a shameful, filthy whisper, she reached the church porch. The girls standing in the porch giggled as she turned and made her way to the farther gate. Swaying drunkenly, she ran home. At the yard gate she took breath and then entered, stumbling over the hem of her skirt, biting her lips till the blood came. Through the lilac darkness the open doorway of the shed yawned blackly. With evil determination she gathered her last strength, ran to the door, and hastily stepped across the threshold. The shed was dry and cold, smelling of leather harness and long-lying straw. Gropingly, without thought or feeling, in a sombre yearning which scratched at her shamed and despairing soul, she made her way to a corner. There she picked up a scythe by the handle, removed the blade (her movements were deliberately assured and precise), and throwing back her head, with all the force and joyous resolution that possessed her she slashed her throat with its point. She fell as though struck down before the burning, savage pain, and feeling, mournfully realizing, that she had not completely carried out her intention, she struggled on to all fours, then on to her knees. Hurriedly (she was terrified by the blood pouring over her chest) with trembling fingers she tore off the buttons of her jacket, and with one hand she drew aside her taut, unyielding breast, with the other she guided the point of the scythe over the floor. She crawled on her knees to the earthen wall, thrust the blunt end of the scythe blade into it, and, throwing her arms above her head, pressed her chest firmly forward, forward. . . . She clearly heard and felt the resisting, cabbage-like scrunch of the rending flesh; a rising wave of intense pain flowed over her breast to her throat and pressed with ringing needles into her ears. . . .

The kitchen door scraped. Lukinichna came down the stairs, feeling for the steps with her feet. From the belfry came the measured beat of the church-bell. With an incessant grinding the giant floes were floating end-up down the Don. The joyous, full-flowing, liberated river was carrying its icy fetters away down to the Sea of Azov.

Chapter 12

Aksinia confessed her pregnancy to Gregor only during the sixth month, when she was no longer able to conceal it from him. She had kept silent so long because she was afraid he would not believe it was his child she was carrying.

She told him agitatedly one evening, anxiously scanning his face the while for any change in its expression. But he turned away to the window and coughed with vexation.

"Why didn't you tell me before?" he demanded.

"I was afraid to, Gregor. I thought you might throw me over. . . ."

Drumming his fingers on the back of the bed, he asked:

"Is it to be soon?"

"The beginning of August, I think."

"Is it Stepan's?"

"No, it's yours."

"So you say."

"Reckon up for yourself. From the day of the wood-cutting it is . . ."

"Don't lie, Aksinia! Even if it was Stepan's, where would you go to now?"

Weeping angry tears, Aksinia sat down on the bench and broke into a burning whisper:

"I lived with him so many years and nothing ever happened! Think for yourself! I'm not an ailing woman. . . . I must have got it from you. . . . And you . . ."

Gregor talked no more about the matter. A new thread of anxious aloofness and a light mocking pity entered into his attitude to Aksinia. She withdrew into herself, asking for no favours. Since the summer she had lost her good looks, but pregnancy hardly affected her shapely figure; her general fullness concealed her condition, and although her face was thinner, it gained a new beauty from her warmly glowing eyes. She easily managed her work as cook, especially as that year fewer labourers were employed on the farm.

Eugene had arranged for Gregor to be freed from the spring training camp, and he worked at the mowing, occasionally drove old Listnitsky to the district centre, and spent the rest of the time hunting with him after bustards. The easy-going, comfortable life began to spoil him. He grew lazy and stout and looked older than his years. He was troubled only by the thought of his forthcoming army service. He had neither horse nor equipment, and he could hope for nothing from his father. He saved the wages he received for himself and Aksinia and spent nothing ever on tobacco, hoping to be able to buy a horse without having to beg from his father. Old Listnitsky also promised to help him. Gregor's presentiment that his father would give him nothing was quickly confirmed. At the end of June, Piotra visited his brother and in the course of conversation mentioned that his father was as angry with him as ever and had declared that he would not help him to get a horse. "Let him go to the local command for one," he had said.

"He needn't worry, I'll go to do my service on my own horse," Gregor declared, stressing "my own."

"Where will you get it from?" Piotra asked.

"I'll beg for it, or dance for it, and if I don't get it that way, I'll steal it."

"Brave lad!"

"I shall buy a horse with my wages," Gregor said more seriously.

Piotra sat on the steps, asking about Gregor's work and chewing the ends of his moustache. Having completed his inquiries, as he turned to go he said to his brother:

"You should come back; there's no point in knocking your head against a brick wall."

"I'm not intending to."

"Are you thinking of staying with her?"

"With who?"

"With this one."

"At present I am, but what of it?"

"Oh, I'm just interested."

As Gregor went to see his brother off, he had to ask at last: "How is everything at home?"

Piotra laughed as he untied his horse from the balustrade of the steps. "You've got as many homes as a rabbit has holes! Everything is all right. Your mother longs to see you. We've got in the hay—three loads of it."

Agitatedly Gregor scanned the old mare his brother was riding. "No foal this year?" he inquired.

"No, brother, she's barren. But the bay which we got from Christonia has foaled. A stallion it is, a good one too. High on the legs, sound pasterns, and strong in the chest. It'll be a good horse."

Gregor sighed. "I pine for the village, Piotra," he said. "I pine for the Don. You never see running water here. It's a dreary place!"

"Come and see us," Piotra replied as he hoisted his body on to the mare's bony spine.

"Some day."

"Well, good-bye."

"A good journey."

Piotra had ridden out of the yard when, remembering something, he called to Gregor, who was still standing on the steps:

"Natalia—I'd forgotten—a misfortune. . . ."

The wind blowing round the farm carried the end of the sentence away from Gregor's ears. Piotra and the horse were enveloped in velvety dust, and Gregor shrugged his shoulders and went off to the stables.

The summer was dry. Rain fell but rarely, and the grain ripened early. As soon as the rye was garnered the barley was ripe and yellow. The four day-labourers and Gregor went out to reap it.

Aksinia had finished work early that day, and she asked Gregor to take her with him. Despite his attempt to dissuade her, she quickly threw a kerchief over her head, ran out, and caught up with the wagon in which the men were riding.

The event which Aksinia anticipated with yearning and joyous impatience, which Gregor awaited with apprehension, happened during the harvesting. Feeling certain symptoms, she threw down the rake and lay under a shock of corn. Her travail came on quickly. Biting her blackened tongue, she lay flat on the ground. The labourers with the reaping machine drove in a circle around her. As they passed, one of them called out to her:

"Hey, you! You've lain yourself down to bake in an awkward spot, haven't you? Get up, or you'll melt!"

Gregor got one of the men to take his place at the machine and went across to her.

"What's the matter?" he asked.

Her lips writhing uncontrollably, she said hoarsely:

"I'm in labour. . . ."

"I told you not to come, you devilish bitch! Now what are we to do?"

"Don't be angry with me, Grishka! . . . Oh! . . . Oh! . . . Grishka, harness the horse to the wagon. I must get home. . . . How could I, here? . . . with the Cossacks . . ." she groaned, gripped in an iron band of pain.

Gregor ran for the horse. It was grazing in a hollow a little way off, and by the time he drove up, Aksinia had struggled on to all fours, thrust her head into a pile of dusty barley, and was spitting out the prickly beards she had chewed in her pain. She fixed her dilated eyes vacantly on Gregor and set her teeth into her crumpled handkerchief to prevent the labourers from hearing her horrible, rending cry.

Gregor tumbled her into the wagon and drove the horse fast towards the estate.

"Oh! Don't hurry. . . . Oh, death! You're—shaking—me. . . ." Aksinia screamed as her head knocked on the bottom of the wagon.

Gregor silently plied the whip and swung the reins around his head, without a glance back at her.

Pressing her cheeks with her palms, her staring, frenzied eyes rolling wildly, Aksinia bounced about in the wagon, tumbling from side to side over the bumpy, unworn road. Gregor kept the horse at a gallop. For a moment Aksinia ceased her shrieking howl. The wheels rattled, and her head thudded heavily against the bottom board. At first her silence did not impress itself on Gregor, but then, taking thought, he glanced back. Aksinia was lying with horribly distorted face, her cheek pressed hard against the side of the wagon, her jaws working like a fish flung ashore. The sweat was pouring from her brow into her sunken eyes. Gregor turned and raised her head, putting his crumpled cap beneath it. Glancing sidelong at him, she said firmly:

"I shall die, Grishka. And that's all there is to it!"

Gregor shuddered; a chill ran down his body to his toes. Suddenly alarmed, he sought for words of encouragement, of comfort, but could not find them. From his trembling lips came:

"You're lying, you fool!" He shook his head and, bending over her, awkwardly squeezed her foot.

"Aksinia, my little pigeon . . ."

The pain died away and left Aksinia for a moment, then returned with redoubled force. Feeling something rending and bending in an arch under her belly, she pierced Gregor's ears with an inexpressibly horrible, rising scream. Gregor frantically whipped up the horse.

"Oh! . . . Ah! . . ." Aksinia shrieked in her agony.

Then above the rattle of the wheels Gregor just heard her thin, yearning voice:

"Grishka!"

He reined in the horse and turned his head. Aksinia lay in a pool of blood, her arms flung out. Below her skirt, between her legs, a white and crimson living thing was stirring. Gregor frenziedly jumped down from the wagon and stumbled to the back. Staring into Aksinia's panting, burning mouth, he rather guessed than caught the words:

"Bite through the cord . . . tie it with cotton . . . from the shirt. . . ."

With trembling fingers he tore a bunch of threads from the sleeve of his own cotton shirt, and screwing up his eyes until they pained him, he bit through the cord and carefully tied up the bleeding end with cotton.

The estate of Yagodnoe lay in a spacious valley. The wind blew changeably from north or south, summer advanced on the valley, the autumn rustled with falling leaves, winter flung its forces of frost and snow against it, but Yagodnoe remained sunk in its wooden torpor. So the days passed, crawling over the high wall that cut off the estate from the rest of the world.

The farmyard was always alive with black ducks wearing red spectacles; the guinea-fowls scattered like a beady rain; gaily-feathered peacocks called hoarsely from the roof of the stables. The old general was fond of all kinds of birds and even kept a maimed crane. In November it wrung the heart-strings with its copper-tongued, yearning cry as it heard the call of the wild cranes flying south. But it could not fly, for one wing hung uselessly at its side. As the general stood at the window and watched the bird stretching out its neck and jumping, fluttering off the ground, he laughed; and the bass tones of his laughter rocked through the empty hall like clouds of tobacco-smoke.

During all the time of Gregor's stay at Yagodnoe only two events disturbed the sleepy, monotonous life: the coming of Aksinia's child, and the loss of a prize gander. The inhabitants of Yagodnoe quickly grew accustomed to the baby girl, and they found some of the gander's feathers in the meadow and concluded that a fox had carried her off.

One day in December Gregor was summoned to the district administration at Vieshenska. There he was given a hundred rubles to buy a horse and was instructed to report on two days after Christmas at the village of Mankovo for the army draft.

He returned to Yagodnoe in considerable agitation. Christmas was approaching, and he had nothing ready. With the money he had received from the authorities plus his own savings he bought a horse for a hundred and forty rubles. He took Sashka with him and they purchased a presentable animal enough, a six-year-old bay with one hidden blemish. Old Sashka combed his beard with his fingers and advised:

"You won't get one cheaper, and the authorities won't see the fault! They're not smart enough!"

Gregor rode the horse bareback to Yagodnoe, trying out its paces.

A week before Christmas Pantaleimon arrived unexpectedly at Yagodnoe. He did not drive into the yard, but tied up his horse and basket sledge at the gate and limped into the servants' quarters, rubbing the icicles off his beard. As through the window he saw his father approaching, Gregor exclaimed in confusion:

"Well I'm— Father!"

For some reason Aksinia ran to the cradle and wrapped up the child. Pantaleimon entered, bringing a breath of cold air with him. He removed his three-cornered cap and crossed himself to the ikon, then gazed slowly around the room.

"Good health!" he greeted his son.

"Good morning, Father!" Gregor replied, rising from the bench and striding to the centre of the room.

Pantaleimon offered Gregor his ice-cold hand and sat down on the edge of the bench, wrapping his sheepskin around him. He would not look at Aksinia.

"Getting ready for your service?" he asked.

"Of course."

Pantaleimon was silent, staring long and questioningly at Gregor.

"Take your things off, Father, and we'll get a samovar going."

"Thank you"; the old man scraped an old spot of mud off his coat with his fingernail, and added: "I've brought your equipment; two coats, a saddle, and trousers. You'll find them all there in the sledge."

Gregor went out and removed the two sacks of equipment from the sledge. When he returned, his father rose from the bench.

"When are you going off?" he asked his son.

"The day after Christmas. You aren't going already, are you, Father?"

"I want to get back early."

He took leave of Gregor and, still avoiding Aksinia's eyes, went towards the door. As he lifted the latch he turned his eyes in the direction of the cradle and said:

"Your mother sends her greetings. She's in bed with trouble in her legs." After a momentary pause he said heavily: "I shall ride with you to Mankovo. Be ready when I come."

He went out, thrusting his hands into warm knitted gloves. Aksinia, pale with the humiliation she had suffered, said nothing. Gregor followed his father, trying to avoid a creaking floorboard and giving Aksinia a sidelong glance as he passed.

On Christmas Day Gregor drove his master to Vieshenska. Listnitsky attended Mass, had breakfast with his cousin, a local landowner, and then ordered Gregor to get the sleigh ready for the return journey. Gregor had not finished his bowl of greasy soup, but he rose at once, went to the stable, and harnessed the grey trotting-horse into the light sleigh.

The wind was blowing the crumbling, tingling snow into spray; a silvery froth whirled hissingly through the yard; on the trees beyond the palisade hung a tender, scalloped hoarfrost. The wind sent it flying, and as it fell and scattered, it reflected a marvelous variety of colours from the sun. On the roof close to the smoking chimney, rooks were chattering coldly. Startled by the sound of footsteps, they flew off, circled round the house like dove-coloured snowflakes, then flew to the east, to the church, clearly outlined against the violet morning sky.

"Tell the master we're ready," Gregor shouted to the maid that came to the steps of the house.

Listnitsky came out and entered the sleigh, his whiskers buried in the collar of his raccoon-fur coat. Gregor wrapped up his legs and buttoned the shaggy wolfskin over him.

They arrived at Yagodnoe within two hours. Listnitsky held no communication whatever with Gregor during the journey, except for an occasional tap on the back with his finger, to order him to stop while he rolled and lit a cigarette. Only as they were descending the hill to the house did he ask:

"Early in the morning?"

Gregor turned sideways in his seat and with difficulty opened his frozen lips. His tongue, bursting and stiff with cold, stuck to the back of his teeth.

"Yes," he managed to reply.

"Received all your money?"

"Yes."

"Don't be anxious about your wife; she'll be all right. Be a good soldier. Your grandfather was a fine Cossack; you must conduct yourself in a manner worthy of your grandfather and father. Your father received the first prize for trick riding at the Imperial Review in 1883, didn't he?"

"Yes, it was my father."

"Well, well!" the old man ended with a stern note in his voice as though admonishing Gregor. And he buried his face once more in his fur coat.

At the yard Gregor handed over the horse to Sashka and turned to go to the servants' quarters.

"Your father's arrived," Sashka shouted after him.

Gregor found Pantaleimon sitting at the table, eating cranberry jelly. "Drunk!" Gregor decided as he glanced at his father's sodden face.

"So you're back, soldier?" Pantaleimon exclaimed.

"I'm all frozen," Gregor answered, clapping his hands together. Turning to Aksinia, he added: "Untie my hood, my fingers are too cold to do it."

On this occasion his father was much more affable and told Aksinia curtly, as though he were master in the house:

"Cut me some more bread; don't spare it!"

When he had finished he rose from the table and went towards the door to have a smoke in the yard. As he passed the cradle he rocked it once or twice, pretending that the action was accidental, and asked:

"A Cossack?"

"A girl," Aksinia replied for Gregor; and catching the expression of dissatisfaction that passed over the old man's face, she hurriedly added:

"She's so handsome! Just like Grishka!"

Pantaleimon attentively examined the dark little head sticking out of the clothes and declared, not without a touch of pride:

"She's of our blood! . . . Ah, you! . . ."

"How did you come, Father?" Gregor asked.

"With the mare and Piotra's horse."

"You need only have used one, and we could have harnessed mine for the journey to Mankovo."

"Let him go light. He's a good horse, too."

Disturbed by the one common thought, they talked about various matters. Aksinia took no part in the conversation, but sat on the bed. She had noticeably grown stouter since the birth of the child and had a new, confidently happy air.

It was late when they went to bed. As she lay pressed against Gregor, Aksinia wet his shirt with her tears.

"I shall die of pining for you. How shall I be able to live without you? The long nights . . . the child awake. . . . Just think, Grishka! Four years!"

"In the old days service lasted twenty-five years, they say."

"What do I care about the old days? Curse your army service, say I."

"I shall come home on furlough."

"On furlough!" Aksinia groaned, blowing her nose on her shift. "Much water will flow down the Don before then."

"Don't whine so! You're like rain in autumn—one continual drizzle."

"You should be in my skin," she retorted.

Gregor fell asleep a little before dawn. Aksinia got up and fed the child, then lay down again. Leaning on her elbows and gazing unwinkingly into Gregor's face, she took a long farewell of him. She recalled the night when she had tried to persuade him to go with her to the Kuban: once more the yard outside the window was flooded with the white light of the moon. So they had lain then, and Gregor was still the same, yet not the same. Behind them both lay a long track trodden out by the passing days.

He turned over, muttered something about Olshansky village, and then was silent. Aksinia tried to sleep, but her thoughts drove all sleep away as wind does a haycock. Until daybreak she lay thinking over his disconnected phrase, seeking its meaning. Pantaleimon awoke as soon as the faintest glimmer of daylight peered through the window.

"Gregor, get up!" he cried.

By the time they had breakfasted and packed, dawn had fully come. Pantaleimon went to harness his horses, while Gregor tore himself away from Aksinia's passionate kisses and went to say good-bye to Sashka and the other servants.

Wrapping the child up warmly, Aksinia took her out with her for a last farewell. Gregor lightly touched his daughter's damp little forehead with his lips and went to his horse.

"Come in the sledge," his father called as he touched up his horses.

"No, I'll ride my horse."

With calculated deliberation Gregor fastened the saddle-girths, mounted his horse, gathered the reins in his hand. More than once Aksinia repeated:

"Grishka, wait—there's something I wanted to say"; and puckering her brow, she tried to remember what it was.

"Well, good-bye. . . . Look after the child. . . . I must be off; see how far Father's got already."

"Wait, dear!" With her left hand Aksinia seized the icy iron stirrup; her right arm pressed the baby to her breast; and she had no free hand with which to wipe away the tears streaming from her staring, unwinking eyes.

Benyamin came to the steps of the house.

"Gregor, the master wants you!" he called.

Gregor cursed, waved his whip, and dashed out of the yard. Aksinia ran after him, stumbling in the drifted snow.

He overtook his father at the top of the hill. Then he turned and looked back. Aksinia was standing at the gate, the child still pressed to her breast, the ends of her crimson shawl fluttering in the wind.

He rode his horse alongside his father's sledge. After a few moments the old man turned his back to his horses and asked:

"So you're not thinking of living with your wife?"

"That old story again? I've already told you . . ."

"So you're not thinking . . ."

"No, I'm not!"

"You haven't heard that she laid hands on herself?"

"Yes, I've heard. I happened to meet a man from the village."

"And in the sight of God?"

"Why, Father, after all—what falls from the wagon is lost."

"Don't use that devil's talk to me. What I'm saying to you I'm saying for your good," Pantaleimon flared up.

"You see I have a child. What is there to talk about? You can't push the other on to me now. . . ."

"Take care you're not feeding another man's child."

Gregor turned pale; his father had touched a sore spot. Ever since the child was born he had tormentedly nursed the suspicion in his mind, while concealing it from Aksinia. At night, when Aksinia was asleep, he had more than once gone to the cradle and stared down at the child, seeking his own features in its swarthily rosy face, and had turned back to bed as uncertain as before. Stepan also was dark red, almost black of complexion, and how was he to know whose blood flowed in the child's veins? At times he thought the child resembled him; at other times she was painfully like Stepan. Gregor had no feeling for her, except perhaps of hostility as he recalled the moments he had lived through as he drove Aksinia back from the steppe. Only once Aksinia was busy elsewhere, and he had had to change the child's wet diaper. As he did so he had felt a sharp, pinching agitation. Afterwards he had bent stealthily over the cradle and pressed the baby's great toe between his teeth.

His father probed mercilessly at the wound, and Gregor, his palm resting on the saddle-bow, numbly replied: "Whose-ever it is, I won't leave the child."

Pantaleimon waved his whip at the horses without turning round. "Natalia's spoilt her good looks. She carries her head on one side like a paralytic. It seems she cut a large tendon." He lapsed into silence.

"And how is she now?" Gregor asked, studiously picking a bur out of his horse's mane.

"She's got over it somehow or other. She lay seven months. On Trinity Sunday she was all but gone. Father Pankraty performed the last rites. Then she got better, rose, and walked. She thrust the scythe at her heart, but her hand trembled, and it missed."

"Quicker up the hill!" Gregor proposed, and waved his whip and outdistanced his father, sending a shower of snow from his horse's hoofs over the sledge. He broke into a trot, standing in his stirrups.

"We're taking Natalia back into our home," Pantaleimon shouted, chasing after him. "The woman doesn't want to live with her own folks. I saw her the other day and told her to come to us."

Gregor made no reply. They drove as far as the first village without exchanging a word, and his father made no further reference to the subject.

That day they covered forty-five miles. They arrived at Mankovo as dusk was falling the next day, and spent the night in the quarters allotted to the Vieshenska recruits.

Next morning the district ataman conducted the Vieshenska recruits before the medical commission. Gregor fell in with the other young men from his own village. In the morning Mitka Korshunov, riding a high bay horse equipped with a new and gaily ornamented saddle, had passed Gregor standing at the door of his quarters, but had gone by without a word of greeting.

The men undressed in turn in the cold room of the local civil administration. Military clerks bustled around, and the adjutant to the provincial ataman hurried past. From an inner room came the sound of the doctors' orders and snatches of remarks.

A clerk came out and curtly called Gregor and another into the examination room. Gregor went in, his back all gooseflesh with the cold. His swarthy body was the colour of oak. He was embarrassed as he glanced down at his hairy legs. The humiliating procedure of the medical examination irritated him. A grey-haired doctor in white overalls sounded him with the aid of a stethoscope. A younger doctor turned up his eyelids, and looked at his tongue. Behind him a third in horn-rimmed spectacles bustled about, rubbing his hands.

"On the scales!" an officer ordered.

Gregor stepped on to the cold platform.

"A hundred eighty-five and a half."

"Wha-a-at? He's not particularly tall, either," the grey-haired doctor drawled, turning Gregor round by the arm.

"Astonishing!" the younger man coughed.

"How much?" an officer sitting at the table asked in surprise.

"A hundred eighty-five and a half pounds," the grey-haired doctor replied.

"How about the Life Guards for him?" the district military commissary asked, bending towards his neighbour at the table.

"He has a brigand's face. . . . Very savage-looking. . . ."

"Hey, turn round! What's that on your back?" an official wearing colonel's epaulets shouted, impatiently tapping his finger on the table. Turning to face the colonel, trying to restrain the trembling of his body, Gregor replied:

"I got frozen in the spring. They're the marks."

Towards the end of the examination the officials at the table decided that Gregor would have to be drafted into an ordinary regiment.

"The 12th Regiment, Melekhov. Do you hear?" he was told. And as he went towards the door he heard a whispered:

"It's impossible. Just consider; the Emperor would see a face like that, and then what? His eyes alone . . ."

"He's a crossbreed. From the East undoubtedly."

"And his body isn't clean. Those marks . . ."

Buttoning up his coat as he went, he ran down the steps. Horses were being mustered in the square. The warm wind breathed of thaw; the road was bare in places, and steaming. Clucking hens fluttered down the street, geese were splashing in a puddle.

The examination of the horses took place the following day. A long line of mounts was drawn up in the square against the church wall. A veterinary surgeon and his assistant passed along the line. The Vieshenska ataman went running from the scales to the table in the middle of the square, where the results of the examination were being entered. The military commissary went by, deep in conversation with a young captain.

When his turn came, Gregor led his horse to the scales. The surgeon and his assistant measured every part of the animal's body, and weighed it. Before it could be led from the platform the surgeon had deftly taken it by the upper lip, looked down its throat, felt its chest muscles, and running his fine fingers like spider's legs over its body, turned to its legs. He felt the knee joints, tapped the tendons, squeezed the bone above the fetlocks. When he had finished his examination he passed on, his white overalls flapping in the wind and scattering the scent of carbolic acid.

Gregor's horse was rejected. Sashka's hopes proved unjustified, and the experienced surgeon discovered the secret blemish of which the old man had spoken. Gregor at once held an agitated consultation with his father, and before half an hour had elapsed he led Piotra's horse on to the scales. The surgeon passed it almost without an examination.

Gregor led the horse a little way off, found a comparatively dry spot, and spread out his saddle-cloth on the ground. His father held his horse. Past them strode a tall, grey-haired general in a light grey cloak and a silver astrakhan-fur cap, followed by a group of officers.

"That's the provincial ataman," Pantaleimon whispered, digging Gregor from behind.

Gregor stared inquisitively at the unfamiliar features of the officers and officials. An adjutant fixed a bored gaze on him and turned away as he met Gregor's attentive eyes. An old captain went by almost at a run, agitated by something and biting his upper lip with his yellow teeth.

On his saddle-cloth Gregor had set out his saddle, adorned with a green ribbon, with its saddlebags at the pommel and the back; two army coats, two pairs of trousers, a tunic, two pairs of leg-boots, a pound and a half of biscuit, a tin of corned beef, grits, and other food in the regulation quantities. In the open saddlebags were four horseshoes, shoe-nails wrapped in a greasy rag, a soldier's sewing-kit with a couple of needles and thread and towels.

He gave a last glance over his accoutrements, and squatted down to rub some mud off the ends of the pack-strings with his sleeve. From the end of the square the army commission slowly passed

along the rows of Cossacks drawn up behind their saddle-cloths.
The officers and the ataman closely examined the equipment, stooping and feeling the edges of the greatcoats, fumbling in the saddlebags, turning out the contents of the sewing-kits, and weighing the
bags of biscuit in their hands.

The talk gradually died away as the commission approached.
Gregor drew himself up. Behind him his father coughed. The wind
carried the scent of horses' urine and melted snow over the square.
The sun looked unhappy, as though after a drinking bout.

The group of officers halted by the man next to Gregor, then
came on to him one by one.

"Your surname, Christian name?"

"Melekhov, Gregor."

The commissary picked up the greatcoat by its edge, smelled at
the lining, and hurriedly counted the fastenings; another officer,
wearing a cornet's epaulets, felt the good cloth of the trousers between his fingers. A third stooped and rummaged in the saddlebags. With his thumb and forefinger the commissary cautiously
poked at the rag of shoe-nails as though afraid it might be hot, and
counted the nails with whispering lips.

"Why are there only twenty-three nails? What is this?" He
angrily pulled at the corner of the rag.

"Not at all, Your Excellency. Twenty-four."

"What, am I blind?"

Gregor hastily turned back a folded corner and revealed the
twenty-fourth nail. As he did so, his hairy black fingers lightly
touched the officer's white hand. The commissary snatched his
hand away as though struck, rubbed it on the edge of his greatcoat,
frowning fastidiously, and drew on his glove.

Gregor noticed his action and smiled evilly. Their eyes met, and
the commissary flushed and raised his voice.

"What's all this, what's all this, cossack? Why aren't your pack-
strings in order? Why aren't your snaffles right? And what does this
mean? Are you a Cossack or a peasant? Where's your father?"

Pantaleimon pulled on the horse's rein and stepped forward a
pace, his lame leg dragging.

"Don't you know the Cossack regulations?" the commissary
poured out the vials of his wrath upon him.

The provincial ataman came up, and the commissary quieted

down. The ataman thrust the toe of his boot into the padding of the saddle and passed on to the next man. The draft officer of the regiment to which Gregor had been drafted politely turned out all his belongings down to the contents of the sewing-kit and passed on last of all.

A day later a train of red wagons loaded with horses, Cossacks and forage left for Voronezh. In one of them stood Gregor. Past the open door crawled an unfamiliar flat landscape; in the distance a blue and tender thread of forest whirled by. Behind him the horses were munching hay and stepping from hoof to hoof as they felt the unstable floor beneath them. The wagon smelt of wormwood, horses' sweat, the spring thaw; and on the horizon lurked the distant thread of forest, blue, pensive, and as inaccessible as the faintly shining evening star.

Chapter 13

It was on a warm and cheerful spring day of March 1914 that Natalia returned to her father-in-law's hut. Pantaleimon was mending the broken wattle fence with puffy dove-coloured twigs. The silvery icicles hanging from the roofs were dripping, and the traces of former runnels showed as black scratches on the cornices. The warm sun caressed the melting hills, and the earth was swelling; an early grass showed a green malachite on the chalky headlands that swept in promontories from the Donside hills.

Natalia approached her father-in-law from behind, bending her mutilated, crooked neck.

"Good health, Father!" she said.

"Natiushka! Welcome, my dear, welcome!" Pantaleimon fussed around her. The twigs dropped out of his hand. "Why haven't you been to see us? Come in; Mother will be glad to see you."

"Father, I've come . . ." Natalia stretched out her hand uncertainly and turned away. "If you don't drive me away, I'd like to stay with you always," she added.

"What then, what then, my dear? Are you a stranger to us? Look, Gregor has written about you in his letter. He's told us to ask about you."

They went into the kitchen. Ilinichna wept as she embraced Natalia. Wiping her nose on the end of her kerchief, she whispered: "You want a child. That would win him. Sit down. I'll get you some pancakes, shall I?"

Dunia, flushed and smiling, came running into the kitchen and embraced Natalia around the knees. "You shameless one! You forgot all about us!" she reproached her.

They all talked together, interrupting one another. Ilinichna, supporting her cheek on her palm, grieved as she looked at Natalia, so changed from what she had been.

"You've come for good?" Dunia asked as she rubbed Natalia's hands.

"Who knows? . . ."

"Why, where else should she live? You'll stay with us," Ilinichna decided, as she pushed a platter of pancakes across the table.

Natalia went to her husband's parents only after long vacillation. At first her father would not let her go. He shouted at her in indignation when she suggested it, and attempted to persuade her against such a step. But it was difficult for her to look her people in the face; she felt that with her own family she was almost a stranger. For his part, after he had seen Gregor off to the army Pantaleimon was continually wheedling her to come, for he was determined to have her back and to reconcile Gregor to her.

From that day of March Natalia lived with the Melekhovs. Piotra was friendly and brotherly; Daria gave little outward sign of her dissatisfaction, and her occasional hostile glances were more than compensated by Dunia's attachment and the parental attitude of the old people.

The very day after Natalia came to them Pantaleimon ordered Dunia to write a letter to Gregor:

Greetings, our own son, Gregor Pantalievich! We send you a deep bow, and from all my fatherly heart, with your mother, Vasilisa Ilinichna, a parental blessing. Your brother, Piotra Pantalievich, and his wife, Daria Matvievna, greet you and wish you health and well-being; also your sister, Dunia, and all at home greet you. We re-

ceived your letter, sent in February, the fifth day, and heartily
thank you for it. And as you wrote that the horse is knocking his legs
smear him with some lard, you know how, and don't shoe his hind
hoofs so long as there is no slipperiness or bare ice about. Your wife,
Natalia Mironovna, is living with us and is well and comfortable.
Your mother sends you some dried cherries and a pair of woollen
socks, and some dripping and other things. We are all alive and well,
but Daria's baby died. The other day I and Piotra roofed the shed,
and he orders you to look after the horse and keep it well. The
cows have calved, the old mare seems to be in foal, we put a stallion
from the district stables to her. We are glad to hear about your
service and that your officers are pleased with you. Serve as you
should. Service for the Czar will not be in vain. And Natalia will
live with us now, and you think that over. And one other trouble,
just before Lent an animal killed three sheep. Now keep well, and
in God's keeping. Don't forget your wife, that is my order to you.
She is a good woman and your legal wife. Don't break the furrow,
and listen to your father.

> Your father, senior sergeant,
> Pantaleimon Melekhov

Gregor's regiment was stationed at a little place called Radzivillovo,
some three miles from the Russo-Austrian frontier. He rarely wrote
home. To the letter informing him that Natalia was living with his
father he wrote a cautiously worded reply and asked his father to
greet her in his name. All his letters were non-committal and ob-
scure in their meaning. Pantaleimon required Dunia or Piotra to
read them to him several times, pondering over the thought concealed between the lines. Just before Easter he wrote and asked
Gregor definitely whether on his return from the army he would live
with his wife or with Aksinia as before.

Gregor delayed with his reply. Only after Trinity Sunday did
they receive a brief letter from him. Dunia read it quickly, swallowing the ends of her words, and Pantaleimon had difficulty in grasping the essential thought among the numerous greetings and inquiries. At the end of the letter Gregor dealt with the question of
Natalia:

*You asked me to say whether I shall live with Natalia or not, but
I tell you, Father, you can't stick on again what has been cut off.
And how shall I make up to Natalia, when you know yourself that
I have a child? And I can't promise anything, it is painful for me
to talk about it. The other day a Jew was caught smuggling goods
across the frontier and we happened to see him. He said there would
be war with the Austrians soon and that their Emperor has come to
the frontier to see where to begin the war from and which land to
seize for himself. When war begins maybe I shan't be left alive, and
nothing can be settled beforehand.*

Natalia worked for her foster-parents and lived in continual hope
of her husband's return. She never wrote to Gregor, but nobody in
the family yearned with more pain and desire to receive a letter
from him.

Life in the village continued in its inviolable order; on work-days
the grey labour imperceptibly consumed the time, on Sunday
mornings the village poured in family droves into the church: the
Cossacks in tunics and holiday trousers, the women in long, varicoloured skirts that swept the dust, and little jackets with puff
sleeves. In the square the empty wagon shafts stuck high into the
air, the horses whinnied; by the fire-shed the Bulgar settlers traded
in fruit set out in long rows; behind them the children ran about in
bands, staring at the unharnessed camels superciliously surveying
the market square. Everywhere were crowds of men wearing red-
banded caps, and women in bright kerchiefs.

In the evening the streets groaned with the tramp of feet, with
song, and dancing to the accordions; and only late at night did the
last voices die away in the outskirts of the village.

Natalia never went visiting neighbours on Sunday evenings, but
sat listening gladly to Dunia's artless stories. Imperceptibly Dunia
was growing into a shapely and in her way a beautiful girl. She
matured early, like an early apple. This year her elder girl friends
forgot that they had reached adolescence before her and took her
back into their circle. She was fifteen now, and her figure was
still girlish and angular. She was a painful and naïve mixture of
childhood and blossoming youth; her little breasts grew and pressed

noticeably against her jacket, and in her long, rather slanting eye-sockets her black eyes still sparkled bashfully and mischievously. She would come back after an evening out and tell only Natalia her innocent secrets.

"Natalia, I want to tell you something."

"Well, tell on!"

"Yesterday Misha Koshevoi sat the whole evening with me on the stump by the village granaries."

"Why are you blushing?"

"Oh, I'm not!"

"Look in the glass; you're all one great flame."

Dunia rubbed her burning cheeks with her swarthy palms, and her young, artless laugh rang out.

"He said I was like a little azure flower."

"Well, go on!" Natalia encouraged her, rejoicing in another's joy and forgetting her own past and downtrodden happiness.

"And I said: 'Don't tell lies, Misha!' And he swore . . ."

Shaking her head, Natalia sent her laughter pealing through the room. The black, heavy plaits of her hair slipped like newts over her shoulders and back.

"What else did he say?"

"He asked me to give him my handkerchief for a keepsake."

"And did you?"

"No. I said I wouldn't. 'Go and ask your woman,' I told him. He's been seen with Yerofievna's daughter-in-law, and she's a bad woman, she plays about with the men."

"You'd better keep away from him."

"I'm going to!" Dunia continued her story. "And then, as the three of us, two other girls and me, were coming home, drunken old father Mikhy came after us. 'Kiss me, my dears!' he shouted. And Nura hit him on the face with a twig and we ran away."

The summer was dry. By the village the Don grew shallow, and where the surging current had run swiftly, a ford was made, and bullocks could cross to the other bank without wetting their backs. At night a heavy, hot exhalation flowed down from the range of hills into the village, and the wind filled the air with the strong scent of burning grass. The dry growth of the steppe was afire, and a sickly-smelling haze hung over the Donside slopes. At night the clouds deepened over the Don, ominous peals of thunder were to be heard; but no rain came to refresh the parched earth, although the lightning tore the sky into jagged, livid fragments.

Night after night an owl screeched from the belfry. The cries surged terrifyingly over the village, and the owl flew from the belfry to the cemetery and groaned over the brown and grass-grown mounds of the graves.

"There's trouble brewing," the old men prophesied as they listened to the owl screeching from the cemetery.

"There's war coming. An owl called just like that before the Turkish campaign."

"Expect no good when it flies from the church to the dead."

As he talked with the old men in the market-place Pantaleimon solemnly announced:

"Our Gregor writes that the Austrian Czar has come to the frontier and has given orders to collect all his troops in one place and to march on Moscow and Petersburg."

The old men remembered past wars and shared their apprehensions with one another.

"But there won't be any war," one objected. "Look at the harvest."

"The harvest has nothing to do with it. It's the students giving trouble, I expect."

"In any case we shall be the last to hear of it. But who will the war be with?"

"With the Turks across the sea. Depend on it, the water won't keep them apart."

The talk turned to jest, and the old men went about their business.

For two nights Martin Shamil, who lived close to the cemetery, watched by the cemetery palisade for the accursed owl, but the invisible, mysterious bird flew noiselessly over him, alighted on a cross at the other end of the cemetery, and sent its alarming cries over the sleepy village. Martin swore unbecomingly, shot at the black, hanging belly of a cloud, and went home. On his return to the hut his wife, a timorous, ailing woman as fruitful as a doe rabbit, welcomed him with reproaches.

"You're a fool, a hopeless fool!" she declared. "The bird doesn't interfere with you, does it? What if God should punish you? Here am I just up from my bed with my last, and supposing I get pregnant again through you?"

"Shut up, woman!" Martin ordered her. "You'll get pregnant all right, never fear! What is the bird doing here, giving us all the cold shivers? It's calling down woe on us, the devil! If war breaks out they'll take me off, and look at the litter you've got!" He waved at the corner where the children were sleeping.

Guards were set to watch over the meadow hay. The grass beyond the Don was inferior to the hay of the steppe and was sickly and scentless. It was the same earth, yet the grass drank in different juices. In the steppe there was a splendid black soil, so heavy and firm that the herd left no traces where they passed over it. On it grew a strong-scented grass standing as high as a horse's belly. But along the Don banks the soil was damp and rotten, growing a joyless and worthless grass which even the cattle would not always look at.

Haymaking was in full swing when an event occurred which shook the village from one end to the other. The district commissary arrived with an investigator and an officer in a uniform never seen before in the village. They sent for the ataman, collected witnesses, and then went straight to cross-eyed Lukieshka's hut. They walked along the path on the sunny side of the street, the village ataman running ahead like a cockerel. The investigator questioned him:

"Is Stockman at home?"

"Yes, Your Excellency."

"What does he do for a living?"

"He's a master locksmith."

"You haven't noticed anything suspicious about him?"

"Not at all."

"Does he ever have visitors?" the investigator asked, pulling the ataman back.

"Yes; they play cards sometimes."

"But who?"

"Chiefly labourers from the mill."

"But who exactly?"

"The engineer, the scalesman, David, and sometimes some of our Cossacks."

The investigator halted and waited for the officer, who had lagged behind. He said something to him, twisting the button of his tunic with his fingers, then beckoned to the ataman. The ataman ran up on tiptoe, with bated breath.

"Take two militia-men and go and arrest the men you mentioned. Bring them to the administration office and we'll be along in a minute or two. Do you understand?"

The ataman drew himself up and turned back to execute his instructions.

Stockman was sitting in his unbuttoned vest, his back to the door, filing a design on veneer. He glanced round as the officials entered, and bit his lip.

"Please get up; you're under arrest," the investigator ordered.

"What's this for?"

"You occupy two rooms?"

"Yes."

"We shall search them."

The officer walked across to the table and with a frown picked up the first book that came to hand. "I want the key of that trunk," he said.

"To what do I owe this visit?"

"There'll be time to talk to you after."

Stockman's wife looked through the doorway from the other room and drew back. The investigator's secretary followed her in.

"What is this?" the officer quietly asked Stockman, holding up a book in a yellow cover.

"A book," Stockman replied with a shrug of his shoulder.

"You can keep your witticisms for a more suitable occasion. Answer the question properly."

With a wry smile Stockman leaned his back against the stove. The commissary glanced over the officer's shoulder at the book and then turned to Stockman.

"You're studying?"

"I'm interested in the subject," Stockman dryly replied.

"So!"

The officer glanced through the pages of the book and threw it back on the table. He looked through a second, put it on one side, and having read the cover of the third, turned to Stockman again.

"Where do you keep the rest of this type of literature?"

Stockman screwed up one eye as though taking aim at the officer, and replied.

"You see all that I have."

"You're lying," the officer retorted, waving the book at him. "I demand—"

"Search the rooms!"

Holding his sabre in his hand, the commissary went across to the trunk, where a pockmarked Cossack militia-man, obviously terrified by the circumstances in which he found himself, had begun to rummage among the clothing and linen. The man turned out everything that it was possible to turn out. The search was conducted in the workshop also. The zealous commissary even knocked on the walls with his knuckles.

When the search was ended Stockman was taken to the administration office. He walked along the middle of the road in front of the militia-men, one arm folded across his old coat, the other waving as though he were shaking mud off it. The others walked along the path by the walls.

Stockman was the last of the prisoners to be examined. Ivan Alexievich, with hands still oily, guiltily smiling David, Valet with his jacket across his shoulders, and Misha Koshevoi were herded together in the anteroom, guarded by militia-men.

Rummaging in his portfolio, the investigator questioned Stockman:

"When I examined you in regard to the murder at the mill why did you conceal the fact that you are a member of the Russian Social-Democratic Labour Party?"

Stockman stared silently over the investigator's head.

"That much is established. You will receive a suitable reward for your work," the investigator shouted, annoyed by the prisoner's silence.

"Please begin your examination," Stockman said in a bored tone, and glancing at a stool, he asked for permission to sit down. The investigator did not reply, but glared as Stockman calmly seated himself.

"When did you come here?" he asked.

"Last year."

"On the instruction of your organization?"

"Without any instructions."

"How long have you been a member of your party?"

"What are you talking about?"

"I ask you how long have you been a member of the Russian Social-Democratic Labour Party?"

"I think that—"

"I don't care what you think. Answer the question. Denial is useless, even dangerous." The investigator drew a document out of his portfolio and pinned it to the table with his forefinger. "I have here a report from Rostov, confirming your membership in the party I mentioned."

Stockman turned his eyes quickly to the document, rested his gaze on it for a moment, and then, stroking his knee, replied firmly:

"Since 1907."

"So! You deny that you have been sent here by your party?"

"Yes."

"In that case why did you come here?"

"They needed a locksmith."

"But why did you choose this particular district?"

"For the same reason."

"Have you now or have you at any time had any contact with your organization during the period of your stay here?"

"No."

"Do they know you have come here?"

"I expect so."

The investigator sharpened his pencil with a pearl-handled penknife and pursed his lips.

"Are you in correspondence with any members of your party?"

"No."

"Then what about the letter which was discovered during the search?"

"That is from a friend who has no connection whatever with any revolutionary organization."

"Have you received any instructions from Rostov?"

"No."

"What did the labourers at the mill gather in your rooms for?"

Stockman shrugged his shoulders as though astonished at the stupidity of the question.

"They used to come in the winter evenings to pass the time away. We played cards. . . ."

"And read books prohibited by law?" the investigator suggested.

"No. Every one of them was almost illiterate."

"None the less the engineer from the mill and the others also do not deny this fact."

"That is untrue."

"It seems to me you haven't the most elementary understanding of—" Stockman smiled at this, and the investigator concluded: "You simply do not possess a sound intelligence. You persist in denials to your own harm. It is quite clear that you have been sent here by your party in order to carry on demoralizing activities among the Cossacks, in order to turn them against the government. I fail to understand why you are playing this game of pretence. It cannot diminish your offence. . . ."

"Those are all guesses on your part. May I smoke? Thank you. And they are guesses entirely without foundation."

"Did you read this book to the workers who visited your rooms?" The investigator put his hand on a small book and covered the title. Above his hand the name Plekhanov was visible.

"We read poetry," Stockman replied, and puffed at his cigarette, gripping the bone holder tightly between his fingers.

The next morning the postal tarantass drove out of the village with Stockman dozing on the back seat, his beard buried in his coat collar. On each side of him a militia-man armed with a drawn sabre was squeezed on the seat. One of them, the pockmarked man who had made the search, gripped Stockman's elbow firmly in his knotty, dirty fingers, casting timorous sidelong glances at him. The tarantass rattled briskly down the street. By the Melekhovs' farmyard a little woman wrapped in a shawl stood waiting for it, her back against the wattle fence. Her grey face was wet with the tears that filled her eyes.

The tarantass sped past, and the woman, pressing her hands to her breast, flung herself after it.

"Osip! Osip Davidovich! Oh, how could they—"

Stockman wanted to wave his hand to her, but the pockmarked militia-man jumped up and clutched his arm and in a hoarse, savage voice shouted:

"Sit down or I'll cut you down!"

For the first time in all his simple life he had seen a man who dared to act against the Czar himself.

The long road from Tatarsk to the little town of Radzivillovo lay somewhere behind him in a grey, intangible mist. Gregor tried occasionally to recall the road, but could only dimly remember station buildings, the wagon-wheels clattering beneath the unstable floor, the scent of horses and hay, endless threads of railway line flowing under the wagons, the smoke that billowed in through the open door, and the bearded face of a gendarme on the station platform either at Voronezh or at Kiev, he was not sure which.

At the place where they detrained were crowds of officers and clean-shaven men in grey overcoats, talking a language he could not understand. It took a long time for the horses to be unloaded, but when this had been accomplished the assistant echelon commander led three hundred or more Cossacks to the veterinary hospital. Here followed a long procedure in connection with the examination of the horses. Then allotment to troops. The first troop was formed of light brown horses, the second of bay and dun, the third of dark brown. Gregor was allotted to the fourth, which consisted of plain brown and golden horses. The fifth was composed entirely of sorrel, and the sixth of black horses.

Their road led them along the macadam highway. The Don horses, which had never seen metalled roads before, at first stepped along gingerly, setting their ears back and snorting; but after a while they grew accustomed to the strange feel of the road. The unfamiliar Polish land was crisscrossed with slices of straggling wood. The day was warm and cloudy, and the sun wandered behind a dense curtain of cloud.

The estate of Radzivillovo was some three miles from the station, and they reached it in half an hour. Stroking his horse's neck, Gregor stared at the neatly-built, two-storeyed house, the wooden fence, and the unfamiliar style of the farm buildings. But as they rode past the orchard the bare trees whispered the same language as those in the distant Don country.

Life now showed its tedious, stupefying side to the Cossacks. Torn away from their field labour, they quickly tired at first and spent most of their free time talking. Gregor's troop was quartered in the great tile-roofed wing of the house and slept on pallet beds under the windows. Gregor's bed was by the farthest window. At night the paper pasted over the chinks of the window sounded in the breeze like a distant shepherd's horn, and as he listened to it he was seized with a well-nigh irresistible desire to get up, go to the stables, saddle his horse, and ride and ride until he reached home again.

Reveille was sounded at five o'clock, and the first duty of the day was to clean and groom the horses. During the brief half-hour when the horses were feeding, there was opportunity for desultory conversation.

"This is a hell of a life, boys!"

"I can't stick it!"

"And the sergeant-major! What a swine! He even makes us wash the horses' hoofs!"

"They're cooking pancakes at home now—today is Shrove Tuesday."

"I bet my wife is saying: 'I wonder what my Michael is doing?' "

During exercise the officers stood smoking at the side of the yard, occasionally intervening. As Gregor glanced at the polished, well-groomed officers in their handsome grey cloaks and closely fitting uniforms, he felt that there was an impassable wall between him and them. Their very different, well-ordered, far from Cossack existence flowed on peacefully, untroubled by mud, fleas, or fear of the sergeant-major's fists.

An incident which occurred on the third day after their arrival at Radzivillovo made a painful impression on Gregor, and indeed on all the young Cossacks. They were being instructed in cavalry drill, and Prokhor Zykov's horse happened to kick the sergeant-major's as it passed. The blow was not very hard and it only slightly cut the skin on the horse's left leg. But the sergeant-major struck Prokhor across the face with his whip and, riding right at him, shouted:

"Why the hell don't you look where you're going, you son of a swine? I'll show you. . . . You'll spend the next three days with me!"

The company commander happened to witness the scene, but he turned his back, rubbing the sword-knot of his sabre and yawning boredly. His lips trembling, Prokhor rubbed a streak of blood from his swollen cheek. As Gregor rode past he glanced across at the officers, but they were talking together unconcernedly, as though nothing untoward had happened.

The dreary, monotonous order of existence crushed the life out of the young Cossacks. Until sundown they were kept continuously at foot and horse exercises, and in the evening the horses had to be groomed and fed. Only at ten o'clock, after the roll-call and stationing of guards, were they drawn up for prayers, and the sergeant-major, his eyes wandering over the ranks before him, intoned a "Pater Noster."

In the morning the same routine began again, and the days were as like one another as peas.

In the whole of the estate there were only two women: the old wife of the steward, and the steward's comely young kitchen-maid, Frania. Frania was often to be seen in the kitchen, where the old, browless army cook was in charge. The various troops watched every movement of the young girl's skirt as she ran across the yard. Feeling the gaze of the officers and Cossacks fixed upon her, she bathed in the streams of lasciviousness that came from three hundred pairs of eyes, and swung her hips provokingly as she ran backward and forward between the kitchen and the house, smiling at each troop in turn, but at the officers in particular. Although all fought for her attentions, rumour had it that only the company commander had won them.

One day in early spring Gregor was on duty all day in the great stables. He spent most of his time at one end, where the officers' horses were excited by the presence of a mare. He had just walked past the stall containing the company commander's horse when he heard a sound of struggling and a muffled cry coming from the dark corner at the far end of the stable. A little astonished by the unusual noise, he hurried past the stalls. His eyes were suddenly blinded as someone slammed the stable door and he heard a voice calling in a suppressed shout:

"Hurry up, boys!"

Gregor hastened his steps and called out:

"Who is that?"

The next moment he knocked against one of his company sergeants, who was groping his way to the door. "That you, Melekhov?" the sergeant whispered, putting his hand on Gregor's shoulder.

"Stop! What's up?" Gregor demanded.

The sergeant burst into a guilty snigger and seized Gregor's

sleeve. Tearing his arm away, Gregor ran and threw open the door.
The light momentarily blinded him; he shaded his eyes with his
hand and turned round, hearing an increasing noise in the dark
corner of the stable. He went towards the sound and was met by
Zharkov buttoning up his trousers.

"What the—what are you doing here?"

"Hurry up!" Zharkov whispered, breathing in Gregor's face.
"They've dragged the girl Frania in there . . . undressed her!"
His snigger suddenly broke off as Gregor sent him flying against
the stable wall. Running to the corner, Gregor found a crowd of
Cossacks of the first troop struggling with one another to get to
the middle. He silently pushed his way through them and saw
Frania lying motionless on the floor, her head wrapped in a horse-
cloth, her dress torn and pulled back above her breasts, her white
legs flung out shamelessly and horribly. A Cossack had just risen
from her; holding up his trousers and not looking at his comrades,
with a sheepish grin he fell back to make way for the next. Gregor
tore his way back through the crowd and ran to the door, shouting
for the sergeant-major. But the other Cossacks ran after him and
caught him at the door, flinging him back and one putting a hand
over his mouth. He sent one man flying and gave another a kick
in the stomach, but the others flung a horse-cloth around his head,
tied his hands behind him, and threw him into an empty manger.
Choking in the stinking horse-cloth, he tried to shout, and kicked
lustily at the partition. He heard whispering in the corner and the
door creaking as the Cossacks went in and out. He was set free some
twenty minutes later. At the door the sergeant-major and two Cossacks from another troop were standing.

"You just keep your mouth shut!" the sergeant-major said to him,
winking hard but not looking at him.

The two Cossacks went in and lifted up the motionless bundle
that was Frania and, climbing on to a manger, thrust it through
a hole left in the wall by a badly-fitting plank. The wall bordered
on the orchard. Above each stall was a tiny grimy window. Some
of the Cossacks clambered on to the stall partitions to watch what
Frania would do, others hastened out of the stables. Gregor also
was possessed by a bestial curiosity, and getting on to a partition
he drew himself up to one of the windows and looked down. Dozens
of eyes were thus staring through the dirty windows at the girl

lying under the wall. She lay on her back, her legs crossing and uncrossing like scissor-blades, her fingers scrabbling in the snow by the wall.

She lay there a long time and at last struggled on to her hands and knees. Gregor could clearly see her arms trembling, hardly able to bear her. Swaying, she scrambled to her feet, and dishevelled, unfamiliar, hostile, she passed her eyes in a long, slow stare over the windows.

Then she went, one hand clinging to the woodbine, the other resting and groping along the wall.

Gregor jumped down from the partition and rubbed his throat, feeling that he was about to choke. At the door someone, afterwards he could not even remember who, said to him in distinct and unequivocal tones:

"Breathe a word . . . and, by Christ, we'll kill you!"

On the parade ground the troop commander noticed that a button had been torn from Gregor's greatcoat and asked:

"Who have you been wrestling with? What style do you call this?"

Gregor glanced down at the little round hole left by the missing button; overwhelmed by the memory, for the first time for many a day he felt like crying.

PART II

War

WAR

Chapter 1

A SULTRY, sunny July haze lay over the steppe. The ripe floods of wheat smoked with yellow dust. The metal parts of the reapers were too hot to be touched with the hand. It was painful to look up at the bluish-yellow flaming sky. Where the wheat ended, a saffron sweep of clover began.

The entire village of Tatarsk had moved out into the steppe. The horses choked in the heat and the pungent dust and were restive as they dragged the reapers. The wind blowing from the river raised clouds of dust from the steppe, and the sun was enveloped in a tingling haze.

Since early morning Piotra, who was forking the wheat off the reaper platform, had drunk half a bucketful of water. Within a minute of his drinking the warm, unpleasant liquid his throat was dry again. His shirt was wet through, the sweat streamed from his face, there was a continual trilling ring in his ears. Her face covered with her kerchief, her shirt unbuttoned, Daria was gathering the corn into stooks. A greyish, granular sweat ran down between her urgent breasts. Natalia was leading the horses. Her cheeks were burned the colour of beet, her eyes were filled with tears because

189

of the glaring sun. Pantaleimon was walking up and down the
swaths of grain, his wet shirt scalding his body. His beard felt as
though it were a stream of melting black cart-grease flowing over
his chest.

At last Daria could stand no more. "Piotra!" she called. "Let's
stop."

"Wait a bit; we'll finish this row," he answered.

"Let's put it off till it's cooler. I've had enough."

Natalia halted the horses; her chest was heaving as though it
were she who had been pulling the reaper. Daria went across to
them, her bare feet slapping carefully over the cut grain.

"Piotra, we're not far from the lake here."

"Not far! Only two miles or so!"

"A bathe would be good!"

"While you're getting there and back . . ." sighed Natalia.

"Why the devil should we walk? We'll unharness the horses and
ride."

Piotra glanced uneasily at his father tying up a sheaf and waved
his hand. "All right, unharness the horses."

Daria unfastened the traces and dextrously jumped on to the
mare's back. Natalia smilingly led her horse to the reaper and tried
to mount from the driver's seat. Piotra went to her aid and hoisted
her by her leg on to the horse. They rode off. Daria, sitting her
horse Cossack-fashion, trotted in front, her skirt tucked up above
her bare knees, her kerchief pressed tightly over the back of her
head.

As they crossed the field path Piotra glanced to his left and
noticed a tiny cloud of dust moving swiftly along the distant highroad from the village.

"Someone riding there," he remarked to Natalia, screwing up
his eyes.

"And fast, too! Look at the dust!" Natalia replied in surprise.

"Who on earth can it be? Daria!" Piotra called to his wife. "Rein
in for a minute and let's watch that rider!"

The cloud of dust dropped down into a hollow and disappeared,
then came up again on the other side. Now the figure of the rider
could be seen through the dust. Piotra sat gazing, his dirty palm
set against the edge of his straw summer hat. He frowned and took
his hand away; an agitated expression passed across his face.

Now the horseman could be seen quite plainly. He was riding his horse at a furious gallop, his left hand holding on his cap, a dusty red flag fluttering in his right. He rode along the path so close to them that Piotra heard his horse's panting breath. As he passed, the man shouted:

"Alarm!"

A flake of yellow soapy foam flew from his horse and fell into a hoof-print. Piotra followed the rider with his eyes. The heavy snort of the horse, and, as he stared after the retreating figure, the horse's croup, wet, and glittering like a steel blade, remained impressed in his memory.

Still not realizing the nature of the misfortune that had come at last upon them, Piotra gazed stupidly at the foam lying in the dust, then glanced around the rolling steppe. From all sides the Cossacks were running over the yellow strips of grass towards the village; across the steppe, as far as the distant upland, little clouds of dust betokening horsemen were to be seen. Along the tracks they were riding in a dense mass, and long trails of dust moved along the roads.

"What is it all about?" Natalia half-groaned, looking fearfully at Piotra. Her gaze, the gaze of a hare in a trap, startled him. He galloped back to the reaper, jumped off his horse before it had halted, hustled into the trousers he had flung off while working, and, waving his hand to his father, tore off to add one more cloud of dust to those which had already blossomed over the sultry steppe.

He found a dense grey crowd assembled in the square. Many were already wearing their army uniforms and equipment. The blue military caps of the men belonging to the ataman's regiment rose a head higher than the rest, like swans among geese.

The village tavern was closed. The military commissary had a gloomy and careworn look. The women, attired in their holiday clothes, lined the fences along the streets. One word was on everybody's lips: "Mobilization." Intoxicated, excited faces. The general anxiety had been communicated to the horses, and they were kicking and plunging and snorting angrily. The square was strewn with empty bottles and the papers of cheap sweets. A low cloud of dust hung in the air.

Piotra led his saddled horse by the rein. Close to the church fence a healthy-looking, swarthy Cossack of the ataman's regiment was buttoning up his blue trousers, his mouth gaping with a smile, while around him a stocky little woman, his wife or lover, was bustling and nagging. Near him a red-bearded sergeant-major was arguing with an artillery-man:

"Nothing will come of it, never fear!" he was assuring him. "We'll be mobilized for a few days, and then back home again."

"But supposing there is a war?"

"Pah, my friend! What power could stand on its feet against us?"

In a neighbouring group a handsome, elderly Cossack was waxing indignant:

"It's nothing to do with us. Let them do their own fighting, we haven't got our grain in yet."

"It's a shame! Here we are standing here, and on a day like this we could harvest enough for a whole year."

"The cattle will get among the stacks."

"And we'd just begun to reap the barley!"

"But the ataman said they'd called us up only in case anything happened!"

"Another twelve months and I'd have been out of the third line of reserves," an elderly Cossack said regretfully.

"Don't you worry, as soon as they start killing the men off, they'll be taking the old ones too," someone reassured him.

Three Cossacks led a fourth, completely drunk, and stained with blood, into the village administration office. He threw himself back, tore his shirt open, and, rolling his eyes, shouted:

"I'll show their peasants! I'll have their blood! They'll know the Don Cossack!"

The circle around him laughed approvingly.

"That's right, give it to them!"

"What have they tied him up for?"

"He went for some peasant!"

"Well, they deserve it; we'll give them some more!"

"I took a hand when they put them down in 1905. That was a sight worth seeing!"

"There's going to be war. They'll be sending us again to put them down."

Outside Mokhov's shop was a surging crowd. In the middle Ivan

Tomilin was drunkenly arguing with Şergei Platonovich. "What's all this?" Mokhov expostulated. "My word, this is an outrage! Boy, run for the ataman!"

Rubbing his sweaty hands on his trousers, Tomilin pressed against the frowning merchant and sneered: "You've squeezed us and squeezed us with your interest, you swine, and now you've got frightened. I'll smash your face in, you serpent!"

The village ataman was busily pouring out the oil of soothing words for thc benefit of the Cossacks surrounding him: "War? No, there won't be any war. Their Excellencies the military commissaries said the mobilization was only against emergency. You needn't get alarmed."

"Good! Back to the fields as soon as we're home!" the chorus arose. Until late at night the square was alive and noisy with excited crowds.

The first-reserve Cossacks from Tatarsk and the neighbouring villages spent the second night after their departure from home in a little village. The Cossacks from the lower end of Tatarsk drew into a separate group from those of the upper end, so Piotra Melekhov, Anikushka, Christonia, Stepan Astakhov, Ivan Tomilin, and others were all billeted in one hut. The Cossacks had lain down to sleep, spreading out their horse-blankets in the kitchen and the front room, and were having a last smoke for the night. The master of the house, a tall, decrepit old man who had served in the Turkish war, sat talking with them.

"So you're off to war, soldiers?"

"Yes, grand-dad, off to war."

"It won't be anything like the Turkish war was, I don't suppose. They've got different weapons now."

"It'll be just the same. Just as devilish. Just as they killed the Turks off then, so we'll have to now," Tomilin barked, angry with no one knew whom.

"My sons, I ask you one thing. I ask you seriously, and you mark what I say," the old man said. "Remember one thing! If you want to come back from the mortal struggle alive and with a whole skin, you must keep the law of humanity."

"Which one?" Stepan Astakhov asked, smiling uncertainly. He

had begun to smile again from the day he heard of the war. The war called him, and the general anxiety and pain assuaged his own.

"This one: don't take other men's goods. That's one. As you fear God, don't do wrong to any woman. That's the second. And then you must know certain prayers."

The Cossacks sat up, and all spoke at once:

"If only we didn't have to lose our own goods—not to speak of taking other people's!"

"And why mustn't we touch a woman? How are we to stand that?"

The old man fixed his eyes sternly on them and answered:

"You must not touch a woman. Never! If you can't stand that, you'll lose your heads or you'll be wounded. You'll be sorry after, but then it will be too late. I'll tell you the prayers. I went right through the Turkish war, death on my shoulders like a saddlebag, but I came through alive because of these prayers."

He went into the other room, rummaged beneath the ikon, and brought back a crumbling, faded brown scrap of paper.

"Get up and write them down!" he commanded. "You'll be off again before dawn tomorrow, won't you?"

He spread the paper out on the table and left it. Anikushka was the first to get up; on his smooth, womanish face the shadows cast by the flickering light played nervously. All except Stepan sat and wrote down the prayers. Anikushka rolled up the paper he had used and fastened it to the string of the cross at his breast. Stepan jeered at him:

"That's a nice home you've made for the lice."

"Young man, if you don't believe, hold your tongue!" the old man interrupted him sternly. "Don't be a stone of offence to others and don't laugh at faith. It's a sin."

Stepan smiled, but he lapsed into silence.

The prayers which the Cossacks wrote down were three, and each could choose which he wished. The Prayer in Time of Attack read:

Supreme Ruler, Holy Mother of God, and our Lord Jesus Christ. Bless, Lord, Thy slave of God entering battle, and my comrades who are with me. Wrap them in cloud, with Thy heavenly, stony hail protect them. Holy Dmitry Soslutsky, defend me, the slave of God, and my comrades on all four sides; permit not evil men to shoot, nor with spear to pierce, nor with pole-axe to strike, nor with butt end of axe to smite, nor with axe to hew down, nor with sword to cut down or pierce, nor with knife to pierce or cut; neither old nor young, swarthy nor black; neither heretic nor wizard nor any magic-worker. All is before me now, the slave of God, orphaned and judged. In the sea, in the ocean, on the island of Buyan stands an iron post; on the post is an iron man resting on an iron staff, and he charms iron, steel, lead, zinc, and all weapons. "Go, iron, into your mother earth away from the slave of God and past my comrades and my horse. The arrow-shafts into the forest, and the feather to its mother bird, and the glue to the fish." Defend me, the slave of God, with a golden buckler from steel and from bullet, cannon-fire and ball, spear and knife. May my body be stronger than armour! Amen.

Very similar were all the prayers which the Cossacks wrote down and concealed under their shirts, tying them to the strings of the little ikons blessed by their mothers and to the little bundles of their native earth. But death came upon all alike, upon those who wrote down the prayers also. Their bodies rotted on the fields of Galicia and East Prussia, in the Carpathians and Rumania, wherever the ruddy flames of war flickered and the tracks of Cossack horses were imprinted in the earth.

Some four days later the red cars of the troop trains were carrying the Cossacks in their regiments and batteries towards the Russo-Austrian frontier.

"War. . . ."

The wagons hummed with talk and song. At the stations the Cossacks were eyed with inquisitive, benevolent looks. The crowds felt the stripes on the Cossacks' trousers.

"War. . . ."

At the stations the women waved their handkerchiefs, smiled, threw cigarettes and sweets. Only once, just before the train reached Voronezh, did an old railway worker thrust his head into the car where Piotra Melekhov was crowded with twenty-nine other Cossacks, and ask:

"You going?"

"Yes. Get in and come with us, grand-dad," one of the Cossacks replied.

"My boy . . . bullocks for slaughter!" the old man shook his head reproachfully.

Chapter 2

During the second week of July 1914 the divisional staff transferred Gregor Melekhov's regiment to the town of Rovno in Volhynia to take part in manœuvres. A fortnight later, tired out with continual manœuvring, Gregor and the other Cossacks of the fourth company were lying in their tents when the company commander, Lieutenant Polkovnikov, galloped furiously back from the regimental staff.

"Another attack I suppose," Prokhor Zykov suggested tentatively, and waited for someone to agree.

The troop sergeant thrust the needle with which he had been mending his trousers into the lining of his cap and remarked:

"I expect so; they won't let us rest for a moment."

A minute or two later the bugler sounded the alarm. The Cossacks jumped to their feet. They had their horses saddled well within regulation time. As Gregor was tearing up the tent-pegs the sergeant managed to mutter to him:

"It'-   this time, my boy!"

"You're lying!" Gregor expressed his disbelief.

"God's truth! The sergeant-major told me."

The company formed in the street, the commander at its head. "In troop columns!" his command flew over the ranks.

The horses' hoofs clattered as they went at a trot out of the village on to the highway. From a neighbouring village the first and fifth companies could be seen riding towards the station.

A day later the regiment was detrained at a station some twenty miles from the Austrian frontier. Dawn was breaking beyond a group of birch trees. The morning promised to be fine. The engine fussed and rumbled over the tracks, which glittered with dew. The Cossacks of the fourth company led their horses by the bridles out of the cars and over the level crossing, mounted, and moved off in column formation. Their voices sounded eerily in the crumbling, lilac darkness. Faces and the contours of horses emerged uncertainly out of the gloom.

"What company is that?" came a challenge.

"And who are you? Are you lost?" one of the Cossacks replied.

"I'll show you who I am! How dare you speak to an officer in that way?"

"Sorry, Your Excellency, I didn't recognize you."

"Ride on! Ride on!"

A little farther on, the fourth company was held up for a while by the first, which had detrained before it. As they sat, the Cossacks sang quietly under their breath. Against the bluish grey of the sky the silhouettes of the horsemen ahead stood out clearly, as though drawn with India ink. The lances swung like bare sunflower stalks. Occasionally a stirrup jingled or a saddle creaked.

Prokhor Zykov was riding at Gregor's side. Prokhor stared into his face and whispered:

"Melekhov, you're not afraid, are you?"

"What is there to be afraid of?"

"We may take part in a battle today."

"Well, what of it?"

"But I'm afraid," Prokhor admitted, his fingers playing nervously with the reins. "I didn't sleep a wink all night."

Once more the company advanced; the horses moved at a measured pace, the lances swayed and flowed rhythmically. Dropping the reins, Gregor dozed. And it seemed to him that it was not the horse that put its legs forward springily, rocking him in the saddle, but he himself who was passing along a warm, dark road and walking with unusual ease, with irresistible joy. Prokhor chattered away at his side, but the voice mingled with the creak of the saddle and the clatter of hoofs and did not disturb his thoughtless doze.

The company turned into a by-road. The silence rang in their ears. Ripe oats hung over the wayside, their heads smoking with dew. The horses tried to reach the low ears and dragged the reins out of their riders' hands. The gracious daylight crept under Gregor's eyelids. He raised his head and heard Prokhor's monotonous voice, like the creak of a cart-wheel.

He was abruptly aroused by a heavy, rumbling howl that billowed across the oatfields.

"Gunfire!" Zykov almost shouted, and tears filled his calfish eyes. Gregor lifted his head. In front of him the troop sergeant's grey greatcoat rose and fell in unison with the horse's back; on each side stretched fields of uncut grain; a skylark danced in the sky at the height of a telegraph pole. The entire company was aroused. The sound of the firing ran through it like an electric current. Lashed into activity, Lieutenant Polkovnikov put the company into a fast trot. Beyond a crossroad, where a deserted tavern stood, they began to fall in with the carts of refugees. A squadron of smart-looking dragoons went by. Their captain, riding a sorrel thorough-bred, stared at the Cossacks ironically and spurred on his horse. They passed a great pockmarked artillery-man carrying an armful of boards probably torn from the fence of the tavern and came upon a howitzer battery stranded in a muddy and swampy hollow. The riders were lashing at their horses, while the gunners struggled with the carriage-wheels.

A little farther on they overtook an infantry regiment. The soldiers were marching swiftly, their overcoats flung back. The sun glittered on their polished helmets and streamed from their bayonets. A corporal in the last company threw a lump of mud at Gregor:

"Here, catch! Chuck it at the Austrians!"

"Don't play about, grasshopper!" Gregor replied, and cut the lump of mud in its flight with his whip.

From now on they were continually passing foot regiments crawl-ing like caterpillars, batteries, baggage-wagons, Red Cross wagons. The deathly breath of imminent battle was in the air.

A little later, as it was entering a village, the fourth company was overtaken by the commander of the regiment, Colonel Kaledin, accompanied by his second in command. As they passed, Gregor heard the latter say agitatedly to Kaledin:

"This village isn't marked on the ordnance map, Vassily Maxi-movich! We may find ourselves in an awkward situation."

Gregor did not catch the colonel's reply.

The regiment was continually changing its pace, and the horses began to sweat. In the distance appeared the huts of a little village lying under a steep slope. On the other side of the village was a wood, its green tree-tops piercing the azure dome of the sky. From beyond the wood came the sound of gunfire, mingled with the frequent rattle of rifle-shots. The horses pricked up their ears. The smoke of bursting shrapnel hovered in the sky a long way off; the rifle-fire came from the right of the company.

Gregor listened tensely to every sound, his nerves tautened into little bundles of sensation. Prokhor Zykov fidgeted in his saddle, talking incessantly:

"Gregor, those shots sound just like boys rattling sticks along railings, don't they?" he remarked.

"Shut up, magpie!"

The company entered the village. Russian soldiers were over-running the yards. The inhabitants of the huts were packing their belongings to flee, their faces impressed with alarm and confusion. As Gregor passed he noticed that soldiers were firing the roof of a shed, but its owner, a tall, grey-haired White Russian, crushed by his sudden misfortune, went past them without paying the slightest attention. Gregor saw the man's family loading a cart with red-covered pillows and ramshackle furniture, and the man himself was carefully carrying a broken wheel-rim, which was of no value to anybody and had probably lain in the yard for years. Gregor was amazed at the stupidity of the women, who were piling the carts with painted pots and ikons and were leaving necessary and valu-able articles behind in the huts. Down the street the feathers from a featherbed blew like a miniature snow-storm.

The company crossed the Austrian frontier at noon. The horses jumped across the overthrown frontier post. From the right came the sound of rifle-fire. In the distance the brick walls of a farm were visible. The sun's rays fell perpendicularly. A bitter-tasting cloud of dust settled on everything. The regimental commander issued orders for advance patrols to be detached and sent ahead. From the fourth company went the fourth troop under the troop officer Semionov. The regiment, dissected into its companies, was left behind in a grey haze. The troop of some twenty Cossacks rode past the farm along the rutted road.

The officer led the reconnaissance patrol a couple of miles, then halted to study his map. The Cossacks gathered in a group to smoke. Gregor dismounted to ease his saddle-girth, but the sergeant shouted:

"What are you up to? Get back on your horse!"

The officer lit a cigarette and diligently swept the country ahead with his binoculars. To the right rose the serrated outline of a wood. Just over a mile away was a little village, beyond it a deep-running rivulet and the glassy surface of water. The officer stared intently through his binoculars, studying the deathly stillness of the village streets, but it was as deserted as a cemetery. Only the blue ribbon of water beckoned challengingly.

"That must be Korolevka." The officer indicated the village with his eyes.

The sergeant took his horse nearer the officer. He made no reply, but the expression of his face said eloquently:

"You know better than I! I'm concerned only with minor questions."

"We'll ride to it," the officer said irresolutely, putting away his binoculars and frowning as though he had toothache.

"Mightn't we run into them, Your Excellency?"

"We'll go cautiously."

They rode fearfully down into the deserted street. Every window suggested an ambush, every open cellar door evoked a feeling of savage isolation and sent an unpleasant shudder down the back. All eyes were drawn as though by magnets to the fences and ditches. They rode in like a band of robbers—or as wolves approach human habitations in the blue winter night—but the streets were empty. The silence howled stupefyingly. From the open window of one house came the naïve striking of a clock. The sounds cut like pistol-shots, and Gregor saw the officer tremble and his hand spasmodically grip his revolver.

There was not a soul in the village. The patrol forded the river; the water reached the horses' bellies. They entered willingly and drank it as they went, while their riders pulled at the reins and urged them on. Gregor stared thirstily down at the turbid water, close yet inaccessible; it drew him almost irresistibly towards itself. If it had been possible he would have jumped out of his saddle and lain without undressing under the drowsy murmur of the stream, so that its coolness could freshen his back and his chest.

From the rise beyond the village they saw a town in the distance: square rows of houses, brick buildings, gardens, and church spires. The officer rode to the top of the rise and put his binoculars to his eyes.

"There they are," he shouted, the fingers of his left hand playing nervously.

The sergeant rode to the sun-baked crest and gazed. He was followed by the other Cossacks in single file. Along the streets they saw people swarming. Wagons dammed up the side streets, horsemen were galloping furiously. With eyes screwed up, gazing from under his palm, Gregor was able even to distinguish the grey, unfamiliar colour of the uniforms. Before the town stretched the freshly-dug brown lines of trenches, with men swarming about them.

The sergeant drove the Cossacks hurriedly back down the rise. The officer made some pencil notes in his field notebook and then beckoned to Gregor:

"Melekhov!"

"Sir!"

Gregor dismounted and went to the officer, his legs feeling like stone after the long ride. The officer handed him a folded paper.

"You've got the best horse. Deliver this to the regimental commander. At the gallop!" he ordered.

Gregor hid the paper in his breast pocket and went back to his horse, slipping the chin-strap under his chin as he went. The officer watched him until he had mounted, then glanced at his wrist-watch.

The regiment had nearly reached the village of Korolevka when Gregor rode up with the report. After reading it the colonel gave an order to his adjutant, who galloped off to the first company.

The fourth company rode through Korolevka and as quickly as though on the parade ground extended over the country beyond, straightening out its horseshoe formation. The horses tossed their heads to shake off the horse-flies, and there was a continual jingle of snaffles. In the midday silence the noise of the first company passing through the village sounded heavily.

Lieutenant Polkovnikov rode on his prancing horse to the front

of the ranks. Gathering the reins tightly in one hand, he dropped
the other to his sword-knot. With bated breath Gregor awaited the
word of command.

The officer drew his sabre from its sheath; the blade gleamed
like blue light.

"Company!" The sabre was swung to the right, then to the left,
and finally brought down in front of him, hanging in the air above
the horse's ears. "In file formation, forward!" Gregor mentally
executed the command. "Lances at the ready! Into the attack . . .
gallop!" The officer snapped out the orders and gave his horse the
rein.

The earth groaned heavily, crushed beneath a thousand hoofs.
Gregor, who was in the front rank, had hardly brought his lance to
the ready when his horse, carried away by a lashing flood of other
horses, broke into a gallop and went off at full speed. Ahead of him
the commanding officer rippled against the grey background of the
field. A black wedge of ploughed land sped irresistibly towards
him. The first company raised a shrieking, quivering shout; the
fourth company took it up. Through the roaring whistle in his ears
Gregor caught the sound of distant firing. The first shell flew high
above them, furrowing the glassy vault of heaven. Gregor pressed
the hot shaft of his lance against his side until it hurt him and his
palm sweated. The whistle of flying shells made him duck his head
down to the wet neck of his horse, and the pungent scent of the
animal's sweat penetrated his nostrils. As though through the misty
glass of binoculars he saw the brown ridges of trenches, and men
in grey running back to the town. A machine-gun incessantly spread
a fan of whistling bullets at the Cossacks; in front of them and under
their horses' feet they tore up woolly spirts of dust.

That which before the attack had sent the blood coursing faster
through his veins now turned to stone within him; he felt nothing
except the ringing in his ears and a pain in the toes of his left foot.
His thought, emasculated by fear, congealed in a heavy mass in
his head.

The ensign was the first to drop from his horse. Prokhor rode
over him. Gregor glanced back, and a fragment of what he saw
was impressed on his memory as though cut with a diamond on
glass. As Prokhor's horse leaped across the fallen officer it bared
its teeth and stumbled. Prokhor flew out of the saddle as though

catapulted and, falling headlong, was crushed under the hoofs of the horse behind him. Gregor heard no cry, but from Prokhor's face, with its distorted mouth and calf's eyes staring out of their sockets, he realized that he must be screaming inhumanly. Others fell, both horses and Cossacks. Through the film of tears caused by the wind in his eyes Gregor stared ahead at the grey, seething mass of Austrians fleeing from the trenches.

The company, which had torn away from the village in an orderly stream, scattered and broke into fragments. Those in front reached the trenches, Gregor foremost among them.

A tall, white-eyebrowed Austrian, his forage cap drawn over his eyes, fired almost point-blank at Gregor. The heat of the bullet scorched his cheek. He struck with his lance, at the same time pulling on the reins with all his strength. The blow was so powerful that it pierced right through the Austrian and ran for half a shaft-length out of his back. Gregor was not quick enough to withdraw the lance. He felt a quivering and convulsion in his hand and saw the Austrian, bent right back so that only the point of his chin was visible, clutching and scratching at the shaft with clawing fingers. Opening his hand, he dropped the shaft and felt with numbed fingers for his sabre-hilt.

The Austrians fled into the streets of the town. Over the grey clots of their uniforms the Cossack horses towered.

Gregor struck at his horse with the flat of his sabre; shaking its neck, it carried him away down the street. Along by the iron railings of a garden an Austrian ran, swaying, without rifle, his cap clutched in his hand. Gregor saw the back of his head and the damp collar of his tunic around his neck. He overtook him and, afire with frenzy, whirled his sabre around his head. The Austrian was running close to the railings on the left-hand side, and it was awkward for Gregor to hew him down. But, leaning over his saddle, holding his sabre aslant, he struck at the man's temple. Without a cry the Austrian pressed his hand to the wound and spun round with his back to the railings. Without reining in his horse, Gregor jumped across him, turned round, and rode back at a trot. The square, fear-contorted face of the Austrian was already turning the hue of cast iron. His arms were stretched down the seams of his trousers, his ashen lips were quivering. The sabre had slipped from his temple, and the flesh was hanging over his cheek like a crimson rag. The blood streamed on to his uniform. Gregor's eyes met the mortally terror-stricken eyes of the Austrian. The man slowly bent at the knees; a gurgling groan came from his throat. Screwing up his eyes, Gregor swept his sabre down. The blow split the cranium in two. The man flung out his arms and fell; his head knocked heavily against the stone of the road. At the sound Gregor's horse took alarm and, snorting, carried him into the middle of the street.

Infrequent shots sounded in the streets. Past Gregor a foaming horse carried a dead Cossack. One foot had come out of the stirrup, and the horse was dragging the bruised and battered body over the stones. Gregor saw only the red band on the trousers and the torn green shirt drawn in a bundle over the head.

Gregor's head felt as heavy as lead. He slipped from his horse and shook his head vigorously. Some Cossacks of the third company trotted past him, carrying a wounded man in their overcoats and driving a crowd of Austrian prisoners before them. The men ran in a dense grey herd, their iron-shod boots clattering joylessly on the stones. In Gregor's eyes their faces blended into a gelid patch of clayey hue. He dropped his horse's reins and went across to the Austrian soldier he had cut down. The man lay where he had fallen, by the wrought-iron-work of the railings, his dirty brown palm stretched out as though begging. Gregor glanced at his face. It seemed small, all but childlike, despite the hanging moustaches and the tortured expression of his harsh, distorted mouth.

"Hey, you!" a strange Cossack officer shouted as he rode down the middle of the street.

Gregor looked up and stumbled across to his horse. His steps were burdensomely heavy and tottering, as though he were carrying an unbearable weight on his back. Loathing and perplexity crushed his spirit. He took the serrated stirrup in his hand, but for a long time he could not hoist his heavy foot into it.

Chapter 3

It was usual for the Cossacks of the upper districts of the Don, including Vieshenska, to be drafted into the 11th and 12th Cossack Regiments and the ataman's Life Guards. But for some reason part of the enrolment of 1914 was assigned to the 3rd Don Cossack Regiment, which was composed mainly of Cossacks from the Ust-Medvedietz district. Among those so drafted was Mitka Korshunov.

The 3rd Don Cossack Regiment was stationed at Vilno, together with certain sections of the Third Cavalry Division. One day in June the various companies rode out from the city to take up country quarters. The day was dull but warm. The flowing clouds coursed in droves across the sky and concealed the sun. The regimental band blared at the head of the column, and the officers in their light summer caps and drill uniforms rode in a bunch at the back, a cloud of cigarette-smoke rising above them.

On each side of the road the peasants and their womenfolk were cutting the hay, stopping to gaze at the columns of Cossacks as they passed. The horses sweated with the heat, a yellowish foam appeared between their legs, and the light breeze blowing from the south-east did not cool, but rather intensified the steaming swelter.

Arrived at its destination, the regiment was broken up by companies among the estates in the district. During the day the Cossacks cut the clover and meadow grass for the landowners, at night they grazed their hobbled horses in the fields assigned to them, and played cards or told stories by the smoke of the camp-fires. The sixth company was billeted on the large estate of a Polish landowner. The officers lived in the house, played cards, got drunk, and paid attentions to the steward's daughter; the Cossacks pitched their tents a couple of miles away from the house. Each morning the steward drove out in a droshky to their camp. The corpulent, estimable gentleman would get out of the droshky and invariably welcome the Cossacks with a wave of his white, glossy-visored cap.

"Come and cut hay with us, sir; it'll shake your fat down a bit," the Cossacks called to him. The steward smiled phlegmatically, wiped his bald head with his handkerchief, and went with the sergeant-major to point out the next section of hay to be cut.

In the hot dusk of the June evening the Cossacks sang around the camp-fires:

> "A Cossack went to a distant land,
> Riding his horse o'er the plain;
> His native village he left for aye";

a silvery tenor voice pined and drooped, expressing a heavy, velvety sorrow:

> "He'll ne'er come back again."

Now the tenor rose a tone higher:

> "In vain did his youthful Cossack bride
> To the north-west gaze each morn and eve;
> Waiting in hope that her Cossack dear
> Would return from the land he ne'er will leave."

Several voices struggled with the song, and it grew brisk and heady like home-brewed beer:

> "But beyond the hills where the snow lies deep,
> The icefields crack, and the tempests blow,
> Where angrily bow the pines and firs
> The Cossack's bones lie beneath the snow."

While they told one another simple stories of Cossack life the tenor would sing in an undertone, like a skylark soaring above the thawed earth of April:

> "As the Cossack lay dying he pleadingly asked
> That above him a mound should be piled for his tomb,
> And a hazel tree from his native land
> Should be planted in brilliant flower to bloom."

At another camp-fire the company's story-teller was spinning stories. The Cossacks listened with unflagging attention. Only occasionally, when the hero of the story cleverly extricated himself from an awkward intrigue plotted against him by the Muscovites and the unclean powers, did someone's hand gleam white in the firelight as it was slapped against the leg of his boot, or a voice would utter a rapturous exclamation. Then the flowing, unbroken tones of the story-teller would continue.

A week or so after the regiment's arrival at its country quarters, the company commander sent for the smith and the sergeant-major. "What condition are the horses in?" he asked.

"All in good order, Your Excellency; in very good order indeed," the sergeant-major replied.

The captain twisted his black moustaches and said:

"The regimental commander has issued instructions for all stirrups and bits to be tinned. There is to be an Imperial review of the regiment. Let everything be polished until it gleams, the saddles and the rest of the equipment. When can you be ready?"

The sergeant-major looked at the smith; the smith looked at the sergeant-major. Then both of them looked at the captain. The sergeant-major suggested:

"How about Sunday, Your Excellency?" and respectfully touched his moustache with his finger.

The preparations for the review were put in hand the same day. The Cossacks groomed their horses, cleaned the bridles, rubbed the snaffles and the other metal parts of the horses' equipment with bathbrick. By the end of the week the regiment was shining like a new threepenny piece. Everything glittered with polish, from the horses' hoofs to the Cossacks' faces. On the Saturday the regimental commander inspected the regiment and thanked the officers and Cossacks for their zealous preparations and splendid appearance.

The azure thread of the July days reeled past. The Cossack horses were in perfect condition; only the Cossacks themselves were uneasy and consumed with questionings. Not a whisper was to be heard of the Imperial review. The weeks passed in unending talk, continual preparation. Then like a bolt from the blue came an order for the regiment to return to Vilno.

They were back in the city by the evening. A second order was at once issued to the companies. The Cossacks' boxes were to be collected and stored in the barracks, and preparations made for a possible further removal.

"Your Excellency, what is it all about?" The Cossacks implored the truth from their troop officers. The officers shrugged their shoulders. They themselves would have been very glad to know.

But on the 1st of August the regimental commander's orderly managed to whisper to a friend:

"It's war, my boy!"

"You're lying!"

"God's truth! But not a word to anyone!"

Next morning the regiment was drawn up in company formation outside the barracks, awaiting the commander. He came round a corner of the barrack buildings and, riding his horse to the front of the regiment, turned the animal sideways. The adjutant drew out his handkerchief to wipe his nose, but had no time to accomplish the manœuvre. Into the soundless, jarring silence the colonel threw his voice:

"Cossacks!"

"Now it's coming!" everyone thought. An impatient agitation kept them all on tenterhooks. Mitka Korshunov's horse was shifting from hoof to hoof, and he irritatedly brought his heel against its flank.

"Germany has declared war on us. . . ."

Along the ranks ran a whisper as though a puff of wind had run across a field of ripe, heavy-eared oats. A horse's neigh cut the Cossacks' ears. Round eyes and gaping mouths turned in the direction of the first company, where the animal had dared to neigh.

The colonel said much more. He chose his words carefully, seeking to arouse a feeling of national pride. But before the mental eyes of the thousand Cossacks it was not the silk of foreign banners that fell rustling at their feet, but their own everyday life, hard, yet native, that fluttered and called: their wives, children, lovers, ungathered grain, orphaned villages.

"In two hours we entrain . . ." was the only thought that penetrated all minds.

The regiment rode singing to the station. The Cossacks' voices drowned the band, and it lapsed into disordered silence. The officers' wives rode in droshkies, a colourful crowd foamed along the pavements, the horses' hoofs raised a cloud of dust. Laughing at his own and others' sorrow, twitching his left shoulder so that his blue strap tossed hectically, the leading singer sang a bawdy Cossack song. Deliberately running the words into one another, to the accompaniment of newly shod hoofs the company carried its song along to the red railway cars at the station. One of the Cossacks winked cynically at the crowd of women seeing them off.

On the track the engine bellowed warningly as it got up steam. Echelons. . . . Echelons. . . . Echelons innumerable.

Along the country's arteries, over the railway tracks to the western frontier, distracted Russia was driving its grey-coated blood.

At a little town on the line the regiment was broken up into its respective companies. On the instructions of the divisional staff the sixth company was assigned to the disposition of the third army infantry corps, and went by forced marches to Pelikalia.

On August 9 the company commander sent for the sergeant-major and a Cossack named Mrikhin, from the first troop. Mrikhin returned to the troop late in the afternoon, just as Mitka Korshunov was bringing the horses back after watering them.

Mrikhin, a massive, swarthy Cossack, went into the hut. At the table Shchegolkov was mending a broken rein by the light of a guttering oil lamp. Kruchkov was standing by the stove with his hands behind him, talking to Ivankov.

"Tomorrow, boys, we go out at daybreak to an outpost at Liubov," Mrikhin announced.

"Who's going?" Mitka inquired, entering at that moment and setting the pitcher down at the door.

"Shchegolkov, Kruchkov, Rvachev, Popov, and Ivankov."

"And what about me?" Mitka asked.

"You stay here, Mitry."

"Well, then the devil take the lot of you!"

The party set out at dawn. After riding steadily for some time, from a rise they saw the large village of Liubov lying stretched along a river valley. Mrikhin chose the last farm in the village for their observation post, as it was nearest to the frontier. The master of the farm, a clean-shaven, bandy-legged Pole in a white sailcloth hat, showed the Cossacks a shed in which they could stable their horses. Behind the shed was a green field of clover. Slopes rolled away to a neighbouring wood, and a white stretch of grain was intersected by a road, grass-land lying beyond. They took turns to watch with binoculars from the ditch behind the shed. The others lay in the cool shed, which smelt of long-stored grain, the dust of chaff, mice, and the sweetish, mouldering scent of earth.

In the evening Ivankov relieved Shchegolkov, who had been on duty all the afternoon, and, adjusting the binoculars, stared in the direction of the north-west, towards the wood. He could see the snowy stretch of grain waving in the wind, and a ruddy flood of sunlight bathing the green headland of fir wood. Beyond the village he saw the white, glowing forms of the lads bathing in the stream. A woman's contralto voice called: "Stassia, Stassia! Come here!" Shchegolkov lit a cigarette and remarked as he went back to the shed:

"Look how the sunset is burning! It's blowing up for wind."

That night the horses stood unsaddled. In the village all lights were extinguished and all sound died away.

The following day passed in idleness. In the afternoon Popov was sent back to the company with a report.

Evening. Night. Over the village rose the yellow brim of the young moon. From time to time a ripe apple dropped with a soft thud from the tree in the garden.

About midnight, while Ivankov was on guard, he heard the sound of horses along the village street. He crawled out of the ditch to look, but the moon was swathed in cloud, and he could see nothing through the impenetrable darkness. He went and awoke Kruchkov, who was sleeping at the door.

"Kozma! Horsemen coming! Get up!"

"Where from?"

"They're riding into the village."

They went out. The clatter of hoofs came clearly from the street, some hundred yards away.

"We'll go into the garden. We can hear better there," Kruchkov suggested.

They ran past the hut into the tiny front garden and lay down by the fence. The jingle of stirrups and creak of saddles came nearer. Now they could see the dim outline of the horsemen, riding four abreast.

"Who goes there?" Kruchkov called.

"And what do you want?" a voice answered in Russian from the leading rank.

"Who goes there? I shall fire!" Kruchkov rattled the bolt of his rifle.

One of the riders reined in his horse and turned it towards the fence.

"We're the frontier guard," he said. "Are you an outpost?"

"Yes."

"From which regiment?"

"The 3rd Cossack. . . ."

"Who are you talking to there, Trishin?" a voice called out of the darkness. The man by the fence replied:

"There's a Cossack outpost stationed here, Your Excellency."

A second horseman rode up to the fence.

"Good luck, Cossacks! Have you been here long?" he asked, striking a match and lighting a cigarette. By the momentary gleam Kruchkov saw an officer of the frontier guard.

"Since yesterday," he replied.

"Our guard is being withdrawn," the officer said. "You must bear well in mind that you are now the farthest outpost. The enemy may advance tomorrow." He turned and gave the order for his men to ride on.

At that moment the wind pitilessly tore the bandage of cloud away from the moon, and over the village, the gardens, the steep roof of the hut, and the detachment of frontier guards riding up the hill fell a flood of deathly yellow light.

Next morning Rvachev rode back to the company with a report. During the night the horses had stood saddled. The Cossacks were alarmed by the thought that they were now left to confront the enemy. They had not experienced the feeling of isolation and loneliness so long as they knew the frontier guard was ahead of them, but the news that the frontier was open had a marked effect upon them.

Mrikhin had a talk with the Polish farmer, and for a small sum the man agreed to let them cut clover for their horses. The Pole's meadow lay not far from the shed. Mrikhin sent Ivankov and Shchegolkov to mow. Shchegolkov mowed while Ivankov raked the dank, heavy grass together and tied it into bundles.

As they were thus occupied, Mrikhin, who was gazing through the binoculars along the road leading to the frontier, noticed a boy running across the fields from the south-west. The lad ran down the hill like a brown hare; when still some distance off, he shouted and waved the long sleeve of his coat. He ran up to Mrikhin, gasping for breath and rolling his eyes, and panted:

"Cossack! Cossack! The Germans! The Germans are coming!"

He pointed with his hand. Holding the binoculars to his eyes, Mrikhin saw a distant group of horsemen. Without removing the binoculars he shouted:

"Kruchkov! Run and call the boys! A German patrol is coming!"

Kruchkov ran to the meadow. Now Mrikhin could clearly see the group of horsemen flowing along beyond the greyish streak of grass-land. He could even distinguish the bay colour of their horses and the dark-blue tint of their uniforms. There were over twenty of them, and they were riding in a compact mass, coming from the south-west, whereas he had been expecting them from the north-west. They crossed the road and went along the ridge above the valley in which the village lay.

Meantime Kruchkov ran across the field to where Ivankov and Shchegolkov were mowing. "Drop it!" he shouted as he came up.

"Now what's the matter?" Shchegolkov asked, thrusting the scythe by the point into the ground.

"The Germans!"

Ivankov threw down the bundle of grass. The Pole, bent almost to the ground, ran off to the hut, followed by the Cossacks. The little party leaped into their saddles and galloped up the rise out of the village. When they reached the crest of the hill, the Germans were already between them and the town of Pelikalia. They were riding at a trot, led by an officer on a dock-tailed roan.

"After them! We'll get them at our second outpost," Mrikhin ordered.

They put their horses into a swift trot. The blue uniforms of the German dragoons were clearly visible. They had caught sight of the

Cossacks following them and were cantering in the direction of the second Russian outpost, which was stationed at a farm some two miles back from the village of Liubov. The distance between the two parties perceptibly diminished.

"We'll fire at them!" Mrikhin shouted, jumping from his saddle. Standing with the reins over their arms, the Cossacks fired. Ivankov's horse reared at the shot and sent him headlong. As he fell he saw one of the Germans first lean to one side, then, throwing out his arms, suddenly tumble from his saddle. The others did not stop or even unsling their carbines from their shoulders, but rode on at a gallop in open formation. Mrikhin was the first to remount his horse. The Cossacks plied their whips. The Germans swung to the left, and the Cossacks, following them, passed close to the fallen dragoon. Beyond stretched an undulating country intersected with shallow ravines. As the Germans rode up the farther side of each ravine, the Cossacks sent shots after them. A little farther on, another German went down.

"Our Cossacks should be coming from that farm in a minute. That's the second outpost," Mrikhin muttered, thrusting a cartridge into the magazine of his rifle with his tobacco-stained finger. As the Cossacks rode past the farm they glanced towards it, but it was deserted. Afterwards they learned that the outpost had withdrawn the previous night, having discovered that the telegraph wires some half a mile away had been cut.

Mrikhin sent another shot after the Germans, firing from the saddle, and one, lagging slightly behind, shook his head and spurred up his horse.

"We'll drive them along to the third outpost," Mrikhin shouted, turning round to the others behind him. Only then did Ivankov notice that Mrikhin's nose was peeling and a piece of skin was hanging from his nostril.

"Why don't they turn and defend themselves?" he asked anxiously, adjusting his rifle on his back.

The Germans dropped into a ravine and disappeared. On the farther side was ploughed land; on this side, scrub and an occasional bush. Mrikhin reined in his horse, removed his cap, and wiped the sweat away with the back of his hand. The Germans did not appear on the other side of the ravine. Mrikhin looked at the others, spat, and said:

"Ivankov, you ride down and see where they've got to."

Ivankov thirstily licked his lips and rode off.

"Oh, for a smoke!" Kruchkov muttered, driving the gadflies off with his whip.

Ivankov rode steadily down into the ravine, rising in his stirrups and gazing across the bottom. Suddenly he saw the glittering points of lances; then the Germans appeared, their horses turned round and galloping back up the slope to the attack. During the moment in which Ivankov was wheeling his horse round, the clean-shaven, moody face of the officer and his statuesque seat in the saddle were impressed on his memory. His back felt the pinching chill of death almost painfully. He silently galloped back towards the others.

Mrikhin did not have time to fold up his tobacco-pouch. Seeing the Germans behind Ivankov, Kruchkov was the first to ride down to meet them. The dragoons on the right flank were sweeping round to cut Ivankov off and were overtaking him with savage swiftness. Ivankov was lashing at his horse, wry shudders passing over his face, and his eyes staring out of his head. Bent to the saddle-bow, Mrikhin took the lead.

Only to get back to his comrades! That one idea possessed Ivankov, and he had no thought of defence. He gathered his great body into a ball, his head touching his horse's mane.

A big, ruddy-faced German overtook him and thrust his lance at his back. The point pierced Ivankov's leather belt and passed sideways for a good inch into his body.

"Brothers, turn back!" he shouted almost deliriously, drawing his sabre. He parried a second thrust aimed at his side, and cut down a German riding at him from the left. But he was surrounded. A German horse struck the side of his own mount, almost knocking it off its feet, and Ivankov saw the terrible face of an enemy at point-blank range.

Mrikhin was the first to reach the group. He was driven off. He swung his sabre and turned like an electric fan in his saddle, his teeth bared, his face changed and deathly. Ivankov was lashed across the neck with the point of a sword. A dragoon towered above him on the left, and the terrifying gleam of steel glittered in his eyes. He countered with his sabre; steel clashed against steel. From behind, a lance caught in his shoulder-strap and thrust insistently, tearing the strap away. Beyond his horse's head appeared the perspiring, fevered face of an elderly German, who tried to reach Ivankov's breast with his sword. But he failed, and, dropping it, he tore his carbine from its saddle-holster, not turning his blinking eyes from Ivankov's face for a moment. He did not succeed in freeing his carbine, for Kruchkov reached at him across his horse with a lance he had torn from the grip of another dragoon. The German, tearing the lance away from his breast, threw himself back, groaning in fear and astonishment:

"*Mein Mutter!*"

Eight dragoons surrounded Kruchkov, trying to capture him alive. But causing his horse to rear, he fought until they had to attempt to strike him down. He wielded his captured lance as though on the parade ground. Beaten back, the Germans now came at him with drawn swords. They bunched together over a small patch of dismal, clayey ploughed land, seething and rocking in the struggle as though shaken by the wind.

Beside themselves with terror, the Cossacks and Germans thrust and cut at whatever came their way: backs, arms, horses, and weapons. The horses jostled and knocked against one another in a frenzy of mortal fear. Regaining some measure of self-command, Ivankov tried several times to strike at the head of a long-faced, flaxen-haired German who had fastened on him, but his sabre fell on the man's helmet and slipped off.

Mrikhin broke through the ring and galloped free, streaming with blood. The German officer chased after him. Tearing his rifle from his shoulder, Mrikhin fired and killed him almost at point-blank range. This proved to be the turning-point in the struggle. Having lost their commander, the Germans, all of them wounded with clumsy blows, dispersed and retreated. The Cossacks did not pursue them. They did not fire after them. They rode straight back to their company at Pelikalia, while the Germans picked up a wounded comrade and fled towards the frontier.

After riding perhaps half a mile, Ivankov swayed in his saddle. "I'm— I shall drop. . . ." He halted his horse. But Mrikhin pulled at his reins, crying:

"Come on!"

Kruchkov wiped the blood from his face and felt his breast.

Crimson spots were showing damply on his shirt. Beyond the farm where the second outpost had been stationed the party disagreed as to the way.

"To the right!" Mrikhin said, pointing towards the green, swampy ground of an alder wood.

"No, to the left!" Kruchkov insisted.

They separated. Mrikhin and Ivankov arrived at the regimental headquarters after Kruchkov and Shchegolkov. They found the Cossacks of their company awaiting them. Ivankov dropped the reins, jumped from the saddle, and swayed and fell. They had difficulty in freeing the sabre-hilt from his stony grasp.

Within an hour almost the entire company rode out to where the German officer lay. The Cossacks removed his boots, clothing, and weapons and crowded around to look at the young, frowning, yellow face of the dead man. One of them managed to capture the officer's watch and sold it on the spot to his troop sergeant. In a pocket-book they found a few coins, a letter, a lock of flaxen hair, and a photograph of a girl with a proud, smiling mouth.

Afterwards this incident was transformed into a heroic exploit. Kruchkov, a favourite of the company commander, told his story and received the Cross of St. George. His comrades remained in shadow. The hero was sent to the divisional staff headquarters, where he lived in clover until the end of the war, receiving three more crosses because influential women and officers came from Petersburg and Moscow to look at him. The ladies "ah'd" and "oh'd," the ladies regaled the Don Cossack with expensive cigarettes and chocolates. At first he cursed them by all the devils, but afterwards, under the benevolent influence of the staff toadies in officers' uniforms, he made a remunerative business of it. He told the story of his "exploit," laying the colours on thick and lying without a twinge of conscience, while the ladies went into raptures and stared admiringly at the pock-marked, brigand face of the Cossack hero.

The Czar visited headquarters, and Kruchkov was taken to be shown to him. The sleepy Emperor looked Kruchkov over as if he were a horse, blinked his heavy eyelids, and slapped the Cossack on the back.

"Good Cossack lad!" he remarked, and turning to his suite, he asked for some Seltzer water.

Kruchkov's shaggy head was continually pictured in the newspapers and journals. There was a Kruchkov brand of cigarettes. The merchants of Nizhnii-Novgorod presented him with a gold-mounted firearm.

And what had really happened? Men had clashed on the field of death and, embraced by mortal terror, had fought, struck, inflicted blind blows on one another, wounded one another's horses; then they had turned and fled, frightened by a shot which had killed one of their number. They had ridden away mortally mutilated.

And it was called a heroic exploit.

Chapter 4

After his first battle Gregor Melekhov was tormented by a dreary inward pain. He grew noticeably thin, lost weight, and frequently, whether attacking or resting, sleeping or waking, he saw the features and form of the Austrian whom he had killed by the railings. In his sleep he lived again and again through that first battle and even felt the shuddering convulsion of his right hand clutching the lance. He would awake and drive the dream off violently, shading his painfully screwed-up eyes with his hand.

The cavalry trampled down the ripened grain and left their hoof-prints on the fields as though hail had rattled over all Galicia. The soldiers' heavy boots tramped the roads, scratched the macadam, churned up the August mud. The gloomy face of the earth was pock-marked with shells; fragments of iron and steel tore into it, yearning for human blood. At night ruddy flickerings lit up the horizon: trees, villages, towns were flaming like summer lightning. In August—when fruits ripen and grain is ready for harvest—the wind-swept sky was unsmilingly grey, the rare fine days were oppressive and sultrily steaming.

August declined to its close. The leaves turned an oily yellow in the orchards, and a mournful purple flooded the stalks. From a distance it seemed as though the trees were rent with wounds and streaming with blood.

Gregor studied with interest the changes that occurred in his comrades. Prokhor Zykov returned from hospital with the marks of a horseshoe on his cheek, and pain and bewilderment lurking in the corners of his lips. His calfish eyes blinked more than ever. Yegor Zharkov lost no opportunity of cursing and swearing, was more bawdy than ever, and imprecated everything under the sun. Yemelian Groshev, a serious and efficient Cossack from Gregor's own village, seemed to char; his face turned dark, and he laughed awkwardly and morosely. Changes were to be observed in every face; each was inwardly nursing and rearing the iron seeds implanted by the war, and the young Cossacks were wilting and drooping like the stalks of mown grass.

The regiment was withdrawn from the line for a three-day rest, and its complement was made up by reinforcements from the Don. The Cossacks of Gregor's company were about to go for a bathe in a neighbouring lake when a considerable force of cavalry rode into the village from the station some two miles away. By the time the men had reached the dam of the lake, the force was riding down the hill. Prokhor Zykov was pulling off his shirt when, looking up, he stared and exclaimed:

"They're Cossacks, Don Cossacks!"

Gregor gazed after the column crawling like a snake into the road leading to the estate where the fourth company was quartered.

"Reinforcements, I expect," he remarked.

"Look, boys; surely that's Stepan Astakhov. There in the third rank from the front," Groshev exclaimed, laughing gratingly.

"And there's Anikushka."

"Gregor! There's your brother. Do you see him?"

Narrowing his eyes, Gregor stared, trying to recognize the horse Piotra was riding. "Must have bought a new one!" he thought, turning his gaze to his brother's face. It was strangely changed since their last meeting.

Gregor went to meet him, taking off his cap and waving mechantally. After him poured the half-undressed Cossacks, avoiding the broken undergrowth of angelica and burdock.

Led by an elderly, corpulent captain with a wooden, fixed expression on his authoritative lips, the detachment swung round the orchard into the estate. "A stickler!" Gregor thought as he smiled with joyous agitation at his brother.

"Hello, Piotra!" he shouted.

"Glory be! We're going to be together. How are you, Gregor?"

"Oh, all right."

"So you're still alive?"

"After a fashion."

"Greetings from the family."

"How are they all?"

"Very well."

Piotra rested his palm on the croup of his horse and turned his entire body round in the saddle, smilingly running his eyes over Gregor's form. Then he rode on and was hidden by the oncoming ranks of other Cossacks, known and unknown.

Yegor Zharkov came from the lake dressed only in his shirt and hopping on one leg, trying to thrust the other into his trousers as he ran.

"Why, here's Zharkov!" rose a shout from the ranks.

"Hello, stallion! Have they had to hobble you, then?"

"How's my mother?" Zharkov asked.

"She's all right. She sent her love, but no presents. Things are difficult enough as it is."

Yegor listened with an unusually serious expression to the reply and then sat down on his bare bottom in the grass, hiding his anxious face and struggling ineffectually to get his trembling leg into his trousers.

The detachment was drawn up in the yard. The other Cossacks returned to their bathe, being joined soon after by the new arrivals. Gregor dropped down at his brother's side. The damp, crumbling clay of the dam smelt raw and deathly. He sat killing the bloodless, flaccid lice in the folds and hems of his shirt and told his brother:

"Piotra, I'm dead in spirit. I'm like a man all but killed. As though

I'd been between millstones; they've crushed me and spat me out."
His voice was complainingly high-pitched, and the furrows (only
now, with a feeling of anxiety, did Piotra notice them) darkened
and streamed across his forehead.

"Why, what's the matter?" Piotra asked as he pulled off his shirt,
revealing his bare white body with the clean-cut line of sunburn
around the neck.

"It's like this," Gregor said hurriedly, and his voice grew strong
in its bitterness. "They've set us fighting one another, but they
don't come themselves. The people have become worse than wolves.
Evil all around you. I think to myself that if I was to bite a man
he'd go mad."

"Have you had to—kill anyone?"

"Yes," Gregor almost shouted, screwing up his shirt and throwing
it underfoot. Then he sat clutching with his fingers at his throat
as though choking with a stranded word and gazed aside.

"Tell me!" Piotra ordered, avoiding his brother's eyes.

"My conscience is killing me. I sent my lance through one man—
in hot blood—I couldn't have done it otherwise. . . . But why did
I cut down the other?"

"Well?"

"It isn't 'well'! I cut down a man, and I'm sick at heart because
of him, the reptile! He comes to me in my dreams, the swine. Was
I to blame?"

"You're not used to it yet; that's what's wrong."

"Are you staying with our company?" Gregor asked abruptly.

"No, we're drafted to the 27th Regiment."

"Well, let's have a bath."

Gregor hastily pulled off his trousers and went to the edge of the
dam. He was clearly older than when they last saw each other,
Piotra thought. Raising his hands, he dived into the water; a heavy
green wave closed over him and billowed away. Gracefully cleaving
the water, lazily moving his shoulders, he swam towards the group
of Cossacks larking about in the middle.

Piotra was slow in removing the cross with the prayer sewn to
it slung round his neck. He thrust the string under his pile of
clothes, entered the water with timorous caution, wet his breast
and shoulders, then pressed forward with a groan and swam to
overtake Gregor. They made for the opposite bank. The movement

through the water cooled and soothed, and Gregor flung himself down on the bank and spoke restrainedly and without his previous passion.

"The lice have eaten me up!" he remarked. "If I was at home now, I'd fly as if I had wings. Only to take one little peep! How are they all?"

"Natalia is living with us."

"How are Father and Mother?"

"All right. But Natalia still waits for you. She still believes you will go back to her."

Gregor snorted and silently spat out water. Piotra turned his head and tried to look into his brother's eyes.

"You might send her a word in your letters. The woman lives only for you."

"What, does she still want to tie up the broken ends?"

"Well, 'hope springs eternal.' . . . She's a fine little woman. Strict too. She won't let anybody play about with her!"

"She ought to get a husband."

"Strange words from you!"

"Nothing strange about them. That's how it ought to be."

"Well, it's your business. I shan't interfere."

"And how's Dunia?"

"She's a woman, brother! She's grown so much this year that you wouldn't know her."

"No!" Gregor said in astonishment.

"God's truth! She'll be getting married next, and we shan't even get our whiskers into the vodka. We'll be killed off, damn them!"

They lay side by side on the sand, bathing in the warm sun. Burying a beetle in the sand, Gregor asked:

"Heard anything of Aksinia?"

"I saw her in the village just before war was declared."

"What was she doing there?"

"She'd come to get some things of hers from her husband."

"Did you speak to her?"

"Only passed the time of day. She was looking well, and cheerful. She seems to have an easy time at the estate."

"And what about Stepan?"

"He gave her her odds and ends all right. Behaved decently enough. But you keep your eyes open! I've been told that when he was drunk he swore to put a bullet through you in the first battle. He can't forgive you."

"I know."

"I got myself a new horse," Piotra changed the conversation.

"Sold the bullocks?"

"For a hundred and eighty. And the horse cost a hundred and fifty. Not a bad one, either."

"What's the grain like?"

"Good. They took us off before we could get it in."

The talk turned to domestic matters, and the intensity of feeling passed. Gregor thirstily drank in Piotra's news of home. For a brief while he was living there again, a simple, restive lad.

They returned with a crowd of Cossacks to the yard. At the fence of the orchard Stepan Astakhov overtook them. As he walked he was combing his hair and adjusting it under the visor of his cap. Drawing level with Gregor, he said:

"Hello, friend!"

"Hello!" Gregor halted and turned to him with a slightly embarrassed, guilty expression on his face.

"You haven't forgotten me, have you?"

"Almost."

"But I remember you!" Stepan smiled and passed by without stopping.

After sundown a telephone message came from the divisional staff for Gregor's regiment to return to the front. The companies were assembled within fifteen minutes and rode off singing to close a breach made in the line by the enemy cavalry.

As they said good-bye to each other, Piotra thrust a folded paper into his brother's hand.

"What's this?" Gregor asked.

"I've written down a prayer for you. Take it. . . ."

"Is it any good?"

"Don't laugh, Gregor!"

"I'm not laughing."

"Well, good-bye, brother. Don't dash away in front of the rest. Death has a fancy for the hot-blooded ones. Look after yourself," Piotra shouted.

"And what about the prayer?"

Piotra waved his hand.

For some time the companies rode without observing any precautions. Then the sergeants gave orders for the utmost possible quiet and for all cigarettes to be put out. Over a distant wood flew rockets adorned with tails of lilac smoke.

During August the Twelfth Cavalry Division took town after town by storm, and by the end of the month they were deployed around the town of Kamenka-Strumilovo. The reconnaissance patrols reported that considerable forces of enemy cavalry were approaching the town. In the woods along the roads little battles broke out where the Cossack outposts came into collision with the enemy advance guards.

During all the days since he saw his brother, Gregor Melekhov had sought to put an end to his painful thoughts and to recover his former tranquillity of spirit. But he was unable. Among the last reinforcements from the second line of reservists a Cossack from the Kazan district, Alexei Uriupin, had been drafted into Gregor's troop. Uriupin was tall, round-shouldered, with an aggressive lower jaw and drooping Kalmyk whiskers. His merry, fearless eyes were always smiling, and he was bald, with only scanty ruddy hair around the edges of his angular cranium. On the very first day of his arrival he was nicknamed "Tufty."

After fighting around Broda the regiment had a few days' respite. Gregor and Uriupin were quartered in the same hut. One evening after feeding their horses they were smoking, their backs against a moss-grown, decrepit fence. Hussars were riding four abreast along the street; dead bodies were littered in the yards, for fighting had occurred in the suburbs. The town was one immense destruction and loathsome emptiness in the colourful early evening hour.

Suddenly Uriupin remarked:

"You know, Melekhov, you're moulting or something."

"What do you mean by 'moulting'?" Gregor asked, his face clouding.

"You're all limp, as though you're ill," Uriupin explained.

"I'm all right," Gregor spat out, not looking at the other.

"You're lying! I've got eyes to see!"

"Well, and what can you see?"

"You're afraid! Is it death you fear?"

"You're a fool!" Gregor said contemptuously, staring at his finger-nails.

"Tell me, have you killed anyone?"

"Yes. What of it?"

"Does it weigh on your mind?"

"Weigh on my mind?" Gregor laughed.

Uriupin drew his sabre from its sheath. "Would you like me to chop your head off?" he asked.

"What for?"

"I can kill a man without sighing over it. I have no pity." Uriupin's eyes were smiling, but by his voice and the rapacious quiver of his mouth Gregor realized that he meant what he said.

"You've got a soft heart," Uriupin added. "Do you know this stroke? Watch!" He selected an old birch tree in the hedge and went straight towards it, measuring the distance with his eyes. His long, venous arms with their unusually broad wrists hung motion-less. "Watch!"

He slowly raised his sabre and suddenly swung it slantwise with terrible force. Completely severed four feet from the ground, the birch toppled over, its branches scraping at the window and claw-ing the walls of the hut.

"Did you see that? I'll teach you the stroke. You could cut a horse in two like that."

It took Gregor a long time to master the technique of the new stroke. "You're strong, but you're a fool with your sabre. This is the way!" Uriupin instructed him. "Cut a man down boldly! Man is as soft as butter! Don't think about the why and the wherefore. You're a Cossack, and it's your business to cut down without asking questions. To kill your enemy in battle is a holy work. For every man you kill, God will wipe out one of your sins, just as He does for killing a serpent. You mustn't kill an animal unless it's necessary, but destroy man! He's a heathen, unclean; he poisons the earth; his life is like a toadstool!"

When Gregor raised objections he only frowned and lapsed into an obstinate silence.

Gregor noticed with astonishment that all horses were afraid of Uriupin. When he went near them, they would prick up their ears and bunch together as though an animal were approaching, and not a man. On one occasion the company had to attack over a wooded and swampy district and took to their feet, the horses being led aside into a dell. Uriupin was among those assigned to take charge of the horses, but he flatly refused.

"Uriupin, why the devil don't you lead away your horses?" The troop sergeant flew at him.

"They're afraid of me. God's truth, they are!" he replied.

He never took his turn at minding the horses. He was kind enough to his own mount, but Gregor observed that whenever he went up to it a shiver ran down the animal's back, and it fidgeted uneasily.

"Tell me, why are the horses afraid of you?" Gregor once asked him.

"I don't know," he replied with a shrug of his shoulders. "I'm kind enough to them."

"They know a drunken man and are afraid of him; but you're always sober."

"I have a hard heart, and they seem to feel it."

"You have a wolf's heart. Or maybe it's a stone you've got and not a heart at all."

"Maybe," Uriupin willingly agreed.

The troop was dispatched on reconnaissance work. The previous evening a Czech deserter from the Austrian Army had informed the Russian command of a change in the disposition of the enemy forces and a proposed counter-attack, and there was need for continual observation over the road along which the hostile regiments must pass.

The troop officer left four Cossacks with the sergeant at the edge of a wood and rode with the others towards a town lying beyond the next rise. Gregor, Uriupin, Misha Koshevoi, and another Cossack were left with the sergeant. They lay smoking by a fallen pine, while the sergeant watched the country through his binoculars. Half an hour they lay there, exchanging lazy remarks. From somewhere to the right came the incessant roar of gunfire. A few paces away a field of ungathered rye, its ears emptied of grain, was waving in the wind. Gregor crawled into the rye and selected some still full ears, husked them, and chewed the grain.

A group of horsemen rode out of a distant plantation and halted, surveying the open country, then set off again in the direction of the Cossacks.

"Austrians, surely!" the sergeant exclaimed under his breath. "We'll let them get closer and then send them a greeting. Have your rifles ready, boys," he added feverishly.

The riders steadily drew closer. They were six Hungarian hussars, in handsome tunics ornamented with white braid and piping. The leader, on a big black horse, held his carbine in his hands and was quietly laughing.

"Fire!" the sergeant ordered. The volley went echoing through the trees. The hussars galloped in single file into the grain. One of them fired into the air. Uriupin was the first to leap to his feet. He sped off, stumbling through the rye, holding his rifle across his chest. Some hundred yards away he found a fallen horse kicking and struggling, and a Hungarian hussar standing close by, rubbing his knee, hurt in the fall. He shouted something to Uriupin and raised his hands in token of surrender, staring after his retreating comrades.

All this had happened so quickly that Gregor hardly had time to take in what was occurring before Uriupin had brought back his prisoner.

"Off with it!" Uriupin shouted at the Hungarian, roughly tearing at the hussar's sword.

The prisoner smiled apprehensively and fumbled with his belt, only too willing to hand over his sword. But his hands trembled, and he could not manage to unfasten the clasp. Gregor cautiously assisted him, and the hussar, a young, fat-cheeked boy with a downy moustache just showing on the upper lip, thanked him with a smile and a nod of the head. He seemed glad to be deprived of the weapon and fumbled in his pocket, pulled out a leather pouch, and muttered something, offering the Cossacks tobacco.

"He's treating us!" the sergeant smiled, and felt for his cigarette papers. The Cossacks rolled cigarettes from the hussar's tobacco and smoked. The strong black tobacco quickly went to their heads.

"He must be escorted to the company. Who'll take him, boys?" the sergeant asked, passing his eyes over his men.

"I will," Uriupin replied quickly.

"All right, off with you!"

The prisoner evidently realized what was to happen to him, for he smiled wrily, turned out his pockets, and offered the Cossacks some broken chocolate.

"*Rusin ich—Rusin—nein Austrische . . .*" he stammered, gesticulating absurdly and holding out the chocolate.

"Any weapons?" the sergeant asked. "Don't rattle away like that, we can't understand you. Got a revolver? A bang-bang?" The sergeant pulled an imaginary trigger. The prisoner furiously shook his head.

He willingly allowed himself to be searched, his fat cheeks quivering. Blood was streaming from his torn knee. Talking incessantly, he tied his handkerchief around it. He had left his cap by his horse, and he asked permission to go and fetch it and his blanket and notebook, in which were photographs of his family. The sergeant tried hard to understand what he wanted, but at last waved his hand in despair:

"Off with him!"

Uriupin took his horse and mounted it. Adjusting his rifle across his back, he pointed to the prisoner. Encouraged by his smile, the Hungarian also smiled and set off at the horse's side. With an attempt at familiarity he patted Uriupin's knee, but the Cossack harshly flung off his hand and pulled on the reins.

The prisoner guiltily drew away from the horse and strode along with a serious face, frequently looking back at the other Cossacks. His lint-white hair stuck up vividly on the crown of his head. So he remained in Gregor's memory: his tunic flung open, his flaxen tuft of hair, and his confident, brave mien.

"Melekhov, go and unsaddle his horse!" the sergeant ordered, regretfully spitting out the end of his cigarette. Gregor went to the fallen animal, removed the saddle, and then for some undefined reason picked up the cap lying close by. He smelled at the lining and caught the scent of cheap soap and sweat. He carried the horse's equipment back to the trees. Squatting on their haunches, the Cossacks rummaged in the saddlebags and stared at the unfamiliar design of the saddle.

"That tobacco he had was good; we should have asked him for some more." The sergeant sighed at the memory and swallowed down his spittle.

Not many minutes had passed when a horse's head appeared

through the pines, and Uriupin rode up.

"Why, where's the Austrian? You haven't let him go?" the sergeant questioned him.

"He tried to run away," Uriupin snarled.

"And so you let him?"

"We reached an open glade, and he—so I cut him down."

"You're a liar!" Gregor shouted. "You killed him for nothing."

"What are you shouting about? What's it to do with you?" Uriupin fixed icy eyes on Gregor's face.

"What?" Gregor's voice slowly rose, and he swung his arms round in readiness to grapple with Uriupin.

"Don't poke your nose in where it isn't wanted! Understand?" the other replied sternly. Gregor snatched up his rifle and threw it to his shoulder. His finger quivered as it felt for the trigger, and his face worked angrily.

"Now then!" the sergeant exclaimed threateningly, running to him. His jostle preceded the shot, and the bullet cut a branch from a tree and went whistling into space. He tore the rifle out of Gregor's hands. Uriupin stood without changing his position, his feet planted apart, his left hand on his belt.

"Fire again!" he remarked.

"I'll kill you!" Gregor rushed towards him.

"Here, what's all this about? Do you want to be court-martialled and shot? Put your arms down!" the sergeant commanded. Thrusting Gregor back, he placed himself with arms outstretched between the two men.

"You lie; you won't kill me!" Uriupin smiled.

As they were riding back in the dusk, Gregor was the first to notice the body of the hussar lying in the path. He rode up in front of the others and, reining in his horse, stared down. The man lay with arms flung out over the velvety moss, his face downward, his palms, yellow like autumn leaves, turned upward and open. A terrible blow from behind had cloven him in two from the shoulder to the belt.

The Cossacks rode past the body and on to the company headquarters in silence. The evening shadows deepened. A breeze was driving up a black, feathery cloud from the east. From a swamp near by came the stagnant scent of marsh grass, of rusty dampness and rot. A bittern boomed. The drowsy silence was broken by the jingle of the horses' equipment and the occasional knock of sabre on stirrup, or the scrunch of pine cones under the horses' hoofs. Through the glade the dark ruddy gleam of the departed sun streamed over the pine trunks. Uriupin smoked incessantly, and the fleeting spark of his cigarette lit up his thick fingers with their blackened nails firmly gripping the cigarette.

The cloud floated over the forest, emphasizing and deepening the fading, inexpressibly mournful hues of the evening shadows on the ground.

The following morning an assault was begun on the next town. Flanked by cavalry, the infantry was to have advanced from the forest at dawn. Somewhere someone blundered; the infantry regiments did not arrive in time; the 211th Sharpshooter Regiment was ordered to cross over to the left flank, and during the offensive movement initiated by another regiment it was raked with fire from its own batteries. The hopeless confusion upset the plans, and the attack threatened to end in failure, if not in disaster. While the infantry was thus being shuffled about, the order came for the Eleventh Cavalry Division to advance. The wooded and marshy land in which they had been held in readiness did not permit of an extended frontal movement, and in some cases the Cossacks had to advance in troops. The fourth and fifth companies of the 12th Regiment were held in reserve in the forest, and within a few minutes of the general advance the roaring, rending sound of the battle began to reach their ears.

The two companies were drawn up in a glade. The stout pine trunks hemmed them in and prevented their following the course of the battle. After the first few moments of shouting a deep silence fell. All strained their ears. From time to time they caught an outburst of cheering; on the right flank the Austrian artillery thundered away at the attacking forces; the roar was interspersed with the rattle of machine-guns.

Gregor glanced around his troop. The Cossacks were fidgeting nervously, and the horses were restive as though troubled by gnats. Uriupin had hung his cap on the saddle-bow and was wiping his bald head; at Gregor's side Misha Koshevoi puffed fiercely at his home-grown tobacco. All the objects around were distinct and exaggeratedly real, as they appear after a night's unbroken watching.

The companies were held in reserve for three hours. All the stocks of tobacco were exhausted and the men were pining in expectation when just before noon an orderly officer galloped up with instructions. The commander of the fourth company led his men off to one side. To Gregor it seemed that they were retreating rather than advancing. His own company was marched off and rode for some twenty minutes through the forest, the sound of the battle drawing nearer and nearer. Not far behind them a battery was firing; the shells flew overhead with a roar. The narrow forest paths broke up the company's formation, and they emerged into the open in disorder. About half a mile away Hungarian hussars were sabring the team of a Russian battery.

"Company, form!" the commander shouted.

The Cossacks had not completely carried out the order when the further command came:

"Company, draw sabres; into the attack, forward!"

A blue shower of blades. From a swift trot the Cossacks broke into a gallop.

Six Hungarian hussars were busily occupied with the horses of the field-gun on the extreme right of the battery. One was dragging at the bits of the excited artillery horses, another was beating them with the flat of his sword, while the others were tugging and pulling at the spokes of the carriage-wheels. An officer on a dock-tailed chocolate mare was superintending the operations. At the sight of the Cossacks he gave an order, and the hussars leaped to their horses.

As Gregor galloped towards them one foot momentarily lost its stirrup, and feeling himself insecure in his saddle, with inward alarm he bent over and fished with his toe for the dangling iron. When he had recovered his foot-hold he looked up and saw the six horses of the field-gun in front of him. The outrider on the foremost, in a blood- and brain-spattered shirt, was lying over the animal's neck, embracing it. Gregor's horse brought its hoof down with a sickening scrunch on the body of a dead gunner. Two more were lying by an overturned case of shells. A fourth was stretched face-downward over the gun-carriage. A Cossack of Gregor's troop was just in front of him. The Hungarian officer fired at almost point-blank range and the Cossack fell, his hands clutching and embracing the air. Gregor pulled on his reins and tried to approach the officer from the right, the better to use his sabre; but the officer saw through his manœuvre and fired under his arm at him. He discharged the contents of his revolver and then drew his sword. Three smashing blows he parried dextrously. Gregor reached at him yet a fourth time, standing in his stirrups. Their horses were now galloping almost side by side, and he noticed the ashen-grey, clean-shaven cheek of the Hungarian and the regimental number sewn on his collar. With a feint he drew off the officer's attention and, changing the direction of his stroke, thrust the point of his sabre between the Hungarian's shoulder-blades. He aimed a second blow at the neck, just at the top of the spine. The officer dropped his sword and reins from his hands and straightened up, then toppled over his saddle-bow. Feeling a terrible relief, Gregor lashed at his head and saw the sabre smash into the bone above the ear.

A fearful blow at his head from behind tore consciousness away from Gregor. He felt a burning, salty taste of blood in his mouth and realized that he was falling; from one side the stubbled earth came whirling and flying up at him. The heavy crash of his body against the ground brought him momentarily back to reality. He opened his eyes; blood poured into them. A trample past his ears, and the heavy breathing of horses. For the last time he opened his eyes and saw the dilated nostrils of horses, and someone's foot in a stirrup. "Finished!" the comforting thought crawled through his mind like a snake. A roar, and then a black emptiness.

Chapter 5

In the middle of August, Eugene Listnitsky decided to apply for a transfer from the ataman's Life Guard regiment to one of the Cossack regular army regiments. He made his formal application and within three weeks received an appointment as he desired. Before leaving Petersburg he wrote to his father informing him of the step he had taken and asking his blessing.

The train for Warsaw left Petersburg at eight p.m. Listnitsky took a droshky and drove to the station. Behind him Petersburg lay in a dove-blue twinkle of lights. The station was clamorous with soldiers. He settled down into his compartment, removed his sword-belt and coat, and spread his Cossack blanket over the seat. By the window sat a priest with the lean face of an ascetic. Brushing the crumbs from his hempen beard, he offered some curd-cake to a swarthy girl sitting in the seat opposite him. As Eugene dozed off he heard the priest's voice, as though coming from a distance:

"It's a miserable income my family gets, you know. So I'm off as a chaplain to the forces. The Russian people cannot fight without faith. And, you know, from year to year the faith increases. Of course there are some who fall away, but they are among the intelligentsia; the peasant holds fast to God."

The priest's bass voice failed to penetrate further into Eugene's consciousness. After two sleepless nights a refreshing sleep came to him. He awoke when the train was a good twenty-five miles outside Petersburg. The wheels clattered rhythmically, the car swayed and rocked, in a neighbouring compartment someone was singing. The lamp cast slanting lilac shadows.

The regiment to which Listnitsky was assigned had suffered considerable losses and had been withdrawn from the front to be remounted and have its complement made up. The regimental staff headquarters were at a large village called Berezniagi. Eugene left the train at some nameless halt. At the same station a field hospital was detrained. Eugene inquired the destination of the hospital from the doctor in charge and learned that it had been transferred from the south-western front to the sector in which his own regiment was engaged. The doctor spoke very unfavourably of his immediate superiors, cursed the divisional staff officers up hill and down dale, and tearing his beard, his eyes glowing behind his pince-nez, poured his jaundiced anger into the ears of his fortuitous acquaintance.

"Can you take me to Berezniagi?" Eugene interrupted him.

"Yes, get into the trap, subaltern," he agreed, and familiarly twisting the button on Eugene's coat, went on with his complaints

Dusk was falling as the field hospital approached Berezniagi. The wind ruffled the yellow stubble. Clouds were massing in the west. At their height they were a deep violet black, but below they shaded into a tender, smoky lilac. In the middle the formless mass, piled like floes against a river dam, was drawn aside. Through the breach the flood of sunset rays poured in a strong orange, spreading in a spirting fan of light and weaving a bacchanalian spectrum of colours below the gap.

A dead horse lay by the roadside ditch. On one of its hoofs, flung weirdly upward, the horseshoe gleamed. Jumping down from the trap, Listnitsky stared at the carcass. The orderly with whom he was riding explained:

"It's overeaten itself. . . . Got among the grain. . . . There it lies, and no one troubles to bury it. That's just like the Russians. The Germans are different."

"And how do you know?" Eugene asked with unreasoning anger. At that moment he was filled with hatred for the orderly's phlegmatic face with its suggestion of superiority and contempt. The man was grey and dreary like a stubble field in September; he was in no way different from the thousands of peasant soldiers whom Eugene had seen on his way to the front. They all seemed faded and drooping, dullness stared in their grey eyes, and they strongly reminded him of well-worn, long-minted copper coins.

"I lived in Germany for three years before the war," the orderly replied unhurryingly. In his voice was the same nuance of superiority and contempt that showed in his face.

"Hold your tongue!" Listnitsky commanded sternly, and turned away.

They drove on. The colours faded in the west, sucked into the clouds. Behind them the leg of the dead horse stuck up like a wayside cross bereft of its arm. As Eugene was staring back at it, suddenly a stream of rays fell on the horse, and, lit up with an orange gleam, the leg with its sorrel hair unexpectedly blossomed like a marvellous leafless branch.

As the field hospital drove into Berezniagi it passed a transport of wounded soldiers. An elderly White Russian, the owner of the first wagon, strode along at his horse's head, the hempen reins gathered in his hands. On the wagon lay a Cossack with bandaged head. He was resting on his elbow, but his eyes were closed wearily as he chewed grain and spat out the black husks. At his side a soldier was stretched out; over his buttocks his torn trousers were horribly shrivelled and taut with congealed blood. He was cursing savagely, without lifting his head. Listnitsky was horrified as he listened to the intonation of the man's voice, for it sounded exactly like a believer fervently muttering prayers.

On the fifth wagon three Cossacks were comfortably seated. As Listnitsky passed they stared silently at him, their harsh faces showing no sign of respect for an officer.

The commander of Listnitsky's new regiment had his headquarters in the house of a priest. The place was very quiet and slack, like all staff headquarters situated away from the front line. Clerks were bent over a table; an elderly captain was laughing down the mouthpiece of a field-telephone. The flies droned around the windows, and distant telephone bells buzzed like mosquitoes. An orderly conducted Eugene to the regimental commander's private room. They were met on the threshold by a tall colonel, who greeted him coldly, and with a gesture invited him into the room. As he closed the door the colonel passed his hand over his hair with a gesture of ineffable weariness and said in a soft, monotonous voice:

"The brigade staff informed me yesterday that you were on your way. Sit down."

He questioned Eugene about his previous service, asked for the latest news from the capital, inquired about his journey, and not once during all their brief conversation did he raise his eyes to Listnitsky's face.

"He must have had a hard time at the front; he looks mortally tired," Eugene thought sympathetically. As though deliberately to disillusion him, the colonel remarked:

"Well, lieutenant, you must make the acquaintance of your brother officers. You must excuse me, I haven't been to bed for three nights running. In this dead hole there's nothing to do except play cards and get drunk."

Listnitsky saluted and turned to the door, hiding his contempt behind a smile. He went out thinking unfavourably over this first meeting with his commanding officer and ironically jesting at the respect which the colonel's tired appearance had instilled in him.

Eugene's division was allotted the task of forcing the river Styr and taking the enemy in the rear. The operations to force the river were carried through brilliantly. The division shattered a considerable concentration of enemy forces on their left flank and reached their rear. The Austrians attempted to initiate a counter-offensive with the aid of cavalry, but the Cossack batteries swept them away with shrapnel, and the Magyar squadrons retreated in disorder, annihilated by flanking machine-gun fire and pursued by the Cossack cavalry.

Listnitsky advanced with his regiment to the counter-attack. The troop he commanded lost one Cossack killed and four wounded. One of them, a young, hook-nosed Cossack, was crushed under his dead horse. He lay quietly groaning and beseeching the Cossacks riding past:

"Brothers, don't leave me. Get me free of the horse, brothers. . . ."

His low, tortured voice sounded faintly, but there was not a sign of pity in the hearts of the other Cossacks, or if there was, a higher will drove them on relentlessly, forbidding them to dismount. The troop rode on at a trot, letting the horses recover their wind. Half a mile away the scattered Magyar squadrons were in full retreat; here and there among them appeared the grey-blue uniforms of the enemy infantry. An Austrian transport crawled along the crest of a hill, and the milky smoke of shrapnel hovered valedictorily above them. From the left a battery was bombarding the transport, and its dull thunder rolled over the fields and echoed through the forest.

The regiment halted for the night in a little village. The twelve officers were all crowded into one hut. Broken with fatigue, they lay down hungry to sleep. The field kitchen arrived only about midnight. Cornet Chubov brought in a pot of soup, and within a few minutes the officers were eating greedily, without exchanging a word, making up for the two days lost in battle. After the late meal their previous sleepiness passed, and they lay on their cloaks talking and smoking.

First Lieutenant Kalmikov, a tubby little officer whose face as well as his name bore the traces of his Mongolian origin, gesticulated fiercely as he declared:

"This war is not for me. I've been born four centuries late. You know, I shan't live to see the end of the war."

"Oh, drop your fortune-telling!"

"It's not fortune-telling. It's my predestined end. I'm atavistic, and I'm superfluous here. When we were under fire today, I trembled with frenzy; I can't stand not seeing the enemy. The horrible feeling I get is equivalent to fear. They fire at you from several miles away, and you ride like a bustard hunted over the steppe. I envy those who fought in the old-time, primitive fashion," he continued, turning to Listnitsky. "To thrust at your opponent in honourable battle and to split him in two with your sword— that's the sort of warfare I understand. But this is the devil knows what."

"In future wars there will be no part left for the cavalry to play. It will be abolished," another officer observed.

"But you can't replace men by a machine. You're going too far."

"I'm not referring to men, but to horses. Motorcycles or motor vehicles will take their place."

"I can just imagine a motor squadron!"

"That's all nonsense!" Kalmikov interposed excitedly. "An absurd fantasy! We don't know what war will be like in two or three centuries' time, but today cavalry are . . ."

"What will you do with the cavalry when there are trenches all along the front? Tell me that!"

"They'll break through the trenches, ride across them, and make sorties far to the rear of the enemy; that will be the cavalry's task."

"Nonsense!"

"Oh, shut up and let us get some sleep," someone demanded.

The argument tailed away, and snores took its place. Listnitsky lay on his back, breathing the pungent scent of the musty straw on which he had spread his cloak. Kalmikov lay down at his side.

"You should have a talk with the volunteer Bunchuk," he whispered to Eugene. "He's in your troop. A very interesting fellow!"

"How?" Eugene asked, as he turned his back to Kalmikov.

"He's a Russianized Cossack. He's lived in Moscow as an ordinary worker, but he's interested in the question of machinery. He's a first-rate machine-gunner, too."

"Let's get to sleep," Listnitsky replied.

Eugene completely forgot Kalmikov's reference to Bunchuk, but
the very next day chance brought him into contact with the volunteer. The regimental commander ordered him to ride at dawn on
reconnaissance work and if possible to establish contact with the
infantry regiment which was continuing the advance on the left
flank. Stumbling about the yard in the half-light and falling over
the bodies of the sleeping Cossacks, Eugene found the troop sergeant and roused him:

"I want five men to go on a reconnaissance with me. Have my
horse got ready. Quickly!"

While he was waiting for the men to assemble, a stocky Cossack
came to the door of the hut.

"Your Excellency," the man said, "the sergeant will not let me
go with you because it isn't my turn. Will you give me permission
to go?"

"Are you out for promotion or what have you done?" Eugene
asked, trying to recognize the man's face in the darkness.

"I haven't done anything."

"All right, you can come," Eugene decided. As the Cossack turned
to go, he shouted after him:

"Hey! Tell the sergeant . . ."

"Bunchuk is my name," the Cossack interrupted.

"A volunteer?"

"Yes."

Recovering from his confusion, Listnitsky corrected his style of
address: "Well, Bunchuk, please tell the sergeant to— Oh, all right,
I'll tell him myself."

Listnitsky led his men out of the village. When they had ridden
some distance, he called:

"Volunteer Bunchuk!"

"Sir!"

"Please bring your horse alongside me."

Bunchuk brought his commonplace mount alongside Eugene's
thoroughbred.

"What district are you from?" Listnitsky asked him, studying the
man's profile.

"Novocherkassk."

"May I be informed of the reason that compelled you to enlist as
a volunteer?"

"Certainly," Bunchuk replied with the slightest trace of a smile. The unwinking gaze of his greenish eyes was harsh and fixed. "I'm interested in the art of war. I want to master it."

"There are military schools established for that purpose."

"I want to study it in practice first. I can get the theory after."

"What were you before the war broke out?"

"A worker."

"Where were you working?"

"In Petersburg, Rostov, and the armament works at Tula. I'm thinking of applying to be transferred to a machine-gun section."

"Do you know anything about machine-guns?"

"I can handle the Bertier, Madsen, Maxim, Hotchkiss, Vickers, Lewis, and several other makes."

"Oho! I'll have a word with the regimental commander about it."

"If you will."

Listnitsky glanced again at Bunchuk's sturdy, stocky figure. It reminded him of the Donside cork-elm. There was nothing remarkable about the man, not one line indicating distinction; all was ordinary, grey, commonplace. Only the firmly pressed jaws and the eyes meeting his distinguished him from the mass of other rank-and-file Cossacks around him. He smiled but rarely, his lips twisting into a bow; but his eyes grew no softer, and they retained their uncertain gleam. Coldly restrained, he was exactly like the cork-elm, the tree of a stern iron hardness that grows on the grey, loose soil of the inhospitable Don earth.

They rode in silence for a while. Bunchuk rested his broad palms on his iron-shod saddle-bow. Listnitsky selected a cigarette, and as he lit it from Bunchuk's match he smelled the pungent scent of horse's sweat on the man's hand. The back of his hand was thickly covered like a horse's skin with brown hair, and Eugene felt an involuntary desire to stroke it.

At a turn of the road into the forest stood a clump of friendly birches. Beyond them the eye was wearied with the joyless yellow of stunted pines, the straggling forest undergrowth and bushes crushed by Austrian transports. On the right the artillery were thundering in the distance, but by the birches it was inexpressibly quiet. The earth was drinking in a rich dew; the grasses were turning rosy, flooded with autumnal colours that cried of the speedy death of colour. Listnitsky halted by the birches and, taking out his binoculars, studied the rise beyond the forest. A bee settled on the honey-coloured hilt of his sabre.

"Stupid!" Bunchuk remarked quietly and compassionately.

"What is?" Eugene turned to him.

With his eyes Bunchuk indicated the bee, and Listnitsky smiled.

"Its honey will be bitter, don't you think?" he observed.

It was not Bunchuk that answered him. From a distant clump of pines a piercing magpie stutter shattered the silence, and a spirt of bullets sped through the birches, sending a branch crashing on the neck of Listnitsky's horse.

They turned and galloped back towards the village, urging on their horses with shout and whip. The Austrian machine-gun rattled without intermission through its belt of bullets.

After this first encounter Listnitsky had more than one talk with the volunteer Bunchuk. On each occasion he was struck by the inflexible will that gleamed in the man's eyes, and could not discover what lay behind the intangible secrecy that veiled the face of one so ordinary-looking. Bunchuk always spoke with a smile compressed on his firm lips, and he gave Eugene the impression that he was applying a definite rule to the tracing of a tortuous path. As he wished, he was transferred to a machine-gun detachment. A few days later, while the regiment was resting behind the front, Listnitsky overtook him walking along by the wall of a burnt-out shed.

"Ah, Volunteer Bunchuk!" he called.

The Cossack turned his head and saluted.

"Where are you going?" Eugene asked.

"To the chief command."

"Then we're going the same way."

For some time they walked along the street of the ruined village in silence.

"Well, are you learning the art of war?" Listnitsky asked, glancing sidelong at Bunchuk, who was slightly behind him.

"Yes, I'm learning it."

"What do you propose to do after the war?"

"Some will reap what is sown . . . but I shall see," Bunchuk replied.

"How am I to interpret that remark?"

"You know the proverb: 'Those who sow the wind shall reap the whirlwind'? Well, that's how."

"But dropping the riddles?"

"It's quite clear as it is. Excuse me, I'm turning to the left here."

He put his fingers to the visor of his cap and turned off the road. Shrugging his shoulders, Listnitsky stood staring after him.

"Is the fellow trying to be original or is he just someone with a bee in his bonnet?" he wondered irritatedly as he stepped into the company commander's earth hut.

Chapter 6

The second and third lines of reserves were called up together. The districts and villages of the Don were depopulated, as though everybody had gone out to mow or reap the harvest.

But a bitter harvest was reaped along the frontiers that year; death carried away the labourers, and more than one straight-haired Cossack's wife sang of the departed one: "Beloved mine, for whom have you deserted me?" Darling heads were laid low on all sides, the ruddy Cossack blood was poured out, and glassy-eyed, un-awakable, they rotted beneath the artillery dirge in Austria, in Poland, in Prussia. . . . So the eastern wind did not carry the weeping of their wives and mothers to their ears.

One pleasant September day a milky gossamer web, fine and cottony, was floating over the village of Tatarsk. The anæmic sun was smiling like a widower, the stern, virginal blue sky was repellently clean and proud. Beyond the Don the forest pined a jaun-diced yellow, the ash gleamed pallidly, the oak dropped rare figured leaves; only the fir remained screamingly green, gladdening the sight with its vitality.

That day Pantaleimon Prokoffievich received a letter from the army on active service. Dunia brought it back from the post office.

As the postmaster handed it to her he bowed, shook his old bald pate, and deprecatingly opened his arms.

"Forgive me, for the love of God, for opening the letter. Tell your father I opened it. I badly wanted to know how the war was going. . . . Forgive me and tell Pantaleimon Prokoffievich what I said." He seemed confused and came out of his office with Dunia, muttering something unintelligible. Filled with foreboding, she agitatedly returned home and fumbled at her breast a long time for the letter. As she drew it out she said breathlessly:

"The postmaster told me he had read the letter and that you mustn't be angry with him."

"The devil take him! Is it from Gregor?" the old man asked, breathing asthmatically into her face. "From Gregor? Or from Piotra?"

"No, Father. I don't know the writing."

"Read it!" Ilinichna cried, tottering heavily to the bench. Her legs were giving her much trouble these days. Natalia ran in from the yard and stood by the stove with her head on one side, her elbows pressed into her breasts. A smile trembled on her lips. She was continually hoping for a message from Gregor or the slightest reference to her in his letters, in reward for her doglike devotion and fidelity.

"Where's Daria?" Ilinichna whispered.

"Shut up!" Pantaleimon shouted. "Read it!" he added to Dunia.

" 'I have to inform you,' " she began; then, slipping off the bench where she was sitting, she screamed:

"Father! Mother! Oh, Mamma! Our Grishka! Oh, oh! Grishka's—been killed."

Entangled among the leaves of a half-dead geranium, a wasp beat against the window, buzzing furiously. In the yard a chicken clucked contentedly; through the open door came the sound of ringing childish laughter.

A shudder ran across Natalia's face, though her lips still wore her quivering smile. Rising, his head twitching paralytically, Pantaleimon stared in frenetic perplexity at Dunia, who was rolling spasmodically on the floor.

The communication read:

I have to inform you that your son Gregor Pantalievich Melekhov, a Cossack in the 12th Don Cossack Regiment, was killed on the

*29th of August near the town of Kamenka Strumilovo. Your son died
the death of the brave; may that be your consolation in your irreplaceable loss. His personal effects will be handed to his brother,
Piotra Melekhov. His horse will remain with the regiment.*

*Commander of the Fourth Company, Lieutenant Polkovnikov.
Field Army August 31, 1914*

After the arrival of the letter Pantaleimon seemed suddenly to
wilt. He grew visibly older every day. His memory began to go
and his mind lost its clarity. He walked about with bowed back,
his face an iron hue; and the feverish oily gleam in his eyes betrayed
his mental stress. He began to go grey, and the dazzling grey hairs
swiftly patched his head and wove threads into his beard. He grew
gluttonous, too, and ate much and ravenously.

He hid the letter among the books under the ikon. Several times
a day he went into the porch to beckon to Dunia. When she came
in he would order her to get the letter and read it to him, fearfully
glancing the while at the door of the kitchen, where his wife was
working. "Read it quietly, to yourself like," he would wink
cunningly. Choking down her tears, Dunia would read the first
sentence, and then Pantaleimon, squatting on his heels, would raise
his brown hand:

"All right. I know the rest. Take the letter back and put it where
you found it. Quickly, or Mother—" and he would wink repulsively,
his whole face contorted like burnt tree-bark.

Nine days after the Requiem Mass, the Melekhovs invited Father
Vissarion and their relations to the repast in memory of the fallen
Gregor. Pantaleimon ate fast and ravenously, and the vermicelli
hung on his beard in ringlets. Ilinichna, who had been anxiously
watching him during the past few days, burst into tears.

"Father, what's the matter with you?" she whispered.

"Eh?" The old man fidgeted, raising his filmy eyes from his plate.
Ilinichna waved her hand and turned away, pressing her handkerchief to her eyes.

"Father, you eat as though you had fasted for three days," Daria
said angrily, her eyes glittering.

"I eat—? All right, I won't," Pantaleimon replied, overcome with embarrassment. He glanced around the table; then, pressing his lips together, sitting with knitted brows, he lapsed into silence, not even replying to questions.

"You're torturing yourself needlessly, Prokoffich! What's the good of grieving so much?" Father Vissarion attempted to rally him when the meal was ended. "Gregor's death was a holy one; don't be angry with God, old man. Your son has received a crown of thorns for his Czar and his fatherland. And you—it's a sin, and God won't pardon you."

"That's just it, holy father! That's my torture. 'Died the death of the brave.' That's what his commander said."

Kissing the priest's hand, the old man fumbled for the door latch, and for the first time since the arrival of the letter he burst into tears, his body shaking violently.

From that day he regained his self-control and recovered a little from the blow.

Each licked the wound in her own way. When Natalia heard Dunia scream that Gregor was dead she ran into the yard. "I'll lay hands on myself. It's the finish of all things for me." Her thought drove her on like fire. She struggled in Daria's arms and gladly swooned, as an alleviation and postponement of the moment when consciousness would return and violently remind her of what had happened. She passed a week in dull oblivion and returned to the world of reality changed, quieter, gnawed by a black impotence.

An invisible corpse haunted the Melekhovs' hut, and the living breathed in its mouldering scent.

On the twelfth day after the news of Gregor's death the Melekhovs received two letters from Piotra by the same post. Dunia read them at the post office and sped like a stalk caught up by the wind, then swayed and stopped, leaning against a fence. She caused no little excitement in the village and carried an indescribable feeling of agitation into the hut.

"Grishka's alive! Our dear's alive!" she sobbed and cried when still some distance away. "Piotra's written. Grishka's wounded, but he isn't dead. He's alive, alive!"

In his letter dated September 2 Piotra had written:

Greetings, dear family! I must tell you that our Grishka all but gave up his soul to God, but now, glory be, he's alive and well, as we wish you, in the name of the Lord God, health and well-being. Close to the town of Kamenka-Strumilovo his regiment was in battle, and in the attack the Cossacks of his troop saw him cut down by a Hungarian hussar, and Gregor fell from his horse and after that nobody knew anything, and when I asked them they could tell me nothing. But afterwards I learned from Misha Koshevoi that Gregor lay till night, but that in the night he came round and started crawling away. He crawled along, making his way by the stars, and came across one of our officers wounded. He picked him up and dragged him for four miles. And for this Gregor has been given the Cross of St. George and has been raised to the rank of corporal. His wound isn't serious, and Mishka told me he would be back at the front soon. You must excuse this letter, I am writing in the saddle.

In his second letter Piotra asked his family to send him some dried cherries from their own orchard and told them not to forget him but to write more often. In the same letter he upbraided Gregor because, so he had been told, he was not looking after his horse properly, and Piotra was ashamed, as the horse was really his. He asked his father to write to Gregor and said he had sent a message to him that if he did not look after the horse he would give him one on the nose that would draw blood, even if he had got the Cross of St. George.

Old Pantaleimon was a pitiful sight to see. He was scalded with joy. He seized both letters and went into the village with them, stopping all who could read and forcing them to read the letters. In his belated joy he bragged all through the village.

"Aha! What do you think of my Grishka?" He raised his hand when the reader came to the passage where Piotra described Gregor's exploit. "He's the first to get the cross in our village," he declared proudly. Jealously taking the letter, he thrust it into the lining of his cap and went off in search of another reader.

Even Sergei Mokhov, who saw him through his shop window, came out, taking off his cap.

"Come in for a minute, Prokoffievich!" he invited him.

Inside, he squeezed the old man's fist in his own puffy white hand and said:

"Well, I congratulate you; I congratulate you. You must be proud to have such a son. I've just been reading about his exploit in the newspapers."

"Is it in the papers?" Pantaleimon's face twisted spasmodically.

"Yes, I've just read it."

Mokhov took a packet of the finest Turkish tobacco down from a shelf and poured out some expensive chocolates into a bag without troubling to weigh them. Handing the tobacco and sweets to Pantaleimon, he said:

"When you send Gregor Pantalievich a parcel, send him a greeting and these from me."

"My God! What an honour for Grishka! All the village is talking about him. I've lived to see . . ." the old man muttered as he went down the steps of the shop. He blew his nose violently and wiped the tears from his cheek with his sleeve, thinking:

"I'm getting old. Tears come too easily. Ah, Pantaleimon Prokoffievich, what has life done with you? You were as hard as a flint once, you could carry two hundred and fifty pounds on your back as easily as a feather, but now . . . Grishka's business has upset you a little!"

As he limped along the street, pressing the bag of chocolates to his chest, again his thought fluttered around Gregor like a lapwing over a marsh, and the words of Piotra's letter wandered through his mind. Gregor's father-in-law, Korshunov, was coming along the road, and he called to Pantaleimon:

"Hey, Pantaleimon, stop a minute!"

The two men had not met since the day war was declared. A cold, constrained relationship had arisen between them after Gregor left home. Miron was annoyed with Natalia for humbling herself to Gregor and for forcing her father to endure a similar humiliation.

Miron went right up to Pantaleimon and thrust out his oak-coloured hand. "How are you?"

"Thanks be to God. . . ."

"Been shopping?"

Pantaleimon shook his head. "These are gifts to our hero. Sergei Platonovich read about his deed in the papers and has sent him some chocolates and tobacco. Do you know, the tears came to his eyes," the old man boasted, staring fixedly into Miron's face in the attempt to discover what impression his words had made.

The shadows gathered under Miron's eyelashes, giving his face a ludicrously smiling twist.

"So!" he croaked, and turned to cross the street. Pantaleimon hurried after him, opening the bag and trembling with anger.

"Here, try these chocolates, they're as sweet as honey," he said spitefully. "Try them, I offer them in my son's name. Your life is none too sweet, so you can have one; and your son may earn such an honour some day, but then he may not."

"Don't pry into my life. I know best what it's like."

"Just try one, do me the favour," Pantaleimon bowed with exaggerated affability, running in front of Miron.

"We're not used to sweets." Miron pushed away his hand. "And we're not used to breaking our teeth on others' hospitality. It was hardly decent of you to go begging alms for your son. If you're in need, you can come to me. Our Natalia's eating your bread. We could have given to you in your poverty."

"Don't you tell those lies, no one has ever begged for alms in our family. You're too proud, much too proud. Maybe it is because you are rich that your daughter came to us."

"Wait!" Miron said authoritatively. "There's no point in our quarrelling. I didn't stop you to have a quarrel. I've some business I want to talk over with you."

"We have no business to talk over."

"Yes, we have. Come on."

He seized Pantaleimon's sleeve and dragged him into a side street. They walked out of the village on to the steppe.

"Well, what's the business?" Pantaleimon asked in more amiable tones. He glanced sidelong at Korshunov's face. Turning the edges of his long coat under him, Miron sat down on the bank of a ditch and pulled out his old tobacco-pouch.

"You know, Prokoffich, the devil knows why you went for me like a quarrelsome cock. As it is, things aren't too good, are they? I want to know"—his voice changed to a hard, rough tone—"how long your son is going to make a laughing-stock of Natalia. Tell me that!"

"You must ask him about it, not me."

"I've nothing to ask him; you're the head of your house and I'm talking to you."

Pantaleimon squeezed the chocolate still held in his hand, and the sticky mess oozed through his fingers. He wiped his palm on the brown clay of the bank and silently began to roll a cigarette, opening the packet of Turkish tobacco and pouring out a pinch. Then he offered the packet to Miron. Korshunov took it without hesitation and made a cigarette from the tobacco intended for Gregor. Above them a cloud hung its white, sumptuous breast, and a tender flying web stretched up towards it, fluttering in the wind.

The day declined to its close. The September stillness lulled peacefully and with inexpressible sweetness. The sky had lost its full summer gleam and was a hazy dove-colour. Over the ditch apple leaves, carried God knows whence, rustled their exuberant purple. The road disappeared over the undulating crest of the hills; in vain did it beckon to pass along it, beyond the emerald, dreamily uncertain horizon into unseen space. Held down to their huts and their daily round, the people pined in their labour, exhausted their strength on the threshing-floor; and the road, a deserted, yearning track, flowed across the horizon into the unseen. The wind trod along it, with aimless elegance stirring up the dust.

"This is weak tobacco, it's like grass," Miron said, emitting a cloud of smoke from his mouth.

"It's weak, but it's pleasant," Pantaleimon half agreed.

"Give me an answer, Pantaleimon," Korshunov asked in a quieter tone, putting out his cigarette.

"Gregor never says anything about it in his letters. He's wounded now. What will come after, I don't know. Maybe he'll be killed, and then what?"

"But how can it go on like this?" Miron blinked distractedly and miserably. "There she is, neither maid nor wife nor honest widow, and it's a disgrace. If I had known it was going to turn out like this I'd never have allowed the matchmakers across my threshold. Ah, Pantaleimon—Pantaleimon—each is sorry for his own child. Blood is thicker than water."

"How can I help it?" Pantaleimon replied with restrained frenzy. "Tell me! Do you think I'm glad my son left home? Was it any gain to me?"

"Write to him," Miron dictated, and the dust streaming from under his hands into the ditch kept time with his words. "Let him say once for all."

"He's got a child by that—"

"And he'll have a child by this!" Korshunov shouted, turning livid. "Can you treat a human being like that? Eh? Once she's tried to kill herself and is maimed for life? And you can trample her into the grave? Eh? . . . His heart, his heart—" Miron hissed, tearing at his breast with one hand, tugging at Pantaleimon's coat-tails with the other. "Is it a wolf's heart he's got?"

Pantaleimon wheezed and turned away.

"The woman's devoted to him, and there's no other life for her without him. Is she a serf in your service?" Miron demanded.

"She's better off with us than with you! Hold your tongue!" Pantaleimon shouted, and he rose from the bank.

They parted without a word of farewell, and went off in different directions.

When swept out of its normal channel, life scatters into innumerable streams. It is difficult to foresee which it will take in its treacherous and winding course. Where today it flows in shallows, like a rivulet over sandbanks, so shallow that the shoals are visible, tomorrow it will flow richly and fully.

Suddenly Natalia came to the decision to go to Aksinia at Yagodnoe and to ask, to beseech her to return Gregor to her. For some reason it seemed to Natalia that everything depended on Aksinia, and if she asked her, Gregor would return, and with him her own former happiness. She did not stop to consider whether this was possible, or how Aksinia would receive her strange request. Driven on by subconscious motives, she sought to act upon her decision as quickly as possible.

At the end of the month a letter arrived from Gregor. After messages to his father and mother he sent his greeting and regards to Natalia. Whatever the reason inciting him to this, it was the stimulus

Natalia required, and she made ready to go to Yagodnoe the very next Sunday.

"Where are you off to, Natalia?" Dunia asked, watching as she attentively studied her features in the scrap of looking-glass.

"I'm going to visit my people," Natalia lied, and blushed as she realized for the first time that she was going towards a great humiliation, a terrible moral test.

"You might have an evening out with me just for once," Daria suggested. "Come this evening, won't you?"

"I don't know, but I don't think so."

"You little thorn! Our turn only comes when our husbands are away," Daria winked, and stooped to examine the embroidered hem of her new pale-blue skirt. Daria's attitude to Natalia had changed of late, and their relations had grown simple and friendly. The dislike which she had felt for the younger woman was gone, and the two, different in every respect, lived together amicably. Daria had altered considerably since Piotra's departure. Unrest showed in her eyes, her movements and carriage. She arrayed herself more diligently on Sundays, and came back late in the evening to complain to Natalia:

"It's woeful, God's truth! They've taken away all the suitable Cossacks and left only boys and old men in the village."

"Well, what difference does that make to you?"

"Why, there's nobody to lark about with of an evening." And with cynical frankness she asked Natalia: "How can you bear it, my dear—so long without a Cossack?"

"Shame on you! Haven't you any conscience?" Natalia blushed.

"Don't you feel any desire?"

"It's clear you do."

Daria laughed, and the arches of her brows quivered. "Why should I hide it? I'd throw any old man on his back this very minute! Just think, it's two months since Piotra went."

"You're laying up sorrow for yourself, Daria."

"Shut up, you respectable old woman! We know you quiet ones! You would never admit it."

"I've nothing to admit."

Daria gave her a ludicrous sidelong glance and bit her lips. "The other day Timothy Manitsev, the ataman's son, sat down beside me. I could see he was afraid to begin. Then he quietly slipped his

hand under my arm, and his hand was trembling. I just waited
and said nothing, but I was getting angry. If he had been a lad now
—but he's only a snot. Sixteen years old, not a day more. I sat without speaking, and he pawed and pawed, and whispered: 'Come
along to our shed.' Then I gave him one!" She laughed merrily. "I
jumped up. 'Oh, you this and that! You yellow-necked whelp! Do
you think you can wheedle me like that? When did you wet the
bed last?' I gave him a fine dressing-down."

Natalia went out. Daria overtook her in the porch.

"You'll open the door for me tonight?" she asked.

"I expect I shall stay the night with my people."

Daria thoughtfully scratched her nose with her comb and shook
her head:

"Oh, all right. I didn't want to ask Dunia, but I see I shall have
to."

Natalia told Ilinichna she was going to visit her people and went
into the street. The wagons were rattling away from the market in
the square, and the villagers were coming from church. She turned
up a side lane and hurriedly climbed the hill. At the top she turned
and looked back. The village lay flooded in sunlight, the little
limewashed huts were white, and the sun glittered on the steep
roof of the mill, making the sheet iron shine like molten ore.

Yagodnoe also had lost men, torn away by the war. Benyamin
and Tikhon had gone, and the place was still sleepier, more dreary
and isolated than ever. Aksinia waited on the general in Benyamin's place, while fat-bottomed Lukeria took over all the cooking
and fed the fowls. There was only one new face, an old Cossack
named Nikitich who had been taken on as coachman.

This year old Listnitsky sowed less and supplied some twenty
horses for army remounts, leaving only three or four for the needs
of the estate. He passed his time shooting bustards and hunting
with the borzois.

Aksinia received only brief, infrequent letters from Gregor, informing her that so far he was well. He had grown stronger, or
else he did not want to tell her of his weakness, for he never let
slip any complaint that he found active service difficult and dreary.
His letters were cold, as though he had written them because he

felt he had to, and only in one did he write: "all the time at the front, and I'm fed up with fighting and carrying death on my back." In every letter he asked after his daughter, telling Aksinia to write about her. Aksinia seemed to bear the separation bravely. All her love for Gregor was poured out on her daughter, especially after she became convinced that the child was really his. Life gave irrefragable proofs of that: the girl's dark ruddy hair was replaced by a black, curly growth; her eyes changed to a dark tint and elongated in their slits. With every day she grew more and more like her father; even her smile was Gregor's. Now Aksinia could see him beyond all doubt in the child, and her feeling for it deepened.

The days passed on, and at the end of each one a caustic bitterness settled in Aksinia's breast. Anxiety for the life of her beloved pierced her mind like a sharp needle; it left her neither day nor night. Restrained during the hours of labour, it burst all dams at night, and she tossed in an inarticulate cry, in tears, biting her hand to avoid awakening the child with her sobs and to kill her mental with a physical pain. She wept her tears into a napkin, thinking in her childish naïveté: "Grishka must feel through his child how I yearn for him."

After such nights she arose in the morning as though she had been beaten unmercifully. All her body ached, little silver hammers knocked incessantly in her veins, and sorrow lurked in the corners of her swollen lips. The nights of yearning aged Aksinia.

On the Sunday of Natalia's visit she had given her master his breakfast and was standing on the steps when she saw a woman approaching the gate. The eyes beneath the white kerchief seemed strangely familiar. The woman opened the gate and entered the yard. Aksinia turned pale as she recognized Natalia. She went slowly to meet her. A heavy layer of dust had settled on Natalia's shoes. She halted, her large, labour-scarred hands hanging lifelessly at her sides, and breathed heavily, trying to straighten her mutilated neck.

"I want to see you, Aksinia," she said, running her dry tongue over her lips.

Aksinia gave a swift glance at the windows of the house and

silently led Natalia into her room. She closed the door and, standing in the middle of the room with her hands under her apron, took charge of the situation, asking stealthily, almost in a whisper:

"What have you come for?"

"I'd like a drink," Natalia asked, staring heavily around the room. Aksinia waited. Natalia began to speak, with difficulty raising her voice:

"You've taken my husband from me. . . . Give me my Gregor back. You have broken my life. You see how I am. . . ."

"Husband to you?" Aksinia grated her teeth, and the words came sharply and freely like raindrops on stone. "Husband to you? Who are you asking? Why did you come? You've thought of it too late. Too late!"

Laughing caustically, her whole body swaying, Aksinia went right up to Natalia. She sneered as she stared in the face of her enemy. There she stood, the lawful but abandoned wife, humiliated, crushed with misery. She who had come between Aksinia and Gregor, separating them, causing a bloody pain like a heavy stone in Aksinia's heart. And while she had been wearing herself out with mortal longing, this other one, this Natalia, had been caressing Gregor and no doubt laughing at her, the unsuccessful, forsaken lover.

"And you've come to ask me to give him up?" Aksinia panted. "You snake in the grass! You took Gregor away from me first! You knew he was living with me. Why did you marry him? I only took back my own. He's mine. I have a child by him, but you—"

With stormy hatred she stared into Natalia's eyes and, waving her arms wildly, poured out a boiling torrent of words.

"Grishka's mine, and I'll give him up to no one! He's mine, mine! Do you hear? . . . Mine! Clear out, you shameless bitch, you're not his wife. You want to rob a child of its father? And why didn't you come before? Well, why didn't you come before?"

Natalia went sideways to the bench and sat down, drooping her head and covering her face with her palms.

"You left your husband. Don't shout like that," she answered.

"Except for Grishka I haven't any husband. No one nowhere in the whole world." Feeling an anger that could not find vent raging within her, Aksinia gazed at the strand of black hair that had slipped from under Natalia's kerchief.

"Does he need you?" she demanded. "Look at your twisted neck! And do you think he longs for you? He left you when you were well, and is he likely to yearn for you as you are now? I won't give Gregor up! That's all I have to say. Clear out!"

Aksinia grew ferocious in defence of her nest. She could see that, despite the slightly crooked neck, Natalia was as good-looking as before. Her cheeks and lips were fresh, untouched by time, while her own eyes were lined with furrows, and all because of Natalia.

"Do you think I had any hope of getting him back by asking?" Natalia raised her eyes, drunk with suffering.

"Then why did you come?" Aksinia asked.

"My yearning drove me on."

Awakened by the voices, Aksinia's daughter stirred in the bed and broke into a cry. The mother took up the child and sat down with her face to the window. Trembling in every limb, Natalia gazed at the infant. A dry spasm clutched her throat. Gregor's eyes stared at her inquisitively from the baby's face.

Weeping and swaying, she walked out into the porch. Aksinia did not see her off. A minute or two later Sashka came into the room.

"Who was that woman?" he asked, evidently half-guessing.

"Someone from our village."

Natalia walked back towards Tatarsk for a couple of miles and then lay down under a wild thorn. Crushed by her yearning, she lay thinking of nothing. Gregor's black, morose eyes, staring out of a child's face, were continually before her own eyes.

Chapter 7

So vivid that it was almost a blinding pain, the night after the battle remained for ever imprinted in Gregor's memory. He returned to consciousness some time before dawn; his hands stirred among the prickly stubble, and he groaned with the pain that filled his head. With an effort he raised his hand, drew it up to his brow.

and felt his blood-clotted hair. He touched the flesh wound with his finger. Then, grating his teeth, he lay on his back. Above him the frost-nipped leaves of a tree rustled mournfully with a glassy tinkle. The black silhouettes of the branches were clearly outlined against the deep blue background of the sky, and stars glittered among them. Gregor gazed unwinkingly, and the stars seemed to him like strange bluish-yellow fruits hanging from the twigs.

Realizing what had happened to him, and conscious of an invincible, approaching horror, he crawled away on all fours, grinding his teeth. The pain played with him, threw him down headlong. He seemed to be crawling an immeasurably long time. He forced himself to look back; the tree stood out blackly some fifty paces away. Once he crawled across a corpse, resting his elbows on the dead man's hard, sunken belly. He was sick with loss of blood, wept like a babe, and chewed the dewy grass to avoid losing consciousness. Close to an overturned case of shells he managed to get on to his feet and stood a long time swaying, then started to walk. His strength began to return; he stepped out more firmly and was even able to take his bearings by the Great Bear, moving in an easterly direction.

At the edge of the forest he was halted by a sudden warning shout:

"Stop or I'll fire!"

He heard the rattle of a revolver and looked in the direction of the sound. A man was reclining by a pine tree.

"Who are you?" he asked, listening to the sound of his voice as though it were another's.

"A Russian? My God! Come here!" The man by the pine slipped to the ground. Gregor went to him.

"Bend down!" the man ordered him.

"I can't."

"Why not?"

"I shall fall and not be able to get up again. I'm wounded in the head."

"What regiment are you?"

"The 12th Don Cossack."

"Help me, Cossack!"

"I shall fall, Your Excellency," Gregor replied, recognizing the officer by his epaulets.

"Give me your hand at least."

Gregor stooped and helped the officer to rise, and they went off together. But with every step the officer hung more heavily on his arm. As they rose out of a dell he seized Gregor by the sleeve and said:

"Let me drop, Cossack. I've got a wound—right across the stomach."

He swooned; but Gregor dragged him along, falling and rising again and again. Twice he dropped his burden and left it; but each time he returned, lifted it, and stumbled on as if in a waking sleep.

At eleven o'clock they were picked up by a patrol and taken to a dressing station.

Gregor secretly left the station the very next day. Once on the road, he tore the bandage from his head and walked along waving the blood-soaked bandage in his relief.

"Where have you come from?" his company commander asked him in amazement when he turned up at regimental headquarters.

"I've returned to duty, Your Excellency," he replied.

His company had halted in Kamenka-Strumilovo for two days and were now preparing to advance again. Gregor found the house in which the Cossacks of his troop were quartered and went to see to his horse. His towels and some underlinen were missing from his saddlebags.

"Stolen before my very eyes, Gregor," Misha Koshevoi admitted guiltily. "The infantry were quartered here, and they stole them."

"Well, they can keep them, damn them! Only I want to bandage my head."

Uriupin came into the shed where they were standing. He held out his hand as though the quarrel between him and Gregor had never occurred.

"Hello, Melekhov! So you're still alive!" he exclaimed.

"More or less."

"Your head's all bleeding. Let me have a look."

He forced back Gregor's head and snorted:

"Why did you let them cut your hair off? The doctors would have made a fine mess of you. Let me heal you."

Without waiting for Gregor's consent he drew a cartridge out of his cartridge-case, broke the bullet open, and poured the black powder into his hand.

"Misha, find me a spider's web," he ordered.

With the point of his sabre Koshevoi scraped up a web and handed it to Uriupin. With the same sabre Uriupin dug up some earth and, mixing it with the web and the powder, chewed it between his teeth. Then he plastered the sticky mess over the bleeding wound and smiled.

"It'll be all right again in three days," he declared. "But here I am looking after you, and yet you would have killed me."

"Thank you for looking after me, but if I had killed you I'd have had one sin the less on my conscience. What's the wound like?"

"It's a cut half an inch deep. You won't forget it in a hurry. The Austrians don't sharpen their swords, and you'll have a scar for the rest of your life."

They turned to leave the shed. Gregor's bay horse whinnied after him, turning up the whites of its eyes.

"He pined after you, Gregor." Koshevoi nodded at the horse. "He wouldn't eat, but was whinnying all the time."

"When I crawled away I kept calling him," Gregor said in a thick voice. "I was sure he wouldn't leave me, and I knew it wouldn't be easy for a stranger to catch him."

"That's true. We had to take him by force. We lassoed him."

"He's a good horse. He's my brother Piotra's." Gregor turned his back to hide his wet eyes.

They went into the house. Yegor Zharkov was lying asleep on a spring mattress in the front room. An indescribable disorder silently witnessed to the haste with which the owners had left the place. Fragments of broken utensils, torn paper, books, scraps of material, children's toys, old boots, scattered flour were all tumbled in confusion about the floor.

Yemelian Groshev and Prokhor Zykov had cleared a space in the middle of the room and were eating their dinner. At the sight of Gregor, Zykov's calfish eyes nearly dropped out of his head.

"Grishka! Where have you dropped from?" he exclaimed.

"From the other world! Don't stare like that!"

"Run and get him some soup," Uriupin shouted.

Prokhor rose and went to the door, chewing as he walked. Gregor sat down wearily in his place. "I don't remember when I ate last." He smiled guiltily.

Prokhor quickly returned with a pot of soup and a bag of buck-wheat gruel.

"What shall I pour the gruel into?" he asked.

Not knowing its purpose, Groshev picked up a bedroom utensil, remarking: "Here's a pot with a handle."

"Your pot stinks," Prokhor frowned.

"Never mind. Pour it out and we'll share it afterwards."

Zykov turned the bag upside-down over the vessel, and the rich, thick gruel fell in a mass, an amber edging of fat running down over it. They talked as they ate. Licking a grease-spot on the faded stripe of his trousers, Uriupin muttered through a mouthful of gruel:

"You should have been here this morning, Melekhov. We were thanked by the divisional commander himself. He reviewed us and thanked us for smashing the Hungarian hussars and saving the battery. 'Cossacks,' he said, 'the Czar and the fatherland will not forget you.'"

As he spoke, there was the sound of a shot outside, and a machine-gun began to stutter. Dropping their spoons, the Cossacks ran out. Overhead an aeroplane was circling low. Its powerful engine roared menacingly.

"Lie down under the fence. They'll be dropping a bomb in a minute. There's a battery billeted next door to us," Uriupin shouted. "Someone go and wake Yegor up. They'll kill him as he lies on a soft mattress!"

Soldiers ran along the street, their bodies bent to the ground. From the next yard came the neighing of horses and a curt order. Gregor glanced over the fence; the gunners were hurriedly wheeling a gun under a shed. Screwing up his eyes at the prickly blue of the sky, he stared at the roaring, swooping bird. At that moment something fell suddenly away from it and glittered sharply in the sunlight.

Uriupin ran down the steps, Gregor behind him, and they threw themselves down by the palings. One wing of the aeroplane glittered as it turned. From the street came irregular shots. Gregor had just thrust a charge of cartridges into the magazine of his rifle when a shattering explosion threw him six feet away from the fence. A lump of earth struck him on the head, filling his eyes with dust and crushing with its weight.

Uriupin lifted him to his feet. A sharp pain in the left eye prevented Gregor from seeing. With difficulty opening the right eyelid, he saw that half the house was demolished; the bricks were scattered in a horrible confusion, a rosy cloud of dust hovered over them.

As he stood staring, Yegor Zharkov crawled from under the steps. His entire face was a cry; bloody tears were raining from his eyes torn out of their sockets. With his head buried in his shoulders he crawled along, screaming without opening his deathly blackening lips.

"A-i-i-i-i. A-i-i-i-i. . . . A—i—i. . . ."

Behind him one leg, torn away at the thigh, dragged along by a shred of skin; the other leg was gone completely. He crawled slowly along on his hands, a thin, almost childish scream coming from his lips. The cry stopped and he fell over on his side, pressing his face right against the harsh, unkind brick- and dung-littered earth. No one attempted to go to him.

"Pick him up!" Gregor shouted, not removing his hand from his left eye.

Infantry ran into the yard; a two-wheeled cart with telephone operators stopped at the gate. Two women, and an old man in a long black coat, came up. Zharkov was quickly surrounded by a little crowd. Pressing through them, Gregor saw that he was still breathing, whimpering and violently shivering. A beady, granular sweat stood out on his deathly yellow brow.

"Pick him up! What are you, men or devils? . . ."

"What are you howling about?" a tall infantryman snapped. "Pick him up, pick him up! But where are we to take him to? You can see he's dying."

"And he's still conscious."

Uriupin touched Gregor on the shoulder from behind. "Don't move him," he whispered. "Come round the other side and look."

He drew Gregor along by the sleeve and pushed the crowd aside. Gregor took one glance, then with huddled shoulders turned away and went to the gate. Under Zharkov's belly the rosy and blue intestines hung smoking. The end of the intertwined mass was poured out on the sand and dung, stirring and swelling. The dying man's hand lay at the side as though raking the ground.

"Cover his face," someone proposed.

Zharkov suddenly rose on his hand and, throwing his head back until it beat between the shoulder-blades, shouted in a hoarse, inhuman voice:

"Brothers, kill me. . . . Brothers! . . . What are you standing looking for? . . . Ah! . . . Ah! . . . Brothers, kill me!"

The wagon rocked easily; the knock of its wheels was lullingly drowsy. A yellow band of light streamed from the lantern. It was good to be stretched out at full length, with boots off, giving the feet their freedom, to feel no responsibility for oneself, to know that no danger threatened your life, and that death was so far away. It was especially pleasant to listen to the varying chatter of the wheels, for with their every turn, with every roar of the engine, the front was farther and farther off. And Gregor lay listening, wriggling the toes of his bare feet, all his body rejoicing in the fresh, clean linen. He felt as though he had thrown off a dirty integument and, spotlessly clean, was entering a new life.

His quiet, tranquil joy was disturbed only by the pain in his left eye. It died away occasionally, then would suddenly return, burning the eye and forcing involuntary tears beneath the bandage. In the field hospital a young Jewish doctor had examined his eye and had told him:

"You'll have to go back. Your eye is in a very unsatisfactory state."

"Shall I lose it, doctor?"

"Why should you think that?" The doctor smiled, catching the unconcealed alarm in Gregor's voice. "But you must have it attended to, and an operation may be necessary. We shall send you to Petersburg or Moscow. Don't be afraid, your eye will be all right." He clapped Gregor on the shoulder and gently drew him outside into the corridor. As he turned back he rolled up his sleeves in readiness for an operation.

After long wanderings Gregor found himself in a hospital train. He lay for days on end enjoying the blessed peace. The ancient engine exerted all its strength to haul the long line of cars. They drew near Moscow and arrived at night. Those who could walk were assembled on the platform. The doctor accompanying the train called out Gregor's name and handed him over to a nurse, instructing her as to his destination.

The nurse led the way out of the station, her dress rustling. Gregor walked uncertainly behind her. They took a droshky. The roar of the great city, the jangle of street-car bells, the blue gleam of electricity had a crushing effect upon him. He leaned against the back of the droshky, staring inquisitively at the crowded streets, and it was strange for him to feel the agitating body of a woman at his side. Autumn had visibly arrived in Moscow. Along the boulevards the leaves of the trees gleamed yellow in the lamplight, the night breathed a wintry chill, the pavements were shining, and above him the stars were autumnally clear and cold. From the centre of the town they turned into a deserted side street. The horse's hoofs clattered over the cobblestones; the driver in his long blue coat swayed on his high seat and waved the ends of the reins at his mare. In the distance railway engines whistled. "Perhaps a train just off to the Don," Gregor thought, pricked with yearning.

They stopped outside a three-storeyed house. Gregor jumped out.

"Give me your hand," the nurse asked, bending down over him. He took her small, soft hand in his and helped her to alight.

"You smell of soldier's sweat." She laughed quietly.

"You ought to spend some time out there, nurse, then you might stink of something else," Gregor replied with suppressed anger.

The door was opened by a porter. They went up a gilt balustraded staircase to the next floor. Passing into an anteroom, Gregor sat down at a round table while the nurse whispered something to a woman in a white overall. After a few minutes an orderly, also dressed in white, led him to a bathroom.

"Strip!" he ordered.

"What for?"

"You've got to have a bath."

While Gregor was undressing and looking in astonishment around the bathroom, the orderly filled the tub with water, measured the temperature, and told him to get in. He assisted him to wash himself thoroughly, then gave him a towel, linen, houseshoes, and a grey, belted overall.

"What about my clothes?" Gregor asked in amazement.

"You'll wear these while you're here. Your clothes will be returned to you when you are discharged from the hospital."

As Gregor passed a wall mirror, he did not recognize himself. Tall, dark of face, with patches of crimson on the cheeks and a growth of moustache and beard, in a dressing-gown, his hair swathed in a cap, he had only a distant resemblance to the former Gregor Melekhov. "I've grown younger." He smiled wanly to himself.

The orderly showed him into a room, and a few minutes later a corpulent nurse with a large, ugly face opened the door.

"Melekhov, we want to have a look at your eyes," she said in a low, chesty voice, and stood aside to let him pass out.

Chapter 8

The army command decided on a big attack on the south-west front with a view to breaking through the enemy lines, destroying his communication lines, and disorganizing his forces with sudden assaults. The command set great store by the plan, and large forces of cavalry were concentrated in the area, among them being Eugene Listnitsky's regiment. The attack was to have begun on September 10, but a rain-storm caused it to be postponed until the following day.

Over a six-mile area the infantry on the right flank made a demonstrative offensive to draw the fire of the enemy. Also sections of one cavalry division were dispatched in a misleading direction.

In front of Listnitsky's regiment, as far as eye could see, there was no sign whatever of the enemy. About a mile away Eugene could see deserted lines of trenches, behind them rye-fields billowing in a wind-driven, bluish early-morning mist. The enemy must have learned of the attack in preparation, for during the night they had retired some four miles, leaving only nests of machine-guns to harass the attackers.

Behind the clouds the sun was rising. The entire valley was flooded with a creamy yellow mist. The order came for the offen-

sive to begin, and the regiments advanced. The many thousands
of horses' hoofs set up a deep rumbling roar that sounded as though
it came from under the ground. A mile was covered, and the level
lines of attacking forces drew near the fields of grain. The rye,
higher than a man's waist and entangled with twining plants and
grasses, rendered the cavalry's progress extremely difficult. Before
them rose continually the ruddy heads of rye; behind them it lay
overthrown and trampled down by hoofs. After three miles of such
riding the horses began to stumble and sweat, but still there was
no sign of the enemy. Listnitsky glanced at his company commander; the captain's face wore an expression of utter despair.

Four miles of terribly heavy going took all the strength out of
the horses; some of them dropped under their riders; even the
strongest stumbled, exerting all their strength to keep moving. Now
the Austrian machine-guns began to work, sprinkling a hail of
bullets. The murderous fire mowed down the leading ranks. A regiment of Uhlans was the first to falter and turn; a Cossack regiment
broke. The machine-gun rain lashed them into a panic-stricken
flight. Thus this extraordinarily extensive attack was overwhelmed
with complete defeat. Some of the regiments lost half their complement of men and horses. Four hundred Cossacks and sixteen officers
were killed and wounded in Listnitsky's regiment alone.

Eugene's own horse was killed under him, and he himself was
wounded in the head and the leg. A sergeant-major leaped from his
horse and picked him up, flung him over his saddle-bow, and
galloped back with him.

The chief of staff of the division, one Colonel Golovachev, took
several snapshots of the attack and afterwards showed them to
some officers. A wounded subaltern struck him in the face with his
fist and burst into tears. Then Cossacks ran up and tore Golovachev
to pieces, made game of his corpse, and finally threw it into the
mud of a roadside ditch. So ended this brilliantly inglorious offensive.

From the hospital in Warsaw Eugene informed his father that
he had been given leave and was coming down to Yagodnoe. The
old man shut himself up in his room and came out again only the
next day. He ordered Nikitich, the coachman, to harness the trot-

ting-horse into the droshky, had breakfast, and drove to Vieshenska. There he sent his son a telegram which was a miniature letter and cost four hundred rubles to dispatch.

Yet there was nothing in Listnitsky's life to write about. It dragged on as before, without variation; only the cost of labour rose, and there was a shortage of liquor. The master drank more frequently and grew more irritable and fault-finding. One day he summoned Aksinia to him and complained:

"You're not working properly. Why was the breakfast cold yesterday? Why wasn't the glass properly clean? If it happens again I shall discharge you. I can't stand slovenliness. Do you hear?"

Aksinia pressed her lips together and burst into tears.

"Nicholai Alexievich!" she exclaimed. "My daughter is ill. Let me have time to attend to her. I can't leave her."

"What's the matter with the child?"

"She seems to be choking."

"What? Diphtheria? Why didn't you speak before, you fool? Run and tell Nikitich to drive to Vieshenska for the doctor. Hurry!"

Nikitich brought the doctor back the next morning. He examined the unconscious, feverish child and without replying to Aksinia's entreaties went straight to the master. The old man received him in the anteroom.

"Well, what's wrong with the child?" he asked, acknowledging the doctor's greeting with a careless nod.

"Diphtheria, Your Excellency!"

"Will it get better? Any hope?"

"Hardly! It's dying."

"You fool!" The old man turned livid. "What did you study medicine for? Cure her!" He slammed the door in the doctor's face and paced up and down the hall.

Aksinia knocked and entered. "The doctor wants horses to take him to Vieshenska," she said.

The old man turned on his heel. "Tell him he's a blockhead! Tell him he doesn't leave this place until the child is well. Give him a room and feed him," he shouted, shaking his fist. He strode over to the window, drummed with his fingers for a minute, and then, turning to a photograph of his son as a baby in his nurse's arms, stepped back two paces and stared hard at it.

As soon as the child had fallen sick Aksinia had decided that

God was punishing her for taunting Natalia. Crushed with fear for the child's life, she lost control of herself, wandered aimlessly about, and could not work. "Surely God won't take her!" the feverish thought beat incessantly in her brain, and not believing, with all her force trying not to believe, that the child would die, she prayed frantically to God for His last mercy, that its life might be spared.

But the fever was choking the little life. The girl lay like marble, a difficult, broken cry coming from her throat. The doctor attended her four times a day and stood of an evening smoking on the steps of the servants' quarters, gazing at the cold sparkle of the autumnal stars.

All night Aksinia remained on her knees by the bed. The child's gurgling rattle wrung her heart.

"My little one, my little daughter," she groaned; "my flower, don't go away, Tania. Look, my pretty one, open your little eyes, come back. My black-eyed darling! Why, O Lord . . . ?"

The child occasionally opened its eyelids, and the bloodshot eyes gave her an errant, intangible glance. The mother caught at the glance greedily. It seemed to be withdrawn into itself, yearning, resigned.

She died in her mother's arms. For the last time the little mouth gaped and the body was racked with a convulsion. The tiny head was thrown back, out of its mother's arm, and the little Melekhov eyes gazed with an astonished, morose stare.

Old Sashka dug a tiny grave under an old poplar by the lake, carried the coffin to the grave, and with unwonted haste covered it with earth, then waited long and patiently for Aksinia to rise from the clayey mound. At last he could wait no longer, and blowing his nose violently, he went off to the stables. He drew a flask of eau-de-Cologne and a little flagon of denatured alcohol out of a manger, mixed the spirits in a bottle, and muttered as he held the concoction up to the light:

"In memory! May the heavenly kingdom open its gates to the little one! The angel soul is dead."

Three weeks later Eugene Listnitsky sent a telegram saying he was on his way home. A troika was sent to meet him at the station.

and everybody on the estate was on tiptoe with expectation. Turkeys and geese were killed, and old Sashka flayed a sheep. The young master arrived at night. A freezing rain was falling, and the lamps flung fugitive little beams of light over the meadow. Throwing his warm cloak to Sashka, Eugene, limping slightly and very agitated, walked up the steps. His father hastened to meet him, sending the chairs flying in his progress.

Aksinia served supper in the dining-room and went to summon them to table. Looking through the keyhole, she saw the old man embracing and kissing his son on the shoulder; old Listnitsky's shoulders were quivering. Waiting a few minutes, she looked again. This time Eugene was on his knees before a great map spread out on the floor. The old man, puffing clouds of smoke from his pipe, was knocking with his knuckles on the arm of a chair and roaring indignantly:

"It can't be! I don't believe it!"

Eugene replied quietly, persuasively running his fingers over the map. The old man answered:

"In that case the supreme command was in the wrong. A narrow shortsightedness on their part. Look, Eugene, I'll give you a similar instance from the Russo-Japanese campaign. Let me! Let me!"

Aksinia knocked. The old man came out animated, gay, his eyes glittering youthfully. With his son he drank a bottle of wine of 1879 vintage. As Aksinia waited on them and observed their cheerful faces, she felt keenly her own loneliness. An unwept yearning rent her. After the death of the child she had wanted to weep, but tears would not come. A cry came to her throat, but her eyes were dry, and so the stony grief oppressed her doubly. She slept a great deal, seeking relief in a drowsy oblivion, but the child's call reached her even in sleep. She imagined the infant was asleep at her side, and she turned and clawed at the pillow with her fingers, hearing the whispered: "Mamma, Mamma." "My darling," she would answer with chilly lips. Even in the oppressive broad daylight she sometimes imagined that the child was at her knee and she caught herself reaching out her hand to stroke the curly head.

The third day after his arrival Eugene sat until late in the evening with old Sashka in the stables, listening to his artless stories of

the former free life of the Don Cossacks. He left him at nine o'clock.
A wind was blowing through the yard; the mud squelched slushily
underfoot. A young, yellow-whiskered moon peered between the
clouds. By its light Eugene looked at his watch, and turned towards
the servants' quarters. He stopped by the steps to light a cigarette,
stood thinking for a moment, then, shrugging his shoulders, went
up the steps. He cautiously lifted the latch and opened the door,
passed through into Aksinia's room, and struck a match.

"Who is that?" she asked, drawing the blanket around her.

"It's only me, Listnitsky."

"I'll be dressed in a minute."

"Don't trouble. I shall only stay for a moment or two."

He threw off his overcoat and sat down on the edge of the bed.

"So your daughter died."

"Died . . ." Aksinia exclaimed echoingly.

"You've changed considerably. I can guess what the loss of the
child meant to you. But I think you are torturing yourself uselessly;
you can't bring her back, and you are still young enough to have
children. Take yourself in hand and be reconciled to the loss.
After all, you haven't lost everything. All your life is still before
you."

He pressed her hand and stroked her caressingly yet authoritatively, playing on the low tones of his voice. He lowered his voice
to a whisper, and hearing Aksinia's stifled weeping, he began to
kiss her wet cheeks and eyes.

Woman's heart is susceptible to pity and kindness. Burdened
with her despair, not realizing what she was doing, Aksinia yielded
herself to him with all her strong, long dormant passion. But as
an unprecedentedly devastating, darkening wave of delight lashed
her spirit, she came to her senses and cried out sharply; losing all
sense of reason or shame, she ran out half-naked, in her shift alone,
on to the steps. Eugene hastily followed her out, leaving the door
open, pulling on his overcoat as he went. As he mounted the steps
to the terrace of the house, he smiled joyously and contentedly.
Lying in his bed, rubbing his soft breast, he thought: "From the
point of view of an honest man, what I have done is shameful,
immoral. I have robbed my neighbour; but, after all, I have risked
my life at the front. If the bullet had gone right through my head
I should have been feeding the worms now. These days one has to

live passionately for each moment as it comes." He was momentarily horrified by his own thoughts; but his imagination again conjured up the terrible moment of attack and how he had raised himself from his dead horse only to fall again, shot down by bullets. As he dropped off to sleep he decided: "Time enough for this tomorrow, but now to rest."

Next morning, finding himself alone with Aksinia in the dining-room, he went towards her, a guilty smile on his face. But she pressed against the wall and stretched out her hands, scorching him with her frenzied whisper:

"Keep away, you devil!"

Life dictates its own unwritten laws to man. Within three days Eugene went again to Aksinia at night, and she did not repel him.

Chapter 9

A small garden was attached to the eye hospital. There are many such clipped, uncomfortable gardens on the outskirts of Moscow, where the eye gets no rest from the stony, heavy dreariness of the city, and as one looks at them the memory recalls still more sharply and painfully the wild freedom of the forest. Autumn reigned in the hospital garden. The paths were covered with leaves of orange and bronze, a morning frost crumpled the flowers and flooded the patches of grass with a watery green. On fine days the patients wandered along the paths, listening to the church-bells of believing Moscow. When the weather was bad (and such days were frequent that year) they went from room to room or lay silently on their beds, boring themselves and one another.

The civilian patients were in the majority in the hospital, and the wounded soldiers were accommodated in one room. There were five of them: Jan Vareikis, a tall, ruddy-faced, blue-eyed Latvian;

Ivan Vrublevsky, a handsome young dragoon; a Siberian sharp-shooter named Kosikh; a restless little yellow soldier; and Gregor. At the end of September another was added to the number. He arrived in the afternoon and underwent an operation the same evening. A few minutes after he had been taken into the operating-room, the other patients heard the muffled sound of singing. While he was under chloroform and the surgeon was removing the remains of one eye shattered by a flying piece of shell, he was singing and cursing. After the operation he was brought into the ward where the other soldiers were quartered. When the effects of the chloro-form passed, he informed the others that he had been wounded on the German front, that his name was Garanzha, he was a machine-gunner, a Ukrainian from Chornigov province. He made a par-ticular friend of Gregor, whose bed was next to his, and after the evening inspection they would talk a long time in undertones.

"Well, how goes it?" he opened their first conversation.

"Like soot and chalk."

"What's wrong with the eye?"

"I'm having injections."

"How many have you had?"

"Eighteen, so far."

"Are they painful?"

"They aren't pleasant!"

"Ask them to cut the eye right out."

"What for? I don't want to be blind."

Gregor's jaundiced, venomous neighbour was discontented with everything. He cursed the government, the war, his own lot, the hospital food, the cook, the doctors, everything he could lay his tongue to.

"What did we peasants go to war for, that's what I want to know," he demanded.

"For the same reason as everybody else."

"Ha! You're a fool! I've got to chew it all over for you! It's the bourgeosie we're fighting for, don't you see? What are the bour-geosie? They're birds among the fruit trees."

He explained the hard words to Gregor, interlarding his speech with peppery swear-words. "Don't talk so fast. I can't understand your Ukrainian lingo. Speak more clearly," Gregor would interrupt him.

"I'm not talking so thickly as that, my boy. You think you're fighting for the Czar, but what is the Czar? The Czar's a nobody, and the Czarina's a chicken; but they're both a weight on our backs. Don't you see? The factory-owner drinks vodka, while the soldier kills the lice. The capitalist takes the profit, the worker goes bare. That's the system we've got. Serve on, Cossack, serve on! Earn a few more crosses, you great oak!"

Day after day he revealed truths hitherto unknown to Gregor, explaining the real causes of war, and jesting bitterly at the autocratic government. Gregor tried to raise objections, but Garanzha silenced him with simple, murderously simple questions, and he was forced to agree.

Most terrible of all was that Gregor began to think Garanzha was right, and that he was impotent to oppose him. He realized with horror that the intelligent and bitter Ukrainian was gradually but surely destroying all his former ideas of the Czar, the country, and his own military duty as a Cossack. Within a month of the Ukrainian's arrival all the system on which Gregor's life had been built up was a smoking ruin. It had already been rotten, eaten up with the canker of the monstrous iniquity of the war, and it needed only a jolt. That jolt was given, and Gregor's mind awoke. He tossed about, seeking a way out, a solution to his predicament, and gladly found it in Garanzha's answers.

Late one night Gregor rose from his bed and awoke Garanzha. He sat down on the edge of the Ukrainian's bed. The greenish light of a September moon streamed through the window. Garanzha's cheeks were dark with furrows, the black sockets of his eyes gleamed humidly. He yawned and wrapped his legs in the blanket.

"Aren't you asleep?" he grumbled.

"I can't sleep," Gregor replied. "Tell me this one thing: war is good for one and bad for another, isn't it?"

"Well?" the Ukrainian yawned.

"Wait!" Gregor whispered, blazing with anger. "You say we are being driven to death for the benefit of the capitalists. But what about the people? Don't they understand? Aren't there any who could tell them, who could go and say: 'Brothers, this is what you are dying for'?"

"How could they? Tell me that! Supposing you did. Here we are whispering like geese in a box, but talk out loud and you'll have a bullet in you. The people are stone deaf. The war will wake them up. After the storm will come the fine weather."

"But what's to be done about it? Tell me, you serpent! You've turned me upside-down."

"Those I can turn aside, I turn aside. You must turn your rifle without any regret. You must shoot those who sent the people into hell. You know who!" Garanzha rose in his bed and, grinding his teeth, stretched out his hand. "A great wave will rise and sweep them all away."

"So you think everything has to be turned upside-down?"

"Ha! The government must be thrown aside like an old rag. The lords must be stripped of their fleece, for they've murdered the people too long already."

"And what will you do with the war when you've got the new government? They'll still go on fighting, and if not us, then our children will. How are you going to root out war, to destroy it, when men have fought for ages?"

"True, war has gone on since the beginning of time, and will go on so long as we don't sweep away the evil government. But when every government is a workers' government they won't fight any more. That's what's got to be done. When the Germans and the French and all the others have got a workers' and peasants' government. What shall we have to fight about then? Away with frontiers, away with anger! One beautiful life all over the world. Ah!" Garanzha sighed, and twisting the ends of his whiskers, his one eye glittering, he smiled dreamily. "Grishka, I'd pour out my blood drop by drop to live to see that day."

They talked on until the dawn came. In the grey shadows Gregor fell into a troubled sleep.

September and October passed. The days dragged by interminably, filled with mortal boredom. In the morning at nine o'clock the patients were served with tea, two miserable, transparent slices of French bread, and a piece of butter the size of a fingernail. After dinner they were still hungry. In the evening they had tea again, carousing with a glass of water to break the monotony. The patients in the military ward changed. First the Siberian went, then the Latvian. At the end of October, Gregor was discharged.

The hospital surgeon examined Gregor's eyes and pronounced their sight satisfactory. But he was transferred to another hospital, as the wound in his head had unexpectedly opened and was slightly suppurating. As he said good-bye to Garanzha, Gregor remarked:

"Shall we be meeting again?"

"Two mountains never meet."

"Well, Hokhol, thank you for opening my eyes. I can see now, and I'm not good to know."

"When you get back to your regiment, tell the Cossacks what I've told you."

"I shall."

"And if you ever happen to be in Chornigov district, in Gorokhovka, ask for the smith Andrei Garanzha and I'll be glad to see you. So long, boy."

They embraced. The picture of the Ukrainian, with his one eye and the pleasant lines running from his mouth across the sandy cheeks, remained long in Gregor's memory.

Gregor spent ten days in the second hospital. He nursed unformulated decisions in his mind. The destructive poison of Garanzha's teaching was working within him, and its jaundice had deeply affected him. He talked but little with his neighbours in the ward, and a certain cautious alarm was manifest in all his movements. For some days he was feverish and lay in his bed listening to the ringing in his ears.

A high personage, one of the Imperial family, came to pay a visit to the hospital. Informed of this in the morning, the personnel of the hospital scurried about like mice in a burning granary. They re-dressed the wounded, changed the bedclothes before the time appointed, and one young doctor even tried to instruct the men how to reply to the personage and how to conduct themselves in conversation with her. The anxiety was communicated to the patients also, and some of them began to talk in whispers long before the time fixed for the visit. At noon a motor horn sounded at the front door, and, accompanied by the usual number of officials and officers, the personage passed through the hospital portals. She went the round of the wards, asking the stupid questions characteristic of one in her position and circumstances. The wounded, their eyes staring out of their heads, replied in accordance with the instructions of the junior surgeon. "Exactly so, Your Imperial Highness," and "Not at all, Your Imperial Highness." The chief surgeon supplied commentaries to their answers, squirming like a grass-snake nipped by a fork. The regal personage distributed little ikons to the soldiers. The throng of brilliant uniforms and the heavy wave of expensive perfumes came towards Gregor. He stood by his bed, unshaven, gaunt, with feverish eyes. The slight tremor of the brown skin over his angular cheekbones revealed his agitation.

"There they are!" he was thinking. "There are the people for whose pleasure we have been driven from our native villages and flung to death. Ah, the reptiles! Curse them! There are the lice on our backs. Was it for them we trampled other people's grain with our horses and killed strangers? And I crawled over the stubble and shouted? And our fear? They dragged us away from our families, starved us in barracks. Their bellies filled till they shine! I'd send you out there, curse you! Put you on a horse, under a rifle, load you with lice, feed you on rotten bread and maggoty meat!"

Gregor's eyes wandered over the officers of the retinue and rested on the marsupial cheeks of the royal personage.

"A Don Cossack, Cross of St. George," the chief surgeon smirked as he pointed to Gregor, and from the tone of his voice one would have thought it was he who had won the cross.

"From what district?" the personage inquired, holding an ikon ready.

"Vieshenska, Your Imperial Highness."

"How did you win the cross?"

Boredom and satiation lurked in the clear, empty eyes of the royal personage. Her left eyebrow was artificially raised, this being intended to give her face greater expression. For a moment Gregor felt cold, and a queer chopping sensation went on inside him. He had felt a similar sensation when going into attack. His lips twisted and quivered irresistibly.

"Excuse me. I badly want to— Your Imperial— Just a little need." Gregor swayed as though broken, and pointed under the bed.

The personage's left eyebrow rose still higher. The hand holding

the ikon half-extended towards Gregor was frozen stiff. Her queru-
lous lips hanging with astonishment, the personage turned to a
grey-haired general at her side and asked him something in English. A hardly perceptible embarrassment troubled the members of
her suite. A tall officer with a snow-white glove thrust under his
epaulet looked askance, a second looked silly; a third glanced inquiringly at his neighbour. The grey-haired general smiled respectfully and replied in English to Her Imperial Highness, and the
personage was pleased to thrust the ikon into Gregor's hand and
even to bestow on him the highest of honours, a touch on the
shoulder.

After the guests had departed, Gregor dropped on his bed and,
burying his face in his pillow, lay for some minutes, his shoulders
shaking. It was impossible to tell whether he was crying or laughing. Certain it is that he rose with dry eyes. He was immediately
summoned to the room of the chief surgeon.

"You're a canaille," the doctor began, grasping his beard in his
fingers.

"I'm not a canaille, you reptile!" Gregor replied, striding towards
the doctor. "You're not at the front." Then, recovering his self-
control, he said quietly: "Send me home."

The doctor turned and went to his writing-table, saying more
gently:

"We'll send you! You can go to the devil!"

Gregor went out, his lips trembling with a smile, his eyes glaring.
For his monstrous, unpardonable behaviour in the presence of the
royal personage he was deprived of his food for three days. But
the cook and his comrades in the ward kept him supplied.

It was evening of November 17 when Gregor arrived at the first
village in his own district. As he passed down the street, children
were singing a Cossack song under the river willows; as he listened
to the familiar words a chill gripped his heart and hardened his
eyes. Avidly sniffing in the scent of the smoke coming from the
chimneys, he strode through the village, the song following him.

"And I used to sing that song, but now my voice is gone and life
has broken off the song. Here am I going to stay with another man's
wife, no corner of my own, no home, like a wolf," he thought, walk-

ing along at a steady, tired pace and bitterly smiling at his own
savagely misdirected life. He climbed out of the village and at the
top of the hill turned to look back. The yellow light of a hanging
lamp shone through the window of the last hut, and in its light he
saw an elderly woman sitting by a spinning-wheel.

He went on, walking through the damp, frosty grass at the side
of the road. He spent the night in a little village and set out again
as soon as dawn was coming in the yard. He reached Yagodnoe in
the evening. Jumping across the fence, he went past the stables.
The sound of Sashka's coughing arrested him. He shouted:

"Old Sashka, you asleep?"

"Wait, who is that? I know the voice. Who is it?"

Sashka came out, throwing his old coat around his shoulders.

"Holy fathers! It's Grishka! Where the devil have you come
from?"

They embraced. Gazing up into Gregor's face, Sashka said:

"Come in and have a smoke."

"No, not now. I will tomorrow. I . . ."

"Come in, I tell you."

Gregor unwillingly followed him in and sat down on the plank
bed while the old man recovered from a fit of coughing.

"Well, dad, so you're still alive, still walking the earth?"

"Ah, I'm like a flint. There'll be no wear with me."

"And how's Aksinia?"

"Aksinia? Praise be, she's all right."

The old man coughed violently. Gregor guessed it was a pretence
to hide his embarrassment.

"Where did you bury Tania?"

"In the orchard under a poplar."

"Well, tell me all the news."

"My cough's been troubling me a lot, Grishka."

"Well?"

"We're all alive and well. The master drinks beyond all sense, the
fool."

"Where is Aksinia?"

"She's in the servants' quarters. You might have a smoke. Try
my tobacco, it's first rate."

"I don't want to smoke. Talk or I'll clear out! I feel—" Gregor
turned heavily, and the pallet creaked under him. "I feel you're

keeping something from me like a stone in the breast. Strike!"

"And I will strike! I haven't got the strength to be silent, Grishka, and silence would be shameful."

"Tell me, then," Gregor said, letting his hand drop caressingly on the old man's shoulder. He waited, bowing his back.

"You've been nursing a snake," Sashka suddenly exclaimed in a harsh, shrill voice. "You've been feeding a serpent. She's been playing about with Eugene."

A stream of sticky spittle ran down over the old man's chin. He wiped it away and dried his hand on his trousers.

"Are you telling the truth?" Gregor demanded.

"I've seen them with my own eyes. Every night he goes to her. I expect he's with her now."

"Oh, well!" Gregor bit his fingernail and sat with hunched shoulders for a long time, the muscles of his face working.

"A woman's like a cat," Sashka said. "She makes up to anyone who strokes her. Don't you trust them, don't give them your trust."

He rolled a cigarette and thrust it into Gregor's hand. "Smoke!" he said.

Gregor took a couple of pulls at the cigarette, then put it out with his fingers. He went out without a word. He stopped by the window of the servants' quarters, panting heavily, and raised his hand several times to knock. But each time his hand fell as though struck away. When at last he did knock he tapped at first with his finger; but then, losing patience, he threw himself against the wall and beat at the window furiously with his fist. The glass rang with the blows, and the blue, nocturnal light shimmered in the pane.

Aksinia's frightened face appeared at the window for an instant; then she opened the door. At the sight of Gregor she screamed. He embraced her.

"You knocked so hard you terrified me. I wasn't expecting you. My dear . . ."

"I'm frozen."

Aksinia felt his body shuddering violently, although his hands were feverishly hot. She fussed about unnecessarily, lighted the lamp and ran about the room, a downy shawl around her shoulders. Finally she lit a fire in the stove.

"I wasn't expecting you. It's so long since you wrote. I thought you would never come. Did you receive my last letter? I was going

to send you a parcel, but then I thought I'd wait to see if I received
a letter. . . ."

Gregor sat down on the bench without taking off his greatcoat.
His unshaven cheeks burned, and a heavy shadow fell from the
cowl of his coat. He began to unfasten the cowl, but suddenly
turned to fidget with his tobacco-pouch and searched his pockets for
paper. With intangible yearning he ran his eyes over Aksinia's face.

She had devilishly improved during his absence, he thought. Her
beautiful head was carried with a new, authoritative poise, and
only her eyes and the large, fluffy ringlets of her hair were the
same. Her destructive, fiery beauty did not belong to him. Hardly,
when she was the mistress of the master's son!

"You don't look like a kitchen-maid, you're more like a housekeeper," he remarked.

She gave him a startled look and laughed forcedly.

Dragging his pack behind him, Gregor went towards the door.

"Where are you going?"

"To have a smoke."

On the steps Gregor opened his pack and from the bottom drew
out a hand-painted kerchief carefully wrapped in a clean shirt. He
had bought it from a Jewish trader in Zhitomir for two rubles and
had preserved it as the apple of his eye, occasionally pulling it out
and enjoying its wealth of rainbow colours, foretasting the rapture
with which Aksinia would be possessed when he should spread it
open before her. A miserable gift! Could he compete in presents with
the son of a rich landowner? Struggling with a spasm of dry sob-
bing, he tore the kerchief into little pieces and pushed them under
the step. He threw the pack on the bench in the porch and went
back to the room.

"Sit down and I'll pull your boots off, Grishka," Aksinia said.

With white hands long divorced from hard work she struggled
with Gregor's heavy army boots. Falling at his knees, she wept long
and silently. Gregor let her weep to her heart's content, then asked:

"What's the matter? Aren't you glad to see me?"

In bed he quickly fell asleep. Aksinia undressed and went out
to the steps. She stood there in the cold, piercing wind, under the
funeral dirge of the northern blast, embracing the damp pillar, not
changing her position, until dawn came.

In the morning Gregor threw his greatcoat across his shoulders and went to the house. The old master was standing on the steps, dressed in a fur jacket and a yellow Astrakhan cap.

"Why, there he is, the Chevalier of St. George! But you're a man, my friend!" He saluted Gregor and stretched out his hand. "Staying long?" he asked.

"Two weeks, Your Excellency."

"We buried your daughter. A pity—a pity. . . ."

Gregor was silent. Eugene came on to the steps, drawing on his gloves.

"Why, it's Gregor. Where have you arrived from?"

Gregor's eyes darkened, but he smiled. "Back on leave, from Moscow."

"You were wounded in the eye, weren't you? I heard about it. What a brave lad he's grown, hasn't he, Papa?"

He nodded to Gregor and turned towards the stables, calling to the coachman:

"The horses, Nikitich!"

Nikitich finished harnessing the horse and, giving Gregor an unfriendly look, led the old grey trotting-horse to the steps. The frostbound earth crumbled under the wheels of the light droshky.

"Your Excellency, let me drive you for the sake of old times." Gregor turned to Eugene, smiling beseechingly.

"The poor chap doesn't guess," Eugene thought, smiling with satisfaction, and his eyes glittered behind his glasses.

"All right, jump up," he assented.

"What, hardly arrived and you're already leaving your young wife?" Old Listnitsky smiled benevolently.

Gregor laughed. "A wife isn't a bear. She won't run off into the forest," he replied.

He mounted the driver's seat, thrust the knout beneath him, and gathered up the reins:

"Ah, I'll give you a drive, Eugene Nicholaivich!"

"Drive well and you shall have tea money."

"Haven't I already got enough to be thankful for? I'm grateful to you for feeding—my Aksinia—for giving her—a piece—"

Gregor's voice suddenly broke, and a vague, unpleasant suspicion troubled Eugene. "Surely he doesn't know? Of course not!

How could he?" He threw himself back in his seat and lit a cigarette.

"Don't be long," old Listnitsky called after them.

Gregor pulled with the reins at the horse's mouth and urged it to
its topmost speed. Within fifteen minutes they had crossed the rise,
and the house was out of sight. In the very first valley they came
to, Gregor jumped down and pulled the knout from under the seat.

"What are you doing?" Eugene frowned.

"I'll show you!"

Gregor waved the knout and brought it down with terrible force
across Eugene's face. Then, seizing it by the lash, he beat the
officer with the butt on the face and arms, giving him no time to
bestir himself. A fragment of the glass from his pince-nez cut
Eugene above the brow, and a little stream of blood flowed into
his eyes. At first he covered his face with his hands, but the blows
grew more frequent. He jumped up, his face disfigured with blood
and fury, and attempted to defend himself; but Gregor fell back
and paralysed his arm with a blow on the wrist.

"That's for Aksinia! That's for me! For Aksinia! Another for Aksinia! For me!"

The knout whistled, the blows slapped softly. At last Gregor
threw Eugene down on the hard ruts of the road and rolled him
on the ground, beating him bestially with the iron-shod heels of
his boots. When he had no strength to do more, he got on to the
droshky seat and, sawing at the horse's mouth, galloped it back.
He left the droshky by the gate, and seizing the knout, stumbling
over the edges of his open greatcoat, he flew into the servants'
quarters.

At the sound of the door flung open, Aksinia glanced round.

"You reptile! You bitch!" The knout whistled and curled around
her face.

Panting, Gregor ran into the yard and, heedless of Sashka's questionings, left the estate. When he had covered a mile he was overtaken by Aksinia. Panting violently, she walked along silently at
his side, occasionally pulling at his sleeve. At a fork in the road,
by a brown wayside shrine, she said in a strange, distant voice:

"Gregor, forgive me!"

He bared his teeth and, hunching his shoulders, turned up the
cowl of his greatcoat. Aksinia was left standing by the shrine. He

did not look back once and did not see her hand stretched out to him.

At the crest of the hill above Tatarsk he noticed in astonishment that he was still carrying the knout; he threw it away, then strode down into the village. Faces were pressed against the windows, amazed to see him, and the women he met bowed low as he passed.

At the gate to his own yard a lanky, black-eyed, good-looking girl ran to meet him, flung her arms around his neck, and buried her face on his breast. Pressing her cheeks with his hands, he raised her head and recognized Dunia.

Pantaleimon Prokofflevich limped down the steps, and Gregor could hear his mother weeping aloud in the hut. With his left hand he embraced his father; Dunia was kissing his right hand.

The almost painfully familiar creak of the steps, and Gregor was in the porch. His ageing mother ran with the activity of a girl, wet the strings of his greatcoat with her tears, and inseparably embraced her son, muttering her own mother language, disconnected, untranslatable into words; while by the door, holding on to it to avoid falling, stood pallid Natalia. With a tortured smile she dropped, cut down by Gregor's hurried, distracted glance.

That night in bed Pantaleimon gave his wife a dig in the ribs and whispered:

"Go quietly and see whether they're lying together or not."

"I made up their bed on the bedstead."

"But go on and look, look!"

Ilinichna got up and peeped through a crack in the door leading to the best room.

"They're together," she said when she returned.

"Well, God be praised! God be praised!" the old man whimpered, raising himself on his elbow and crossing himself.

Chapter 10

1916. October. Night. Rain and wind. The trenches in the alder-grown marshes of Polesie. Barbed-wire entanglements in front. A freezing slush in the trenches. The wet sheet-iron of an observation post gleams faintly. Lights here and there in the dug-outs.

At the entrance to one of the officers' dug-outs a thickset officer halted for a moment, his wet fingers slipping over his greatcoat fasteners. He hurriedly unfastened them, shook the water from the collar, wiped his boots on the heap of straw trampled into the mud at the entrance, and only then pushed open the door, stooped, and entered the dug-out.

A yellow band of light streaming from a little paraffin lamp gleamed oilily on his face. An officer in an open jacket rose, passed his hand over his rumpled grey hair, and yawned.

"Raining?" he asked.

"Yes," the visitor replied, and, removing his greatcoat, hung it together with his sopping wet cap on a nail by the door. "You're warm in here!"

"We've had the fire lighted recently. It's bad, though, that the water is oozing up through the floor. The rain will outlast us. What do you think, Bunchuk?"

Rubbing his hairy hands, Bunchuk stooped and squatted down by the stove.

"Put some planks down over the floor," he replied. "We're fine and dry in our dug-out. We could walk about with bare feet. Where's Listnitsky?"

"He's asleep. He came back from a round of the guards and lay down at once."

"All right to wake him up?"

"Go ahead. We'll have a game of chess."

Bunchuk stroked the rain from his heavy brows with his index finger, examined the finger attentively, and called quietly:

"Eugene Nicholaivich!"

"Well?" Listnitsky raised himself on his elbow.

"Have a game of chess?"

Eugene dropped his legs from the bed and rubbed hard with his soft white palm at his chest.

As the first game was nearing its end, two officers of the fifth company, Captain Kalmikov and Subaltern Chubov, entered.

"News!" Kalmikov cried as he crossed the threshold. "The regiment will probably be withdrawn."

"Where did you hear that?" the grey-haired officer, Lieutenant Merkulov, smiled disbelievingly.

"The commander of the battery has just informed us over the telephone. How did he know? Well, he only returned from the divisional staff yesterday."

"It would be great to have a bath," Chubov said, with a note of ecstasy in his voice.

"You're damp in here, gentlemen, very damp," Kalmikov grumbled, looking around the log-timbered walls and the squelching earthen floor.

"We've got the marsh right at our side," Merkulov said apologetically.

"Thank the Almighty that here in the marsh you're as comfortable as if you were in Abraham's bosom!" Bunchuk intervened. "In other districts they're attacking, but here we fire one round a week."

"Better to be attacking than rotting in this hole."

"They don't keep the Cossacks to get them wiped out in attacks. You ought to know better, Captain Merkulov," Bunchuk observed.

"Then what are we kept for, in your opinion?"

"At the right moment the government will play its old game of maintaining itself on the backs of the Cossacks."

"Now you're talking heresy." Kalmikov waved his hand.

"How is it heresy? You can't deny the truth!"

"How is it the truth?"

"Why, everybody knows it's the truth. Why don't you admit it too?"

"Attention, gentlemen!" Chubov shouted, and, bowing theatrically, pointed to Bunchuk. "Cornet Bunchuk will now begin to interpret the Social-Democratic dream-book!"

"You don't like the Social Democrats, do you?" Bunchuk laughed as he caught Chubov's eye. "1 tell you that as soon as the trench warfare began, the Cossack regiments were distributed in sheltered spots and are being kept quietly until the right moment arrives."

"And then?" Listnitsky asked as he gathered up the chessmen.

"And then, when unrest sets in at the front—and that is inevitable; the soldiers are beginning to get fed up with the war, the growth of desertion shows that—then the Cossacks will be called upon to suppress the revolts. The government holds the Cossacks like a stone in its hand. At the right moment it will attempt to break the head of the Revolution with that stone."

"Your assumptions are rather shaky," Listnitsky objected. "To begin with, it is impossible to predict the course of events. How do you know about the coming unrest and so on? But put this case: supposing the Allies shatter the Germans and the war ends brilliantly, then what role will you assign to the Cossacks?"

Bunchuk smiled dryly. "Something not at all like an end, but all the more brilliant. . . ."

"When did you get back from leave?" Kalmikov asked.

"Two days ago," Bunchuk replied.

"Where did you spend it?"

"In Petersburg."

"And what is the situation like there? Ah, what the devil wouldn't I give to spend just one short week in Petersburg!"

"You'd find little to comfort you," Bunchuk said, weighing his words carefully. "There's a shortage of food. In the workers' districts there is hunger, discontent, and seething unrest."

"We shan't come happily out of this war. What do you think, gentlemen?" Merkulov looked interrogatively around.

"The Russo-Japanese war gave birth to the Revolution of 1905. This war will end with a new revolution, and not only revolution, but civil war," Bunchuk replied.

Listnitsky made an indefinite gesture as though about to interrupt him, then rose and paced up and down the dug-out, frowning. With restrained anger in his voice he said:

"I'm astonished to find such men as he among us officers." He pointed to Bunchuk. "I'm astonished because to this very day I cannot clearly gather what is his attitude to his country, and to the war. The other day he spoke very vaguely, yet sufficiently clearly to let us understand that he wants to see us defeated. Did I understand you aright, Bunchuk?"

"I am in favour of our being defeated."

"But why? In my view, no matter what your political opinions may be, to wish the defeat of your own country is state treason. It is dishonourable to any decent man."

"Do you remember that the Social-Democratic members of the Duma agitated against the government and so have conduced to the country's defeat?" Merkulov intervened.

"Do you share their views, Bunchuk?" Listnitsky asked.

"If I say I am in favour of our being defeated it is obvious that I do, and it would be absurd for me, a member of the Social-Democratic Bolshevik Party, not to share the view of my fellow party-members in the Duma. I am very surprised that you, Eugene Nicholaivich, with your intelligence, are so ignorant politically."

"First and foremost I am a soldier devoted to the monarchy. I am revolted by the very sight of 'Socialist comrades,'" Listnitsky declared.

"First and foremost you are a blockhead, and after that a self-satisfied military brute," Bunchuk thought, and the smile faded from his face.

"We officers have been placed in an exceptional situation," Merkulov said as though apologizing. "We have all held ourselves apart from politics; we live on the outskirts of the village, so to speak."

Captain Kalmikov sat stroking his drooping whiskers, his burning Mongolian eyes gleaming. Chubov lay on a bed, staring at a drawing by Merkulov fastened to the wall. It represented a half-naked woman with the face of a Magdalen, languorously and depravedly smiling as she gazed at her bare breasts. With two fingers of her left hand she was drawing aside one nipple, and the little finger was cocked back cautiously. Under her half-closed eyelids lay a shadow and the warm gleam of her translucent pupils. One slightly raised shoulder held up her slipping chemise, and a soft shade of light fell into the hollows below her collar-bones. There was so much natural grace and real truth in her pose, so unexpectedly beautiful were the soft tones, that Chubov involuntarily smiled, delighting in the masterly sketch and not following the drift of the conversation at all.

"That's fine!" he exclaimed, tearing his eyes away. His remark came at a very inopportune moment, for Bunchuk had just said:

"Czarism will be destroyed, you can rest assured."

Rolling a cigarette and smiling caustically, Listnitsky stared first at Bunchuk, then at Chubov.

"Merkulov, you're a real artist!" Chubov winked.

"It's only the merest sketch. . . ."

"We may lose a few hundred thousand soldiers, but it is the duty of everyone whom this country has nurtured to defend his fatherland from enslavement." Listnitsky puffed at his cigarette and removed his pince-nez to clean the glasses, staring the while at Bunchuk with his shortsighted eyes.

"The workers have no fatherland," Bunchuk stamped the words out. "There is the deepest of truth in those words of Marx. We never have had, and we still have no fatherland. This accursed country gave you your food and drink, but we workers grow like the wormwood on the steppe. . . . We and you can't flourish together."

He drew a large packet of papers from his pocket and rummaged among them, standing with his back to Listnitsky. Then, going to the table, he spread open a newspaper yellow with age.

"Would you like to listen?" He turned to Eugene.

"What to?"

"This is an article on the war. I'll read an extract. I'm not very well educated, as you know, and it puts it much better than I could:

"The bourgeoisie is deluding the masses by cloaking the imperialist spoliation with the old ideology of a 'national' war. The working class exposes this deception, raising the cry of transforming the imperialist into civil war. Of course, such a transformation is not easy and cannot be accomplished 'at the wish' of individual parties. But that is the transformation which lies in the objective conditions of capitalism, and of the period of the end of capitalism in particular. And in this direction, and this direction alone, must the Socialists carry on their activities. No votes for war credits, no support of the chauvinism of 'their own' country, no restriction to legal forms of struggle when a crisis has arisen and the bourgeoisie has itself repealed the legality it itself created: that is the line of

activity which leads to civil war and which will lead to it sooner or later in the European conflagration.

"The war is no accident, it is not a 'sin,' as the Christian parsons think, preaching patriotism, humanity, and peace no worse than the opportunists, but an inevitable stage of capitalism, just as natural a form of capitalist life as is peace. The war of our times is a war of peoples. But from that truth it follows not that we must swim with the 'popular' current of chauvinism, but that in wartime, and in the war, and in warlike fashion the class contradictions rending the peoples continue to exist and will manifest themselves. Refusal of military service, striking against the war, and suchlike are simple stupidity, a poor and cowardly dream of unarmed struggle against the armed bourgeoisie, a sighing after the destruction of capitalism without a desperate civil war or series of wars. The duty of the Socialist is the propaganda of class struggle even in the war; activity directed to the transformation of the people's war into civil war is the only work for Socialists in the period of the imperialist armed clash of the bourgeoisie of all nations. Down with the sanctimonious sentimental and stupid sighs for 'peace at any price.' Raise the banner of civil war! Imperialism has put the destiny of European culture to the hazard; after the present war, if it is not followed by a series of successful revolutions, will quickly come further wars; the legend of the 'last war' is an empty, dangerous legend, a petty suburban myth. . . ."

Bunchuk had read slowly and quietly, but as he came to the last sentences he raised the heavy, iron ring of his voice and ended:

"If not today, then tomorrow; if not during the present war, then after it; if not during this war, then in the next that follows, the proletarian banner of civil war will gather round it not only the hundreds of thousands of class-conscious workers, but the millions of semi-proletariat now deluded with chauvinism, and the petty bourgeoisie whom the horrors of war will not only terrify and crush, but educate, teach, awaken, organize, temper, and prepare for the war against the bourgeoisie both of 'their own' country and of 'alien countries.'"

When he had finished there was a long silence. Then Merkulov asked:

"That wasn't printed in Russia, was it?"

"No"

"Where, then?"

"In Geneva. It appeared in the thirty-third number of the *Social-Democrat* for 1914."

"And who wrote the article?"

"Lenin."

"He's the leader of the Bolsheviks, isn't he?"

Bunchuk did not reply. He carefully folded up the paper, his fingers trembling a little. Merkulov let loose the impending storm by remarking:

"He has a great gift of persuasion. . . . Damn it, there's a lot to think about in what he says."

Obviously greatly agitated, Listnitsky buttoned up the collar of his shirt and, pacing swiftly up and down from corner to corner, poured out a fine hail of words.

"That article is a pitiful attempt on the part of a man flung out of his native country to influence the course of history. In our age of reality prophecy does not enjoy much success, still less when it is of that sort. The true Russian passes by these hysterical babblings with contempt. 'The transformation of the war of peoples into civil war'! Damn it, what contemptible rot!"

Listnitsky stared with knitted brows at Bunchuk, who was still bent over his packet of papers. Eugene spoke fierily, but his low, thin voice made no impression.

"Bunchuk!" Kalmikov exclaimed. "One moment, Listnitsky! Bunchuk, listen! Let us admit that this war will be transformed into a civil war. But then what? You'll overthrow the monarchy. But what sort of government do you propose to set up in its place?"

"The government of the working class."

"A Parliament, do you mean?"

"Hardly!" Bunchuk smiled.

"Well, what, then?"

"A workers' dictatorship."

"Now we've got it! But the intelligentsia, the peasantry? What part will they play?"

"The peasantry will follow us, and part of the intelligentsia also. The others—this is what we shall do with the others." With a swift movement he screwed up a paper in his hand and threw it away, saying through his teeth: "That's what we'll do with them!"

"What the devil did you volunteer for the front and even reach officer's rank for? How can you reconcile that with your views? Here's a man against the war, against the destruction of his class brothers, and he's an officer!" Kalmikov slapped his hands against the legs of his boots and laughed out loud.

"How many German workers have you slaughtered with your machine-guns?" Listnitsky inquired.

Bunchuk rapidly turned over his packet of papers and, still bent over the table, replied:

"How many German workers have I shot? That's—a question. I came voluntarily because I'd have had to come in any case. I think the knowledge I have gained here in the trenches will be of some service later on. Listen:

"Take the modern army. It is one of the splendid examples of organization. And that organization is good only because it is flexible and because it simultaneously knows how to give millions of men a single will. Today those millions of men are sitting at home in various parts of the country. Tomorrow the mobilization order is issued, and they are assembled at the appointed centres. Today they lie in the trenches, and lie for sometimes months on end. Tomorrow they go into the attack. Today they perform miracles, hiding from bullets and shrapnel. Tomorrow they perform miracles in open battle. Today their leading detachments lay mines under the earth. Tomorrow they march for miles at the direction of aeroplanes flying above the earth. That is what is called organization, when in the name of a single purpose, inspired by a single will, millions of men change the forms of their social life and their activity, change the place and the methods of their activity, change their weapons and arms in accordance with the modified circumstances and demands of the struggle. The same thing applies to the struggle of the working class against the bourgeoisie. Today a revolutionary situation is not present. . . ."

"But what do you mean by 'situation'?" Chubov interrupted.

Bunchuk stared at him as though he had only just been awakened from sleep and rubbed his brow with his finger, trying to grasp the question.

"I asked, what do you mean by 'situation'?"

"I understood all right, but it's difficult for me to explain." Bunchuk smiled a simple, childlike smile. It was strange to see it on his big, moody face. It was as though a ray of sunlight had danced across an autumnal, rain-swept field. "A situation is a position, a combination of circumstances. That's clear, isn't it?"

Listnitsky waved his hand vaguely. "Read on," he said.

"Today a revolutionary situation is not present, there are not the conditions for ferment among the masses, for an intensification of their activity. Today they hand you a ballot—take it. Know how to organize yourselves in order to strike your enemies with it, and not in order to introduce into Parliament, into the comfortable jobs, men who grip their chairs in fear of prison. Tomorrow they have deprived you of your electoral rights and have given you arms and a quick-firing gun splendidly equipped in accordance with all the latest developments of technique. Take this weapon of death and destruction; don't listen to the sentimental vapourings of those afraid of war. There is still too much left in the world that has to be destroyed with fire and sword for the sake of the emancipation of the working class; and if indignation and despair increase in the masses, if a revolutionary situation develops, prepare to create new organizations and to put into motion such serviceable weapons of death and destruction against your government and your bourgeoisie. . . ."

Bunchuk was interrupted by a knock and the entry of the sergeant-major of the fifth company.

"Your Excellency," he turned to Kalmikov, "an orderly from the regimental staff."

Kalmikov and Chubov threw on their greatcoats and went out. Merkulov sat down to draw. Listnitsky continued his pacing up and down the dug-out, fingering his moustaches and deep in thought. Shortly afterwards Bunchuk also took his departure. He made his way through the slippery mud of the trenches, his left hand holding the edges of his collar together, his right keeping down his greatcoat. The wind streamed along the narrow trench, clinging to the ledges, whistling and eddying. His face wore a sad smile. When he reached his dug-out he was again wet through with the rain and smelling of decaying alder leaves. The commander of the machine-gun detachment was asleep, his face still showing the

traces of three sleepless nights spent at cards. Bunchuk rummaged
in the kit-bag he had kept since the days of his service as a private
soldier, arranged a pile of papers close to the door, and set fire to
them. He put two tins of meat and some handfuls of revolver bullets
into his pocket, then went out again. The wind caught at the momentarily opened door, sent the grey ash of the burnt papers flying,
and blew out the smoking lamp.

After Bunchuk's departure Listnitsky strode up and down for
some time in silence, then went across to the table. Merkulov was
still drawing, and from under his pencil-point the face of Bunchuk,
wearing his customary thin smile, was beginning to stare from the
white square of paper.

"He's got a strong face!" Merkulov remarked, turning to Listnitsky.

"Well, what do you think?" Eugene asked.

"The devil knows!" Merkulov replied, guessing the significance
of the question. "He's a strange fellow. He's given himself away
completely now, but previously I didn't know how to decipher
him. You know he enjoys tremendous popularity with the Cossacks,
especially among the machine-gunners. Have you noticed that?"

"M, yes," Listnitsky answered, a little indefinitely.

"The machine-gunners are Bolsheviks to the last man. He's certainly succeeded in winning them over. I was astonished when he
showed his hand today. What did he do it for? He knows that none
of us can share his views. Yet he gives himself away like that. And
he isn't a hot-head either. He's dangerous."

Still pondering on Bunchuk's strange behaviour, Merkulov
pushed away his drawing and began to undress. He hung his grey
stockings over the stove, wound up his watch, and lay down, smoking a cigarette. He quickly fell asleep. Listnitsky sat down on the
stool Merkulov had vacated, and on the other side of the drawing
of Bunchuk wrote in his flowing hand:

Your Excellency:

*The suppositions which I previously communicated to you have
now been completely confirmed. In a talk today with the officers
of our regiment (Captain Kalmikov and Subaltern Chubov of the*

fifth and Lieutenant Merkulov of the third company being present in addition to myself) Cornet Bunchuk, for reasons which I have to admit I do not fully understand, explained the tasks which he is carrying out in accordance with his political convictions and undoubtedly on the instruction of his party. He had with him a number of papers of an illegal nature. Without doubt Cornet Bunchuk is carrying on underground activities in our regiment (we may suppose that that is why he joined the regiment as a volunteer), and the machine-gunners have been the first object of his attentions. They have been demoralized. His dangerous influence is beginning to tell on the morale of the regiment. There have been cases of refusal to carry out military tasks, as I have already informed the divisional staff. He has only just returned from leave, bringing back with him a large quantity of subversive literature. He will now endeavour to carry on his work with greater intensity.

On the basis of the foregoing I come to the conclusions: (1) That Cornet Bunchuk's guilt is fully established. (2) In order to stop his revolutionary activities it is necessary to arrest him immediately and to bring him before a field court martial. (3) The machine-gun detachment must be broken up quickly, the more dangerous of them being removed and the others either sent to the rear or dispersed over other regiments.

I ask you not to overlook my sincere desire to serve my country and the monarchy.

Captain Eugene Listnitsky

Sector No. 7
November 2, 1916

Early next morning Listnitsky sent his report by orderly to the divisional staff and after breakfast went out into the trenches. Beyond the slippery bank of the earthworks a mist was swaying over the marsh, hanging in shreds as though caught on the barbs of the wire entanglements. A sticky mud covered the bottom of the trench to the depth of an inch. Little brown streams were crawling out of the embrasures. The Cossacks, in wet, mud-plastered greatcoats, were boiling pots of tea on sheet iron from the earthworks, smoking, and squatting on their heels, their rifles leaned against the walls of the trench.

"How many times have you been told not to dare to light fires on the sheet iron? Don't you understand, you swine?" Eugene shouted as he reached the first group of Cossacks.

Two of them rose unwillingly; the others continued to squat and smoke, the edges of their greatcoats gathered up under them. A swarthy, bearded Cossack, with a silver ear-ring swinging at his ear, replied as he thrust a handful of brushwood under the pot:

"We'd be very glad to do without the sheet iron. But how are we to light a fire otherwise, Your Excellency? Look at the mud."

"Pull that iron out at once!"

"What, so we're to sit here hungry? Is that it?" a broad-faced, pockmarked Cossack asked, frowning and not looking the officer in the face.

"I tell you to pull that iron out!" With the toe of his boot Eugene kicked away the burning brushwood from under the pot.

Smiling angrily and confusedly, the Cossack with the ear-ring poured the water out of the pot, muttering:

"You've had your tea, boys. . . ."

The Cossacks stared silently after the captain as he strode off. Little fires gleamed in the bearded Cossack's eyes.

In the sector manned by the first troop Listnitsky was overtaken by Merkulov. He came up panting, his new leather jerkin creaking and exuding the strong scent of home-grown tobacco. He called Eugene aside and said hurriedly:

"Heard the news? Bunchuk deserted last night."

"Bunchuk? What's that?"

"Deserted. Understand? The commander of the machine-gun detachment, who is in the same dug-out, told me he didn't return after leaving us. So he must have cleared out on leaving our dug-out. What do you think of that?"

Listnitsky stood polishing his glasses and frowning.

"You seem to be disturbed." Merkulov stared inquisitively into his face.

"I? Are you in your senses? Why should I be disturbed? I was only taken aback by the unexpected news."

A couple of days later the sergeant-major came with a worried look on his face into Listnitsky's dug-out and with much humming and hawing informed him:

"This morning, Your Excellency, the Cossacks found these papers in the trenches. It's a bit awkward. . . . And I thought it best to report to you. . . ."

"What papers?" Listnitsky asked, rising from his bed.

The sergeant-major handed him some crumpled typewritten leaflets. Listnitsky read:

Proletariat of all countries, unite!
Comrade Soldiers:

Two years this accursed war has lasted. Two years you have rotted in the trenches, defending other men's interests. Two years the blood of the workers and peasants of all nations has been poured out. Hundreds of thousands of killed and wounded, hundreds of thousands of widows and orphans—these are the results of this slaughter. What are you fighting for? Whose interests are you defending? The Czarist government has sent millions of soldiers into the firing line in order to seize new lands and to oppress the peoples of those lands as it already oppresses enslaved Poland and other nationalities. The world industrialists are dividing the markets by armed force, and you, in the struggle for their interests, are going to death and are killing toiling men like yourselves.

Enough of shedding your brothers' blood! Awake, toilers! Your enemy is not the Austrian and German soldiers, but your own Czar, your own industrialist and landowner. Turn your rifles against them. Fraternize with the German and Austrian soldiers. Across the wire entanglements which separate you as though you were animals, stretch out your hands to one another. You are brothers in labour, the bloody calluses of your toil are still on your hands. Down with the autocracy! Down with the imperialist war! Hurrah for the unity of the toilers of all the world!

Listnitsky read the leaflet with rising anger. "Now it's begun!" he thought, gripped by a senseless hatred and overwhelmed with his presentiments. He at once communicated the discovery by telephone to the regimental commander.

"What are your instructions in the matter, Your Excellency?" he asked.

"Take the sergeant-major and the troop officers and carry out a search at once. Search everybody, not excluding the officers. I'll ask the divisional staff today when they propose to relieve the regiment. I'll hurry them up. If you find anything in the course of the search, inform me at once."

"I think it's the work of the machine-gunners," Eugene said.

"You do? I'll order the commander at once to search his Cossacks."

Assembling the troop officers in his dug-out, Listnitsky informed them of the regimental commander's order.

"How monstrous!" Merkulov exclaimed indignantly. "Are we going to search one another?"

"Your turn first, Listnitsky," a young subaltern remarked.

"No, we'll throw dice for it."

"Joking aside, gentlemen," Listnitsky interrupted. "Our old man's gone too far, of course; the officers in our regiment are as pure as Cæsar's wife. There was only Cornet Bunchuk, and he's deserted. But we must search the Cossacks. Someone fetch the sergeant-major."

The sergeant-major, an elderly Cossack with three bars to his Cross of St. George, entered. He coughed and glanced uneasily from one to another of the officers.

"Who are the suspicious characters in the company? Who do you think would have left these leaflets about?" Eugene demanded.

"There's no one in our company, Your Excellency," the man replied confidently.

"But the leaflets were found in our sector. Have any men from another company been in our trenches?"

"No, sir."

"We'll go and search every man." Merkulov waved his hand and turned towards the door.

The search began. The Cossacks' faces expressed every shade of feeling. Some frowned in amazement, others looked at the officers in alarm, yet others laughed as the officers rummaged in their miserable belongings. The search yielded almost no results. Only one Cossack had a crumpled copy of the manifesto in his greatcoat pocket.

"Have you read this?" Merkulov demanded.

"I picked it up for a smoke." The Cossack smiled without raising his downcast eyes.

"What are you grinning at?" Listnitsky shouted furiously, turning livid and striding towards the man. His eyelids blinked nervously beneath his glasses.

The Cossack's face turned crimson, and the smile vanished as though swept away by the wind:

"Excuse me, Your Excellency. I can hardly read. I picked it up because I haven't any paper for cigarettes, and I saw this lying about and I picked it up." The man spoke in a loud, aggrieved, almost angry tone.

Listnitsky spat and turned away, the other officers trailing after him.

The next day the regiment was withdrawn and stationed some seven miles behind the front line. Two of the machine-gun detachment were arrested and court-martialled, some of the others were transferred to reserve regiments, and some distributed over the regiments of the Second Cossack Division. After some days' rest the regiment was brought into comparatively good order. The Cossacks washed and cleaned themselves up thoroughly and even shaved. Nor did they have to resort to the method used in the trenches, which consisted in setting light to the hair on the face, and as soon as the flame began to burn the cheek passing a wet towel over it and wiping the burnt hair off. This method had come to be called "singeing the pig," after a troop barber had asked one of his clients: "Shall I singe you like a pig, or how?"

The regiment rested, and the Cossacks seemed outwardly light-hearted and in splendid fettle. But Listnitsky and the other officers knew that the mood was only superficial and fleeting, like a fine day in November. As soon as any rumour of a return to the front ran through the regiment, the facial expressions changed, and discontent, strain, and morose unfriendliness came uppermost. The mortal weariness and strain made themselves felt and engendered moral instability and apathy.

Listnitsky knew well how terrible man can be when, dominated by such a mood, he struggles to some purpose. In 1915 he had seen a company of soldiers sent five times into attack, suffering terrible losses and still receiving again and again the command to renew the offensive. The remnants of the company had at last arbitrarily withdrawn from the sector and had marched towards the rear. Listnitsky's company had been ordered to stop them, and when, spreading out in a chain, the Cossacks had attempted to halt the movement, the soldiers had opened fire. Not more than sixty of them were left, and Listnitsky had noted the senselessly desperate bravery with which these sixty had defended themselves, had fallen under the Cossacks' sabres, marching on to death, to destruction, resolved that it mattered not where death came to them.

The incident had left its menacing memory, and Listnitsky anxiously and fearfully studied the Cossacks' faces, wondering whether they also would turn round one day and retreat, restrained by nothing but death. And as he noticed their tired, sullen glances he had to admit that they would.

The Cossacks had changed radically since the early days of the war. Even their songs were new, born of the war and expressing a sombre joylessness. As he passed by the spacious shed of the factory in which his company was quartered he most frequently heard one yearning, indescribably mournful song. Listnitsky would stop to listen, and the simple sorrow of the song would move him strongly. A string was tautened with the increasing beat of his heart, and the low timbre of the voice plucked the string, setting it vibrating painfully. Listnitsky would stand a little way off, staring into the autumnal gloom of the evening and feeling his eyes moisten with tears.

Only once during the whole time the regiment was resting did Listnitsky hear the brave words of an old Cossack song. He was returning from his usual evening stroll, and as he passed the shed a noise and the sounds of half-drunken voices reached his ears. He guessed that the quartermaster-sergeant, who had been to the neighbouring town for provisions, had brought back some illicit spirits and had treated the Cossacks. And now they were quarrelling and laughing at something or other. He heard the wild and piercing whistle of the Cossacks and the strong melody of the song when still some way off.

He involuntarily smiled as he listened, and tried to bring his steps into time with the rhythm. "I don't suppose the infantry yearn for home so strongly as the Cossacks," he thought; but cold reason objected that the infantry soldier was no different. Yet undoubtedly the Cossacks reacted more painfully to the enforced sitting in the

trenches, for the very nature of their service had accustomed them
to continual movement. And for two years they had been engaged
in trench warfare, or in marking time in one spot, in continual,
fruitless attempts to advance. Even so they would hold out; if they
did break down, they would be the last to do so. They were a little
nation in themselves, military by tradition, and not factory or
peasant riffraff.

As though deliberately to undeceive him, a strained voice began
to sing another song. Other Cossacks took it up, and once more
Listnitsky heard the Cossacks' yearning translated into song:

> The young officer prays to God.
> The young Cossack asks to go home.
> "Oh, young officer,
> Let me go home,
> Let me go home
> To my father.
> To my father and mother
> And my young wife."

Chapter 11

The zone from Vladimir-Volhynsk to Kovel in Volhynia was held
by the Special Army. The Special Army was really Number Thir-
teen, but as even generals of high rank suffered from superstitious
prejudices, it was called the "Special Army." During the early days
of October 1916, plans were made for an advance in this area, and
the way was prepared with artillery operations.

The command of the eightieth army corps of the Special Army
was instructed to throw two divisions into the area of the offensive.
Among those transferred was the 318th Chornogorsk Regiment.
The regiment was withdrawn from the front line on the Stokhod
River at night and, after a demonstrative movement in the opposite
direction, turned round and marched back behind the lines towards
the active zone.

Next morning the regiment was distributed through a forest, in abandoned dug-outs, and here for four days they were instructed in the French method of attack, advancing in half-companies instead of battalions. Then they marched on again. For three days they passed through forests, through glades, along wild woodland paths scarred with the marks of cannon-wheels. A light, patchy mist, stirred by the wind, flowed and clung to the tops of the pines and eddied among the firs over the blue-green of the steaming marshes. A drizzling rain fell continually, and the men were wet through and in sullen mood. They reached a village not far from the zone of the offensive and rested for some days, preparing for the mortal journey.

At the same time a special Cossack company, accompanied by the staff of the Eightieth Division, was moving down towards the scene of the battle. In the company were second-reserve Cossacks from Tatarsk village, and the second troop was entirely composed of them. There were the two brothers of one-armed Alexei Shamil, the former mill engine-man Ivan Alexievich, Afonka Ozierov, the former ataman Manitskov, and many others.

Early on the morning of October 16 the company entered a village just as the first battalion of the Chornogorsk regiment was preparing to march out. The soldiers were running out of the abandoned, half-ruined huts and assembling in the street. The Cossacks came down the left side of the street. Ivan Alexievich, the engine-man, was on the outside file in one of the ranks of the second troop. He was marching with his eyes fixed on the ground in an attempt to avoid the puddles. Someone called to him from the ranks of the infantry, and he turned his head and passed his eyes over the soldiers.

"Ivan Alexievich, old friend. . . ."

A little soldier broke away from his platoon and came running towards him, throwing his rifle back over his shoulder. But the sling slipped and the butt jangled against his mess-tin.

"Don't you know me? Forgotten me already?" the soldier cried.

With difficulty Ivan Alexievich recognized Valet in the soldier with mouth and chin covered with a bristling, smoky-grey beard.

"Where've you sprung from?" he asked.

"I'm in this regiment, the 318th Chornogorsk. I never, never hoped to meet any of my old friends here."

Still gripping Valet's dirty little hand in his own bony fist, Ivan Alexievich smiled gladly and agitatedly. Valet hurried to keep up with the Cossack stride and began to trot, looking up into Ivan's eyes, while the gaze of his own close-set, evil little eyes was unusually tender and moist.

"We're going into an attack."

"And so are we."

"Well, how are you getting on, Ivan Alexievich?"

"There's nothing to tell."

"The same here. I haven't been out of the trenches since 1914."

"Do you remember Stockman? He was a lad, was our Osip Davidovich! He'd tell us what it was all about. He was a man, if ever there was one. . . ."

"Do I remember him!" Valet cried, shaking his tiny fist and crinkling his little bristly face into a smile. "I remember him better than my own father. You never heard how he got on, did you?"

"He's in Siberia," Ivan Alexievich sighed.

"How?" Valet asked, bobbing up and down beside his friend and turning up his foxy ear.

"He's in prison. For all I know, he may be dead now."

Valet walked along without speaking for a moment or two, now looking back to where his company was assembling, then gazing up at Ivan's chin and the deep round dimple right under the lower lip.

"Good-bye!" he said, releasing his hand from Ivan's. "I don't suppose we shall be seeing each other again."

With his left hand the Cossack removed his cap, and bending down, he put his arms round Valet's shoulders. They kissed each other strongly, as though saying good-bye for ever, and Valet dropped back. His head suddenly sank on his breast, so that only the dark rosy tips of his ears emerged from his grey greatcoat. He turned back, huddled up and stumbling over his feet.

Ivan Alexievich broke away from the rank and called, with a quiver in his voice:

"Hey, brother! Brother! You were bitter, weren't you! Do you remember? You were a strong one . . . eh?"

Valet turned his tear-stained face and beat his fist on his bony breast through his open greatcoat and torn shirt.

"I was! I was hard! But they've crushed me now. . . . They've driven the old horse to death!"

He shouted something else, but the Cossack company turned into a side street, and Ivan lost sight of him.

As the Cossacks marched out of the village they began to fall in with wounded, at first in ones and twos, then in groups of several at a time, at last in entire droves. Several carts filled to overflowing with serious cases dragged slowly along. The mares pulling at the traces were terribly emaciated. Their skinny backs revealed the marks of incessant whipping, and in places the bones showed through the wounds. They hauled the carts along with difficulty, snorting and straining, with their nostrils almost touching the mud. Occasionally one would stop, her sunken sides heaving impotently and her head hanging despondently. A blow of a whip would stir her from the spot, and she would drag on again, swaying from side to side. All around the carts wounded men were clinging, assisting themselves along.

The Cossack company turned off the road and entered the forest. Until evening they were huddled together under the streaming pines. The rain leaked beneath their collars and wandered down their backs; they were forbidden to strike any lights, but in any case it would have been difficult to do so in the rain. As dusk was falling they were led off into a trench. Not very deep, hardly more than a man's height, it was flooded with water and stank of slime, of sodden pine-cones and the moist, velvety soft smell of rain. From the trench the company was led on again through the darkling pine forest. They marched along endeavouring to encourage one another with jest. Someone began to whistle.

In a small glade they came upon a long trail of corpses. The bodies lay flung down shoulder to shoulder in various, frequently horrible and indecent postures. A soldier armed with a rifle, a gasmask hanging from his belt, stood on guard over them. The Cossacks were led close to the bodies, and they caught the cloying scent of decay already coming from them. The company commander halted the company, went with the troop officers up to the soldier, and stood talking to him for a minute or two. Meantime the Cossacks broke rank and went over to the bodies, removing their caps and staring down at the forms with that feeling of secret, fluttering fear and bestial curiosity which all living beings experience before the mystery of the dead. The bodies were those of officers, and the Cossacks counted forty-seven of them. The majority were youngsters between twenty and twenty-five years old, judging by their looks. Only the one on the extreme right, who was wearing the epaulets of a staff captain, was elderly. His mouth was wide open, concealing the mute echoes of his last cry in its yawning depths; above it hung heavy black whiskers; the broad brows frowned across his deathly pallid face. Two or three of them had no covering to their heads. The Cossacks stood staring long at the figure of one lieutenant, handsome even in death. He lay on his back, his left arm pressed against his chest, his right flung out and holding a pistol in an everlasting grip. Evidently someone had tried to take the weapon away; his broad yellow wrist was scratched; but the steel had fused to his hand and they would never be separated. On his curly flaxen hair was a broken cap. His face was pressed cheek-downward to the earth, as though fondling it, and his orange-bluish lips were contemptuously, amazedly writhed. His right-hand neighbour lay face-downward, his greatcoat hummocked on his back with its tail torn away, revealing his strong legs with their tautened muscles in khaki-coloured trousers and short chrome-yellow boots, the heels twisted to one side. He had no cap, nor had he the upper part of his cranium, for it had been cut clean away by a shard of shrapnel. In the empty brain-pan, framed by damp strands of hair, glimmered rose-coloured rain-water. Next to him lay a stout little officer in an open leather jerkin and a torn shirt. His lower jaw rested crookedly on his bare breast; below the hair of his head glimmered a narrow white band of forehead with the skin burned and shrivelled into a little tube. Between the brow and the jaw were merely pieces of bone and a thick black and crimson mash. Beyond these were carelessly gathered pieces of limbs, rags of overcoats, a crushed leg where the head should have been. Then came a boy with full lips and a charming oval face. A stream of machine-gun bullets had swept across his chest, his greatcoat was holed in four places, and burnt knobs of flesh were sticking through the holes.

"Who—who was he calling for in his hour of death? His mother?" Ivan Alexievich stuttered with chattering teeth, and turned sharply away, stumbling as though blind.

The Cossacks hurriedly returned to their places, crossing themselves and not glancing back. They preserved a long silence as they passed on through the narrow glades, hastening to get away from the memory of what they had seen. After some time the company was halted close to a dense network of abandoned dug-outs. The officers entered one of the dug-outs, and the men stood at ease. Darkness closed over the forest. The wind sent the clouds scurrying and tore them apart to reveal the lilac points of the distant stars. Meantime the commander assembled the officers in the dug-out and, opening a packet by the light of a stump of candle, acquainted them with the instructions of the staff command.

While the Cossacks were resting in the dug-outs, the first battalion of the Chornogorsk regiment passed in front of them. The dense forest was heavily holed with shells. The soldiers marched cautiously, feeling the ground with their feet; occasionally someone would fall and curse under his breath. Valet was in the company on the extreme right, and was sixth from the end of the long file.

"Hey, neighbour!" someone suddenly whispered to the left of him.

"Hello?" he replied.

"Going all right?"

"All right!" Valet said, immediately stumbling and sitting down in a shell-hole filled with water.

"It's dark, devilish dark!" he heard on his left.

They went on for a minute or two, invisible to one another, then unexpectedly the same hissing voice whispered right into Valet's ear:

"Let's go together. It isn't so bad then. . . ."

They went on in silence, setting their waterlogged boots cautiously down on the slippery earth. Suddenly a horned and spotted moon broke from behind the clouds, breasting the misty waves like a boat; emerging into clear sky, it poured down a flood of uncertain light. The damp pine needles gleamed phosphorescently in its light, and the cones seemed to smell more strongly and the wet soil to breathe more coolly.

They hurried along to overtake the file of men. But in the darkness they missed them and somehow got in front. After wandering on for some time they jumped down into a dark cleft of trench zigzagging off into the darkness.

"Let's search the dug-outs. We may find something to eat," Valet's comrade proposed irresolutely.

"All right."

"You go to the right, I'll take the left. We'll search while the others are coming up."

Valet struck a match and stepped through the open doorway of the first dug-out he found. But he flew out again as though expelled by a catapult; inside, two dead bodies lay crossed one on the other. He searched three dug-outs fruitlessly and flung open the door of a fourth, all but collapsing as he heard a strange metallic voice speaking German:

"Who is that?"

His body tingling, Valet silently jumped back.

"Is that you, Otto? Why have you been so long?" the German asked, stepping out of the dug-out and carelessly adjusting his greatcoat across his shoulders.

"Hands up! Hands up! Surrender!" Valet shouted hoarsely.

Mute with astonishment, the German slowly raised his hands, turned sideways, and stared fixedly at the gleaming point of the bayonet presented at him. His greatcoat fell from his shoulders, his big, work-scarred hands trembled above his head, and the fingers stirred as though playing on invisible strings of fear. Valet stood without changing his position, gazing at the tall, stalwart form of the German, the metal buttons of his tunic, the short boots, and the peakless cap set slightly on one side. Suddenly changing his attitude, he swayed as though being shaken out of his greatcoat, emitted a curt, throaty sound, neither cough nor wheeze, and stepped towards the German.

"Run!" he said in a hollow, broken voice. "Run, German! I've got no grudge against you! I won't shoot!"

He leaned his rifle against the wall of the trench and, rising on tiptoe, stretched his hand up to the right hand of the German. His confident movements reassured the man, who dropped his hand and listened intently to the unfamiliar intonation of the Russian's voice.

Without hesitation Valet gave him his own hairy, labour-worn hand and squeezed the German's cold, limp fingers. Then he lifted the palm. The light of the moon fell on it and revealed the brown calluses.

"I'm a worker," Valet said, trembling with his smile as though with the ague. "What should I kill you for? Run!" He gently pushed the German's shoulder and pointed to the black outline of the forest. "Run, you fool! Our men will be here soon. . . ."

The German stood staring at Valet's outflung hand, his body a little forward, his ears straining to catch the sense of the incomprehensible words. So he stood for a second or two, his eyes meeting Valet's; then suddenly a joyous smile quivered on his lips. Stepping backward a pace, he threw out his arms, strongly squeezed Valet's hands, and shook them, smiling agitatedly and staring into the Russian's eyes.

"You're letting me go? Oh, now I understand. . . . You're a Russian worker? A Social Democrat like me? Yes? . . . My brother, how can I ever forget? . . . I cannot find words . . . but you're a fine lad. . . . I . . ."

Amid the boiling torrent of foreign words Valet caught the one familiar "Social Democrat." He swept his yellow palm across and slapped it against his chest.

"Yes. I'm a Social Democrat. You've guessed right, old man. And now, run! . . . Good-bye, brother. Give me your hand. We're brothers, you know, and brothers shouldn't part like this."

Strongly moved, intuitively understanding each other, they stood with clasped hands, staring into each other's eyes. From the forest came the sounds of the approaching chain of Russians. The German whispered:

"In the coming class struggle we shall be in the same trenches, shan't we, comrade?" Then he leaped like a great grey animal on to the breastwork.

A moment or two later the file of Russian soldiers came up, a Czech reconnaissance party with the officers at their head. They all but fired at Valet's companion as he crawled out of a dug-out.

"I'm a Russian, can't you see?" he cried frantically, hugging a loaf of black bread to his breast as he saw the barrel of a rifle pointed at him.

Just before dawn the Czech reconnaissance party ran up against a German observation post. The Germans shattered the silence with a volley of shots. At equal intervals they fired two more volleys. Over the trenches soared a crimson rocket, and its purple sparks had hardly died away when the German artillery opened fire. The sound of the exploding shells came from far behind the Russian forces, somewhere by the Stokhod River.

As soon as the first shot was fired, the company, moving up nearly a hundred yards behind the Czechs, threw itself down headlong. The rocket shed a ruddy glow over the ground. By its light Valet saw the soldiers crawling like ants among the bushes and trees, no longer careful of the muddy soil, but pressing against it in their search for protection. The men heaped around every rut, disappeared behind every tiny earthy mound, thrust their heads into every little hole. Nevertheless, when the stuttering machine-gun fire luxuriantly flooded the forest like a May downpour, they could not hold their positions. Their heads buried between their shoulders, clinging like caterpillars to the ground, moving without stirring an arm or a leg, creeping like snakes and leaving their traces in the mud behind them, they crawled back. Some jumped to their feet and ran. Lashing up the cones, splintering the pines, the exploding bullets skipped and tore through the forest, rending into the earth, hissing like serpents.

Seventeen men were missing from the first half-company of the Chornogorsk regiment when it reached the second line of trenches again. A little way off, the Cossacks of the special company were also assembling. They had advanced on the right of the Chornogorsk half-company, had moved cautiously, and might have taken the Germans by surprise, overwhelming the outposts. But when the fire was opened on the Czechs the Germans were put on the alert along the entire sector. Firing at random, the enemy had killed two Cossacks and wounded another.

Within half an hour a further order came from the regimental staff. After the ground had been prepared by an artillery bombardment, the Chornogorsk regiment and the special Cossack company were again to attack the enemy and to drive him out of the first line of trenches.

Chapter 12

Twenty-five miles lower down the Stokhod, the river of a hundred ways, the battle was raging. For three weeks the roar of the artillery had continued without ceasing. At night the distant violet heaven was shredded with the rays of searchlights sowing dim rainbow beams, infecting with inexplicable uneasiness those who watched from afar the flames and explosions of war.

Meantime the 12th Cossack Regiment, to which Gregor's company belonged, was holding a wild and swampy sector. By day they fired occasional shots at the Austrians lining the shallow trenches opposite. By night, protected by the marsh, they slept or played cards. Only the guards watched the fitful orange outbursts of light where the struggle was being continued, some twenty-five miles lower down the Stokhod River.

On one of those tingling frosty nights when the distant reflections flickered more clearly than usual against the sky, Gregor Melekhov left his dug-out and made his way along a communication trench into the forest, which stood out behind the trenches in a grey brush over the black skull of a low hill. He flung himself down on the spacious, scented earth. The air was stifling and oppressive in the dug-out; a brown tobacco-smoke hung like a shaggy blanket over the table around which eight Cossacks were playing cards. But through the forest on the hill-crest a breeze was blowing, quietly as though fanned from the wings of invisible passing birds. A mournful scent arose from the frost-bitten grasses. Above the shell-sheared forest gathered the darkness; the smoking fire of the Pleiades was burning out in the sky, the Great Bear lay to one side of the Milky Way like an overturned wain with the shaft sticking up, in the north the Pole Star gleamed with a steady, fading light.

Gregor stared up at the star, and its icy light, dim, yet strangely prickling to his eyes, caused cold tears to spring beneath his eyelashes. A rush of memory brought all the past years of the war vividly before him. He recalled the night when he had gone to Aksinia at Yagodnoe. He remembered her with sudden pain, the dear yet alien outlines of her face appearing uncertainly before

him. With beating heart he tried to recall that face as he had seen
it for the last time, distorted with pain, the livid mark of the knout
on her cheek. But memory persistently suggested another face, held
slightly on one side, and smiling pallidly. Now again Aksinia turned
her face confidently and amorously, looking up at him with fierily
black eyes, her depravedly avid, crimson lips whispering something
inexpressibly caressing; then she slowly turned her eyes, her head,
away from him, and he saw the two fluffy curls on her swarthy neck.
How he had loved to kiss them!

Gregor shuddered. For a moment he thought he could even
smell the fine, intoxicating aroma of Aksinia's hair, and he dilated
his nostrils. But no! It was the troubling scent of fallen leaves. The
oval of Aksinia's face faded and passed. He closed his eyes, pressed
his palm to the rough skin of the earth, and lay staring unwinkingly beyond the broken pines, at the Pole Star hanging like a blue
butterfly in motionless flight.

Other memories obscured Aksinia's features. He recalled the
weeks he had spent at Tatarsk with his family after his break with
Aksinia; at night Natalia's greedy, ravaging embraces, as though
she were trying to make up for her previous virgin iciness; during
the days the watchful and almost challenging attitude of his family,
and the respect with which the villagers greeted their first
"chevalier" of St. George. Everywhere, even in his own home,
Gregor caught sidelong astonished and respectful glances. They
examined him as though they could not believe it was the same
Gregor who had been such a self-willed and merry lad. The old men
talked to him as an equal and took off their hats when they met him;
the girls and women stared with unconcealed admiration at his
trim, slightly stooping figure and the cross on his breast. He noticed
how obviously proud his father was of him as they walked together to church or to the square. And all this subtle, complex poison
of flattery, respect, and admiration gradually submerged and erased
from his consciousness the truth which Garanzha had implanted.
Gregor returned to Tatarsk one man and went back to the front
another. His own Cossack national traditions, sucked in with his
mother's milk and loved all his life, rose above the greater human
truth.

"I knew you'd make a good Cossack, Gregor," old Pantaleimon
had said, stroking his black and silver beard, as they parted. "When

you were twelve months old I carried you out into the yard and sat you bareback on a horse, as is the good old Cossack custom, and you, you little devil, you just seized him by the mane with your tiny hands; I said then you'd make good. And so you have."

Gregor returned to the front a good Cossack. Mentally still unreconciled to the senselessness of war, none the less he faithfully defended his Cossack honour.

In May 1915 the 13th German Iron Regiment had advanced over a brilliantly green meadow close to the village of Olkhovshchik. The machine-guns rattled away like cicadas. The heavy machine-gun of the Russian regiment ensconced along the rivulet stuttered powerfully. The 12th Cossack Regiment bore the brunt of the German attack. While waiting for the oncoming enemy, Gregor glanced back and saw the molten orb of the sun in the midday sky, and another sun in the reedy rivulet. Beyond the river, beyond the poplars were the Cossack horses, and in front was the German line, the yellow gleam of the copper eagles on the helmets. A wind billowed the bluish wormwood smoke of the gunfire. Gregor fired unhurriedly, taking careful aim and listening between his shots to the troop commander shouting the range. He cautiously dislodged a ladybird that settled on his sleeve. Then came the attack. With his rifle-butt Gregor knocked a tall German lieutenant off his feet, took three prisoners, and, firing over their heads, forced them to run towards the rivulet.

In July 1915, with a Cossack troop he had recovered a battery captured by the Austrians. During the same battle he had worked his way to the rear of the enemy and had opened fire on them with a portable machine-gun, putting the advancing Austrians to flight. Then he had taken a corpulent officer prisoner, flinging him across his saddle-bow as if he had been a sheep.

As he lay on the hillside, Gregor particularly remembered one incident in which he had met his deadly enemy Stepan Astakhov. The 12th Regiment had been withdrawn from the front and flung into East Prussia. The Cossack horses had trampled the orderly German fields, the Cossacks had fired the German habitations. Along the road they travelled, a ruddy smoke had risen, and the charred walls and the tiled roofs had crumbled to dust. Near the town of Stolypin the regiment went into attack at the side of the 27th Don Cossack Regiment. Gregor caught a momentary glimpse of his brother, of clean-shaven Stepan and other Cossacks from his own village. The regiments suffered defeat and were surrounded by the Germans. When the twelve companies, one after another, were flinging themselves into the attack in order to break through the enemy ring, Gregor saw Stepan leap from the horse killed beneath him and circle around like a wolf. Fired by a sudden joyous resolve, Gregor reined in his horse, and when the last company had galloped past, all but trampling on Stepan, he rode up to him and shouted:

"Catch hold of my stirrup!"

Stepan seized the stirrup-strap and ran for half a mile at the side of Gregor's horse. "Don't ride too fast, not too fast, for the love of Christ!" he pleaded, his mouth gaping and panting.

They passed successfully through the breach in the German ring. Not more than two hundred yards separated them from the forest to which their companies had retreated when a bullet whipped Stepan off his feet and he fell headlong. The wind tore the cap from Gregor's head and sent his hair into his eyes. Brushing it back, he looked round and saw Stepan limp towards a bush, tear off his Cossack cap, sit down, and hurriedly unbutton his trousers. From beyond the hill the Germans came running. Gregor realized that Stepan had no wish to die and so was tearing off his trousers, knowing that the Germans would show a Cossack no mercy. Mastering the beating of his heart, he turned his horse round and galloped back to the bush, jumping off while the horse was moving.

"Get on my horse!" he ordered Stepan.

Unforgettable was the curt sweep of Stepan's eyes as Gregor helped him to mount, then ran at his side, holding on to the stirrup. A stream of bullets whistled over their heads, and on either side and behind them sounded the spirting shots, like the splitting of overripe acacia pods.

In the forest Stepan, his face twisted with pain, slipped down from the saddle and limped away. Through the leg of his right boot blood was flowing, and at every step a cherry-red little stream spirted from his broken sole. He leaned against the trunk of a spreading oak and beckoned to Gregor.

"My boot's full of blood," he said when Gregor went across to him.

Gregor was silent, gazing aside.

"Grishka! When we went into the attack today— Do you hear, Gregor?" Stepan said, attempting to look into his enemy's eyes. "When we went into the attack I fired three times at you from behind. . . . God stopped me from killing you."

Their eyes met.. Stepan's keen pupils gleamed insufferably in their sunken sockets. He spoke almost without stirring his lips.

"You've saved me from death. . . . Thank you. . . . But I can't forgive you for Aksinia . . . my soul won't try. . . . Don't force me, Gregor. . . ."

"I shan't force you," Gregor answered. They had parted enemies as before.

In May the regiment with other sections of the Brusilov army had broken through the front at Lutsk and had carrouselled in the enemy's rear, striking and being struck. By Lvov, Gregor had himself drawn his company into an attack and had beaten back an Austrian howitzer battery. One night nearly a month later he had swum across the Bug River and had sent a sentry flying, and they had struggled a long time in the darkness before Gregor could bind him.

Strongly had Gregor defended his Cossack honour, seizing every opportunity of displaying immortal prowess, risking his life in madcap adventures, changing his clothes and making to the rear of the enemy, capturing outposts, and feeling that the pain for other men which had oppressed him during the first days of the war had gone for ever. His heart had grown hard, dry like a salt-marsh in drought; as a marsh will not absorb water, so Gregor's heart would not absorb compassion. With cold contempt he played with his own and others' lives, and covered himself with glory. He had won four St. George crosses and four other medals. On the occasional parades he stood by the regimental banner, seasoned with the gunpowder-smoke of innumerable wars. But he knew that he no longer laughed as in former days, that his eyes were sunken and his cheekbones stood out sharply. He knew what price he had paid for his crosses and medals.

He lay on the hillside, the edges of his greatcoat turned under him, resting on his left elbow. His memory obediently resurrected the past, and among the throng of memories some distant incident of his youth was entwined like a fine blue thread. For a moment he rested his mental eye upon it sadly and lovingly, then returned to the present. In the Austrian trenches someone was playing a mandolin. The fine wind-billowed strains hurried across the Stokhod River, scattering lightly over the earth so often washed with human blood. In the zenith the stars flamed, but the darkness was deepening and a midnight mist was bowed over the marsh. He smoked two cigarettes in succession, then rose from the hospitable earth and went back to the trenches.

In his dug-out the men were still playing cards. Gregor dropped on his pallet and fell off to sleep. In his sleep he dreamed of the parched, interminable steppe, the rosy lilac of the immortelles, the traces of unshod horses' hoofs among the shaggy lilac thyme. The steppe was empty and terrifyingly quiet. He was walking over the hard, sandy ground, but he could not hear his own footfalls, and this alarmed him. . . . He awoke for a moment and raised his head, chewing his lips like a horse that has momentarily caught the aroma of some unusual herb. Then he fell asleep again, into an untroubled, dreamless sleep.

Next day he awoke with an inexplicable, sucking yearning troubling him.

"What are you fasting for today? Dreamed about home last night?" Uriupin asked him.

"You guessed right. I dreamed of the steppe. . . . I'm so worn out in spirit. . . . I'd like to be back home. I'm fed up with the Czar's service. . . ."

Uriupin smiled condescendingly. He had lived continually in one dug-out with Gregor and had that respect for him which one strong animal feels for another. Since their quarrel in 1914 there had been no conflict between them, and Uriupin's influence was clearly discernible in Gregor's changed character and psychology. The war had strongly modified Uriupin's outlook. He dully but unswervingly turned towards an anti-war attitude, talked a great deal about traitor generals and the Germans in the Czar's palace. Once he had muttered: "Don't expect any good to come of it when the Czaritsa herself is of German blood. . . ." Gregor had tried to explain Garanzha's teaching to him, but Uriupin would have none of it.

"The song's all right, but the voice is throaty," he had said with a humorous smile. "Misha Koshevoi is always crowing the same story like a cock on a wall. There's no sense ever comes from these revolutions, only mischief. You remember that what the Cossacks need is their own government, and not any other! We need a strong Czar like Nicholai Nicholaich; we've got nothing in common with the peasants, the goose and the swine are not comrades. The peasants want to get the land for themselves, the workers want to have higher wages. But what will they give us? Land we've got in plenty. . . . Oho! And what else do we need? Our Czar's a horse-radish, there's no use denying it! His father was stronger, but this one will wait till revolution is knocking at the door as it did in 1905, and then they'll go rolling down to the devil together. That's not to our good; once they've driven the Czar out, they'll be coming down on us. Here the old fights will break out again, there they'll begin to take our land away for the peasants. We must keep our ears pricked."

"You always think one-sidedly," Gregor frowned.

"You're talking nonsense. You're young yet, you've not seen the world. But you wait a little and you'll find out who's right."

The argument usually ended at that, Gregor lapsing into silence and Uriupin attempting to talk about something else.

That day Gregor was drawn into an unfortunate incident. At midday the field kitchen stopped on the farther side of the hill as usual. The Cossacks pressed on one another along the communication trench to the kitchen. Misha Koshevoi went to get the food for the third troop and came back carrying the steaming pots on a long pole. He had hardly entered the dug-out when he shouted:

"This isn't good enough, brothers! Are we dogs, or what?"

"What's up?" Uriupin asked.

"They're feeding us on dead horse," Koshevoi exclaimed indignantly. Throwing back his head of golden hair, he set the pots down on a bed and suggested, glancing sidelong at Uriupin:

"Smell for yourself what the soup stinks like!"

Uriupin bent over his pot and distended his nostrils. He started back and pulled a wry face. Koshevoi also frowned, and his nostrils quivered in involuntary imitation of Uriupin.

"The meat's gone bad," Uriupin decided.

He pushed the pot away fastidiously and looked at Gregor. Gregor rose from his bed, bent his already hooked nose over the soup, then flung himself away and with a lazy movement sent the nearest pot to the ground.

"What have you done that for?" Uriupin asked irresolutely.

"Don't you see what for? Look! Are you half-blind? What's that?" Gregor pointed to the muddy wash oozing over the floor.

"Here! Worms! My old mother! And I didn't see them! There's a fine dinner for you! That's not cabbage soup, that's vermicelli. Worms instead of giblets!" Uriupin exclaimed.

For a moment there was silence. Gregor spat through his teeth. Then Koshevoi drew his sabre and said:

"We'll arrest this soup and report it to the company commander."

"That's the idea!" Uriupin approved. "We'll take the soup, and you, Gregor, must come behind and make the report."

With their bayonets Uriupin and Koshevoi picked up a pot of soup, then drew their sabres. Gregor followed behind them, and as they passed along the trenches a line of inquisitive Cossacks gathered in a grey-green wave and followed them. They halted outside the officers' dug-out. Gregor stooped and, holding his cap on with his left hand, entered the "fox-hole."

After a moment the company commander came out, buttoning up his overcoat and looking back at Gregor in astonishment mingled with a hint of anxiety.

"What's the matter, boys?" The officer ran his eyes over the assembled Cossacks.

Gregor stepped in front of him and replied:

"We've brought a prisoner."

"What prisoner?"

"That." He pointed to the pot of soup at Uriupin's feet. "There's the prisoner. Smell what your Cossacks are being fed on."

"They've started to serve out dead horse," Misha Koshevoi exclaimed fiercely.

"Change the quartermaster! The soup's got worms in it," other shouts arose.

The officer waited until the howl of voices had died down, then said sternly:

"Silence! You've said enough! I'll change the quartermaster to-day. I'll appoint a commission to investigate his activities. If the meat isn't good . . ."

"Court-martial him!" came a shout from behind, and the officer's voice was drowned in a new storm of cries.

The quartermaster had to be changed while the regiment was on the march. A few hours after the Cossacks had arrested the soup and brought it before the company commander, the order was re-ceived to withdraw from the front and to move by forced marches into Rumania. During the night the Cossacks were relieved by Siberian sharpshooters. The next day the regiment was mounted and on its way.

The march took seventeen days. The horses were exhausted with shortage of fodder. There was no food anywhere along the devas-tated zone immediately behind the front; the inhabitants had either fled into the interior or hidden in the forests. The gaping doors of the huts gloomily revealed bare walls. Occasionally the Cossacks would fall in with a sullen, terrified villager in a deserted street, but as soon as he saw the soldiers he hastened to hide himself. Worn out with their unbroken march, frozen, and irritable because of all they had had to endure, they tore off the straw roofs of the build-ings. In villages still unrifled by others they did not hesitate to steal the miserable food, and no threats on the part of their officers could stop them.

Not far from the Rumanian frontier Uriupin succeeded in stealing some barley from a barn in some more affluent village. The owner caught him in the act, but he knocked the peaceable, elderly Bess-arabian down and carried the barley to his horse. The troop officer found him filling his horse's basket and with trembling fingers strok-ing the animal's sunken, bony sides.

"Uriupin! Hand over that barley, you swine! You'll be shot for this!" the officer shouted.

Uriupin gave the officer a sidelong glance and threw his cap down on the ground. For the first time during all his life in the regiment he raised a heart-rending cry:

"Court-martial me! Shoot me! Kill me on the spot, but I won't give up the barley. . . . Is my horse to die of hunger, eh? I won't hand over the barley, not a single grain!"

The officer stood without replying, staring at the horse's terribly emaciated flanks and shaking his head. Finally he remarked, with a note of perplexity in his voice:

"What are you giving the horse grain for when he's still hot?"

"But he's cooled down, now," Uriupin replied almost in a whisper, gathering up the grains fallen on the ground and putting them back in the basket.

The regiment arrived at its new position in the middle of November. The winds were howling over the Transylvanian mountains, a freezing mist gathered in the valleys, and the tracks of animals were frequently seen on the early snows. Terrified by the war, the wolves, elks, and goats were abandoning their wild fastnesses and making for the interior of the country.

On November 20 the regiment attempted to storm height "320." The previous evening the trenches had been held by Austrians, but on the morning of the attack they were relieved by Saxons freshly transferred from the western front. The Cossacks marched on foot up the stony, slightly snow-covered slopes, sending the stones rolling down and raising a fine snowy dust. As Gregor strode along, he smiled guiltily and sheepishly and told Uriupin:

"I'm quite nervous this morning, for some reason. I feel just as though I was going into battle for the first time."

The Cossacks marched up the slope in irregular chain formation. Not a shot was fired. The enemy trenches were ominously silent. Gregor was smiling anxiously. His hook-nose and his sunken cheeks with their black harvest of whisker were a yellowish blue; his eyes gleamed dully like pieces of anthracite beneath his rime-covered brows. His accustomed composure had deserted him. Today as never before he was anxious for himself and for his comrades. He felt as though he wanted to throw himself on the ground and weep, complaining with childish phrases to the earth as if it were his mother. He fixed a distrustful gaze on the grey, snow-fringed line of trenches ahead, and struggling with the terrible feeling, mastering his tears, he talked away to Uriupin.

The very first volley from the enemy knocked Gregor over, and he fell to the ground with a groan. He tried to reach the first-aid dressing in his pack, but the hot blood pouring from the elbow inside his sleeve left him too weak. He lay flat and, shielding his head behind a boulder, licked the downy fringe of snow with his parched tongue and thirstily caught at the snowy dust with quivering lips. He listened with unusual fear and trembling to the dry, sharp crack of the rifles and the dominating thunder of the guns. Raising his head, he saw the Cossacks of his company running back down the slope, slipping, falling, aimlessly firing backward and upward. An inexplicable and irrational fear brought him to his feet and forced him also to run down towards the serrated edging of the pine forest whence the regiment had opened the attack. The companies poured in torrents into the forest. On the grey slopes behind them lay little grey bundles of dead; the wounded crawled down unaided, whipped along by the fierce machine-gun fire.

Leaning on Misha Koshevoi's arm, Gregor entered the forest. The bullets ricocheted off the sloping ground. On the Germans' left flank a machine-gun was spitting out a fine hail, sounding as though stones flung by a strong hand were ringingly bouncing off the thin ice of a frozen river.

"They're giving us a warm time!" Uriupin shouted almost exultantly. Leaning against the ruddy breast of a pine, he fired lazily at the Germans pouring over the ridge of the trenches.

"This will teach the fools, this will teach them!" Koshevoi shouted, tearing his arm away from Gregor. "The people are swine, swine! When they've poured out all their blood, then they'll learn what they're being shot down for!"

"What are you raving about?" Uriupin frowned.

"If you're wise you can understand for yourself. But the fools, what of them? You can't drive sense into their heads even with a hammer."

"Do you remember your oath? Did you take the oath or not?" Uriupin demanded.

Instead of replying, Koshevoi fell to his knees and with fumbling hands raked up some snow. He swallowed it greedily, shivering and coughing the while.

Chapter 13

Through the sky, flecked with a grey ripple of cloud, the autumn
sun rolled over Tatarsk. In the heaven a gentle breeze urged the
clouds slowly on towards the west; but over the village, over the
dark green plain of the Don Valley, over the bare forest it blew
strongly, bending the crowns of the willows and poplars, ruffling
the Don, and chasing droves of crimson leaves along the streets. In
Christonia's threshing-floor it tousled a badly stacked rick of wheat-
straw, tearing away its top and sending the thin ridge-pole flying.
Suddenly snatching up a golden load of straw as if on a pitchfork,
it carried the burden out into the yard, sent it whirling across the
street, and scattered it munificently over the deserted road, finally
throwing the untidy bundle on to the roof of Stepan Astakhov's hut.
Christonia's wife ran out into the yard and stood for a minute or
two watching the wind lording it about the threshing-floor, then
went in again.

The third year of the war had left noticeable marks in the village. Where the huts had been deprived of all male hands, the sheds
gaped wide open, the yards were shabby, and gradual decay was
leaving its traces everywhere. Christonia's wife had only her little
nine-year-old son to help her. Anikushka's wife was no hand whatever at farm work and, because of her lonely situation, paid redoubled attention to her own appearance, painted her face with a
veneer of beauty, and as there were not enough grown-up Cossacks,
accepted lads of fourteen or so. The state of her long untarred gates
witnessed eloquently to the neglect of the farm. Stepan Astakhov's
hut was completely abandoned; the owner had boarded up the
windows, the roof was falling in and was overgrown with bur-
docks, the door lock was rusting, and wandering cattle strayed
through the open gate, seeking shelter from the heat or rain in the
weedy, grass-grown yard. The wall of Ivan Tomilin's hut was falling into the street, being kept from doing so only by a forked
wooden prop. Fate seemed to be wreaking its vengeance on the

hardy artillery-man for the German and Russian houses he had destroyed.

And so in all the streets and alleys of the village. At the lower end only Pantaleimon Melekhov's hut and yard had their usual appearance; there everything seemed sound and in order, yet it was not entirely so. On the granary roof the sheet-iron cocks had fallen, eaten away with age; the granary was sinking on one side; and an experienced eye would have detected other signs of neglect. The old man could not manage everything. He sowed less and less, and only the Melekhov family itself did not diminish. To make up for Piotra and Gregor's absence Natalia gave birth to twins in the autumn of 1915. She was clever enough to please both Pantaleimon and Ilinichna by having a girl and a boy. Natalia's child-bearing was a painful one; there were whole days when she could hardly walk, owing to the tormenting pains in her legs, and tottered about, dragging her feet one behind the other. But she bore the pain stoically, and it never found any reflection in her swarthy, lean, and happy face. Only the sweat stood out on her temples when the pain was more intense, by which Ilinichna would guess at her suffering and tell her to go and lie down.

One fine September day Natalia, feeling her time near at hand, turned to go out into the street.

"Where are you off to?" Ilinichna asked her.

"Into the meadow. I'll see the cows out."

Groaning and holding her hands beneath her belly, she walked hurriedly out beyond the village, made her way into a wilderness of wild thorn, and lay down. Dusk was falling when she returned by side ways to the hut, carrying twins in her canvas apron.

"My dear! You little devil! What's all this? And where have you been?" Ilinichna found her voice.

"I was ashamed, so I went out. . . . I didn't like to . . . in front of Father. . . . I am clean, Mother, and I've washed them. Take them . . ." Natalia replied, turning pale.

Dunia ran for the midwife, and Daria busied herself lining a trough. Ilinichna, laughing and weeping for joy, shouted at her:

"Daria, put that trough down. Are they kittens, that you want to put them in a trough? Lord, there's two of them! Oh Lord, one's a boy! Natalia—put them to bed!"

When Pantaleimon heard that his daughter-in-law had given birth to twins he opened wide his arms with astonishment, then wept happily and combed his beard. He shouted irrationally at the approaching midwife.

"You're a liar, you old hag!" He shook his fist in front of the old crone's nose. "You're a liar! The Melekhov line hasn't died out yet! My daughter's got a Cossack and a girl. There's a daughter-in-law for you! Lord, my God! For such kindness how can I repay her?"

Fruitful was that year; the cow gave birth to twins, the sheep had twins, the goats. . . . Astonished at the circumstance, Pantaleimon reasoned to himself:

"This is a lucky year, and profitable! Everything having twins! What a fruitful time for us, oho!"

Natalia kept her children at the breast for twelve months. She weaned them in the September, but she did not get really well again until late in the autumn. Her teeth gleamed milkily in her emaciated face, and her eyes, seeming unnaturally large because of her thinness, shone with a warm light. All her life was devoted to the children. She grew negligent of herself and spent all her spare time with them, washing them, binding them, mending for them; frequently, sitting on the bed with one leg hanging, she would lift them out of the cradle and, with a movement of her shoulders releasing her full, large melon-yellow breasts, would feed them both at once.

"They've sucked enough at you already. You feed them too often," Ilinichna would remark, slapping the full little legs of her grandchildren.

"Feed them! Don't spare the milk! We don't want it for cream!" Pantaleimon would intervene with jealous roughness.

During these years life declined to its ebb, like flood water in the Don. The days were dreary and exhausting and passed unobtrusively, in continual activity, in work, in petty needs, in little joys and a great, unsleeping anxiety for those who were at the war. Rare letters in envelopes covered with postmarks arrived from

Piotra and Gregor. Gregor's last letter had fallen into someone else's hands; half of it was carefully obliterated with violet ink, and an incomprehensible sign had been made in ink in the margin of the grey paper. Piotra wrote more frequently than Gregor, and in his letters to Daria he implored and adjured her to give up her goings on. Evidently rumours of his wife's unseemly life had reached his ears. With his letters Gregor sent home money, his pay and allowances for his crosses, and indicated that he had tried to get leave, but had failed. The two brothers' roads ran in very different directions. Gregor was oppressed by the war, and the flush was sucked out of his face, leaving a yellow jaundice. He did not expect to live to see the end. But Piotra climbed swiftly and easily upward; he wormed his way into the good graces of his company commander, was awarded two crosses, in the autumn of 1916 was made a corporal, and he was now talking in his letters of attempting to get himself sent to an officers' school. During the summer he sent home a German officer's helmet and cloak and his own photograph. His ageing features stared complacently from the grey card, his twisted, flaxen moustaches stuck upward, and under the snub nose the well-known grin parted his lips. Life was smiling on Piotra, and the war delighted him because it opened up unusual prospects. But for its coming how could he, a simple Cossack, ever have dreamed of an officer's commission and a different, sweeter life? Only in one respect did Piotra's life have an unpleasant feature: ugly rumours concerning his wife circulated in the village. Stepan Astakhov was given leave in the autumn of 1916 and on his return to the regiment boasted to all the company of his splendid time with Piotra's wife. Piotra would not believe the stories; his face went dark, but he smiled and said:

"Stepan's a liar! He's trying to get his own back for Gregor."

But one day, as Stepan was coming out of his dug-out, whether by accident or design he dropped an embroidered lace handkerchief. Piotra, who was just behind him, picked it up and at once recognized his wife's handiwork. Again the old hostility broke out between them. Piotra watched for his opportunity; death watched over Stepan. If Piotra could, he would have had Stepan lying on the bank of the Dvina with Piotra's mark on his skull. But ere long it happened that Stepan went out on an expedition to get rid of a German outpost and did not come back. The Cossacks who went with him said the German heard them cutting the barbed wire and flung a grenade. The Cossacks managed to get up to him and Stepan knocked him down with his fist, but a supporting guard opened fire, and Stepan fell. The Cossacks bayoneted the second guard, dragged away the German stunned by Stepan's blow, and attempted to pick Stepan up also. But he was too heavy and they had to leave him. Stepan pleaded: "Brothers, don't let me go! Comrades! What are you leaving me for?" But a hail of machine-gun bullets spattered through the wire, and the Cossacks crawled away. "Brothers!" Stepan called after them, but what of that? Your own skin has to be saved before another's. When Piotra heard of Stepan's fate he felt relieved, like a sore on the bottom after anointing it with dripping, but he resolved none the less that when he got leave he would have Daria's blood. He wasn't Stepan! He wouldn't stand for that! He thought of killing her, but at once rejected the idea. "Kill the serpent, and ruin all my life because of her? Rot in a prison, lose all my labours, lose everything?" He decided merely to beat her, but in such a fashion that it would deprive her of all desire ever to raise her tail again. "I'll knock her eyes out, the snake!" he thought as he sat in the trenches not far from the steep, clayey bank of the Dvina River.

That autumn Daria made up for all her hungry, husbandless life. One morning Pantaleimon Prokoffievich awoke as usual before the rest of the family and went out into the yard. He clutched his head, overcome by what he saw. The gates had been removed from their hinges and had been flung down in the middle of the road. It was an insult, a disgrace! The old man immediately put the gates back in their place and after breakfast called Daria outside into the summer kitchen. What they talked about was never known to the others, but a few minutes later Dunia saw Daria run dishevelled and crying out of the kitchen, her kerchief awry. As she passed Dunia she swung her shoulders, and the black arches of her eyebrows quivered in her tear-stained, angry face.

"You wait, you old devil! I'll pay you back for this!" she hissed between her swollen lips.

Dunia saw that her jacket was torn at the back, and a fresh livid bruise showed on her bare shoulders. She ran up the steps and disappeared into the porch, while from the summer kitchen Pantaleimon came limping, as evil as the devil, and folding up some new leather reins as he walked. Dunia heard her father say:

"I'll teach you to play those games, you bitch! You whore!"

Order was restored in the hut. For some days Daria went about quieter than water, lower than the grass, went to bed before anybody else each night, and smiled coldly at Natalia's sympathetic glances, shrugging her shoulders and raising her eyebrows as though saying: "All right, we shall see!" On the fourth day after, an incident occurred of which only Daria and old Pantaleimon knew. Afterwards Daria went about laughing triumphantly, but the old man was embarrassed for a whole week and as disconcerted as a doctored cat. IIe did not tell his wife what had occurred, and even at confession kept the incident and his own sinful thoughts about it a secret from Father Vissarion.

What happened was this: Pantaleimon was not sure of Daria's complete conversion, and he told his wife Ilinichna:

"Don't spare Daria! Make her work harder. She'll never go wrong at work, and she's a slippery hussy; all she thinks of is nights out."

He himself made Daria clean out the threshing-floor and gather up the wood chips in the back yard and helped her to clear the chaff-shed. Later the same afternoon he thought he would shift the winnowing machine from the barn into the chaff-shed and called his daughter-in-law to help him.

Adjusting her kerchief and shaking off the chaff which had worked beneath the collar of her jacket, Daria came out and passed through the threshing-floor into the barn. Pantaleimon, in a padded woollen workday coat and ragged trousers, went in front. The yard was empty. Dunia was helping her mother spin the autumn's wool, and Natalia was setting the dough for the morrow's bread. The evening sunset was glowing beyond the village. The bell was ringing for vespers. A little raspberry-coloured cloud hung motionless in the zenith of the translucent sky, the rooks were hanging in black, burning knobs on the bare branches of the grey poplars beyond the Don. In the empty silence of the evening every sound was sharp and distinct. The heavy scent of steaming dung and hay came from the cattle-yard. Pantaleimon and Daria carried the faded-red winnowing machine into the chaff-shed and set it down in a corner. He raked away some fallen chaff and turned to go out.

"Father!" Daria called in a low whisper.

He went back to the winnowing machine, asking:

"What's the matter?"

"Here, Father, here's something. .... Come and look," she said, bending sideways and stealthily glancing across the old man's shoulder at the open door. He went right up to her. Suddenly she flung out her arms, and embracing his neck and interlocking her fingers, she stepped back, dragging him after her and whispering:

"Here, Father. . . . Here. . . . It's softer. . . ."

"What's the matter with you?" Pantaleimon asked in alarm. Wriggling his head from side to side, he tried to free himself of her arms; but she drew his head more strongly towards her own face, breathing hotly in his beard and laughing and whispering.

"Let me go, you bitch!" The old man struggled, feeling his daughter-in-law's straining belly right against him. Pressing still closer, she fell backward and drew him down on top of herself.

"The devil! She's gone silly! Damn you! Let me go!" he spluttered.

"Don't you want to?" Daria panted. Opening her hands, she shoved the old man in the chest. "Or perhaps you can't? Then don't judge me! Do you hear?"

Jumping to her feet, she hurriedly adjusted her skirt, brushed the chaff off her back, and shouted into the frenzied old man's face:

"What did you beat me for the other day? Am I an old woman? Weren't you the same when you were young? My husband . . . ? I haven't seen him for a year! And what am I to do—lie with a dog? A fig for you, one-leg! Here, take this!" She made an indecent gesture, and, her eyebrows working, went towards the door. At the door she once more carefully examined her clothes, brushed the dust from her jacket and kerchief, and said without looking back at Pantaleimon:

"I can't do without it. I need a Cossack, and if you don't want to . . . I'll find one for myself, and you keep your mouth shut!"

With a furtive, hurried gait she went to the door of the threshing-floor and disappeared without a glance back, while Pantaleimon remained standing by the winnowing machine, chewing his beard and staring guiltily and disconcertedly around the chaff-shed. "Perhaps she's right after all. Maybe I should have sinned with her?" he thought in his perplexity, flabbergasted by what had happened to him.

In November the frost gripped icily. An early snow fell. At the bend by the upper end of the village the Don was frozen over. Occasionally someone ventured over the dove-blue ice to the farther side. Lower down only the edges of the river were sheeted with thin ice, and the stream ran turbulently in the middle, the green waves tossing their grey heads. In the pool below the Black Cliff the sheat-fish had long since sunk in a wintry somnolence to a depth of seventy feet. The carp lay near by. Only the pike struggled up-stream and shied at the dam in its chase after whitebait. The sterlet lay above the gravel. The fishermen waited for a strong frost, in order to drag the river for fish.

In November the Melekhovs received a letter from Gregor. He wrote from Rumania, saying he had been wounded; a bullet had shattered the bone of his left arm, and so he was being sent back to his own district while the wound was healing. A further woe came upon the Melekhov household hard on the heels of the first. Eighteen months previously Pantaleimon had had need of money and had borrowed a hundred rubles from Sergei Mokhov, giving him a bill of sale as security. During the summer the old man had been called into Mokhov's shop and had been asked whether he intended to pay or not. Pantaleimon's gaze had wandered distractedly around the half-empty shelves and the shining counters, and he had hesi-tated.

"Wait a bit; give me time to turn round a little and I'll pay it back," he had said at last.

But the old man had not been able to "turn round." The harvest had been poor, and the cattle were not worth selling. Suddenly, like snow in June, the bailiff arrived at the village administration office, sent for Pantaleimon, and demanded in so many words:

"Put down a hundred rubles."

Pantaleimon asked permission to go home, promising to bring the money the very same day. But he made straight for Korshunov's hut. On the square he met one-armed Alexei Shamil.

"Still limping, Pantaleimon?" Shamil greeted him.

"A little."

"Going far?"

"To Korshunov on business."

"Oh! You'll find them merry. Their son Mitka has come back from the front, I hear."

"Is that so?"

"So I've been told," Shamil replied, winking with his eye and cheek. Pulling out his pouch, he added: "Have a smoke, old boy. My paper, your tobacco."

Pantaleimon lit a cigarette and stood hesitating whether to go to see Korshunov or not. Finally he decided to go and limped on.

"Mitka's got a cross, too. He's trying to catch up with your sons. We've got as many crosses in the village now as sparrows in the bushes," Shamil called after him.

Pantaleimon walked slowly to the end of the village, glanced through the window of Korshunov's hut, and went to the wicket gate. He was met by Miron himself. The old man's freckled face was shining with joy.

"Heard about our luck?" Korshunov asked, linking his arm in Pantaleimon's.

"I've just been told about it by Alexei Shamil. But I've come on other business. . . ."

"Let it wait! Come into the house and meet the lad. We've been having a little to drink in our joy."

"You needn't have told me." Pantaleimon smiled and dilated his nostrils. "I've smelled it already."

Miron flung open the door and stood aside to let Pantaleimon pass in. He stepped across the threshold and at once fixed his gaze on Mitka, who was sitting behind the table.

"Here he is, our soldier boy!" Grand-dad Grishaka exclaimed with tears in his eyes, falling on Mitka's shoulder.

Pantaleimon took Mitka's long hand in his and stepped back a pace, looking him over in astonishment.

"Well, what are you staring at?" Mitka asked hoarsely, with a smile on his face.

"I can't help looking, I'm so astonished. I saw you and Gregor off at the same time, and you were children. And now look at you! A Cossack, and fit for the ataman's regiment, at that."

Lukinichna gazed at Mitka with eyes filled with tears, at the same time attempting to pour out vodka into a glass. Not watching what she was doing, she let it spill over the edge.

"Hey, you scab! What are you doing, wasting good spirit!" Miron bawled at her.

"To your joy, and to you, Mitka, on your happy homecoming!"

Pantaleimon said, passing his eyes round the room. Without taking breath he sipped down the vodka. Slowly wiping his lips and whiskers with his palm, he fixed his eyes on the bottom of the glass, threw his head back, tossed an orphaned drop of vodka into his gaping mouth, and only then took a breath and bit at a pickled cucumber, blinking beatifically. Lukinichna poured him out a second glass, and the old man at once got ludicrously fuddled. Mitka watched him with a smile. The lad had certainly changed beyond recognition during his years of absence. In this healthy, black-whiskered Cossack almost nothing remained of the fine, elegant Mitka who had gone off to do his service three years previously. He had grown considerably, his shoulders had broadened, he had filled out, and certainly weighed not less than a hundred and eighty. His face and voice were coarser, and he looked older than his years. Only the eyes were the same, just as disturbing and restless.

Mitka lived a thoughtless, birdlike existence; life today was good, and tomorrow would take care of itself. He was not too keen on soldiering, and despite his fearless heart he did not go out of his way to earn distinction, although when he was mentioned in dispatches it was just as well for him. He had been twice court-martialled, once for raping a Russian-born Polish woman and once for stealing. During the three years of war he had received innumerable punishments, and on one occasion the field court-martial had all but sentenced him to be shot. But he had managed somehow to extricate himself, and although he was one of the worst characters in the regiment, the Cossacks liked him for his gay, smiling morals and his bawdy songs, for his comradeship and straight-forward nature, while the officers liked him for his brigand ardour. Smilingly Mitka trod the earth with light, wolfish feet: there was a good deal of the wolf breed in him. For Mitka life was simple and direct, stretching away like a furrow, and he walked along it the absolute master. Just as primitively simple and direct were his thoughts. If you were hungry you could and should steal even from your comrades; and Mitka stole when he was hungry. If your boots were worn out it was the simplest thing in the world to take a pair from a German prisoner. If you were punished you must make up somehow for your crime; and Mitka did make up for it, going out and bringing back half-strangled German outposts and volunteering for the most dangerous enterprises. In 1915 he had been wounded and taken prisoner; but the same night, tearing his fingernails to pieces, he had broken through the roof of the shed and fled, picking up some wagon harness for a keepsake as he went. And in such ways Mitka got away with a good deal.

"So you've won the cross?" Pantaleimon said, smiling drunkenly.

"Who hasn't got a cross among the Cossacks?" Mitka frowned.

"He's proud," old Grishaka hurried to intervene. "He's just like me. He can't bow his back."

"They don't give them crosses for that," Pantaleimon was about to reply angrily, but Miron drew him into the kitchen, sat down on a chest, and asked him:

"How's Natalia and the grandchildren? All alive and well? Praise God! You said you'd come on business, didn't you? What is it? Speak up, or we'll be drinking again and you'll be too drunk to talk."

"Give me money! For the love of God! Help me, or I'll be ruined by these—by this money matter," Pantaleimon implored with expansive, drunken abasement. Miron interrupted:

"How much?"

"A hundred rubles."

Korshunov rummaged in the chest, pulled out a greasy kerchief, untied it, and counted out ten ten-ruble notes.

"Thank you, Miron Gregorievich. You've saved us from misery," Pantaleimon said.

"No, don't thank me. When it's our own flesh and blood. . . ."

Mitka spent five days at home. He passed his nights with Anikushka's wife, having pity on woman's bitter need and even more on her, a helpless and simple grass-widow. The days he spent wandering among his kinsfolk and friends. Dressed in a single light overcoat, he swung down the streets with his cap pushed back on his head, vaunting his strength against the cold. One evening he looked in on the Melekhovs. He brought the scent of frost and the unforgettable, pungent smell of the soldier with him into the overheated kitchen, sat talking about the war, the village news, then narrowed his green eyes at Daria and rose to go. Daria flickered like the flame of a candle when the door banged behind him, and, pressing her lips together, was about to put on her kerchief. But Ilinichna asked:

"Where are you off to, Daria?"

"I want to go outside."

"I'll come with you."

Pantaleimon sat without raising his head, as though he had not heard the question and reply. Daria went past him to the door, her eyelids drooping over the wolfish gleam in her eyes, her mother-in-law tottering heavily after her. Mitka was coughing and scrunching his feet at the gate. At the sound of the door latch he turned to come back to the steps.

"That you, Mitka? You haven't lost your way in our yard?" Ilinichna called spitefully. "Fasten the gate behind you or it will be banging all night in this wind."

"No, I'm not lost. I'll fasten the gate!" Mitka replied in a tone of chagrin, and strode straight across the street towards Anikushka's yard.

On the sixth day Miron drove his son to Millerovo station and stood watching as the line of green boxes rattled away, then dug long at the platform with his whip, not raising his bleary eyes. Lukinichna wept for her son; old Grishaka coughed and blew his nose into his hand, then wiped his palm on his coat. And Anikushka's grass-widow wept as she recalled Mitka's great body, so feverish in caresses, and as she suffered with the clap she had caught from him.

Time entangled the days as the wind a horse's mane. Just before Christmas a thaw unexpectedly set in, rain fell for days on end, the water raged down from the hills along the dry courses, the last year's grass showed green on the bared headlands, the edges of the Don foamed, and the ice turned a cadaverous blue and swelled. An inexpressibly sweet scent was exuded by the bare black earth. The water bubbled in the wheel-tracks of the highroad. The clayey cliffs beyond the village yawned with fresh landslides and ruddy wounds. The southerly wind brought the heavy scent of rotten grass, and at noonday dove-blue, tender shadows lurked on the horizon as in springtime. In the village rippling pools stood on the top of the ashes heaped up against the fences. The earth melted around the ricks in the threshing-floors, and the cloying sweetness of damp straw pricked the noses of passers-by. In the day-time a tarry water ran off the straw, icicle-hung roofs and down the cornices; the magpies chattered incessantly on the fences, and the village bull wintering in Miron Korshunov's yard bellowed, enraged by the premature languor of spring. He tore at the fence with his horns and kicked up the crumbling, watery snow.

⌐ The Don broke on the second day after Christmas. The ice floated off down the middle of the stream with a mighty grinding and groaning. Like sleepy, monstrous fish the floes were driven on to the banks. Beyond the Don, urged on by the agitating southern wind, the poplars fled in immobile, flexible flight.

But towards nightfall the hills began to roar; the ravens fluttered and squawked in the square, Christonia's pig ran past the Melekhovs' yard with a bunch of hay in its jaws, and Pantaleimon decided that the spring was nipped off again, a frost would set in on the morrow. During the night the wind veered round to the east, a light frost veneered the puddles with a crystal ice. By the morning the wind was blowing from Moscow, and the frost had set hard again. Winter reigned once more. Only fragments of floes floated down the middle of the Don in great white sheets, and the bared earth smoked frostily on the rise.

Shortly after Christmas the village secretary informed Pantaleimon at a meeting that he had seen Gregor in Kamenska, and that he had asked the official to inform his parents that he would soon be coming over to visit them.

PART III

Revolution

REVOLUTION

Chapter 1

With his small, swarthy, hairy hands Sergei Mokhov felt all the pulses of life. Sometimes life played with him, sometimes it hung on him like a stone round the neck of a drowned man. He foresaw a great deal. During his lifetime Sergei Platonovich had been in many troubles. Long since, when he was still running the elevator, he had had to buy grain from the Cossacks at a few groschen the pood,[1] and afterwards cart four thousand poods of wheat out of the village and pour it into the river. He remembered 1905, too. Mokhov had grown rich and had accumulated sixty thousand rubles, depositing them in the Volga-Kama Bank, but he scented from afar that times of great commotion were coming. He awaited the dark days, and was not mistaken.

Already in February echoes of the city talk of Rasputin and the Czar's family were circulating through the villages of the Don. And in March, Sergei Platonovich announced the news of the overthrow of the autocracy. The Cossacks received the information with restrained anxiety and expectation. That day the old and young Cossacks crowded around the closed doors of Mokhov's shop. The new village ataman, a red-haired and cross-eyed Cossack, was completely crushed by the news and took almost no part in the animated

[1] *Pood:* 36 pounds avoirdupois.

discussions going on outside the shop, only occasionally exclaiming disconcertedly:

"Well, things have come to a pretty pass! Now what shall we do?"

Seeing the crowd outside the shop, Mokhov decided to go out and talk with the old men. He put on his raccoon-skin coat and went down the front steps of his house, leaning on his stick with its modest silver initials.

"Well, Mokhov, you're an educated man, tell us ignorant ones what's going to happen now," Matvei Kashulin asked, smiling anxiously.

At Mokhov's bow the old men respectfully removed their caps, and stood back to let him pass into the middle of the group.

"We shall live without the Czar," Mokhov began tentatively.

All the old men started speaking at once. "But how, without the Czar?" "Our fathers and grandfathers lived under the Czars. And now isn't a Czar necessary?" "Take off the head, and the legs won't go on living!" "What sort of government shall we have?" "Out with it, Sergei Platonovich! Speak up, what is there to be afraid of?"

"Maybe he doesn't know, himself," one remarked with a smile.

Sergei Platonovich stared stupidly at his old boots and said, uttering the words with difficulty:

"The State Duma will govern. We shall have a republic."

He smiled forcedly and looked around the troubled faces of the old men. With his usual gesture he divided his beard in two and spoke out, angry at no one knew whom:

"Now you see what they've brought Russia to! They'll make you equal to the peasants, deprive you of your privileges, and recall the old affronts into the bargain. Bad times are coming. . . . It depends on whose hands the government falls into, otherwise we shall be brought to utter disaster."

"If we're alive, we shall see!" Bogatiriev shook his head and eyed Mokhov distrustfully from under his bushy eyebrows. "You go your own way, Sergei Platonovich, but maybe we shall be better off now."

"How will you be better off?" Mokhov asked venomously.

"The new government may put an end to the war. That may be, mayn't it?"

Mokhov waved his hand and shuffled away to his house, thinking disconnectedly of his personal affairs, of the mill and the worsening trade, and remembering that Elizabeth was in Moscow and Vladimir was shortly to come home from Novocherkassk. The blunt prick of anxiety for his children did not disturb the restless disorder of his thoughts. Glancing back at the old men, he spat across the balustrade of the stairs and went along the veranda to his room.

"My God!" he was thinking, "how everything changes! Right down to my old age I've remained a fool. I believed in the possibility of my life getting better, and in reality I am as lonely as a man on sentry duty. I've got my money by shady means, but you can't get it by clean. . . . I've squeezed others, and now the revolution is coming, and tomorrow my own servants may turn me out of my house. Curse the lot of them! And my children? Vladimir's a fool. . . . And where's the sense of it all? Nothing matters, perhaps. . . ."

He slept badly that night, turning over and over, gripped by disconnected thoughts and subconscious desires. Next morning, hearing that Eugene Listnitsky had arrived home from the front, he resolved to drive to Yagodnoe to find out the real situation and to relieve his mind of its bitter accumulation of anxious presentiments. So Yemelian harnessed the horse to the light sleigh and drove his master to Yagodnoe.

The sun was ripening like a yellow apricot above the village, clouds were smoking above and below it. The keen frosty air was saturated with a juicy, fruity scent. The ice on the road crumbled beneath the horse's hoofs, the steam from the animal's nostrils was carried away by the wind and settled in rime on its mane. Soothed by the swift motion and the cold, Mokhov dozed.

He arrived at Yagodnoe at midday. He was welcomed on the steps by the grey borzoi bitch, who stood in his path, stretching her long legs and yawning, while the other dogs lying around the steps rose lazily after her.

The dry, well-lighted anteroom smelt strongly of dogs and vinegar. An officer's Caucasian fur cap, a cowl with a silver tassel, and a Caucasian cloak lay on top of a trunk. A plump, black-eyed woman came out of a side room, gave Mokhov an attentive stare, and without changing the serious expression of her swarthily ruddy face, asked him:

"You want Nicholai Alexievich? I'll tell him."

Sergei Platonovich had difficulty in recognizing Aksinia in this rather stout, handsome woman. But she had immediately recognized him, had squeezed her lips together, and held herself unnaturally erect. She entered the hall without knocking and closed the door behind her. After a minute or two she came out again, followed by old Listnitsky. With a grave, welcoming smile he said condescendingly:

"Ah, Mokhov the merchant! What brings you here? Come in." He stood aside and with a wave of the hand invited his guest into the hall.

Sergei Platonovich bowed with the respect he had long since learned to adopt towards his social superiors and went in. Eugene Listnitsky came forward to meet him, screwing up his eyes behind his glasses. Smiling and revealing the golden crowns of his teeth, he took Mokhov by the arm and led him to a chair. Old Listnitsky gave Aksinia instructions for tea to be brought in, then came and stood by Mokhov with his hand resting on the table, and asked:

"How are things with you in the village? Have you heard—the good news?"

Mokhov looked up at the clean-shaven fold of flesh beneath the general's chin and sighed:

"How could one help hearing?"

"With what a fatal predetermination things have come to this pass!" the old man said, his Adam's apple quivering. "I foresaw this at the very beginning of the war. Well, the dynasty was doomed."

"We haven't any real news of what has happened," Mokhov said agitatedly. He fidgeted in his chair and lit a cigarette, then went on: "We haven't seen a newspaper for a week. And as I heard that Eugene Nicholaivich had come home on leave, I decided to drive over and ask what has really happened and what we have to expect next."

Now no longer smiling, Eugene replied:

"Menacing events. . . . The soldiers are literally demoralized. They don't want to go on fighting, they're tired of it. To tell the truth, this year we simply haven't had soldiers in the accepted meaning of the word. They have become bands of criminals, licentious and savage. Father simply cannot understand it. He cannot realize the extent to which our army has become demoralized. They arbitrarily abandon their positions, rob and kill the civilians, kill their officers, maraud. . . . Refusal to carry out military orders is now an everyday occurrence."

"The fish rots from the head," old Listnitsky puffed out with a cloud of tobacco-smoke.

"I wouldn't say that," Eugene frowned, one eyelid twitching nervously. "I wouldn't say that. The army is rotting from below, disintegrated by the Bolsheviks. Even the Cossack divisions, especially those which have been in close contact with the infantry, are morally unreliable. A terrible weariness and desire to get back home. . . . And the Bolsheviks—"

"What is it they want?" Mokhov asked, unable to possess himself in patience.

"Oh—" Eugene laughed. "What do they want! . . . They're worse than cholera germs. Worse in this sense, that they attach themselves more easily to a man and penetrate right into the very midst of the soldiers. I mean their ideas, of course . . . there's no quarantine that will save you from them. Undoubtedly there are some very clever men among the Bolsheviks. I've had to come into contact with some of them. There are simple fanatics among them, too, but the majority are licentious, immoral animals. These are not interested in the essence of the Bolshevik teaching, but only in the possibility of pillaging and getting away from the front. They want first of all to get power into their own hands, and on any conditions to end the 'imperialist' war, as they call it, even by way of a separate peace, and then to hand the land over to the peasants, and the factories to the workers. Of course this is as Utopian as it is silly, but it is by such primitive methods that they have succeeded in demoralizing the soldiers."

Mokhov listened with his whole body leaning forward as though he were about to jump out of his chair. Old Listnitsky paced up and down the hall, biting at his black, shaggy cloak and chewing his greenish-grey whiskers.

Eugene went on to tell how even before the Revolution broke out he had been forced to flee from his regiment, afraid of the vengeance of the Cossacks, and related the story of the events in Petrograd of which he had been witness. For a moment the talk lapsed into silence. Then, staring at Mokhov's nose, old Listnitsky abruptly asked:

"Well, will you buy the grey horse that you looked over in the autumn?"

"How can you talk about such matters at a time like this, Nicholai Alexievich?" Mokhov frowned miserably and waved his hand with a gesture of despair.

Meantime Mokhov's driver, Yemelian, was warming himself and drinking tea in the servants' room, wiping the sweat from his beet-red cheeks with a red handkerchief, and telling the news of the village. Wrapped in a downy shawl, Aksinia stood by the bed, her breast against its carved back.

"I suppose our hut has fallen down by now?" she asked.

"No, why should it?" Yemelian replied laconically.

"And our neighbours, the Melekhovs, how are they getting on?"

"They're getting on all right."

"Piotra hasn't returned on leave?"

"I haven't heard tell of it."

"And Gregor?"

"Gregor came home after Christmas. His wife gave him twins last year. And Gregor was wounded."

"Wounded?"

"Yes, in the arm. He was marked all over like a bitch after a fight. I don't know whether he had more crosses or gashes."

"And how did he look—Grishka, I mean?" Aksinia asked. Suppressing a dry sob, she coughed and wiped her nose.

"Just the same as ever; hook-nosed and dark. A Turk of the Turks, as you'd expect."

"I didn't mean that. . . . But does he look any older?"

"How should I know? Maybe he's a little older. His wife gave birth to twins. So he can't have aged very much."

"It's cold in the house," Aksinia said with a shiver, and she went out.

"A poisonous, stinking nit if ever there was one!" Yemelian snorted. "Not so long ago she was running about the village in bast shoes, and now she's quite the lady. 'It's cold in the house'! Pah, you lady from the lower end, your mother gave birth to a bitch, she did! Such women are dangerous. I'd show them, the carrion! . . . 'Cold in the house'! The crawling serpent! The snotty mare! Pah!"

He was so offended that he could not finish his eighth cup of tea, but got up, crossed himself, and went out, staring arrogantly about him and deliberately soiling the clean floor with his boots. The whole of the journey back he was as gloomy as his master. He poured out the vials of his wrath on the horse, flicking its hind-quarters indecently with the end of the whip and calling it names. Contrary to his wont, he did not exchange a single word with his master. And Sergei Platonovich also maintained a frightened silence.

Chapter 2

Before the March Revolution took place, the first brigade of one of the infantry divisions held in reserve on the south-west front, together with the 27th Don Cossack Regiment attached to it, was withdrawn from the front, in order to be transferred to Petrograd to suppress the disorders which had broken out. The brigade was led to the rear, equipped with new winter outfits, fed well for some days, then was entrained and dispatched. But events moved faster than the regiments, and on the very day of departure insistent rumours were circulating that the Czar had signed a decree abdicating the throne, at the headquarters of the commander-in-chief.

The brigade was turned back half-way. At the station of Razgon the 27th Cossack Regiment was ordered to detrain. The railway lines were blocked with transports. Soldiers with red bands on their coats, well-made new rifles of Russian pattern but English manufacture on their shoulders, were scurrying about the platform. Many of them seemed to be excited, and stared anxiously at the Cossacks being formed up in companies.

The day was rainy and exhausting. Water was rippling off the roofs of the station buildings. The oily puddles in between the tracks reflected the grey, fleshy sheepskin of the sky. The roar of the shunting engines sounded muffled. Beyond the freight warehouse the regiment was met by the commander of the brigade on a raven horse. Accompanied by the regimental commander, he rode up to the Cossacks, reined in his horse, stared hard at the companies, and made a speech, stumbling and faltering in his choice of words:

"Cossacks! By the will of the people the reign of the Czar Nicholai II has been—er—overthrown. The government has passed into the hands of the Provisional Committee of the State Duma. The army, and you among them, must take this—er—news calmly. . . . The duty of the Cossacks is to defend their native land from the attacks of external and—er—and, so to speak—from external enemies. We shall hold ourselves apart from the troubles now begun and leave it to the civil population to choose a way of organizing a new government. We must stand apart! For the army, war and politics are —er—incompatible. In times when the foundations are being—er— shaken, we must be as hard—" at this point the old, impotent brigadier-general, unused to speech-making, hesitated over the choice of a simile, while the regiment waited patiently—"as hard as steel. It is your Cossack military duty to obey your officers. We shall struggle against the enemy as brilliantly as before, while back there" (he made a vague, sweeping gesture behind him) "let the State Duma decide the fate of the country. When we have ended the war we shall take part in the internal life of the country, but for the present—we must not, we cannot betray the army. . . . There must be no politics in the army."

The Cossacks remained at the station for some days, taking the oath of allegiance to the Provisional Government, attending meetings, gathering in large local groups, but keeping themselves apart from the soldiers swarming at the station. Among themselves they discussed the speeches they had heard at the meetings, distrustfully turning over every doubtful word, until all of them somehow or other reached the conclusion that if there was freedom now, that meant the end of the war. It became difficult for the officers to struggle with that conviction and to maintain that Russia was bound to fight on to the end.

The bewilderment which took possession of the higher command of the army had a serious effect on the lower ranks. It was as though the brigade staff had completely forgotten the existence of the division stranded on the line half-way to Petrograd. The soldiers

ate up the eight days' rations which had been issued, then crowded
to the neighbouring villages. Liquor appeared miraculously for sale,
and drunken soldiers and officers became a common sight.

Torn out of the normal round of duties, the Cossacks crowded in
their railway cars, awaiting transport to the Don. For the rumour
that the second reservists were to be demobilized was very per-
sistent. They grew negligent in the care of their horses and spent
the day in the market squares, trading with German helmets,
bayonets, overcoats, and the tobacco they had brought back from
the trenches.

When at last an order arrived for the regiment to return to the
front, it was received with open discontent. The second company
at first flatly refused to go, and the Cossacks would not allow the
engine to be coupled to the transport train. But the regimental commander threatened to have them disarmed, and the agitation died
away. The transport dragged slowly towards the front, while in
every car the situation was excitedly discussed.

At a certain railway junction the Cossacks poured out of the train
as though by previous agreement and, taking no notice of the
promises and threats of the commander, began a meeting. In vain
did the ancient station-master mingle with the grey Cossack greatcoats, imploring them to go back to their train and let the tracks be
cleared. The Cossacks listened with unflagging attention to the
speeches of a sergeant and a little rank-and-file Cossack. The latter
had difficulty in giving vent to his angry feelings:

"Cossacks! This isn't good enough! They've mucked everything
up again! They're trying to make fools of us! If there's been a revolution and all the people have been given their freedom, they ought to
stop the war. Do the people and us Cossacks want war? Am I right?"

"You're right!"

"We can't keep our trousers up over our bottoms! And is that
what they call war?"

"Down with the war! Let's go back home."

"Uncouple the engine! Come on, boys!"

"Cossacks! Wait a bit! Cossacks! Brothers! You devils! Hold on!
Brothers!" The little Cossack shouted away, attempting to raise his
voice above the thousand. "Wait! Don't touch the engine! We're
only out to stop this fooling. Let His Excellency the regimental
commander show us the document, let us see whether they really

want us at the front or whether it is only another of their little games."

After the regimental commander, almost beside himself, his lips trembling, had read aloud the telegram from the divisional staff ordering the regiment to the front, the Cossacks consented again to entrain.

Six of the Tatarsk men were in one car. There were Piotra Melekhov, Nicholai Koshevoi (Mitka's uncle), Anikushka, Fiodot Bodovskov, Merkulov (a gypsy-looking Cossack with black curly beard and blazing hazel eyes), and Maksim Griaznov, a dissolute and merry Cossack known throughout the Don district as a fearless horse-stealer. A cross-wind pierced through the car, the horses stood with their horse-cloths over them at hastily built mangers, damp wood smoked on a mound of earth in the middle of the floor, and the pungent smoke was drawn towards the chinks of the door. The Cossacks sat on their saddles around the fire, drying the smelly rags wound round their legs. Bodovskov was warming his bare feet at the fire, a contented smile lurking on his Kalmyk, angular face. Griaznov was hurriedly sewing his gaping sole to the upper with a wax thread. In a husky voice he remarked to no one in particular:

"When I was a lad I used to climb up on the stove in winter-time, and my grandmother (she was a hundred years old then) would search for lice in my head with her fingers, and tell me: 'My little Maksim, my darling! In the old days the people didn't live like they do now; they lived well, lawfully, and nobody dared attack them. But you, my little child, will live to see a time when all the earth is covered with wire, and birds with iron noses will fly through the air and peck at the people as a rook pecks at a watermelon. And there will be hunger and plague among men, brother will rise against brother, and son against father. The people will be left like grass after a fire.'" Griaznov paused a moment, then continued: "Well, it's all come to pass as she said it would. They've invented the telegraph, and there's your wire. And the iron birds are aeroplanes. And there'll be a famine, all right. My own folk have only sown half their land during these years, and there's little left of the reserve stocks. Everywhere it's the same. And if the harvest fails you'll have your hunger."

"But brother against brother—that's a bit far-fetched, isn't it?" Piotra Melekhov asked.

"You wait a bit, and the people will come to that too!"

Anikushka wrinkled his hairless face into an expression of feigned terror and exclaimed:

"By our hairy-legged Czaritsa, and how long yet shall we have to go on fighting?"

"Until you grow a beard, you eunuch," Koshevoi mimicked him.

There was an outburst of laughter, and Anikushka was put to confusion. But in the middle Griaznov unexpectedly broke out:

"No, we've had enough! We've had more than we can stand! Here we are in misery, perishing with lice, and our families at home are also feeling the pinch so much that if you cut them they wouldn't bleed."

"What are you bellowing about?" Piotra asked jokingly, chewing his whiskers.

"You know what!" Merkulov answered for Griaznov, burying his smile in his curly beard. "You know what the Cossack needs, what he longs for. . . . You know how it is; sometimes the shepherd drives the herd out to pasture, and as long as the sun hasn't dried the dew off the grass, the cattle are all right; but as soon as the sun gets overhead, the gadflies begin to bite. And so it is here." He turned round to face Piotra. "Then, mister corporal, the cattle begin to bellow and kick. Yes, and you know it! You needn't be uppish! You've driven bullocks yourself. . . . You know how it happens. Some calf sends its tail swishing over its back and off it goes, scratching away like hell! And the whole herd after it! The shepherd runs to stop them, but they're off like a flood, like we poured in a flood against the Germans. And then you try to stop them!"

"What's the point of all this?"

Merkulov did not reply at once. He wound a curl of his beard around his finger and tugged it cruelly, then said, now serious and unsmiling:

"Four years we've been fighting—that's right, isn't it? We're in the fourth year now since they drove us into the trenches. What for, and why? No one knows. But what I am saying is that sooner or later some Griaznov or Melekhov will break away from the front, and after him the regiment, and after the regiment the army. . . . That's what will happen."

"So that's what you're getting at!"

"Yes, that! I'm not blind, and I see that everything hangs by a hair. Only let someone shout 'Shoo!' and they'll all slip off like an old coat from the shoulders."

"You should be more careful," Bodovskov advised him. "Remember Piotra's a corporal."

"I've never brought trouble on any comrade of mine," Piotra exploded.

"All right, don't get angry. I was only joking."

Bodovskov was put out of countenance by Piotra's outburst, and he rose and pattered off to the horses. In another corner of the car Cossacks from other villages were talking in whispers. After a time they struck up a tune. Koshevoi invited the group to join them at the fire, they threw the fragments of a fence broken away at the station on to it, and the song was raised again, now more joyously.

But above blood-soaked White Russia the stars wept mournfully. The nocturnal darkness yawned smokily and fluidly. The wind fawned on the earth, saturated with the scent of fallen leaves, of damp, clayey mouldiness, of March snows.

Within twenty-four hours the regiment was again close to the front. The transport train was halted at a railway junction. The corporals brought the order to detrain. The horses were hurriedly led down planks on to the track, there was a scurrying backward and forward after forgotten articles, ragged bundles of hay were flung straight on to the damp sand of the roadbed.

An orderly from the regimental commander called out to Piotra Melekhov as he passed:

"The commander wants you at the station."

Adjusting a strap on his greatcoat, Piotra went slowly towards the platform. "Anikushka, give an eye to my horse," he asked as he went by.

Anikushka stared silently after him, anxiety mingling with the usual expression of boredom on his sullen face. As Piotra walked along, staring at his muddy boots and wondering why the regimental commander had sent for him, his attention was attracted by a small group gathered at the end of the platform by the hot-water shed. He went up and listened to the conversation. Some score of soldiers stood surrounding a tall, ruddy-faced Cossack who was standing with his back to the shed in an awkward, hunted attitude.

Piotra stared at his bearded face, at the figure 52 on his blue, sergeant's epaulet, and felt sure he had seen the man before somewhere.

"What's the matter?" he asked inquisitively, touching the shoulder of a man standing in front of him.

The soldier turned his head and answered unwillingly:

"Caught a deserter—one of your Cossacks."

Piotra tried to recall where he had seen the Cossack before. The prisoner made no reply to the importunate questionings of the soldiers around him, but with great gulps drank hot water out of a copper mug made from a shell-case and chewed at a dry biscuit soaked in the water. His widely spaced, dilated eyes narrowed as he chewed and swallowed, and his eyebrows quivered as he glanced down and around. An elderly, thickset soldier stood on guard with rifle and fixed bayonet at his side. The Cossack finished his drink and passed his tired eyes over the soldiers unceremoniously examining him. His blue, childishly simple eyes suddenly hardened. Hurriedly swallowing, he licked his lips and shouted in a coarse, deep, inflexible voice:

"Am I an animal? Won't you let a man eat, you swine? Damn you, haven't you ever seen a man before?"

The soldiers burst into a roar of laughter; but Piotra had hardly heard the first words when the identity of the man came back to him in a flash.

"Fomin! Yakob!" he shouted, pushing his way through the crowd

The man put the mug down with a clumsy, bewildered movement and, gazing at Piotra with smiling, embarrassed eyes, replied, as he chewed:

"I can't say I know you, brother!"

"You're from Rabiezhin, aren't you?"

"Yes. And you're surely from Zhelanska?"

"No, from Vieshenska. But I know you all right. You sold my father a bullock at the market four years ago."

Still smiling the same childish smile, Fomin tried to remember.

"No, I've forgotten it. I can't remember you," he said with evident regret.

"You were in the 52nd?"

"Yes."

"You ran away? How could you, brother?"

Fomin took off his fur cap and fished out an ancient pouch. He bent and slowly pushed his cap under his arm, tore off a corner of paper, and only then fixed Piotra with a stern, moistly twinkling gaze.

"Couldn't stand any more, brother," he said gruffly.

Transfixed by the man's stare, Piotra coughed and bit at his yellow whisker.

"Well, finish your talk or I'll be getting into trouble through you," the soldier escort remarked, picking up his rifle. "Come on, old boy."

Fomin hurriedly pushed the mug into his pack, said good-bye to Piotra with eyes averted, and with a heavy bearish, swaying gait went with his escort towards the station commandant's office.

Piotra found the regimental commander with the two company commanders bent over a table in the former first-class buffet.

"You've kept us waiting, Melekhov." The colonel frowned with tired, irritable eyes.

Piotra listened to the information that his company was being placed at the disposition of the divisional staff, and that it was necessary to keep a sharp watch on the Cossacks, informing the company commander of any noticeable change in their attitude. He stared unwinkingly at the colonel's face, listening attentively, but Fomin's twinkling eyes and the quiet "Couldn't stand any more, brother," stuck ineradicably in his memory.

He left the warm, steaming buffet and went back to the company. As he approached his car he saw a group of Cossacks gathered around the company smith. He promptly forgot Fomin and their conversation and hurried his steps, intending to have a word with the smith about the reshoeing of his horse. The petty cares and anxieties of the daily round rose uppermost. But it was only for a moment. From behind a car came a woman decked in a white fluffy shawl and dressed differently from the women in White Russia. The strangely familiar shape of her figure fixed Piotra's attention. The woman suddenly turned her face towards him and hastened in his direction, swinging her shoulders and her fine youthful body. And, although not yet close enough to distinguish her features, by that light, crisp walk of hers Piotra recognized his wife. A pleasant prickly cool penetrated to his heart. His joy was the greater because unexpected. Deliberately slowing his steps, so that the others should not think he was particularly pleased, he went to meet her. He embraced Daria, kissed her the customary three times, and was about to ask her something. But his deep inward agitation broke through to the surface, his lips trembled, and he lost his voice.

"I wasn't expecting you," he choked up at last.

"My dove! How you have changed!" Daria clapped her hands. "You're quite a stranger! You see I've come to visit you. They didn't want to let me go at home. But I thought I must go and see my dear one." She stumbled out the words, pressing against her husband and gazing at him with moist eyes.

Around the cars the Cossacks crowded, staring at them, quacking and winking:

"Piotra's happy all right!"

"My old wolf-bitch wouldn't come to visit me!"

"He might lend his wife to his own troop for a night. In pity on our poverty. . . ."

At that moment Piotra forgot that he had promised himself to punish his wife ruthlessly, and he caressed her in front of everybody, stroking the arches of her eyebrows with his great tobacco-stained finger and rejoicing. Daria also forgot that only two nights previously she had slept in a car with a veterinary surgeon of the dragoons, who had been on his way from Kharkov to rejoin his regiment. The surgeon had unusually fluffy black moustaches; but that had been two nights ago, and now with tears of sincere joy in her eyes she embraced her husband, gazing at him with true, clear eyes.

Chapter 3

On his return from leave Eugene Listnitsky did not report to his old regiment, but went straight to the divisional staff. The chief of staff, a young general from a famous Don Cossack noble family, willingly arranged for his transfer to the 14th Don Cossack Regiment in view of his difficulties with the Cossacks of his previous regiment.

Listnitsky was glad of the transfer. The same day he travelled to Dvinsk, where the 14th Regiment was stationed, and reported to the regimental commander. He was satisfied to find that the majority of the officers were monarchists, while the Cossacks were by no means revolutionarily disposed. They had taken the oath of allegiance to the Provisional Government very reluctantly, and took no part in the events seething around them. Cringing and peaceable Cossacks had been elected to the regimental and company committees. Listnitsky breathed more easily in his new circumstances.

The regiment had been stationed some two months in Dvinsk, assembled into a single unit and resting. Previously the two companies had been attached to infantry divisions and had wandered about the front from Riga to Dvinsk, but in April a careful hand had brought the companies together, and the regiment was now prepared for anything. Protected by the officers' strict supervision, the Cossacks spent their days at exercise, fed their horses well, and lived a temperate, sluggish existence, removed from all outside influence. Unpleasant rumours circulated among them as to the future purpose of the regiment, while the officers talked openly of their intention, guided by reliable hands, to turn back the wheel of history in the not distant future.

The front extended a little farther to the west. There the armies breathed in a mortal fever; there was a shortage of military supplies, of food. With innumerable hands the soldiers reached out to the phantasmal word "peace." In the armies a ripened anger flowed and bubbled like water in a spring. . . . But in Dvinsk the Cossacks lived peaceably, quietly, and the miseries they had endured at the front were overgrown in their memories. The officers regularly attended the officers' meetings, lived well, and ardently discussed the future of Russia.

So till the early days of July. On the 16th the order came to advance without losing an instant. The regiment moved towards Petrograd. On the 20th the hoofs of the Cossack horses were clattering over the wood-paved streets of the capital.

The regiment was quartered in houses on the Nevsky Prospect, and Listnitsky's company was assigned an empty commercial building. The Cossacks had been awaited with impatience and joy; the care which the city authorities had taken to fit up the quarters assigned to them witnessed eloquently to that. The walls gleamed with fresh whitewash, the clean floors shone like new pins, it was almost comfortable in the light, tidy semi-basement. Listnitsky carefully examined the quarters and decided that they could hardly have been better. Satisfied with his inspection, he turned towards the door leading to the yard, accompanied by the little, elegantly dressed representative of the city administration who had been assigned to show him the building.

Listening inattentively to the chatter of the city representative, he crossed the yard and inspected the warehouse allotted for stables. "We must have another doorway made in these stables," he pointed out. "Three doors for a hundred and twenty horses are insufficient. In the event of an alarm it would take us half an hour to get the horses out. It's strange that this circumstance was not taken into consideration beforehand. I shall have to report the matter to the regimental commander."

He left the man making protestations that the work would be put in hand at once, and went upstairs to the rooms temporarily assigned to the company officers. He threw himself down on his camp-bed and lay silent, feeling the damp sweat of his shirt cooling pleasantly on his skin. Worn out with his journey, he was disinclined to rise and wash, but mastering his lassitude, he rose at last, stripped, and washed thoroughly, then rubbed himself dry with the towel. The wash freshened him, and he was about to pick up the newspaper to read about the disturbances of a few days before in the city, when an invitation came for him to call on the regimental commander. Rising unwillingly from his bed, he dressed and went on to the Nevsky Prospect. Lighting a cigarette, he strolled along the pavement. A dense throng foamed with men's straw hats, derbies, and caps and women's artificially simple and trimmed hats. Occasionally the democratic green cap of a soldier appeared and disappeared, engulfed in the flood of colours.

A fresh, stimulating breeze was blowing from the sea, but it broke against the blocks of buildings and was scattered into thin, unequal gusts. Clouds were floating southward over the steely,

violet-tinted heaven; their milky-white masses were sharply and
distinctly serrated. A steaming sultriness heralding rain hung over
the city. The air was scented with the smell of warm asphalt, burnt
gasoline, the near-by sea, the indefinite aroma of perfumes, and
the myriad other odours characteristic of every large town.

The awnings of the shops cast lazy, olive-yellow patches on the
pavement. The wind sent the blinds billowing and bellying, and
the patches stirred, tearing away from the feet of the passers-by.
Despite the afternoon hour, the Nevsky was crowded with people.
With joyous satisfaction Listnitsky, grown unaccustomed to towns
during the years of war, drank in the myriad-voiced roar, the motor-
horns, the shouts of the newspaper-sellers. Feeling among his own
people in this crowd of well-dressed, well-fed people, nevertheless
he could not but think:

"How satisfied, how glad and happy you are now! All of you:
merchants, stock-brokers, officials, landowners, people of blue
blood! But how did you feel only three days ago when the workers
and soldiers were pouring in a molten stream along this very street?
Truly, I am glad for you, yet not glad. And I don't know how to
rejoice in your well-being. . . ."

He tried to analyse his mingled feelings, to find their source, and
had no difficulty in deciding that he thought and felt so because
the war and all he had had to live through had drawn him apart
from this crowd of well-fed and satisfied men and women.

"Now, you, for instance," he thought, as his eyes met those of a
plump, rosy-cheeked young man, "why aren't you at the front? I
suppose he's the son of a factory-owner or some commercial giant
and has got out of military service, the scum! And he's growing
fat in work 'for the defence of the fatherland.'"

He went slowly up the steps of the house in which the regimental
staff was quartered. On the landing of the second floor he smoked
a cigarette, cleaned his eyeglasses, and then ascended to the third
floor, where the staff was quartered.

The regimental commander opened a map of Petrograd before
him and pointed out the area in which Listnitsky's company was
to guard the government offices. He specified the buildings one by
one and informed him with the utmost detail of the time and manner
of posting the guards. He concluded with:

"In the Winter Palace Kerensky. . . ."

"Not a word of Kerensky!" Listnitsky muttered fiercely, turning a deathly pallor.

"Eugene Nicholaivich, you must take yourself in hand."

"Colonel, I ask you—"

"Now, my dear fellow . . ."

"I ask you!"

"Your nerves . . ."

"Am I to send out patrols in the direction of the Putilov works immediately?" Eugene asked quietly, breathing heavily.

The colonel bit his lips, smiled, shrugged his shoulders, and replied:

"At once! And invariably in charge of a troop officer."

Listnitsky turned and went out, crushed by the memory of his talk with the colonel. Almost outside the main door he saw a patrol of the 4th Don Cossack Regiment. Fresh flowers drooped gloomily from the snaffles of the officer's horse, and a smile twisted the man's flaxen-whiskered face.

"Hurrah for the saviours of the country!" some sententious elderly gentleman shouted, stepping off the pavement and waving his hat.

The officer courteously saluted, and the patrol trotted on. Listnitsky stared at the agitated, slobbering-lipped face of the civilian who had cheered the Cossacks, at the man's carefully tied coloured cravat, and, frowning, huddled hurriedly into the gateway of his company quarters.

General Kornilov's appointment as commander-in-chief of the south-western front was highly approved by the officers of the 14th Cossack Regiment. They spoke of him with esteem and respect as a man with an iron character and undoubtedly capable of getting the country out of the mess into which the Provisional Government had plunged it. Listnitsky especially welcomed the appointment. Through the younger officers of the company and trusted Cossacks he tried to find out how the lower ranks reacted to it, but the information he obtained hardly pleased him, for the Cossacks were either silent or replied apathetically:

"It makes no difference to us."

"If he tried to bring peace, then of course . . ."

"We shan't be any better off by his advancement."

Within a few days of Kornilov's appointment, rumours were circulating among the officers that he was putting pressure on the government to restore the death-sentence at the front and to introduce other resolute measures on which the successful prosecution of the war depended, but that Kerensky was resisting him and was trying to have him replaced by a more compliant general. So the government communiqué of August 1, appointing Kornilov as supreme commander-in-chief, came as a great surprise. On the evening of the same day Listnitsky, in conversation with other officers of the regiment, raised the question sharply and directly: on whose side were they?

"Gentlemen," he said, restraining his agitation, "we are living like one family, yet so far a number of important questions have remained unsettled among us. And now that we are clearly moving towards a clash between the supreme command and the government, we must settle the question on whose side we are. Let's talk like comrades, hiding nothing from one another."

The first to reply to his invitation was Lieutenant Atarshchikov:

"For General Kornilov I am ready to give my own blood, and that of others also. He is a man of transparent honesty, and only he is capable of putting Russia on her feet. Look what he's done already with the army. Thanks to him, the hands of the commanders have been untied somewhat, whereas before it was continual committees, fraternizations, desertions. How can there be any discussion about it?"

He spoke fierily, and when he had ended, looked around the group of officers and tapped a cigarette challengingly on his case.

"If we've got to choose between the Bolsheviks, Kerensky, and Kornilov, of course we're for Kornilov," said another.

"It's difficult to judge what Kornilov wants; is it the restoration of order, or the restoration of something else? . . ." a third remarked.

"That's no answer! Or if it is, it's a silly one! What is it you're afraid of: the restoration of the monarchy?"

"I'm not afraid of that; on the contrary."

"Well then, what are you arguing about?"

"Gentlemen," spoke up Dolgov, who had only recently been raised from corporal to cornet for his military distinction, "what are you quarrelling about? Say frankly that we Cossacks must hold by General Kornilov as a child clings to its mother's skirt. If we break with him, we're lost. Russia will bury us in dung. The position is clear: where he goes, we go also."

"That's exactly it!"Atarshchikov exclaimed, clapping Dolgov on the back. "Now, gentlemen," he raised his voice, "are we for Kornilov or aren't we?"

"Why, of course we are."

Laughing and kissing one another, the officers drank their tea. The tense feeling which had prevailed was dissipated, and the conversation turned to the events of the past few days.

"We're all for the commander-in-chief, but the Cossacks are a bit down in the mouth," Dolgov remarked irresolutely.

"How 'down in the mouth'?" Listnitsky asked.

"Why, they're in the dumps, and that's all there is to it. The swine want to go home to their wives. Their life isn't too easy or pleasant."

"It's up to us to carry the Cossacks with us," another officer declared, bringing his fist down with a bang on the table. "That's what we're officers for."

Listnitsky rattled his spoon against his glass, and when he had secured attention, said deliberately:

"I ask you to remember, gentlemen, that our work at the moment consists in explaining to the Cossacks the true state of affairs. We must get the Cossacks away from the influence of the committees. We must have a different approach to them now. Formerly—in 1916, for instance—I could thrash a Cossack and risk his sending a bullet through my back in the next battle. But after the March Revolution we had to act differently, because if I struck some idiot, he might easily have killed me on the spot without waiting for a convenient opportunity. And now the situation has changed again. Now we must fraternize with the Cossacks. Everything depends on that," he declared emphatically. "You know what is happening at present in the 1st and 4th Regiments? Their officers continued to cut themselves off from the Cossacks with the old walls, and as a result the Cossacks almost to a man have come under the influence of the Bolsheviks. It's clear that we shall not be able to avoid the menacing events that are coming. The risings of July 16 and 18 were only a harsh forewarning to all who are heedless. . . . Either we shall have to struggle with Kornilov against the army of the revolutionary democracy or the Bolsheviks will bring about yet another revolution. They are having a breathing-space, a concentration of their strength, and meantime we are slacking. Is that good enough?"

"That's true, Listnitsky."

"Russia has one foot in the grave."

"I say that when the coming struggle arrives—the civil war, I mean —and I've only just begun to realize that it is inevitable—we shall have need of trusty Cossacks. We must struggle to win them away from the committees which are inclining towards the Bolsheviks. That is a bloody necessity! Remember that in the event of new disturbances the Cossacks of the 1st and 4th Regiments will shoot down their own officers. . . ."

"That's true; they won't stand on ceremony."

". . . And by their experience—a very bitter one— we must profit. The Cossacks of the 1st and 4th Regiments (for that matter, they're no longer Cossacks!) will have to be dealt with summarily. The weeds must be cleared from the field! And we must save our own Cossacks from mistakes for which they would afterwards have to pay."

After Listnitsky one of the company commanders, an elderly officer who had been nine years in the regiment and had been wounded four times, spoke of the difficulties of service in the Cossack regiments before the war. The Cossack officers had been kept in the back yard, in the shade; promotion had been slow; and in his view this explained the inertia of the Cossack leaders at the time of the Czar's overthrow. But even so, it was necessary to support Kornilov at all costs and to maintain closer contacts with him through the Soviet of the Alliance of Cossack Troops and the Chief Committee of the Officers' Alliance. "Let Kornilov become dictator!" he ended. "For the Cossacks that will be salvation. Maybe we shall be better off under him than under the Czar."

The officers sat talking till dawn. It was decided to have talks with the Cossacks three times a week on political subjects, and the troop officers were to occupy the troops daily with gymnastics and reading, in order to fill up spare time and to win the Cossacks away from the disintegrating atmosphere of politics. Before breaking up, toasts were jestingly proposed, to the ring of their glasses of tea, and Dolgov and Atarshchikov raised the tune of the old Cossack song:

. . . But our Don is proud, our gentle Don, our father dear;
Never did he bow to heathen, never asked of Moscow how to live;
And the Turks—with the sword-point for ages he greeted them;
And from year to year the Donland steppe, our motherland,
For the Immaculate Holy Mother and its own true faith,
Yes, for the Don so free, with its billowing waves, battled with
the enemies. . . .

Atarshchikov sat with hands crossed on his knees, singing without faltering, his face unusually stern. Only towards the end of the song Listnitsky noticed a tear running down his cheeks.

After the officers of the other companies had departed, Atarshchikov came and sat down on Listnitsky's bed and, fiddling with the faded blue braces on his chest, whispered:

"You know, Eugene—I am devilishly fond of the Don, of all that old, age-old style of Cossack life. I love my Cossacks, and the Cossack women. I love them all! I want to weep when I smell the scent of the steppe wormwood. . . . And when the sunflower blossoms and the perfume of the rain-washed grapevines is in the air, I love it all so deeply and painfully . . . you understand. . . . And now I'm thinking: mayn't we be fooling these same Cossacks with all this? Is this the road we want them to take?"

"What are you getting at?" Listnitsky asked cautiously.

"I'm wondering whether this is the best for the Cossacks."

"But if not, what is best for them?"

"I don't know. . . . But why are they so elementally turning away from us? The Revolution has literally divided us into sheep and goats; our interests seem to be different."

"Don't you see?" Listnitsky began carefully. "Here we get a difference in the understanding of events. We have the greater culture, and we can critically estimate the situation, but for them everything is more primitive and simple. The Bolsheviks are continually driving into their heads that the war must be ended, or rather must be transformed into civil war. They are poisoning the Cossacks against us, and as they are tired, as there is more of the animal in them and they don't have that strong moral consciousness of their duty and responsibility to their fatherland which we have, it is natural that the Bolsheviks should find them a favourable soil for their doctrines. After all, what does the fatherland really mean to the Cossacks? It is an abstract conception at the best. 'The Don district is far from the front,' they reason, 'and the Germans will never get so far.' That's the whole trouble. We must explain to them the consequences that would follow from the transformation of the war into a civil war."

Even while he spoke, Eugene felt that his words were not reaching their aim, and that Atarshchikov was closing himself up again like an oyster. When he had finished, the other man sat for a long time without speaking, and try as he would, Listnitsky could not discover the secret train of thought Atarshchikov was pursuing. "I should have let him speak his mind out to the end . . ." he thought regretfully.

Atarshchikov wished him a good-night and went to his own bed. Listnitsky lay smoking for a while, troubled and angered by his inability to get to the bottom of what was disturbing his friend. As he stared tensely into the grey velvety darkness, he suddenly remembered Aksinia and his days of leave, filled to the brim with her. He fell asleep soothed by the change of thought and the fortuitous, fragmentary recollection of the women whose roads at various times had crossed his road.

In Listnitsky's company was a Cossack, Ivan Lagutin, who had been one of the first to be elected to the regimental Military Revolutionary Committee. Until the regiment arrived in Petrograd, he displayed no outstanding characteristics, but at the beginning of August the troop officer informed Eugene that the man was in the habit of attending the military section of the Petrograd Soviet of Workers' and Soldiers' Deputies, was always talking to the other Cossacks of the troop, and had an unfortunate influence over them. There had been two cases of refusal to undertake guard and patrol duty, and the troop officer attributed them to Lagutin's influence. Listnitsky decided that he must get to know the man better and find out what he was thinking. An opportunity quickly presented itself. A few nights later Lagutin's troop was assigned patrol duty in the streets around the Putilov works, and Listnitsky informed the troop officer that he would take charge on this occasion. He gave instructions to his orderly to get his horse ready and went out into the yard.

The troop was already mounted and waiting. He led it out, and they rode along several streets through the misty darkness. Eugene deliberately dropped behind and called Lagutin to him. The man turned his horse and rode up, glancing inquiringly at the captain.

"Well, what's the latest news in the committee?" Listnitsky asked.

"Nothing much just now," the man replied.

"What district are you from, Lagutin?"

"Bukanovsk."

"And the village?"

"Mitkin."

"Are you married?" the captain asked, after a silence during which he studied the man's face.

"Yes. I've got a wife and two children."

"And a farm?"

"A farm, do you call it?" Lagutin replied, with a sneer and a note of self-pity in his voice. "We live from hand to mouth, and all our life is one long grind and struggle." He paused for a moment, then added harshly: "Our land is sandy."

Listnitsky had once driven through the Bukanovsk district, and he vividly remembered the remote, isolated region, bounded on the south by level, worthless marsh-land and belted by the capricious windings of the river Khopra.

"I expect you'd like to get back home," he asked.

"And why not, sir? Of course I'd like to get back as soon as I can. We've had to put up with a lot through this war."

"I'm afraid you won't be getting back yet awhile, my lad."

"I think we shall," Lagutin answered.

"But the war isn't ended yet."

"It'll be over soon. We'll be going home soon," the Cossack replied obstinately.

"We'll be fighting among ourselves first. Don't you think so?"

Without raising his eyes from his saddle-bow, Lagutin replied after a moment:

"Who are we going to fight, then?"

"We'll have plenty on our hands. . . . The Bolsheviks perhaps."

Again Lagutin was silent, as though he were dozing to the firm, rhythmic clatter of the hoofs. Then he slowly answered:

"We haven't any quarrel with them."

"But what about the land?"

"There's enough land for everybody."

"You know what the Bolsheviks are after?" Eugene inquired.

"I've heard a little about it."

"Well then, what ought we to do if the Bolsheviks attack us in order to seize our land and to enslave the Cossacks? You've been fighting the Germans in defence of Russia, haven't you?"

"The Germans are different."

"And the Bolsheviks?"

"Why, sir—" Lagutin spoke up. Evidently he had come to some decision; he raised his eyes and tried to catch Listnitsky's gaze. "The Bolsheviks won't take my last bit of land from me. I've only got one share, and they won't need that. . . . But—only you won't be offended, will you? There's your father, now, he has twenty thousand acres."

"Not twenty, but eight."

"That doesn't make any difference. Eight thousand isn't a little. And where's the right of that? And there's a lot like your father all over Russia. Then you think what every mouth needs. You want to eat and everybody else wants to eat. Under the Czar everything was wrong, and the poor had a lean time. They gave your father eight thousand as his share of the pie, but he can't eat two men's food any more than I can. It's a shame. And the Bolsheviks are on the right track, yet you want us to fight them."

At first Listnitsky listened with inward agitation. But as the Cossack developed his argument, he could not control himself and lost his temper.

"Are you a Bolshevik, then?" he demanded.

"The name doesn't matter," Lagutin replied. "It's not a question of names, but of right. The people want their rights, but they're always being buried and the earth heaped over them."

"It's obvious what the Bolsheviks are teaching you! You haven't wasted the time you have spent in their company."

"Ah, captain, it's life itself that has taught us patient ones, and the Bolsheviks have only set fire to the tinder."

"You can drop those stories," Listnitsky ordered, now thoroughly angry. "Answer me! You were speaking just now of my father's land, and of the landowners' land generally, but you know as well as I do that it is private property. If you have two shirts and I haven't even one, do you think I ought to take one from you?"

Eugene could not see the Cossack's face, but from his reply he guessed that he was smiling.

"I'd give up my extra shirt of my own accord. At the front I gave up not one extra shirt but my very last shirt and wore my greatcoat against my bare back. And nobody would be hurt by losing a little bit of land."

"Haven't you enough land already?" Listnitsky raised his voice. Lagutin almost shouted his answer:

"And do you suppose I'm only thinking about myself? We've been in Poland—you saw how the people were living there? And how the peasants are living all around us in the Don? I've seen it! It's enough to make your blood boil! Do you think I'm not sorry for them?"

Eugene was about to make a biting reply, but from the looming grey buildings of the Putilov works ahead came a sudden shout of "Hold him!" There was a clatter of hoofs and the sound of a shot. Plying his whip, Listnitsky put his horse to a gallop. He and Lagutin rode up side by side and found the troop halted and gathered at a corner. Several of the Cossacks were dismounted, and in the middle of the ring a man was struggling. The troop sergeant, Arzhanov, was hanging out of his saddle and holding a little man in a Russian shirt by his collar, while three dismounted Cossacks were twisting his arms.

"What's the matter?" Listnitsky thundered, urging his horse into the crowd.

"This serpent has been throwing stones. . . ."

"He struck one of us and ran away."

"Give it to him, Arzhanov!" another Cossack shouted.

Almost beside himself with rage, Listnitsky shouted at the man: "Who are you?"

The prisoner raised his head, but in his white face the lips remained pressed firmly together.

"Who are you?" Eugene repeated his question. "Throwing stones were you, you scum? Silence! Arzhanov, give it to him!" he ordered, turning his horse away.

Three or four of the dismounted Cossacks threw the man down and swung their knouts. Lagutin flung himself out of the saddle and ran to Listnitsky.

"Captain—what are you doing? . . . Captain!" He seized Listnitsky's knee with his trembling fingers and shouted: "You can't go on like that! He's a man. . . . What are you doing?"

Eugene shook his reins over his horse's neck and made no reply. Running back to the Cossacks, Lagutin seized Arzhanov around the waist and tried to drag him away. But the sergeant resisted, muttering:

"Don't take on so! Don't take on! Is he to throw stones and us not say a word? Let me go! Let me go, I tell you for your own good!"

One of the Cossacks bent and, swinging his rifle from his shoulder, brought the butt down against the man's soft body. A low, primitively savage cry crept over the roadway. "Ah-ah-ah-ah! They're killing me!" There was silence for a few seconds, then again the voice arose, but now young and choking, quivering with pain. After each blow he muttered curt exclamations between his groans:

"Swine! Counter-revolutionaries! Beat on! O-oh!"

Lagutin ran back to Listnitsky, and pressing against his knee, scratching with his fingernails at the saddle, he choked:

"Let him go!"

"Stand back!" Eugene ordered.

"Captain—Listnitsky! Do you hear? . . . You'll answer for this!" He turned and ran to the Cossacks standing apart from the group around the man. "Brothers!" he shouted. "I am a member of the Revolutionary Committee. . . . I order you to save that man from death! . . . You will have to answer for it! It's not the old days now!"

An unreasoning, blinding hatred carried Listnitsky away. He struck his horse between the ears with his whip and rode at Lagutin. Thrusting his black, well-greased pistol into the Cossack's face, he howled:

"Silence, traitor! Bolshevik! I'll shoot you!"

With a supreme effort of will he mastered himself, removed his finger from the trigger, swung his horse round on its hind legs, and rode off.

A few minutes later three Cossacks set out after him. Two of them dragged the prisoner along between their two horses. The man's blood-soaked shirt was sticking to his body. Supported under the armpits by the Cossacks, he swayed helplessly, his feet dancing over the cobbles. His bloody face, beaten almost to a pulp, hung back loosely between his raised shoulders. The third Cossack rode some distance away. At the corner of a street he saw a droshky-driver and, standing in his stirrups, cantered towards him. Expressively striking his boot-leg with his knout, he gave the man a curt order, and with servile haste the droshky-driver drove up to the two Cossacks halted in the middle of the street.

The next morning Listnitsky awoke with the feeling that he had committed a great and irreparable blunder. He bit his lips as he recalled the scene of the previous night and all that had passed between himself and Lagutin. As he dressed he decided that for the present Lagutin had better be left alone, in order to avoid any worsening of relationships with the regimental committee. It would be advisable to wait until the other Cossacks of the troop had forgotten the incident, and then quietly remove him.

"And that's what we mean when we talk about fraternizing with the Cossacks," he thought with bitter irony.

One fine sunny day in the middle of August, Listnitsky and Atarshchikov went into the city. Since the conversation after the officers' meeting nothing had happened to resolve the uncertainty which had arisen between them. Atarshchikov kept his own counsel, and whenever Eugene attempted to draw him into the open, he dropped the impenetrable curtain which most men employ to protect their true features from other eyes. Eugene could only conclude that in his struggle to find a way out from the antagonisms dividing the various sections of the nation, Atarshchikov was linking up the Cossack national aspirations with those of the Bolsheviks. And this supposition led him to cease his attempts to become more friendly with Atarshchikov.

They strolled down the Nevsky Prospect, exchanging casual remarks.

"Let's go and have something to eat," Listnitsky proposed, with his eyes indicating a restaurant.

"All right!" the other man agreed.

They entered and sat down at a table by the window. Through the lowered curtain the broken sunrays stuck like yellow needles into the tablecloth. The smell of cooking overpowered the subtle perfume of the flowers set out on the tables. Listnitsky ordered some iced beet soup and sat thoughtfully fiddling with the rusty-yellow nasturtium he had taken from the vase. Atarshchikov wiped his perspiring brow with his handkerchief. His drooping, weary eyes, blinking incessantly, watched the sunlight playing on the legs of the neighbouring table. They had not finished eating when two officers, talking loudly, entered the restaurant. As the first looked for a free table, he turned his sunburnt face in Listnitsky's direction, and his black eyes lit up gladly.

"Why, it's Listnitsky! Surely?" he cried, and came with confident and unhesitating steps towards Eugene.

Listnitsky at once recognized Captain Kalmikov and his companion Chubov. They shook hands heartily. After introducing them to Atarshchikov, Eugene asked:

"What fate has brought you here?"

Twisting his whiskers, Kalmikov replied:

"We've been ordered to Petrograd. I'll tell you later. But first tell us all about yourself. How do you find life in the 14th Regiment?"

They left the restaurant together. Kalmikov and Listnitsky dropped behind the others, turned down the first side street, and walked along towards a quiet part of the city, talking almost in whispers.

"Our third corps is held in reserve on the Rumanian front," Kalmikov told Eugene. "About ten days ago I received instructions from the regimental commander to hand over my company to another officer and to go with Chubov to place ourselves at the disposition of the divisional staff. Wonderful! We go to the divisional staff. There we are confidentially informed that we are to go at once to report to General Krimov. So we go to corps headquarters. Krimov sees me, and as he has been informed which officers are being sent to him, he tells me frankly: 'The government is in the hands of men who are deliberately leading the country to destruction. The group at the head of the government must be replaced, and possibly the Provisional Government will have to be dismissed in favour of a military dictatorship.' He mentioned Kornilov as a probable candidate, and then proposed that I should go to Petrograd, to put myself at the disposition of the Central Committee of the Officers' Alliance. And now several hundred reliable officers are gathered in the city. You can guess what our role is to be? The Central Committee of the Officers' Alliance is working in close contact with our Soviet of the Alliance of Cossack Troops, and shock battalions are being organized at railway junctions and among the divisions."

"And what will come of it? What do you think?"

"That's the point! But do you mean to say that you, living here, still don't know the situation? Undoubtedly there will be a governmental coup, and Kornilov will seize power. The whole army is on his side. We think there are two equated forces: the Bolsheviks and Kornilov. Kerensky is between the upper and nether millstones. One or the other will crush him. He is caliph for an hour. Of course we officers are like pieces on a chessboard; we don't know where the player will move us to. I, for instance, don't understand all that is happening at staff headquarters. But I do know that there is some secret understanding among the generals. . . ."

"But the army—? Will the army follow Kornilov?" Eugene asked.

"Of course the soldiers won't. But we must lead them."

"You know that under pressure from the left Kerensky is trying to dismiss the commander-in-chief?"

"He won't dare. Tomorrow he will himself be on his knees. The Central Committee of the Officers' Alliance has expressed its opinion quite categorically on that matter," Kalmikov replied. "There can't be any talk of dismissing Kornilov. But did you see his arrival in the city yesterday? It was classic! His guard was a squadron of Tekke. There were machine-guns placed in every motor-car. And they all rode to the Winter Palace, where Kerensky was. An unequivocal warning enough! You should have seen the mugs of the Tekke in their shaggy cowls! They're worth looking at!"

The two officers walked back to the centre of the city and took leave of each other.

"We mustn't lose sight of each other, Eugene," Kalmikov said as he shook hands. "Difficult times are coming! Keep your feet on the ground, or you'll be lost."

As Listnitsky walked away Kalmikov called after him:

"Oh, I'd forgotten to tell you. You remember Merkulov—the artist fellow?"

"Yes?"

"He was killed in May. Quite unexpectedly. You couldn't have seen a more silly death. A grenade burst in the hands of a patrol and blew off the man's arms at the elbow, while all we found of Merkulov, who was at his side, was part of his entrails. For three years death had spared him. . . ."

He shouted something else, but the wind raised the grey dust and brought only the ends of his words to Listnitsky's ears. Eugene waved his hand and strode away, giving an occasional glance back.

On August 26 Kornilov left staff headquarters for a State Conference at Moscow. It was a warm, rather cloudy day. The sky looked as though cast of aluminum. In the zenith hung a clearly defined, fluffy violet cloud. From it fell a slanting rain, broken with rainbow hues, and falling on the train flying over the rails, the distant, clean outlines of birches, and all the widow's weeds of the early autumn earth. The train sped on, leaving behind a ruddy scarf of smoke. General Kornilov sat by the open window of his car, staring out at the landscape, and the warm drops of rain spattered munificently over his sunburnt face and the black, hanging whiskers. The wind fluttered and blew back the strand of hair that had fallen over his forehead.

The day before Kornilov's arrival in Moscow, Captain Listnitsky had come to the city with important documents entrusted to him by the Soviet of Cossack Troops at Petrograd. When he handed the packet over to the staff of the Cossack regiment stationed in Moscow, he learned that Kornilov was expected to arrive next day.

At noon the following day Listnitsky was at the station to meet the commander-in-chief. A dense crowd of people, chiefly military, was assembled in the waiting-rooms and buffets. A guard of honour from the military academy was drawn up on the platform, and the Moscow women's death battalion was arrayed outside. Kornilov's train arrived about three o'clock. Listnitsky saw Kornilov, accompanied by several officers, alight from the train, inspect the guard of honour, and receive deputations from the Alliance of Chevaliers of St. George, the Alliance of Army and Navy Officers, and the Soviet of the Alliance of Cossack Troops.

As Kornilov approached he was bombarded with flowers thrown

by the well-dressed women standing at the end of the platform. One rosy blossom caught in his epaulets and hung there. He brushed it off with a slightly embarrassed, uncertain gesture. A bearded, elderly officer began to stammer out greetings in the name of the Cossack regiments, but Listnitsky could not hear what was said, for the crowd pushed him against the wall. After the speeches Kornilov moved on, the way being cleared by officers with joined hands. But the crowd swept them away. Dozens of hands were stretched out to Kornilov. A stout, dishevelled woman hovered at his side, trying to press her lips to his sleeve. At the station entrance Kornilov was lifted shoulder-high and carried out, to a tumult of acclamation. With a strong thrust of the shoulder Listnitsky managed to push aside some dignified elderly gentleman, caught at Kornilov's feet, and put the general's legs across his shoulder. Unconscious of the weight, panting with his agitation, endeavouring to keep his feet, he moved slowly forward, deafened by the roar of the crowd and the blare of a band. Down the steps they went into the square. In front was the crowd, the green ranks of soldiers, and a Cossack company. Listnitsky set his hand to the visor of his cap, blinking his tear-filled eyes and trying to restrain the irresistible trembling of his lips. Afterwards he had a confused memory of the rattle of cameras, the frenzy of the crowd, the ceremonial march of the Junkers, and the little, erect figure of General Kornilov taking the salute.

Next day Listnitsky returned to Petrograd. He climbed into the upper berth of his compartment, unbuttoned his tunic, and smoked, thinking of Kornilov.

At about the same time, during a break in the session of the Moscow State Conference, two generals, one short and with the face of a Mongol, the other stout, with a thick growth of close-cropped hair on his square head, were strolling up and down one of the corridors of the Grand Theatre, talking in whispers.

"Does any point of the declaration provide for the abolition of committees in the army?" Kornilov asked.

"Yes," replied Kaledin.

"A united front and complete solidarity are absolutely indispensable," Kornilov declared. "Without the enforcement of the measures I have indicated, there can be no salvation. The army is quite incapable of fighting. Such an army not only cannot bring victory, but will not even be able to withstand any considerable attack. The divisions have been disintegrated by the Bolshevik propaganda. And here in the rear? You see how the workers react to any attempt to apply measures to bridle them. Strikes and demonstrations! The members of the conference have to go on foot. . . . It's scandalous! The militarization of the rear, the establishment of a harsh, punitive regime, the ruthless extermination of all the Bolsheviks—these are our immediate tasks. Can I count on your support in the future, General Kaledin?"

"I am absolutely with you."

"I was sure of that. Thank you. You see how, when it is necessary to act resolutely and firmly, the government confines itself to half-measures and resounding phrases. We soldiers are accustomed to acting first and talking afterwards. They do the opposite. Well—the time is coming when they will eat the fruits of their half-measures. But I have no desire to take part in this dishonourable game. I remain an adherent of the open struggle. I am no double-dealer."

He halted and, twisting a button of Kaledin's tunic, stuttered in his agitation:

"They've removed the muzzle, and now they're afraid of their own revolutionary democracy and are asking me to move reliable troops nearer to the capital, although at the same time they're afraid to take any real measures themselves. One step forward, one step back. . . . Only by a complete consolidation of our forces and strong moral pressure can we win concessions from the government. And if not—we shall see. I shall not hesitate to lay the front open. Let the Germans bring them to their senses!"

He stood thinking for a moment, then added: "I shall expect you and the rest in my room after the session. What is the situation like on the Don?"

Kaledin's square head sank on his chest and he stared down in front of him with a morose, lowering look. His lips trembled as he replied:

"I haven't my former confidence in the Cossacks. And it is difficult to judge of the situation at the moment. A compromise is necessary; the Cossacks must be conceded something in order to hold them. We are taking certain steps in this direction, but I cannot guarantee their success. I am afraid of a clash of interest between the Cossacks and the settlers. The land . . . all their thoughts are centred on that at the moment."

"You must have reliable Cossack divisions ready to hand, in order to safeguard yourself. When I return to the staff, we shall find some way of sending several regiments from the front back to the Don."

"I shall be very grateful to you if you can."

"Well then, this evening we shall discuss the question of our future co-operation. I firmly believe in the successful accomplishment of our plan. But fortune is a fickle jade, general. If she turns her back on me despite everything, can I count on finding refuge with you in the Don?"

"Not only refuge, but defence. The Cossacks are famous for their hospitality." For the first time during the conversation Kaledin smiled.

An hour later Kaledin, the ataman of the Don Cossacks, announced to a hushed audience the historic Declaration of the Twelve Cossack Regiments. From that day on, the threads of a great conspiracy, like a black spider-web, were flung throughout the Don, the Kuban, the Urals, throughout the Cossack lands from end to end, from one village to another.

Chapter 4

About a mile from the ruins of a little town that had been wiped out by gunfire during the July offensive, the monstrously winding zigzag of the trenches ran past a forest. The sector along the outskirts of the forest was held by the special company.

Behind them, beyond the impenetrable green of a fir wood and young birches, stretched the rusty mud of peat marsh, and the crimson berries of dog-rose bushes shore gaily. To the right, beyond a protruding cape of forest, stretched a shell-holed macadam road. At the fringe of the forest grew miserable, bullet-rent bushes, and charred trunks huddled forlornly. Here the yellow-brown clay of the breastworks was visible, and the trenches ran like frowns across the open fields into the distance. Behind them even the marsh with its remains of former peat-works, and even the broken road were an eloquent testimony to life and abandoned labour; but by the forest edge the earth presented a joyless and bitter picture to the eye.

One day in August, Ivan Alexievich, the former employee at Mokhov's mill, went off to the neighbouring town where the company baggage train was quartered, and did not return until early evening. As he made his way into his dug-out he ran into Zakhar Koroliov. Zakhar was almost running, aimlessly waving his arms, his sabre catching in the edges of the sandbags. Ivan Alexievich stepped aside to let him pass, but Zakhar seized him by a button of his tunic and, rolling the unhealthy yellow of his eyes, whispered:

"Have you heard? The infantry to our right are leaving the front. Maybe they're running away."

"What do you mean? Perhaps they're being relieved. Let's go to the troop officer and find out."

Zakhar turned back, and they went along to the troop officer's dug-out, slipping and stumbling over the slippery wet earth.

But within an hour the company was relieved by infantry and was on its way to the town. Next morning they took to their horses and were riding by forced marches to the rear.

A fine rain was falling. The birches were bowed gloomily. The road plunged into a forest, and scenting the dampness and the mouldering, pungent scent of fallen leaves, the horses snorted and quickened their pace. The rain-washed spurge-flax hung in rosy beads, the foamy caps of the white clover gleamed an unearthly pallor. The wind sprinkled heavy granular water-drops from the trees over the riders. Their greatcoats and caps were dark with wet spots, as though spattered with shot. The smoke of tobacco curled and flowed above the ranks. An excited discussion of their unknown destination went on. After a while they struck up a song, rejoicing that they had been snatched out of the "wolves' cemetery," as they called the trenches. The same evening they were loaded into freight cars at a station. The train dragged towards Pskov. And only some time later did they learn that the company was being transferred, together with other sections of the third army corps, to Petrograd to suppress outbreaks of disorder. Then the talk died away in the train, and a drowsy silence reigned.

"Out of the frying-pan . . ." one of them at last expressed their general opinion.

At the first halt Ivan Alexievich, who since March had been permanent chairman of the company committee, went to the company commander.

"The Cossacks are in a state of excitement, captain," he reported.

The captain stared at the deep dimple in Ivan's chin and replied with a smile:

"I am in a state of excitement myself, my friend."

"Where are we being taken to?"

"To Petrograd!"

"To put down risings?"

"Well, you didn't think you were going to assist the disorders, did you?"

"We don't want either the one or the other."

"As it happens, they're not asking our opinion."

"But the Cossacks—"

"What about the Cossacks?" the officer interrupted him angrily. "I know myself what the Cossacks are thinking. Do you think I like the job? Take this and read it to the company. And at the next station I'll talk to the Cossacks."

The commander handed him a folded telegram, frowning with evident distaste.

Ivan Alexievich returned to his car, carrying the telegram gingerly in his hand as though it were a burning brand. "Call the Cossacks from the other cars," he said.

The train was already in motion, but Cossacks came jumping into Ivan's car until some thirty were collected.

"The commander's given me a telegram to read," Ivan told them. In a deathly silence he read aloud the manifesto of the commander-in-chief, Kornilov:

I, the supreme commander-in-chief Kornilov, before all the nation declare that my soldierly duty, my devotion as a citizen of free Russia, and my supreme love for the country have compelled me in these serious moments of the fatherland's existence to refuse to carry out the instructions of the Provisional Government and resign the supreme command of the army and the fleet. Supported in this decision by the commands of all the fronts, I declare to all the Russian people that I prefer death to removal from my post. A true son of the Russian people will always die at his post and sacrifice his life for the fatherland.

It is not for me, a blood son of my people, who have given all my life to their service, to refuse to defend the great liberties of my people. An impudent enemy is among us, by bribery and treachery bringing ruin not only to freedom, but to the very existence of the Russian people. Awake, Russian people, and glance into the bottomless pit into which our country is falling!

Avoiding all disturbance, averting all shedding of Russian blood, ignoring mutual reproaches and all my shame and humiliation at their hands, I address myself to the Provisional Government and say: "Come to me at the staff headquarters, where your freedom and safety are assured by my word of honour, and together with me work out and organize such a form of national defence as will safeguard freedom and lead the Russian nation towards the great future worthy of a mighty, free people."

General Kornilov

At the next station the train was halted for some time. The Cossacks gathered outside their cars, talking over Kornilov's telegram and another from Kerensky, read by the company commander, declaring Kornilov a traitor and counter-revolutionary. The Cossacks discussed the situation distractedly, and even the officers were in bewilderment.

"Everything's all mixed up," Martin Shamil complained. "How the devil are we to know who is guilty?"

"They're plaguing one another and plaguing the soldiers!"

"They all want to be at the top."

A group of Cossacks came up to Ivan Alexievich and demanded: "Come to the commander and find out what we are to do."

They went in a body to the company commander and found the officers in conference in his car. Ivan Alexievich went in.

"Captain, the Cossacks are asking what they're to do," he declared.

"I'll come out to them in a minute," the commander replied.

The entire company waited by the end car. The commander joined the crowd, made his way to the middle, and raised his hand.

"We are subordinate, not to Kerensky, but to the commander-in-chief and our immediate superiors," he said. "That's correct, isn't it? And so unquestionably we must carry out the orders of our superior command and go on to Petrograd. In the last resort we can discover what is the situation when we reach the station of Dno, where we shall find the commander of the First Don Division. I ask you not to get agitated. Such are the times we are living through."

The commander went on to talk about the soldiers' duty, the country, and the Revolution, seeking to soothe the Cossacks and replying evasively to their questions. He achieved his aim. While he was talking to the Cossacks an engine was coupled to the train (the Cossacks were not to know that two officers had speeded up their departure by threatening the station-master with revolvers), and the men dispersed to their cars.

The troop train set off again, drawing near the station of Dno. The Cossacks fed their horses and slept, or sat at the half-open doors, smoking and staring out at the sky. Ivan Alexievich lay gazing through the door-chink at the stars flowing past. During the last few hours he had been thinking over the situation and had come to the firm decision to resist the further movement of the company towards Petrograd by all means in his power. As he lay he considered how best to bring the Cossacks to his own way of thinking.

His thoughts turned to Stockman. Osip Davidovich had once said to him: "Ivan Alexievich, once let this national rottenness peel off you, and you will be a piece of good human steel, a little grain in the general mass of our party. And the rottenness will peel off! All dross is burned away in the forging." And he wasn't mistaken, Ivan thought. Although he was somewhere outside the party, yet he had struggled vigorously and youthfully towards the party and its work. He had been forged into a reliable Bolshevik, seared with an unshakable hatred for the old system. Among the obdurate Cossacks it was hard for him, without a single comrade to help him. He felt keenly his own political ignorance, and so he moved gropingly, testing each step by his own class instinct. During the years of war he had formed the habit, whenever any difficulty arose, of asking himself: "How would Stockman act in this case?" and then trying to do what he thought Stockman would have done. So it had been during the summer when he heard of the proposed Constitutional Assembly. At first he had been drawn gladly towards the idea, but then he hesitated, remembering Stockman's words: "You must never put any trust in those who talk big in the name of the people, but who in reality are serving the bourgeoisie and by their double-faced politics are weakening the militant revolutionary movement of the masses." Then, no longer hesitating, he had turned his back on the proposal and had rejoiced to find his decision confirmed in the Bolshevik trench newspaper.

So in this new case: even before Kornilov's proclamation he realized that the Cossacks' road did not coincide with that of the commander-in-chief, yet instinct warned him that it was not for them to defend Kerensky. He turned the problem over and over and resolved not to let the company get to Petrograd. If a clash had to come with anybody, it must be with Kornilov; yet it must not be in favour of Kerensky, nor for his government, but for the one which would arise after him. He was more than confident that the real government he desired would come when Kerensky went. During the summer he had been in the military section of the Party Executive Committee in Petrograd, whither he had been sent by the company for advice in regard to a conflict that had arisen with the company commander. There he had seen the work of the committee, had talked to several Bolshevik comrades, and had thought: "Let this backbone be clothed with our workers' meat, and then there will be a government! Die, Ivan, but hang on to that, hang on like a child to its mother's nipple!"

As he lay on his horse-cloth, he thought again and again with a great burning affection of the man under whose guidance he had first found his hard new road. He remembered what Stockman had said about the Cossacks: "The Cossacks are conservative to the backbone. Don't forget that when you are trying to convince one of them of the truth of the Bolshevik ideas, but act cautiously, thoughtfully, and adapt yourself to the situation. At first they will be as contemptuous of you as you and Misha Koshevoi were of me, but don't let that trouble you. Chisel away stubbornly—the final success is ours."

Ivan reckoned that he would meet with some objection from the Cossacks when in the morning he tried to persuade them not to go with Kornilov. But when he began to talk to his companions and suggested that they ought to demand their return to the front and not go on to Petrograd to fight their own brothers, the Cossacks willingly agreed and were fully prepared to refuse to travel farther. Zakhar Koroliov and a Cossack named Turilin were closest to Ivan in their outlook, and they spent all day going from car to car and talking to the others. Towards evening, while the train slowed up at a wayside station, a sergeant of the third troop jumped into Ivan's car.

"The company is detraining at the first stop," he shouted at Ivan. "What sort of chairman of committee are you if you don't know what the Cossacks want? We won't go any farther! The officers are putting a noose round our necks, and you're neither fish nor flesh. Is that what we elected you for?"

"You should have said that long ago," Ivan smiled.

At the first stop he jumped out of the car and, accompanied by Turilin, went to the station-master.

"Don't send our train any farther," he ordered him. "We're going to detrain here."

"How is that?" the man asked in bewilderment. "I have instructions to send you on. . . ."

"Close your mouth!" Turilin harshly interrupted.

They found the station committee and explained to the chairman, a heavy-built, grey-haired telegrapher, what was afoot. Within a few minutes the engine-driver had willingly shunted the train on to a siding.

Hurriedly laying down planks from the cars to the roadbed, the Cossacks began to lead out their horses. Ivan stood by the engine with feet planted wide apart, wiping the sweat from his smiling face. The company commander came running to him.

"What are you doing? You know that—"

"I know," Ivan interrupted. "And don't you kick up any fuss, captain." Turning pale, his nostrils quivering, he said meaningly: "You've done enough shouting, my lad. Now we shall do the ordering."

"The commander-in-chief, Kornilov . . ." the officer stuttered, turning livid. But Ivan stared down at his boots pressed firmly into the sand of the roadbed and, waving his hand with relief, counselled the captain:

"Hang him round your neck instead of a crucifix; we haven't any use for him."

The officer turned on his heels and ran back to his wagon. Within an hour the company, not accompanied by one officer, but in perfect order, rode away from the station in a south-westerly direction. At the head of the first troop rode Ivan Alexievich in command, with the short, lop-eared Turilin as his assistant.

With difficulty making their way by the map taken from the commander, the company reached a village and halted for the night. In a general meeting it was resolved to return to the front, and if anyone tried to stop them, to fight. Hobbling the horses and setting guards, the Cossacks lay down to wait for the dawn. No fires were lit. It was evident that the majority were in a depressed mood; they lay without their usual talking and joking, concealing their thoughts from one another.

"What if they think better of it and go back and submit?" Ivan thought anxiously as he huddled under his greatcoat. As though he had heard the thought, Turilin came up.

"Are you asleep, Ivan?" he asked.

"Not yet."

Turilin squatted down by his side and, lighting a cigarette, whispered:

"The Cossacks are troubled. . . . They've done the damage, and now they're afraid. We've cooked a fine meal for ourselves. What do you think?"

"We shall see," Ivan answered calmly. "You're not afraid, are you?"

Turilin scratched his head and smiled wryly. "To tell the truth, I am. At first I wasn't, but now I'm a little scared."

They lapsed into silence. A gentle, gracious nocturnal stillness enwrapped the meadows. The dew besprinkled the grass. A breeze brought the mingled scents of the marsh-grass and the mouldering rushes, the muddy soil and the dewy grass to the Cossacks' nostrils. Occasionally a horse's hobble jingled, or there was a snort and a heavy thud as one of the animals lay down. Then again the sleepy silence, the distant, hoarse, hardly audible call of a wild drake and the nearer answering quack of its mate. The hurried, scribbling whistle of invisible wings in the darkness. A misty, meadow rawness. To the west in the nadir hung a rising, heavily violet billow of cloud. And in the zenith, over the ancient lands of Pskov, like a broad, well-trodden track the Milky Way stretched in unsleeping reminder.

At dawn the company set out again. They passed through the village, followed by the slow stares of women and the children driving the cattle to pasture. They mounted a rise flushed a brick-red by the dawn. Turilin happened to look back and touched Ivan's stirrup with his foot:

"Look round! There are horsemen galloping after us."

Ivan gazed back at the village and saw three riders galloping along in a flying cloud of rosy dust.

"Company, halt!" he commanded.

With their accustomed speed the Cossacks ranged themselves in a grey square. When about half a mile away, the riders dropped into a trot. One of them, a Cossack officer, pulled out a white handkerchief and waved it above his head. The Cossacks kept their eyes fixed on the approaching horsemen. The Cossack officer, in a khaki tunic, came on in front; the two others, in Circassian uniform, kept a little behind him.

Riding forward to meet them, Ivan Alexievich asked:

"What do you want with us?"

"We have come to enter into negotiations," the officer replied with a touch of his cap. "Who has taken charge of the company?"

"I have."

"I am a plenipotentiary from the First Don Cossack Division, and these officers are representatives of the Native Division," the officer explained, pulling on his reins and stroking the neck of his sweating horse. "If you are willing to enter into a discussion of the situation, order the company to dismount. I have to transmit the verbal instructions of the chief of the division, Major-General Grekov."

The Cossacks dismounted, and the officers also. Pushing into the crowd, they made their way to the middle. The company made room for them and formed a small circle. The Cossack officer spoke:

"Cossacks! We have come to persuade you to think over what you are doing and to avert the serious consequences of your action.

Yesterday the divisional staff learned that you had given way to someone's criminal persuasions and had arbitrarily abandoned your train, and we have been sent today to instruct you to return imme· diately to the station. The soldiers of the Native Division and other cavalry forces occupied Petrograd yesterday; we have received a telegram to that effect today. Our advance guard has entered the city, has occupied the government buildings, banks, telegraph and telephone stations, and all the important points. The Provisional Government has fled and is overthrown. Think, Cossacks! If you do not submit to the orders of the divisional commander, armed forces will be sent against you. Your conduct will be regarded as treachery, as refusal to fulfil your military obligations. Only if you submit unconditionally can you avoid bloodshed."

As the officers rode up, Ivan Alexievich realized that it would not be possible to avoid entering into discussion with them, for that would have only contrary results to those he desired. When the company dismounted he winked to Turilin and quietly pushed close up to the officers. The Cossacks stood with downcast, gloomy faces listening attentively to the captain's words; some began to whisper among themselves. Ivan's own closest friends shuffled and stirred uneasily, while the entire second troop stood without raising their heads, as though at prayers.

Ivan realized that the Cossacks were on the point of submitting. A few more minutes and the officer's eloquence would win them to his side. At all costs the impression he had made must be dispelled. Ivan raised his hand and swept the crowd with dilated, strangely white eyes.

"Brothers! Wait a bit!" he cried, and turning to the officer, he asked: "Have you got the telegram with you?"

"What telegram?" the captain asked in astonishment.

"The telegram saying Petrograd has been taken."

"Of course not. What do you want with the telegram?"

"Aha! He hasn't got it!" came a single sigh of relief from the entire company. Many of the Cossacks lifted their heads and fixed their eyes hopefully on Ivan. Raising his hoarse voice, he shouted jestingly and assuredly:

"You haven't got it, you say? And so we've got to take your word? You can't catch us so easily as that!"

"It's a trick!" the company roared in unison.

"The telegram wasn't addressed to us. Cossacks!" The officer pressed his hand persuasively against his chest.

But they would not listen to him. Feeling that he had again won the company's sympathy and confidence, Ivan cut like a diamond on glass.

"And even if you had got it, our roads don't run with yours. We don't want to fight our own folk! We won't march against the people. No! The fools have been dragged out into the open. We're not going to help set up a government of generals. And that's that!"

The Cossacks shouted their assent. "He's giving it to them!" "That's right, Ivan!" "Send them to the rightabout!"

Ivan glanced at the emissaries. The Cossack officer was waiting patiently with lips pressed together; behind him the others stood shoulder to shoulder. One of them, a handsome young Ingush, stood with folded arms, his slanting almond eyes glittering; the other, an elderly, grey-haired Osset, had his hand resting negligently on his sabre-hilt and was surveying the Cossacks with smiling eyes. Ivan was on the point of breaking off further discussion; but he was forestalled by the Cossack officer, who, after whispering to the Ingush, cried stentoriously:

"Don Cossacks! Will you allow the representative of the Savage Division to speak?"

Without waiting for permission the Ingush stepped forward, nervously fiddling with his narrow ornamental belt.

"Brother Cossacks! What's all the noise about? You don't want General Kornilov? You want war? All right. We will give you war. We're not frightened! Not at all frightened! We shall smash you today. There are two regiments at our backs! So!" He began with ostensible calm, but as he went on he poured out his words more passionately, phrases from his own language mingling with his broken Russian. "It's that Cossack there that's upsetting you! He's a Bolshevik, and you're following him! So! Don't I see it? Arrest him! Disarm him!"

He pointed boldly at Ivan Alexievich and swept his eyes around the circle, gesticulating fiercely, his face flushed swarthily. His companion maintained an icy calm, and the Cossack officer played with his sword-knot. The Cossacks were again silent, embarrassed and agitated. Ivan stared fixedly at the Ingush officer and thought regretfully that he had let slip the moment when with one word he could have ended the talk and led away the Cossacks. Turilin saved the situation. Waving his arms desperately, he leaped into the middle of the ring and roared, while the spittle dribbled from his lips:

"You crawling serpents! Devils! . . . Skunks! . . . They wheedle you like whores, and you prick up your ears! The officers will make you do as they want. What are you doing? What are you doing? They ought to be cut down, and you stand listening to them! Cut their heads off, let the blood out of them! While you're palavering they're surrounding us. They'll mow us down with machineguns! You won't be holding meetings long when they start rattling! They're deliberately pulling the wool over your eyes until their soldiers arrive. Ha, call yourselves Cossacks? You're a lot of petticoats!"

"To horse!" Ivan Alexievich thundered.

His shout burst like shrapnel over the crowd. The Cossacks flung themselves towards their horses. Within a minute the company was again drawn up in troop columns.

"Listen, Cossacks!" the captain shouted.

Ivan Alexievich unslung his carbine from his shoulder and, putting his finger firmly to the trigger, exclaimed:

"The talk is ended! Now if we have to talk to you it will be in this language!"

He expressively shook his rifle.

Troop after troop they rode off down the road. Looking back, they saw the emissaries, mounted on their horses, conferring among themselves. The Ingush was arguing fiercely, frequently raising his hand; the lining of his cuff shone snowily white. As Ivan looked round for the last time, he noticed this dazzlingly gleaming band of silk, and abruptly before his eyes appeared the wind-lashed bosom of the Don, its foaming green waves, and the white wing of a seagull slanting across their crests.

Chapter 5

The various sections of the army flung by Kornilov against Petrograd were scattered over an enormous stretch of eight railway lines
running from the west, south, and east. All the main stations and
even halts and sidings were packed with the slowly moving troop
trains. The regiments were beyond the moral control of the senior
command, and the scattered companies lost touch with one another. The confusion was made worse by the changing of instructions while en route and by uncoordinated orders, and this intensified the already tense and nervous mood of the troops. Meeting
with the elemental opposition of the railway workers, overcoming
difficulty after difficulty, the Kornilov armies slowly moved on
towards Petrograd.

In the red cages of the cars half-starved Cossacks from all the
Cossack districts crowded beside their half-starved horses. The
trains stood for hours at the stations waiting to be dispatched, and
the men poured out of them and streamed into the waiting-rooms,
or gathered on the roadbeds, eating everything left by previous
trains, stealing from the inhabitants, and pillaging the food warehouses.

Held up on the railways, the commanders hesitated to take to
the road and remained in their trains.

Together with the other regiments composing the First Don Cossack Division, the regiment in which Eugene Listnitsky had formerly served was flung against Petrograd along the Revel-Narva
railway line. Two companies of the regiment arrived at Narva at
five in the afternoon of September 10. The commander learned
that it would be impossible to travel farther that night, as the
tracks beyond Narva had been destroyed. A gang of track-layers
had been dispatched to the spot, and if they could restore the
line in time, the train would be sent on early in the morning. Willy-
nilly, the commander had to accept this. He clambered cursing

into his car, communicated the news to the other officers, and sat down to drink tea.

The night was overcast. A harsh, piercing wind was blowing from the Gulf of Finland. In the train and beside it the Cossacks gathered to talk. At the end of the train a young Cossack voice struck up a song, complaining in the darkness to no one knew whom.

A man emerged from beyond the grey bulk of the warehouse. He stopped and listened to the song, looked up and down the track gleaming with yellow patches of light, and strode confidently towards the cars. His steps echoed hollowly on the sleepers, but were muffled when he walked down the sandy path between the tracks. He passed round the end car, and the Cossack standing at its door stopped singing and shouted to him:

"Who's that?"

"And what do you want?" the man answered reluctantly, without stopping.

"What are you wandering about at night for? We'll give you tramps a good hiding!"

The man walked along until he came to the middle of the train, and thrusting his head through a car door, asked:

"What company are you?"

"Prisoners!" someone laughed in the darkness.

"No, I'm asking seriously."

"We're the second."

"And where's the fourth troop?"

"The sixth car from the front."

Three Cossacks, one squatting and the others standing, were smoking at the door of the sixth car. They stared silently at the man coming up to them.

"Good luck, Cossacks!" he said.

"Praise be!" one of them replied, gazing into the newcomer's face.

"Is Nikita Dugin alive? Is he here?"

"Here I am," the man squatting answered, and rose to his feet, treading out his cigarette with his heel. "But I don't know you. Who are you?" He poked his bearded face forward in the attempt to examine the stranger in greatcoat and soiled soldier's cap. Suddenly seizing his beard in his fist, he cried in astonishment: "Ilia!

Bunchuk! Where the devil have you sprung from, old man?"

Gripping Bunchuk's hairy hand in his own and bending over him, he said more quietly:

"These are our boys, you needn't be afraid. How did you get here? Tell me, the devil curse you!"

Bunchuk shook hands with the other Cossacks and replied in a broken, iron-hollow voice:

"I've come from Petrograd, and I've been looking for you. There's work on hand. We must have a talk. I'm glad to see you alive and well, brother. Let's go into the car."

They clambered inside. Dugin prodded someone with his foot and whispered:

"Get up, my boy! A useful guest has arrived. Hurry up! Get a move on!"

The Cossack stirred and rose. A couple of great hands, smelling of tobacco and horses' sweat, carefully felt Bunchuk's face in the darkness, and their owner asked:

"Bunchuk?"

"That's right. And is it you, Chikamasov?"

"Yes. Glad to see you, friend. Shall I run and fetch the boys of the third troop?"

"That's a good idea."

The third troop arrived almost to a man, only two remaining with the horses. The Cossacks went up to Bunchuk and thrust their hands into his, bent over him, and examined his face by the light of the lantern. In all their greetings was a single tone of warm, comradely welcome.

They made him sit down facing the lantern and crowded around him, those closest squatting on their heels, the others standing in a dense circle. Dugin coughed:

"We received your letter the other day, Ilia, but all the same we wanted to see you and have your advice what to do. They're sending us to Petrograd."

"It's like this, Ilia," a Cossack standing near the door said. An ear-ring was hanging from the lobe of an ear; it was the same man whom Listnitsky had once affronted by forbidding him to boil water on the sheet iron. "All sorts of agitators come along and try to get us not to go on to Petrograd, telling us we ought not to fight among ourselves, and all that sort of thing. We listen to them, but we don't trust them too much. They're not our people. They may be misleading us, for all we know. If we refuse to go to Petrograd, Kornilov will send his Native divisions against us, and that will lead to bloodshed too. But you're a Cossack like us, and we have more trust in you, and we're very thankful that you wrote to us and sent us newspapers—we were getting short of paper for cigarettes. . . ."

"What are you telling those lies for, you blockhead?" another interrupted angrily. "You can't read, and so you think of that. But we aren't all like you. As if we only used the newspapers for cigarettes! We read them from front to back, Ilia."

Bunchuk smiled as he gazed at the Cossacks. He found it difficult to talk sitting down; so he stood up, turned his back to the lantern, and spoke slowly and assuredly:

"There's nothing for you to do in Petrograd. There aren't any risings there. Do you know what they are sending you there for? In order to overthrow the Provisional Government. And who is leading you? The Czarist General Kornilov. What does he want to kick Kerensky out for? In order to sit in his place. Listen, Cossacks! They want to throw the wooden yoke off your necks, but they'll put a steel one in its place! Of two evils you must choose the lesser. Isn't that so? Think it over for yourselves: under the Czar they put their fists in your face and used you to fight the war. Under Kerensky they're still wanting you to fight, but they don't use their fists on you any longer. It's only a little better under Kerensky, but still it is better. But it will be much better after Kerensky, when the power gets into the hands of the Bolsheviks. Let them get the government and there'd be peace at once. I'm not on Kerensky's side, the devil take him; they're all tarred with the same brush!" He smiled, wiped the sweat from his brow with his hand, and continued: "But I call on you not to shed the blood of the workers and for the present to defend the Provisional Government. Why defend it? Because if Kornilov gets in its place, Russia will begin to wade knee-deep in the workers' blood, and it will be more difficult to tear the power from him and hand it over to the toiling people."

"Wait a bit, Ilia"; a little Cossack, as thickset as Bunchuk himself emerged from the back rows. The man coughed and rubbed his hands, long and like the rain-washed roots of an ancient oak.

Gazing at Bunchuk with smiling eyes as green as young leaves, he asked him: "You said something just now about yokes. But when the Bolsheviks get the power, what yokes will they put on us?"

"What, are you going to put yokes on yourselves?"

"What do you mean, 'put them on ourselves'?"

"Well, under the Bolsheviks who will be the government? You will, if they elect you, or Dugin, or this old boy here. It will be an elected government, a soviet. Understand?"

"But who will be at the top?"

"Why, whoever is elected. If they choose you, you will be at the top."

"Surely? You're not lying, Ilia?"

The Cossacks laughed, and all began to speak at once. Even the guard posted at the door left his place for a moment in order to join in.

"But what do they want to do with the land?"

"They won't take it from us?"

"Will they stop the war? Or will they at once want us to fight for them."

"Tell us the truth. We're all in the dark here."

Bunchuk turned this way and that, studying the Cossacks attentively and waiting until they were quiet. His first feeling of uncertainty as to the success of his enterprise had gone, and realizing the mood of the Cossacks, he knew of a surety that, whatever happened, the troop train would be halted at Narva. When the previous day he had suggested himself to the Petrograd Regional Party Committee for agitation work among the Cossack detachments, he had been quite confident of success, but on arrival at Narva he had been stricken with doubts. He knew that the Cossacks must be talked to in their own language, and he was afraid that he might not be able to do that; for since leaving the front he had mingled only with workers and had once more thoroughly assimilated their habits and turns of speech.

When he first began to speak to the Cossacks, he caught the stumbling uncertainty in his own voice and tormentedly racked his brains for words which would convince and shatter. But only empty phrases had come like soap-bubbles from his lips, while the emasculated, elusive thoughts were entangled in his mind. He stood sweating heavily, breathing heavily, thinking: "I've been entrusted with this big job, and I'm ruining it myself. Another man would have spoken a thousand times better. Oh hell, what an idiot I am!"

The Cossack who asked about the yokes knocked him out of his stupid impotence, and the talk that followed his reply gave him an opportunity to pull himself together. He felt an unusual flow of strength and a rich choice of clear, pointed, cutting words coming to him. He grew enthusiastic and, concealing his agitation under a semblance of calm, dealt weightily and sharply with the questions, guiding the conversation like a rider who has mastered an unbroken horse.

"Tell us, why is the Constitutional Assembly a bad thing?" the fire of questions continued. "Your Lenin—the Germans sent him here, didn't they?" "Bunchuk, did you come of your own free will, or were you sent?" "And aren't the Mensheviks also of the people?" "We have our own Military Council and people's government. What do we want soviets for?"

He dealt with the questions one after another. The little meeting broke up after midnight, having decided to call both companies to a general meeting in the morning. Bunchuk spent the night in the train, and Chikamasov proposed that he should share his blankets. As the Cossack crossed himself and lay down, he warned Bunchuk:

"You can lie and sleep without fear, Ilia. . . . But we're eaten up with lice. If you lie with us, you mustn't get fed up. The lice are so thick and fat, every one is as big as an egg. . . ." He was silent for a moment, then quietly asked: "Bunchuk, what race is Lenin? I mean, where was he born and did he grow up?"

"Lenin? He's a Russian."

"Ho?"

"It's true; he's Russian."

"No, brother, you're wrong there! It's clear you don't know much about him," Chikamasov said with a touch of superiority in his voice. "Do you know where he's from? He's of our blood. He's come from the Don Cossacks, and was born in Salskov province, Vielikokniazoe district—understand? They say he was in the army as an artillery-man. And his face fits: he's like the lower Cossacks—strong cheekbones and the same eves."

"How do you know?"

"The Cossacks have talked it over among themselves, and I've heard so."

"No, Chikamasov. He's Russian, and was born in Simbirsk province."

"I don't believe you. And it's very simple why. There's Pugachov; was he a Cossack? And Stenka Razin? And Timofievich Yermak? That's it! There's not a man who has ever raised the poor people against the Czar who wasn't a Cossack. And you say he was from a Siberian province! I'm ashamed to hear such words, Ilia. . . ."

Bunchuk asked with a smile:

"So they say he's a Cossack?"

"Yes, and he is a Cossack, only he won't say so at present. As soon as I see his face I shall know." Chikamasov lit a cigarette and breathed the pungent scent of the uncured tobacco into Bunchuk's face. He coughed thoughtfully. "It's a miracle I'm telling, and we came to blows over it. You see, if Vladimir Ilich is one of us Cossacks, and an artillery-man, where did he get all his knowledge from? Well, they say that he was taken prisoner by the Germans at the beginning of the war and learned it all there, but when he began to get their workers to revolt they got frightened. 'Clear out, you big-head!' the Germans said to him. 'Clear out to your own people, by Christ; you're giving us so much trouble we shall never be able to stop it.' And so they sent him to Russia, because they were afraid he would get their workers to rise. Oho! He's a molar, brother!" Chikamasov said the last words vauntingly and laughed happily in the darkness. "You haven't ever seen him, have you? No? Pity! They say he has an enormous head." He coughed and sent a grey scroll of smoke out of his nostrils. "He's never let any Czar talk him down! No, Ilia, don't try to argue with me. Ilich is a Cossack. What do you want to doubt it for? Such men never came out of Siberian province."

Bunchuk remained silent, a smile on his face. He was long in getting to sleep; the lice swarmed over him, spreading a fiery, tormenting itch beneath his shirt. Chikamasov sighed and snored at his side, and a restless horse drove away sleep. He turned over and over and, angrily realizing that he was wide awake, began to think of the morrow's meeting. Involuntarily he recalled an episode during an attack in 1915, and as if rejoicing to find itself on an unknown track, his memory insistently began to conjure up

fragments of reminiscence: the faces and hideous postures of dead
Russian and German soldiers; the colourless, uncertain aspects of
landscapes; the echoes of gun cannonades; the well-known sputter of machine-guns and the rattle of the belts; a brave melody,
beautiful almost to pain; the faint outline of the mouth of a woman
he had once loved; and then again scraps of the war; the graves
of his brothers lying over a hill. . . .

He sat up and said aloud, or maybe only thought: "Until I
die I shall carry these memories, and not I alone but all who come
through. Our whole life has been mutilated, cursed! Damn
them! . . . Damn them! Not even with death will their guilt be
wiped out. . . ."

He grated his teeth and groaned, almost choking with the poisonous hatred that filled him. He sat rubbing his hairy chest, feeling that his hatred was boiling in his breast, preventing him from
breathing, and paining him under the heart.

He did not drop off to sleep until morning was at hand. And at
dawn, yellow and more morose than usual, he went to the railwaymen's committee, persuaded them not to send the Cossack troop
train out of Narva, then searched for the garrison committee in
order to ensure their assistance.

He returned to the train at eight o'clock, rejoicing sadly at the
probable success of his mission, at the sun pouring across the
rusty roof of the warehouse, and the musical, singing timbre of a
woman's voice. A brief but luxuriant rain had fallen late in the
night. The sandy earth of the roadbed was wet and furrowed with
the traces of little streams; it smelt of dampness and still retained
the pitted holes of the raindrops on its surface, as though it had
had smallpox.

As he passed round the train an officer in a greatcoat and muddy
leg-boots came towards him. Bunchuk recognized Captain Kalmikov and slowed his steps. As he came up, Kalmikov halted, and
his slanting black eyes gleamed coldly:

"Cornet Bunchuk? Are you still at liberty? Excuse me, I can't
offer you my hand. . . ."

"You spoke too quickly; I had no intention of offering you mine,"
Bunchuk replied banteringly.

"What are you doing here? Saving your skin? Or— You haven't come from Petrograd? You're not from friend Kerensky?"

"Is this a cross-examination?"

"It is merely justifiable curiosity as to the fate of a deserter who was once a colleague."

Bunchuk shrugged his shoulders. "I can reassure you. I have not come from Kerensky," he smiled.

"But you are facing great danger here. And you are touchingly alone. But all the same, who and what are you? No epaulets, and wearing a soldier's greatcoat." Kalmikov contemptuously and commiseratingly examined Bunchuk's figure. "A political travelling salesman? Have I guessed right?" Without waiting for an answer, he turned on his heel and strode away.

Bunchuk found Dugin waiting for him in the car.

"Where have you been?" the Cossack shouted. "The meeting's already begun."

"Already begun?"

"Yes. Our company commander, Kalmikov, has been away in Petrograd and returned this morning and called a meeting of the Cossacks. He's just gone along to talk to them."

He went with Dugin to the place where the meeting was being held. Beyond the warehouse was a dense grey-green ring of Cossack tunics and greatcoats. In the middle, surrounded by officers, Kalmikov was mounted on a barrel and shouting sharply and emphatically:

". . . . carry on to a victorious conclusion. They trust us, and we will justify their trust. The agents of the Bolsheviks and Kerensky are preventing the movement of our troops along the railway. We have received instructions from the commander-in-chief that in the event of its being impossible to travel by the railway we are to take to horse and march to Petrograd. We advance today. Get ready to detrain."

Roughly working his way through the crowd with his elbows, Bunchuk burst into the middle of the ring and, without approaching the group of officers, shouted stentoriously:

"Comrade Cossacks! I have been sent to you by the Petrograd workers and soldiers. Your officers are leading you on to war with your brothers, to the defeat of the Revolution. If you want to attack the people, if you want to restore the monarchy and to continue the war until you are all turned into corpses and cripples, carry on! But the Petrograd workers and soldiers hope that you will not be Cains. They send you a flaming brotherly greeting and want to see you not as enemies, but as allies."

He was not allowed to continue. An indescribable uproar arose, and the storm of shouts seemed to tear Kalmikov down from the barrel. He strode across towards Bunchuk, but halted a few steps away and turned to the Cossacks:

"Cossacks! Last year Cornet Bunchuk deserted from the front; you know that. And are we going to listen to this coward and traitor?"

The commander of the sixth company, Major Sukin, outshouted Kalmikov with his deep voice:

"Arrest him, the scum! We have poured out our blood, and he has saved himself in the rear! Seize him!"

"Wait a bit, brother!" "Let him speak!" "We don't want any deserters!" "Go on, Bunchuk!" "Down with them!" "Give it to them, Bunchuk, give it to them!" A chorus of conflicting shouts arose from the Cossacks.

A tall, capless Cossack, a member of the regimental Revolutionary Committee, jumped on to the barrel. His clean-shaven head turned like a snake's this way and that on his slender neck. In fiery words he called upon the Cossacks not to obey the orders of General Kornilov, the traitor to the Revolution, and spoke of the ruinous consequences of a war with the people. At the end of his speech he turned to Bunchuk:

"And you, comrade," he cried, "don't think that we despise you as the officers do. We are glad of you and respect you, because when you were an officer you did not crush the Cossacks, but were with them as a brother. We never heard a rough word from you; but don't think that we, uneducated men, don't understand good treatment. Even the cattle understand a kindly word, and far more man. We bow to the earth before you, and ask you to tell the Petrograd workers that we shall not raise a hand against them."

There was a roar of approving shouts like the roll of kettle-drums. It rose to an extraordinary pitch, slowly fell, and died away.

Kalmikov again jumped up on to the barrel, his handsome form swaying towards the Cossacks. Panting and deathly pale, he spoke of the glory and honour of the Don, of the historic mission of the Cossackry, of the blood which officers and men had all shed.

Kalmikov was followed by a Cossack with a lint-white head of hair. His indignant words attacking Bunchuk were shouted down by the crowd, and they dragged him off the barrel. At once Chikamasov jumped up. Waving his arms as though cleaving a log, he barked:

"We won't go! We won't detrain! Kalmikov says the Cossacks promised to help Kornilov; but who asked us whether we would? We've made no promises to Kornilov! The officers of the Cossack Alliance made the promises. Let them help him!"

One after another, at an increasing rate, the speakers clambered on to the barrel. Bunchuk stood with head bowed, a swarthy flush in his cheeks, the pulse beating strongly in his face and neck. The atmosphere was charged with electricity. A little more, and some hasty action would have led to bloodshed. But the soldiers of the garrison came along in a crowd, and the Cossack officers abandoned the meeting.

Half an hour later Dugin came running to Bunchuk.

"Ilia, what shall we do?" he panted. "Kalmikov has thought of something. They're unloading the machine-guns, and they've sent mounted couriers off somewhere."

"We'll go along. Collect twenty Cossacks or so. Hurry!"

By the officers' car Kalmikov and three other officers were loading machine-guns on to horses. Bunchuk strode up to them, glanced round at the Cossacks behind him, and, thrusting his hand into his greatcoat pocket, pulled out a revolver.

"Kalmikov, you are arrested!" he declared. "Hands up! . . ."

Kalmikov leaped away from the horse and bent to pull his revolver out of its holster. But over his head whistled a bullet, and in a heavy, ominous voice Bunchuk shouted:

"Hands up!"

The hammer of his revolver slowly rose to the half-cock. Kalmikov watched it with narrowed eyes and slowly raised his hands, his fingers twitching. The officers unwillingly handed over their weapons. The Cossacks unloaded the horses and carried the machine-guns back into the car.

"Set guards over these," Bunchuk told Dugin. "Chikamasov, you arrest the other officers and bring them here. Dugin and I will take Kalmikov along to the garrison Revolutionary Committee. Captain Kalmikov, please step forward."

"That was smart—smart!" one of the officers remarked in admiring tones, jumping into the car and watching Bunchuk, Dugin, and Kalmikov march off.

"Gentlemen! For shame, gentlemen! We behaved like children! No one thought of striking that scoundrel down! When he raised his revolver against Kalmikov we should have gone at him, and it would have been all over." Major Sukin stared at the other officers indignantly and fumbled with a cigarette in his case. The officers silently lit cigarettes, occasionally exchanging glances. The speed with which Bunchuk had acted had crushed them.

For a little way Kalmikov walked along without speaking, biting the end of his black whisker. His left cheek burned as though it had been scrubbed with a brush. The passers-by stopped and stared in amazement, whispering to one another. Above the town the evening sky was clouded. Fallen birch leaves lay in ruddy ingots along the roads. Rooks were circling around the green cupola of the church. Beyond the station, beyond the darkling fields night had already fallen, breathing coldly; but to the south torn, leaden-white clouds were still to be seen scudding along. Crossing invisible frontiers, night pressed on the shadows.

By the station Kalmikov turned sharply round and spat in Bunchuk's face.

"Scoundrel!" he shouted.

Bunchuk dodged the spittle and raised his eyebrows. His fingers itched to seize his revolver; but he restrained himself and curtly ordered the officer to walk on.

Kalmikov moved on, cursing horribly, pouring out a stream of oaths born of mortal pain, fear, desperation, and yearning during the years of war.

"You're a traitor! You'll pay for this!" he shouted, frequently stopping and turning on Bunchuk.

"Get on, I ask you! . . ." Bunchuk urged again and again.

And again Kalmikov would step out, clenching his fists and straining like an excited horse. They drew near to the water-tower. Grinding his teeth, Kalmikov screamed:

"You're not a party, but a gang of scurrilous dregs of society.

Who is your leader? The German staff command! Bolsheviks—ha-ha! Mongrels! Your party can be bought like prostitutes. The cads! The cads, blast them all! . . . They've betrayed their fatherland! I'd hang you all from one tree. . . . But the time will come! Didn't your Lenin sell Russia for thirty silver marks? He took his bribe . . . and hid himself . . . the convict. . . ."

"Stand up against the wall!" Bunchuk shouted deliberately, panting out the words.

Dugin began to get agitated. "Ilia! Bunchuk! Wait a bit!" he exclaimed. "What are you going to do? Stop!"

His face distorted and livid with rage, Bunchuk leaped at Kalmikov and struck him on the temple. He trampled on the cap that went flying from the officer's head, and dragged the prisoner towards the dark brick wall of the water-tower.

"Stand up!"

"What are you going to do? You—won't dare—won't dare to shoot me?" Kalmikov roared, struggling to resist him.

He was flung with his back against the wall, and straightened up, abruptly understanding.

"So you're going to kill me!"

He took a step forward, swiftly buttoning up his greatcoat.

"Shoot, you son of a swine! Shoot! And see how Russian officers can die! In the face of death I— Oh!"

The bullet struck him in the mouth. The echo of the shot went ringing round the water-tower. Kalmikov clutched at his head with his left hand, stumbled, and fell. He bowed in a half-circle, spat out bloodstained teeth on his breast, and licked his lips with his tongue. His back had hardly touched the damp ground when Bunchuk fired again. Kalmikov shuddered convulsively, turned over on his side, then like a drowsy bird huddled his head on his chest and sobbed once or twice.

Bunchuk turned away. Dugin ran after him.

"Ilia! . . . What did you shoot him for, Bunchuk?"

Bunchuk shook him by the shoulder, fixing his gaze firmly into the Cossack's eyes, and said with a strangely calm, gentle voice:

"It's either us or them! There's no middle way. There are no prisoners in this war. Blood for blood. War to extermination. . . . Understand? Such men as Kalmikov have to be wiped out, crushed like serpents. And those who slobber with pity for them must be

shot too. Understand? What are you slobbering for? Pull yourself
together! Be hard! If Kalmikov had had the power he would have
shot us without removing the cigarette from his mouth; and you—
Ah, you cry-baby!"

But Dugin's head shook and his teeth chattered, and he went
stumbling along over his great feet.

They walked along the deserted street without speaking. Bunchuk glanced back. The funereally sombre clouds moving towards
the east foamed low in the sky. Out of a small space of clear September heaven the horned, rain-washed moon gazed with the green,
slanting eye of a corpse. At a corner a soldier and a woman with
a white shawl over her shoulders stood pressed to each other. The
soldier embraced the woman and strained her towards him, whispering something. But she pushed with her hands at his chest and
flung her head back, muttering in a choking voice: "I don't believe
you! I don't believe you!" And a youthful, hollow laugh came from
her lips.

Summoned to Petrograd by Kerensky, on September 13 General Krimov shot himself.

Delegations and the commanders of the sections of Krimov's army
began to pour to the Winter Palace to make their submission.
Men who only recently had been marching to open war on the
Provisional Government now obsequiously bowed and scraped
to Kerensky, assuring him of their feelings of utter devotion.
Morally shattered, Krimov's army struggled in its death-agony.
From sheer inertia some sections still rolled on towards Petrograd,
but the movement had lost all purpose, for the Kornilov putsch
was at an end, the Bengal lights of this outburst of reaction were
dying out, and the temporary ruler of the country was strutting
like a Napoleon and speaking at government meetings of the
"complete political stabilization" of Russia.

The day prior to Krimov's suicide General Alexeev was appointed commander-in-chief. Realizing the equivocal nature of his
position, the scrupulous and squeamish Alexeev at first categorically
refused the post offered to him; but afterwards he accepted, being
governed by the desire to mitigate the fate of Kornilov and those
who had been implicated in the organization of his anti-govern-

mental revolt. Alexeev entered into direct telephonic communication with Kornilov at staff headquarters, trying to ascertain the late commander's attitude to his appointment and imminent arrival. The negotiations dragged on, with interruptions, until late at night.

On September 14 Alexeev arrived at staff headquarters. The same evening, on the instruction of the Provisional Government, he arrested Kornilov, Lukomsky, and Romanovsky. The next day the commander-in-chief of the south-western front, General Denikin, together with Generals Markov, Vannovsky, and Erdeli, were arrested at Berdichev. So ended the Kornilov revolt. But in its end it engendered a new revolt; for the first beginnings of the plans for the coming civil war and the extended attack on the Revolution were born in the "Kornilov days."

Chapter 6

Early one morning at the beginning of November, Captain Listnitsky received instructions from the regimental commander to take his company on foot to the Winter Palace Square. He gave the necessary orders to the sergeant-major and hurriedly dressed. The other officers rose also, yawning and cursing. They went into the yard. The company was drawn up in troop columns. Listnitsky led them at a swift march into the street. The Nevsky Prospect was deserted. Occasional shots sounded in the distance. An armoured car was driving about the Winter Palace Square, and Junkers were on patrol. A desert silence reigned in the streets. At the gates of the Winter Palace the Cossacks were met by a detachment of Junkers and the Cossack officers of the fourth company. One of them, the company commander, led Listnitsky to one side.

"Have you all the company with you?" he asked.

"Yes. Why?"

"The second, fifth, and sixth companies refused to march, but we've got the machine-gun detachment with us. How are your Cossacks?"

Listnitsky curtly waved his hand and replied:

"Bad! But how about the 1st and 4th Regiments?"

"They're not here. They won't come. You know an attack from the Bolsheviks is expected today? The devil knows what is afoot." He sighed sadly and added: "I'd be glad to get back to the Don and away from all this. . . ."

Listnitsky led his company into the palace yard. The Cossacks piled their arms and wandered over the spacious courtyard, while the officers gathered in one corner and smoked and talked.

Some time later a regiment of Junkers and the women's battalion arrived. The Junkers took up their position with machine-guns in the vestibule of the palace. The women crowded in the yard. The Cossacks drew towards them, making filthy jests. A sergeant clapped one of the women on the back, remarking:

"It's your job to have children, aunty, and not mix in men's business."

"Bear children yourself!" the unfriendly "aunty" snapped back.

The Cossacks roared with laughter. But towards noon their gay spirits evaporated. The women broke up into platoons and barricaded the gates with great pine beams. They were commanded by a big woman of masculine build, wearing a medal of St. George on her well-fitting greatcoat. The armoured car drove more frequently around the square, and the Junkers carried in boxes of cartridges and machine-gun ribbons.

A group of sympathizers and men from his own district was gathered around Lagutin discussing something. The officers had disappeared, and there was no one but the Cossacks and the women in the yard. Several abandoned machine-guns stood by the gates, their shields shining wetly.

Towards evening a light frost set in. The Cossacks began to grumble at being left without food.

"We must send someone for the field kitchen," one of them suggested.

Two men were sent. The Cossacks waited another couple of hours, but neither field kitchen nor messengers appeared. Just as dusk was falling the women's battalion, gathered by the gates, lay down in a long chain behind the beams and began to fire across the square. The Cossacks took no part in the shooting, but stood smoking and getting more and more fed up. At last Lagutin gathered the company by the wall and, apprehensively watching the windows of the palace, spoke to the crowd:

"This is the position, Cossacks! There's nothing for us to do here. We must go out or we'll suffer without cause. They'll begin to fire at the palace, and where shall we be then? The officers have vanished. . . . And are we to stop and die here? Let's go home; why should we rub our backs against this wall? As for the Provisional Government, what good have they been to us? What do you think, Cossacks?"

"If we go out of the yard the Bolsheviks will start firing at us," a Cossack objected.

"Then let us break up. . . ."

"No, let us stay here to the end."

"We're like sheep in a pen waiting for the butcher here."

"Do what you like, our troop is going out."

"And we're going too!"

"Send men out to the Bolshies. Let them leave us alone and we'll leave them alone."

The Cossacks of the first and fourth companies came up and joined in the meeting. After a little more discussion three Cossacks, one from each company, went out through the gates. After some time they returned, accompanied by three sailors. The sailors leaped across the stockade of beams and strode across the yard with a deliberately jaunty air. They joined the Cossacks, and one of them, a handsome young, black-whiskered sailor in a sailor jacket, his cap thrust to the back of his head, pushed into the middle of the crowd.

"Comrade Cossacks!" he addressed them. "We, the representatives of the revolutionary Baltic fleet, have come to propose that you leave the Winter Palace. Why should you defend an enemy bourgeois government? Let their own bourgeois sons, the Junkers, defend them! Not a single soldier has come out in defence of the Provisional Government, and your brothers of the 1st and 4th Regiments have joined with us. All those who want to go with us, step over to the left."

"Wait a bit, brother!" A sergeant of the first company stepped forward. "We'll go with pleasure, but supposing the Bolsheviks start shooting at us?"

"Comrades! In the name of the Petrograd Military Revolutionary

Committee we promise that you will leave in absolute safety. No one will touch you," the sailor replied.

The Cossacks hesitated. Some of the women's battalion approached and stood listening for a moment, then went back to the gates.

"Hey, you women, coming out with us?" a bearded Cossack shouted after them.

"Pick up your rifles and march!" Lagutin said resolutely.

The Cossacks willingly seized their arms and arranged themselves in line.

"Shall we take the machine-guns?" one of the gunners asked the black-whiskered sailor.

"Yes. Don't leave them for the Junkers."

Just as the Cossacks were about to leave the courtyard, their officers appeared. They stood in a dense group, not removing their eyes from the sailors. The companies began to march off. The machine-gun detachment went in front with its guns. The wheels scraped and rattled against the wet stones. The sailor in the jacket went with the leading troop of the first company. A tall, lint-white Cossack tugged at his sleeve and said in a guilty voice:

"Brother, you don't think we wanted to go against the people, do you? They got us here by a trick, but if we'd known we shouldn't have come." He shook his head violently. "Believe my word, we wouldn't! God's truth!"

The Cossacks paused at the gate, where the entire women's battalion was drawn up in a solid mass. One of the men mounted the stockade and, persuasively and significantly shaking his dirty finger, declared:

"You listen to me! We're going out, but you in your women's foolishness are staying here. Well then, no tricks! If you start firing at our backs we shall turn and cut you all into little bits. Is that clear? Well then, good-bye for the present."

He jumped down from the stockade and ran to catch up with his troop, occasionally looking back. The Cossacks had almost reached the centre of the square when one of them glanced round and anxiously cried out:

"Look, boys! There's an officer running after us!"

Many of the men turned their heads. Over the square a tall officer was running, holding his cap on and waving his hand.

"It's Atarshchikov of the third company."

"Surely he wants to come with us?"

"He's a brave fellow!"

Atarshchikov ran swiftly after the company, a smile flickering on his face. The Cossacks waved their hands and laughed.

"Run, captain! Quicker!" they shouted.

From the palace gates came the single dry crack of a shot. Atarshchikov threw out his hands and stumbled, then fell on his back, kicking out his legs and struggling to get up. As though by command the whole company turned back towards the palace. The machine-gunners trained their guns on the gates. There was a rattle of belts. But not a soul was visible behind the pine beams. The company hastily drew up in ranks again and marched away at a hurried pace. Two Cossacks from the last troop, who had gone back to Atarshchikov, caught up with them, and loudly, so that all the company could hear, one of them shouted:

"They caught him under the left shoulder. He's done for!"

The companies' steps rang out firmly and strongly. The black-whiskered sailor gave the order:

"Left wheel—march!"

They wheeled and marched away to the left, leaving the deserted, huddled mass of the palace wrapped in silence.

Chapter 7

The 12th Cossack Regiment had been retreating for two days. Slowly, and fighting all the way, but retreating. The transport wagons of the Russian and Rumanian armies rolled over the raised, unpaved roads. The combined Austrian and German divisions embraced the retiring armies with a deep enveloping flank movement and sought to close the ring.

Towards evening the news was general that the 12th Regiment and the Rumanian brigade next to it were threatened with encirclement. In the night the 12th Regiment, reinforced by a battery of the Mountaineers' Division, received the order to occupy rear-guard positions in the lower levels of a valley. Setting guards the regiment prepared for the advancing enemy.

The same night Misha Koshevoi and another man from Tatarsk village, Alexei Bieshniak, were posted on secret guard. They concealed themselves in the open, close to a disused well, and breathed in the frosty air. From time to time a flock of wild geese sped over the clouded sky, marking their flight with anxious cries. Angry at the order that there was to be no smoking, Misha quietly whispered to his companion:

"It's a strange life, Alexei! Men walk along groping, as though they were blind; they come together and part again, and sometimes they tread on one another. . . . Here you are living on the edge of death, and you can't but ask yourself savagely, what is it all about? I don't think there is anything more terrible in the world than human beings; do what you like you can't get to the bottom of them. . . . Here am I lying by your side, and I don't know what you're thinking, and never did know, and what sort of a life lies behind you I don't know, and you know no more about me. . . . Maybe I am wanting to kill you now, and here you are giving me a biscuit and haven't any idea of what I'm thinking. . . . People know little about themselves. In the summer I was in the hospital. At my side was a soldier from Moscow. And all the time he was asking how the Cossacks live and the Lord knows what else. They believe the Cossacks think of nothing except knouts; they think the Cossack is a savage, and that instead of a soul he's got bottle-glass. And yet we're men like them, and we're just as fond of women and girls; we weep over our sorrows, but don't rejoice at others' gladness. What do you think, Alexei? I'm only a young fellow, but I'm hungry for life; when I remember how many beautiful women there are in the world, my heart begins to pinch. . . . I've grown so tender to women that I could love them all to pain. I could lie with them all, tall or short, lean or fat, so long as they were pretty. And life only lets you have one at a time, and you've got to stay with her till death, until you're fed up with her. And then they thought of making war, and . . ."

He threw himself on his back and was silent, staring up at the emptiness of sky and dreamily smiling, his hands caressing the cold, inaccessibly tranquil earth.

An hour before they were due to be relieved, the Germans

caught them. Bieshniak managed to fire one shot, then fell, grinding his teeth and writhing in his death-agony. A German bayonet minced his entrails, pierced his bladder, and quivered as it struck against his backbone. Koshevoi was sent down by a butt end. A stout conscript carried him on his back for half a mile. Misha came to, felt the blood choking him, sighed, and, collecting his strength, had little difficulty in dropping off the German's back. They fired a volley after him, but the darkness and clumps of bushes helped him, and he escaped.

After the retreat had been stayed and the Russo-Rumanian forces had extricated themselves from the enveloping movement, the 12th Regiment was withdrawn to the rear. It was instructed to block the roads, setting outposts on them in order to prevent deserters from getting through. If necessary they were to be halted by fire, and any caught were to be sent under guard to the staff.

Misha Koshevoi was among the first to be sent on outpost duty. He and three other Cossacks left their village in the morning and disposed themselves at the end of a cornfield, close to the road. The road ran along the edge of a wood and vanished into a rolling, well-cultivated valley. They took turns to watch. In the afternoon they saw a group of some ten soldiers coming along the road towards them. As they came up to the wood they halted and lit cigarettes, evidently discussing their route, then came on and turned sharply to the left.

"Shall we shout to them?" Koshevoi asked the others as he rose from the corn-stalks.

"Fire over their heads."

"Hey, you! Stop!"

The soldiers, now some hundred yards away from the Cossacks, heard the shout and halted for a moment, then again slowly moved on.

"Stop!" one of the Cossacks shouted, firing into the air.

With rifles trailed, they ran to overtake the slowly moving soldiers.

"Why the devil didn't you stop? Where are you from? Where are you going? Show us your documents!" the Cossack sergeant in charge of the outpost shouted.

The soldiers halted. Three of them slowly unslung their rifles. One man bent and refastened the wire holding the sole on to the upper of one of his boots. They were all incredibly ragged and filthy. Evidently they had spent the night in the undergrowth of a forest, for there was a dense brush of brown burs on their great-coats. Two of them were wearing forage caps; the others had fur caps with unbuttoned ear-flaps and fluttering strings. His sunken cheeks trembling, a tall, bowed soldier, evidently their leader, shouted in an evil voice:

"What do you want? Have we done you any harm? What are you following us for?"

"Your documents!" the sergeant interrupted, assuming a stern tone.

One soldier, blue-eyed and as ruddy as a freshly baked brick, drew a hand-grenade from his pocket. Shaking it in the face of the sergeant, he looked round at his comrades and said hurriedly in Yaroslav dialect:

"There's my document, my boy! There! That will serve as a mandate for all the year. Look after yourself, for if I throw it there'll be no collecting your insides afterwards. Understand? Did you understand? Is that clear?"

"Don't play about!" The sergeant frowned and dug him in the breast. "Don't play about and don't try to frighten us, we're fright-ened enough already. But if you're deserters, come back with us to the staff. They're collecting men like you there."

Exchanging glances, the men unslung their rifles. One of them, dark-haired and lean, and evidently a miner, turned his desperate eyes from one to another of the Cossacks and whispered:

"We'll give you a taste of the bayonet, by God! Clear off! By God, I'll put a bullet through the first one to come on."

The blue-eyed soldier waved his grenade around his head; the tall bowed man in front scraped with his rusty bayonet against the cloth of the sergeant's greatcoat; the miner measured and swung the butt-end of his rifle in Misha Koshevoi's direction. One of the Cossacks seized a little soldier by the edge of his greatcoat and dragged him along at arm's length, nervously looking back at the others in his fear of a blow from behind.

The dry leaves rustled on the corn-stalks. Beyond the rolling valley emerged a blue, undulating line of hills. Ruddy-brown cows were wandering over the pasture-land close to the village. The wind sent a frozen dust whirling beyond the wood. Sleepy and peaceful was the dull November day; a blessed calm and silence lay over the pallidly sunlit countryside. But just off the road men were trampling in meaningless anger, preparing to poison the seeded, fertile, rain-satiated land with their blood.

Their passions died down a little, and the soldiers and Cossacks began to talk more peaceably.

"It's only three days since we were withdrawn from our positions," Koshevoi said indignantly. "We haven't run away to the rear. And you're deserting, shame on you! You're leaving your comrades! Who will hold the front? My own comrade was bayoneted at my side, and you say we haven't tasted war! Taste it as we have tasted it!"

"What is there to talk about?" another of the Cossacks interrupted him. "Come on to the staff, and without any argument."

"Stand out of the road, Cossacks, or we'll shoot—by God, we'll shoot!" one of the soldiers said persuasively.

The sergeant helplessly flung out his arms. "We can't do it, brother! Kill us if you like, but all the same you won't get through; our company is quartered in that village there. . . ."

The tall, bowed soldier now threatened, now cajoled, now began to plead humbly. At the end he bent, drew a bottle out of his filthy pack, winked at Koshevoi, and whispered:

"We'll give you money, Cossacks; and look—German vodka. . . . And we'll collect something more. Let us pass, for the love of Christ. We've got children at home, you know how it is yourselves. . . . We're all beaten down, eaten up with yearning. . . . How long are we to stand it? God! Surely you won't stop us?" He hurriedly pulled his pouch out of the leg of his boot, shook two soiled Kerensky ruble notes out of it, and insistently pushed them into Koshevoi's hand. "Take them! Take them! My God! . . . Don't you worry—we'll break through somehow. The money is nothing. We can do without it. Take it! We'll gather some more. . . ."

Flaming with shame, Koshevoi stepped back, hiding his hand behind him and shaking his head. The blood flushed into his cheeks, and tears started to his eyes. "Bieshniak's death has made me mad!" he thought. "Here am I myself against the war, and I'm trying to arrest these men. What right have I got? What am I doing here? What a low swine I am!"

He went to the sergeant, drew him aside, and said, not looking into his eyes:

"Why not let them go? What do you think? Let them go, by God!"

His eyes wandering as though he were doing something shameful, the sergeant replied:

"Let them go! What the devil shall we do with them? We'll be doing the same ourselves soon. Why try to hide it?"

Turning to the soldiers, he angrily shouted:

"You scum! We treat you decently, with all respect, and you offer us money! Do you think we're short ourselves?" He turned livid and shouted: "Put your pouches away, or we'll drag you to the staff."

The Cossacks stepped aside. The soldiers walked on. Glancing back at the distant empty streets of the village, Koshevoi shouted after the retreating deserters:

"Hey! You fillies! What are you marching along in broad daylight for? There's a wood over there; get into it for the day, and go on at night, or you'll run into another outpost and they'll take you!"

The soldiers glanced around irresolutely; then, like wolves, in a dirty grey chain they dragged towards the aspen wood.

About the middle of November rumours of the Revolution in Petrograd began to reach the Cossack troops. The staff orderlies, who were usually better informed than the others, confirmed that the Provisional Government had fled to America; Kerensky, they said, had been captured by sailors, who had shaven him absolutely bare, tarred him as though he were a prostitute, and dragged him for two days through the streets of Petrograd.

Later, when the official news of the overthrow of the Provisional Government and the transfer of power to the Bolsheviks arrived, the Cossacks grew anxiously quiet. Many were glad, in the expectation that the war would be ended. But the echoes of rumours that the third cavalry corps was marching with Kerensky on Petrograd, and Kaledin was pressing with Cossack regiments from the south, instilled alarm.

The front broke to pieces. In October the soldiers had deserted in scattered, unorganized groups; but by the beginning of December entire companies, regiments, divisions were retiring from their positions in good order, sometimes marching with only light equipment, but more frequently taking the regimental property with them, breaking into the warehouses, shooting their officers, pillaging en route, and pouring in an unbridled, stormy flood-tide back to their homes.

In the new circumstances the 12th Regiment's task of holding up deserters became senseless. After being flung back into the front in the useless attempt to close the holes and breaches formed by the infantry abandoning their sectors, in December it was again withdrawn, marched to the nearest station, and, loading all the regimental property, machine-guns, reserves of ammunition, and horses into cars, set off into the heart of struggle-racked Russia.

Through the Ukraine the troop trains of the 12th Regiment dragged towards the Don. Not far from Znamenka the Bolsheviks endeavoured to disarm them. The negotiations lasted half an hour. Koshevoi and five other Cossacks, the chairmen of the company Revolutionary Committees, asked for permission to pass through with their arms.

"What do you want the arms for?" the members of the station soviet asked.

"To kill our own bourgeoisie and generals! To twist Kaledin's tail!" Koshevoi answered for them all.

The trains were allowed to go on. At Kremenchug a further attempt was made to disarm them. They were allowed to pass only when the Cossack machine-gunners set up their guns at the open doors of the cars and directed them against the station, while one of the companies lay in a chain along the tracks and made ready to fight. By Yekaterinoslav not even an exchange of shots with a Red Guard detachment availed; the regiment was partly disarmed, and the machine-guns, more than a hundred cases of cartridges, the field-telephone apparatus, and several reels of wire were confiscated. To the proposal that they should arrest their officers the Cossacks replied with a refusal. Throughout the journey they lost only one officer, the regimental adjutant, and he was sentenced to death by the Cossacks themselves.

Close to Chaplin the regiment was accidentally drawn into the struggle which had broken out between the anarchists and the Ukrainians. It lost three men and broke through by sheer force, with great difficulty clearing the lines occupied by the troop trains of some sharpshooters' division.

Within three days the first section of the regiment was detraining at Millerovo station. Half of them broke away and rode straight home from the station, while the remainder rode in good order to Kargin village. There next day they traded their trophies and the horses captured from the Austrians and divided the regimental funds and equipment.

Koshevoi and the other Cossacks from Tatarsk village set off home in the evening. They rode up a hill. Below, on the icy white, winding banks of the Chir, lay the village of Kargin, the most beautiful of all the villages of the upper Don. Smoke was rising in scattered clumps from the chimney of the steam mill, a black crowd of people was gathered in the square, the bell was ringing for vespers. Beyond the slopes of Kargin the crowns of the willows by Klimovsky village could just be seen. Beyond them, on the wormwood blue of the snow-clad horizon, the spreading sunset sparkled and smoked in cloudy glooms.

The eighteen riders passed by a mound nurturing three wild apple-trees, and at a swift trot, their saddles creaking, rode off to the north-east. The frosty night lurked thievishly behind the range of hills. Wrapping their faces in their cowls, from time to time the Cossacks urged their horses into a sharp gallop. The horseshoes rang out almost painfully on the hard road. Southward the road flowed from under the horses' hoofs. On each side stretched an icy ribbon of snow, smoothed by a recent thaw and gleaming and flowing with a chalky, fluid reflection of the moonlight.

The Cossacks silently urged on their horses. The road fled to the south. A forest girdled the east. The tiny marks of hares' feet showed on the snow at the side of the road. Over the steppe the Milky Way girdled the sky like an ornamented, chased Cossack belt.

Chapter 8

The Cossacks began to come home from the front in the late autumn of 1917. Ageing Christonia and three others who had served with him in the 52nd Regiment returned. Smooth-cheeked Anikushka returned, the artillery-man Ivan Tomilin, and Yakob Podkova. After them came Martin Shamil, Ivan Alexievich, Zakhar Koroliov, and the ungainly long Borshchev. In December, Mitka Korshunov unexpectedly turned up, and a week later a whole party of Cossacks who had served in the 12th Regiment: Misha Koshevoi, Prokhor Zykov, Yepifan Maksaev, Andrei Koshulin, and Yegor Sinilin. Fiodot Bodovskov got separated from his regiment and rode direct from Voronezh on a handsome dun horse taken from an Austrian officer. Afterwards he was always telling the story of how he had made his way through the revolutionarily seething villages of Voronezh province and had got away from right under the noses of Red Guard detachments, trusting to the mettle of his mount. Then came Merkulov, Piotra Melekhov, and Nicholai Koshevoi, who had run off from the Bolshevized 27th Regiment. It was they who brought the news that Gregor Melekhov, who had recently been serving in the 2nd Reserve Regiment, had gone over to the Bolsheviks and remained in Kamenka. They had also left behind them the incorrigible horse-stealer Maksim Gryaznov, who had been attracted to the Bolsheviks by the novelty of the troublous days and the possibility of living in clover. They told of Maksim that he had acquired a horse of extraordinary ugliness and as extraordinary mettle, that a band of silver hair stretched right along its back, that it was not particularly high-standing, but long and as red as a cow. They did not refer much to Gregor. Evidently they were reluctant to, knowing that his roads ran counter to those of the village, and whether they would run together again was uncertain.

The huts to which the Cossacks returned as masters or expected guests were filled with rejoicing. The rejoicing was emphasized more sharply and ruthlessly by the deep misery of those who had lost their relatives and dear ones for ever. There were many Cossacks missing, scattered over the fields of Galicia, the Bukovina, East Prussia, the Carpathians, Rumania—their bodies lying and

rotting under the gunfire dirge. And now the hillocks of the brotherly graves were overgrown with vegetation, rain pressed down
on them, and the drifting snow enwrapped them. No matter how
often the straight-haired Cossack women ran to the corner and
gazed under their palms, they would never live to see their dear
ones come riding home. No matter how much the tears streamed
from their swollen and faded eyes, they could not wash away the
pain. No matter how much they cried on the anniversaries and
remembrance days, the eastern wind would not carry their cries
to Galicia and East Prussia, to the grass-grown hillocks of the
brotherly graves.

The grass grows over the graves, time overgrows the pain. The
wind blew away the traces of those who had departed; time blows
away the bloody pain and the memory of those who did not live
to see their dear ones again—and will not live, for brief is human
life, and not for long is any of us granted to tread the grass.

The wife of Prokhor Shamil beat her head against the hard
ground and chewed the earthen floor of her hut with her teeth as
she saw her brother-in-law, Martin Shamil, caressing his pregnant
wife or giving his children presents and dandling them. She writhed
and crawled on hands and knees over the floor, while around her
her little children clung like a drove of sheep, howling as they
watched their mother, their eyes dilated with fear.

Tear the collar of your last shirt at your throat, dear heart! Tear
the hair of your head, thin with your joyless, heavy life; bite your
lips till the blood comes; wring your work-scarred hands and beat
yourself against the floor on the threshold of your empty hut! The
master is missing from your hut, your husband is missing, your
children are fatherless; and remember that no one will caress you
or your orphans, no one will press your head to his breast at night,
when you drop worn out with weariness; and no one will say to
you as once he said: "Don't worry, Aniska, we'll manage somehow!"
You will not get another husband, for labour, anxieties, children
have withered you and lined you. No father will come for your
half-naked, snivelling children. You yourself will have to do all the
ploughing, the dragging, panting with the over-great strain. You
will have to pitchfork the sheaves from the reaper, to throw them
on to the wagon, to raise the heavy bundles of wheat on the pitchfork, feeling the while that something is rending beneath your

belly. And afterwards you will writhe with pain, covering yourself with your rags and issuing with blood.

As Alexei Bieshniak's mother turned over his old underwear, she wept bitter tears as she sniffed at it; but only in the folds of his last shirt, brought back by Misha Koshevoi, could she smell the traces of his sweat. Dropping her head on to it, the old woman rocked and lamented grievously, soiling the stained and dirty cotton shirt with her tears.

The families of Manitskov, Ozierov, Kalinin, Likhovidov, Yermakov, and many other Cossacks were orphaned.

Only for Stepan Astakhov did no one weep; for there was no one. His boarded-up hut, tumbledown and gloomy even in summertime, was left empty. Aksinia lived in Yagodnoe, and little was heard of her; she never set foot in the village and had no inclination towards it.

The Cossacks of the upper districts of the Don returned home in local waves. By December almost all had returned to the villages of Vieshenska district. Day and night the bands of riders passed through Tatarsk in groups of from ten to forty, making their way to the left bank of the Don.

"Where are you from, soldiers?" the old men would go out and ask.

"From Chorna Rechka"; "From Zimovna"; "From Dubrovka"; "From Gorokhovska," would come the replies.

"Finished fighting, then?" an old man would ask with a sneer.

Some of the riders, more honest and peaceable, would reply: "We've had enough, daddy! We're finished!"

But the more desperate and evil would curse and advise the old men:

"Go home, old men, and mind your own business! What are you asking for? There are too many of you busybodies about."

By the end of the winter the beginnings of civil war had broken out close to Novocherkassk, but in the villages in the upper districts of the Don reigned a graveyard silence. Only an internal, hidden dissension raged in the huts, and sometimes it broke through to the surface. The old men could not get on with the Cossacks returned from the front.

Of the war which was raging close to the capital of the Don province they knew only by hearsay. Only hazily understanding the various political tendencies that had arisen, they waited on event, listening attentively.

Until January life flowed quietly in the village of Tatarsk. The Cossacks who had returned from the front rested at the sides of their wives and ate their fill, little recking that still more bitter woes and burdens than those they had had to bear during the war were on guard at the threshold of their huts.

Chapter 9

In January 1917 Gregor Melekhov was promoted to officer's rank in recognition of his distinguished services in the field and was appointed to the 2nd Reserve Regiment as a troop commander. In the following September he went home on leave, after an illness with inflammation of the lungs. He spent six weeks at home, then was passed as fit by the district medical commission and returned to his regiment. After the November Revolution he was promoted to the rank of company commander. About this time his opinions underwent a considerable change as the result of the events occurring around him and the influence of one of the officers in the regiment, Captain Yefim Izvarin.

Gregor made Izvarin's acquaintance the day he returned from leave and afterwards met him frequently both on and off duty. Yefim Izvarin was the son of a well-to-do Cossack. He had been educated in the Novocherkassk Junkers Training College, went straight from college to the 10th Don Cossack Regiment at the front, served in this regiment for about a year, received the Cross of St. George and fourteen pieces of hand-grenade in various convenient and inconvenient parts of his body, and was then transferred to the 2nd Reserve Regiment.

A man of many abilities, highly talented, educated considerably above the level of the average Cossack officer, Izvarin was a fervent Cossack nationalist. The March Revolution afforded him opportunities for development; he associated with Cossack separationist circles and carried on an intelligent agitation for the complete autonomy of the Don region and the establishment of the form of government which had existed before the enslavement of the Cossacks by Great Russia. He was well acquainted with history, was ardent, yet clear-sighted and sober, in intellect, and with compelling eloquence painted a picture of the future free life of the Don Cossacks when they would have their own government, when there would not be a Russian left in the province, and the Cossackry, setting guards along their own frontiers, would talk as equals, without any cap-raising, with the Ukraine and Great Russia, and carry on commerce and exchange with them. Izvarin turned the heads of the simple-minded Cossacks and the poorly educated officers, and Gregor also fell under his spell. At first heated arguments went on between them, but the half-educated Gregor was no match for his opponent, and Izvarin easily triumphed in the verbal duels. The discussion usually took place in some corner of the barracks, and the listeners were always on Izvarin's side. He impressed the Cossacks with his views, touching their innermost, deeply cherished feelings.

"But how shall we be able to live without Russia, when we've got nothing except wheat?" Gregor would ask.

Izvarin would patiently explain:

"I am not thinking of an independent and completely isolated existence for just the Don region. We shall live together with the Kuban, the Terek, and the mountaineers of the Caucasus on the basis of federation—that is, association. The Caucasus is rich in minerals; you can find everything there."

"And coal too?"

"The Don basin is right at hand."

"But it belongs to Russia."

"Whom it belongs to and on whose territory it is is a matter of dispute. But even if the Don basin goes to Russia we shall lose very little. Our federative alliance will not be based on industry. We are an agrarian country, and as that is so, we shall supply our small industry with coal bought from Russia. And not only coal! There are many other things we shall have to buy from Russia:

timber, metal articles, and so on; and in return we shall supply them with good-quality wheat and oil."

"And what advantage shall we get by being separate?"

"That's simple! In the first place we shall be free from their political protection. We shall restore the order destroyed by the Russian Czars and turn out all the foreigners. Within ten years by importing machinery we shall raise our agriculture to such a level that we shall be ten times as rich. The land is ours. It was washed with our fathers' blood and fertilized with their bones; but for four hundred years we have been in subjection to Russia, defending her interests and not thinking of ourselves. We have a way out to the sea. We shall have a strong fighting army, and neither the Ukraine nor even Russia will dare to violate our independence. Life will be like a fairy-tale then!"

Izvarin, with his average height, handsome figure, and broad shoulders, was a typical Cossack. He had curly hair the colour of unripened oats, a swarthy face, a white, receding forehead, and was sunburnt only on his cheeks and along his bleached eyebrows. He spoke in a high, flexible tenor voice and, when talking, had a habit of suddenly raising his left eyebrow and wrinkling his hook-nose, so that he seemed to be sniffing at something. His energetic walk, self-confident carriage, and the open gaze of his black eyes marked him out from the other officers of the regiment. The Cossacks had a frank respect for him, more perhaps than for the regimental commander himself.

He and Gregor had long talks together, and Gregor, feeling that the ground was quaking beneath his feet, passed through an experience similar to that in the hospital at Moscow when he met Garanzha. He compared the words of Izvarin and Garanzha, and tried to decide where the truth was to be found. But he could not. Nevertheless, almost involuntarily and subconsciously he adopted the new faith.

Shortly after the November Revolution he had a long conversation with Izvarin. Torn by contradictory impulses, he cautiously asked the captain what he thought of the Bolsheviks.

"Tell me, Yefim Ivanich," he said; "do you think the Bolsheviks are right or not?"

Raising his eyebrow and humorously crinkling his nose, Izvarin replied:

"Are the Bolsheviks right? Ha-ha! My boy, you're like a new-born babe. The Bolsheviks have their own program, their own plans and hopes. They are right from their point of view, and we are right from ours. Do you know the real name of the Bolsheviks' party? No? It is the Russian Social-Democratic Workers' Party. Understand? 'Workers'! They're flirting now with the peasantry and the Cossacks, but the working class is their basis. They are bringing emancipation to the workers, but perhaps even worse enslavement to the peasants. In real life it never works out that everybody gets an equal share. If the Bolsheviks get the upper hand it will be good for the workers and bad for the rest. If the monarchy returns it will be good for the landowners and suchlike and bad for the rest. We don't want either the one or the other. We need our own, and first of all we need to get rid of all our protectors, whether Kornilov or Kerensky or Lenin. God save us from our friends and we'll manage our enemies ourselves."

"But you know the majority of the Cossacks are drawn towards the Bolsheviks?"

"Gregor, my friend, understand this, for it is fundamental: At the moment the roads of the peasants and the Cossacks coincide with that of the Bolsheviks. That's true, but do you know why? It is because the Bolsheviks stand for peace, for an immediate peace, and at the moment this is where the Cossacks feel the war!" He gave himself a sounding slap on his swarthy neck and, straightening his lifted eyebrow, shouted:

"And that is why the Cossacks are reeking with Bolshevism and are going step by step with the Bolsheviks. But—as soon as the war is over and the Bolsheviks stretch out their hands to touch the Cossacks' possessions, the roads of the Cossacks and the Bolsheviks will part! That is basic, and historically inevitable. Between the present order of Cossack existence and Socialism, which is the final consummation of the Bolshevik Revolution, there is an uncrossable Rubicon, an abyss. Well, what do you say to that?"

"I say that I don't understand it," Gregor mumbled. "It's hard for me to make head or tail of it. I'm all over the place, like drifting snow in the steppe."

"You won't get out of it like that. Life itself will force you to make something of it, and will drive you to one side or the other," Izvarin clinched his argument.

This conversation took place at the beginning of November. Later in the same month Gregor happened to meet another Cossack who played a large part in the history of the Revolution in the Don. A freezing rain had been falling since midday. Towards evening the weather cleared, and Gregor decided to call on Drozdov, a subaltern of the 28th Regiment who came from his own district. He found Drozdov had company: a healthy, sturdy Cossack with the epaulets of a sergeant-major in the Guards' battery was sitting on the camp-bed with his back to the window. He sat with bowed back, his legs in their black cloth trousers set wide apart, his large, hairy hands resting on his broad knees. His tunic fitted him tightly and was rucked up under the arms. At the scrape of the door he turned his short neck, stared coldly at Gregor, and dropped his puffy eyelids over the chilly light of his eyes.

"Let me introduce you to each other. Gregor, this is Podtielkov from Ust-Khopersk, almost a neighbour of ours," said Drozdov.

The two men silently shook hands, and Gregor sat down. He offered his new acquaintance a cigarette. Podtielkov fumbled a long time with his great red fingers at the closely packed case, flushing with confusion and cursing in his vexation. Finally he managed to pick out a cigarette and raised his smiling eyes to Gregor's face. His easy manner pleased Gregor, who asked:

"What village are you from?"

"I was born in Krutovsky, but I've recently been living in Ust-Klinovsky. You've heard of Krutovsky, I expect."

Podtielkov's face was slightly pockmarked. His whiskers were twisted tightly; his hair was plastered down over his little ears and raised elegantly over his left eyebrow. He would have made a pleasant impression but for his large upturned nose and his eyes. At first glance there was nothing extraordinary about his eyes, but as he looked more closely, Gregor almost felt their leaden heaviness. Small like grapeshot, they gleamed through narrow slits as though out of embrasures and fastened their gaze on one spot with a heavy, cadaverous obstinacy.

Gregor stared at the man curiously, noting one characteristic feature: Podtielkov almost never blinked. As he talked he fixed his cheerless gaze on his audience or shifted his glance from object to object, but all the time his curly, sun-bleached eyelashes were drooped and motionless. Only occasionally did he drop his puffy eyelids and suddenly raise them again.

"Here's an interesting point, brothers," Gregor opened the conversation. "The war will end and we shall begin to live again. The Ukraine will have a separate government, and the Military Council will rule in the Don."

"You mean Ataman Kaledin," Podtielkov quietly corrected him.

"It's all the same. Where's the difference?"

"Oh, there's no difference," Podtielkov agreed.

"We've said good-bye to Mother Russia," Gregor continued his paraphrase of Izvarin's argument, curious to see how Drozdov and this stranger from the Guards' battery reacted to these ideas. "We shall have our own government and our own style of life. Out with the Ukrainians from the Cossack lands; we'll establish frontier guards and keep the Hokhols out! We shall live as our forefathers lived in the old days. I think the Revolution is all to our good. What is your opinion, Drozdov?"

Drozdov smiled ingratiatingly. "Of course it will be better for us," he replied. "The 'peasants' robbed us of our strength and we couldn't live under them. And all the atamans were Germans: von Taube, von Grabbe, and the devil knows what else. They gave our land to all these staff officers. Now we shall get time to breathe, at any rate."

"But will Russia agree to all this?" Podtielkov quietly asked of no one in particular.

"She'll have to," Gregor assured him.

"In any case it will be just the same. The same old soup, only thicker."

"How do you make that out?"

'Of course it will." Podtielkov shifted his tiny eyes more swiftly and threw a heavy glance at Gregor. "The atamans will go on just the same as before, oppressing the people who have to work. You will go before some 'Excellency,' and he'll give you one on the snout. A fine life indeed! A millstone round the neck, and nothing else."

Gregor rose and began to pace up and down the room. Finally he halted in front of Podtielkov and asked:

"Then what are we to do?"

"Go on to the end!"

"To what end?"

"Once you've started ploughing, you must furrow on to the end. Once you've overthrown the Czar and the counter-revolution, you must work for the government to pass into the hands of the people. That story about the old times is all fairy-tales. In the old days the Czars oppressed us, and now if the Czars don't, somebody else will."

"Then what is your way out, Podtielkov?"

"A people's government, elected. If you get into the hands of the generals there'll be war again, and we can do without that. If only we could get a people's government set up all over the world, so that the people were not oppressed and we didn't have war! But what have we got now? If you turn a pair of old trousers inside out, you're still left with the holes. We'd better keep free of the old days, or they'll be harnessing us up so that we shall be worse off than under the Czar."

Gregor clutched at the air with his hand and asked in a mournful voice:

"Are we to give up our land? Divide it up among everybody?"

"No—why should we?" Podtielkov seemed confused and embarrassed by the question. "We shan't give up our land. We shall divide it up among ourselves, among the Cossacks, first taking the landowners' land away from them. But we mustn't give any to the peasants. They're a whole coat to our sleeve. Once we start dividing it with them, they'll beggar us."

"And who will govern us?"

"We shall govern ourselves," Podtielkov replied more animatedly. "We shall have our own government. Only let the Kaledins loosen the saddle-girths a little and we shall soon throw them off our backs."

Gregor halted before the steaming window and stared out into the street, at children playing some game, at the wet roofs of the houses opposite, at the pale grey branches of a bare poplar in the fence, and listened no more to the argument between Podtielkov and Drozdov. He was struggling painfully to see daylight through the jumble of thoughts oppressing him, to come to some decision.

For some ten minutes he stood drawing initials with his finger on the window-glass. Beyond the window the faded, early winter sunset was smouldering on a level with the roof of the low house opposite. The sun hung as though set edgeways on the rusty crown of the roof and about to roll down on one or the other side. Rustling leaves came chasing along the street from the town garden, and the strong wind blowing from the Ukraine raided the town again and again.

PART IV

Civil War

CIVIL WAR

Chapter 1

THE town of Novocherkassk became the centre of attraction for all who had fled from the Bolshevik Revolution. Important generals who formerly had been arbiters of the destiny of the Russian armies poured down into the lower regions of the Don, hoping to find support for their activities among the reactionary Don Cossacks and to develop an offensive against Sovietized Russia. On November 15 General Alexeev arrived in the town. After talks with Kaledin he set to work to organize volunteer detachments. The backbone of the future Volunteer Army was provided by officers, Junkers, and others who had fled from the north. Within three weeks an unwholesome flesh had grown around this framework, consisting of students, soldiers, the most active of the counter-revolutionary Cossacks, and men seeking adventure and higher pay even in Kerensky rubles.

At the beginning of December more generals arrived, and on December 19 Kornilov himself appeared in the town. By this time Kaledin had succeeded in withdrawing almost all the Cossack regiments from the Rumanian and Austro-German fronts and had distributed them along the main railway lines of the Don province. But the Cossacks, wearied with three years of war and returning from the front in a revolutionary mood, showed no great desire

417

to fight the Bolsheviks. The regiments were left with hardly a third of their normal complement, for the home fires beckoned powerfully, and there was no power on earth that could have restrained the Cossacks from their elemental movement homeward.

When Kaledin made a first attempt in December to send front-line detachments against revolutionary Rostov, the Cossacks refused to attack and turned back after going a little distance. But the widely developed organization for consolidating the fragmentary divisions began to have its results. By the middle of December, Kaledin had several reliable volunteer detachments at his command.

But from three sides columns of Red Guards were approaching the province. In Kharkov and Voronezh forces were being assembled to strike a blow against the counter-revolutionaries in the Don. Clouds hung and deepened and blackened over the Don. The winds from the Ukraine were already bringing the sound of the gun-thunder accompanying the first clashes. Gloomy days were coming to the Don; an evil time was approaching.

Yellow-white, billowing clouds were floating slowly over Novocherkassk. In the height of the heaven right above the glittering dome of the Cathedral, a grey, fluffy scrawl of feathery cloud hung in an expanse of cloudless blue, its long tail drooping and gleaming a rosy silver.

One morning in November, Ilia Bunchuk arrived at Novocherkassk by the Moscow train. He was the last to leave the car, pulling down the edges of his old overcoat and feeling a little awkward and strange in his civilian clothing.

He went out into the town, carrying his cheap, shabby suitcase under his arm. He met hardly anyone along the whole of the road, although he crossed the town from one side to the other. After half an hour's walk he halted before a small, dilapidated house. It had not been repaired for years; time had set its hands upon it, and the roof was sinking, the walls were awry, the shutters hung loosely, and the windows squinted. As he opened the wicket gate Bunchuk ran his eyes over the house and the tiny yard; then he hurried up the steps.

He found half the narrow corridor of the house occupied by a chest piled with lumber. In the darkness he knocked his knee against one corner, but threw open the door, not feeling the pain. There was no one in the first, low room. He went towards the second, halting on the threshold. His head swam with the terribly familiar scent peculiar to this one house. His eyes took in all the room: the ikon in the corner, the bed, the table, the small, speckled mirror above it, some photographs, several rickety chairs, a sewing-machine, and a tarnished samovar standing on the stove. With heart suddenly, violently beating, he threw down his suitcase and stared around the kitchen. The tall, green-washed stove had a welcoming look; from behind a blue cotton curtain peeped an old tabby-cat, its eyes gleaming with almost human curiosity. An un-washed utensil lay untidily on the table, and a ball of wool and four gleaming knitting-needles carrying an unfinished stocking had been left on a stool.

He ran out on the steps. From the door of a shed in the far corner of the yard emerged an old, bowed woman. "Mother! But is it? Is it she?" His lips trembling, he ran to meet her, tearing the cap from his head as he went.

"Who do you want?" the old woman asked cautiously, standing with her palm shading her eyes.

"Mother!" the words burst hoarsely from Bunchuk's throat. "Don't you know me?"

He went stumbling towards her and saw her sway at his shout as though before a blow. She wanted to run, but her strength failed her and she came in little spurts, as though battling against a wind. He caught her in his arms, he kissed her furrowed face and her eyes, dull with fear and gladness, while his own eyes blinked helplessly.

"Ilia! Iliusha! My little son! I didn't know you. . . . Lord, where have you come from?" the old woman whispered.

They went into the house. He threw off his overcoat with a sigh of relief and sat down at the table.

"I never thought I should see you again. . . . It's so many years. . . . My dear—how could I know you when you had grown so much and looked so much older?" she said.

"Well, but how are you, Mother?" he asked with a smile.

As she disconnectedly replied she bustled about, clearing the table, putting charcoal into the samovar. With streaming eyes she

ran back again and again to her son to stroke his head and press
him to her. She boiled water and gave him a meal, herself washed
his head, took some clean underwear, yellow with age, from the
bottom of the chest, and sat until midnight with her eyes fixed on
him, questioning him and bitterly shaking her head.

Two o'clock had just struck in the neighbouring belfry when
Bunchuk lay down to sleep. He dropped off at once, and dreamed
that he was once more a pupil at the craft school, tired out with
play and dozing over his books, while his mother opened the door
from the kitchen and asked sternly: "Ilia, have you learned your
lessons for tomorrow?" He slept with a fixed, tensely happy smile
on his face.

His mother went to him more than once during the night,
straightening the blanket and pillow, kissing his great forehead,
and quietly going out again.

He spent only one day at home. In the morning a comrade in
a soldier's greatcoat came and talked with him in undertones. After
the man had gone he bustled about, swiftly packed his suitcase,
and drew on his ill-fitting overcoat. He took a hurried farewell of
his mother, promising to see her again within a month.

"Where are you off to now, Ilia?" she asked.

"To Rostov, Mother, to Rostov. I'll be back soon. . . . Don't you
fret, Mother . . . don't fret," he cheered her.

She hurriedly removed a small cross from her neck, and as she
kissed her son she slipped the string over his head. As with trembling fingers she adjusted it around his neck, she whispered:

"Wear this, Ilia. Defend him and save him, Lord; cover him with
Thy wings. He is all I have in the world. . . ." As she passionately
embraced him she could not control herself, and the corners of
her lips quivered and drooped bitterly. Like spring rain one warm
tear after another fell on to Bunchuk's hairy hand. He unfastened
her hands from his neck and ran with clouded face out of the
house.

The crowd was packed like sardines at Rostov station, and the
floors were littered ankle-deep with cigarette-ends and the husks
of sunflower-seeds. In the station square the soldiers from the town
garrison were trading their equipment, tobacco, and articles they

had stolen. A swarming throng of the many nationalities to be found in the southern seaport towns moved slowly about. Bunchuk pressed through the crowd, sought out the party committee room, and made his way upstairs. His further progress was barred by a Red Guard armed with a rifle of Japanese pattern. A knife was tied to its barrel instead of a bayonet.

"Who do you want, comrade?" the guard asked.

"I want Comrade Abramson. Is he here?"

"Third room on the left."

Bunchuk opened the door of the room indicated, and found a short, big-nosed, black-haired man talking to an elderly railwayman. His left hand was thrust into his jacket, his right waved methodically in the air.

"That's not good enough!" the black-haired man was declaring. "That isn't organization! If you carry on your agitation like this you'll get exactly opposite results to those we want."

Judging from the anxiously guilty look on the railwayman's face, he wanted to say something in justification, but the other man would not let him open his mouth. Evidently irritated to the last degree, he shouted:

"Remove Mitchenko from the work at once! This is not to be endured! We cannot allow what is going on among you. Vierkhovietsky will have to answer for it to the revolutionary tribunal. Is he arrested? Yes? I shall insist on his being shot!" he ended harshly. Still not completely in control of himself, he turned his angry face in Bunchuk's direction and asked sharply: "What do you want?"

"Are you Comrade Abramson?" Bunchuk asked.

"Yes."

Bunchuk handed him documents from the Petrograd party committee and sat down on the window-ledge. Abramson carefully read the letters, then said, smiling morosely:

"Wait a bit; we'll have a talk in a moment or two."

He dismissed the railwayman and went out, returning a few minutes later with a well-built, clean-shaven, non-commissioned officer bearing the mark of a sabre-cut across his lower jaw.

"This is a member of our Military Revolutionary Committee," Abramson said to Bunchuk. "And you, Comrade Bunchuk, are a machine-gunner, aren't you?"

"Yes."

"You're just the man we're wanting," the non-commissioned officer smiled.

"Can you organize machine-gun detachments from the worker
Red Guards for us? As soon as possible?" Abramson asked.

"I'll try. It's a question of time."

"Well, how long do you need? A week—two, three?" Smiling expectantly, the other man bent towards Bunchuk.

"Several days."

"Excellent!"

Abramson rubbed his forehead and said with obvious annoyance:

"Part of the town garrison is badly demoralized, and they are
not to be relied on. Like everywhere else, I suppose, Comrade
Bunchuk, our hopes here are in the workers. The sailors too; but
as for the soldiers—" He tugged at his beard, and asked: "How are
you off in regard to supplies? Well, we'll arrange that. Have you
had anything to eat today? No, of course not."

"You must have starved a bit in your time, brother, if you can
tell at a glance whether a man is full or hungry," Bunchuk thought.
As he went with a guide to Abramson's room, his mind still turned
on him: "He's a brave lad, he's a true Bolshevik! Hard, yet there's
something good and human in him. He doesn't think twice about
the death-sentence for some saboteur, yet he can see to the needs
of his comrades."

Still under the warm impression of his meeting, he reached
Abramson's quarters and had some dinner, then lay down to rest
on the bed in the little book-filled room. He fell straight off to
sleep.

For the next four days Bunchuk was occupied from early morning till nightfall with the workers assigned to him by the party
committee. There were sixteen all together, men of the most varied
peace-time occupations, ages, and even nationalities. There were
two stevedores, a Ukrainian named Khvilichko, and a Russianized
Greek, Mikhalidze; a compositor, Stepanov; eight metal-workers;
a miner, Zelenkov, from the Paramonov mines; a weak-looking
Armenian baker, Gievorkiantz; a Russianized German and skilled

locksmith named Rebinder; and two workers from the railway workshops.

A seventeenth requisition was brought to Bunchuk by a woman attired in a padded soldier's greatcoat and boots too large for her feet. As he took the sealed letter from her, he asked: "On your way back can you call at the staff for me?"

She smiled, embarrassedly tidied a thick lock of hair that had fallen below her kerchief, and replied nervously:

"I have been sent to you—" then, overcoming her momentary confusion, she added: "as a machine-gunner."

Bunchuk flushed heavily. "Have they gone out of their minds? Is it a woman's battalion I've got to organize? Excuse me, but this isn't fit work for you; it's heavy and calls for a man's strength. No, I can't accept you."

Still frowning, he opened the letter and hurriedly scanned its contents. The requisition itself merely stated that the party member Anna Pogoodko had been assigned to the machine-gun section, but attached to it was a letter from Abramson, which read:

Dear Comrade Bunchuk:

We are sending you a good comrade in Anna Pogoodko. We have yielded to her insistent demand, and hope that you will make a fighting machine-gunner of her. I know the girl. I can warmly recommend her, she is a valuable worker, and I ask you only to watch one thing: she is fiery and a little exalted in temperament (she hasn't yet outgrown her youth). Keep her from thoughtless actions, and look after her.

Speed up the training. We hear that Kaledin is preparing to attack us.

With comradely greeting,

Abramson

Bunchuk stared at the girl standing before him. The dim light of the cellar which had been allotted to him for headquarters shadowed her face and concealed its lines.

"Oh well," he said ungraciously, "if it's your own wish—and Abramson asks, you can stay."

They crowded around the machine-gun, hung in clusters over it, leaning on one another's backs and watching with inquisitive eyes as under Bunchuk's skilful hands it came to pieces. Then he reassembled it, explaining the nature and function of each section, showing them how to handle it, to load it, sight it, determine the trajectory and the range. Then he showed them how to protect themselves from the enemy fire, pointed out the necessity of setting up the gun at a point of vantage and of arranging the ammunition-cases correctly.

All seventeen learned quickly with the exception of the baker, Gievorkiantz. No matter how many times Bunchuk showed him, he could not remember, and he lost his head, muttering in his confusion:

"Why doesn't it come out right? Ah—I'm a fool—this bit ought to be there. . . . And now it isn't right!" he cried in despair. "Why isn't it?"

"This is why!" The swarthy Bogovoi imitated his tone. "It doesn't come right because you're stupid. That's how it goes." He confidently put the section in its proper place.

"He's extraordinarily stupid," the phlegmatic German, Rebinder, agreed.

Only Stepanov shouted with annoyance, his face flushing:

"You ought to show your comrade and not snarl at him!"

He was supported by Krutogorov, a great, big-limbed worker from the railway workshops:

"You stand there laughing, you fools, and the work can wait! Comrade Bunchuk, instruct your waxwork gallery or else send them packing! The Revolution is in danger, and they stand there laughing! And they're party men too!" He waved his sledge-hammer fist.

Anna Pogoodko inquired about everything with keen curiosity. She attached herself importunately to Bunchuk, seized his sleeve, and could not be displaced from the side of the machine-gun.

"And what would happen if the water were to freeze in the water-jacket?" "What deviation has to be allowed for in a strong wind?" she plied him with questions, expectantly raising her black eyes to his.

In her presence he felt awkward, and as though in revenge he grew more exacting in regard to her and was exaggeratedly cool in his manner. But when each morning punctually at seven she entered the cellar, her hands thrust into the sleeves of her jacket, the soles of her great soldier's boots shuffling, he was troubled with an unusual, agitating feeling. She was rather shorter than he, of a full, healthy figure, perhaps a little round-shouldered, and not particularly beautiful except for her great, strong eyes, which endowed all her face with a wild beauty.

During the first four days he hardly had an opportunity to look at her. The cellar was badly lighted, and even if he had had time to study her face he would have felt too uncomfortable to do so. On the evening of the fifth day they left together. She went in front, but as she stood on the topmost step, she turned back to him with some query. She stood waiting for the answer, her head slightly tilted, her eyes bent on him, her hand brushing back her hair. But he did not catch her question. He slowly mounted the stairs, gripped by a pleasantly painful feeling. He knew it well: he had experienced its prick at all important turns in his life. Now he felt it again as he stared at the swarthily rosy cheeks of this girl, at the June azure in the whites of her eyes, and the bottomless depths of her black irises. She found it difficult to adjust her hair without removing her kerchief, and in her concentration her rosy nostrils quivered a little. The lines of her mouth were strong, yet childishly tender. On her raised upper lip there was a fine down, which showed dark against her skin. As simple as a fairy-story she stood before him, holding her hairpins in her silvery-white teeth, her arched brow quivering; and it seemed that she would melt away like a sound at dawn in a pine wood.

A wave of rapture and heavy joy carried Bunchuk away. He bowed his head as though before a blow and said half-seriously, half in jest:

"Anna Pogoodko, you're as good as someone's happiness."

"Nonsense!" she said firmly, and smiled. "Nonsense, Comrade Bunchuk! I was asking at what time we go to shooting practice tomorrow."

Her smile made her appear more simple, approachable, and earthly. He stopped at her side, gazing abstractedly down the street to where the stranded sun was flooding everything with a livid hue. He quietly replied:

"Tomorrow at eight. Which way do you go? Where do you live?"

She mentioned the name of some little street on the outskirts of the town. They went together, walking for some distance without speaking. At last she gave him a sidelong glance and asked:

"Are you a Cossack?"

"Yes."

"And you've been an officer?"

"Me an officer!"

"What is your native district?"

"Novocherkassk."

"Have you been long in Rostov?"

"Several days."

"And before that?"

"I was in Petrograd."

"When did you join the party?"

"In 1913."

"And where is your family?"

"In Novocherkassk," he said hurriedly, and imploringly stretched out his hand. "Stop a minute and let me do some questioning now. Were you born in Rostov?"

"No. I was born in Yekaterinoslav province, but I have lived here for some time."

"Are you a Ukrainian?"

She hesitated for a moment, then firmly replied:

"No."

"A Jewess?"

"Yes. But how did you know? Do I talk like one?"

"No."

"Then how did you guess I was a Jewess?"

He reduced the length of his stride in an attempt to fall into step with her and answered:

"Your ear—the shape of your ears, and your eyes. Otherwise you show little sign of your nationality." He thought for a moment, then added: "It's good that you're with us."

"Why?" she asked inquisitively.

"Well, the Jews have a certain reputation. And I know that many workers believe it to be true—you see I am a worker, too—that the Jews only do all the ordering and never go under fire themselves. That is not true, and you will prove splendidly that it isn't true."

They walked slowly. She deliberately took a longer way home and, after telling him a little more about herself, began to question him again about the Kornilov attack, the attitude of the Petrograd workers, and the November Revolution. From somewhere on the quays came the sound of a rifle-shot, then a machine-gun disturbed the silence. She at once asked him:

"What make is that?"

"A Lewis."

"How much of the belt has been used?"

He did not reply. He was admiring the orange feeler of a search-light stretching from an anchored trawler into the height of the flaming evening sky.

They wandered about the deserted town for some three hours and separated at last at the gate of her dwelling.

He returned home glowing with an inward satisfaction.

"She's a fine comrade and an intelligent girl! It was good to have a talk with her. I've grown boorish during these last years, and friendly intercourse with people is necessary, otherwise one gets as worm-eaten as soldiers' biscuit," he thought, deliberately deceiving himself.

Abramson, just returned from a session of the Military-Revolutionary Committee, began to question him about the training of the machine-gun detachments and asked about Anna.

"How is she getting on? If she isn't suitable we can easily put her to other work," he said.

"Oh no!" Bunchuk took alarm. "She's a very capable girl."

He felt an almost irresistible desire to go on talking about her and mastered his inclination only with a great effort of his will.

On December 8 Kaledin began to fling troops into an attack upon Rostov. Thin chains of Alexeev's officers' detachment moved along the railway line, supported on the right flank by a denser body of Junkers, and on the left by partisans of Popov's detachment.

The line of Red Guards scattered around the outskirts of the town was possessed with restless anxiety. Some of the workers, many of whom had rifles in their hands for the first time in their lives, were terror-stricken and pressed close to the muddy ground; while others raised their heads and stared at the distant tiny figures of the oncoming Whites.

Unable to endure the tense silence, the Red Guards opened fire without waiting for the word of command. When the first shot rang out, Bunchuk, kneeling at the side of his machine-gun, cursed, jumped to his feet, and shouted:

"Cease fire!"

His cry was lashed by the sputter of shots. He waved his hand, tried to outshout the firing, and ordered Bogovoi to open fire with the machine-gun. Bogovoi set his smiling, muddy face close to the breech and put his hand on the firing lever. The familiar sound of the spirting machine-gun bullets penetrated Bunchuk's ears. He stared in the direction of the enemy, attempting to determine the accuracy of the range, then ran along the line towards the other machine-guns.

"Fire!" he shouted.

"Right-o! Ho-ho-ho-ho!" Khvilichko howled, turning a frightened but happy face towards him.

The third machine-gun from the centre was manned by not altogether reliable elements. Bunchuk ran towards it. He stopped half-way and, bending, stared through his glasses. He could clearly see the spirting grey mounds cast up by the bullets in the distance. He lay down and assured himself that the range of the third machine-gun was hopelessly inaccurate.

"Lower, you devils!" he cried, crawling along the line. Bullets whistled close above him. The enemy was firing as perfectly as if at exercise.

The gun muzzle was tilted at a ridiculous angle; around it the gunners lay on top of one another. The Greek Mikhalidze was firing without pause, uselessly expending all his reserves of ammunition. Close to him was the terrified Stepanov, and behind, with head thrust into the ground and back humped like a tortoise, was one of the railwaymen.

Thrusting Mikhalidze aside, Bunchuk took long and careful sight. When the bullets began to spirt once more from the gun, they immediately had effect. A group of Junkers who had been coming on at a run turned and fled back down the slope, leaving one of their number on the clayey ground.

Handing the machine-gun over, Bunchuk returned to his own gun and found Bogovoi lying on his side, cursing and binding up a wound in his leg. Rebinder had taken his place and was firing intelligently and economically, without a trace of excitement.

From the left flank Gievorkiantz came leaping like a hare, dropping at every shot that passed over his head, groaning and shouting:

"I. can't. . . . I can't. . . . It won't shoot! It's jammed!"

Bunchuk ran along the line to the disabled gun. When still a little way off, he saw Anna on her knees at its side, staring under her palm at the advancing enemy chain.

"Lie down!" he shouted, his face darkening with fear for her. "Lie down, I tell you!"

She glanced at him and continued to kneel. Curses as heavy as stones fell from his lips. He ran up to her and flung her forcibly to the ground.

Krutogorov was wheezing by the shield.

"It's had enough! It won't work!" he muttered to Bunchuk and, looking round for Gievorkiantz, burst into a shout: "He's run away, damn him! Your antediluvian monster has run away. . . . He's completely upset me with his groans. . . . He wouldn't let a man work properly!"

Gievorkiantz crawled up, writhing like a serpent, mud clinging to the black scrub of his beard. Krutogorov stared at him for a moment, then howled above the roar of the firing:

"What have you done with the ammunition belts? You animal! Bunchuk, take him away or I shall kill him!"

Bunchuk examined the machine-gun. A bullet struck hard against the shield, and he removed his hand as though burned. He put the gun in order, and himself directed the firing, forcing the oncoming Alexeev men to lie down. Then he crawled away, looking for cover.

The chains of the enemy drew closer. Their fire grew heavier. In the Red Guard ranks three men were hit, and their comrades took their rifles and cartridges: dead men have no need of weapons. Right in the eyes of Anna and Bunchuk, as they lay at the side of Krutogorov's gun, a young Red Guard was struck by a bullet. He writhed and groaned, digging into the earth with his feet, and finally, raising himself on his hands, coughed and gasped in air for the last time. Bunchuk glanced sidelong at Anna. A fleeting terror lurked in her great, dilated eyes as she stared unwinkingly at the feet of the dead lad, not hearing Krutogorov's shout:

"A belt—a belt! Girl, give me a fresh belt!"

By a deep flanking movement the Kaledin troops pushed the Red Guard ranks back. The black greatcoats and tunics of the retreating workers began to dribble through the streets of the suburb. The machine-gun on the extreme right fell into the hands of the

Whites. The Greek Mikhalidze was shot down by a Junker, a second gunner was transfixed with bayonets, and only the compositor, Stepanov, managed to escape.

The retreat was halted when the first shells began to fly from the Red trawlers in the port. The Red Guards hesitated and turned, then advanced into the attack. Bunchuk had gathered Anna, Krutogorov, and Gievorkiantz around him. Suddenly Krutogorov pointed to a distant fence with little grey human figures assembled behind it.

"There they are!" he shouted.

Bunchuk swung the gun round in that direction. Anna sat down and saw all movement die away behind the fence. After a moment the Whites opened a measured fire, and the bullets sped over them, tearing invisible holes in the misty canvas of the sky. The belt rattled like a kettle-drum as it ran through the machine-gun. The shells fired by the Black Sea fleet sailors in the trawlers went screaming overhead. The sailors had now got the range and were carrying on a concentrated fire. Isolated groups of the retreating Kaledin troops were covered by the bursting shrapnel. One of the shells burst right in the midst of one group, and the brown column of the explosion scattered the men in all directions. Anna dropped her field-glasses and groaned, covering her terror-stricken eyes with dirty palms.

"What's the matter?" Bunchuk shouted, bending towards her.

She compressed her lips, and her dilated eyes glazed.

"I can't . . ."

"Be brave! You—Anna, do you hear? Do you hear? You mustn't do that! You mustn't . . ." the authoritative voice of command beat at her ear.

On the right flank some of the enemy had gathered in a valley and on the slopes of a rise. Bunchuk noticed them, ran with the machine gun to a more convenient spot, and opened fire on the valley.

Towards evening a first fine snow began to whirl down over the harsh earth. Within an hour the wet, sticky snow had completely enveloped the field and the muddy black bundles of the dead. The Kaledin troops withdrew.

Bunchuk spent the night in the machine-gun outpost. Krutogorov chewed away at some stringy meat, spitting and cursing. Huddled in the gateway of a yard, Gievorkiantz warmed his blue hands over a cigarette. Bunchuk sat on an ammunition-case, wrapping the trembling Anna in his greatcoat, tearing her damp hands from her eyes and kissing them. The words of unaccustomed tenderness came with difficulty from his lips.

"Now, now; how could you take on so? . . . You were hard. . . . Anna, listen, take yourself in hand! Anna—dear—you'll get used to it. If your pride will not allow you to go back, you must be different. You can't look on the dead like that. Don't let your thoughts turn that way! Take them in hand. You see now; although you said you were brave, the woman in you has won."

Anna was silent. Her hands smelt of the wintry earth and of womanly warmth.

The falling snow concealed the sky in a dense gracious blanket. The yard, the fields, the town lurking like a beast in the darkness were wrapped in drowsy slumber.

Six days the struggle continued around and in Rostov. Fighting went on in the streets and at the crossroads. Twice the Red Guards surrendered the station, and twice they drove the enemy out again. During those six days there were no prisoners taken by either side.

Late one afternoon Bunchuk and Anna were passing the freight station and saw two Red Guards shoot a captured officer. Bunchuk said almost challengingly to Anna, who had turned away:

"That's sensible! They must be killed, wiped out without mercy. They show us no mercy, and we don't ask for it. So why should we show them mercy? This filth must be raked off the earth. There can be no sentimentality, once it is a question of the fate of the Revolution. Those workers are right!"

On the third day of the struggle he was taken ill. But he kept on his feet for some days, feeling a continually increasing nausea and weakness in all his body. His head rang and was unbearably heavy.

The Red Guard detachments abandoned the town at dawn on December 15. Bunchuk, supported by Anna and Krutogorov, walked behind a wagon containing wounded and a machine-gun. He bore his helpless body along with the utmost difficulty, put forward his iron-heavy feet as though asleep, and heard Anna say from a great distance off:

"Get into the wagon, Ilia. Do you hear? Do you understand what I say? I ask you to get in; you're ill."

But he did not understand her words, nor did he understand that he was broken and in the grip of typhus. He clutched his head and pressed his hairy hands to his burning, flaming face. He felt as though blood were dripping from his eyes, and all the world, boundless and unstable, cut off from him by an invisible curtain, were rearing and tearing under his feet. In his delirium his imagination began to conjure up incredible visions. He stopped again and again, struggling with Krutogorov, who was trying to put him into the wagon.

"No! Wait! . . . Who are you? . . . Where's Anna? Give me a bit of earth. . . . And destroy these. . . . I order you to turn the machine-gun on them. . . . Stop! It's hot!" he shouted hoarsely, tearing his hand from Anna's grip.

They lifted him forcibly into the wagon. For a moment more he could smell a pungent mixture of various scents, he saw a chaotic confusion of colour effects and struggled fearfully to retain command of himself. But he could not. A black, soundless emptiness closed over him; only somewhere in the height burned a point of opal and azure blue, and zigzags and fires of ruddy lightning intercrossed before his eyes.

Chapter 2

The icicles were falling from the cornices and shattering with a glassy tinkle. In the village the thaw blossomed into pools and denuded earth. The cattle went wandering with sniffing nostrils along the streets. The sparrows chattered as though it were springtime as they pecked among the heaps of brushwood in the yards. Martin Shamil chased across the square after a sorrel horse that had escaped from his stable. Its stringy tail raised high, its unkempt mane tossing in the wind, it bucked and sent the clods of half-melted snow flying from its hoofs, circled round the square, halted by the church wall, and sniffed at the bricks. It allowed its master to get fairly close, glanced askance at the bridle in his hand, and broke again into a gallop.

January was caressing the earth with warm, cloudy days. The Cossacks watched the Don in expectation of a premature flood. Miron Korshunov stood in his back yard staring at the snow deep on the fields, at the icy grey-green of the Don, and thought: "It's piling up this year just like last. Snow, snow, nothing but snow! I fear the earth will be heavy underneath."

Mitka, in a khaki tunic, was cleaning out the cattle-yard. His white fur cap stuck to the back of his head by a miracle. His straight hair, dank with sweat, fell over his brow, and he brushed it back with his dirty, smelly palm. A heap of frozen cattle-dung lay by the gate, and a fluffy goat was treading over it. The sheep were huddled against the fence. A lamb bigger than its mother tried to suck at her, but she put her head down and drove it off. A ring-horned black sheep was scratching itself against a plough.

Miron went to the threshing-floor and with professional eyes estimated the quantity of hay still left. He began to rake together some millet straw scattered about by the goats, but unfamiliar voices reached his ears. He threw the rake on the pile and went into the yard.

His feet planted apart, Mitka was standing rolling a cigarette, holding his richly embroidered pouch, the gift of some village sweetheart, in two fingers. With him were Christonia and Ivan Alexievich. Christonia was pulling some cigarette paper out of his cap. Ivan Alexievich was leaning against the fence, rummaging in his trouser pockets. His clean-shaven face wore a look of vexation: evidently he had forgotten something.

"Had a good night, Miron Gregorievich?" Christonia greeted him.

"Praise be!"

"Come and join us in a smoke."

"No, I've just had one."

Miron shook hands with the Cossacks, removed his three-cornered cap from his head, stroked his bristly white hair, and smiled.

"And what may you be wanting with us today, brothers?" he asked.

Christonia looked him up and down, but did not reply at once. He spat on his paper, slowly drew his great rough tongue along it, and, after rolling the cigarette, replied:

"We've got business with Mitka."

Grand-dad Grishaka passed by, carrying a fish-net over his shoulder. Ivan and Christonia took off their caps and greeted him. He carried the net to the steps and then turned back.

"Why are you staying at home, soldiers? Having too good a time with your wives?" he asked.

"Why, what's up?" Christonia inquired.

"Shut up, Christonia! Don't tell me you don't know!"

"God's truth, I don't know!" Christonia replied. "By the cross I don't, old dad!"

"A man arrived the other day from Voronezh, a merchant, a friend or relation or something of Sergei Mokhov—I don't know exactly. Well, he comes and says that strange soldiers, the Bolshies themselves, are at Chertkov. Russia is going to make war on us. And you're staying at home! You scum. . . . Do you hear, Mitka? Haven't you anything to say? What do you think about it?"

"We don't think at all about it!" Ivan Alexievich smiled.

"That's the shame, that you don't think!" old Grishaka waxed indignant. "They'll take you in a snare like partridges! The peasants will take you prisoners and smash your snouts!"

Miron Gregorievich smiled discreetly. Christonia rasped over his long-unshaven cheeks with his hand. Ivan Alexievich stood smoking and looking at Mitka, and little fires sparkled in Mitka's eyes. It was impossible to judge whether he was laughing, or burning with repressed annoyance.

After a little more talk Ivan Alexievich and Christonia took their leave of Miron and called Mitka to the wicket gate.

"Why didn't you come to the meeting yesterday?" Ivan sternly asked.

"I hadn't time."

"But you had time to go along to the Melekhovs'!"

With a jerk of his head Mitka brought his cap down over his forehead and said with restrained anger:

"I didn't come, and that's all there is to it. Why should we waste time talking about it?"

"All the men from the front in the village were there except you and Piotra Melekhov. We've decided to send delegates from the village to Kamenska. There is to be a congress of front-line men there on January 23. We cast dice and it was settled that I, Christonia, and you should go."

"I'm not going," Mitka announced resolutely.

"What's your game?" Christonia frowned and took him by the button of his tunic. "Are you breaking away from your own comrades?"

"He's hand in glove with Piotra Melekhov," Ivan Alexievich said. He shook the sleeve of Christonia's jacket and added, turning noticeably pale: "Come on. There's nothing we can do here. So you won't go, Mitry?"

"No! I've said no, and I mean no."

With eyes averted Mitka stretched out his hand and said goodbye, then turned and went to the kitchen.

"The snake!" Ivan Alexievich muttered, and his nostrils quivered. "The snake!" he said aloud, staring at Mitka's back.

On their way home they informed some of the front-line men that Mitka had refused to go and that the two of them would set out the following day for the congress.

They left Tatarsk at dawn on January 21. Yakob Podkova had volunteered to drive them to Kamenska. His pair of good horses drew them swiftly out of the village and up the slope. The thaw had laid the road bare, and where the snow had melted, the sledge-runners stuck to the earth, the sledge jerked along, and the horses strained at the traces. The Cossacks walked behind the sledge. Red with the light morning breeze, Podkova strode along, his boots scrunching the fine ice. Christonia panted up the hill over the granular snow at the roadside, gasping because of the German poison gas he had drawn into his lungs at Doobno in 1916.

At the hilltop the wind was stronger and the air keener. The Cossacks were silent. Ivan Alexievich wrapped his face in the collar of his sheepskin. They drew near to a wood, through which the road pierced to emerge on a mounded ridge. The wind rippled in streams through the wood. The trunks of the sappy oaks were stained with scaly layers of gold-green rust. A magpie chattered in the distance, and it fluttered across the road. The wind was carrying it out of its course, and it flew violently, lop-sidedly, its pied feathers ruffling.

Podkova, who had not said a word since leaving the village, turned

to Ivan Alexievich and remarked deliberately, evidently giving
voice to thoughts long pondered:

"At the congress work for things to be arranged without war.
There'll be no volunteers for a war."

"Of course," Christonia agreed, enviously staring after the magpie's free flight and mentally comparing the bird's thoughtlessly
happy life with human existence.

They arrived at Kamenska in the early evening of the 23rd.
Crowds of Cossacks were making their way through the streets
towards the centre of the town. There was a noticeable animation
everywhere. Ivan and Christonia sought out the quarters of Gregor
Melekhov, but learned that he was not at home. The mistress of the
house, an elderly, white-haired woman, informed them that he had
gone to the congress.

When they arrived they found the congress in full swing. The
great, many-windowed room could hardly hold all the delegates,
and many of the Cossacks were crowded on the stairs, in the corridors, and in adjacent rooms.

"Hold on behind me!" Christonia whispered to Ivan, working his
elbows vigorously. Ivan followed in the narrow cleft he made. The
Cossacks smiled and stared with involuntary respect at Christonia,
who was a good head taller than any of them. They found Gregor
by the wall at the back. He was squatting, smoking and talking to
another delegate. When he saw his fellow-villagers his raven whiskers quivered with his smile.

"Why, what wind has blown you here? Hallo, Ivan Alexievich!
How are you, Daddy Christonia?" he exclaimed.

"Not too bad," Christonia laughed back, gathering all Gregor's
hand in his own great fist.

"And how is everybody in the village?"

"All well. They sent their greetings. Your father has sent you
orders to come and visit them."

"And how's Piotra?"

"Piotra—" Ivan Alexievich smiled awkwardly. "Piotra doesn't mix
with us."

"I know. And how's Natalia? And the children? Did you happen
to see them?"

"All well, and they send their greetings. . . ."

As he talked Christonia stared at the group sitting behind the table on the platform. Even from the back he could see better than anyone else. Gregor continued to ply them with questions, taking advantage of a momentary break in the session. Ivan Alexievich gave him the news of the village and briefly told him of the front-line men's meeting which had sent them to Kamenska. He in turn began to inquire about events in Kamenska, but someone sitting at the table shouted:

"Cossacks, a delegate from the miners will now speak. I ask you to listen carefully to him and to keep order."

A thick-lipped man of average height stroked his fair hair back and began to speak. The hum of voices died away at once.

From the very first words of the miner's burning, passionate speech Gregor and the other Cossacks came under the spell of his convincing eloquence. He spoke of the treacherous policy of Kaledin, who was driving the Cossacks into a war against the workers and peasants of Russia, of the common interests of the Cossacks and the workers, of the aims of the Bolsheviks, who were carrying on a struggle against the Cossack counter-revolutionaries.

"We stretch out our brotherly hands to the toiling Cossacks, and hope that in the struggle against the White Guard bands we shall find faithful allies among the front-line Cossacks," his trumpet-voice thundered. "At the fronts of the Czarist Russian-German war the workers and Cossacks jointly poured out their blood; and in the war against the nests of the bourgeoisie we must stand together. And we shall stand together! Hand in hand we shall go into the struggle against those who have enslaved the toilers for many centuries."

"That's right! Ay, that's right!" Ivan Alexievich muttered again and again as he listened with half-open mouth.

After other speakers, a delegate from the 44th Regiment stood up. He was burdened with his own clumsy, involved phrases and found it as difficult to make a speech as to set a mark on the air. But the Cossacks listened to him with great sympathy, only rarely interrupting with approving cries. Evidently his words found a vivid response among them!

"Brothers, we must take our congress to this serious business so that it should not be shameful to the people and so that everything should end quietly and well. What I mean is that we must find a way out without a bloody war. As it is we've had three and a half years of being buried in the trenches, and if we've got to go on fighting, the Cossacks will be worn to death. . . ."

"That's true!"

"We don't want war."

"We must talk it over with the Bolsheviks and the Military Council."

The chairman, Podtielkov, thundered on the table with his fist, and the roar died away. The delegate of the 44th Regiment went on:

"We must send delegates to Novocherkassk and ask the volunteers and the partisans to clear out of here. And the Bolsheviks haven't anything to do here either. We can settle with the enemies of the working people ourselves. We don't need other people's help from anyone, and if we do need it we'll ask them to give us help."

Lagutin, the Cossack who had been in Listnitsky's regiment, followed the delegate of the 44th Regiment with a challengingly fiery speech. He was frequently interrupted with shouts. The proposal was made to suspend the meeting for ten minutes, but as soon as silence was established Podtielkov shouted to the excited crowd of Cossacks:

"Brother Cossacks! Here we are arguing and discussing, but the enemy of the toiling people is not asleep. We would all like the wolves to be full and the sheep whole, but that isn't what Kaledin thinks. We have captured a copy of an order signed by him for all those taking part in this congress to be arrested. I will read it aloud."

As he read the order, a wave of agitation ran through the delegates, and a tumult arose still greater than before. At last the roar of voices sang, and from the platform the Cossack Krivoshlikov's girlishly thin tones pierced through the growing lull:

"Down with Kaledin! Hurrah for the Cossack Military Revolutionary Soviet!"

The crowd groaned. In the heavy, lashing braid of sound, cries of approval were to be heard. Krivoshlikov remained standing with upraised hand. His fingers were trembling a little, like the leaves of an aspen. Hardly had the deafening roar subsided when he cried in the same thin, flowing voice:

"I propose that we elect a Cossack Military Revolutionary Committee from among the delegates present, and that it be instructed to carry on the struggle against Kaledin and the organs of . . ."

"Ha-a-ah!" a shout like a bursting shell arose, sending flakes of whitewash from the ceiling.

The meeting at once began to elect the members of the committee. A small section of the Cossacks, led by the delegate of the 44th Regiment and others, continued to call for a peaceful settlement of the conflict with the Kaledin government. But the majority no longer supported them. The Cossacks had been enraged by Kaledin's order for their arrest, and demanded active resistance to him.

Gregor did not stay to the end of the election, as he was summoned urgently to the regimental staff. As he turned to go out he asked Christonia and Ivan:

"When it's over come along to my room. I shall be curious to know who is elected."

Ivan Alexievich turned up after nightfall.

"Podtielkov is chairman, Krivoshlikov secretary," he informed Gregor as he stood on the threshold.

"And the members?"

"Ivan Lagutin and Golovachev, Minaev, Kudinov, and some others."

"But where is Christonia?" Gregor asked.

"He went with several other Cossacks to arrest the Kamenska authorities. He got all worked up and I couldn't stop him."

Christonia did not return till dawn. He stood in the room breathing heavily and mumbling something under his breath. Gregor lit the lamp and noticed that his face was bloody and a gunshot scratch ran across his forehead.

"Who did that to you? Shall I tie it up? Wait a moment, I'll find a bandage." Gregor jumped up and turned out his first-aid kit.

"It'll heal quickly enough, like a dog does," Christonia rumbled. "The military commander fired at me with his pistol. We went to him like guests, with all due respect, and he tried to defend himself. He wounded another Cossack too. I wanted to drag the soul out of him to see what an officer's soul is like, but the other Cossacks wouldn't let me or I'd have given him a good time!"

Gregor's friend Lieutenant Izvarin fled from his regiment just before the congress of front-line Cossacks was held at Kamenska. The night before he left he visited Gregor and hinted vaguely at the step he was about to take.

"I find it difficult to serve in the regiment in the present situation," he said. "The Cossacks are wavering between two extremes. the Bolsheviks and the former monarchic system. No one wishes to support Kaledin's government, if only because he is behaving like a child with a new toy. What we want is a firm, resolute man who will put the foreigners in their proper place. But I think it is better to support Kaledin at the moment, otherwise we shall lose the game entirely." After a silence, during which he lit a cigarette, he asked: "I gather you have accepted the Red faith?"

"Almost," Gregor assented.

"Sincerely? Or are you like Golubov, out to get popular with the Cossacks?"

"I am not in need of popularity. I am myself seeking a way out."

"You're in a blind alley, and you haven't found a way out."

"We shall see. . . ."

"I'm afraid we shall meet as enemies, Gregor."

"No enemies are friends on the field of battle," Gregor smiled.

Izvarin sat talking a little while longer, then departed. Next morning he had disappeared like a stone into water.

The next day the 10th Don Cossack Regiment, sent by Kaledin to arrest all the members of the congress and to disarm the most revolutionary of the Cossack divisions, arrived at Kamenska, detraining just as a meeting was being held at the station. The newly arrived Cossacks crowded around the meeting and mingled with the men of other regiments. The yeast of the vigorous agitation which the Bolshevik adherents at once began among them worked quickly, and when the regimental commander called on them to carry out Kaledin's orders they refused.

Meantime Kamenska was feverish with activity; hurriedly assembled divisions of Cossacks were being sent out to occupy stations; troop trains were being dispatched. Elections of officers were taking place in the detachments. The Cossacks anxious to avoid war slipped quietly out of the town. while belated delegates from various villages were still arriving. Never before had the Kamenska streets been so animated.

On January 26 a delegation from the Don Military Government arrived in the town to open negotiations. A large crowd met it at the station. An escort of Cossacks from the ataman's Life Guard regiment conducted it to the post-office building, where the Military Revolutionary Committee spent most of the night in session with the government delegation.

The conference failed to reach any settlement. About two o'clock in the morning, when it was evident that no agreement could be achieved, a member of the delegation proposed that the Military Revolutionary Committee should send a delegation to Novocherkassk, in order to come to some final decision on the issue of the future government. The proposal was adopted.

The Don government delegation departed, and the representatives of the Military Revolutionary Committee set out immediately after it for Novocherkassk. Podtielkov was at their head. The officers of the ataman's regiment, who had been arrested in Kamenska, were held as hostages.

A snow-storm was raging outside the car windows. Wind-driven snowdrifts were visible above the half-ruined snow-fences. The railway cabins, the telegraph poles and all the illimitable, dreary, snowy monotony of the steppe sped away to the north. The compartment was foggy with tobacco-smoke, and cold. The members of the delegation felt by no means confident of their mission to Novocherkassk. They talked but little, and the silence was dreary. At last Podtielkov expressed the general conviction:

"Nothing will come of it. We shan't agree."

Again they sat silent. They drew near to Novocherkassk. Minaev began to relate:

"When in the old days the Cossacks of the ataman regiment had served their time, they were equipped to return home. They'd load their chests, their horses and goods into the train. The train would set out, and just by Voronezh, where the line crosses the Don for the first time, the engineer would go slowly, as slowly as possible —he knew what was coming. And as soon as the train got on to the bridge—my grandfathers! What a scene! The Cossacks would go quite mad: 'The Don! The Don! The gentle Don! Our father; giver of our food! Hurrah!' and through the window, over the bridge, straight into the water would go caps, old tunics, trousers, shirts, and the Lord knows what else! They would give presents to the Don on their return from service. Sometimes as you looked at the water you would see blue ataman caps floating like swans or flowers. . . . It was a very old custom."

The train reduced speed and finally stopped. The Cossacks rose. As he buttoned his tunic Krivoshlikov said with a wry smile:

"Well, here we are, at home!"

"They're not giving their guests a very hospitable welcome!" Skachkov tried to jest.

A tall captain threw open the door without knocking and entered the compartment. He surveyed the members of the delegation with eyes expressive of his hostility and said with deliberate roughness:

"I have been instructed to accompany you. Please leave the car as quickly as possible, mister Bolsheviks. I cannot guarantee the crowd and—your safety."

"There they are, the scoundrels, the betrayers of the Cossacks!" a long-whiskered officer standing among the crowd on the platform shouted as they got out. Podtielkov turned pale and glanced back at Krivoshlikov with disconcerted eyes. A strong escort of officers guarded the delegation. To the very door of the government head-quarters they were accompanied by a frenzied crowd demanding that they should be lynched on the spot. Not only officers and Junkers, but elegantly dressed women and students, and even a few Cossacks hurled abuse at them.

The hall of the government administration was not large enough to accommodate all the crowd that had gathered. While the members of the delegation were seating themselves on one side of a table, the members of the government arrived. Accompanied by Bogaevsky, Kaledin, stooping slightly, approached the table with a firm wolfish stride. He pulled back his chair and sat down, setting his cap with its officer's cockade calmly on the table, brushing back his hair, and buttoning up the great side-pocket of his tunic. Then he bent towards Bogaevsky and whispered something to him. His every movement and gesture were expressive of resolute, deliberate confidence, of mature strength. Bogaevsky seemed more agitated in face of the coming negotiations. He sat whispering, hardly moving his lips, his slanting eyes glittering behind his glasses. He betrayed his nervousness by restless movements of his hands, adjusting his collar, feeling his chin, and raising his eyebrows. The rest of the government delegates seated themselves on either side of Kaledin, and the general stared across at Podtielkov opposite him and said: "I think we can begin."

Podtielkov smiled and, speaking in audible tones, stated the reasons for the arrival of the delegation. Krivoshlikov picked up the ultimatum prepared by the Military Revolutionary Committee and stretched it across the table, but Kaledin rejected it with a movement of his white hand and said firmly:

"There is no point in wasting time while every member of the government separately studies the document. Please read your ultimatum aloud. Then we shall discuss it."

Krivoshlikov stood up. His girlishly thin voice flowed indistinctly through the crowded hall as he read the committee's demand for the abdication of the military ataman and his government. Hardly had his voice died away when Kaledin loudly asked:

"What troops have given you authority for this ultimatum?"

Podtielkov exchanged glances with Krivoshlikov and began to calculate aloud:

"The ataman Life Guards, the Cossack Life Guards, the 6th and 32nd batteries, the 44th Regiment . . ." as he mentioned each division he bent down the fingers of his left hand, and a jeering titter ran through the hall. He frowned, set his hairy hands down on the table, and raised his voice: "the 28th Regiment, the 28th battery, the 27th Regiment, the 14th Regiment. . . ."

When he had finished, Kaledin asked a few unimportant questions; then, pressing his chest against the edge of the table, he stared at Podtielkov and demanded:

"Do you recognize the authority of the Soviet of People's Commissars?"

Podtielkov gulped down a glass of water, set the glass back on the table, wiped his whiskers with his sleeve, and replied evasively:

"Only all the people can reply to that."

Afraid that the more simple Podtielkov might say too much, Krivoshlikov intervened:

"The Cossacks will not condemn any government in which there are representatives of the parties of national freedom. But we are Cossacks, and the government should be our own Cossack government."

"How are we to interpret that remark, when Bronstein and such men are at the head of the Soviet?"

"Russia has trusted them, and we shall trust them."

"Will you have relations with them?"

"Yes."

Kaledin drummed with his fingers and asked inquiringly:

"What have you in common with the Bolsheviks?"

"We want to have Cossack self-government in the Don region."

"Yes, but surely you know that on February 17th a Military Council is to be called? The members will be re-elected. Will you agree to joint control?"

"No!" Podtielkov raised his eyes and replied firmly. "If you are in the minority we shall dictate our will to you."

"But that will be coercion!"

"Yes."

Bogaevsky turned his eyes from Podtielkov to Krivoshlikov and asked:

"Do you recognize the Military Council?"

"Only in so far as—" Podtielkov shrugged his shoulders. "The regional Military Revolutionary Committee will call a congress of representatives of the people. It will work under the control of the military forces. If the congress doesn't satisfy us we shall not recognize it."

"And who are to be the judges in this matter?" Kaledin raised his eyebrows.

"The people!" Podtielkov proudly threw back his head.

After a short interval Kaledin spoke again. All noise died away in the hall, and the low, autumnally lack-lustre tones of his voice sounded clearly in the silence:

"The government cannot abdicate its powers at the demand of the regional Military Revolutionary Committee. The present government has been elected by all the population of the Don, and only they, and not individual sections, can demand that we abdicate our powers. You are blind instruments in the hands of the Bolsheviks. You are doing the will of German mercenaries, not realizing the colossal responsibility to the Cossacks which you are taking on yourselves. I advise you to reconsider the matter, for you are bringing terrible misery on your native land by entering into conflict with the government which reflects the will of the entire population. I shall not cling to my authority. A great Military Council is to be called, and it will accomplish the destinies of the country. But until it meets I must remain at my post. For the last time I advise you to think over your position."

Podtielkov pushed back his chair and replied tensely, stuttering with agitation, seeking words expressing an overwhelming power of conviction:

"If the Military Government could be trusted I would willingly renounce all our demands. But the people do not trust it! It is not us, but you who are beginning the civil war. Why have you given the shelter of the Cossack land to these runaway generals? That is why the Bolsheviks are coming to make war on our gentle Don. I will not submit to you! You will pass over my dead body first! I do not believe that the Military Council can save the Don. Why are you sending your partisans against the miners? Tell me, what guarantee is there that the Military Government will avoid civil war? The people and the front-line Cossacks are on our side!"

A laugh like a rustling wind ran through the hall, and angry exclamations against Podtielkov were heard. He turned his flushed face in their direction and shouted, making no attempt to hide his bitter anger:

"You're laughing now, but you'll be weeping before you're finished!" He turned back to Kaledin and fixed his eyes on him: "We demand that you hand over the government to us, the representatives of the toiling people, and clear out all the bourgeoisie and the Volunteer Army."

With Kaledin's permission several speakers from the Don Military Government attempted to talk the members of the Revolutionary Committee over to a different point of view. The hall grew blue and heavy with tobacco-smoke. Beyond the windows the sun was drawing near the end of its daily journey. Frozen fir branches clung to the outer panes.

At last Lagutin could endure it no longer. Interrupting one of the speakers, he turned to Kaledin:

"Come to a decision: it's time to end this!"

Bogaevsky whispered reprovingly:

"Don't get agitated, Lagutin! Take a drink of water. It's danger‹
ous for anyone prone to epilepsy to get agitated. And besides, it's
not the thing to interrupt speakers; this isn't a soviet here!"

After a moment Kaledin rose. His reply had been previously prepared, and he had already issued instructions for a large force to
advance in the direction of Kamenska. But he was playing for time,
and he ended the conference with a procrastinating suggestion:

"The Don government will consider the Revolutionary Committee's proposals and will give an answer in writing by ten o'clock
tomorrow morning."

The reply of the Military Government, handed to the delegates
of the Military Revolutionary Committee the next morning con-
stituted a complete rejection of the committee's proposals and
called for the dissolution of the committee and the submission of its
forces to the existing regional Military Council. It further proposed that the Military Revolutionary Committee should partici-
pate in a joint deputation to the Bolshevik forces, with a view to
negotiating for a peaceful settlement of the question of their ad‹
vance into the Don. This last proposal was accepted by the delegates, and Lagutin and Skachkov became members of the deputation sent to Taganrog. Podtielkov and the others were detained, for
the time being, in Novocherkassk, but meantime Kaledin's forces
under the command of Colonel Chornetsov had occupied the station of Likhi and continued their advance towards Kamenska,
occupying that town on January 30.

The revolutionary forces had to evacuate Kamenska in a hurry.
The depleted Cossack companies crowded pell-mell into the trains,
abandoning everything that could not easily be carried. The lack of
organization, of a resolute officer who would assemble and order
their really quite considerable forces, was making itself felt. During those days a captain named Golubov was outstanding among the
elected commanders. He took command of the militant 27th Cossack Regiment and at once ruthlessly restored order. The Cossacks
submitted to him implicitly, recognizing that he had qualities that
the regiment lacked: the ability to weld it into a unity, to allot
duties, and to take command. During the evacuation he shouted at
the Cossacks who were slow in loading the wagons:

"What's the matter with you? Are you playing hide-and-seek, damn you? Get on with it! In the name of the Revolution I order you to submit immediately. . . . What? Who's that demagogue? I'll shoot him, the scum! Silence! . . . You're a saboteur and secret counter-revolutionary, and no comrade!"

And the Cossacks did submit. Many of them even liked his hectoring ways, for they still had hankerings after the past. In the old days the biggest bully had always been the best commander in the Cossacks' eyes.

The detachments of the Military Revolutionary Committee retreated to Gluboka. The virtual command passed into the hands of Golubov. In less than two days he had reorganized the scattered forces and taken the necessary steps to hold Gluboka. At his demand Gregor Melekhov was placed in command of a division consisting of two companies of a reserve regiment and one company of the ataman regiment.

As twilight was falling on February 2, Gregor went out to make the round of the outposts set along the railway line. The night promised to be frosty, and a light breeze was blowing from the east. The sky was clear. The snow scrunched beneath his feet. The moon rose slowly and one-sidedly, like an invalid going upstairs. Beyond the houses the steppe smoked, a dusky lilac. It was the evening hour when all outlines, colours, and distances are obliterated, when daylight is still inextricably entangled with the night, and everything seems unreal and fluid. At this hour even scents have their own more subtle shades.

After making the round he returned to his quarters. His host, an employee on the railway, prepared the samovar and sat down at the table.

"Are you going to attack?" he asked.

"I don't know," Gregor replied.

"Or are you going to wait for them here?"

"We shall see."

"That's quite sound. I don't think you've anything to attack with, and then it's better to wait. I went through the German war as a sapper, and I know tactical strategy thoroughly. Your forces are small?"

"They'll be enough." Gregor endeavoured to avoid the disagree-able conversation.

But the man maintained a zealous fire of questions, hovering about the table and scratching his lean belly beneath his waistcoat.

"Plenty of artillery? Guns, cannon?"

"You've been in the army; don't you know a soldier's duty?" Gregor said with cold anger, and he rolled his eyes so violently that the man started back. "What right have you to question me as to the numbers of our troops, and our plans? I'll have you arrested and cross-examined. . . ."

"Lord—officer! My dear fellow—" The man turned pale and almost choked with anxiety. "I was stupid—stupid. Pardon me!"

Soon afterwards six Cossacks of the 2nd Reserve Regiment, who were also billeted in the house, returned and sat down to drink tea, laughing and talking noisily. Gregor was half-asleep, but he caught snatches of their conversation. One of them was telling of an incident of the same day:

"I was present when it happened. Three miners from Gorlovka came along from mine number eleven and said they had collected a force, but they hadn't any weapons. So they asked us to give them what we could spare. And Podtielkov—I heard him myself—tells them: 'Go and ask elsewhere, comrades, we haven't any here.' But how does he make out that we haven't any? I know we've got re-serves of rifles. That wasn't the point. He was jealous of the peasants interfering. . . ."

"And quite right too!" another exclaimed. "Give them weapons and they may fight or they may not, but as soon as the question of the land comes up they'll be laying their hands on it."

The first speaker thoughtfully tapped his spoon against his glass, keeping time to his words as he replied deliberately:

"No, that sort of thing won't do. The Bolsheviks will meet us half-way for the sake of all the people, and we're Bolsheviks of a kind. First we must kick Kaledin out, then we shall see. . . ."

"But my dear fellow," a high-pitched voice remarked with con-viction, "don't you see that we've got nothing to give away? We get perhaps three acres of good land in the share-out, and the rest is good for nothing. So what can we give them?"

"They won't take from you, but there are others with too much land."

As he dozed off, Gregor heard the Cossacks settling down on the floor for the night, still arguing about the land and how it should be divided.

They were awakened before daybreak by the sound of a shot fired right outside the window. Gregor drew on his shirt, fumbling a moment with the sleeve, seized his tunic, and put on his boots as he ran. Shots rattled out in the street. A cart rumbled by. Someone cried in a voice of fear outside the door:

"To arms—to arms . . . damn you!"

The Chornetsov forces had driven back the outposts and were pouring into the town. Riders dashed past in the grey misty darkness. Men were running, their boots clattering. A machine-gun had been set up at the corner of the street. A chain of some thirty Cossacks barred the road. Another group ran off down the street. A battery thundered by, the horses galloping, the outriders waving their whips. Machine-guns suddenly started to sputter somewhere close at hand. In the next street a field kitchen had been overturned in its headlong flight by one wheel hooking against a fence-post. "You blind devil! Couldn't you see it?" roared a mortally terrified voice.

With difficulty Gregor collected his company and led it at a gallop towards the station. They found the Cossacks already retreating in a dense stream.

"Where are you going?" Gregor seized one of the foremost by his rifle.

"Let go!" The Cossack pulled. "Let go, you swine! What are you stopping me for? Can't you see we're retreating?"

"Knock him over! . . . Sweep the fool aside!" others shouted.

Close to a long warehouse at the end of the station Gregor tried to deploy his company in extended formation, but a fresh wave of fleeing Cossacks swept them aside. The Cossacks of Gregor's company began to mingle with the crowd and fled back with them into the streets.

"Stop! Halt, or I'll fire!" Gregor roared, trembling with fury.

But they paid no attention to him. A hail of machine-gun bullets raked the street. The Cossacks dropped to the road for a moment, crawled closer to the walls, and fled into the side-turnings.

"You won't hold them now, Melekhov!" a troop officer shouted as he ran past. Gregor followed him, grinding his teeth and waving his rifle.

The panic which had taken possession of the Cossacks ended in complete and disorderly flight from Gluboka, most of the equipment being left behind. Only at daybreak was it possible to reassemble the companies and throw them into a counter-attack.

Livid and sweating, Golubov, in an open sheepskin jacket, ran along the files of his own 27th Regiment, shouting in a metallic, steely voice:

"Step out! No lying down! March, march!"

The battle began at six. The mixed forces of Cossacks and Red Guards from Voronezh swept on in a dense mass, trimming the snowy ground with a dark lacework of figures. A freezing wind was blowing from the east. Beneath the wind-driven clouds the dawn showed blood-red. Gregor sent off half the ataman company to cover the 14th battery, and led the others into the attack.

The first shell fell far beyond the Chornetsov forces. The tattered orange and blue flag of the explosion was flung upward. A second shell whistled overhead. A moment of tense silence, emphasized by rifle-fire, then a distant echo as it burst. The enemy forces in front began to lie down. Screwing up his eyes against the wind, Gregor thought with a feeling of satisfaction: "We've got the range!"

On the right flank were the companies of the 44th Regiment. Golubov was leading his own regiment in the centre. Gregor was on his left. Beyond were Red Guard detachments covering the left flank. Three machine-guns had been allotted to Gregor's companies. Their commander, a thickset Red Guard, with morose face and hairy hands, directed their fire excellently, paralysing the enemy's attempts at an offensive. He remained the whole time close to the machine-gun that was moving forward with the ataman Cossacks. At his side was a stocky woman in a soldier's tunic. As Gregor passed along the file of Cossacks he thought angrily: "The petticoat! Going into battle, and he can't leave his woman behind! He should have brought his children and his feather bed with him too!"

The commander of the machine-gun detachment came up to him.

"Are you in command of this section?" he asked.

"Yes."

"I'll direct a barrage fire in front of the ataman half-company. The enemy are preventing their advance."

"All right!" Gregor assented. At a shout from the direction of the momentarily silent machine-gun he turned and heard the bearded machine-gunner roar furiously:

"Bunchuk! We shall melt the gun! You human devil, you can't go on like that!"

The woman in a soldier's tunic went down on her knees. Her black eyes, burning under her kerchief, reminded Gregor of Aksinia, and for a second he stared at her with an unwinking gaze, holding his breath.

At noon an orderly galloped up from Golubov, with instructions for Gregor to withdraw his two companies from their positions and to encircle the right flank of the enemy, doing so unobserved if possible. He was to strike from the flank immediately the main forces opened a decisive attack. Gregor at once drew off his companies and, after mounting them, led them in a semicircle for eight miles along a valley. The horses stumbled and floundered in the deep snow, which sometimes reached to their chests. Gregor listened to the sound of firing and looked anxiously at his watch, a trophy taken from the hand of a dead German officer in Rumania. He directed their course by a compass, but even so deviated rather more to the left than necessary. They emerged into the open field over a broad down. The horses were smoking with sweat and wet in the groins. Gregor gave the order to dismount and was the first to climb the hill. The horses were left in the valley. The Cossacks crawled after him up the steep slope. He looked back, saw more than a company of Cossacks scattered over the snowy rise, and felt stronger and more confident. Like most other men, in battle he was strongly possessed by the herd instinct.

Taking in the situation of the battle at a glance, he realized that he was late by half an hour at the least. With a daring strategic manœuvre Golubov had almost cut off the rear of the Chornetsov forces, sending out flanking detachments on both sides, and was now striking at them from in front. The rifle-fire was rattling like shot in a frying-pan, shrapnel was sweeping the demoralized ranks of the enemy, and the shells were falling thickly.

"Forward!" Gregor shouted.

He struck with his companies on the flank. The Cossacks advanced as though on parade, but a dextrous Chornetsov machine-gunner sprayed them so healthily with bullets that they were glad to lie down, after losing three of their number.

In the early afternoon Gregor was struck by a bullet which pierced the flesh above the knee. Feeling a burning pain and the familiar nausea from loss of blood, he grated his teeth. He crawled out of the line and jumped to his feet, half-delirious with the shock and shaking his head. The pain was all the greater as the bullet had not passed out, but remained buried in the muscle. The burning, lacerating agony prevented all movement, and he lay down again. As he lay, his mind vividly recalled the attack of the 12th Regiment in the Transylvanian mountains, when he had been wounded in the arm. . . .

Gregor's assistant took charge of the companies and ordered two Cossacks to lead Gregor back to the horses. As they sat him on his horse they sympathetically advised him to tie up the wound. Gregor was already in his saddle, but he slipped down and, dropping his trousers, frowning with pain, hurriedly bandaged the inflamed, bleeding hole. Then, accompanied by his orderly, he rode back by the same circuitous route through the valley, to the spot where the counter-attack had begun. Drowsy with sleep, he stared at the traces of horse-hoofs in the snow, at the familiar outlines of the valley; and the incidents on the hillside already seemed to have happened a long time ago.

For two miles they rode through the valley. The horses began to tire with the heavy going.

"Make for the open!" Gregor snorted to his orderly, and turned his own horse up the drifted slope of the down. In the distance they saw the scattered figures of the dead lying like settled crows. On the very horizon a tiny riderless horse was galloping. Gregor saw the main forces of the enemy, shattered and thinned, break away from the battle, turn, and retreat towards Gluboka. He put his bay into a gallop. Some way off were several scattered groups of Cossacks. As he rode up to the nearest of them, Gregor recognized Golubov. The commander was sitting huddled in his saddle. His sheepskin jacket was flung open, his fur cap was pushed back on his head, his brows were wet with sweat. Twisting his sergeant-major whiskers, he hoarsely shouted:

"Melekhov, brave lad! What, are you wounded? The devil! Is the bone whole?" Without awaiting an answer he broke into a smile. "We've completely smashed them! Completely! We've smashed the officers' division so that they'll never be able to assemble them again."

Gregor asked for a cigarette. Over all the steppe Cossacks and Red Guards were streaming. A Cossack on horseback came galloping from a dense crowd approaching in the distance.

"Forty men taken, Golubov!" he shouted when still a little way off. "Forty officers, and Chornetsov among them!"

"You're lying!" Golubov turned anxiously in his saddle and rode off to meet the prisoners, ruthlessly plying his whip across his white-stockinged horse.

Gregor waited a moment, then trotted after him.

The crowd of captured officers was escorted by a convoy of thirty Cossacks. Chornetsov strode in front of the others. In an endeavour to escape he had thrown away his sheepskin coat and was wearing only a light leather jerkin. The epaulet had been torn from his left shoulder, and a fresh abrasion was bleeding above his left eye. He walked quickly and firmly. His fur cap, set on one side, gave him a carefree and youthful appearance. There was not a shadow of fear on his rosy face. Evidently he had not shaved for some days, for a growth of hair gilded his cheeks and chin. He harshly and swiftly surveyed the Cossacks running towards him, and a bitter, hateful frown darkened between his brows. He struck a match and lit the cigarette held in one corner of his firm lips.

The majority of the officers were young, only one or two having traces of grey hair. One, wounded in the leg, hung back and was driven on with a butt end by a small, pockmarked Cossack. Almost at Chornetsov's side was a tall, dashing captain. Two more walked arm in arm, smiling; behind them came a stocky, capless Junker. Another officer had hurriedly flung a soldier's tunic around his shoulders. Yet another was hatless and had an officer's red cowl pulled down over his handsome eyes.

Golubov rode behind them. He halted and shouted to the Cossack escort:

"Listen! You will answer with all the discipline of the military-revolutionary times for the safety of these prisoners. See that they reach staff headquarters unharmed."

He called a mounted Cossack to him, wrote a note, and ordered the man to give it to Podtielkov. Then he turned to Gregor and asked:

"Are you going to the staff, Melekhov?"

Receiving an affirmative reply, Golubov rode up close to him and said:

"Tell Podtielkov that I will be responsible for Chornetsov. Understand? All right, off you go!"

Gregor outdistanced the crowd of prisoners and rode off to the Revolutionary Committee staff, which was stationed near a small village. He found Podtielkov surrounded with staff officers, couriers, and Cossack orderlies. Minaev and Podtielkov had both only just returned from the scene of the battle. Gregor called Podtielkov aside.

"The prisoners will be here in a minute," he reported. "Have you received Golubov's note?"

Podtielkov waved his whip violently and, dropping his blood-shot eyes, shouted:

"Damn Golubov! It's a fine thing he's asking for! He'll take charge of Chornetsov, will he? Take charge of that counter-revolutionary and brigand! Well, he won't! I'll have them all shot and be done with them!"

"Golubov said he would be responsible for him," Gregor objected.

"I won't give him up! I've said that, and I mean it. That's all! He will be tried by a revolutionary court and the sentence carried out immediately. As an example to others! You know—" he spoke more quietly, staring keenly at the crowd of approaching prisoners—"you know how much blood he has made to flow? Oceans! . . . How many miners has he had shot?" And again stuttering with fury, his eyes rolling frenziedly, he shouted: "I won't hand him over!"

"There's nothing to shout about!" Gregor also raised his voice. He was inwardly trembling, as though Podtielkov had communicated his frenzy to him. "You have enough judges here. You go back there!" His nostrils quivering, he pointed behind him to the battlefield. "There are too many of you wanting to settle accounts with the prisoners!"

Podtielkov retreated, tightly gripping his whip in his hands. From a safe distance he shouted:

"I've been there! Don't think I've been saving my skin by this cart. You keep your mouth shut, Melekhov! Understand? Who are you talking to? Get rid of those officer ways of yours! So! The Revolutionary Committee will judge, and not any . . ."

Gregor set his horse at him, and jumped out of his saddle, forgetting his wound for the moment. But he doubled up with pain and fell headlong. The blood poured from his leg. He rose without assistance, dragged himself somehow or other to a cart, and dropped with his back against the rear spring.

The prisoners came up. Some of the escort mingled with the orderlies and Cossacks acting as bodyguard to the staff. The fire of the battle had not yet burned itself out in them, and their eyes glittered feverishly and evilly as they exchanged opinions on the recent struggle.

Stepping heavily over the deep snow, Podtielkov went towards the prisoners. Chornetsov, still a little way in front, stared at him with his clear, desperate eyes screwed up contemptuously, his left leg carelessly swinging, his upper teeth clenched over his lower lip. Podtielkov, trembling violently, went right up to him, his unwinking gaze wandering over the untrodden snow. He raised his eyes, and his stare crossed with Chornetsov's hateful, fearless, scornful gaze.

"So we've caught you, you serpent!" he said in a low, gurgling voice, stepping a pace backward. A wry, sombre smile gashed his cheeks like a sabre-stroke.

"Betrayer of the Cossacks! Hound! Traitor!" Chornetsov spat through his teeth.

Podtielkov shook his head as though avoiding a blow, his face darkened, and his open mouth gasped in air.

What followed occurred with astonishing speed. Chornetsov, his teeth bared, his face pale, his fists pressed against his chest, all his body bent forward, strode towards Podtielkov. Unintelligible words mingled with curses fell from his quivering lips. Only the slowly retreating Podtielkov caught what he said.

"Your time will come . . . you know that!" he raised his voice suddenly, so that the words were heard by the prisoners, the escort, and the staff officers.

"Well—" Podtielkov hoarsely choked, fumbling for his sword-hilt.

There was an abrupt silence. The snow scrunched clearly beneath the feet of Minaev, Krivoshlikov, and half a dozen others who threw themselves in Podtielkov's direction. But he outdistanced them. Turning his entire body to the right, and crouching, he tore his sword from its scabbard, flung himself violently forward, and struck Chornetsov with terrible force across the head.

Gregor saw the officer shudder and raise his left hand to ward off the blow; he saw the sword cut through the wrist as though it were paper and come down on Chornetsov's defenceless head. First the fur cap fell; then, like grain broken at the stalk, Chornetsov slowly dropped, his mouth twisted wryly, his eyes agonizingly screwed up and frowning as if before lightning.

As the officer lay, Podtielkov sabred him again, then turned and walked away with an aged, heavy gait, wiping his bloodstained sword. Stumbling against the cart, he turned to the escort and shouted in a choking, howling voice:

"Cut them down. . . . Damn them! All of them! We take no prisoners! In their hearts, in their blood!"

Shots rang out feverishly. The officers turned and fled in a disorderly, jostling mob. The lieutenant with beautiful, womanish eyes and a red cowl ran with his hands clutching his head. A bullet sent him jumping high as though over a barrier. He fell and did not rise again. Two Cossacks cut down the tall captain. He caught at the blade of one sword, and the blood poured out of his hand over his sleeve. He screamed like a child, fell on his knees, on to his back, his head rolling over the snow, his face all bloodshot eyes and a black mouth lacerated with a cry. The flying blades played over his face, his mouth, but still he shrieked in a voice thin with pain and horror. Straddling over him, a Cossack finished him off with a bullet. The Junker all but broke through the ring; he was overtaken and struck down by an ataman Cossack. The same man sent a bullet through the back of an officer running with his coat flapping in the wind. The officer squatted down and grabbed with his fingers at his breast until he died. A grey-haired lieutenant was killed on the spot; as he parted with life he dug a deep hole in the snow with his feet and would have gone on kicking like a mettlesome, haltered horse if a Cossack had not taken pity on him and ended his struggles.

Immediately the execution began, Gregor had burst up from the cart and, fixing his eyes on Podtielkov, had limped swiftly towards him. But Minaev seized him from behind, twisted his arms, tore the pistol out of his hand, and, gazing into his eyes with a dull stare, pantingly demanded:

"And you—what game are you playing?"

Chapter 3

Flooded with a sunny glare and the blue of a cloudless sky, the blindingly brilliant, snowy spine of the hill whitened and sparkled like sugar. Below the hill a scattered village lay like a tattered blanket. To the right, little hamlets and German settlements nestled in blue patches. To the east of the village straddled another sloping hill, rent with gulleys. Over its brow ran a palisade of telegraph posts. The day was unusually clear and frosty. Pillars of haze smoked in rainbow hues around the sun. The wind was blowing from the north, and driving up the snow from the steppe. But the snowy expanse was clear to the horizon: only to the east, right on the skyline, did a violet haze lurk over the steppe.

Pantaleimon Prokoffievich had been to Millerovo to bring Gregor home. He decided not to stop at the village, but to drive on to Kashara and spend the night there. He had set out from Tatarsk in reply to a telegram from Gregor and had found his son awaiting him at a peasants' tavern. After being wounded at Gluboka, Gregor had been a week travelling in a field-hospital wagon to Millerovo. When his leg had healed a little, he resolved to go home. He went with feelings of mingled dissatisfaction and gladness: dissatisfaction because he had abandoned his regiment at the very height of the struggle for power in the Don, and gladness at the thought that he would see his own people again. He concealed even from himself his desire to see Aksinia, yet he could not help thinking of her.

His meeting with his father was attended by a feeling of estrangement. Pantaleimon (Piotra had been whispering in his ear) stared moodily at Gregor, and discontent and expectant anxiety lurked in his eyes. In the evening he questioned Gregor at some length about the events occurring in the Don region, and evidently his son's replies did not content him. He chewed at his grey beard, stared at his felt boots, and snorted. He entered reluctantly into argument, but flared up in defence of Kaledin, told Gregor to shut up as in the old days, and even stamped with his lame leg.

"Don't try to tell me! Kaledin was in Tatarsk in the autumn. We had a meeting in the square, and he climbed on to a table and talked with the old men, and prophesied like the Bible that the peasants would come, there would be war, and if we didn't make up our minds what we were going to do they would take everything from us and begin to live on our land. Even then he knew there would be war. And what do you think about it, you son of a swine? Does he know less than your lot? An educated general like that, who's led the army, and who is it he knows less than? The men in Kamenska are uneducated talkers like you, and they're troubling the people. Your Podtielkov—who is he? A sergeant-major? Oho! A man who served with me. That's what we've come to!"

Gregor entered unwillingly into argument with him. He knew beforehand what attitude his father would take. And a new element had entered into the situation for him: he could not forget, he could not forgive the death of Chornetsov and the slaughter of the officer prisoners without trial.

The two horses easily drew the basket-sleigh along. Gregor's saddled horse was tied behind. The well-known villages and settlements unfolded along the road. All the way to his own village Gregor was thinking disconnectedly and aimlessly of the recent happenings and trying at least to discern some landmarks in the future. But his mind could see no farther than a rest at home. "When I get back I'll take a little rest and get my wound healed, and after that—" he mentally shrugged his shoulders. "We shall see. Time will show."

He was broken by weariness engendered of the war. He wanted to turn his back upon all the tempestuous, hate-filled, hostile, and incomprehensible world. Behind him everything was entangled, contradictory. With difficulty he had found the right path; but as soon as he had set foot upon it the ground had risen up beneath him, the path had dwindled to nothing, and he had lost all confidence that he was on the right course. He had been drawn towards the Bolsheviks, had led others after him, then had hesitated, his heart had turned cold. "Is Izvarin right after all? Who are we to trust?" But when he thought that soon it would be time to get the harrows ready for spring, mangers would have to be woven of willows, and that when the earth was unclothed and dry he would be driving out into the steppe, his labour-yearning hands gripping the plough-handles; when he remembered that soon he would be breathing in the sweet scent of the young grass and the damp-smelling earth turned over by the ploughshare, his heart warmed within him. He longed to collect the cattle, to toss the hay, to smell the withered scent of the clover, the twitch, the pungent smell of dung. He wanted peace and quietness; and so his harsh eyes nursed a constrained gladness as they gazed at the steppe, at the horses, at his father's back. Everything reminded him of his half-forgotten former life: the scent of sheepskin from his father's coat, the homely appearance of the ungroomed horses, and a cock crowing from some farmyard. Life here, in this retirement, seemed sweet and heavily intoxicating.

They arrived at Tatarsk towards evening of the following day. From the hill Gregor glanced towards the Don: there were the backwaters fringed with a sable fur of reeds; there was the withered poplar; and the crossing over the Don was not where it used to be. The village, the familiar blocks of farms, the church, the square. . . . As he fixed his eyes on his own farm the blood rushed to his head, and a flood of memories overwhelmed him. The crane of the well in the yard seemed to be beckoning to him with its uplifted willow arm.

"A sight for tired eyes!" Pantaleimon smiled, glancing round. Making no attempt to conceal his feelings, Gregor replied:

"Yes . . . and how much!"

"What a lot home means!" the old man sighed contentedly.

He made for the centre of the village. The horses ran swiftly down the hill, and the sleigh skidded along, bouncing from hummock to hummock. Gregor guessed his father's intention, but he asked none the less:

"What are you going to drive through the village for? Make for our own end."

Pantaleimon turned and winked, smiling into his beard. "I saw my sons off to the war as rank-and-file Cossacks, and they fought their way to officers' rank. Don't you think I'm proud to drive my son through the village? Let them look and be jealous! My heart is oiled with butter!"

In the main street he called to the horses and played with his whip; and the horses, knowing they were near home, ran freshly and swiftly as though they had not done twenty-five miles that day. The passing Cossacks bowed, the women stared under their palms from the yards and the windows, and the hens scattered squawking over the road. Everything went as smoothly as clockwork. They drove through the square. Gregor's horse glanced sidelong at another horse tied up by Mokhov's palings, snorted, and raised its head high. The end of the village and the roof of Astakhov's hut were in sight. But at the first crossroad there was an awkward incident. A young pig running across the road lost its head, fell under the horses' hoofs, grunted, and rolled over, squealing and trying to raise its broken back.

"The devil take you!" Pantaleimon cried, giving the pig a taste of his whip.

Unfortunately it belonged to Aniutka, the widow of Afonka Ozierov, an ill-tempered and long-tongued woman. She ran out of her yard and poured out such a stream of curses that Pantaleimon reined in the horses and turned back.

"Hold your tongue, you fool!" he shouted. "What are you roaring about? We'll pay you for your mangy pig."

"You unclean spirit! . . . You devil! You're mangy yourself, you limping hound! I'll have you before the ataman at once!" she screamed, waving her arms. "I'll teach you to crush a poor widow's animal!"

Pantaleimon had heard enough, and turning livid, he croaked:

"Filthy mouth!"

"You cursed Turk!" the woman replied energetically.

"You bitch, a hundred devils were mother to you!" Pantaleimon raised his voice.

But Aniutka Ozierov was never at a loss for abuse:

"Foreigner! Whoremonger! Thief! Who stole a harrow? Who runs after the grass-widows?" she chattered away like a magpie.

"I'll give you one with this whip, you slut! Close your mouth!" the old man retorted.

But now Aniutka shouted something so evil that even Pantaleimon, who had seen and heard much in his time, went red with embarrassment and began to sweat.

"Drive on! What did you stop for?" Gregor said angrily, seeing a crowd collecting and listening attentively to this fortuitous exchange of compliments between old Melekhov and the honest widow Ozierova.

"What a tongue! As long as a pair of reins!" Pantaleimon spat out, pulverized, and whipped up the horses as though he intended to ride down Aniutka herself. The blue shutters of their own hut sped past. Piotra, with bare head and unbelted shirt, opened the gate. There was a glimmer of a white kerchief, and Dunia, with gleaming, smiling black eyes, ran down the steps.

As Piotra kissed his brother he glanced into Gregor's eyes:

"Are you well?"

"I've been wounded."

"Where?"

"Near Gluboka."

"Did you have to shed some more blood there? You should have come home long since."

He gave Gregor a warm and friendly shake and handed him on to Dunia. Gregor embraced his sister's broad shoulders and kissed her on the lips and the eyes, then stepped back in astonishment.

"Why, Dunia, the devil himself wouldn't know you! Look at the girl you've turned out to be, and I thought you would be so stupid and ugly!"

"Now, now, brother!" Dunia turned away from his pinch, and smiling the same white-toothed smile as Gregor, she ran off.

Ilinichna brought the children out in her arms, and Natalia ran in front of her. Gregor's wife had blossomed and improved astonishingly. Her smoothly combed, gleaming black hair, gathered in a heavy knot at the back, shadowed her gladly crimson face. She pressed herself against Gregor, brushed her lips awkwardly several times against his cheeks and whiskers, and, snatching her son from Ilinichna's arms, held him out to her husband.

"Look what a fine son you have!" she cried with happy pride.

"Let me have a look at *my* son!" Ilinichna agitatedly pushed her aside. She pulled down Gregor's head, kissed his brow, and stroked his face with her rough hand, weeping with excitement and joy.

"And your daughter, Gregor! Here, take her!"

Natalia set the girl in Gregor's other arm, and in his embarrassment he did not know whom to look at: Natalia, or his mother, or his children. The little boy, with morose eyes and knitted brows, was cast in the Melekhov mould: the same long slits of black, rather stern eyes, blue, swollen whites, the spreading line of brows, and swarthy skin. He thrust his dirty little fist into his mouth and stared stubbornly and unyieldingly at his father. Gregor could see only the tiny, attentive black eyes of his daughter; the rest of her face was wrapped in a kerchief.

Holding them both in his arms, he moved towards the steps; but his leg was shot through with pain.

"Take them, Natalia," he laughed wryly and guiltily, "or I shan't be able to get up the steps."

Daria was standing in the middle of the kitchen, tidying her hair. She smiled and came jauntily towards Gregor, closed her laughing eyes, and pressed her moist warm lips against his.

"You taste of tobacco!" She worked the delicate arches of her brows humorously.

Gregor took off his sheepskin and tunic and hung them at the foot of the bed, then combed his hair. He sat down on a bench and called his son:

"Come to me, Misha! Why, don't you know me?"

His fist still in his mouth, the child approached sideways, but came to a halt by the table. His mother gazed fondly and proudly at him. She bent down and whispered something into her daughter's ear and gently pushed her forward. "Go on!" she said.

Gregor gathered them both up, set them on his knee, and asked:

"Don't you know me, you woodnuts? Polia, don't you know your daddy?"

"You're not our daddy," the boy said, feeling more confident now that his sister was with him.

"Then who am I?"

"You're some other Cossack."

"And that's that!" Gregor laughed aloud. "Then where is your daddy?"

"He's away in the army," the girl said with conviction in her voice.

"That's right, children, give it to him! He's been away all these years and it's high time he came home!" Ilinichna intervened with feigned harshness, and smiled at Gregor. "Even your wife will be giving you up soon! We were already looking for a man for her!"

"What do you say to that, Natalia?" Gregor turned jokingly to his wife.

She blushed, but overcoming her embarrassment, went across to him and sat down at his side. Her boundlessly happy eyes drank him in, and her burning hand stroked his dry, brown arm.

"Daria, set the table!" Ilinichna called.

"He's got a wife of his own!" Daria laughed, and turned with her jaunty step towards the stove.

She was as slender and elegant as ever. Her lilac woollen stockings clung tightly to her beautiful legs, her shoes fitted her feet as though made for her. The flounced, raspberry-coloured skirt embraced her closely, and her embroidered apron was of an irreproachable whiteness. Gregor turned his eyes to his wife and noticed that she had changed somewhat. She had decked herself out for his homecoming: a blue satin jacket with lace sleeves tight at the wrists displayed her shapely figure and swelled over her soft large breasts; a blue skirt with a full, crinkled, embroidered hem clasped her waist. Gregor looked at her sturdy legs, her swollen belly, and her broad bottom, like that of a well-fed mare, and thought: "You can tell a Cossack woman among a thousand. She dresses herself to show everything: 'Look if you want to, and don't if you don't!' But you can't tell the back from the front of a peasant woman, she covers her body in a sack. . . ."

Ilinichna caught his gaze and vaingloriously boasted:

"See how officers' wives dress among us Cossacks! They could rub shoulders with any town lady!"

"How can you talk like that, Mother?" Daria interrupted her.

"We should look fine among the town ladies! One of my ear-rings is broken, and the other isn't worth a grosch," she ended bitterly.

Gregor put his arm across his wife's broad back and thought: "She's good-looking, anybody can see that. How did she live without me? I expect the Cossacks ran after her, and maybe she ran after one of them. Suppose she did!" At this unexpected thought his heart beat violently, and he stared searchingly at her rosy, shining face.

Natalia flushed beneath his attentive gaze and whispered:

"What are you looking at me like that for? Glad to see me again?"

"Why, of course!"

He drove away his unpleasant thought, but for a moment he almost hated his wife.

Pantaleimon came in coughing, crossed himself before the ikon, and croaked:

"Well, good health to you all once more!"

"Praise be, old man! Are you frozen? We've been waiting for you. The soup's hot." Ilinichna bustled around clattering the spoons.

He untied the red handkerchief around his neck, pulled off his sheepskin, shook the icicles from his beard and whiskers, and sitting down by Gregor, said:

"I'm all frozen; but we were warm enough coming through the village. We drove over Aniutka Ozierova's pig. How she came running out, the bitch! How she carried on! 'I'll give it to you,' and 'You're this, that, and the other,' and 'Who stole a harrow?' The devil knows what harrow!"

He detailed all the nicknames Aniutka had called him, ignoring only her reference to his "whoremongering." Gregor laughed and sat down at the table. Seeking to justify himself in his son's eyes, Pantaleimon ended fierily:

"I'd have given her a taste of the whip, but Gregor was with me, and it wasn't a good moment."

Piotra opened the door and Dunia entered, leading in a handsome young calf by a girdle.

"We shall be having pancakes with cream at Shrovetide," Piotra cried gaily, thrusting the calf forward with his foot.

After dinner Gregor untied his sack and distributed his presents. "That's for you, Mother," he said to her, giving her a warm shawl

Frowning and blushing like a young girl, Ilinichna took the shawl and threw it around her shoulders. She spent so much time admiring herself in the glass that even Pantaleimon was riled:

"You old hag, fussing about in front of the glass! Pah!" he exclaimed.

"And that's for you, Father," Gregor said hurriedly, untying a new Cossack cap with a raised front and a flaming red band.

"God save you! I was needing a new cap. There haven't been any in the shop all this past year. I don't like going to church in my old one. It was only fit for a scarecrow, but I went on wearing it," he said in indignant tones, looking around as though afraid someone would take away his son's present.

He turned to go to the glass to see how it fitted, but caught Ilinichna's eyes, wheeled suddenly round, and limped to the samovar. He stood before it to try his cap on, setting the peak jauntily to one side.

"What are you doing there, you old wire?" Ilinichna rounded on him. But Pantaleimon barked back:

"Lord, what a fool you are, woman! This is a samovar, not a looking-glass."

Gregor gave his wife a length of woollen cloth for a skirt; his children received a pound of honey cake, Daria a pair of silver earrings, Dunia material for a jacket, and Piotra cigarettes and tobacco. While the women were chattering away over their gifts, Pantaleimon strutted about the kitchen like a lord, with his chest thrown out.

"There's a fine Cossack of the Life Guard regiment for you!" Piotra said admiringly. "Took prizes too! Won the first prize at the Imperial review. A saddle and all its equipment! Oh, you—!"

Gregor laughed, the men lit cigarettes, and Pantaleimon, glancing uneasily at the window, said to him:

"Before the relations and neighbours begin to come, tell Piotra what's happening back there."

Gregor waved his hand. "They're fighting," he replied.

"Where are the Bolsheviks?" Piotra immediately asked as he seated himself more comfortably.

"Coming from three sides: from Tikhoretsk, from Taganrog, and Voronezh."

"Well, and what does your Revolutionary Committee think about that? Why are they letting them come on to our land? Christonia and Ivan Alexievich came back and told us all sorts of yarns, but I don't believe them. It's not as they say."

"The Revolutionary Committee is helpless. The Cossacks are running home."

"And is that why it's leaning on the Soviets?"

"Of course that's why."

Piotra was silent while he puffed at his cigarette, then he opened his eyes wide at his brother.

"And on what side are you?" he asked.

"I want a Soviet government."

"The fool!" Pantaleimon exploded like gunpowder. "Piotra, you tell him!"

Piotra smiled and clapped his brother on the shoulders. "He's as fiery as an unbroken horse," he said. "Can anyone tell him anything, Father?"

"There's nothing to tell me!" Gregor grew angry. "I'm not blind. What are the front-line men in the village saying?"

"What have the front-line men to do with us? Don't you know that fool of a Christonia by now? What can he understand? The people are all lost and don't know which way to turn. It's only misery everywhere!" Piotra waved his hand and bit at his whisker. "Try to see what will happen in the spring and you won't have a notion. At the front we played at being Bolsheviks, but now it's time we came back to our senses. 'We don't want anything belonging to anybody else, but don't you touch ours!' that's what the Cossacks ought to say to all who come whining to us. It's a dirty business that's been going on at Kamenska. They've got friendly with the Bolsheviks and they'll set up their system."

"You think it over, Gregor," his father said. "You're not a fool! You must understand that once a Cossack, always a Cossack. Stinking Russia ought not to govern us. And do you know what the foreigners are saying now? All the land ought to be divided up equally among all. What do you think of that?"

"We'll give land to those foreigners who have been living in the Don for years."

"Not an inch!" Pantaleimon swore, setting his hook-nose close to Gregor's face.

There was a tramp of feet on the steps outside, and Anikushka,

Christonia, and Ivan Tomilin entered.

"Hello, Gregor! Pantaleimon Prokoffievich, what about a drink to celebrate his homecoming?" Christonia roared.

At his shout the calf dozing by the stove started up in alarm, tottering on its still feeble legs and gazing with agate eyes at the newcomers. In its fright it let a fine stream on to the floor. Dunia stopped it with a tap on the back, wiped up the pool, and set a dirty pot under the animal.

"You frightened the calf, you trumpet!" Ilinichna angrily exclaimed.

Gregor shook hands with the Cossacks and invited them to sit down. Soon other Cossacks from the far end of the village arrived. As they talked, they smoked so much that the lamp began to sputter and the calf to choke.

"The fever take you!" Ilinichna cursed them as she sent the guests packing at midnight. "Go out into the yard and smoke, you chimneys! Clear out, clear out! Our Gregor hasn't had any rest yet after his journey. Clear off, in God's name!"

Next morning Gregor was the last to awake. He was aroused by the noisy, springlike chatter of the sparrows in the eaves and outside the windows. A golden drift of sunlight was sifting through the chinks in the shutters. The church-bell was ringing for matins, and he remembered that it was Sunday. Natalia was not at his side, but the feather bed still retained the warmth of her body. Evidently she had not long been up.

"Natalia!" he called.

Dunia entered. "What do you want, brother?" she asked.

"Open the window and call Natalia. What is she doing?"

"She's helping mother. She'll come in a minute."

Natalia came in, screwing up her eyes in the twilight of the room. Her hands smelt of fresh dough. Without rising he embraced her, and laughed as he recalled the night.

"You overslept yourself!" he said.

"Aha! The night . . . tired me out." She smiled and blushed, hiding her head against Gregor's hairy chest.

She helped him to dress his wound, then drew his best trousers out of the chest and asked:

"Will you wear your officer's tunic with the crosses?"

"No, why?" He waved her off in alarm. But she pleaded importunately:

"Do wear it! Father will be pleased. Why did you win them if you're going to let them lie in the chest?"

He yielded to her entreaties. He rose, borrowed his brother's razor, shaved, and washed his face and neck.

"Shaved the back of your neck?" Piotra asked.

"Oh, the devil! I forgot!"

"Well, sit down and I'll do it."

The cold lather burned his neck. Reflected in the glass he saw his brother wielding the razor, his tongue sticking out at one corner of his mouth.

"Your neck's got thinner, like a bull does after ploughing," Piotra smiled.

"Well, you don't grow fat on army victuals."

Gregor put on his tunic with its officer's epaulets and row of heavy crosses, and when he glanced into the steaming mirror he hardly recognized himself: a tall, gaunt officer as swarthy as a gypsy stared back at him.

"You look like a colonel!" Piotra exclaimed in delight, without the least trace of envy in his voice as he admired his brother. The words pleased Gregor despite himself. He went into the kitchen. Daria stared at him admiringly, while Dunia cried:

"Pfooh! How elegant you look!"

At this Ilinichna could not restrain her tears. Wiping them away with her dirty apron, she replied to Dunia's banter:

"You have children like that, you hussy! I've had two sons and they've both got on in the world."

Gregor threw his greatcoat around his shoulders and went out into the yard. Because of his wounded leg he found it difficult to get down the steps. "I'll have to use a stick," he thought as he held on to the balustrade. The bullet had been removed at Millerovo, but the scab had drawn the skin tight and he could not bend his leg properly.

The cat was sunning itself on the ledge of the hut wall. The snow was melting into a pool around the steps. Gregor stared gladly and observantly around the yard. Right by the steps stood a post with a wheel fastened across its top. It had been there ever since he was a child, being used by the women. At night they stood at the top of the steps and placed the milk-jugs on it, and during the day the pots and household utensils dried on it. Certain changes in the yard struck his eyes at once: the door of the granary had been painted with brown clay instead of paint, the shed had been re-thatched with still yellow rye straw; the pile of stakes seemed smaller—probably some had been used to repair the fence. The hummock of the earthen cellar was blue with ashes; a raven-black cock surrounded by a dozen or so variegated hens was perched on it with one leg raised limply. The farm implements were stored under the shed for the winter; the ribbed side-frames of the wagons were stood up, and some metal part of the reaping machine burned in a ray of sunlight that pierced through a hole in the roof. Geese were squatting on a pile of dung by the stable, and a crested Dutch gander squinted arrogantly at Gregor as he limped past.

He went all over the farm, then returned to the hut. The kitchen smelt sweetly of warmed butter and hot bread. Dunia was washing some pickled apples. He glanced at her and asked with sudden interest:

"Is there any salted watermelon?"

"Go and get him some, Natalia," Ilinichna called.

Pantaleimon returned from church. He divided the wafer into nine parts, a bit for each member of the family, and distributed it around the table. They sat down to breakfast. Piotra, also dressed up for the occasion, even his moustaches greased with some fat, sat at Gregor's side. Opposite them Daria balanced herself on the edge of a stool. A pillar of sunrays poured over her rosy, shining face, and she screwed up her eyes and discontentedly lowered the black arches of her gleaming brows. Natalia fed the children with baked pumpkin, Dunia sat at her father's side, Ilinichna was at the end of the table nearest the stove.

As always on holidays, they ate a hearty meal. The cabbage soup with lamb was followed by home-made vermicelli, then mutton, a chicken, cold lamb's trotters, potatoes baked in their jackets, wheat gruel with butter, vermicelli with dried cherries, pancakes and clotted cream, and salted watermelon. After the heavy meal Gregor rose with difficulty, drunkenly crossed himself, puffed, and lay down on the bed. Pantaleimon was still tackling the gruel; making a hole with his spoon, he poured the amber melted butter into

it and drew up a spoonful of the greasy mess. Piotra, who was very
fond of children, sat feeding Misha and playfully anointing the lad's
cheeks and nose with sour milk.

"Uncle, don't fool around!" the boy objected.

"Why, what's the matter?"

"What are you putting it all over my face for?"

"Well, what of it?"

"I'll tell Mamma." Misha's morose eyes glittered angrily, and
tears of vexation trembled in them. He wiped his nose with his fist
and shouted, in despair of persuading Piotra with fair words: "Don't
do it! Stupid! Fool!"

Piotra only burst into a roar of laughter and again anointed his
nephew on the nose and mouth.

Dunia sat down by Gregor and told him: "Piotra's just a big
stupid! He's always up to some new trick. The other day he went
with Misha out into the yard, and the boy badly wanted to go, and
asked: 'Uncle, can I go by the steps?' But Piotra said: 'No, you
mustn't. Go a little farther off.' Misha ran a little way and asked:
'Here?' 'No, no; run to the granary.' From the granary he sent him
to the stable, from the stable to the threshing-floor. He made the
poor boy run and run until he did it in his trousers. And Natalia did
go on at him!"

Gregor listened with a smile to Piotra and Misha and rolled himself a cigarette. His father came across to him.

"I'm thinking of driving to Vieshenska today," the old man confided.

"What for?"

Pantaleimon belched heavily from the food he had eaten and
stroked his beard. "I've got some business with the saddler; he's
had two yokes of ours to mend."

"Coming back today?"

"Why not? I'll be back in the evening."

After a rest the old man harnessed the mare, which had gone
blind that year, into the shafts of the sledge and drove off. In two
hours or so he was at Vieshenska. He went to the post office, then
to the saddler and collected the yokes. Then he drove to an old

acquaintance and gossip who lived by the new church. The man, a thoroughly hospitable sort, made him stay to dinner.

"Been to the post office?" he asked as he poured something into a glass.

"Yes," Pantaleimon answered, staring in astonishment at the bottle and sniffing the air like a hound tracking an animal.

"Then you've heard the news?"

"News? No, I've heard nothing. What is it?"

"Kaledin, Alexei Maximovich Kaledin, has gone to his rest."

"What are you saying?" Pantaleimon turned noticeably green, forgot the suspect bottle and its scent, and threw himself back in his chair.

Blinking moodily, his host told him:

"We've had the news by the telegraph that he shot himself the other day in Novocherkassk. And he was the one real general in all the province. What a spirit the man had! He wouldn't have let any shame come on the Cossacks."

"Wait a bit! What's going to happen now?" Pantaleimon asked distractedly, pushing away the glass offered him.

"God knows. Bad days are coming. I fear a man wouldn't put a bullet into himself if the times were good."

"What made him do it?"

His host, a man as conservative as Pantaleimon himself, waved his hand angrily. "The front-line men had deserted him and had let the Bolsheviks into the province; and so the ataman went. I doubt we'll find any more like him. Who will defend us? A Revcom or something has been set up in Kamenska, with front-line Cossacks in it. And here—have you heard? We've had an order from Kamenska to get rid of the atamans and to elect Revcoms in their place. The peasants are beginning to raise their heads. All these carpenters, smiths, and job-hunters—they're as thick in Vieshenska as midges in a meadow."

Pantaleimon sat a long time silent, his grey head drooping. When he looked up, his gaze was stern and harsh.

"What is that you've got in the bottle?" he asked.

"Liquor. A relation brought it from the Caucasus."

"Well, pour it out, friend. We'll drink to the memory of the dead ataman. May the heavenly kingdom open to him!"

They drank. The daughter of the house, a tall, long-lashed girl, brought in food. At first Pantaleimon glanced at the mare standing morosely by the sledge, but his host assured him:

"Don't worry about the horse. I'll see that she's fed and watered."

Over the burning conversation and the bottle Pantaleimon soon forgot his horse and all else in the world. He talked disconnectedly about Gregor, fell into an argument with his tipsy host, went on arguing, and then quite forgot what it was all about. It was evening when he started to his feet. Ignoring an invitation to stay the night, he decided to set off home. His friend's son harnessed the horse, and his host assisted him into the sledge. Then the man thought he would see him out of the village. They lay down together in the bottom of the sledge and embraced. Their sledge first hooked against the gatepost, then caught in every projecting corner until they drove out into the steppe. There his host burst into tears and fell voluntarily out of the sledge. For a long time he remained on all fours, cursing and unable to rise to his feet. Pantaleimon whipped the horse into a trot and saw no more of his host crawling along the road with nose thrust into the snow, laughing happily and hoarsely pleading: "Stop tickling. . . . Please stop tickling."

Warmed up with the whip, the mare moved swiftly but uncertainly at a blind trot. Soon her master, overcome by a drowsy intoxication, fell back with his head against the side of the sledge and was silent. The reins happened to fall underneath him, and the horse, unguided and helpless, dropped into an easy walk. At the first fork she turned off the right road and made for a little village. After a few minutes she lost this road also. She struck across the open steppe, was stranded in the deep snow lying in a wood, and dropped down into a hollow. The sledge hooked against a bush, and she came to a halt. The jerk awoke the old man for a second. He raised his head and hoarsely shouted: "Now, you devil—" then lay down again.

The horse moved on and passed the wood without mishap, successfully made her way down to the bank of the Don, and, guided by the scent of smoke brought by the easterly wind, made for the next village.

Some half-mile from the village there is a gap in the left bank of the river. Around the gap springs emerge from the sandy bank, and here the water is never frozen, even in the depth of winter, but lies in a broad, semicircular pool. The road along the river-side carefully avoids the water, making a sharp turn to one side. In springtime, when the field water pours in a mighty flood back through the gap to the Don, a roaring whirlpool is formed. All the summer the carp lie at a great depth close to piled driftwood fallen from the bank.

The old mare directed her blind steps towards the left edge of the pool. When it was some fifty yards away Pantaleimon turned over and half-opened his eyes. Out of the black heaven the yellow-green, unripe cherries of stars stared down at him. "Night . . ." he mistily realized, and pulled violently at the reins.

"Now! I'll give you one, you old horseradish!" he shouted at the horse.

The mare broke into a trot. The scent of the near-by water entered her nostrils. She pricked up her ears and turned a blind, uncomprehending eye in the direction of her master. Suddenly the splash of swirling water came to her ears. Snorting wildly, she turned aside and tried to back. The half-melted ice at the edge of the pool scrunched softly beneath her hoofs, and the snowy fringe broke away. The mare gave a snort of mortal terror. With all her strength she resisted with her hind feet, but her forefeet were already in the water, and the thin ice began to break under her hind hoofs. Groaning and crackling, the ice gave way. As the pool swallowed up the mare, she convulsively kicked out with one hind leg and struck the shaft. At that very moment Pantaleimon, hearing that something was wrong, jumped from the sledge and tumbled backward. He saw the back of the sledge rise, laying bare the gleaming runners as the front was drawn down by the weight of the mare; then it slipped away into the green-black depths. The water, mingled with pieces of ice, hissed softly and rolled in a wave almost to his feet. With incredible swiftness he crawled backward and jumped firmly to his feet, roaring:

"Help, good people! We're drowning!"

His drunkenness passed from him as though cut away by a sabre. He ran to the pool. The freshly broken ice gleamed sharply. The wind drove bits of ice over the broad black half-circle of the pool; the waves shook their green manes and muttered. All around was a deathly silence. The lights of the distant village shone yellow through the darkness. The stars, granular as though freshly winnowed, burned ecstatically in the plush of the sky. The breeze raised the snow from the field, and it flew hissingly in a floury dust into the black depths of the pool. And the pool steamed a little and remained menacingly, yawningly black.

Pantaleimon realized that it was useless and foolish to shout now. He looked around, discovered where he had got to in his drunken torpor, and shook with anger at himself and at what had happened. His knout was still in his hand; he had jumped out of the sledge with it. Cursing frightfully, he whipped away at his back with the lash, but it did not pain him, for his stout sheepskin softened the blows. And it seemed senseless to undress just for that pleasure. He tore a handful of hair out of his beard, and mentally counting the purchases he had lost, the value of the mare, the sledge, and the yokes, he swore frenziedly and went still closer to the pool.

"You blind devil, your mother was . . ." he said in a trembling, moaning voice, addressing the drowned mare. "You chicken! Drowned yourself and all but drowned me! Where has the unclean spirit taken you? The devils will harness you up and drive you, but they won't have anything to touch you up with! Here, take the whip, too!" He waved the cherry knout desperately around his head and flung it into the middle of the pool.

It smacked and pierced the water stock-first and disappeared into the depths.

Chapter 4

The first sight to meet Bunchuk's gaze when he returned to consciousness was Anna's black eyes glittering with tears and a smile. For three weeks he had been delirious. For three weeks he had wandered in another, intangible and fantastic world. His senses returned to him towards the evening of January 6. He stared at Anna with serious, filmy eyes, trying to recall all that was associated with her, but only partly succeeding. Much of his recent past was still inflexibly concealed in the depths of his memory.

"Give me a drink . . ." he heard his own voice coming from afar off, and he smiled with amusement at it. He stretched out his hand for the cup held by Anna, but she pushed it aside.

"You must drink from my hand," she said.

He felt a stirring of gratitude towards her. Trembling with the effort of lifting his head, he drank, then fell wearily back on the pillow. He lay staring at the wall, wanting to say something. But his weakness took the upper hand, and he dozed off.

When he awoke, it was again Anna's anxious, troubling eyes that first met his own; then he noticed the saffron light of the lamp and the white circle cast by it on the bare planks of the ceiling.

"Anna, come here!"

She approached and took his hand. He replied with a feeble pressure.

"How do you feel?" she asked.

"My tongue belongs to someone else, my head belongs to someone else, and my legs too; and I feel as though I was two hundred years old," he carefully enunciated every word. After a silence he asked: "Have I had typhus?"

"Yes."

His eyes wandered around the room, and he asked indistinctly,

"Where are we?"

"In Tsaritsyn."

"And you—how is it you're here?"

"I stayed with you," and as though justifying herself or trying to avert some unexpressed thought of his, she hastened to add:

"We couldn't leave you entirely to strangers. So Abramson and the comrades of the committee asked me to look after you. . . . And so you see I had quite unexpectedly to come with you."

He thanked her with a look and a weak movement of his hand.

"And Krutogorov?" he asked.

"He's gone to Lugansk."

"And Gievorkiantz?"

"He—you see—he died of typhus."

They were both silent, as though paying respect to the memory of the dead.

"I was afraid for you. You were very ill," she said quietly.

"And Bogovoi?"

"I've lost touch with them all. Some of them went to Kamenska. But is it all right for you to talk? And wouldn't you like a drink of milk?"

Bunchuk shook his head. He turned awkwardly over; his head swam and the blood rushed to his eyes. Feeling her cool palm on his brow, he opened his eyes. One question was tormenting him: he had been unconscious, and who had attended to his needs? Surely not she? A faint flush coloured his cheek, and he asked:

"Did you have to look after me all by yourself?"

"Yes."

The fever had left him with the complication of slight deafness. The doctor sent by the Tsaritsyn Party Committee told Anna that it would be possible to cure it only when he was thoroughly well again. He made slow progress. He had a wolfish appetite, but Anna strictly apportioned his diet. There was more than one quarrel between them on this account.

"Give me some more milk," he would ask.

"You can't have any more."

"I ask you—give me some more. Do you want me to die of starvation?"

"Ilia, you know that I mustn't give you more than a certain amount."

He lapsed into an injured silence, turned his face to the wall, sighed, and refused to talk. Although suffering with an almost motherly tenderness for him, she would not yield. After a little while he turned back, his face clouded and so looking even more unhappy, and pleaded:

"Can't I have some pickled cabbage? Please, Anna dear. . . . Listen to me. . . . It's all doctor's fairy-stories that it's not good for you."

Always meeting with a decided refusal, he sometimes wounded her with harsh remarks:

"You have no right to make sport of me like this. You're an unfeeling and heartless woman. I'm beginning to hate you."

"That would be the best payment I could have for what I have gone through in nursing you," she could not restrain herself from saying.

"I didn't ask you to stay with me. It's not fair to reproach me with that. You're exploiting your position. All right! Don't give me anything. Let me die! Great is pity!"

Her lips trembled, but she kept her self-command and patiently endured all. Once, however, after they had quarrelled over an extra helping of dinner, with tightened heart she noticed tears glittering in his eyes. "Why, you're a perfect child!" she exclaimed, and ran to the kitchen to bring back a full plate of patties.

"Eat, eat, Ilia dear. Don't get angry any more. Here's an extra nice one." With trembling fingers she thrust a patty into his hands.

Suffering intensely, Bunchuk attempted to refuse. But he could not hold out; wiping away his tears, he sat up and ate the patty. A guilty smile slipped over his emaciated face, and asking forgiveness with his eyes, he said:

"I'm worse than a child. You see, I almost cried. . . ."

She looked at his terribly thin neck, at the sunken, fleshless chest visible through the open shirt-collar, at his bony arms. Troubled by a deep love and pity, for the first time she simply and tenderly kissed his dry, yellow brow.

Only after a fortnight was he able to move about the room without assistance. His spidery legs collapsed under him, and he had to learn to walk.

"Look, Anna, I can walk," he exclaimed, and tried to move more quickly. But his legs could not support the weight of his body, and the floor broke from his feet. Compelled to lean against the first support to hand, he smiled broadly, and the skin on his translucent cheeks tightened into furrows. He laughed an agedly jarring, miserable little laugh and, weak with his efforts, fell back on the bed.

Their rooms were close to the quay. From the window they could see the snowy stretch of the Volga, beyond it forests sweeping in a dark half-circle, and the soft, undulating outlines of distant fields. Anna often stood by the window thinking over the strange and violent change that had occurred in her life. Bunchuk's illness had brought them very close together. But even before that, after their first meetings in Rostov, she had realized with an inward chill and tremor that she was bound to this man by inseverable bonds. Out of due season, in a time of menacing events, in the nineteenth spring of her life as brief as a dream, her feelings had taken charge of her and driven her towards Bunchuk. Plain and simple as he was, her heart had chosen him; in battle struggles she had become one with him; she had robbed death of him, had pulled him through.

At first, when after a long and arduous journey they had arrived at Tsaritsyn, her life had been burdensome and bitter to the point of tears. Never before had she had to look so closely and nakedly at the reverse side of living with one beloved. Clenching her teeth, she had changed his linen, combed the insects out of his lousy head, and with shuddering and aversion glanced stealthily at his naked, masculine body, at the envelope beneath which the dear life was hardly warm. Everything in her had risen up and revolted, but the external filth could not crush the deeply and faithfully preserved feeling. Under its powerful command she had learned to overcome her pain and incomprehension. And at last all that was left was compassion and a deep well of love which beat and soaked through to the surface.

Once Bunchuk happened to ask her:

"I suppose I'm repellent to you after all this—am I not?"

"It was a hard test."

"What of? Your self-control?"

"No. My feelings."

He turned away and for long could not restrain his lips from trembling. They did not refer again to the subject. Words would have been superfluous and colourless.

When he returned to health their friendly relations were not troubled by a single misunderstanding. He seemed to be trying to compensate her for all she had suffered for him, and was exceptionally attentive, anticipating her every wish, but doing it unobtrusively, with an unwonted gentleness. With eyes rough, yet humble and full of boundless devotion he watched her.

At the end of January they went to Voroniozh. As she stared from the rear platform of the car at the retreating town of Tsaritsyn, she laid her hand on his shoulder and said, as though completing the conversation they had left unfinished:

"We came together in extraordinary circumstances. . . . Perhaps it would have been better not to. . . . I say that with my head, and not with my heart, of course. And do you know why I say it? Look." She pointed to the snowy steppe, lying like an enormous, glittering silver ruble. "Out there life is fermenting. It calls for the application of all one's strength, and I think at such times feeling dissipates our concentration on the struggle. We should have met earlier or else later."

"That's not true!" He smiled and pressed her to himself. "You and I will be one, and that will not only not weaken our concentration, but on the contrary it will strengthen it. It's easy to break one twig, but more difficult to break two intertwined."

"Not a very good example, Ilia."

"Perhaps not . . . but all this talk leads nowhere."

"That's true, and besides, I'm not so very sorry that we—" she was embarrassed, and hesitated—"have half come together. The personal cannot stifle our desire to struggle—"

"And conquer, damn it!" he finished for her, squeezing her little, militantly closed fist in his hand.

The fact that they had not yet come together physically gave their relationship a childlike, agitatingly tender quality. They were not oppressed by the desire to cross the last barrier to their complete union. This circumstance gave Anna cause for agitated joy, and as she thought of it she asked:

"Our relations are not at all like what they usually are in such cases, are they? Our landlady in Tsaritsyn and everybody else thought we were man and wife, didn't they? How good it is, if only because we have got beyond the petty restrictions of the everyday! In the struggle you and I came to love each other, and succeeded in preserving our feeling without soiling it with anything bestial, earthly. . . ."

"Romanticism!" he laughed.

"What?" she inquired.

He silently stroked her head.

She stared with misty eyes at the snowy expanse, at the distant, indistinct outlines of villages, at the lilac contours of copses, at the gashes of ravines. She spoke hurriedly, and her voice was low and crooning in timbre like a violoncello:

"And besides, how poisonous and petty seems any care for the achievement of one's own individual little happiness at the present time! What does it signify in comparison with the uncompassable human happiness which suffering humanity will achieve through the Revolution? Isn't that so? We must be wholly absorbed in this struggle for liberation, we must—must fuse with the collective group and forget ourselves as isolated parts." Gently, like a child in sleep, she smiled at the corners of her tender yet strong mouth, and a wavering shadow lay on her upper lip because of her smile. "You know, Ilia, I perceive the future life like a distant, distant, magically beautiful music. Just as one sometimes hears it in sleep. . . . Do you hear music in your sleep? It is not a separate, slender melody, but a mighty, growing, perfectly harmonized hymn. Who doesn't love beauty? I love it in all, even its smallest manifestations. . . . And won't life be beautiful under Socialism! No more war, no more poverty or oppression or national barriers—nothing! How human beings have sullied, have poisoned the world! How much human misery has been poured out!" She turned passionately towards Bunchuk and sought for his hand. "Tell me, wouldn't it be sweet to die for that? Tell me! Yes? What is there to believe in if not in that? What is one to live for? It seems to me that if I die in the struggle—" She pressed his hand to her chest so that he felt the muffled beating of her heart, and gazing up at him with a deep, darkened glance, she whispered: ". . . and if death is not instantaneous, then the last thing I shall feel will be that triumphant, disturbingly beautiful music of the future."

Bunchuk listened with bowed head. He was inflamed by her youthful, passionate outburst; and through the rhythmic clatter of the wheels, through the scrape of the car and the ring of the rails he thought he heard a great, intangible melody. A shiver ran down his back. He went to the outer door and threw it open with a kick of his boot. The wind burst whistling into the platform, bringing with it steam, a prickly, snowy dust, and the incessant, powerful roar of the engine.

Bunchuk and Anna arrived at Voroniozh on the evening of January 29. They spent two days there; then, learning that the Don Revolutionary Committee had been driven out of Kamenska by the Chornetsov troops, they followed it to Millerovo.

Millerovo was alive and active with people. Bunchuk remained there only a few hours and left by the next train for Gluboka. The next day he resumed command of the machine-gun detachment and the following morning took part in the battle which ended in the defeat of the Chornetsov forces.

After Chornetsov had been smashed Bunchuk had unexpectedly to part from Anna. One morning she came running from staff headquarters, excited and a little sad.

"Do you know, Abramson's here. He badly wants to see you. And I've some more news—I'm going away today."

"Where to?" he asked in amazement.

"Abramson, I, and several other comrades are going to Lugansk on agitation work."

"So you're deserting our detachment?" he asked coldly.

She laughed and pressed her flushed face against his chest.

"Confess! You aren't sad because I'm deserting the detachment, but because I'm deserting you! But it's only for a time. I'm sure that I shall be of more service in that work than with you. Agitation is more in my line than machine-guns"—she gave him a roguish look— "even under so experienced a commander as Bunchuk."

She went behind a screen to change her clothes. When she returned she was wearing a soldier's khaki tunic girdled with a leather belt, and her old black skirt, patched in places, but spotlessly clean. She had recently washed her hair, and it fluffed and broke away from the knot. She put on her overcoat and asked, in a voice which had lost all its previous vivacity and was dull and pleading:

"Will you be taking part in the attack today?"

"Why, of course! I'm not going to sit with folded hands."

"I only ask you. . . . Listen, do be careful. You'll do that for my sake, won't you? I'm leaving you an extra pair of woollen socks. Don't catch cold, and try to keep your feet dry. I'll write to you from Lugansk."

The light suddenly faded from her eyes. As she said good-bye she confessed:

"You see, it's very painful for me to leave you. When Abramson proposed that I should go to Lugansk I was delighted, but now I feel that it will be desolate there without you. Another proof that feeling is only in the way at present. Well, in any case, good-bye."

She was cold and constrained in her farewell, but he understood that she was afraid of breaking down in her resolution.

He went to the door to see her off. She walked away hurriedly, swinging her shoulders and not looking round. He wanted to call her back, but he had noticed a moist glitter in her eyes as she said good-bye for the last time, and mastering his desire, he shouted with feigned cheerfulness:

"I hope to see you in Rostov. Keep well, Anna!"

She glanced round across her shoulder and hastened her steps.

After she had gone, Bunchuk suddenly realized all his terrible loneliness. He turned back into the house, but ran out again at once as though it were on fire. Everything there spoke of her. Everything retained her scent: the forgotten handkerchief, the soldier's wallet, the copper mug, everything her hands had touched.

Until nightfall he wandered about the station, experiencing an unusual anxiety and a feeling that something had been cut away from him. He could not get accustomed to his new situation. He abstractedly stared into the faces of Red Guards and Cossacks, recognizing some and being recognized by many others. He was stopped by a Cossack who had been in the army with him during the Russian-German war. The man dragged him to his home and invited him to join in a game of cards with a number of other Red Guards and sailors. Enveloped in tobacco-smoke, they slapped the cards down, rustled their Kerensky ruble notes, and cursed and shouted incessantly. Bunchuk longed for air, and under the pretext that he had to take part in an attack within the hour, he left without saying good-bye to anyone.

Chapter 5

The last hopes of the counter-revolutionary forces were collapsing like rotten wood. The Bolshevik noose was lashing and tightening round the throat of the Don province. The revolutionary forces were drawing near to Rostov, and Kornilov, realizing that it was dangerous to remain in the town, decided on February 22 to retreat. Towards evening of that day a long column of soldiers wound its way out of Rostov, marching heavily over the half melted snow.

The majority were wearing officers' uniforms, and captains and colonels were in command of the platoons. In the ranks were Junkers and officers of all degrees from ensigns to colonels. Behind the numerous wagons of the baggage train came crowds of refugees: elderly, well-dressed men in overcoats and galoshes, and women wearing high-heeled shoes. In one of the companies of soldiers was Captain Listnitsky.

The evening shadows gathered. A frost set in. A salty, humid breeze was blowing from the mouth of the Don. Yellow puddles appeared here and there on the heavily trodden road. The going was difficult, and the damp penetrated inside the boots. As he walked Listnitsky listened to the conversation of the men in front of him. An officer in a fur jacket and an ordinary Cossack fur cap was saying:

"Did you see him, lieutenant? Rodzianko, the president of the State Duma, and an old man, forced to go on foot. . . ."

"Russia is going to her Golgotha. . . ."

Someone remarked ironically:

"A Golgotha, truly—with the one difference that instead of a stony road we have snow and a devilish cold."

"Have you anything to smoke?" a lieutenant asked Listnitsky. The man took the cigarette Eugene offered, thanked him, and blew his nose on his hand soldier-fashion, afterwards wiping his fingers on his coat.

"You're acquiring democratic habits, lieutenant," a lieutenant-colonel smiled sarcastically.

"One has to. willy-nilly. What do you do? Have you managed to salvage a dozen handkerchiefs?"

The lieutenant-colonel made no reply. Tiny green icicles were clinging to his reddish-grey moustache. Occasionally he snorted, frowning with the cold which pierced through his overcoat.

"The flower of Russia!" Listnitsky thought, glancing with keen commiseration over the ranks of the column winding along the road. As he listened unattentively to the conversation, he recalled his departure from Yagodnoe, his father, and Aksinia. He was choked by a sudden feeling of yearning. He put his feet forward limply, stared at the rifle-barrels and bayonets swinging in front of him, at the fur caps and cowls swaying to the rhythm of the march, and thought:

"Every one of these five thousand ostracized are like me, carrying with them a charge of hatred and boundless anger. The swine have thrown us out of Russia and think to crush us here. We shall see! Kornilov will yet lead us into Moscow!"

Until the 24th of March the Volunteer Army was concentrated in the district of Olginsk, a few miles to the south-east of Rostov. Kornilov delayed any further movement, as he was expecting the arrival of General Popov, the newly appointed ataman of the Don Cossack army, who had retreated from Novocherkassk into the steppes to the east of the Don with a detachment of sixteen hundred men, five field-guns, and forty machine-guns. Popov, accompanied by his chief of staff, Sidorin, and a Cossack escort, rode into Olginsk on the 26th. He reined in his horse in the square in front of the house occupied by Kornilov, dismounted, and slowly walked towards the porch, followed by Sidorin.

Entering the hall, the two newcomers greeted the generals assembled for the conference and went to the table. Alexeev asked a few unimportant questions concerning their journey and the evacuation of Novocherkassk. Kutepov entered, accompanied by several line officers whom Kornilov had invited to the conference.

Staring fixedly at Popov, who had seated himself calmly at the table, Kornilov asked:

"General, tell us the size of your detachment."

"Fifteen hundred swords, a battery, and forty machine-guns with their complement."

"You know the circumstances which have compelled the Volunteer Army to evacuate Rostov. We held a conference yesterday and took the decision to march to the Kuban, in the direction of Yekaterinodar, where volunteer detachments are already in action. We shall take this route." He passed the blunt end of his pencil over the map and went on hurriedly: "We shall draw in the Kuban Cossacks as we march, shattering the few unorganized and feeble Red Guard bands which may attempt to impede our movement. We propose that you join the Volunteer Army with your detachment and march with us to Yekaterinodar. It is not to our interests to split up our forces."

"I cannot do that," Popov announced sharply and resolutely.

Alexeev bent a little in his direction. "Why not, if I may ask?" he said.

"Because I cannot abandon the territory of the Don province and retire into the Kuban. Covered on the north by the Don, we shall await events in the steppe. We cannot count on any active movement on the part of the enemy, because the thaw will set in soon and it will be impossible to send artillery or cavalry beyond the Don. From the area we have chosen, well supplied with forage and provisions, we can develop guerrilla activities at any moment and in any direction."

He stopped for breath, but seeing that Kornilov was about to speak, obstinately shook his head.

"Let me finish. In addition there is one very important factor, and we of the command have got to take it into account. That is the attitude of our Cossacks. If we retreat to the Kuban, there is a danger of our detachment breaking up. The Cossacks may refuse to go. It must not be overlooked that the permanent and the strongest contingent of my detachment consists of Cossacks, and they are by no means so morally reliable as—as your own men, for instance. And I cannot risk losing all my detachment. You must pardon me: I have told you our decision and must assure you that we are not in the position to change it. Of course it is not to our interest to split our forces, but there is one way out of the difficulty. I suggest that, taking what I have said into account, it would be more sensible for the Volunteer Army not to retreat into the Kuban, but to join the Don detachment in the steppe beyond the Don. There it will be able to rest and recuperate and in the spring will be reinforced by fresh volunteers from Russia. . . ."

Kornilov looked at Alexeev, evidently uncertain which course to take and seeking support from another authority. Alexeev, accustomed to decide a question quickly and with exhaustive clarity, expressed himself in few words in favour of the march to Yekaterinodar.

"In that direction it will be easier for us to break through the Bolshevik ring and to join forces with the detachment already in action there," he ended.

"But if we don't succeed?" Lukomsky cautiously asked.

Alexeev ran his finger over the map. "Even if we are not successful," he said, "we still have the possibility of retreating to the Caucasus Mountains and there dispersing the army."

The discussion went on for some time longer, but, supported by the majority of the generals, Kornilov held to his decision to march by a devious route into the Kuban, collecting horses for the equipment of cavalry as he went. The conference broke up. Kornilov exchanged a few words with Popov, coldly said good-bye, and went to his room, followed by Alexeev. Colonel Sidorin went out on the porch and cried cheerfully to his aide-de-camp:

"The horses!"

A young, swarthy-faced Cossack captain came up to him. He halted on the lowest step and asked in a whisper:

"Well, what decision, colonel?"

"Not bad!" Sidorin replied in an undertone, with exaggerated cheerfulness. "We have refused to march to the Kuban. We're leaving at once. Are you ready, Izvarin?"

"Yes. They're bringing the horses."

The escort brought up the horses, and Izvarin, Gregor Melekhov's old friend, mounted his and gave the order to ride into the street. Popov and Sidorin, accompanied by some of the generals, came down the front steps. One of the escort held General Popov's horse and helped him to find his stirrup. Waving his homely Cossack knout, Popov put his horse into a trot, and behind him, standing in the stirrups and leaning a little forward, came Sidorin, the other officers, and the Cossacks.

Chapter 6

After Kaledin's death a Military Council was summoned in Novocherkassk, at which General Nazarov was appointed provincial ataman. Only a few delegates were present. Assured of the support of this depleted council, Nazarov proclaimed the mobilization of all Cossacks from seventeen to fifty-five years of age. But the Cossacks obeyed reluctantly, despite threats and the dispatch of armed bands into the villages to enforce the order.

The Council was feeble in action. All felt that the result of the struggle against the Bolsheviks was a foregone conclusion. During the sessions of the Council Nazarov, formerly an energetic and vigorous general, sat with his head in his hands, as though tortuously thinking of something.

Golubov's detachment was sent by the Revolutionary Committee in a wide encircling movement to capture Novocherkassk, and Bunchuk went with it. Golubov led the division at a swift pace, riding at its head and bringing his whip impatiently down across his horse's croup. At daybreak they passed through a little village. It was still deserted, but near the square an old Cossack was breaking the ice in a trough by a well. Golubov rode up to him, while the division halted.

"Good morning, old man," the commander greeted the Cossack.

The man slowly raised his mittened hand to his fur cap and replied in an unfriendly tone:

"Good morning."

"Well, daddy, have your Cossacks gone off to Novocherkassk? Has there been a mobilization in your village?"

Without answering, the old man hurriedly picked up his axe and disappeared through the gateway of his yard.

"Forward!"Golubov cried, and rode off cursing.

That same day the Military Council was preparing to evacuate Novocherkassk. The newly appointed field ataman of the Don army, General Popov, had already withdrawn the armed forces from the town and removed all the military supplies. Meeting with no opposition, Golubov's cavalry entered Novocherkassk unexpectedly. Golubov himself, accompanied by a large detachment of Cossacks, galloped up to the headquarters of the Military Council. A crowd of gaping sightseers was gathered at the gate, and a courier was waiting with General Nazarov's saddled horse.

Bunchuk jumped from his horse and seized his hand machine-gun. With Golubov and the other Cossacks he ran into the house. At the sound of the door being flung open, the delegates assembled in council in the spacious hall turned their heads and went white.

"Stand up!" Golubov commanded tensely, as though on parade. Surrounded by Cossacks, he hurried to the head of the table. At the authoritative shout the members of the Council rose with a rattle of their chairs, only Nazarov remaining seated.

"How dare you interrupt a session of the Military Council?" the general demanded in an angry voice.

"You are arrested! Silence!" Golubov turned livid. He ran to Nazarov, tore the epaulets from the general's uniform, and roared hoarsely: "Stand up, I tell you! Take him away! Who am I talking to? Brass-hat!"

Bunchuk had set up his machine-gun at the door. The members of the Council herded together like sheep. Past Bunchuk the Cossacks dragged Nazarov, Voloshinov, the chairman of the Council, and several others. His sword clattering, his face crimson, Golubov followed them. One of the members of the Council caught at his sleeve:

"Mister colonel, where are we to go?"

Another thrust his head across Golubov's shoulder. "Are we free?" he asked.

"Go to the devil!" the commander shouted, pushing them away; as he reached Bunchuk he turned on them and stamped his foot; "Clear off to hell! I don't want you! Well, what are you waiting for?"

Bunchuk spent the night in his mother's house. Next day the news came that Rostov had been captured. He at once obtained Golubov's permission to go to Rostov and rode off the next morning.

Arrived in Rostov, he worked two days in the staff headquarters and visited the offices of the Revolutionary Committee. But neither Abramson nor Anna was there. On the third day he went again to the Revolutionary Committee. As he was going up the stairs he heard Anna's deep voice coming from a room. The blood rushed to his heart. He slowed his steps and pushed open the door.

The room was thick with tobacco-smoke. He saw Anna standing at the window with her back to the door. Abramson was sitting on the window-ledge with hands clasped beneath his knee, and a tall Red Guard with Lettish features was standing at his side. As the man rolled a cigarette he was talking, evidently telling of some humorous incident, for Anna had her head thrown back in a hearty laugh, and Abramson's face was furrowed like a melon-skin with his smile.

Bunchuk walked across and laid his hand on Anna's shoulder. "Hello, Anna!"

She looked round. The blood flooded her face and flowed down to her collar-bones, and tears started to her eyes.

"Where have you sprung from? See, Abramson! He's looking like a new coin, and you were anxious about him!" she stammered without raising her eyes. Unable to control her agitation, she turned and walked towards the door.

Bunchuk squeezed Abramson's hot hand, exchanged a few words with him, and then, with a foolish, boundlessly happy smile on his face, went to Anna. She had recovered her self-control and welcomed him with a smile, a little angry at her own embarrassment.

"Well, and how are you?" she asked. "When did you arrive? Are you from Novocherkassk? Were you in Golubov's division? Well, and what is the news?"

He replied to her questions without removing his unwinking, heavy gaze from her face. Her own eyes faltered and turned away from his.

"Let's go out into the street for a minute," she proposed.

As they turned to go, Abramson called after them: "You'll be back soon? I've got work for you, Comrade Bunchuk. We're already thinking of making use of you."

"I shall be back in an hour," he replied.

In the street Anna gazed right into Bunchuk's eyes and waved her hand angrily.

"Ilia, Ilia, how badly I lost control of myself! Just like a girl! It was because of the unexpectedness of seeing you, and also because of our half-and-half relation to each other. Really, though, what is my relation to you? That of idyllic 'husband and wife'? You know, at Lugansk Abramson once asked me: 'Are you living with Bunchuk?' I denied it, but he's a very observant man and cannot but see what happens right under his eyes. He didn't say anything, but I could see by his look that he didn't believe me."

"But tell me all about yourself."

"Oh, how we made the work go at Lugansk! We gathered a detachment of two hundred and eleven bayonets. We carried on organizational and political activities . . . but I can't tell you all about it in two words! I am still upset with your unexpected arrival. Where are you—where are you sleeping?" she asked.

"At a comrade's house." He stammered over the lie, for he had spent his nights in the staff headquarters.

"You'll transfer to our house this very day! Do you remember where I live? You took me home once."

"I'll find it. But—isn't it rather crowding you?"

"Don't be silly! You'll be crowding nobody, and in any case don't talk about it."

So it was decided. In the evening he collected his belongings into his capacious soldier's kit-bag and went to the street on the outskirts where Anna lived. On the threshold of a small brick house he was met by an old woman. Her features had some distant resemblance to Anna's; she had the same bluish-black glitter in her eyes and a slightly hooked nose, but her furrowed and earthy skin and her fallen mouth betrayed her age.

"Are you Bunchuk?" she asked.

"Yes."

"Come in, will you? My daughter has told me about you."

She led him into a small room, showed him where to put his things, and with rheumatically contorted fingers pointed around the room:

"This is where you will sleep. That is your bed."

She spoke with a noticeably Jewish accent. Beside her in the house there was a young girl, deep-eyed like Anna.

A little while later Anna herself arrived, bringing life and animation with her.

"Has anyone been here? Has Bunchuk arrived?" she asked.

Her mother replied in Yiddish, and Anna strode firmly to the door of Bunchuk's room.

"May I come in?" she called.

"Yes, yes." He rose from the chair and went to meet her.

She looked him over with a satisfied, smiling glance and asked:

"Have you had anything to eat? Come into the other room."

She led him by his sleeve into the larger room and said:

"Mother, this is my comrade." And she smiled.

During the night shots cracked like acacia seed-pods over Rostov. Occasionally a machine-gun rattled; then the sound died away, and the night, the gracious, sombre March night, wrapped the streets again in silence. Bunchuk sat up till late in his scrupulously tidy little room.

"I lived here with my little sister," she told him. "You see how modestly we lived—just like nuns. No cheap pictures or photographs, nothing to show that I was a student in the high school."

"How did you manage?" he asked her.

Not without pride she replied: "I worked at a factory and gave lessons."

"And now?"

"Mother takes in sewing. The two of them need very little."

He told her details of the capture of Novocherkassk and the battles in which he had taken part since she left him. She gave him impressions of her work in Lugansk and Taganrog. At eleven o'clock, as soon as her mother had put out the light in her room, she said good-night and left him.

Bunchuk was assigned to work in the Revolutionary Tribunal attached to the Don Revolutionary Committee. The tall chairman of the Tribunal, hollow-cheeked and faded of eye with incessant activities and sleepless nights, led him to the window of his room and asked:

"When did you join the party? Aha, good! Well, you will be our commandant. Last night we sent our previous commandant to join Kaledin, because he was taking bribes. He was nothing but a sadist, a bestial swine, and we don't want that type in our ranks. It's dirty work we're doing, but we must retain full consciousness of our responsibility to the party. Understand rightly what I am saying." (He laid extra emphasis on this phrase.) "And we must preserve humanity. Of necessity we are physically exterminating the counter-revolutionaries, but we mustn't make a circus of the job. You understand me? Well, that's good. Now go and take over."

That same night Bunchuk, in charge of a squad of Red Guards, shot sixteen counter-revolutionaries at midnight, taking them some three miles outside the town. Among them were two Cossacks, the rest being inhabitants of Rostov. Almost every night thereafter they carried those sentenced to death out of the town, and hasty graves were dug, some of the Red Guards and the condemned working side by side. Then Bunchuk would draw up his squad of Red Guards and in an iron-hollow voice would give the command:

"At the enemies of the Revolution—" A wave of his revolver. "Fire!"

After a week of this work he withered and darkened, as though drawn by the earth. His eyes became sunken, and the nervously twitching eyelids failed to hide their cold and yearning glitter. Anna saw him only at night, for she was working in the Revolutionary Committee and came home late. But she always waited up until the familiar knock at the window told of his arrival.

One night he returned as usual after midnight. She opened the door and asked:

"Will you have some supper?"

He did not reply, but passed into his own room, stumbling drunkenly. He flung himself just as he was, in greatcoat, boots, and cap, on his bed. Anna went to him and glanced into his face: his eyes were stickily filmed, spittle was dribbling from his bared teeth, and his hair, thin after typhus, lay in a damp strand over his brow.

She sat down at his side. Pity and pain clawed at her heart. She whispered:

"It is hard for you, Ilia?"

He squeezed her hand, ground his teeth, and turned to the wall. So he fell asleep, saying not a word. He muttered indistinctly and miserably in his sleep and tried to jump up. She watched him in terror and shuddered with unaccountable fear. He slept with eyes half-closed, and the yellow of the swollen whites gleamed feverishly below the lids.

"Go away from here!" she told him in the morning. "You'd better go to the front. You're looking like nothing on earth, Ilia. You'll perish at this work."

"Shut up!" he shouted, his eyes blinking with his rage.

"Don't shout! Have I offended you?"

He was quiet at once, as though his shout had released the fury pent up in his breast. He looked wearily at his palms and said:

"The destruction of human filth is a filthy business. To shoot them down is injurious to the health and to the mind, you see. Damn it all . . ." for the first time he cursed indescribably in her presence. "For such filthy business volunteer either fools and beasts or fanatics. We all want to live in a flower-garden, but . . . to the devil with them! Before the flowers and trees can be planted the dirt must be cleared away. The earth must be dunged! The hands must be soiled!" He raised his voice, although Anna had turned silently away. "The filth must be exterminated, and yet they are fastidious about the job!" he shouted, thundering his fists on the table and blinking his bloodshot eyes.

Anna's mother glanced into the room, and he recollected himself and spoke more quietly:

"I will not give up this work! I see, I feel positively, that I am being of service here. I shall rake away the filth, dung the earth so that it will be more fertile. More fruitful! Some day happy people will walk over it. . . . Perhaps my own son, that I haven't got, will walk there too!" He laughed gratingly and joyously. "The music of the future . . . do you remember, Anna? How many of these serpents, these ticks, have I shot! The tick is an insect that eats into the body. I've killed dozens with these hands." He stretched out his long-nailed, black-haired hands, clenched like a vulture's talons, then dropped them to his knees and said in a whisper: "To the devil with it all! Let it burn so that the sparks fly and no smoke comes. . . . Only, I am tired—that's true. A little more, and then I'll go to the front. . . . You're right. . . ."

She quietly said:

"Yes, go to the front or get on to other work. Do, Ilia, or you'll—go out of your mind."

He turned his back to her and drummed on the window.

"No. I'm strong. Don't think that there are any men made of iron. We're all cast of one material. In real life there isn't a man who is without fear in battle, and not a man who can kill people without carrying—without getting morally scratched. I don't feel any regret for the officers. They're class-conscious like you and me. But yesterday I had to shoot three Cossacks among the rest—three toilers. I began to bind one . . ." his voice became hollow and indistinct, as though he were going farther and farther away. "I happened to touch his hand, and it was as hard as sole-leather,

covered with calluses. A black palm, all cuts and lumps. . . . Well,
I must be going." Seized by a harsh spasm, he sharply broke off and
rubbed his throat.

He put on his boots, drank a glass of milk, and went out. In the
passageway Anna overtook him. She stood long holding his heavy,
hairy hand in her own; then she pressed it to her flaming cheek and
ran out into the yard.

Time swept on in lengthening days. The weather turned warmer.
Spring came knocking at the lands of the Don. At the beginning
of April, Red Guard detachments driven back by the Ukrainians
and the Germans began to arrive in Rostov. Murders, pillaging,
unauthorized requisitions occurred in the town. The Revolutionary
Committee was compelled to disarm certain completely demoralized units. The task was not accomplished without conflicts and
exchanges of fire. Around Novocherkassk the Cossacks were stirring. In March, like buds on the poplars, clashes broke out in the
villages between the Cossacks and the Russian settlers, risings
rumbled here and there, counter-revolutionary conspiracies were
discovered. But Rostov went on living a passionate, full-blooded
life. Crowds of soldiers, sailors, and workers promenaded up and
down the main street of an evening. They held meetings, they
husked sunflower-seeds, spat into the little streams running over
the pavements, and flirted with the women. As before, they worked,
ate, drank, slept, died, gave birth, made love, hated, breathed the
salty sea-breeze, and lived in the grip of great and petty passions.
Days sown with menace were approaching Rostov. The air was
laden with the scent of the thawing black earth and the blood of
imminent battles.

One sunny, pleasant day Bunchuk returned home earlier than
usual and was surprised to find Anna already there.

"But you are always so late; why are you early today?" he asked
her.

"I am not feeling very well."

She followed him into his room. He removed his outdoor clothes
and said with a smile of tremulous joy:

"Anna, after today I shall not be working in the Tribunal."

"What are you saying? Where are you going?"

"To the Revolutionary Committee. I had a talk with Krivoshlikov today. He promised to send me somewhere into the district."

They had supper together, and afterwards he lay down to sleep. In his agitation he could not get to sleep for a long time, but lay smoking, tossing on the hard mattress. He was greatly satisfied to leave the Tribunal, for he felt that a little more and he would not last, but would break down under the strain. He was finishing his fourth cigarette when he heard the light scrape of the door. Raising his head, he saw Anna. Barefoot, and only in her shift, she slipped across the threshold and quietly approached his bed. Through a clink in the shutter the misty green light of the moon fell on her bare shoulders. She bent over him and laid a warm hand on his lips.

"Move over. Not a word. . . ."

They lay down together. Her burning legs were trembling at the knees. She raised herself on her elbow and passionately whispered into his ear:

"I've come to you . . . only quieter—quieter . . . Mother's asleep."

She impatiently brushed back a strand of hair, as heavy as a bunch of grapes, from her forehead. Her eyes smoked with a bluish fire, and she whispered roughly, tormentedly:

"If not today, then tomorrow I may be deprived of you. . . . I want to love you with all my strength." She shuddered violently with her own resolution. "Well, quickly!"

Bunchuk kissed her cool, tightly swelling, drooping breasts and stroked her compliant body. But with horror, with a great shame that whipped his consciousness, he realized that he was impotent. His head shook and his cheeks flamed with his torture. After a moment Anna released herself and angrily thrust him off. Pulling down her shift, with loathing and aversion in her voice she asked in a contemptuous whisper:

"You—are you impotent? Or are you—ill? Oh, how abominable! . . . Leave me alone!"

He squeezed her fingers so tightly that they cracked a little, fixed his gaze on her dilated, mournfully darkened, hostile eyes, and stammeringly asked, his head twitching paralytically:

"Why? What are you condemning me for? Yes, I'm burnt up to the very depths of me! . . . Even for this I am impotent at the moment. I am not ill. . . . Understand. . . . Understand! I am only completely emptied. . . ."

He bellowed stupidly, jumped up from the bed, and lit a cigarette. He huddled by the window as though shattered. Anna arose, silently embraced him, and as calmly as a mother kissed him on the brow.

But after a week, when that happened which they both desired, Anna, hiding her burning face beneath his arm, confessed:

"I thought—you had been with some other—I didn't realize that the work had exhausted you so much."

And for long afterwards Bunchuk felt not only the caress and fire of a woman beloved, but the warm, full-flowing care of a mother.

He was not sent into the country. Podtielkov insisted that he should be retained in Rostov. The Don Revolutionary Committee was boiling with activity, preparing for a provincial congress of Soviets and for a struggle against the counter-revolution raising its head in the Don area.

Chapter 7

The frogs were croaking beyond the river-side willows. The sun streamed over the hillside across the rapids. The cool of evening was soaking into the village of Sietrakov. Enormous slanting shadows cast by the huts fell athwart the dusty road. The village cattle were straggling slowly black from the steppe. The Cossack women drove them on with wattles, exchanging gossip as they went. The barefoot and already sunburnt children were playing leapfrog in the side alleys. The old men were sitting in rows on the ledges of the hut walls.

The village had finished the spring sowing. Only here and there were they still sowing sunflowers and millet.

A group of Cossacks were sitting on a fallen oak close to one of the huts on the outskirts of the village. The master of the hut, a freckled artillery-man, was telling of some incident in the Russian-German war. His audience, an old neighbour and his son-in-law, were listening in silence. The artillery-man's wife, a handsome woman as corpulent as a noblewoman, came down the steps. Her rose-coloured bodice, gathered into her skirt, was torn at the elbows and revealed her swarthy, shapely arms. She was carrying a pitcher and went to the cattle-yard with that free and sweeping, elegant stride peculiar to Cossack women. Her hair was escaping from its white kerchief, and the shoes on her bare feet slapped along, lightly pressing down the young green overgrowing the yard.

The sound of milk streaming against the sides of the pitcher came to the ears of the Cossacks. The mistress finished milking the cows and returned to the hut, a little bowed and carrying the full pitcher of milk in her left hand.

"Simion, you'd better go and look for the calf," she called from the steps.

"And where's Mitka?" her husband asked.

"The devil knows; he's run off somewhere."

The Cossack rose unhurriedly and went to the corner of the street. The old man and his son-in-law turned to go home. But the Cossack called to them from the corner:

"Look, Dorofei Gavrilich! Come here!"

The two men went across to the Cossack, who silently pointed out into the steppe. A ruddy cloud of dust raised by ranks of infantry, cavalry, and wagons was advancing along the road.

"Soldiers, surely." The old man screwed up his eyes in astonishment and set his palm to his white eyebrows.

"What are they?" the Cossack wondered.

His wife came out of the yard gate, her jacket flung across her shoulders. She gazed into the steppe and groaned anxiously:

"Who are they? Jesus Christ, how many there are!"

"They're not out for any good, that's certain. . . ."

The old man turned and went to his yard, crying to his son-in-law:

"Come into the yard; there's no point in standing and staring."

Children and women came running to the corner, followed by crowds of Cossacks. The column of soldiers was winding along the road across the steppe about a mile from the village. The wind brought the sound of their voices, the snorting of horses, the rumble of wheels.

"They're not Cossacks; they're not our folk," the artillery-man's wife said to him. He shrugged his shoulders.

"Of course they're not Cossacks. Maybe they're Germans? No, they're Russians. Look, you can see their red flag. . . ."

A tall Cossack came up. He was evidently suffering from malaria, for he was a sandy yellow and was wrapped up in a sheepskin and felt boots. He raised his shaggy fur cap and said:

"You see that flag? They're Bolsheviks."

"It's them right enough."

Several riders broke away from the head of the column and galloped towards the village. The Cossacks exchanged glances and silently began to melt away; the girls and children scattered in all directions. Within a minute or two the street was deserted. The group of riders galloped into the village and rode up to the oak where a few minutes earlier the three Cossacks had been sitting. The artillery-man was standing by his gate. The leader of the riders, in Kuban uniform and with a great crimson silk scarf across his khaki shirt, rode up to him.

"Good health, Cossack! Open the gate!"

The Cossack turned pale and removed his cap.

"And who may you be?" he asked.

"Open the gate!" the soldier shouted.

The horse, glancing askance with evil eyes and champing at the bit, struck its forefeet against the wattle fence. The Cossack opened the wicket gate, and the riders rode into the yard in single file. Their leader jumped nimbly from his saddle and strode towards the hut steps. While the others were still dismounting he had reached the steps, had seated himself, lit a cigarette, and offered the Cossack his case. The man refused.

"Do you smoke?"

"Thank you."

"You're not Old Believers here?"

"No, we're Greek Church. And who may you be?"

"We're Red Guards of the Second Socialist Army."

The other riders hurried towards the steps, leading their horses. They tied them up to the balustrade. One of them, a spindle-shanked man with hair falling like a horse's mane over his brow, went to the sheep-pen. He threw open the gate as though he were the master, bent down, fumbled at the partition of the pen, and pulled out a large sheep by its horns.

"Piotra, come and give me a hand," he cried in a high falsetto voice.

A soldier in an Austrian tunic ran to help him. The Cossack master stroked his beard and looked about him as though he were in someone else's yard. He said nothing and only went up the steps into the hut when the sheep, its throat slit by a sabre, doubled up its thin legs.

The Kuban soldier and two others, one a Chinese, the other a Russian, followed him into the kitchen. "Don't take offence, Cossack," the leader cried as he crossed the threshold. "We'll pay for all we have."

He clapped his hand against the pocket of his trousers and laughed aloud. But the laugh suddenly died away as his eyes fell on the Cossack's wife. She was standing by the stove, her lips compressed, staring at him with terrified eyes. His eyes shifting restlessly around the kitchen, he turned to the Chinese and said:

"You go with the old man." He pointed to the Cossack. "Go with him, he'll give you hay for the horses. Let us have some hay." He turned to the Cossack. "We'll pay handsomely for it. The Red Guard never pillages. Off you go, Cossack, off you go!" A steely note sounded in his voice.

Accompanied by the Chinese and the other soldier, the Cossack went out of the hut. He was going down the steps when he heard his wife calling in a weeping voice. He ran back into the porch. The soldier had seized the woman's arm above the elbow and was dragging her into the twilit front room. She was resisting, pushing at his chest with her hands. He was on the point of putting his arms around her waist and carrying her off bodily, but at that moment the door flew open. The Cossack strode across the kitchen and placed himself in front of his wife. His voice was hard and low:

"You came as a guest into my hut. . . . What are you doing shame to my wife for? Clear out! I'm not afraid of your guns. Take whatever you want, steal everything, but don't lay hands on my wife. You'll do that across my body. And you, Nura—" his nostrils quivering, he turned to his wife—"you go along to Daddy Dorofei.

There's no point in your staying here."

Adjusting the straps across his shirt, the soldier smiled wryly:

"You get upset easily, Cossack. You won't even let a man have his little joke. I'm the joker of the whole regiment, don't you know? I did it on purpose. 'I'll see what the woman's like,' I thought; but she started bawling. Have you let us have some hay? You haven't any? Well, has your neighbour?"

He went out whistling, vigorously waving his whip. Soon afterwards the entire detachment entered the village. There were about eight hundred bayonets and swords in all. The Red Guards, a good third of them Chinese, Letts, and other foreign nationalities, prepared to spend the night outside the village. Evidently their commander did not trust his nondescript and undisciplined soldiers in the village that night.

Shaken in battles against the Ukrainian troops and the German army of occupation, this detachment of the Second Socialist Army had fought its way back to the Don and was trying to make its way through to Voroniozh in the north. Demoralized under the influence of the criminal elements that flourished in the detachment, the Red Guards were roistering along the road. That night, despite the threats and orders of their command, they poured in crowds into the village, began to kill sheep, ravished two Cossack women on the outskirts, opened causeless fire on the square, and wounded one of their own number. During the night they got drunk on the liquor they were carrying with them.

But meantime three mounted Cossacks had been dispatched from the village to give the alarm in the neighbouring villages. In the darkness of the night the Cossacks saddled their horses, armed themselves, and hastily assembled detachments of front-line Cossacks and elder men. Under the command of officers and sergeant-majors living in the villages, they hurried towards Sietrakov, concealing themselves in ravines and behind rises all round the Red Guard camp. During the night groups of men arrived from all the surrounding villages.

The Milky Way was burning out in the sky, the black, velvety fur of night was moulting and fading. At dawn the avalanches of Cossack horsemen flung themselves with a roar from all sides on

the Red Guards. A machine-gun rattled, and died away; broke
into fire again, then was silent.

Within an hour the deed was accomplished; the detachment
was completely shattered; more than two hundred were shot and
hewn down, some five hundred were taken prisoner. Two batteries
of four field-guns apiece, twenty-six machine-guns, thousands of
rifles and a large store of military equipment fell into the hands of
the Cossacks.

Next day the red flags of couriers galloping along the roads and
tracks burst into blossom throughout the district. The villages
seethed with excitement. The Soviets were thrown out head over
heels, and atamen were hurriedly appointed. By the beginning of
May the upper districts of the Don province had completely
broken away from the Don Revolutionary Committee. The popu-
lous Vieshenska was elected the centre of the new district, which
was called the "Upper Don." And the Upper Don region, drawing
twelve Cossack and one Ukrainian district into its orbit, began to
live its own life, cut off from the main centre of the Don province.
A Cossack from the Yelansk district, a general named Zakhar
Akimovich Alferov, was hurriedly elected regional ataman. It was
said of him that he had made his way upward from indigent Cossack officer to the rank of general only thanks to his wife, an energetic and intelligent woman. It was said that she had dragged her
ungifted consort by the ears and had given him no peace until,
after failing three times, at the fourth examination he passed into
the military college.

But if Alferov was talked about at all in these days, it was very
little. The Cossacks' minds were occupied with other things.

Chapter 8

The flood water was beginning to abate from the fields. By the
garden fences the brown earth was laid bare and edged with
borders of dry reeds, branches, and dead leaves left behind by
the flood. The pussy-willows of the flooded Donside woods were

beginning to turn green, and the catkins hung in tassels. The poplars were ready to burst into bud. In the village farmyards the
sprigs of the alders hung low down to the pools at their feet, and
their yellow buds, fluffy like the down of ducklings, dabbled in
the wind-ruffled water. At dawn and sunset flights of wild geese
and ducks swam up to the fences in search of food, the copper-
tongued grebes called in the backwaters. At noonday the wind-
driven surface of the Don was flecked and fondled by white-
feathered teal.

There were many birds in transit that year. The Cossack fishermen rowing out to their nets at dawn, when the wine-red sunrise
was staining the water with blood, frequently saw swans resting
in the wooded stretches of water. But the news brought back to
the village by Christonia and old Matvei Kashulin was the greatest
miracle of all. They had driven into the government forest to select
a couple of young oaks for their farm needs, and as they were
making their way through a thicket they disturbed a wild goat
with a young kid. The lean, yellow-brown goat jumped out of a
dell overgrown with thistles and thorns and stood gazing for some
seconds at them, her thin legs dancing nervously, the kid pressing
against her. Hearing Christonia's gasp of astonishment, she sped
off so fast through the oak saplings that the Cossacks hardly caught
sight of her blue-grey hoofs and the camel-hue of her short tail.

"What was that?" Matvei Kashulin asked, dropping his axe in
his astonishment.

With inexplicable pride Christonia roared through the magically
silent forest:

"It must have been a goat. A wild goat! I've seen them in the
Carpathians."

"Then the war must have driven it into our steppe."

There was nothing left for Christonia but to agree. "That must
be it," he said. "And did you see the kid with her? A pleasant sight,
damn it! Just like a child with its mother."

All the way back to the village they were discussing this unprec-
edented visitor to the district. Old Matvei began to have his doubts.

"But if it was a goat, where was its horns?" he asked.

"And what do you want horns for?"

"I don't want the horns! I simply asked if it was a goat why
wasn't it like a goat? Have you ever seen a goat without horns?

That's the point. Maybe it's some sort of wild sheep."

"Old man, you've lived past your time!" Christonia took offence. "Go and call on the Melekhovs. Their Gregor's got a whip made out of goat's legs. Then will you admit it or not?"

It happened that old Matvei had occasion to visit the Melekhovs the same day. Certainly the stock of Gregor's whip was covered with leather made from a wild goat's leg; even the tiny hoof at the end was there in its entirety and was ingeniously shod with a copper shoe.

On the Wednesday of the last week in Lent, Misha Koshevoi went early one morning to examine the nets he had set in the river by the forest. He left his hut before dawn. The earth, crumbled by the morning frost, was crusted with fine ice, and scrunched beneath his feet. Misha walked along with a great oar over his shoulder, his cap thrust on the back of his head, his trousers gathered into white woollen stockings, breathing in the intoxicating morning air and the scent of the raw dampness. He pushed off his boat and rowed swiftly, standing and pulling strongly at the oar.

He examined his nets, took a fish from the last, dropped the net back into the water, and then, as he rowed easily back, decided to have a smoke. The sky was reddening with the sunrise. In the east the mistily blue heaven looked as though splashed from below with blood. The blood flowed over the horizon and turned a rusty gold. As he lit his cigarette Misha watched the slow flight of a grebe. The smoke curled and clung to the branches of the trees and drifted off in clouds. Examining his catch—three young sterlet, some eight pounds of carp, and a heap of whitefish—he thought:

"Must sell some of it. Squinting Lukieshka will take it in exchange for some dried pears. Mother can make jam from them."

He rowed up to the wharf. By the garden fences where he kept the boat a man was sitting. When he got a little nearer, he saw that it was Valet squatting on his haunches and smoking an enormous cigarette made of newspaper. His sly little eyes gleamed sleepily, and his cheeks were overgrown with a scrub of hair.

"What do you want?" Misha shouted to him. His voice went bouncing over the water like a ball.

"Row closer."

"Do you want some fish?"

"What should I want fish for?"

Valet shook with a fit of coughing, spat violently, and reluctantly stood up. His ill-fitting greatcoat hung on him like a coat on a scarecrow. His sharp, unwashed ears were covered by the hanging flaps of his cap. He had only recently returned to the village, accompanied by the doubtful fame of a Red Guard man. The Cossacks asked him where he had been since he was demobilized, but Valet gave evasive answers, avoiding the dangerous questions. To Ivan Alexievich and Misha Koshevoi he admitted that he had spent four months in a Red Guard detachment in the Ukraine, had been captured by the Ukrainian national troops, had escaped and joined the Red Army close to Rostov, and had given himself furlough to get a rest and re-equip himself.

Valet took off his cap, stroked his bristling hair, looked around, then went to the boat and muttered:

"There's bad business afoot—bad! Stop your fishing for fish, or we'll go on fishing and fishing and forget everything else."

"What's your news? Tell me!" Misha asked, squeezing Valet's hand with his own fishy paw and smiling warmly. They had long been close friends.

"Yesterday Red Guards were smashed up at Migulinsk. The struggle has begun, brother! The fur's beginning to fly!"

"What Red Guards? How did they get to Migulinsk?"

"They were marching through the district, and the Cossacks set upon them and have driven the prisoners to Kargin. They've already begun a field court-martial there. Today they're going to mobilize everybody in Tatarsk."

Koshevoi tied up his boat, poured his fish into a basket, and walked away with great strides. Valet danced along in front like a young horse, his coat-tails flying, his arms swinging.

"Ivan Alexievich told me. He's just relieved me; the mill's been working all night. And he had it straight from the horse's mouth. An officer from Vieshenska has called at Mokhov's."

Across Misha's face, matured and faded with the years of war, passed a look of anxiety. He glanced sidelong at Valet. "Now what's going to happen?" he asked.

"We must clear out of the village."

"Where to?"

"To Kamenska."

"But the Cossacks are White there."

"Then more to the left."

"How are you going to get through?"

"It can be done if you want to. And if not, stay behind and the devil take you!" Valet suddenly snarled. " 'Where to,' and 'where to'! How am I to know? Look around a bit and you'll find a hole through for yourself."

"Don't get angry. What does Ivan say?"

"While you're getting Ivan to move—"

"Not so loud! There's a woman looking."

They glanced fearfully at a young woman driving cows out of a yard. At the first crossroad Misha turned back.

"Where are you going?" Valet asked in surprise.

Without looking back Misha muttered:

"I'm going to get my nets out."

"What for?"

"I don't want to lose them."

"So we'll be going?" Valet said in delight.

Misha waved his oar and said as he walked away:

"Go along to Ivan Alexievich, and I'll take my nets home and come along after."

Ivan Alexievich had already succeeded in passing the news on to the Cossacks who were friendly. He sent his little son to the Melekhovs, and Gregor came back with him. Christonia turned up without being warned, as though he had had a presentiment of impending trouble. Soon Koshevoi also arrived, and they began to discuss the situation. They all talked at once, hurriedly, every moment expecting to hear the tocsin bell.

"We must clear out at once. They'll be bridling us this very day," Valet incited them with burning words.

"Give us your reasons? Why must we?" Christonia queried.

"How, 'why must we?' They'll be ordering a mobilization, and do you think you'll escape it?"

"I won't go, and that's all there is to it."

"They'll carry you!"

"Let them try! I'm not a bullock at the plough."

Ivan Alexievich sent his cross-eyed wife out of the hut, then angrily snorted:

"They'll take you! Valet's right there. Only where are we to go? That's the question."

"That's what I've already told him," Misha sighed.

"Well, do as you like. Do you think I want the lot of you?" Valet snarled. "I'll clear out by myself. I don't want any white-livers with me. 'Yes, but why'! And 'Yes, but where'! They'll give it to you hot and shove you into prison for Bolshevism. How can you sit there joking? In such times as these! Everything will go to the devil!"

Concentratedly and with quiet anger turning over in his hands a rusty nail torn out of the wall, Gregor Melekhov poured cold water over Valet:

"Not so much talk! Your position is different, you can go where you like! But we must think it over carefully. I've got a wife and two little children. I can't look at it in the same way as you." He narrowed his black, angry eyes, bared his stout teeth, and shouted: "You can wag your tongue, you whipper-snapper! As you were, so you still remain! You've got nothing but your jacket. . . ."

"What are you bellowing about?" Valet cried. "Showing off your officer's ways! Don't shout! I don't care a spit for you!" His little nose went white with rage and his tiny, evil eyes glittered balefully.

Gregor had vented on him the anger he felt at having his peace disturbed by the news of the Red Guards' irruption into the district. He jumped up as though struck, strode across to where Valet was fidgeting on his stool, and restraining with difficulty his desire to strike him, he said:

"Shut up, you reptile! Lousy snot! You stump of a man! Who are you ordering about? Go where your arse takes you! Clear out so that you don't stink here! Don't speak, you needn't say goodbye!"

"Drop it, Gregor! That's not the way!" Koshevoi shouted, pushing Gregor's fist away from Valet's nose. "You ought to drop those Cossack habits! Aren't you ashamed? Shame on you, Melekhov! Shame on you!"

Coughing guiltily, Valet rose and went to the door. But at the threshold he could no longer contain himself and, turning round, stabbed the smiling Gregor with his tongue:

"And he was in the Red Guards! You policeman! We shot men like you. . . ."

At that, Gregor also could not restrain himself. He jumped up as though made of rubber, thrust Valet into the porch, treading on the heels of his boots, and in an unpleasant voice promised him:

"Clear out, or I'll tear your legs from your bottom!"

Ivan Alexievich disapprovingly shook his head and gave Gregor an unfriendly look. Misha sat silently biting his lips, evidently struggling to keep back the angry words that were on the tip of his tongue.

"Well, why did he take on himself to tell other people what they'd got to do? What did he disagree with us for?" Gregor embarrassedly tried to justify his behaviour. Christonia gave him a sympathetic look, and beneath his gaze, Gregor smiled a simple, childlike smile. "I all but struck him! And hit him once and he'd bleed!"

"Well, what do you think? We must come to some decision."

Ivan Alexievich fidgeted under the steely gaze of Misha Koshevoi, who had asked the question, and answered with an effort:

"Well, what, Mikhail? Gregor's right in a way. How can we just pick up our things and fly? We've got our families to think of. Now wait a bit," he said hurriedly as he caught Misha's impatient gesture. "Maybe nothing will happen—who is to know? They've broken up the detachment at Sietrakov, and others won't come. We can wait a bit. I've got a wife and child, our clothes are worn out, and we've got no flour. So how can I go off? Who's going to look after them?"

Misha irritatedly raised his eyebrows and fixed his eyes on the earthen floor.

"So you're not thinking of clearing out?" he said slowly.

"I think it's better to wait. It's never too late to clear out. What do you think, Gregor, and you, Christonia?"

Finding unexpected support from Ivan and Christonia, Gregor spoke more animatedly:

"Why of course; that's just what I said. That's what I fell out with Valet over. Are we to break with everything? One, two, and off we go? We've got to think it over—think it over, I say."

As he finished speaking, there was a sudden clang from the bell in the church tower, and the sound flooded the square, the streets, the alleys. Over the brown surface of the flood waters, over the damp, chalky slopes of the hills the clangour rolled, disintegrating into fragments and dying away in the forest. Then once more it broke out incessantly and uneasily:

"Dong, dong, dong, dong. . . ."

"There it goes!" Christonia blinked. "I'm off to my boat. Over to the other side and into the forest. Then let them find me!"

"Well, and what now?" Koshevoi rose heavily like an old man.

"We're not going at once," Gregor answered for the others.

Misha once more raised his brows and brushed a heavy lock of golden hair off his forehead.

"Good-bye . . ." he said. "It's clear our roads lie in different directions."

Ivan Alexievich smiled apologetically.

"You're young, Misha, and fiery. You think they won't run together again? They will! Be sure of that!"

Koshevoi took leave of the others and went out. He struck across the yard to the neighbouring threshing-floor. In the ditch Valet was huddled. He must have sensed that Misha would go that way. He rose to meet him, and asked:

"Well?"

"They've refused."

"I knew they would all along. They're weak. . . . And Grishka—that friend of yours is a cur! He's only in love with himself. He insulted me, the swine! Just because he's stronger. I hadn't a weapon with me or I'd have killed him," he said in a choking voice.

Striding along at his side, Misha glanced at his bristling scrub of hair and thought: "And he would have killed him too, the skunk!"

They walked swiftly, every beat of the bell whipping them along. "Come along to my hut," Misha proposed. "We'll get some victuals and be off. We'll go on foot; I shall leave my horse behind. You've got nothing to take?"

"I've got nothing," Valet said wryly. "I've not saved enough money to buy a mansion or an estate. I haven't even received my wages for the last fortnight. But let old pot-belly Mokhov get fatter on them! He'll dance with joy at not having to pay them."

The bell stopped ringing. The drowsy silence was undisturbed. The chickens were pecking in the ashes along the roadside, calves were looking for herbage under the fences. Misha looked back: Cossacks were hurrying to the meeting in the square, some of them buttoning up their uniform tunics as they went. A rider sped across the square. A crowd was gathered by the school, the women in white kerchiefs and skirts, the men a mass of black.

A woman carrying pails halted in their path, superstitiously refusing to cross in front of them. She said angrily:

"Come on, come on! I don't want to cross your path."

Misha greeted her, and with a gleaming smile she said:

"The Cossacks are all going to the meeting. Where are you off to? You're going the wrong way, Misha."

"I've got something to do at home," he replied.

They turned down a side-alley. They could see the roof of Misha's hut, the starling-box with a dry cherry-branch tied to it rocking in the wind. The sails of the windmill on the rise were slowly turning, the torn sailcloth flapping and striking the sheet iron of the steep roof.

The sun was not strong, but warm. A fresh breeze was blowing from the Don. In one yard some women were plastering a large hut with clay and whitewashing it in readiness for Easter. One of them was kneading the clay with dung. She walked round in a circle, her skirt raised high, with difficulty pulling her full, white legs out of the sticky mess. She held her skirt in the ends of her fingers; her cotton garters were pulled above her knees and cut tightly into the flesh. The two other women, their faces wrapped to the eyes in kerchiefs, had clambered on ladders right under the reed-thatched roof and were whitewashing. With sleeves tucked up above the elbows they worked the brushes backward and forward, and splashes of whitewash spattered over them. They sang as they worked. The elder, Maria, a widow of one of Bogatiriev's sons, was openly setting her cap at Misha. She was a freckled but good-looking woman. She sang away in a low voice, almost masculine in strength and famed throughout the village:

"Ah, there's no one suffers more. . . ."

The other women took up the words, and the three voices tunefully carried on the bitter, naïvely complaining song:

"Than my darling at the war.
An artillery-man is he,
And he always thinks of me."

Misha and Valet passed close to the fence, listening to the song.

"Then a letter came which said
That my darling had been killed.
Oh, he's killed, my darling's killed.
Now under a bush he's dead."

Maria, her warm grey eyes glittering beneath her kerchief, looked down and stared at Misha. Her bespattered face lighting up with a smile, she sang in a deep, amorous voice:

"And his curls, his golden curls,
In the wind were tossed about.
And his eyes, his deep black eyes—
A black raven pecked them out."

Misha smiled the tender smile he always kept for women. Maria glanced around, then bent down from the ladder and said:

"Where have you been, dear?"

"Fishing."

"Don't go far, and we'll go into the barn and have a cuddle."

"You shameless hussy!"

Maria clicked her tongue and with a laugh waved the wet brush at Misha. The drops of whitewash scattered over his jacket and cap.

"You might lend us Valet at least. He could help us clean up the hut," the other woman cried after them, smiling and revealing her milky-white teeth. Maria muttered something to her and they burst into laughter.

"Lewd bitches!" Valet frowned, hastening his steps. But Misha corrected him with a languishing and gentle smile.

"Not lewd, only merry. I'm going off, but I'm leaving my darling behind," he added as he passed through the wicket gate of his yard.

After Koshevoi's departure the others sat on for a little while without speaking. The tocsin bell rocked over the village and rattled the little window-panes of the hut. Ivan Alexievich stared out through the window. A crumbly morning shadow cast by the shed fell over the ground. The dew lay greyly on the young grass. Even through the glass the sky showed azure. Ivan glanced at Christonia's hanging head.

"Maybe that will be the end of it? The Migulinsk people have broken up the Reds, and they won't come farther. . . ."

"No!" All Gregor's body twitched. "They're started, and they'll keep on. Well, shall we go to the square?"

Ivan Alexievich reached for his cap and, resolving his doubts, asked:

"Well, maybe we've got rusty after all. Mikhail's hot-headed, but he's an active lad. He's a reproach to us."

No one answered. They went out silently and turned towards the square.

Ivan Alexievich walked along pensively staring at the ground. He was oppressed with the thought that he had taken the wrong path and had not followed the dictates of his conscience. Valet and Misha were right, they all ought to have gone without hesitating. His attempts to justify his conduct were fruitless, and a deliberate, sneering voice inside him shattered them as a horse's hoof crushes the thin ice in the meadow. The one thing he firmly resolved upon was to desert to the Bolsheviks at the first opportunity. His resolve was definitely taken while he was walking to the square, but he told neither Gregor nor Christonia, mournfully realizing that they were passing through different struggles from his, and already in the depths of his heart afraid for them. They had all three jointly turned down Valet's proposal, each giving his family as the excuse. But each of them knew that the excuse was inconclusive and did not justify their decision. Now each was feeling awkward in the others' company, as though they had done something dirty, shameful. They were silent, but as they passed Mokhov's house Ivan Alexievich could endure the sickening silence no longer, and he said:

"There's no point in hiding it. We came back from the front Bolsheviks, and now we're crawling into the bushes. Let others fight for us, but we'll stay with our women!"

"I've done my share of fighting; let others have a go," Gregor snarled, and turned away.

"And what are they?" Christonia added. "A lot of robbers!

Ought we to join such? What sort of Red Guards do they call that? Raping women, robbing the Cossacks! We've got to see what we're doing. The blind man always falls over the chair."

"And have you seen all this, Christonia?" Ivan sternly asked.

"The people are talking about it. . . ."

"Ah—the people. . . ."

The square was a rich blossom of Cossack striped trousers, caps, and here and there a shaggy black fur cap. All the men of the village were gathered. No women were there, only the old men, the Cossacks who had been in the war, and still younger men. The very oldest stood in front, leaning on their sticks: honorary judges, the members of the church council, the school managers, and the churchwarden. Gregor's eyes searched for his father's black and silver beard and found him standing at the side of Miron Gregorievich. In front of them, in his grey, full-dress tunic and medals, old Grishaka was leaning on his knobbly stick. Together with Pantaleimon and Miron were all the elders of the village. Behind them stood the younger men, many of them comrades-in-arms with Gregor. On the other side of the ring he noticed his brother Piotra, his Russian shirt adorned with the orange and black ribbons of the Cross of St. George. On his left was Mitka Korshunov, lighting a cigarette from that in the hand of Prokhor Zykov. Behind were crowded the youngest Cossacks. In the centre of the ring, at a rickety table with all four legs pressed into the soft, still damp earth, sat the chairman of the village Revolutionary Committee. At his side stood a lieutenant unknown to Gregor, dressed in a khaki cap with a cockade, a leather jacket with epaulets, and khaki breeches. The chairman of the Revolutionary Committee was talking agitatedly to him, and the officer stooped a little to listen with his ear close to the chairman's beard. The meeting hummed like a beehive. The Cossacks were talking and joking among themselves, but on all faces were looks of anxiety. Someone could wait no longer and shouted:

"Begin! What are you waiting for? Almost everybody's here."

The officer straightened up, removed his cap, and said, as simply as though in his own family circle:

"Elders of the village, and you, front-line Cossack brothers, you have all heard what has happened at the village of Sietrakov? A day or two ago a detachment of Red Guards arrived at the village. The Germans have occupied the Ukraine, and as they moved towards the Don province they threw the Red Guards back from the railway. The Reds entered Sietrakov and began to pillage the Cossacks' possessions, to ravish their women, to carry out illegal arrests, and so on. When the neighbouring villages heard what had happened, they fell on them with arms in hand. Half the detachment was destroyed, the remainder taken prisoner. The Migulinsk and Kazansk districts have flung the Bolshevik government out of their areas. From small to great the Cossacks have risen in defence of the peaceable Don. In Vieshenska the Revolutionary Committee has been flung out neck and crop, and a district ataman has been elected; and the same in the majority of the villages."

At this point in the speech the old men gave vent to a restrained mutter, and the chairman of the Revolutionary Committee fidgeted on his seat like a wolf caught in a trap.

"Everywhere detachments are being formed. You also ought to form a detachment of front-line Cossacks, in order to defend the district from the arrival of new savage robber hordes. We must set up our own administration. We don't want the Red government; they bring only debauchery, and not liberty! And we shall not allow the peasants to violate our wives and sisters, to make a mockery of our Greek Church faith, to desecrate our holy temples, to plunder our possessions and property. Don't you agree, elders?"

The meeting thundered with the sudden "Agreed." The officer began to read out a proclamation. Forgetting his papers, the chairman slipped away from the table. The crowd of elders listened without uttering a word. The front-line men behind whispered lifelessly among themselves.

As soon as the officer began to read, Gregor slipped out of the crowd and turned to go home. Miron Gregorievich noticed his departure and nudged Pantaleimon with his elbow.

"Your younger son—he's slipping off!" he whispered.

Pantaleimon limped out of the ring and shouted imperatively: "Gregor!"

His son half turned round and halted without looking back.

"Come back, my son!"

"What are you going away for? Come back!" came a roar of

voices from the crowd, and a wall of faces turned in Gregor's
direction.

"And he's been an officer!"

"He was among the Bolsheviks himself."

"He's shed Cossack blood!"

"The Red devil!"

The shouts reached Gregor's ears. He listened with grating teeth,
evidently struggling with himself. It seemed as though in another
minute he would go off without a look back. But Pantaleimon and
Piotra gave sighs of relief as he wavered and then with downcast
eyes returned to the crowd.

The old men overwhelmingly carried the day. With savage haste
Miron Gregorievich was elected ataman. His freckled face greying,
he went into the middle of the ring and confusedly received the
symbol of his authority, the ataman's copper-headed staff, from
his predecessor. He had never been ataman before, and when they
called for him he hesitated and at first refused the position, saying
that he had not deserved such an honour and that he was illiterate.
But the old men insisted, and so unusual were the circumstances
of the election and the state of semi-war in the district that at last
he agreed. The election was not carried out as in former days,
when the district ataman had arrived in the village, the Cossack
heads of families had been summoned to a meeting, and a ballot
had been taken. Now it was simply: "Those for Korshunov, step to
the right," and the entire crowd had surged that way. Only the
cobbler, who had a grudge against Korshunov, had remained
standing alone in his place like a blasted oak in a meadow.

Miron had hardly had time to blink when the staff was thrust
into his hand, and a roar went up:

"Now how about treating us?"

"Up into the air with the new ataman!"

But the officer intervened and cleverly directed the meeting towards a businesslike settlement of the problems remaining. He
raised the question of electing a commander for the village detachment, and must have heard about Gregor in Vieshenska, for he
began by praising him, and through him the village.

"It would be well," he said, "to have a commander who has been
an officer. In the event of a fight it will be more successful, and
there will be fewer losses. And you've got plenty of heroes in your

village. I cannot impose my will upon you, but for my part I recommend you elect Cornet Melekhov."

"Which one? We've got two of them."

The officer ran his eyes over the crowd and shouted with a smile:

"Gregor Melekhov! What do you think, Cossacks?"

"A good man!"

"Gregor Melekhov! He's a tough nut!"

"Come into the middle of the ring. The elders want to look at you."

Thrust forward from behind, Gregor, his face crimson, emerged into the middle of the ring and looked around him venomously.

"Lead our sons!" Matvei Kashulin stamped his stick and crossed himself with a flourish of his arm. "Lead and guide them so that they will be with you like geese with a gander. As the gander defends its family and saves them from both man and beast, so you watch over them! Earn four more crosses, may God grant it!"

"Pantaleimon Prokoffievich, you've got a son!"

"And a fine brain in his head!"

"You lame devil, how about a drink?"

"Elders! Silence! Shall we carry out a mobilization without calling for volunteers? Volunteers may go or they may not. . . ."

"No, let's have volunteers!"

"You go yourself; what's holding you back?"

Meantime four elders from the upper part of the village were having a whispered consultation with the newly appointed ataman. They turned to the officer. One of them, a little, toothless old man, advanced from the group to speak to him, while the others hung back.

"Your Excellency," the old man said, "it's clear you don't know very much about our village, or you wouldn't have chosen Gregor Melekhov for a commander. We elders don't agree with the selection. We've got a complaint to make against him."

"What complaint? What's the matter?"

"Well, how can we trust him when he's been himself in the Red Guards, was a commander of them, and it's only two months since he came back from them with a wound."

The officer flushed a rosy red, and his ears seemed to swell with the influx of blood.

"Is that really true? I hadn't heard that. No one said anything about it to me."

"It's true, he's been with the Bolsheviks," another elder harshly confirmed. "We can't trust him!"

"Change him! What are our young Cossacks saying? They're saying that in the first battle he'll betray them."

"Elders!" the officer shouted to the meeting, raising himself on his toes. "Elders! We've just elected Gregor Melekhov to be commander, but isn't there a danger in that? I've just been told that during the winter he was himself with the Red Guards. Can you entrust your sons and grandsons to him? And you, front-line brothers, can you follow his lead with quiet hearts?"

The Cossacks were silent for a moment, then a tumult of conflicting shouts arose, and it was impossible to understand a word. When it died away, old Bogatiriev stepped into the middle, took off his cap, and looked around.

"In my foolish mind I think this way. We can't give Gregor Pantalievich this position. He's been on the wrong road, and we've all heard of that. Let him first earn our trust, atone for his guilt, and then we'll see. He's a good fighter, we know. . . . But we can't see the sun for mist; we can't see his past services; his work for the Bolsheviks prevents us."

"Let him go in the ranks," young Andrei Kashulin shouted fierily. "Make Piotra Melekhov commander."

"Let Grishka go in the herd."

"Yes, and I don't want the position! What the devil did you put me forward for?" Gregor shouted, flushing with excitement. Waving his hand he repeated: "I won't take the position if you want me to!" He thrust his hands into the depths of his trouser pockets and with bowed back stalked away. Shouts followed him:

"Stinking filth! That's his Turkish blood coming out!"

"He won't keep quiet! He wouldn't keep his mouth shut even to the officers in the trenches."

"Come back!"

"After him! Hoo! Boo!"

It was long before the meeting quieted down again. In the heat of argument someone jostled someone else, someone's nose began to bleed, one of the youngsters was suddenly enriched with a swelling beneath his eye. When silence was at last restored, they elected Piotra Melekhov commander, and he almost glowed with pride. But now, like a mettlesome horse confronted with too high a fence, the officer came up against an obstacle. When the next step of calling for volunteers was taken, no volunteers were forthcoming. The front-line men, who had been restrained in their attitude throughout the meeting, hesitated and were unwilling to enrol, although they urged others on:

"Why don't you go, Anikei?"

But Anikushka muttered:

"I'm too young. I haven't any whiskers yet."

"None of your jokes! Trying to make a laughing-stock of us?" old Kashulin howled right into his ear.

"You enrol your own son!" Anikushka retorted.

"Prokhor Zykov!" came a shout from the table. "Shall we put your name down?"

"I don't know—" he replied.

Mitka Korshunov went with a serious face up to the table and breathlessly ordered:

"Write my name down."

"Well, who else? How about you, Fiodot Bodovskov?"

"I'm ruptured," Fiodot muttered, modestly dropping his eyes. The front-line men roared with laughter and chaffed him unmercifully:

"Take your wife with you. Then if the rupture's troublesome she'll cure it!"

But the elders began to get annoyed, and swore:

"Enough, enough! What are you so merry for?"

"A good time for making jokes!"

"Shame on you, boys!" one of them shouted. "What of God? God won't overlook it! There are people dying, and you— Think of God!"

"Ivan Tomilin!" the officer looked around.

"I'm an artillery-man," Tomilin replied.

"Shall we put you down? We need artillery-men."

"Oh, all right; write me down, then."

Anikushka and several others began to rally Tomilin. "We'll carve you a gun out of a willow trunk. You'll fire pumpkins and potatoes instead of grapeshot."

With jesting and laughter some sixty men enrolled. The last was Christonia. He went up to the table and said deliberately:

"Write my name down. Only I warn you that I shan't fight."

"Then why put yourself down?" the officer asked irritatedly.

"I'll look on, officer. I want to have a look!"

"Put him down!" The officer shrugged his shoulders.

The meeting was not ended until nearly noonday. It was decided to dispatch the detachment the very next day to the support of the Migulinsk villagers.

Next morning, out of the sixty volunteers only some forty turned up on the square. Piotra, elegantly dressed in a greatcoat and high leg-boots, reviewed the Cossacks. Many of them had shoulder-straps with the numbers of their old regiments on them. Their saddles were loaded with saddle-bags containing victuals, linen, and cartridges brought back from the front. Not all of them had rifles, but the majority had cold steel.

A crowd of women, children, and old men gathered in the square to see them off. Piotra, on his prancing horse, drew up his half-company in ranks, reviewed the varicoloured horses, the riders in greatcoats, tunics, and sailcloth raincoats, and gave the order for departure. He walked the detachment up the hill. The Cossacks stared gloomily back at the village; someone in the last file fired a shot. At the top Piotra drew on his gloves, stroked his wheaten whiskers, and turning his horse so that it advanced sideways, holding his cap on with his left hand, he shouted:

"Company, trot!"

Standing in their stirrups, waving their whips, the Cossacks put their horses into a trot. The wind beat in their faces, shook the horses' tails and manes, and scattered a fine rain. They began to talk and joke. Christonia's raven horse stumbled, and he cursed and warmed it up with lashes of the whip. The horse arched its neck, broke into a gallop, and burst out of the ranks. Their gay mood did not desert the Cossacks until they reached Kargin. They rode in the full conviction that there wouldn't be any war, that the Migulinsk affair was only a fortuitous irruption of the Bolsheviks into Cossack territory.

They reached Kargin in the late afternoon. There were no front-line men left in the district; they had all gone to Migulinsk. Piotra dismounted his detachment on the square, and went to the district ataman to arrange for quarters. He found him smoking on the steps of his house. The man's massive figure, the swelling, steely-strong chest and arm muscles showing beneath his shirt, testified to his unusual strength.

"Are you the district ataman?" Piotra asked.

Puffing out a cloud of smoke from beneath his drooping whiskers, the man replied:

"Yes, I'm the district ataman. Whom do I have the honour of speaking to?"

Piotra gave his name.

Squeezing his hand, the ataman slightly bowed his head:

"My name is Fiodor Dmitrievich Likhovidov."

Likhovidov was elected district ataman in the spring of 1918, immediately after the Sietrakov affair. Sternly the new ataman carried out his duties. His first step was to dispatch every front-line man in the district to Sietrakov the very next day after the massacre of the Red Guards. The foreigners, who composed a third of the inhabitants of the district, at first did not wish to go, while the soldiers, ardent Bolsheviks many of them, protested. But Likhovidov insisted on having his way, and the elders signed the decree he proposed for all peasants who took no part in the defence of the Don to be ejected from the district. The following day dozens of carts filled with soldiers singing and playing accordions were dragging along in the direction of Migulinsk. Of the foreigners only a few young soldiers fled to join the Red Guards.

As Piotra approached, Likhovidov guessed by his walk that he was an officer risen from the ranks. So he did not invite him into his house, and he spoke to him with a hint of benevolent familiarity:

"No, my lad, there's nothing for you to do in the Migulinsk district. They've managed without you; we received a telegram yesterday evening. Ride back and await further orders. Stir up the Cossacks well! A large village like Tatarsk, and only forty fighters? Wring their withers, the scum! It's their skins that are at stake. Good-bye, and good journey."

He went into his house, carrying his heavy body with unexpected ease, his boots creaking. Piotra returned to his Cossacks on the square. They overwhelmed him with questions. Not attempt ing to hide his satisfaction, he smiled and answered:

"Home! They've done without us!"

The Cossacks grinned and went in a crowd towards their horses. Christonia even sighed as though a great load had fallen from his back and clapped Tomilin on the shoulder:

"So we're going home, cannoneer!"

After considering the situation they decided not to spend the night in Kargin, but to return at once. In scattered and disorderly groups they rode out of the village. They had ridden unwillingly to Kargin, rarely breaking into a trot, but on the way back they rode their horses hard, galloping their fastest. The earth, cracked with lack of rain, thundered beneath their horses' hoofs. Beyond the Don and the distant range of hills lightning was playing.

They arrived in Tatarsk at midnight. As they galloped down the hill, Anikushka fired from his Austrian rifle, and a salvo of shots rang out to announce their return. The dogs in the village gave tongue in reply, and scenting its home, one of the horses snorted and neighed. Through the village they scattered in various directions.

As he said good-bye to Piotra, Martin Shamil croaked with relief:

"Well, the fighting's over! That's good!"

Piotra smiled in the darkness and rode off to his hut. Pantaleimon came out and took his horse, unsaddled it and led it into the stable. He and Piotra entered the hut together.

"Is it all over?" he asked.

"Ah-ha!"

"Well, praise be! May we hear no more of it!"

Daria arose, hot from sleep. She went to get her husband some supper. Gregor came out half-dressed from the kitchen, scratching his hairy chest, and winked humorously at Piotra.

"So you've beaten them?" he remarked.

"I can beat any soup that's left!"

"You can beat the soup all right, especially if I give you a hand!"

Until Easter there was not a sound or smell of war. But on Easter Saturday a messenger galloped into the village from Vie shenska, left his foaming horse at Korshunov's gate, and ran into the porch.

"What news?" Miron Gregorievich greeted him.

"I want the ataman. Are you he?"

"Yes."

"Arm the Cossacks at once. Podtielkov is leading the Red Guards into Nagolinsk district. Here's the order." He turned the sweaty lining of his cap inside out to get the packet.

At the sound of talking, old Grishaka came out, harnessing his spectacles to his nose. They read the order from the regional ataman. Leaning against the balustrade, the messenger rubbed the dust from his face with his sleeve.

On Easter Sunday, after breaking their fast, the mobilized Cossacks rode out of the village. General Alferov's order was strict: he threatened that all who refused to go would be deprived of the title of Cossack. So the detachment was composed not of forty men, as at first, but a hundred and more, including a number of older men who were possessed with the desire to have a smack at the Bolsheviks. The young men went willy-nilly; the older in the heat of the hunt.

Gregor Melekhov rode in the last rank. A rain was sprinkling from the clouded heaven. The clouds rolled above the brilliantly green steppe. An eagle was floating high above the hills. With deliberate flaps of its wings it flew before the wind to the east, a dark brown speck diminishing in the distance.

The steppe was a shining green with the rain. Here and there were snapdragons and clumps of last year's wormwood. On the slope single grey bushes stood on guard.

As they dropped down into Kargin they were met by a youngster driving bullocks out to graze. He went slapping along with bare feet, waving his whip. Seeing the riders, he halted and attentively examined their mud-splashed horses.

"Where are you from?" Tomilin asked.

"Kargin," the lad boldly replied, smiling under the coat thrown over his head.

"Have your Cossacks gone?"

"They've gone. They've gone to smash the Red Guards. Have you got any tobacco for a cigarette, daddy?"

"Tobacco for you?" Gregor reined in his horse.

The lad went up to him. His tucked-up trouser legs were wet
and the stripes were a shining red. He stared boldly into Gregor's
face and said:

"You'll be seeing dead bodies in a moment, as soon as you go
downhill. Yesterday our Cossacks drove the Red prisoners out and
killed them. I was minding cattle over there by that bush and saw
them cut down. Oh, it was terrible! When the swords began to
swing they roared and ran. . . . Afterwards I went and looked;
they were mostly Chinese. One of them was cut down through the
shoulder, and I could see the heart beating in his chest, and the
blue kidneys. . . . It was terrible!" he repeated, astonished that
the Cossacks were not frightened by his story. So at least he judged
as he stared at the cold and unmoved faces of Gregor, Christonia
and Tomilin.

He lit his cigarette, stroked the wet neck of Gregor's horse, said:
"Thank you," and ran off to his bullocks.

By the roadside, in a shallow hole washed with rain-water, only
lightly sprinkled with earth, lay the bodies of the Red Guards.
One leaden-blue face was visible; the blood had baked on its lips.
And a bare foot with blue woollen trousers below it stuck out of
the ground.

"They might bury them better! The swine!" Christonia muttered. He abruptly brought his whip down across his horse, overtook Gregor, and galloped downhill.

"Well, so blood has flowed on the Don earth too!" Tomilin smiled,
but his cheeks were twitching. "Gregor, can you smell how the
blood stinks? Can you smell it?"

Chapter 9

In the morning the weather took a strange turn. It had been noticeably hot by nine o'clock, but towards midday a wind sprang up
from the south, the clouds sped across the heavens, and on the
outskirts of Rostov there was an intoxicating scent from the juicy
young poplar leaves and the sunburnt bricks and earth.

On the previous day Bunchuk and Anna, with a selected detachment, had disarmed an insurgent anarchist band at the station. On the previous day frowns had furrowed Bunchuk's ageing brow. But now the wind from the south had driven away his cares, and he was domesticatedly tackling a kerosene stove on the doorstep and coldly staring at Anna's face, which was warm with a taunting smile.

Before breakfast he had muttered something about being a good hand at cutlets with sauce.

"Are you serious?" Anna doubted.

"Quite."

"Where did you learn?"

"Well, you know, a Polish woman taught me during the war."

"Go and try your hand. I still have my doubts."

Hence the kerosene stove. Hence Bunchuk's furrowed brow and Anna's smile, with so much sly roguishness in it that he could not stand it. He vigorously shook the potatoes in the frying-pan, and frowned.

"Of course, if you're going to stand over me and jeer, nothing will come of it. And do you call this a kerosene stove? It's a blast-furnace, if you want to know."

Anna spoke slowly and almost dreamily:

"Why weren't you a cook? What dishes you would have prepared! With what authority you would have ruled in the kitchen! Really, why did you neglect the culinary department?"

"Listen, you're going too far!"

Anna played with a lock of her hair, twisting it in her fingers. Glancing up under her eyelids at him, she burst into a peal of laughter. "I'll tell the boys this very day that you're only a humbug as a machine-gunner, and that you used to be a cook in the household of some great personage."

He was sincerely mortified when, instead of the sauce, he turned out something smelly and evil-tasting. But Anna devotedly ate it and even found words of praise for it.

"Not at all bad! Very nice sauce. A little bitter, that's all."

"Is it really all right?" he cheered up. "But if we had some horse-radish to add to it now, then . . ." he smacked his lips, not observing Anna's bravely compressed mouth.

Towards the end of breakfast she seemed to darken in features, yawned limply, and sat thinking, not answering him. Afterwards she stood in the sun at the garden fence, abstractedly chewing a straw between her teeth.

Bunchuk pressed her head against his shoulder, breathing in the pleasant scent of her hair, and asked:

"Why are you so quiet? What's the matter?"

She stared at him with drooping eyelashes, then stood unbuttoning and buttoning the collar of her blouse.

"Are you going into town?" she asked. Without waiting for a reply she said through closed lips: "I shall be dropping out of the ranks soon, Ilia."

"Why?"

She shrugged her shoulders and watched the dance of the sunspots scattered under a poplar. Resting her breast against the low fence, she said with unexpected irritation:

"I waited. . . . I didn't believe it at first. Now I know. In seven, in seven and a half months I shall be a mother."

The wind from the sea played with the leaves of the poplar and blew Anna's hair over her face. She made no attempt to brush it back. Bunchuk was silent. He stroked her hand, but as though she felt some sense of injury against him, she did not reply to the caress, but with faltering step turned back to the house.

He followed her into his room and shut the door, then asked, unable to struggle with his impatience:

"And what now?"

"Oh, nothing," she replied indifferently.

The silence was torturous. He sought for words, but felt only a stupid jumble of thoughts.

"Let it come. By that time we shall have finished with the counter-revolution. Why, is it so very bad to have children?" Suddenly he instinctively sensed the line to take and, smiling a little embarrassedly, hastened to add: "Of course you must bear the child. Anna, give birth to a boy: a strong, healthy, fat little boy! I shall be a locksmith, and you know life will be fine! In three years or so you will begin to grow fat, and I shall get such a big belly. We'll buy a little house of our own. And of course we shall have a geranium in the window and a canary in a cage. On Sundays we shall have visitors and shall visit other respected citizens. You will make cakes, you will weep if the dough doesn't come up to expectations. We shall save up. . . ."

At first Anna smiled unwillingly and sadly, but towards the end she snorted:

"Pfooh, what an idealist!"

"Don't you like it?"

"It sounds all right!"

They went into the town together. Rostov was swarming with crowds of soldiers, workers, and poorly dressed people. The wind was fluttering the torn proclamations and orders on the fences. The unswept streets smelt of horse-dung and hot stones. The changes in the aspect of the town struck Anna in the eyes.

"See, Ilia, how simple the town looks! You won't see a derby hat anywhere, or a troika. Everything is the colour of stone."

"A town is like a chameleon. If the Whites were to come, how it would change its colour!" He smiled.

They walked silently along, and as silently separated. Towards evening, when Podtielkov interrupted a session of the Don Executive Committee in order to collect a detachment and lead it against an approaching band of Novocherkassk Cossacks, they met again and marched in the same column.

"Turn back!" Bunchuk pleaded with her, touching her hand.

But she obstinately pressed her lips together.

They marched on beyond the last houses of the suburb and opened fire on the slowly advancing Cossacks. Podtielkov strode up and down the chain of Red Guards, encouraging them:

"Don't stint the ammunition, brothers! There's enough and to spare!"

Bunchuk licked the bitter sweat from his lips, hurriedly dug a shallow hole with his trenching tool, and helped to set up the machine-gun. The gunner loaded a cartridge-belt into the gun.

Bunchuk's gunner was Maksim Gryaznov, the Cossack from Tatarsk village. He had lost his horse in a struggle against Kutepov's volunteer detachment and since then had taken to heavy drinking and card-playing. When his horse was killed under him he had unfastened the saddle and carried it three miles or so, then, seeing that at this rate he would not escape alive from the volunteers, he had torn off the valuable metal pommel, had taken the snaffles also, and had voluntarily abandoned the fight. He had turned up in

Rostov, quickly gambled away the silver-hilted sword he had borrowed from a captain cut down in battle, lost also the horse's equipment he had carried away with him, and even his trousers and kid boots. He was almost naked when he joined Bunchuk's command. He might have pulled himself together then, but in this very first battle a bullet struck him in the face, his blue eye fell on to his breast, and from the back of his head, shattered like matchwood, the blood spirted. It was evident that the Tatarsk Cossack Gryaznov, former horse-stealer and recent drunkard, had departed this life.

Bunchuk glanced at his body writhing in the throes of death and carefully wiped the blood off the barrel of the machine-gun. Almost immediately afterwards it became necessary to retreat. Bunchuk dragged back the machine-gun, leaving Maksim to grow cold as he lay on the hot earth, exposing to the sun his swarthy body with the shirt pulled over his head.

A platoon of Red Guards made a stand at the first crossroads of the suburb. A soldier in a half-rotten fur cap helped Bunchuk set up the machine-gun, and the others built a rough barricade across the street. Anna lay down at Bunchuk's side.

Suddenly there was a patter of feet along the next street to the right, and nine or ten Red Guards poured round the corner. One managed to shout:

"They're coming!"

In a moment the crossing became deserted and still. Then there was a storm of dust, and a mounted Cossack with a white band across his cap, a carbine pressed to his side, appeared round the corner. He pulled up his horse with such force that the animal sat down on its hind legs. Bunchuk fired a shot from his revolver. Bending low over his horse's neck, the Cossack galloped back. The soldiers behind the barricade hesitated irresolutely; two of them ran along under the wall and lay down by a gate. It was evident that in another minute the men would waver and retreat. The tense silence and their apprehensive glances did not induce steadiness. . . .

Of all that followed Bunchuk remembered one moment indelibly and palpably. Anna, her kerchief thrust on the back of her head, dishevelled and agitated beyond recognition, jumped up with rifle at the trail, looked round, pointed to the house behind which the

Cossack had disappeared, and in an unrecognizable, broken voice
shouted: "Follow me!" With uncertain, stumbling feet she ran towards the corner.

Bunchuk raised himself off the ground. An unintelligible cry
broke from his mouth. He seized a rifle from the nearest soldier and
ran after Anna, panting, feeling an uncontrollable trembling in his
legs, his face darkening with a fearful and impotent attempt to
shout, to call to her and turn her back. Behind him he heard the
gasping breath of several men following him. In all his being he
felt that something terrible, irreparable would follow this beautiful
yet surely useless gesture.

By the time he reached the corner he was at Anna's side. He ran
full tilt towards the Cossacks galloping up and firing haphazardly
as they came. The whistle of bullets. A thin, miserable shriek from
Anna. Then he saw her crumpling to the road with outstretched
hand and vacant eyes. He did not see the Cossacks turn back, he
did not see the Red soldiers chasing them, afire with belated en-
thusiasm for Anna's impulsive action. She, she alone was in his eyes
as she struggled at his feet. He turned her over to lift her and carry
her away. But he saw a stream of blood coming from her left side
and the rags of her blue blouse fluttering around the wound; he
realized that she had been struck by a dumdum bullet; he realized
that she was dying: he saw death lurking in her fading eyes.

With what passion he kissed those eyes and the almost masculine
hands, tried to arouse her, roughly pulled her about in the endeavour to bring her back to life! . . . Someone thrust him aside,
and they carried her into a yard and laid her in the cool under a
shed.

A soldier pressed wads of cotton into the wound and hurled away
the blood-soaked scraps. Mastering himself, Bunchuk unbuttoned
the collar of her jacket, tore off a piece of his own shirt, and pressed
it in a pad against the wound. But the blood came soaking through;
he saw her face turning blue and her blackened lips quivering with
agony. Her mouth gulped at the air, and her lungs heaved; the air
came out again by her mouth and through the wound. He cut away
her torn shirt and unashamedly laid bare her body clothed with
the sweat of death. They managed to plug the wound a little, and
a few minutes later she returned to consciousness. Her sunken eyes
stared at Bunchuk out of their dark sockets for a moment, then the

trembling eyelashes closed over them.

"Water! It's hot!" she groaned, tossing herself about. She burst into tears. "I want to live! Ilia! Beloved! . . . Aah!"

Bunchuk put his swollen lips to her flaming cheek. He poured water over her chest. It brimmed the hollows beneath her collar-bones, but dried away in a moment. She was aflame with a mortal fire. She struggled and tore herself out of his hands.

"It's hot. . . . Fire! . . ."

Her strength forsook her; she grew a little cooler and said articulately:

"Ilia, but why? Well, you see how simple it is. . . . You're a strange fellow. . . . It's terribly simple. . . . Ilia, dearest, you'll . . . there's Mother." She half-opened her eyes and, striving to master her pain and horror, began to talk unintelligibly, as though oppressed by something. "At first the feeling . . . a blow and a burning . . . now everything's on fire. . . . I feel . . . I am dying." She frowned as she noticed his bitter gesture of denial. "Don't! I am bleeding internally. My lungs are filling with blood. . . . It's hard . . . ah, how hard it is to breathe!"

She talked much and frequently in spasmodic outbursts, as though trying to tell him all that was burdening her. With boundless horror he noticed that her face was lighting up, becoming more translucent, turning yellow at the temples. He turned his eyes to her hands lying lifelessly alongside her body and saw the nails flooding with a rosy blue like ripening black plums.

"Water! On my chest. . . . It's so hot!"

He ran to the house for water. As he returned he could not hear Anna's snorting breath under the shed. The setting sun was shining on her mouth contorted with a last spasm, on the still warm, waxen hand pressed to the wound. Slowly putting his arms around her shoulders, he raised her, stared for a moment at the pinched nose and the tiny dark lines between the eyes, and caught the fading gleam of the pupils beneath the black brows. Her helplessly droop-ing head dropped lower, and in her slender, girlish neck the pulse beat out its last beats.

He pressed his cold lips to the black, half-closed eyelids and called:

"Dearest! Anna!"

Then he straightened up, turned sharply on his heel, and walked away unnaturally erect, not moving the arms pressed against his sides. As though blind he knocked against the gatepost, howled chokingly, and, pursued by a spectral cry, dropped on all fours. Inarticulate sounds broke from his foaming lips. He crawled along under the wall like a half-killed animal, tensely and swiftly, his face amost touching the ground. The three Red Guards stared after him apprehensively, silently exchanging glances, crushed by so repellent and naked a manifestation of human misery.

During the following days Bunchuk lived as though in the delirium of typhus. He went about, did things, ate, slept, but always as if in a stupefying, narcotic doze. With frenetic, dilated eyes he stared uncomprehendingly out at the world around him, failed to recognize his friends, and looked as though heavily intoxicated or only just recovering from a wasting illness. From the moment of Anna's death feeling was temporarily atrophied in him; he wanted nothing, and thought of nothing. "Eat, Bunchuk!" his comrades would suggest; and he ate, his jaws working slowly and harshly. When it was time to sleep they said to him: "Time to sleep!" and he lay down.

He spent four days in this withdrawal from the world of reality. On the fifth day Krivoshlikov met him in the street and caught hold of his arm.

"Aha, there you are! I've been looking for you," he said. Not knowing what had happened to Bunchuk, he gave him a friendly slap on the back and smiled anxiously. "What's the matter with you? You haven't been drinking, have you? Have you heard that we're sending an expedition into the northern Don district, to mobilize the Cossacks there? Podtielkov will lead it. Our only hope is in the Cossacks of the north. Otherwise we'll be caught here. Will you go? We need agitators. You will go, won't you?"

"Yes," Bunchuk replied shortly.

"Well, that's fine. We're leaving tomorrow."

In the same state of complete mental prostration Bunchuk prepared for departure and rode off with the expedition the next day.

At this time the situation in the southern Don was extremely menacing for the Don Soviet government. The German army of

occupation was marching eastward from the Ukraine, the districts
of the lower Don were seething with counter-revolutionary revolts.
Popov was lurking in the steppes beyond the Don and threatening
to attack Novocherkassk at any moment. The Provincial Congress
of Soviets held at the beginning of May was more than once interrupted in order to repel the revolting Cossacks threatening Rostov.
Only in the north were the fires of the Revolution still burning, and
towards those fires Podtielkov and the others were involuntarily
drawn as they lost hope of support in the lower Don. On Lagutin's
initiative, Podtielkov, recently elected chairman of the Don Council
of People's Commissars, decided to go northward to mobilize three
or four regiments of front-line men and to throw them against the
Germans and the counter-revolution in the lower districts. An
Extraordinary Mobilization Commission of five, with Podtielkov at
its head, was appointed; ten million rubles in gold and Czarist
money were withdrawn from the exchequer for the needs of the
mobilization; a detachment consisting mainly of Cossacks from
the Kamenska district was hastily scraped together to act as guard,
and on May 14 the expedition set out northward.

The railroads were crowded with Red Guards retreating from
the Ukraine. The insurgent Cossacks were breaking down the
bridges and organizing train-wrecking activities. Every morning
squadrons of German aeroplanes flew along the railway from Novocherkassk to Kamenska, swooped low like bands of vultures, and
opened machine-gun fire on the Red Guard detachments. Everywhere were the signs of boundless destruction: burnt-out and shattered wagons, broken wires festooned around the telegraph poles,
ruined houses, and snow-fences swept away as though by a hurri-
cane.

For five days the expedition travelled slowly along the railway
line in the direction of Millerovo. On the sixth day Podtielkov called
a meeting of the Mobilization Commission in his car.

"We can't go on like this. I think we ought to leave the train and
march the rest of the way," he proposed.

"What are you suggesting?" Lagutin exclaimed. "While we're
struggling along by forced marches the Whites will sweep right
across us."

"It's too far," Mrikhin doubted.

Krivoshlikov sat silent, wrapped in his greatcoat and yellow with malaria and quinine. He took no part in the discussion, but sat huddled like a sack of sugar.

"Krivoshlikov, you've got a tongue; what do you think?" Podtielkov dryly asked him.

"What's the question?"

"Aren't you listening? We must march on foot, otherwise we'll be overtaken. What do you think? You're more educated than the rest of us."

"We can march," Krivoshlikov deliberately pronounced.

"Good!" Podtielkov said.

He unfolded a map, and Mrikhin held it up by two corners. "We'll take this road," he ran his cigarette-stained fingers over the map. "It might be a hundred and fifty miles. Is that right?"

"That's about it," Lagutin agreed.

Krivoshlikov provokingly shrugged his shoulders. "I make no objection," he said.

"I'll tell the Cossacks to detrain at once. There's no point in losing time." Mrikhin looked around expectantly and, meeting with no opposition, jumped down from the car.

Bunchuk was lying in his car with his head covered by his greatcoat. He was living over and over again the incidents of the past, feeling the same pain. Before his filmy eyes the snow-covered steppe lay like a great silver ruble, fringed with the brown spines of forests on the horizon. He thought he could feel the cold wind and that Anna was standing at his side. He could see her black eyes, the strong yet tender lines of her mouth, the tiny freckles above her nose, the thoughtful furrow of her brow. He could not catch the words that came from her lips: they were inarticulate and interrupted by strange voices and laughter. But by the gleam of her eyes and the flutter of the eyelashes he guessed what she was saying.

But then he saw a different Anna, her face a bluish yellow, the traces of tears on her cheeks, her nose pinched, and her lips torturously writhing. He bent to kiss the dark hollows of her eyes. He groaned and clutched his throat to suppress his sobs. Anna did not leave him for a moment. Her features did not fade or darken with the passing of time. Her face, figure, walk, gestures, the sweep

of her brows, all united to compose her living and whole. He recalled her words, her sentimentally romantic speeches, all he had
lived through with her. And through the vitality of his re-creation
of her his torment was intensified tenfold.

He made no attempt to analyse his present state of mind, but un-
reasoningly, bestially gave himself over to his grief. Thus fettered,
he was perishing—perishing like an oak eaten from the root by
worms.

When the order came to detrain they aroused him. He arose, indifferently pulled himself together, and went out. He helped to
unload the baggage. With the same indifference he clambered on to
a cart and rode off.

A freezing rain was falling. The low-growing grass along the
roadside was wet. The open steppe, the wind freely wandering over
the slopes and hollows. Behind them the smoke of locomotives, the
red blocks of the station buildings. The forty carts hired from the
nearest village dragged along the road. The horses moved slowly.
Soaked with rain, the clayey black earth hindered their movement.
The mud clung to the wheels and dropped off in black woolly clods.
Before and behind them went crowds of miners fleeing with their
wives and families and their miserable belongings eastward from
the Cossack vengeance.

For several days the expedition marched into the heart of the
Don province. The inhabitants of the Ukrainian villages welcomed
them with invariable hospitality, willingly selling them provisions
and provender and giving them shelter.

But as they drew nearer to the Cossack lands Podtielkov and the
other leaders began to be apprehensive. They noticed a change in
the attitude of the people, who began to manifest open ill-will and
alarm, selling their food reluctantly and avoiding questions. Reduced to desperation by their chilly reception, one of the Cossacks
of the expedition struck his sword against the ground in the square
of one village and roared:

"Are you men or devils? What are you standing silent for, damn
you? We're pouring out our blood for your rights, and you won't
come near us! There is equality now, comrades, there aren't any
more Cossacks and Hokhols, and nobody will lay hands on you.

Bring us eggs and chickens at once, and we'll pay for everything in Czarist rubles."

Six Ukrainians stood listening to him, their heads drooping gloomily like horses harnessed to ploughs. Not one of them responded to his burning speech. "You needn't howl!" was all they said as they dispersed in various directions.

In the same village a Ukrainian woman questioned one of the Cossacks:

"Is it true that you will steal everything and cut up everybody?"

Without quivering an eyelash the Cossack replied:

"Yes, it's true. Maybe not everybody, but we'll cut up all the old men."

"Oi, my God! And what do you want to cut them up for?"

"We eat them with gruel. Mutton isn't a good flavour, it isn't sweet enough yet, so we put the daddies into our pots and make a fine stew of them. . . ."

"But aren't you joking, maybe?"

"He's lying, woman!" Mrikhin intervened, and turned on the jester: "You learn how to joke and who to joke with! What are you spreading those stories for? They'll go and tell everybody that we cut up the old men!"

Consumed with anxiety, Podtielkov shortened the length of the halts and the nightly rest and hurried the expedition onward. The day before their arrival in the upper Don district he had a long talk with Lagutin.

"There's no point in our going too far, Ivan," he said. "We'll begin the mobilization as soon as possible. We'll proclaim an enrolment, offer good wages, and gather men as we go along. By the time we get to Mikhailovskoe we shall have a division at our command. You think we shall get them, don't you?"

"We'll get them, provided everything is still quiet there."

"So you think the Whites may have begun already?"

"Who knows?" Lagutin stroked his thin beard and added despondently: "We're late. . . . I'm afraid we shall fail. The officers are already doing their work there. We must hurry."

"We are hurrying! And don't you be afraid! You mustn't be afraid!" Podtielkov replied, his eyes gleaming harshly. "We'll break through! Within two weeks we shall be sweeping the Germans and the Whites out of the Don." Puffing hard at his cigarette, he gave expression to his own secret thoughts: "If we're too late, we're lost, and the Soviet rule in the Don with us. We mustn't be too late! If the officers have organized a rising before we get there, then that's the end!"

Towards evening of the following day they set foot on Cossack territory. As they approached the first village, Podtielkov, who was riding with Lagutin and Krivoshlikov on one of the foremost carts, saw a herd of cattle in the steppe. "We'll go and question the herds-man," he proposed to Lagutin.

They jumped down from the cart and strode towards the herd. Podtielkov greeted the herdsman:

"Good health, old man!"

"Praise be!" the man replied.

"Well, and what's the news in your parts?"

"There's nothing to tell. But who may you be?"

"We're soldiers going home."

"That Podtielkov isn't with you, is he?"

"Yes."

The herdsman was obviously alarmed by the answer, and he turned pale.

"What's the matter, old man?" Podtielkov inquired.

"Why, they say you're going to kill off all the Orthodox."

"Nonsense! Who is telling such stories?"

"The ataman said so at a meeting two days ago."

"So you've got atamen again?" Lagutin asked, glancing at Pod-tielkov.

"We elected an ataman some days ago. The soviet has been closed down."

Podtielkov strode back to the cart and shouted to the driver: "Whip up your horses!" He sat huddled in the cart, urging the Cos-sack driver continually to greater speed.

Rain began to fall. The sky was overcast. Only to the east an ultramarine, sunlit scrap of sky peered through the clouds. As they were descending a slope into a little settlement, they saw people running and several carts racing along out of the farther side.

"They're running away. They're afraid of us . . ." Lagutin said distractedly, eyeing the others.

The carts of the expedition rattled down into the settlement. The wind was eddying along the broad, deserted street. In one of the yards an old Ukrainian woman was throwing pillows into a cart, while her husband, barefoot and hatless, was holding the horses' bridles.

Here they learned that the man they had sent on ahead to arrange for quarters had been taken prisoner by a Cossack patrol and carried off. Evidently the Cossacks were not far away. The leaders of the expedition held a brief consultation to consider whether to turn back. At first Podtielkov insisted on continuing their advance, but after a time even he began to waver. His arguments were roughly interrupted by one of the Cossack agitators:

"You've taken leave of your senses! Where do you want to lead us to? To the counter-revolutionaries? We're going back! We've got no desire to die! What's that? See there?" He pointed to the slope above the village.

They all turned and gazed up the hill. On the crest the figures of three riders were clearly silhouetted against the sky.

"That's one of their patrols!" Lagutin exclaimed.

"And there; look!"

More groups of horsemen appeared, vanished beyond the hill, and reappeared.

Podtielkov gave the order to turn back. They rode to the first Ukrainian village, only to find its inhabitants, evidently forewarned by the Cossacks, preparing to hide and flee.

Dusk began to fall. The fine, chilly rain wet them through to the skin. The men walked alongside the carts, holding their rifles at the ready. The road wound down into a valley, ran through it, and climbed the rise beyond. On the hill-tops the Cossack patrols were appearing and disappearing continually, accompanying the expedition and increasing the already nervous tension of the retreating Reds.

Close to one of the streams crossing the valley Podtielkov jumped from his cart and curtly called to the men: "Be ready!" The spring flood water showed blue in the stream. It ran into a pond formed by a dam. The dam was overgrown with bushes, and beneath it the pond was densely covered with sedges. Podtielkov was expecting an ambush at this spot, but the advance patrol could not discover anybody.

"You needn't expect them here," Krivoshlikov whispered to him. "They won't attack now. They'll wait for night."

The clouds gathered heavily in the west. Night fell. Far away towards the Don lightning was flickering, and the orange sheet-lightning quivered like the wings of a half-dead bird. The sunset gleamed pallidly beneath the heavy pall of cloud. The steppe was brimming with silence and dampness; mournful glimmers of the ebbing daylight lurked in the folds of the valley. There was an autumnal quality in that May evening. Even the grasses exuded an inexpressible odour of decay. Podtielkov sniffed in the mingled aroma of the saturated grasses as he walked along. Occasionally he halted and stooped to clean the mud from his boots, straightening up again heavily, and wearily bearing onward his massive body.

They arrived at the next village after nightfall. The Cossacks of the expedition abandoned their carts and wandered from hut to hut in search of quarters. Podtielkov gave orders for pickets to be posted, but they had difficulty in getting men for the duty. Three flatly refused to go.

"Hold a comrades' court-martial on them at once! Shoot them for refusing to obey orders!" Krivoshlikov fumed. But Podtielkov made a bitter gesture:

"They've been demoralized by the journey. They won't defend themselves. We're done for, Misha!"

Somehow Lagutin managed to collect several Cossacks, and posted sentries outside the village. Podtielkov made a round of the huts and spoke to the Cossacks upon whom he could most rely.

"Don't sleep, lads! Otherwise they'll get us!" he told them.

All through the night he sat at a table, his head on his hands, breathing heavily and hoarsely like a wounded animal. Just before dawn he was overcome with sleep and dropped his head to the table. But almost immediately he was aroused to prepare for the further retreat. Day was breaking. He went out into the yard. The mistress of the hut met him in the porch.

"There are horsemen riding on the hill," she informed him unconcernedly.

He ran into the yard and gazed: on the hill, beyond the pall of mist hanging over the village and the willows of the leas, large forces of Cossacks were visible. They were riding at a fast trot, encircling the village and closing in an iron ring.

The Cossacks from the other huts began to stream into the yard where Podtielkov was standing. One of them came up to him and called him aside.

"Comrade Podtielkov . . . delegates arrived from them just now." He waved his hand towards the hill. "They told us to tell you that we are to lay down our arms and surrender at once. Otherwise they'll attack."

"You—son of a swine! What are you daring to tell me?" Podtielkov seized the man by his greatcoat collar, threw him aside, and ran to the cart. He clutched his rifle by the barrel, and turned and shouted to the Cossacks in a hoarse, rough voice:

"Surrender? What talk can we have with the counter-revolution? We shall fight them! Follow me! To arms!"

A number of Cossacks rushed out of the yard behind him and ran in a bunch to the end of the village. As they reached the last huts Podtielkov was overtaken by Mrikhin.

"For shame, Podtielkov!" he cried. "Are we to shed the blood of our brothers? Come back!"

Seeing that only a small section of the expedition's force had followed him, his sober reason foreseeing the inevitability of defeat in the event of a struggle, Podtielkov silently and limply waved his cap. "It's no good, lads! Back to the village!"

They turned back. The entire expedition assembled in three adjacent yards. A few minutes later a group of forty Cossack horsemen entered the village. The main forces of the enemy remained in their positions on the surrounding hills. Podtielkov went to the end of the village to discuss the terms of the surrender. As he walked along the road he was overtaken by Bunchuk, who ran after him and stopped him.

"Are we surrendering?" Bunchuk asked.

"Force will break a straw. What else are we to do?"

"Do you want to die?" Bunchuk shuddered from head to foot. "Tell them we won't surrender!" he cried in a dull, toneless voice. "You're no longer our leader. Whom have you discussed the question with? By whose permission are you going to betray us?"

He turned on his heel and strode back, waving his revolver. On his return to the yards he tried to persuade the Cossacks to attempt to break through and fight their way to the railway. But the majority were openly in favour of surrender. Some turned away, and others angrily declared:

"You go and fight; we're not going to shoot our own brothers!"

"We'll trust ourselves to them without our arms."

"Today's Easter Sunday, and you want us to shed blood?"

Bunchuk turned and went to his cart, threw his greatcoat underneath it, and lay down, gripping his revolver-butt tightly in his hand. At first he thought of trying to escape. But he could not reconcile himself to secret flight and desertion, and he waited for Podtielkov's return.

Podtielkov came back some three hours later, bringing a great crowd of Cossacks with him into the village. He strode along firmly with head high. At his side was the commander of the White Cossack forces, Spiridonov, who happened to be a former artillery comrade of his. Behind him rode a Cossack pressing the staff of a white flag to his chest.

The streets and the yards where the carts of the expedition were gathered were dammed up with the Cossack newcomers. A roar of voices at once arose. Many of them were former comrades-in-arms of the Podtielkov Cossacks, and as they recognized one another, joyous exclamations and laughter broke out.

"Hello, is that you, Prokhor? What wind has brought you here?"

"We came very near to fighting you," Prokhor replied. "And do you remember how we chased the Austrians under Lvov?"

"Why, there's Cousin Danilo! Christ has risen, cousin!"

"Truly He has risen!" Danilo replied to the Easter greeting. There was the loud smack of kissing. Then the two Cossacks stood stroking their whiskers and staring at each other, smiling and clapping each other on the back.

"We haven't broken our fast yet . . ." one of the Red Cossacks remarked.

"But you're Bolsheviks; what have you got to break your fast for?"

"Hm! Bolsheviks we may be, but we believe in God all the same."

"Ho! You're lying!"

"It's God's truth!"

"And do you wear a cross?"

"Of course. Here it is." The Red Guard unbuttoned the collar of his tunic and pulled out a copper cross from his shirt.

The old men who had come out with pitchforks and axes to hunt the "rebel Podtielkov" looked at one another in amazement. "Why, they told us you had given up the Christian faith!" one of them declared. "We heard you were pillaging the churches and killing the priests."

"That's all lies!" the broad-faced Red Guard assured them confidently. "They've been telling you lies. Why, before I came away from Rostov I went to church and took the sacrament."

A buzz of animated talk went on in the street and the yards. But after half an hour several Cossacks strode down the street, jostling aside the solid mass of men. "Those belonging to Podtielkov's detachment, get ready to fall in," they shouted.

Behind them came Lieutenant Spiridonov. He removed his officer's cap and called:

"All those belonging to Podtielkov's detachment, step to the left towards the fences. The others to the right. Brothers, front-line men! Together with your leaders we have decided that you must surrender all your weapons, for the people are afraid of you while you are armed. Put your rifles and the rest of your arms on your carts. We shall guard them jointly. We are going to send you to Krasnokutsk, and there you will receive your arms back again."

A deep growl of discontent arose among the Red Guard Cossacks, and one of them shouted:

"We won't give up our arms!"

The Cossacks under Spiridonov's command moved over to the right, leaving the Red Guards in a disorderly and spiritless mob in the middle of the street. Krivoshlikov looked around him venomously, while Lagutin writhed his lips. Bunchuk, who was firmly resolved not to surrender his weapons, strode swiftly across to Podtielkov, carrying his rifle at the trail.

"We mustn't give up our arms! Do you hear?" he muttered.

"It's too late now," Podtielkov whispered back.

He was the first to unfasten his revolver holster. As he gave it up, he said huskily:

"My sword and rifle are in the cart."

The Red Guards languidly handed over their arms, some of them attempting to hide their revolvers in the fences and yards. Led by Bunchuk, a number refused to give up their rifles, and the weapons were taken from them by force. One machine-gunner tried to escape from the village, taking the gun-trigger with him. In the general confusion several others hid themselves. Spiridonov at once set guards over Podtielkov and the rest, searched them, and attempted to call a roll. But the prisoners answered reluctantly and called out:

"What are you checking the list for? We're all here."

"Drive us to Krasnokutsk."

"Put an end to this game."

The money-chest was sealed up and sent off under a strong guard. Then Spiridonov assembled the prisoners and, at once changing the tone of his voice and the expression on his face, gave the command:

"In double file! By the left! Quick march! Silence in the ranks!"

A roar of voices rolled along the ranks of the Red Guards. They marched away unwillingly, quickly broke their ranks, and walked along in a disorderly crowd.

When Podtielkov had called on his men to surrender their weapons, undoubtedly he still hoped for a favourable issue to the affair. But as soon as the prisoners were driven out of the village the Cossacks escorting them began to press on the outside men with their horses. Bunchuk was striding along on the left, and an old Cossack, with a flaming red beard and an ear-ring black with age in his ear, needlessly struck him with his whip. The end lashed Bunchuk's cheek. He turned and clenched his fist, but a second, still stronger lash forced him to push his way into the crowd of prisoners. He did so involuntarily, driven by the elemental instinct for self-preservation; and for the first time since Anna's death a wry smile twisted his lips as he realized with astonishment how strong and vital in man is the desire to live.

The Cossack escort began to beat up the prisoners. The old men, infuriated at the sight of their helpless enemies, rode their horses at them and, leaning out of their saddles, struck at them with their whips and the flat of their swords. Involuntarily the prisoners struggled to get into the middle, jostling one another and crying out. Shaking his arms above his head, a tall Red Guard shouted:

"If you're out to kill us, kill us off at once, damn you! What are you torturing us for?"

After a while the old men grew less truculent. In reply to a prisoner's question, one of the escort muttered:

"Our orders are to drive you to Ponamariov. Don't be afraid, brothers; no worse will happen to you."

When they arrived at the village of Ponamariov, Spiridonov stood at the door of a little shop, and as the prisoners passed inside one by one, he asked:

"Your surname? Christian name? Where were you born?"

It came to Bunchuk's turn. "Your surname?" Spiridonov asked, his pencil set expectantly to the paper. He glanced at the Red Guard's moody face, and seeing the man's lips pursed up ready to spit, he dodged swiftly and shouted:

"Move on, you swine! You'll die nameless."

Inspired by Bunchuk's example, others following him refused to give their names, preferring to die unknown. When the last man had passed into the shop Spiridonov locked it up and posted guards around it.

While the spoils taken from the expedition's carts were being shared out close by the shop, a hurriedly organized field court-martial, composed of representatives from all the villages participating in the capture was sitting in a house close at hand. The chairman was a thickset, yellow-haired captain. He sat with elbows sprawled over the table, his cap pushed to the back of his head. His oily, pleasant eyes turned interrogatively from one to another of the members of the court, and he repeated his question:

"What shall we do with them, elders?" he asked. "What shall we do with these traitors to their country, who were coming to pillage our homes and destroy the Cossacks?"

An old man jumped to his feet like a released jack-in-the-box:

"Shoot them! Every one of them!" He shook his head as though possessed and glanced around with fanatical eyes. Spittle dribbling from his lips, he shouted: "No mercy for them, the Judases! Kill them! Smash them! Set them against a wall!"

"Send them into exile?" one of the members irresolutely proposed.

"Shoot them!"

"The death-sentence!"

"Public execution!"

"Of course they must be shot. Why stop to discuss it?" Spiridonov declared indignantly.

At the shouts the good-natured, self-satisfied expression faded from the chairman's face. His lips set stonily.

"To be shot! Write that down!" he ordered the secretary.

"And Podtielkov and Krivoshlikov? Are they to be shot too? That's too good for them," a corpulent elderly Cossack sitting by the window shouted fierily.

"They, as the leaders, must be hanged!" the chairman curtly replied. Turning to the secretary, he ordered: "Write this: 'Decree. We, the undersigned . . .'"

The lamp began to gutter for want of oil, and the wick smoked. In the silence the buzzing of a fly caught in a spider-web on the ceiling, the scraping of the pen over the paper, and the heavy asthmatic breathing of one of the members of the court-martial were clearly to be heard.

The secretary finished writing out the list of those condemned and thrust the pen into the hand of his neighbour.

"Sign!" he said.

The man took the pen in stiff fingers. "I'm not a good hand at writing," he said with a guilty smile.

When all the members of the court had signed, the chairman rose to his feet, mopping his brow with his handkerchief.

"Kaledin in the next world will thank us for this," one man smiled, watching as the secretary fixed the sheet of paper to the wall.

Nobody responded to the jest. They silently went out of the hut.

"Lord Jesus . . ." someone sighed in the darkness of the porch.

There was little sleep that night for any of the prisoners locked up in the hut. Conversation quickly tailed away. The lack of air and their own anxiety choked them. In the evening one of them had asked the guard:

"Open the door, comrade. I want to go outside. . . ."

"None of your 'comrade,'" one of the guard replied at last.

"Open, brother!" the prisoner changed his style of address.

The guard set down his rifle, finished his cigarette, then put his lips to the door-chink and called:

"You can piss yourself, you swine! Your trousers won't rot in the night, and at dawn we'll be sending you in them wet to the heavenly kingdom. . . ."

The prisoners sat shoulder to shoulder. In one corner Podtielkov turned out his pockets and tore up a heap of paper money, muttering curses. Then he touched Krivoshlikov's arm and whispered:

"It's clear now—they've tricked us. Tricked us, the scum! It's insulting, Mikhail. When I was a boy I used to go hunting in the forest with my father's flint-lock. When I saw the ducks sitting I would mess up the shot, and I used to get so annoyed with myself. I could have cried for shame. And here I have messed things up badly. If we'd left Rostov three days earlier we shouldn't have been facing our death here. We'd have turned everything upside-down."

Torturously baring his teeth, Krivoshlikov whispered back:

"Damn them, let them kill us! I'm not afraid to die. The only thing I am afraid of is that in the next world we shan't recognize each other. You and I will be there, Fiodor, and we'll meet as strangers. . . . It's horrible! . . ."

"Drop that!" Podtielkov howled touchily. "That's not the trouble!"

Bunchuk was against the door, eagerly gasping in the draught that came through the chink. As his mind dwelt on the past he momentarily thought of his mother. Pierced with a sharp prick of pain, he forced his thoughts in another direction and turned to memories of Anna and more recent days. He found great relief and assuagement in this. He had none of the usual shiver down his spine or the accompanying yearning at the thought that they were about to deprive him of life. He looked forward to death as a cheerless rest after a bitter and painful road: when one's weariness is so great and the body aches so much that it is impossible to feel any gladness at its end.

A little way off, a group of prisoners was talking gaily and sadly of women, of love, of the great and petty joys which each had experienced. They talked of their families, their relations, their friends. They remarked on the good quality of the young grain: the crows could already get into the wheat and be hidden to sight. They longed for vodka and freedom, they cursed Podtielkov. But drowsiness covered many with its black wing: worn out physically and morally, they fell asleep lying, sitting, standing.

Even as dawn was breaking, one of them, whether awake or asleep, broke into tears. It is terrible when rough, grown-up men, who have forgotten the taste of salty tears since childhood, begin to weep. At once several voices disturbed the drowsy silence:

"Shut up, curse you!"

"What a woman!"

"Here are men asleep, and he's lost all sense of conscience!"

The man snuffled, blew his nose, and lapsed into silence. Here and there the gleaming red points of cigarettes shone out, but nobody made a sound. The air was heavy with the scent of men's sweat, of many healthy bodies pressed close together, of cigarette-smoke and the dew which had fallen during the night.

In the village a cock heralded the sunrise. Outside the shop was the sound of footsteps and the clink of iron.

"Who goes there?" one of the guards called out.

"Friends! We're going to dig a grave for the Podtielkov men."

In the hut everybody began at once to stir.

The detachment of Tatarsk Cossacks led by Piotra Melekhov arrived in Ponamariov at dawn of the same day. They found the village alive with the clatter of Cossack boots, with horses being led to drink. Crowds were pouring towards the far end of the village. Piotra halted his men in the centre of the village and gave the order to dismount. Several Cossacks came up to them.

"Where are you from?" one of them asked.

"Tatarsk."

"You're a bit too late. We've caught Podtielkov without your help. They're shut up over there, like chickens in a coop." He laughed and waved his hands towards the shop.

Christonia, Gregor, and several others went closer to the man.

"Where are they going to send them?" Christonia inquired.

"To join the dead."

"What? You're lying!" Gregor seized the man by his greatcoat.

"Speak a little more civilly, Your Excellency!" the man sharply retorted, pulling his coat away. "Look there; they've already built the gallows for them." He pointed to two ropes hanging from a cross-beam running between two stunted willows.

Clouds overcast the sky. A fine rain was falling. A dense mass of

Cossacks and women was gathered outside the village. Informed that the execution would take place at six o'clock, the inhabitants of Ponamariov went along willingly as though to a rare and merry spectacle. The women were dressed in holiday clothes; many of them had their children with them. The crowd swarmed over the pasture-land, crowded around the gallows and the six-foot-long pit. The children clambered over the raw clay of the mound thrown up on one side of the pit; the women whispered drearily among them-selves.

The court-martial chairman arrived, smoking and chewing his cigarette. He hoarsely ordered the Cossack guard:

"Drive the people back from the hole. Tell Spiridonov to send along the first batch." He glanced at his watch and stood on one side, looking at the crowd, driven back by the guards, surrounding him in a colourful half-circle.

Spiridonov led a squad of Cossacks swiftly towards the shop. On the road he met Piotra Melekhov.

"Any volunteers from your village?" he asked.

"Volunteers for what?" Piotra inquired.

"To act as a firing party."

"No, there aren't, and there won't be!" Piotra roughly answered, passing round Spiridonov as he barred the road.

But there were volunteers from Tatarsk: Mitka Korshunov, strok-ing the hair falling below the visor of his cap, went awkwardly up to Piotra and said, screwing up his green eyes:

"I'll volunteer. What did you say no for? I'll be one. Give me some cartridges. I've only got one round."

He was joined by Andrei Kashulin, an evil expression on his pale face, and Fiodot Bodovskov.

A roar and muffled howl went up from the closely packed crowd when the first party of ten condemned prisoners, surrounded by a Cossack escort, set out from the shop. Podtielkov walked in front, barefoot, dressed in broad black cloth breeches and his leather jerkin, flung wide open. He set his great feet confidently in the mud, and when he slipped flung out his left arm to keep his balance. At his side Krivoshlikov, deathly pale, could hardly drag himself along. His eyes gleamed feverishly, his mouth twitched with suffering. He adjusted the greatcoat hanging around his back, and shrugged his shoulders as though terribly cold. For some reason these two were left their clothes, but the others had been stripped down to their underlinen. Lagutin walked at the side of Bunchuk. Both of them were barefoot and wearing little more than their shirts. Lagutin's ragged drawers revealed his hairy shanks, and he sheepishly drew them around him. Bunchuk stared over the heads of the guards at the grey shroud of clouds in the distance. His cold, sober eyes twinkled expectantly and tensely; his broad palm stroked his chest beneath the open collar of his shirt. One would have thought he was looking forward to something unattainable, yet pleasant to think upon. Some of the others maintained expressions of stolid indifference; one man scornfully waved his hand and spat at the feet of the Cossack guards. But two or three had such a dumb yearning in their eyes, such boundless terror in their distorted faces, that even the guards turned their eyes away as they met their gaze.

They strode along swiftly. Podtielkov gave his arm to the stumbling Krivoshlikov. They drew near the white kerchiefs and red and blue caps of the crowd. As he stared at them Podtielkov cursed aloud. Catching Lagutin's eyes fixed on him, he abruptly asked:

"What's the matter?"

"You've gone grey during these last few days. . . ."

"Isn't it enough to make you?" Podtielkov breathed heavily, wiped the sweat from his narrow brow, and repeated: "Isn't it enough to make you? Even a wolf goes grey in a cage; and I'm a man."

Not another word did they say. The crowd surged forward in a solid mass. To the right stretched the long dark scar of the grave. Spiridonov commanded:

"Halt!"

Podtielkov immediately took a step forward, and wearily ran his eyes over the foremost ranks of the people. Most of them were grey-haired. The front-line men were somewhere at the back, pricked with conscience. Podtielkov's drooping moustaches stirred but the slightest, as he said ponderously, yet distinctly:

"Elders, allow me and Krivoshlikov to watch how our comrades will face their deaths. Hang us afterwards, but now we should like to see our friends and comrades and to strengthen those who are weak of spirit."

The crowd was so quiet that the rain pattered audibly on their caps.

Behind him the captain smiled, baring his tobacco-stained teeth, but made no objection. The elders raggedly shouted their consent. Krivoshlikov and Podtielkov stepped through the crowd, which divided and opened a narrow lane before them. A little way off from the pit they halted, hemmed in on all sides, watched by hundreds of eyes. They gazed as the Cossacks drew up the Red Guards in a line with their backs to the pit. Podtielkov could see perfectly, but Krivoshlikov had to stretch his lean neck and rise on his toes.

They recognized Bunchuk on the extreme left, standing with huddled shoulders, breathing heavily, not raising his eyes from the ground. At his side stood Lagutin, still fumbling with his drawers. The man next in the line was changed almost beyond recognition, and had aged at least twenty years. Two more approached the pit and turned round. One of them was smiling challengingly and impudently, furiously cursing and threatening the silent crowd with his fist. The last of the eight had to be carried. He threw himself back, dragged his feet lifelessly over the ground, clung to the Cossack guards, then, shaking his tear-stained face, started up and bellowed:

"Let me go, brothers! Let me go, for the love of God! Brothers! Little brothers! What are you doing? I won four crosses in the German war. I have children. God, I'm innocent. Oh, why are you doing this? . . ."

A tall Cossack thrust his knee into the man's chest and drove him towards the pit. Only then did Podtielkov recognize him, and his heart turned cold: it was one of the most fearless of his Red Guards, a man who had won all four stages of the Cross of St. George, a handsome, fair-haired youth. The Cossacks raised him upright; but he fell again and scrabbled at their feet, pressing his lips to their boots—to the boots which were kicking him in the face—and bellowing in a fearful, choking voice:

"Don't kill me! Have mercy! I have three little children, one of them a girl . . . my brothers, my friends!"

He embraced the tall Cossack's knees, but the man tore himself away, leaped back, and gave him a swinging kick with his iron-shod heel on the ear. Blood poured from the other ear and ran down his white collar.

"Stand him up!" Spiridonov shouted furiously.

Somehow they raised him, set him up, and ran back. In the opposite rank the firing party brought their rifles to the ready. The crowd groaned and froze into stillness. Some woman whined stupidly.

Bunchuk wanted once more and yet once more to look at the grey pall of the sky, at the mournful earth over which he had wandered twenty-nine years. He raised his eyes and saw the close rank of Cossacks some fifteen paces away. He saw one man, tall, with screwed-up green eyes, a lovelock falling over his narrow white brow, his lips compressed, his body leaning forward, aiming straight at Bunchuk's breast. Just before the volley rang out, Bunchuk's ears were pierced by a protracted shriek. He turned his head: a young, freckled woman ran out of the crowd and fled towards the village, one arm clutching a baby to her breast, the other hand covering its eyes.

After the irregular volley, when the eight men standing at the pit had fallen in a ragged line, the firing party ran towards the hole. Seeing that the Red Guard he had aimed at was still writhing and gnawing at his shoulder, Mitka Korshunov put another shot into him, and whispered to Andrei Kashulin:

"Look at that devil! He's bitten his shoulder until it's bleeding, and died like a wolf, without a groan."

Ten more of the condemned approached the hole, urged on by butt ends.

After the second volley the women in the crowd screamed and fled, jostling one another and dragging their children behind them. The Cossacks also began to disperse. The loathsome scene of extermination, the shouts and groans of the dying, the howling of those awaiting their turn, were overwhelmingly oppressive, and the moving spectacle was too much for the crowd. There remained only the front-line men, who had looked on death to their fill, and the most hardened of the elders.

Fresh groups of barefoot and unclothed Red Guards were brought up, new lines of volunteers confronted them, volleys spirted out, and single shots dryly shook the air as the half-dead were finished off. Hurriedly earth was shovelled over the first group of bodies in the trench. Podtielkov and Krivoshlikov went across to those awaiting their turn and endeavoured to encourage them. But their words had lost all their significance: another power dominated these men whose lives in a minute or two were to be broken off like ripe fruit from a tree.

Gregor Melekhov pushed through the crowd to go back to the village and came face to face with Podtielkov. His former leader stepped back and stared at him:

"You here too, Melekhov?"

A bluish pallor overspread Gregor's cheeks and he halted.

"Here. As you see."

"I see. . . ." Podtielkov smiled wryly, staring with explosive hatred at Gregor's face. "Well, so you're shooting down your brothers? You've turned your coat? What a . . ." He strode closer to Gregor and whispered: "So you serve us and them too, whoever pays most? Pah, you . . ."

Gregor seized his sleeve and pantingly asked:

"Do you remember the battle at Gluboka? Do you remember how they shot down the officers? Shot them down by your order? Eh? And now it's your turn. Don't cry! You're not the only one allowed to tan others' hides! You're finished, chairman of the Muscovite commissars! You filthy swine, you sold the Cossacks to the Jews! Need I say any more?"

Christonia put his arm around the raging Gregor and led him away. "Let's get back to the horses," he said. "There's nothing we can do here. God, what is coming over the people?"

But they halted as they heard Podtielkov's voice raised passionately. Surrounded by old and front-line men, he was shouting:

"You're blind—ignorant! The officers have tricked you, have forced you to kill your blood brothers. Do you think it will end with our death? No! Today you are on top, but tomorrow it will be your turn to be shot. The Soviet government will be established all over Russia. Remember my words! In vain are you shedding our blood! You're a lot of fools!"

"We'll manage any others who come!" an old man retorted.

"You won't shoot them all, daddy!" Podtielkov smiled. "You won't hang all Russia on the gallows! Look after your own head. You'll think better of it some day, but it will be too late."

Gregor did not stop to listen to any more, but almost ran to the yard where his horse was tethered. Tightening the saddle-girths, he and Christonia galloped out of the village and rode over the hill without a backward glance.

By the time all the Red Guards had been executed the trench was filled with bodies. Earth was heaped over them and stamped down with feet. Two officers in black masks took Podtielkov and Krivoshlikov and led them to the gallows. Bravely, proudly lifting his head, Podtielkov mounted the stool beneath the noose, unbuttoned the collar around his stout, swarthy neck, and without the tremor of a muscle, himself set the soapy rope around his throat. One of the officers helped Krivoshlikov to mount his stool and put the rope over his head.

"Allow us to say a last word before our deaths," Podtielkov requested.

"Speak up! Go ahead!" the front-line men shouted.

He stretched his hands towards the little group that remained.

"See how few are left who wish to look on at our death!" Podtielkov began. "Their consciences have pricked them. On behalf of the toiling people, in their interests we have struggled against the rats of generals, not sparing our lives. And now we are perishing at your hands! But we do not curse you. You have been bitterly deceived. The revolutionary government will come, and you will realize on whose side was the truth. The finest sons of the gentle Don have you laid in that hole. . . ."

There was an increasing roar of voices, and his words were lost in the hubbub. Taking advantage of this, one of the officers kicked the stool from under his feet. His great body fell and dangled, but his feet touched the ground. The knot gripping his throat choked him and forced him to draw himself upward. He rose on tiptoe, the toes of his bare feet digging into the damp earth, and gasped for air. Running his protruding eyes over the crowd, he said quietly:

"And you haven't even learned how to hang a man properly. . . . If I had the job, you wouldn't touch the ground, Spiridonov! . . ."

The spittle dribbled freely from his mouth. The masked officers and the nearest men raised the helpless, heavy body with difficulty on to the stool.

Krivoshlikov was not allowed to finish his speech. The stool flew from under his feet and crashed against an abandoned shovel. The lean, muscular body swung to and fro for a long time, contracting into a huddled mass until the knees touched his chin, then stretching again with a convulsive shudder. He was still struggling, his black, protruding tongue was still writhing, when the stool was kicked a second time from under Podtielkov. Again the body fell heavily, the seam of the leather jerkin burst on the shoulder; but again the ends of the toes reached the ground. The crowd of Cossacks groaned; some of them crossed themselves and hurried away. So great were the dismay and confusion that for a minute all stood as though rooted to the spot, staring fearfully at Podtielkov's stone-stiff body.

But he was speechless; the knot gripped his throat too tightly. He only rolled his eyes, from which streams of tears were falling, and his mouth writhed. Striving to lighten his suffering, his entire body stretched terribly and torturously upward.

Someone at last bethought himself of a solution and began with a shovel to dig away the earth beneath him. With each swing the body hung more stiffly, the neck lengthened and lengthened, and the head fell back on to his shoulders. The rope could hardly bear his great weight; it swung gently, creaking at the cross-beam. Yielding to its rhythmic movement, Podtielkov swung also, turning in all directions as though showing his murderers his livid, blackening face and his chest, flooded with burning streams of spittle and tears.

Chapter 10

Misha Koshevoi and Valet left Kargin the second night after they had fled from Tatarsk. A mist enveloped the steppe, gathering in the ravines and crawling over the spurs of the hills. The quails were calling in the young grass. But in the crepe of the sky the moon was floating like the fully opened blossom of a water-lily in a lake overgrown with reeds and sedges.

They kept on until the dawn. The Milky Way began to fade in the sky. A dew arose. They drew near to a village. But a couple of

miles from the village they were overtaken by six Cossack horsemen. Misha and Valet would have turned off the road, but the
grass was short, the moon was shining.

The Cossacks caught them and drove them back towards Kargin.
They went some three hundred yards without speaking. Then a
shot rang out. Valet stumbled over his feet and went sideways, sideways, like a horse afraid of its own shadow. He did not fall, but
awkwardly crumpled to the ground, with his face against the grey
wormwood.

For five minutes Misha walked on, no feeling in his body, but a
ringing in his ears. Then he asked:

"Why don't you shoot, you swine? Why pile on the agony?"

"Get on, get on! Hold your tongue!" one of the Cossacks said
kindly enough. "We killed the peasant, but we've had pity on you.
You were in the 12th Regiment during the German war, weren't
you?"

"Yes."

"Well, you'll serve again in the 12th. You're young yet. You've
gone wrong a bit, but that's no great sin. We'll cure you."

Misha was cured three days later by a field court-martial held at
Kargin. During those times the court had two forms of punishment:
shooting, and the birch. Those sentenced to be shot were driven out
into the steppe at night. But those for whom there was hope of
correction were birched publicly in the square.

On the Sunday morning the people began to assemble, filling all
the square and climbing on to benches, sheds, roofs of houses and
shops.

The first to be punished was the son of a priest. The man was an
ardent Bolshevik and they would have shot him; but his father was
a good priest, respected by all, and they decided to give his son a
score of strokes. They pulled down his trousers, laid him bare over
a bench, tied his hands together underneath it, a Cossack sat on his
legs, and two others with bunches of willow switches stood at his
side. They laid on. When they had finished, the man rose, shook
himself, pulled up his trousers, and bowed in all four directions.
He was very glad to have escaped being shot, so he bowed and
expressed his gratitude:

"Thank you, elders!"

"May it do you good!" someone answered.

And such a roar of laughter broke over the square that even the prisoners sitting a little way off under a shed also smiled.

In accordance with the sentence, they gave Misha twenty strokes good and hot. But still hotter was his burning shame. All the district, old and young, had assembled to watch. Misha pulled up his trousers and, all but weeping, said to the Cossack who had birched him:

"It isn't right!"

"What isn't?"

"It was my head that thought of it, and my arse has had to pay for it. I'm shamed for the rest of my life."

"Don't worry, shame isn't smoke; it won't eat out your eyes," the Cossack consoled him, and in the desire to cheer his victim he added:

"You're strong, my boy! Two of the strokes I gave you were real good ones. I wanted to see whether you would cry out, but I couldn't make you. Now, the other day they were birching a man and he couldn't hold himself. He must have had weak bowels."

The next day Misha was marched off to the front.

Valet was not buried until two days later. A couple of Cossacks from the nearest village were sent out by the ataman to dig a shallow grave. They sat smoking, their legs dangling in the hole.

"The earth's hard here," one said.

"Like iron. It's never been ploughed in my time. It's been set hard like this these many years."

"Yes, the lad will be lying in good earth, on a hill. There's wind here, and sun. It's dry. He won't rot quickly."

They glanced at Valet's body huddled over the grass, and rose.

"Undress him?"

"Of course. He's got good boots on his feet."

They laid him in the grave Christian-fashion, with his head to the east, and shovelled the rich black earth on top of him.

"Stamp it down?" the younger of the two asked when the earth was level with the edges.

"No need, let it be!" the other sighed. "When the angels sound the last trump he will be able to get to his feet more quickly."

Within two weeks the little mound was overgrown with burdock and wormwood; wild oats were dancing on it, rape was yellowing gaily at the side, clover was raising its head, and the air was scented with thyme, spurge, and honey-dew.

Soon afterwards some old man drove out from the village, dug a little hole at the head of the grave, and set up a shrine on a freshly cut oaken pole. In the shadow beneath the triangular coping appeared the sorrowful features of the Mother of God, and on the base below her was painted an inscription in Old Slavonic:

> In the years of trouble and pother,
> Brothers, judge not your brother.

The old man drove off, leaving the shrine in the steppe to depress the passers-by, to arouse a dumb yearning in their hearts with its everlastingly despondent look.

Later on, in June, two bustards fought around the shrine. They beat out a little bare patch in the blue wormwood, crushing the green flood of ripening speargrass, fighting for the female, for the right to life, for love and fertility. And again after a little while, under the mound, right by the shrine, in the shaggy shelter of the old wormwood, a female bustard laid nine speckled, smoky-blue eggs and sat on them, warming them with her body, protecting them with her glossy wings.

ABOUT THE AUTHOR

MIKHAIL SHOLOKHOV was born in 1905 in a village in the Don region, of a family that had been living there for many generations. Despite poverty, he was able to attend school in Moscow. At the age of fifteen he returned to his native village to become a schoolteacher, then a statistician, a food inspector, and held various other jobs.

He began writing when he was eighteen years old. Today he is the Soviet Union's most famous and widely honored living novelist. *And Quiet Flows the Don* was published in 1928 in the Soviet Union, and in the United States in 1934. Its sequel, *The Don Flows Home to the Sea* (available in Vintage Books), was finished in 1939, and appeared in America in 1940. Although each is complete in itself, the two books are often referred to under the title *The Silent Don*. Other volumes by Sholokhov that have been translated into English are *Harvest on the Don, Seeds of Tomorrow,* and *Tales of the Don.*

In 1965 Mr. Sholokhov was awarded the Nobel Prize for Literature.

VINTAGE FICTION, POETRY, AND PLAYS

VINTAGE BELLES—LETTRES